"An exercise in audacity. . . . Ellroy is either our greatest obsessive writer or our most obsessive great writer. Either way, he is turning the crime novel's mean streets into superhighways. . . . A remarkable accomplishment."
—*Financial Times*

"Garrote-tight prose. . . . [Ellroy is] a force of nature, stringing together words into barbed-wire lariats which he then uses to choke the bejeezus out of you. . . . A coherent, ultimately gorgeous and electrifying mess."   —*The Austin Chronicle*

"A dazzling panorama of the '60s as seen through the eyes of some colorful thugs. . . . Ellroy isn't the first to argue that American history is written behind the scenes by violent brutes, but only a mad genius like him could make those monsters lovable."   —*Us*

"Ambitious. . . . Ellroy is a unique American literary voice."
—*USA Today*

"With riveting style and substance, *The Cold Six Thousand* is Ellroy's biggest score."   —*Playboy*

"An ambitious, extravagant book about history as obsession. . . . Richer and darker than ever, this story . . . reminds us how far ahead of his peers Ellroy is."   —*New Statesman*

JAMES ELLROY

THE COLD
SIX THOUSAND

James Ellroy was born in Los Angeles in 1948. His L.A.
Quartet novels—*The Black Dahlia, The Big Nowhere,
L.A. Confidential,* and *White Jazz*—were international
bestsellers. His novel *American Tabloid* was *Time*
magazine's Best Book (fiction) of 1995; his memoir, *My
Dark Places,* was a *Time* Best Book of the Year and a
New York Times Notable Book for 1996. He lives in
Kansas City.

THE COLD
SIX THOUSAND

THE COLD
SIX THOUSAND

a novel

JAMES ELLROY

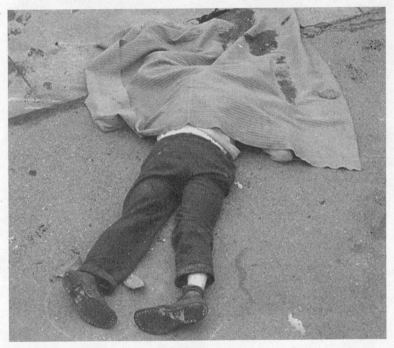

VINTAGE BOOKS
A DIVISION OF RANDOM HOUSE, INC.   NEW YORK

FIRST VINTAGE BOOKS EDITION, JUNE 2002

Copyright © 2001 by James Ellroy

All rights reserved under International and Pan-American Copyright Conventions.
Published in the United States by Vintage Books, a division of Random House, Inc.,
New York, and simultaneously in Canada by Random House of Canada Limited,
Toronto. Originally published in hardcover in the United States by Alfred
A. Knopf, a division of Random House, Inc., New York, in 2001.

Vintage and colophon are registered trademarks of Random House, Inc.

The Library of Congress has cataloged the Knopf edition as follows:
Ellroy, James, 1948–
The cold six thousand : a novel / by James Ellroy.—1st ed.
p. cm.
ISBN 0-679-40392-2
I. Title.
2001088561

Vintage ISBN: 0-375-72740-X

Book design by Virginia Tan

www.vintagebooks.com

Printed in the United States of America
10 9 8 7 6 5 4 3 2 1

Title page photograph by Mell Kilpatrick,
courtesy of Jennifer Dumas

To

BILL STONER

Part I

EXTRADITION

November 22–25, 1963

Wayne Tedrow Jr.

(Dallas, 11/22/63)

They sent him to Dallas to kill a nigger pimp named Wendell Durfee. He wasn't sure he could do it.

The Casino Operators Council flew him. They supplied first-class fare. They tapped their slush fund. They greased him. They fed him six cold.

Nobody *said* it:

Kill that coon. Do it good. Take our hit fee.

The flight ran smooth. A stew served drinks. She saw his gun. She played up. She asked dumb questions.

He said he worked Vegas PD. He ran the intel squad. He built files and logged information.

She loved it. She swooned.

"Hon, what you doin' in Dallas?"

He told her.

A Negro shivved a twenty-one dealer. The dealer lost an eye. The Negro booked to Big D. She loved it. She brought him highballs. He omitted details.

The dealer provoked the attack. The council issued the contract—death for ADW Two.

The preflight pep talk. Lieutenant Buddy Fritsch:

"I don't have to tell you what we expect, son. And I don't have to add that your father expects it, too."

The stew played geisha girl. The stew fluffed her beehive.

"What's your name?"

"Wayne Tedrow."

She whooped. "You just *have* to be Junior!"

He looked through her. He doodled. He yawned.

She fawned. She just loooooved his daddy. He flew with her oodles. She knew he was a Mormon wheel. She'd looove to know more.

Wayne laid out Wayne Senior.

He ran a kitchen-help union. He rigged low pay. He had coin. He had pull. He pushed right-wing tracts. He hobnobbed with fat cats. He knew J. Edgar Hoover.

The pilot hit the intercom. Dallas—on time.

The stew fluffed her hair. "I'll bet you're staying at the Adolphus."

Wayne cinched his seat belt. "What makes you say that?"

"Well, your daddy told me he always stays there."

"I'm staying there. Nobody consulted me, but that's where they've got me booked."

The stew hunkered down. Her skirt slid. Her garter belt gapped.

"Your daddy told me they've got a nice little restaurant right there in the hotel, and, well . . ."

The plane hit rough air. Wayne caught it low. He broke a sweat. He shut his eyes. He saw Wendell Durfee.

The stew touched him. Wayne opened his eyes.

He saw her hickeys. He saw her bad teeth. He smelled her shampoo.

"You were looking a little scared there, Wayne Junior."

"Junior" tore it.

"Leave me alone. I'm not what you want, and I don't cheat on my wife."

1:50 p.m.

They touched down. Wayne got off first. Wayne stamped blood back into his legs.

He walked to the terminal. Schoolgirls blocked the gate. One girl cried. One girl fucked with prayer beads.

He stepped around them. He followed baggage signs. People walked past him. They looked sucker-punched.

Red eyes. Boo-hoo. Women with Kleenex.

Wayne stopped at baggage claim. Kids whizzed by. They shot cap pistols. They laughed.

A man walked up—Joe Redneck—tall and fat. He wore a Stetson. He wore big boots. He wore a mother-of-pearl .45.

"If you're Sergeant Tedrow, I'm Officer Maynard D. Moore of the Dallas Police Department."

They shook hands. Moore chewed tobacco. Moore wore cheap cologne. A woman walked by—boo-hoo-hoo—one big red nose.

Wayne said, "What's wrong?"

Moore smiled. "Some kook shot the President."

Most shops closed early. State flags flew low. Some folks flew rebel flags upright.

Moore drove Wayne in. Moore had a plan: Run by the hotel/get you set in/find us that jigaboo.

John F. Kennedy—dead.

His wife's crush. His stepmom's fixation. JFK got Janice wet. Janice told Wayne Senior. Janice paid. Janice limped. Janice showed off the welts on her thighs.

Dead was dead. He couldn't grab it. He fumbled the rebounds.

Moore chewed Red Man. Moore shot juice out his window. Gunshots overlapped. Joyous shit in the boonies.

Moore said, "Some people ain't so sad."

Wayne shrugged. They passed a billboard—JFK and the UN.

"You sure ain't sayin' much. I got to say that so far, you ain't the most lively extradition partner I ever had."

A gun went off. Close. Wayne grabbed his holster.

"Whoo! You got a case of the yips, boy!"

Wayne futzed with his necktie. "I just want to get this over with."

Moore ran a red light. "In good time. I don't doubt that Mr. Durfee'll be sayin' hi to our fallen hero before too long."

Wayne rolled up his window. Wayne trapped in Moore's cologne.

Moore said, "I been to Lost Wages quite a few times. In fact, I owe a big marker at the Dunes this very moment."

Wayne shrugged. They passed a bus bench. A colored girl sobbed.

"I heard of your daddy, too. I heard he's quite the boy in Nevada."

A truck ran a red. The driver waved a beer and revolver.

"Lots of people know my father. They all tell me they know him, and it gets old pretty quick."

Moore smiled. "Hey, I think I detect a pulse there."

Motorcade confetti. A window sign: *Big D loves Jack & Jackie.*

"I heard about you, too. I heard you got leanings your daddy don't much care for."

"For instance?"

"Let's try nigger lover. Let's try you chauffeur Sonny Liston around when he comes to Vegas, 'cause the PD's afraid he'll get himself in trouble with liquor and white women, and you *like* him, but you *don't* like the nice Italian folks who keep your little town clean."

The car hit a pothole. Wayne hit the dash.

Moore stared at Wayne. Wayne stared back. They held the stare. Moore ran a red. Wayne blinked first.

Moore winked. "We're gonna have big fun this weekend."

The lobby was swank. The carpets ran thick. Men snagged their boot heels.

People pointed outside—look look look—the motorcade passed the hotel. JFK drove by. JFK waved. JFK bought it close by.

People talked. Strangers braced strangers. The men wore western suits. The women dressed faux-Jackie.

Check-ins swamped the desk. Moore ad-libbed. Moore walked Wayne to the bar.

SRO—big barside numbers.

A TV sat on a table. A barman goosed the sound. Moore shoved up to a phone booth. Wayne scoped the TV out.

Folks jabbered. The men wore hats. Everyone wore boots and high heels. Wayne stood on his toes. Wayne popped over hat brims.

The picture jumped and settled in. Sound static and confusion. Cops. A thin punk. Words: "Oswald"/"weapon"/"Red sympath—"

A guy waved a rifle. Newsmen pressed in. A camera panned. There's the punk. He's showing fear and contusions.

The noise was bad. The smoke was thick. Wayne lost his legs.

A man raised a toast. "Oughta give Oswald a—"

Wayne stood down. A woman jostled him—wet cheeks and runny mascara.

Wayne walked to the phone booth. Moore had the door cracked.

He said, "Guy, listen now."

He said, "Wet-nursing some kid on some bullshit extradition—"

"Bullshit" tore it.

Wayne jabbed Moore. Moore swung around. His pant legs hiked up.

Fuck—knives in his boot tops. Brass knucks in one sock.

Wayne said, "Wendell Durfee, remember?"

Moore stood up. Moore got magnetized. Wayne tracked his eyes.

He caught the TV. He caught a caption. He caught a still shot: "Slain Officer J. D. Tippit."

Moore stared. Moore trembled. Moore shook.

Wayne said, "Wendell Durf—"

Moore shoved him. Moore ran outside.

. . .

The council booked him a *biggg* suite. A bellboy supplied history. JFK loved the suite. JFK fucked women there. Ava Gardner blew him on the terrace.

Two sitting rooms. Two bedrooms. Three TVs. Slush funds. Six cold. Kill that nigger, boy.

Wayne toured the suite. History lives. JFK loved Dallas quail.

He turned the TVs on. He tuned in three channels. He caught the show three ways. He walked between sets. He nailed the story.

The punk was Lee Harvey Oswald. The punk shot JFK and Tippit. Tippit worked Dallas PD. DPD was tight-knit. Moore probably knew him.

Oswald was pro-Red. Oswald loved Fidel. Oswald worked at a school-book plant. Oswald clipped the Prez on his lunch break.

DPD had him. Their HQ teemed. Cops. Reporters. Camera hogs all.

Wayne flopped on a couch. Wayne shut his eyes. Wayne saw Wendell Durfee. Wayne opened his eyes. Wayne saw Lee Oswald.

He killed the sound. He pulled his wallet pix.

There's his mother—back in Peru, Indiana.

She left Wayne Senior. Late '47. Wayne Senior hit her. He broke bones sometimes.

She asked Wayne who he loved most. He said, "My dad." She slapped him. She cried. She apologized.

The slap tore it. He went with Wayne Senior.

He called his mother—May '54—he called en route to the Army. She said, "Don't fight in silly wars." She said, "Don't hate like Wayne Senior."

He cut her off. Binding/permanent/4-ever.

There's his stepmom.

Wayne Senior ditched Wayne's mom. Wayne Senior wooed Janice. Wayne Senior brought Wayne along. Wayne was thirteen. Wayne was horny. Wayne dug on Janice.

Janice Lukens Tedrow made rooms tilt. She played indolent wife. She played scratch golf. She played A-club tennis.

Wayne Senior feared her spark. She watched Wayne grow up. She torched reciprocal. She left her doors open. She invited looks. Wayne Senior knew it. Wayne Senior didn't care.

There's *his* wife.

Lynette Sproul Tedrow. Perched in his lap. Grad night at Brigham Young.

He's shell-shocked. He got his chem degree—BYU/'59—summa cum laude. He craved action. He joined Vegas PD. Fuck summa cum laude.

He met Lynette in Little Rock. Fall '57. Central High desegregates. Red-necks. Colored kids. The Eighty-Second Airborne.

Some white boys prowl. Some white boys snatch a colored boy's sandwich. Lynette hands him hers. The white boys attack. Corporal Wayne Tedrow Jr. counters.

He beats them down. He spears one fuck. The fuck screams, "Mommy!"

Lynette hits on Wayne. She's seventeen. He's twenty-three. He's got some college.

They fucked on a golf course. Sprinklers doused them. He told Janice all.

She said, "You and Lynette peaked early. And you probably liked the fight as much as the sex."

Janice knew him. Janice had the home-court advantage.

Wayne looked out a window. TV crews roamed. News vans double-parked. He walked through the suite. He turned off the TVs. Three Oswalds vanished.

He pulled his file. All carbons: LVPD/Dallas County Sheriff's.

Durfee, Wendell (NMI). Male Negro/DOB 6-6-27/Clark County, Nevada. 6'4"/155.

Pander beefs—3/44 up. "Well-known dice-game habitue." No busts outside Vegas and Dallas.

"Known to drive Cadillacs."

"Known to wear flamboyant attire."

"Known to have fathered 13 children out of wedlock."

"Known to pander Negro women, white women, male homosexuals & Mexican transvestites."

Twenty-two pimp busts. Fourteen convictions. Nine child-support liens. Five bail jumps.

Cop notes: Wendell's smart/Wendell's dumb/Wendell cut that cat at Binion's.

The cat was mobbed up. The cat shanked Wendell first. The council set policy. The LVPD enforced it.

"Known Dallas County Associates":

Marvin Duquesne Settle/male Negro/Texas State custody.

Fenton "Duke" Price/male Negro/Texas State custody.

Alfonzo John Jefferson/male Negro/4219 Wilmington Road, Dallas 8, Tex. "Gambling partner of Wendell Durfee."

County Probation: (Stat. 92.04 Tex. St. Code) 9/14/60–9/14/65. Employed: Dr Pepper Bottling Plant. Note: "Subject to make fine payments for term of probation, i.e.: every 3rd Friday (Dr Pepper payday) County Prob. Off."

Donnell George Lundy/male Negro/Texas State custody.

Manuel "Bobo" Herrara/male Mexican/Texas State cust—

The phone rang. Wayne grabbed it.

"Yeah?"

"It's me, son. Your new best buddy."

Wayne grabbed his holster. "Where are you?"

"Right now I'm noplace worth bein'. But you meet me at eight o'clock."

"Where?"

"The Carousel Club. You be there, and we'll find us that burrhead."

Wayne hung up. Wayne got butterflies.

Wendell, I don't want to kill you.

Ward J. Littell

(Dallas, 11/22/63)

There's the limo. It's on the runway. It's late-model FBI black. The plane taxied up. It passed Air Force One. Marines flanked the tailhatch. The pilot cut the engine. The plane fishtailed. The ramp popped and dropped.

Littell got out. His ears popped. His legs uncramped.

They worked fast. They rigged his flight plan. They flew him two-seat non-deluxe.

Mr. Hoover called him—D.C. to L.A.

He said, "The President was shot and killed. I want you to fly to Dallas and monitor the investigation."

The hit occurred at 12:30. It was 4:10 now. Mr. Hoover called at 12:40. Mr. Hoover got the news and called fast.

Littell ran. The limo driver popped the door. The backseat was stuffy. The windows were smoked. Love Field was all monochrome.

Stick figures. Baggage crews. Newsmen and charter planes.

The driver pulled out. Littell saw a box on the seat. He opened it. He emptied it out.

One special agent's shield. One FBI photo ID card. One Bureau-issue .38/holster.

His old photo. *His* old gun.

He gave them up in '60. Mr. Hoover forced him out. He had cover tools now—new and old—he had cosmetic reinstatement.

Mr. Hoover stashed said tools. *In Dallas.* Mr. Hoover predicted the hit.

He knew the locale. He sensed the time frame. He was passively complicit. He sensed Littell's involvement. He sensed Littell's need to quash talk.

Littell looked out his window. The tint made funhouse distortions. Clouds imploded. Buildings weaved. People blipped.

He brought a radio. He played it flying in. He got the basic stats:

One suspect caught—a kid—a sheep-dipped leftist. Guy Banister dipped him. The kid killed a cop. Two cops were set to kill him. Phase Two went bad. The second cop botched his assignment.

Littell holstered up. Littell studied his ID.

Cop/lawyer then. Mob lawyer now. Hoover foe to Hoover ally. A one-man law firm with three clients:

Howard Hughes/Jimmy Hoffa/Carlos Marcello.

He called Carlos. Ten a.m. L.A. time. Carlos was happy. Carlos beat Bobby K.'s deportation bill.

Bobby tried Carlos in New Orleans. Carlos *owned* New Orleans. Carlos was jury-proof there.

Kennedy hubris:

The jury acquits Carlos. Bobby sulks. Jack dies one hour on.

The streets were dead. Windows zipped by. Ten thousand TVs glowed. It was *his* show.

He developed the plan. Pete Bondurant helped. Carlos okayed it and went with Guy Banister's crew. Guy embellished *his* plan. Guy revised it. Guy botched it.

Pete was in Dallas. Pete just got married. Pete was at the Adolphus Hotel. Guy B. was here. Guy B. was somewhere close.

Littell counted windows. All tint-distorted. Smudges and blurs. His thoughts blew wide. His thoughts cohered:

Talk to Pete. Kill Oswald. Ensure a one-shooter consensus.

The limo hit downtown Dallas. Littell pinned on his shield.

There's Dealey Plaza. The PD building's close. Look for:

The book building/a Hertz sign/Greek columns.

There—

The columns. The sign. Mourners at Houston and Elm. A hot-dog vendor. Nuns sobbing.

Littell shut his eyes. The driver turned right. The driver pulled down a ramp. The driver stopped hard and fast. The back windows slid down.

Somebody coughed. Somebody said, "Mr. Littell?"

Littell opened his eyes. Littell saw a basement garage. There's a kiddy Fed standing there. He's all uptight.

"Sir, I'm Special Agent Burdick, and . . . well, the ASAC said you should come straight up and see the witnesses."

Littell grabbed his briefcase. The gun chafed his hip. He got out. He stretched. He cleaned his glasses.

Burdick stuck close. Burdick rode him tight. They walked to a freight lift. Burdick pushed 3.

"Sir, I have to say it's a madhouse. We've got people saying two shooters, three, four, they can't even agree where the shots—"

"Did you isolate them?"

"Well . . . no."

"Who's interviewing them?"

The boy stuttered. The boy gulped.

"Which *agencies,* son?"

"Well, we've got us, DPD, the Sheriff's, and I—"

The door opened. Noise boomed in. The squadroom was packed.

Littell looked around. Burdick got antsy. Littell ignored him.

The witnesses were antsy. The witnesses wore name tags. The witnesses perched on one bench.

Thirty-odd people: Talking. Fretting. Contaminating facts.

Back-wall cubicles. Cops and civilians—holed up in interview slots. Flustered cops and civilians in shock.

Forty desks. Forty phones. Forty cops talking loud. Odd badges on suitcoats. Wastebaskets dumped. Inter-agency chaos and—

"Sir, can we—"

Littell walked over. Littell checked the bench. The wits squirmed. The wits smoked. Full ashtrays jumped.

I saw this/I saw that/his head went pop! A talkathon—bad work—pure mass-witness slop.

Littell looked for standouts. Solid types/credible wits.

He stood back. He framed the bench. He saw a woman: Dark hair/handsome/thirty-five-plus.

She sat still. She stayed calm. She watched an exit door. She saw Littell. She looked away. She never blinked.

Burdick walked a phone up. Burdick mimed "*Him.*" Littell grabbed the phone. The cord stretched taut.

Mr. Hoover said, "Be concise."

Littell cupped his free ear. The room noise half died.

"The preliminary stage of the investigation has been ineptly executed. That's all I'm certain of at this point."

"I'm not surprised and I'm not disappointed, and I'm thoroughly convinced that Oswald acted without assistance. Your job is to cull the names of potentially embarrassing witnesses who might contradict that thesis."

Littell said, "Yes, sir."

Burdick held up a clipboard. Note slips were clamped in. A witness log/clamped witness statements/driver's licenses attached.

The phone went dead. Burdick grabbed it. Littell grabbed the clipboard. It bulged. The clip wobbled.

He skimmed the slips.

Two-line statements. Confiscated DLs. Detainment insurance. Ambiguous data: 3/4/5/6 shots/1/2/3 directions.

The stockade fence. The book building. The triple underpass. Head-on shots. Missed shots. Shots from behind.

Littell checked DL pix.

Wit #6: Shots at Houston and Elm. Wit #9: Shots off the freeway. The calm woman: 2 shots/2 directions. Her stats: Arden Smith/West Mockingbird Lane.

The smoke was bad. Littell stepped back. The smoke made him sneeze. He bumped a desk. He dropped the log. He walked to the interview slots.

Burdick tailed him. The room noise doubled. Littell checked the slots. Shoddy work—no tape machines/no stenos.

He checked slot #1. A thin cop braced a thin kid. The kid laughed. What a gas. My dad voted for Nixon.

Littell checked slot #2. A fat cop braced a fat man.

The cop said, "Mr. Bowers, I'm not disputing what you told me."

Mr. Bowers wore a railroad cap. Mr. Bowers squirmed.

"For the tenth time then, so I can go home. I was up in the tower behind that fence on the knoll. I saw two cars cruising around there about . . . shit . . . a half hour before the shooting, and two men standing right at the edge of the fence, and then just as I heard the shots, I saw a flash of light from that very spot."

The cop doodled. Mr. Bowers tapped a cigarette. Littell studied him. Littell got queasy.

He didn't know the shooter plan. He *did* know credible wits. Bowers was intractably firm. Bowers was *good.*

Burdick tapped Littell. Littell swung around. Littell knocked him back. *"What?"*

Burdick stepped back. "Well, I was just thinking that DPD pulled these three guys, bums or something, out of a railroad car behind the fence, about a half hour after the shooting. We've got them in the tank."

Littell went more queasy.

Littell said, "Show me."

Burdick walked point. They passed the slots. They passed a coffee-break room. Hallways crossed. They veered left. They hit a mesh-front pen.

An intercom popped: "Agent Burdick. Front desk, please."

Burdick said, "I should catch that."

Littell nodded. Burdick fidgeted. Burdick took off from a crouch. Littell grabbed the mesh. The light was bad. Littell squinted hard.

He saw two bums. He saw Chuck Rogers.

Chuck was Pete's man. Wet arts/CIA. Chuck was tight with Guy B.

Rogers saw Littell. The bums ignored him. Rogers smiled. Littell touched his shield. Rogers mimed a rifle shot.

He moved his lips. He went "Pow!"

Littell backtracked.

He walked down the hall. He turned right. He hit a bisecting hall. He made the turn. He saw a side door.

He pushed it open. He saw fire steps and rungs. Across the hall: A men's room and a door marked "Jailer."

The men's room door opened. Mr. Bowers walked out. He stretched. He zipped his fly. He settled his nuts.

He saw Littell. He squinted. He keyed on his shield.

"FBI, right?"

"That's right."

"Well, I'm glad I ran into you, 'cause there's something I forgot to tell the other guy."

Littell smiled. "I'll pass it along."

Bowers scratched his neck. "Okay, then. You tell him I saw some cops rousting these hoboes out of a hay car, and one of them looked like one of the guys I saw by the fence."

Littell pulled his notebook.

He scribbled. He smeared some ink. His hand shook. The book shook.

Bowers said, "I sure feel sorry for Jackie."

Littell smiled. Bowers smiled. Bowers tipped his cap. He jiggled some coins. He ambled. He walked away sloooooow.

Littell watched his back.

Bowers ambled. Bowers turned right. Bowers hit the main hall. Littell flexed his hands. Littell caught his breath.

He worked the Jailer door. He jiggled the knob. He forced it.

The door popped. Littell stepped in.

A twelve-by-twelve space—dead empty. A desk/a chair/a key rack.

Paperwork—tacked to a corkboard:

Vagrant sheets—"Doyle"/"Paolino"/"Abrahams"—no mug shots attached.

Call it: Rogers packed fake ID. Rogers booked in with it.

One key on the rack—cell-size/thick brass.

Littell grabbed the sheets. Littell pocketed them. Littell grabbed the key. He gulped. He walked out brazen. He walked to the pen.

He unlocked the door. Rogers primed the bums. He pumped them up. He went "Ssshh now." He gave a pep talk.

We got ourselves a savior—just do what I say.

The bums huddled. The bums stepped out. The bums hugged the wall. Littell walked.

He hit the main hall. He faced the squadroom. He blocked the view. He signaled Rogers. He pointed. The fire door—go.

He heard footsteps. The bums squealed. The bums giggled loud. The fire door creaked. A bum yelled, "Hallelujah!" The fire door slammed.

Littell caught a breeze. His sweat froze. His pulse went haywire.

He walked to the squadroom. His legs fluttered and dipped. He grazed desks. He bumped walls. He bumped into cops.

The wit bench was smoked in. Twenty cigarettes plumed. Arden Smith was gone.

Littell looked around. Littell scanned desks. Littell saw the wit log.

He grabbed it. He checked statements and DLs. Arden Smith's package—gone.

He checked the slots. He checked the halls. He checked the main window.

There's Arden Smith. She's on the street. She's walking fast. She's walking *away*.

She crossed Houston. Cars swerved by her. She made Dealey Plaza.

Littell blinked.

He lost her. Jack's mourners shadowed her up.

3

Pete Bondurant

(Dallas, 11/22/63)

The bridal suite. The fuck pad supreme.

Gilt wallpaper. Cupids. Pink rugs and chairs. A fake-fur bedspread—baby-ass pink.

Pete watched Barb sleep.

Her legs slid. She kicked wide. She thrashed the sheets.

Barbara Jane Lindscott Jahelka Bondurant.

He got her back early. He sealed up the suite. He closed out the news. She'll wake up. She'll *get* the news. She'll *know*.

I fucked Jack in '62. It was lackluster and brief. You bugged some rooms. You got his voice. You taped it. The shakedown failed. Your pals regrouped. You killed Jack instead.

Pete moved his chair. Pete got fresh views. Barb tossed. Her hair swirled.

She didn't love Jack. She serviced Jack. She cosigned extortion. She wouldn't cosign death.

6:10 p.m.

Jack should be dead. Guy's boy ditto. Chuck Rogers had a plane stashed. The crew should be out.

Barb twitched. Pete fought a headache. Pete popped aspirin and scotch.

He got *bad* headaches—chronic—they started with the Jack squeeze. The squeeze failed. He stole some Mob heroin. A CIA man helped.

Kemper Cathcart Boyd.

They were *très* tight. They were mobbed up. They shared spit with

Sam G. They worked for Carlos M. They worked for Santo Trafficante. They all hated Commies. They all loved Cuba. They all hated the Beard.

Money and turf—dual agendas. Let's pluck the Beard. Let's repluck our casinos.

Santo and Sam played both ends. They sucked up to Castro. They bought "H" off Brother Raúl. Carlos stayed pure. Carlos did not fuck *la Causa.*

Pete and Boyd stole the dope. Sam and Santo nailed them. Pete got the word. They did biz with Fidel.

Carlos stayed neutral. Biz was biz. Outfit laws overruled causes.

They *all* hated Bobby. They *all* hated Jack. Jack fucked them at Pigs. Jack raided Cuban exile camps. Jack nuzzled the Beard.

Bobby deported Carlos. Bobby fucked with the Outfit *très* large. Carlos hated Jack and Bobby—*molto bravissimo.*

Ward Littell hated them. Ward smuggled Carlos back. Ward played factotum. Ward ran his deportation case.

Ward said, Let's clip Jack. Carlos liked it. Carlos talked to Santo and Sam.

They liked it.

Santo and Sam had plans. They said let's clip Pete and Boyd. We want our dope back. We want revenge.

Ward talked to Sam and Carlos. Ward pressed Pete's case. They quashed said clip plan.

The catch:

We let you live. You *owe* us. Now whack Jack the K.

Guy Banister was working up a hit plan. His plan resembled Littell's. Hit plans were running epidemic. Jack pissed off mucho hotheads. The cocksucker was doomed.

Guy had pull. Guy knew Carlos. Guy knew Cuban exiles. Guy knew fat cats with coin. Guy dipped a geek in sheep shit. Guy preempted Ward's plan.

He pitched it to Carlos. Carlos okayed it. Carlos scotched Ward's plan. Shit went sideways. Personnel shifted. Some Pete and Ward guys joined Guy's crew.

Glitches glitched—last-minute—Pete and Boyd unglitched them.

Santo and Sam hated Boyd. They reissued their death decree. Kemper Boyd—*mort sans doute.*

Barb stirred. Pete held his breath. The aspirin hit. His headache fizzled.

Santo and Sam let *him* live. Carlos liked him. He loved *la Causa.* The Boys had plans. He *might* fit in.

He worked for Howard Hughes—'52 to '60. He pimped for him. He scored his dope. He did his strongarm work.

Ward Littell lawyered for Hughes. Hughes wanted to buy up Las Vegas. Hughes craved the Vegas Strip. Hughes craved *all* the hotel-casinos.

Hughes had a buyout plan. Said plan would take years. The Boys had a plan too:

Let's sell Las Vegas. Let's bilk Howard Hughes. We'll keep our work crews. We'll skim Hughes blind. We'll *still* own Las Vegas.

Carlos owned Ward. Ward's job to be: Broker the deal and tailor it *our* way.

The Boys owned Pete. The Boys implied:

Go to Vegas. Work with Ward. Pre-pave the Hughes deal. You know muscle work. You know heroin. We might rescind our no-dope rule. We might let you push to the spooks.

We *might* not kill you. We *might* not kill your Twist queen.

Barb left her gowns out. Blue spangles and green. Two shows tonite. His wife and her ex-hubby's trio.

A sad room. Sad Barb. Let's send one up to Jack.

Hit news preceded the hit. Outfit guys talked. Outfit guys *knew*. Hesh Ryskind checked into the Adolphus. Hesh had cancer. Hesh came to gloat and die.

Hesh watched the motorcade. Hesh died at 1:00 p.m. Hesh kicked with Jack concurrent.

Pete touched the bed. Pink sheets met red hair—one loud color clash.

The doorbell chimed—the B-flat "Eyes of Texas." Barb slept through it. Pete walked over. Pete cracked the door.

Fuck—there's Guy Banister.

Guy popped sweat. Guy was sixty-plus. Guy had heart attacks.

Pete stepped outside. Pete shut the door. Guy waved a highball glass.

"Come on. I rented a room down the hall."

Pete followed him over. The floor rugs sent sparks up. Guy unlocked his door and bolted them in.

He grabbed a jug—Old Crow bond—Pete snatched it quick.

"Tell me they're both dead, and this isn't about some fuck-up."

Guy twirled his glass. "King John the First is dead, but my boy killed a cop and got arrested."

The floor dipped. Pete dug his legs in.

"The cop who was supposed to kill him?"

Guy eyeballed the jug. Pete tossed it back.

"That's right, Tippit. My boy pulled a piece and popped him out in Oak Cliff."

"Does *your boy* know your name?"

Guy uncorked the jug. "No, I worked him through a cutout."

Pete slapped the wall. Plaster chips flew. Guy spilled some booze.

"But your boy knows the cutout's name. The cutout knows *your* name, and your boy'll name names sooner or later. Is that a fucking accurate assessment?"

Guy poured a drink. His hand shook. Pete straddled a chair. His headache retorqued. He lit a cigarette. *His* hand shook.

"We have to kill him."

Guy blotted the spill. "Tippit had a backup man, but he wanted to go in alone. It was a two-man job, so we're paying the price now."

Pete squeezed the chairback. The slats shimmied. One slat sheared loose.

"Don't tell me what we should have done. Tell me how we get to your boy."

Guy sat on the bed. Guy stretched out comfy.

"I gave the job to Tippit's backup."

Pete said, "And?"

"And he's got access to the jail, and he's mean enough for the job, and he owes some casino markers, which means he's in hock to the Outfit."

Pete said, "There's more. You're trying to sell me a bill of goods."

"Well . . ."

"Well, shit, *what?*"

"Well, he's a tough nut, and he doesn't want to do it, and he's stuck on a liaison job with some Vegas cop."

Pete cracked his knuckles. "We'll convince him."

"I don't know. He's a tough nut."

Pete flipped his cigarette. It hit Guy clean. He yipped. He snuffed it out. He burned his pillow.

Pete coughed. "You're the first one Carlos will clip if your boy talks."

A TV kicked on—one room down. The walls leeched sound: "Nation mourns"/"valiant first lady."

Guy said, "I'm scared."

"That's your first fucking sensible comment."

"We got him, though. We made the world spin."

The old fuck *glowed.* Sweats and shitty grins.

"Tell me the rest of it."

"What about a toast to the fallen—"

"What about Rogers and the pro shooter?"

Guy coughed. "Okay, first things first. Mr. Hoover flew Littell in as soon as he heard, and I saw him over at DPD. The cops got Rogers on a sweep, but Littell let him out and misplaced the paperwork. He was carrying fake ID, so I think we're clear there."

Glitches/reglitches—

"The pro. Did he get out?"

"Heads up on that. He got down to McAllen and walked across the border. He left a message at my place in New Orleans, and I called him and got the all-clear."

"What about Rog—"

"He's at a motel in Fort Worth. Littell said the witnesses are confused and telling different stories, and Mr. Hoover's hell-bent to prove that it was all my boy. Littell said we've only got one guy to worry about."

Pete said, "Keep going. Don't make me work so hard."

"Okay, then. Littell said a railroad man put a half-ass ID on Rogers, so it's my considered opinion that we should clip him."

Pete shook his head. "It's too close to the hit. You want him to go back to work like nothing happened."

"Then you throw some fear into him."

"No. Let the backup do it. Have him pull a cop number."

That TV blared—"Nation grieves"/"sole killer."

Guy folded his arms. "There's one more thing."

"I'm listening."

"Okay, then. I talked to the pro. He thinks there's a chance that Jack Ruby put it together."

Ruby: Bagman/pimp/Littell's old snitch/strip-club entrepre—

"I had the crew at a safe house up in Oklahoma. Rogers called Ruby and arranged for some entertainment. The pro said he showed up with two girls and some flunky, and they saw the rifles out back and—wait now—don't get your tits in a twist—I told the backup to brace Ruby and see what he knows."

The room dipped. Crash dimensions. Pete rode out the drop.

Guy said, "We might have to clip them."

Pete said, "No."

Guy reglowed. Guy previewed Heart Attack 3.

"No? The big man says no? The big man says no, like he doesn't know the Boys are talking, and they're saying he's lost his taste for the Life?"

Pete stood up. Pete cracked his thumbs. Pete flexed his hands. Pete grabbed the chair slats. Pete pulled. Pete ripped the chair to sticks.

Guy pissed his britches. Guy fucking plotzed. The stain spread. His crotch seeped. He doused the sheets.

Pete walked out. The hall dipped. The walls balanced him. He walked back to his suite. He stopped ten feet short. He heard his TV.

He heard Barb sob. He heard Barb throw chairs at a wall.

4

(Dallas, 11/22/63)

A dog shit on the runway. A stripper dodged turds. Welcome to the Carousel Club.

Cops clapped. Cops whooped. Cops ruled the room. The club was closed to the public. The owner loved Jackie. The owner loved JFK.

Let's mourn. Let's ride out this tsuris. Let's show some respect.

You badged in. The owner loved cops. Your host—Jack Ruby.

Wayne walked in. Wayne dropped Maynard Moore's name. Ruby seated him. Dallas cops ran tall. Boot heels did it. Wayne was six-one. The cops dwarfed him.

A bandstand adjoined the runway. A sax and drum worked. Two strippers stripped. The blonde looked like Lynette. The brunette looked like Janice.

Moore was late. The club was loud. The combo played "Night Train." Wayne sipped 7-Up. The music fucked with him. The drum pops set up pix.

Pop—he caps Wendell Durfee. Pop—he plants a throwdown piece.

A stripper swayed by. She wore a pastie-patch. Her crotch stubble showed. A cop snapped her G-string. She swayed his way.

Ruby worked the room.

He dumped ashtrays. He tossed scraps. He lured his dog off the ramp. He poured drinks. He lit cigarettes. He laid out some grief.

A fuck killed his President. The fuck was a beatnik. His bookkeeper split. She blew the coop. She blew him off. She wouldn't blow his friends.

He owed the IRS. Arden said she'd help. Arden was skunk cooze. Arden lied and stole. Arden had a fake address. A beatnik shot his hero.

Maynard Moore walked in.

He whooped. He rebel-yelled. He sailed his hat. A stripper snagged it.

Moore walked up to Ruby. Ruby went oh shit. The dog jumped in. Moore grabbed him. Moore kissed him. Moore tweaked his tail.

Ruby yukked. Boychik—you slay me!

Moore dropped the dog. Moore manhandled Ruby. He shoved him. He flicked his mezuzah. He knocked off his hat.

Wayne watched. Moore *squeezed* Ruby.

He jerked his necktie. He snapped his suspenders. He jabbed at his chest. Ruby squirmed. Ruby bumped a rubber machine.

Moore dressed him down. Ruby pulled a handkerchief. Ruby pat-dried his head.

Wayne walked over. Wayne caught Moore in tight.

"Pete's in town. People ain't gonna like what you might know, so you may be owin' some favors."

Wayne coughed. Moore turned around. Ruby squeezed his mezuzah chain.

Moore smiled. "Wayne, this is Jack. Jack's a Yankee, but we like him anyway."

Moore had pressing shit in Plano. Wayne said okay. Fuck it. Let's stall— let's postpone Wendell D.

Traffic was dead. A breeze stirred. Moore drove his off-duty sled. A Chevy 409—lake pipes and slicks—Stemmons Freeway faaaast.

Wayne gripped the dash-bar. Moore sipped Everclear. The fumes stung bad.

The radio howled. A preacher proselytized:

John F-for-Fruitcake Kennedy loved Pope Pinko. He sold his soul to the Jewnited Nations. God bless Lee H-for-Hero Oswald.

Wayne doused the volume. Moore laughed.

"You got a low capacity for the truth, unlike your daddy."

Wayne cracked his wind wing. "Are all the DPD guys like you, or did they waive the IQ test in your case?"

Moore winked. "DPD runs to the right side of the street. We got some Klan and we got some John Birch. It's like that pamphlet your daddy puts out. 'Do you score red or red, white, and blue?' "

Wayne felt rain. "His pamphlets make money. And you won't see him wearing a sheet in Pigshit, Texas."

"You certainly won't, to his everlasting discredit."

The rain came. The rain went. Wayne fugued on out. The fumes tickled. The car droned. He rehashed recent shit.

West Vegas: Assault One/eight counts. A white man beats up colored whores.

He picked them up. He took them home. He beat them and took snapshots—and LVPD didn't care.

He cared. He told Wayne Senior. Wayne Senior pooh-poohed it.

Moore pulled off the freeway. Moore trawled side streets. He hit his brights. He scanned curb plates. He drove down a tract row.

He grazed curbs. He read mailbox names. He found *the* box. He pulled over and stopped.

Wayne squinted. Wayne saw the name: "Bowers."

Wayne stretched. Moore stretched. Moore grabbed a sandwich bag.

"This won't take no more than two minutes."

Wayne yawned. Moore got out. Wayne got out and leaned on the car.

The house was drab. The lawn was brown. The house had peeled paint and chipped stucco.

Moore walked to the porch. Moore rang the bell. A man opened up. Moore badged him. Moore shoved him inside. Moore kicked the door shut.

Wayne stretched some kinks out. Wayne dug on the car.

He kicked the slicks. He touched the pipes. He popped the hood. He sniffed the fuel valves. He nailed the smell. He broke down the oxide components.

You're a cop now. You're a good one. You're a chemist still.

Somebody screamed. Wayne slammed the hood. It muffled scream #2.

Dogs barked. Curtains jerked. Neighbors scoped the Bowers pad.

Moore walked out.

He grinned. He weaved a tad. He wiped blood off his shirt.

They drove back to Big D. Moore chewed Red Man. He tuned in Wolfman Jack. He mimicked his howl. He lip-synced R&B.

They hit Browntown. They found the guy's shack: Four walls—all plywood and glue.

Moore parked on the lawn. Moore grazed a boss Lincoln. The windows were down. The interior glowed.

Moore spat juice. Moore sprayed the seats good.

"You best believe they'll name a car after Kennedy. And every nigger in captivity'll rob and rape to get one."

Wayne walked up. Moore trailed back. The door stood open. Wayne looked in. Wayne saw a colored guy.

The guy crouched. The guy *worked.* The guy fucked with his TV set. He tapped the dials. He tweaked the cord. He raised static and snow.

Wayne knocked. Moore walked in. Moore scoped this shrine shelf:

A plug-in JFK. Bobby cutouts. A Martin Luther King doll.

The guy saw them. He stood up. He shivered. He double-clutched.

Wayne walked in. "Are you Mr. Jefferson?"

Moore sprayed juice. Moore doused a chair.

"He's the boy. Aka 'Jeff,' aka 'Jeffy,' you think I don't do my homework?"

Jeff said, "That's me. Yessir."

Wayne smiled. "You're in no trouble. We're looking for a friend of—"

"How come you people got all these President names? Half the boys I take down got names more distinguished than mine."

"Yessir, that's true, but I don't know what answer to tell you, so—"

"I popped a boy named Roosevelt D. McKinley, and he didn't even know where his mama stole them names from, which is one sorry-ass state of affairs."

Jeff shrugged. Moore mimicked him. He went slack. He bugged his eyes. He pulled a beavertail sap.

The TV sparked. A picture blipped. There's Lee H. Oswald.

Moore spat on the screen. "There's the boy you should name your pickaninnies after. He killed my friend J. D. Tippit, who was one dick-swingin' white man, and it offends me to be in the same room as you on the day he died."

Jeff shrugged. Jeff looked at Wayne. Moore twirled his sap. The TV popped off. Bum tubes crackled.

Jeff twitched. His knees shook. Wayne touched his shoulder. Moore mimicked him. Moore swished.

"You boys are *suuuch* the pair. You'll be holdin' hands any damn second."

That tore—

Wayne shoved Moore. Moore tripped. Moore knocked a lamp down. Jeff shook nelly-style. Wayne shoved him in the kitchen.

They fit tight. The sink cramped them. Wayne toed the door shut.

"Wendell Durfee's running. He always runs to Dallas, so why don't you tell me what you know about that."

"Sir, I don't—"

"Don't call me 'sir,' just tell me what you know."

"Sir, I mean mister, I don't know where Wendell's at. If I'm lyin', I'm flyin'."

"You're shucking me. Stop it, or I'll hand you up to that cracker."

"Mister, I ain't woofin' you. I don't know where Wendell's at."

The walls shook. Shit cracked one room over. Wayne made the sounds:

Sap shots. Hard steel meets plywood and glue.

Jeff shook. Jeff gulped. Jeff picked a hangnail.

Wayne said, "Let's try this. You work at Dr Pepper. You got paid today."

"That's right. If I'm lyin', I'm—"

"And you made your probation payment."

"You ain't woofin' I did."

"Now, you've got some money left. It's burning a hole in your pocket. Wendell's your gambling buddy. There's some kind of payday crap game that you can point me to."

Jeff sucked his hangnail. Jeff gullllped.

"Then how come I ain't at that game right now?"

"Because you lent Wendell most of your money."

Glass broke. Wayne made the sound: One sap shot/one TV screen fucked.

"Wendell Durfee. Give him up, or I tell Tex that you've been porking little white kids."

Jeff lit a cigarette. Jeff choked on it. Jeff coughed smoke out.

"Liddy Baines, she used to go with Wendell. She knowed I owed him money, an' she came by an' said he was lookin' to get down to Mexico. I gave her all but five dollars of my check."

Wood cracked. The walls shook. The floor shook.

"Address?"

"Seventy-first and Dunkirk. The little white house two up from the corner."

"What about the game?"

"Eighty-third and Clifford. The alley by the warehouse."

Wayne opened the door. Jeff stood behind him. Jeff got in a runner's crouch. Moore saw Wayne. Moore bowed. Moore winked.

The TV was dead. The shelf shrine was dust. The walls were pulp and spit.

It got real.

Moore had a throwdown piece. Moore had a pump. A coroner owed him. He'd fudge the wound text.

Wayne went dry. Wayne got pinpricks. Wayne's nuts shriveled up.

They drove. They went Darktown-deep. They went by Liddy Baines' shack. Nobody was home—Liddy, where you at?

They hit a pay phone. Moore called Dispatch. Moore got Liddy Baines' stats: No wants/no warrants/no vehicle extant.

They drove to 83rd and Clifford. They passed junkyards and dumps. Liquor stores and blood banks. Mohammed's Mosque #12.

They passed the alley. They caught a tease: Streetlights/faces/a blanket spread out.

A fat man rolled. A plump man slapped his forehead. A thin man scooped cash.

Moore stopped at 82nd. Moore grabbed his pump. Wayne pulled his piece. Moore popped in earplugs.

"If he's there, we'll arrest him. Then we'll take him out to the sticks and cap him."

Wayne tried to talk. His throat closed. He squeaked. Moore winked. Moore yukked haw-haw.

They walked over. They cleaved to shadows. They crouched. The air dried up. The ground dropped. Wayne lost his feet.

They hit the alley. Wayne heard jive talk. Wayne saw Wendell Durfee.

His legs went. He stumbled. He toed a beer can. The dice men perked up.

Say *what?*

Who *that?*

Mama, that *you?*

Moore aimed. Moore fired. Moore caught three men low. He sprayed their legs. He diced their blanket. He chopped their money up.

Muzzle boom—twelve-gauge roar—high decibels in tight.

It knocked Wayne flat. Wayne went deaf. Wayne went powder blind. Moore shot a trashcan. The sucker *flew.*

Wayne rubbed his eyes. Wayne got partial sight. Dice men screamed. Dice men scattered. Wendell Durfee ran.

Moore aimed high. Moore sprayed a wall. Pellets bounced and whizzed. They caught Durfee's hat. They sliced the band. They blew the feather up.

Durfee ran. Wayne ran.

He aimed his piece up and out. Durfee backward-aimed his. They fired. Blips lit the alley. Shots cut the walls.

Wayne *saw* it. Wayne *felt* it. Wayne didn't *hear* shit.

He fired. He missed. Durfee fired. Durfee missed. Barrel flames. Sound waves. No *real* sound worth shit.

They ran. They stopped. They fired. They sprinted full-out.

Wayne popped six shots—one full cylinder. Durfee popped eight shots—one full-load clip.

The flares stopped. No light. No directional signs—

Wayne stumbled.

He slid. He fell. He hit gravel. He ate alley grit. He smelled cordite. He licked cigar butts and dirt.

He rolled over. He saw roof lights. He saw cherry lights twirl. Two prowl cars—*behind* him—DPD Fords.

He caught some sounds. He stood up. He caught his breath. He walked back. His feet scraped. He heard it.

Moore stood there. Cops stood there. The dice men lay prone. They were cuffed/shackled/fucked.

Shredded pants. Pellet burns and gouges—cuts to white bone.

They thrashed. Wayne heard partial screams.

Moore walked over. Moore said something. Moore yelled.

Wayne caught "Bowers." His ears popped. He caught whole sounds.

Moore flashed his sandwich bag. Moore spread the flaps. Wayne saw blood and gristle. Wayne saw a man's thumb.

5

(Dallas, 11/23/63)

Window wreaths / flags / ledge displays. 8:00 a.m.—one day later—the Glenwood Apartments loves Jack.

Two floors. Twelve front windows. Flowers and JFK toys.

Littell leaned on his car. The facade expanded. He got the sun. He got Arden Smith's car. He got her U-Haul.

He borrowed a Bureau car. He ran Arden Smith. She came back clean. He got her vehicle stats. He nailed her Chevy.

She felt dirty. She saw the hit. She ran from the PD. That U-Haul said *RUNNER*.

She lived in 2-D. He'd checked the courtyard. Her windows faced in— no flags/no trinkets/no shrine.

He worked to midnight. He cleared an office space. Floor 3 was bedlam. Cops grilled Oswald. Camera crews roamed.

His bum ploy worked. Rogers walked. The bums escaped clean. He saw Guy B. He told him to brace Lee Bowers.

He read the wit statements. He read the DPD notes. They played ambiguous. Mr. Hoover would issue a mandate. Agents would secure it. Single-shooter evidence would cohere.

Lee Oswald was trouble. Guy said so. Guy called him "nuts."

Lee didn't shoot. The pro shooter did. Said pro shot from Lee's floor perch. Rogers shot from the fence.

Lee knew Guy's cutout. Cops and Feds worked him all night. He named no names. Guy said he knew why.

The kid craved attention. The kid was fucked-up. The kid craved the solo limelight.

Littell checked his watch—8:16 a.m.—sun and low clouds.

He counted flags. He counted wreaths. The Glenwood loved Jack. He knew why. He used to love Jack. He used to love Bobby.

He never met Jack. He met Bobby once.

He tried to join them. Kemper Boyd pushed his case. Bobby disdained his credentials. Boyd spread his loyalty. Boyd worked for Jack and Bobby. Boyd worked for the CIA.

Boyd got Littell a job. Ward, meet Carlos Marcello.

Carlos hated Jack and Bobby. Jack and Bobby spurned Littell. He built his own hate. He fine-tuned the aesthetic.

He hated Jack. He *knew* Jack. Scrutiny undermined image. Jack was glib. Jack had pizzazz. Jack had no rectitude.

Bobby defined rectitude. Bobby *lived* rectitude. Bobby punished bad men. He hated Bobby now. Bobby dismissed him. Bobby spurned his respect.

Mr. Hoover bugged Mob hangouts. Mr. Hoover picked up hints. He smelled the hit. He never told Jack. He never told Bobby.

Mr. Hoover knew Littell. Mr. Hoover dissected his hatred. Mr. Hoover urged him to hurt Bobby.

Littell had evidence. It indicted Joe Kennedy for long-term Mob collusion. He met Bobby—for one half hour—just five days back.

He stopped by his office. He played him a tape. The tape nailed Joe Kennedy. Bobby was smart. Bobby might link tape to hit. Bobby might gauge the tape as a threat.

Do not talk Mob Hit. Do not stain the name Kennedy. Do not stain sainted Jack. Feel complicitous. Feel guilty. Feel baaaad.

Your Mob Crusade killed your brother. We killed Jack to fuck you.

Littell watched a newscast. Late last night—Air Force One hits D.C. Bobby walks out. Bobby walks calm. Bobby consoles Jackie.

Littell killed Kemper Boyd. Carlos ordered it. Littell shot Boyd on Thursday. It hurt. He owed the Boys. It cancelled his debt.

He saw Bobby with Jackie. It hurt more than Boyd.

Arden Smith walked out.

She walked out fast. She lugged a satchel. She carried skirts and sheets. Littell walked over. Arden Smith looked up. Littell flashed his ID.

"Yes?"

"Dealey Plaza, remember? You witnessed the shooting."

She leaned on the U-Haul. She dropped the satchel. She weighed down the skirts.

"I watched you at the squadroom. You measured your chances and made your move, and I have to say I'm impressed. But you'll have to explain why you—"

"My information was redundant. Five or six people heard what I did, and I wanted to put the whole thing behind me."

Littell leaned on the car. "And now you're moving."

"Just temporarily."

"Are you leaving Dallas?"

"Yes, but that has nothing to do—"

"I'm sure it has nothing to do with what you saw in the motorcade, and all I'm interested in is why you stole your preliminary statement and driver's license from the witness log and left without permission."

She brushed her hair back. "Look, Mr.—"

"Littell."

"Mr. Littell, I tried to do my citizen's duty. I went to the police department and tried to leave an anonymous statement, but an officer detained me. Really, I'd had a shock, and I just wanted to go home and start packing."

Her voice worked. It was firm and southern. It was educated.

Littell smiled. "Can we go inside? I'm uncomfortable talking out here."

"All right, but you'll have to forgive my apartment."

Littell smiled. She smiled. She walked ahead. Kids ran by. They shot toy guns. A boy yelled, "Don't shoot me, Lee!"

The door was open. The front room was chaos. The front room was packed and dollied.

She shut the door. She squared off chairs. She grabbed a coffee cup. They sat down. She lit a cigarette. She balanced the cup.

Littell pulled his chair back. Smoke bothered him. He pulled his notebook. He tapped his pen.

"What did you think of John Kennedy?"

"That's an odd question."

"I'm just curious. You don't seem like someone who's easily charmed, and I can't picture you standing around to watch a man drive by in a car."

She crossed her legs. "Mr. Littell, you don't know me. I think your question says more about you and Mr. Kennedy than you might be willing to admit."

Littell smiled. "Where are you from?"

"Decatur, Georgia."

"Where are you moving to?"

"I thought I'd try Atlanta."

"Your age?"

"You know my age, because you checked me out before you came here."

Littell smiled. She smiled. She dropped ash in her cup.

"I thought FBI men worked in pairs."

"We're short-handed. We weren't planning on an assassination this weekend."

"Where's your gun? All the men in that office had revolvers."

He squeezed his pen. "You saw my identification."

"Yes, but you're taking too much guff from me. Something isn't quite right here."

The pen snapped. Ink dripped. Littell wiped his hands on his coat.

"You're a pro. I knew it yesterday, and you just pushed too hard and confirmed it. You're going to have to convince me—"

The phone rang. She stared at him. The phone rang three times. She got up. She walked to the bedroom. She shut the door.

Littell wiped his hands. Littell smeared his trousers and coat. He looked around. He broke down the room. He quadrant-scanned.

There—

A chest on a dolly. Four drawers all packed.

He got up. He checked the drawers. He brushed socks and underwear. He brushed a slick surface—card-size plastic—he pulled it out.

There—

A Mississippi driver's license—for Arden Elaine *Coates*.

A P.O. box address. Date of birth: 4/15/27. Her *Texas* DL listed 4/15/26.

He put it back. He shut the drawers. He sat down fast. He crossed his legs. He doodled. He made mock notes.

Arden Smith walked out. Arden Smith smiled and *posed*.

Littell coughed. "Why did you watch the motorcade from Dealey Plaza?"

"I heard you had the best view there."

"That's not quite true."

"I'm just saying what I heard."

"Who told you?"

She blinked. "I wasn't told. I read it in the paper when they announced the route."

"When was that?"

"I don't know. A month ago, maybe."

Littell shook his head. "That isn't true. They announced the route ten days ago."

She shrugged. "I'm bad at dates."

"No, you're not. You're good at them, just like you're good at every-thing you try."

"You don't know that. You don't know *me*."

Littell stared at her. She popped goose bumps.

"You're scared, and you're running."

"*You're* scared, and this isn't a real FBI roust."

He popped goose bumps. "Where do you work?"

"I'm a freelance bookkeeper."

"That's not what I asked you."

"I structure deals to get businessmen out of trouble with the IRS."

"I asked, '*Where do you work?*' "

Her hands jumped. "I work at a place called the Carousel Club."

His hands jumped. The Carousel/Jack Ruby/Mob guy/bent cops.

He looked at her. She looked at him. Their brainwaves crossed.

6

(Dallas, 11/23/63)

S hit security. Fucked-up / negligent / weak.

Pete toured the PD. Guy scored him a pass. He didn't need it. Some geek sold dupes. Said geek sold weed and pussy pix.

The ground doors stood open. Geeks hobnobbed. Door guards posed for pix. Camera cords snaked up the sidewalk. News vans jammed up the street.

Reporters roamed. Let's bug the DA. Let's bug the cops. *Lots* of cops—Feds/DPD/Sheriff's—all motormouthed.

Oswald's pink. Oswald's Red. Oswald loves Fidel. He loves folk music. He loves dark trim. He loves Martin Lucifer Coon. We know it's him. We got his gun. He did it alone. I think he's queer. He can't piss with men in the room.

Pete roamed. Pete checked hall routes. Pete sketched floor plans. He nursed a headache—a looong one—the fucker had legs.

Barb KNEW.

She said, "You killed him. You and Ward and those Outfit guys you work for."

He lied. He bombed. Barb looked through him.

She said, "Let's leave Dallas." He said, "No." She split to her gig.

He walked to the club. Biz was bad. Barb sang to three drag queens. She looked straight through him. He walked back alone.

He slept alone. Barb slept in the john.

Pete roamed. Pete passed Homicide. Pete stopped at room 317. Geeks cruised for looks. Geeks framed the door. A cop cracked it wide and obliged.

There's Oswald. He looks beat-on. He's cuffed to a chair.

The crowd closed in. The cop shut the door. Talk fired up:

I knew J.D. J.D. was *Klan*. J.D. was *not*. They got to move him soon. They sure will—to the County Jail.

Pete roamed. Pete dodged geeks with carts. Geeks sold poorboys. Geeks snarfed them. Geeks slurped ketchup.

Pete sketched hall routes. Pete took notes.

One bunco pen. One holding tank adjacent. Basement cells. A press room adjacent. Briefings/newsmen/camera crews.

Pete roamed. Pete saw Jack Ruby. Jack's hawking pens shaped like dicks.

He saw Pete. He seized up. He freaked. He dropped his dick pens. He bent loooow and scooped up.

His pants ripped. Dig those plaid BVDs.

Maynard Moore rubbed him wrong.

His bad breath. His bad teeth. His Klan repartee.

They met at a parking lot. They sat in Guy's car. They faced a nigger church and a blood bank. Moore brought a six-pack. Moore sucked one down. Moore tossed the can out.

Pete said, "Did you brace Ruby?"

Moore said, "Yeah, I did. And I think he knows."

Pete slid his seat back. Moore raised his knees.

"Whoa, now. You're crowdin' me."

Guy dumped his ashtray. "Let's have the details. You can't shut Jack up once he starts talking."

Moore cracked beer #2. "Well, everybody—the crew, I mean—is up at Jack Zangetty's motel in Altus, Oklahoma, where men are men and cows are scared."

Pete cracked his knuckles. "Cut the travelogue."

Moore belched. "Schlitz, breakfast of champions."

Guy said, "Maynard, goddamnit."

Moore giggled. "Okay, so Jack R. gets a call from his old friend Jack Z. It seems that the pilot guy and the French guy want some cooze, so Jack R. says he'll bring some up."

The pilot: Chuck Rogers. The French guy: the pro. Let's observe the no-names policy.

Pete said, "Keep going."

Moore said, "Okay, so Ruby goes up there with his buddy Hank Killiam and these girls Betty McDonald and Arden something. Betty agrees to put out, but Arden don't, which pisses off the French guy something fierce. He slaps her, she burns him with a hot plate, then hightails. Now, Ruby don't know where Arden lives, and he thinks she's got a string of aliases. And the worst part is that everybody saw the rifles and targets, and they might've seen a map of Dealey Plaza layin' around."

Guy smiled. Guy made the finger-throat sign. Pete shook his head. Pete flashed *waaaay* back.

A bomb hits. Flames whoosh. A woman's hair ignites.

Moore belched. "Schlitz, Milwaukee's finest beer."

Pete said, "You're going to clip Oswald."

Moore gagged. Moore sprayed beer suds.

"Uuuh-*uuuuh*. Not this boy. That's a kamikaze mission that you ain't sendin' me on, not when I got an extradition job and a candy-ass partner who won't pull his weight."

Guy dipped his seat. Guy pushed Moore back.

"You and Tippit fucked up. You owe that marker, so you have to pay it off."

Moore cracked beer #3. "Uuuh-*uuuuh*. I'm not flushin' my life down the shitter 'cause I owe some *eye*-talians a few dollars that they won't even miss."

Pete smiled. "It's all right, Maynard. You just find out when they're moving him. We'll do the rest."

Moore burped. "I'll do that. That's a job that won't interfere with the other affairs I got goin'."

Pete reached back. Pete popped the rear hatch. Moore climbed out. Moore stretched. Moore waved bye-bye.

Guy said, "Peckerwood trash."

Moore shagged his 409. Moore laid rubber large.

Pete said, "I'll kill him."

Betty McDonald lived in Oak Cliff—Shitsville, U.S.A.

Pete called DPD. Pete played cop. Pete got her rap sheet: Four prosty beefs/one hot-check caper/one dope bounce.

He tapped out on "Arden." He had no last name.

He went by the Moonbeam Lounge. Carlos owned points. Joe Campisi ran the on-site handbook.

Joe owned the DPD. Cops placed bets. Cops lost. Cops made Joe's collections. Joe shylocked large—vig plus 20%.

Pete schmoozed with Joe. Pete borrowed ten cold. Pete tagged it a margin risk. Nobody said clip them. Nobody said scare them off. Nobody said shit. Guy wasn't Outfit. Guy's wishes meant shit.

Joe supplied a calzone. Pete ate on the freeway. The cheese fucked up his teeth.

He got off. He toured Oak Cliff. He found the address: A shotgun shack/dingy/three small rooms tops.

He parked. He dropped five G's in the calzone box. He schlepped it on up. He knocked on the door. He waited. He checked for eyewits.

Nobody home—zero eyewits.

He got out his comb. He flexed the tines. He picked the lock clean. He walked in and closed the door slow.

The front room smelled—maryjane and cabbage—window light squared him away.

Front room/kitchen/bedroom. Three rooms in a row.

He walked to the kitchen. He opened the fridge. A cat rubbed his legs. He tossed him some fish. The cat scarfed it up. Pete scarfed some Cheez Whiz.

He toured the pad. The cat followed him. He paced the front room. He pulled the drapes. He pulled up a chair and sat by the door.

The cat hopped in his lap. The cat clawed the calzone box. The room was cold. The chair was soft. The walls torqued him back.

Memory Lane. L.A.—12/14/49.

He's a cop. He breaks County strikes. He works *goooood* sidelines. He pulls shakedowns. He extorts queers. He raids the Swish Alps.

He's a card-game guard. He's a scrape procurer. He's Quebecois French. He fought the war. He got green-card Americanized.

Late '48—his brother Frank hits L.A.

Frank was a doctor. Frank had bad habits. Frank made bad friends. Frank whored. Frank gambled. Frank lost money.

Frank did scrapes. Frank scraped Rita Hayworth. Frank was Abortionist to the Stars. Frank played cards. Frank lost money. Frank dug Mickey Cohen's regular game.

Frank partied with scrape folks. Frank met Ruth Mildred Cressmeyer. Ruth did scrapes. Ruth loved her son Huey. Huey did heists.

Huey robbed Mickey's game. Huey's face mask slipped. The players ID'd him. Pete had the flu. Pete took the night off. Mickey told Pete to kill Huey.

Huey laid low. Pete found his pad: An ex-brothel in El Segundo.

Pete torched the pad. Pete stood in the backyard. Pete watched the house flames. Four shapes ran out. Pete shot them. Pete let them scream and burn.

It was dark. Their hair plumed. Smoke blitzed their faces. The papers played it up—FOUR DEAD IN BEACH TORCH—the papers ID'd the vics:

Ruth. Huey. Huey's girlfriend.

And:

One Canuck doctor—François Bondurant.

Someone called their dad. Someone snitched Pete off. His dad called him. His dad begged: Say NO. Say it wasn't YOU.

Pete stammered. Pete tried. Pete failed. His parents grieved. His parents sucked tailpipe fumes. His parents decomped in their car.

The cat fell asleep. Pete stroked him. Time schizzed. He dug on the dark.

He dozed. He stirred. He heard something. The door opened. Light shot straight in.

Pete jumped up. The cat tumbled. The calzone box flew.

There's Betty Mac.

She's got blond hair. She's got curves. She's got harlequin shades.

She saw Pete. She yelled. Pete grabbed her. Pete kicked the door shut. She scratched. She yelled. She clawed his neck. He covered her mouth. She drew her lips back. She bit him.

He stumbled. He kicked the calzone box. He tripped a wall switch. A light went on. The cash fell out.

Betty looked down. Betty saw the money. Pete let his hand go. Pete rubbed his bite wound.

"There, Jesus Christ. Just get out before someone hurts you."

She eased up. He eased up. She turned around. She saw his face.

Pete hit the wall switch. The room light died. They stood close. They caught their breath. They leaned on the door.

Pete said, "Arden?"

Betty coughed—a smoker's hack—Pete smelled her last reefer.

"I'm not going to hurt her. Come on, you know what we've got—"

She touched his lips. "Don't say it. Don't put a name—"

"Then tell me where—"

"Arden Burke. I think she's at the Glenwood Apartments."

Pete brushed by her. Her hair caught his face. Her perfume stuck to his clothes. He got outside. His hand throbbed. The sun killed his eyes.

Traffic was bad. Pete knew why.

Dealey Plaza was close. Let's take the kids. Let's dig on history and hot dogs.

He split Oak Cliff. He found Arden's building. It ran forty units plus. He parked outside. He checked access routes. The courtyard ruled B&Es out.

He checked the mail slots—no Arden *Burke* listed—Arden *Smith* in 2-D.

Pete toured the courtyard. Pete scanned doorplates: 2-A/B/C—

Stop right—

He made the suit. He made the build. He made the thin hair. He stepped back. He crouched. He *looked.*

Right there—

Ward Littell and a tall woman. Talking close and closing out the world.

DOCUMENT INSERT: 11/23/63. Verbatim FBI telephone call transcript. Marked: "Recorded at the Director's Request"/"Classified Confidential 1-A: Director's Eyes Only." Speaking: Director Hoover, Ward J. Littell.

   JEH: Mr. Littell?

   WJL: Good afternoon, Sir. How are you?

   JEH: Forgo the amenities and tell me about Dallas. The metaphysical dimensions of this alleged tragedy do not interest me. Get to the point.

   WJL: I would call things encouraging, Sir. There has been a minimum of talk about a conspiracy, and a very strong consensus seems to have settled in, despite some ambiguous statements from the witnesses. I've spent a good deal of time at the PD, and I've been told that President Johnson has called both Chief Curry and the DA personally, and has expressed his wish that the consensus be confirmed.

   JEH: Lyndon Johnson is a blunt and persuasive man, and he speaks a language those cowpokes understand. Now, continuing with the witnesses.

   WJL: I would say that the contradictory ones could be intimidated, discredited and successfully debriefed.

   JEH: You've read the witness logs, observed the interviews and have been through the inevitable glut of lunatic phone tips. Is that correct?

   WJL: Yes, Sir. The phone tips were especially fanciful and vindictive. John Kennedy had engendered a good deal of resentment in Dallas.

   JEH: Yes, and entirely justified. Continuing with the witnesses. Have you conducted any interviews yourself?

   WJL: No, Sir.

   JEH: You've turned up no witnesses with especially provocative stories?

   WJL: No, Sir. What we have is an alternative consensus pertaining to the number of shots and their trajectories. It's a confusing text, Sir. I don't think it will stand up to the official version.

   JEH: How would you rate the investigation to date?

   WJL: As incompetent.

JEH: And how would you define it?

WJL: As chaotic.

JEH: How would you assess the efforts to protect Mr. Oswald?

WJL: As shoddy.

JEH: Does that disturb you?

WJL: No.

JEH: The Attorney General has requested periodic updates. What do you suggest that I tell him?

WJL: That a fatuous young psychopath killed his brother, and that he acted alone.

JEH: The Dark Prince is no cretin. He must suspect the factions that most insiders would.

WJL: Yes, Sir. And I'm sure he feels complicitous.

JEH: I hear an unseemly tug of compassion in your voice, Mr. Littell. I will not comment on your protractedly complex relationship with Robert F. Kennedy.

WJL: Yes, Sir.

JEH: I cannot help but think of your blowhard client, James Riddle Hoffa. The Prince is his bête noire.

WJL: Yes, Sir.

JEH: I'm sure Mr. Hoffa would like to know what the Prince really thinks of this gaudy homicide.

WJL: I would like to know myself, Sir.

JEH: I cannot help but think of your brutish client, Carlos Marcello. I suspect that he would enjoy access to Bobby's troubled thoughts.

WJL: Yes, Sir.

JEH: It would be nice to have a source close to the Prince.

WJL: I'll see what I can do.

JEH: Mr. Hoffa gloats in an unseemly manner. He told the New York Times, quote, Bobby Kennedy is just another lawyer now, unquote. It's a felicitous sentiment, but I think there are those in the Italian aggregation who would appreciate more discretion on Mr. Hoffa's part.

WJL: I'll advise him to shut his mouth, Sir.

JEH: On a related topic. Did you know that the Bureau has a file on Jefferson Davis Tippit?

WJL: No, Sir.

JEH: The man belonged to the Ku Klux Klan, National States' Rights Party, National Renaissance Party and a dubious new splinter group called the Thunderbolt Legion. He was a close associate of a Dallas PD officer named Maynard Delbert Moore, a man of similar ideological beliefs and a reportedly puerile demeanor.

WJL: Did you get your information from a DPD source, Sir?

JEH: No. I have a correspondent in Nevada. He's a conservative pamphleteer and mail-order solicitor with very deep and diverse connections on the right flank.

WJL: A Mormon, Sir?

JEH: Yes. All the Nevadan führer manqués are Mormons, and this man is arguably the most gifted.

WJL: He sounds interesting, Sir.

JEH: You're leading me, Mr. Littell. I know full well that Howard Hughes wets his pants for Mormons and has two greedy eyes on Las Vegas. I'll always share a discreet amount of information with you, if you broach the request in a manner that does not insult my intelligence.

WJL: I'm sorry, Sir. You understood my design, and the man does sound interesting.

JEH: He's quite useful and diversified. For example, he runs a hate-tract press covertly. He's planted a number of his subscribers as informants in Klan groups that the Bureau has targeted for mail-fraud indictments. He helps eliminate his hate-mail competition in that manner.

WJL: And he knew the late Officer Tippit.

JEH: Knew or knew of. Judged or did not judge as ideologically unsound and outré. I'm always amusingly surprised by who knows who in which overall contexts. For example, the Dallas SAC told me that a former Bureau man named Guy Williams Banister is in town this weekend. Another agent told me, independently, that he's seen your friend Pierre Bondurant. Imaginative people might point to this confluence and try to link men like that to your mutual chum Carlos Marcello and his hatred of the Royal Family, but I am not disposed to such flights of fancy.

WJL: Yes, Sir.

JEH: Your tone tells me that you wish to ask a favor. For Mr. Hughes, perhaps?

WJL: Yes, Sir. I'd like to see the main Bureau file on the Las Vegas hotel-casino owners, along with the files on the Nevada Gaming Commission, Gaming Control Board, and the Clark County Liquor Board.

JEH: The answer is yes. Quid pro quo?

WJL: Certainly, Sir.

JEH: I would like to forestall potential talk on Mr. Tippit. If the Dallas Office has a separate file on him, I would like it to disappear before my less trusted colleagues get an urge to take the information public.

WJL: I'll take care of it tonight, Sir.

JEH: Do you think the single-gunman consensus will hold?

WJL: I'll do everything I can to insure it.

JEH: Good day, Mr. Littell.

WJL: Good day, Sir.

7

(Dallas, 11/23/63)

Glut. Waste. Bullshit.

The hotel copped pleas. The hotel blamed Lee Oswald.

The joint bulged—capacity-plus—newsmen shared rooms. They hogged the phone lines. They sapped the hot water. They swamped the room-service crew.

The hotel copped pleas. The hotel blamed Lee Oswald.

Our guests mourn. Our guests weep. Our guests watch TV. They stay in. They call home. They hash out The Show.

Wayne paced his suite. Wayne nursed an earache—that muzzle boom stuck.

Room service called. They said we're sorry—we're running late. Maynard Moore *didn't* call. Durfee escaped. Moore let it ride.

Moore didn't issue warrants. Moore didn't issue holds. Moore wrote up the crap-game snafu. One guy lost a kneecap. One guy lost two pints of blood. One guy lost a toe.

Mr. Bowers lost a thumb. Wayne nursed the picture—all-nite reruns.

He tossed all night. He watched TV. He made phone calls. He called the Border Patrol. He issued crossing holds. Four units grabbed look-alikes and called him.

Wendell Durfee had knife scars—too fucking bad—the look-alikes had none.

He called Lynette. He called Wayne Senior. Lynette mourned JFK. Lynette said trite shit. Wayne Senior cracked jokes.

Jack's last word was "pussy." Jack groped a nurse and a nun.

Janice came on. Janice extolled Jack's style. Janice mourned Jack's hair. Wayne laughed. Wayne Senior was bald. Janice Tedrow—touché!

Room service called. They said we're sorry. We know your supper's late.

Wayne watched TV. Wayne goosed the sound. Wayne caught a press gig.

Newsmen lobbed questions. One cop went wild. Oswald was a "lethal loner!" Wayne saw Jack Ruby. He carried his dog. He passed out dick pens and French ticklers.

The cop calmed down. He said we'll move Oswald tomorrow—late morning looks good.

The phone rang. Wayne killed the sound.

He picked up. "Who's this?"

"It's Buddy Fritsch, and it took me all day to get a call in to you."

"Sorry, Lieutenant. Things are a bit crazy here."

"So I gathered. I also gathered that you had a run-in with Wendell Durfee, and you let him get away."

Wayne made fists. "Who told you?"

"The Border Patrol. They were checking on your fugitive warrant."

"Do you want to hear my version?"

"I don't want to hear excuses. I don't want to know why you're enjoying your luxury hotel suite when you should be out shaking the trees."

Wayne kicked a footrest. It hit the TV.

"Do you know how *big* the border is? Do you know how many crossing posts there are?"

Fritsch coughed. "I know you're sitting on your keester waiting for callbacks that won't come if that nigger went to ground in Dallas, and for all I know you're living it up with that six thousand dollars the casino boys gave you, without doing the job that they paid you for."

Wayne kicked a rug. "I didn't ask for that money."

"No, you sure didn't. And you didn't refuse it, either, 'cause you're the type of boy who likes to have things both ways, so don't—"

"Lieutenant—"

"Don't interrupt me until you outrank me, and let me tell you this now. You can go either way in the Department. There's boys who say Wayne Junior's a white man, and there's boys who say he's a weak sister. Now, if you take care of this, you'll shut the mouths on those latter boys and make everyone *real* proud of you."

His eyes teared up. "Lieutenant . . ."

"That's better. That's the Wayne Junior I like to hear."

Wayne wiped his eyes. "He's down at the border. All my instincts tell me that."

Fritsch laughed. "I think your instincts are telling you lots of things, so I'll tell you this. That file I gave you was Sheriff's, so you see if DPD has a file. That nigger's got to know some other niggers in Dallas, or my name isn't Byron B. Fritsch."

Wayne grabbed his holster. His blocked ear popped.

"I'll give it my best."

"*No.* You find him and kill him."

A door guard let him in. Some Shriners tagged along. The stairs were jammed. The halls were crammed. The lifts were sardine-packed.

People bumped. People chomped hot dogs. People spilled coffee and Cokes. The Shriners pushed through. They wore funny hats. They waved pens and autograph books.

Wayne followed them. They plowed camera guys. They pushed their way upstairs.

They made floor 3. They made the squadroom. It was *double*-packed.

Cops. Newsmen. Misdemeanants cuffed to chairs. Pinned-out ID: shields/stars/press cards.

Wayne pinned his badge on. The noise hurt. His blocked ear repopped. He looked around. He saw the squad bay. He saw cubicles and office doors.

Burglary/Bunco. Auto Theft/Forgery. Homicide/Arson/Theft.

He walked over. He tripped on a wino. A newsman laughed. The wino shook his cuff chain. The wino soliloquized.

Jackie needs the big *braciole*. Widows crave it. *Playboy* magazine says so.

Wayne hit a side hall. Wayne read door plates. Wayne saw Maynard Moore. Moore missed him. Moore stood in a storeroom. Moore cranked a mimeo press.

Wayne ducked by. Wayne passed a break room. Wayne heard a TV blare. A cop watched a press-room feed—live from downstairs.

Wayne checked doorways. Jack Ruby brushed by—leeched to a *very* big cat. He hung on him. He bugged him. He kvetched:

"Pete, Pete, *pleeease.*"

Wayne veered by a fish tank. Fish howled within. A perv stuck his dick through the mesh. He stroked it. He wiggled it. He sang "Some Enchanted Evening."

Wayne doubled back. Wayne found the file room. A stand-up space with twelve drawers—two marked "KAs."

He shut the door. He popped the "A to L" drawer. He found a blue sheet:

Durfee, Wendell (NMI).

He skimmed it. He got repeat shit and one new KA:

Rochelle Marie Freelon—DOB 10/3/39. Two kids by Whipout Wendell. 8819 Harvey Street/Dallas.

Two file notes:

12/8/56: Rochelle harbors Wendell/the Sheriff wants him/he's got nine bench warrants due. 7/5/62: Rochelle violates *her* parole.

She leaves Texas. She drives to Vegas. She visits Wistful Wendell D. No vehicle stats/recent contact/two cubs by Wendell D.

Wayne copied the data. Wayne replaced the file. Wayne drawered loose sheets up. He walked out. He cruised hallways. He passed the break room.

The TV snagged him. He saw *something weird.* He stopped. He leaned in. He looked.

There's a fat man. He's facing a mike. One hand's in a splint. *One* hand—tight gauze—no *thumb.*

A band ID'd him: "Witness Lee Bowers."

Bowers talked. Bowers' voice broke.

"I was in the tower right before he was shot . . . and . . . well . . . I sure didn't see anything."

Bowers blipped off. A cartoon ad blipped on. Bucky Beaver yap-yap-yapped. The fuck hawked Ipana toothpaste.

Wayne went cold—Popsicle chills—ice down his shorts.

A cop said, "You okay, hoss? You look a little green at the gills."

Wayne borrowed a DPD car. Wayne went out alone.

He got directions. Harvey Street was Darktown. Cops called it the Congo and Coonecticut.

Bowers and Moore—reprise that—do it very slooow.

Wayne tried—it was easy—it was shortbread cake.

Moore was crazy. Moore was bent. Moore drank jar brew. He might push uppers. He might book bets. Bowers might be bent too. They fell out. Moore got pissed. Moore cut hisself a thumb.

Wayne hit Darktown. Wayne found Harvey Street. It was the shits—shacks and hen coops—connected dirt yards.

8819: Dead still and dark.

He parked out front. He hit his brights. He nailed the one window: No window shades/no furniture/no drapes.

Wayne got out. Wayne grabbed a flashlight. Wayne circled the shack. He cut through the backyard. He bumped furniture.

Big piles—yard-sale dimensions. Sofas and chairs—all cheap stuff.

He strafed it. His light roused a hen. She fluffed full. She made claws. She squawked.

Wayne kicked a cushion. A light hit *him*. A man laughed.

"It's my property now. I got a receipt that says so."

Wayne covered his eyes. "Did Wendell Durfee sell it to you?"

"That's right. Him and Rochelle."

"Did he say where they were going?"

The man coughed. "Out of your redneck jurisdiction."

Wayne walked up. The man was fat and high yellow. He twirled his flashlight. The beam jumped.

Wayne said, "I'm not DPD."

The man tapped his badge. "You're that Vegas guy looking for Wendell."

Wayne smiled. Wayne unpinned his coat. Wayne repinned his belt. The man flipped a porch switch. The yard lit up. A pit bull materialized.

Brindle flecks and muscle. Jaw power for two.

Wayne said, "Nice dog."

The man said, "He liked Wendell, so I liked him too."

Wayne walked up. The pit licked his hand. Wayne scratched his ears.

The man said, "I don't always go by that rule, though."

The pit made a fuss. The pit reared and batted his paws.

"Because I'm a policeman?"

"Because Wendell told me how your town works."

"Wendell tried to shoot me, Mr. . . ."

"It's Willis Beaudine, and Wendell tried to shoot you because you tried to shoot him. Now, tell me that Casino Council didn't give you some recreation money when they put that bounty on Wendell."

Wayne sat on a porch step. The pit nuzzled him.

Beaudine said, "Dogs can be fooled, just like anyone else."

"You're saying Wendell and Rochelle made a run for Mexico."

Beaudine smiled. "Them and their kids. You want my guess? They're decked out in sombreros and having a ball this very second."

Wayne shook his head. "It's bad for coloreds down there. The Mexicans hate them like some people in Vegas do."

Beaudine shook his head. "Like most or all, you mean. Like that dealer guy that Wendell cut. The same guy who won't let coloreds piss in his washroom, the same guy who beat up an old woman for selling *Watchtowers* out of his parking lot."

Wayne looked around. The yard furniture trapped dirt. The yard furniture stunk.

Spilled food. Liquor. Dog fumes. Chipped wood and stuffing exposed.

Wayne stretched. His blocked ear popped. He got This Craaazy Idea.

"Can you place a long-distance call for me?"

Beaudine hiked his belt. "Sure . . . I guess I could."

"The Border Patrol station at Laredo. Make it person-to-person. Ask for the watch commander."

Beaudine hiked his belt. Wayne smiled. Beaudine *snapped* his belt—hard.

Craaazy—

Beaudine walked inside. Beaudine hit some lights. Beaudine dialed a phone. Wayne nuzzled the pit. The pit kissed him. The pit swiped his tongue.

Beaudine pulled the phone out. The cord twanged. Wayne grabbed the receiver.

"Captain?"

"Yes. Who's this?"

"Sergeant Tedrow, Las Vegas PD."

"Oh, shit. I was hoping you'd call when we had some good news."

"Is there *bad* news?"

"Yes. Your fugitive, a woman, and two children tried to cross at McAllen an hour ago, but were turned back. Your boy was intoxicated, and nobody made him in time. Lieutenant Fritsch sent us a teletype with his picture, but we didn't make the connection until—"

Wayne hung up. Beaudine grabbed the phone. Beaudine snapped his belt—*hard.*

"This better be good. That was a two-dollar call."

Wayne pulled out his wallet. Wayne forked up two bucks.

"If he tries to cross again, they'll get him. But if he comes back here, you tell him I'll walk him over myself."

Beaudine hiked his belt. "Why would you take that kind of risk for Wendell?"

"Your dog likes me. Leave it at that."

The Adolphus bar—all male at midnight. The big Jack postmortem.

Pro-Jack stools. Anti-Jack stools adjacent. Youth. Outer space. *Ich bin ein Berliner.*

Wayne sat between factions. Wayne heard hi-fi bullshit in stereo sound.

Cowboy trash—faux tall—big boots don't count. They called Jack "Jack." They took liberties—like they all fucked leprechauns in Hyannis.

Fuck them. *He* slept in Jack's bed. *He* thrashed on Jack's sheets.

Wayne got drunk. Wayne *never* got drunk. Wayne drank small-batch bond.

Shot 1 burned. Shot 2 played a picture: Lee Bowers' thumb. Shot 3 gored his gonads. Dig *these* pix: Janice in halters and shorts.

Jack had hound blood. Wayne Senior said so. Martin Luther King fucked white chicks.

Shot 4—more pix:

Durfee tries to cross. The border cops lose him. Wayne fucked up. Wayne gets called home. Buddy Fritsch recruits a new man. Said man kills Wendell D.

Wayne fucked up. Fritsch fucks him for it. Fritsch fucks him off LVPD. Wayne Senior says don't fuck my boy. The fucking ascends triumphant.

Shot 5:

The thumb/the alley chase/the crap-game snafu.

Jack put a man in orbit. Jack played chicken with Khrushchev. Jack put that shine in Ole Miss.

Maynard Moore walked in. He brought company. That Pete guy—the big guy with Jack Ruby.

Moore saw Wayne. Moore detoured up. Pete tagged along.

Moore said, "Let's go find us that spook. My pal Pete hates spooks, don't you, sahib?"

Pete smiled. Pete rolled his eyes. Pete goofed on dipshit Moore.

Wayne chewed ice cubes. "Fuck off. I'll find him myself."

Moore leaned on the bar. "Your daddy wouldn't like that. It'd let him know the apple falls *real* far from the tree."

Wayne tossed his drink. Moore caught it—hard in the eyes. Bourbon burned him—hi-test sting—triple-digit proof.

The cocksucker rubbed his eyes. The cocksucker squealed.

8

(Dallas, 11/24/63)

Pete was late. Littell voyeurized.

His room was high up. The window framed a church. A midnight mass convened.

Littell watched. A poster marked the mass—Jack K. in black borders.

Kids defaced it. Littell watched them—late this afternoon. He went to dinner later. He saw the work up close.

Jack had fangs. Jack had devil horns. Jack said, "I'm a homo!"

Mourners filed in. A breeze dumped the poster. A woman picked it up. She saw Jack's picture. She cringed.

A car cruised by. An arm shot out. A stiff finger twirled. The woman sobbed. The woman crossed herself. The woman squeezed rosary beads.

The Statler was low-rent. The Bureau booked cheap rooms. The view compensated.

Pete was late. Pete was with the backup cop. The cop had details. The cop had a map printed up.

Littell watched the church. It diverted him. It subsumed Arden.

They talked for six hours. They skirted IT. He coded a message: I KNOW. I KNOW you KNOW. I don't care how you KNOW. I don't care what you DID.

She coded a message: *I won't probe your stake.* No one said, "Jack Ruby."

They talked. They omitted. They codified.

He said he was a lawyer. He was ex-FBI. He had an ex-wife and an ex-daughter somewhere. She studied his facial scars. He told her flat-out: My best friend put them there.

Le frère Pete—un Frenchman sanglant.

She said she traveled. She said she held jobs. She said she bought and sold stocks and made money. She said she had an ex-husband. She did not state his name.

She impressed him. She knew it. He coded a response: You're a pro. You dissemble. I don't care.

She knew Jack Ruby. She used the word "roust." He skirted it. He offered advice. He told her to find a motel.

She said she would. He gave her *his* hotel number. Please call me. Please do it soon.

He wanted to touch her. He didn't. She touched his arm once. He left her. He drove to the Bureau.

The office was empty—no agents about—Mr. Hoover made sure. He rifled drawers. He found the Tippit file.

Pete was late. Littell skimmed the file. It rambled and digressed.

Dallas PD was far right: Klan kliques and John Birch. Diverse splinter groups: The NSRP/the Minutemen/the Thunderbolt Legion.

Tippit was "klanned up." Tippit joined the Klarion Klan Koalition for the New Konfederacy. The DPD boss was Maynard D. Moore. Moore was an FBI snitch. Moore's handler was Wayne Tedrow Sr.

Tedrow Senior: "Pamphleteer"/"Fund Raiser"/"Entrepreneur"/"Extensive Las Vegas holdings."

Unique stats—familiar—Mr. Hoover's "Führer manqué."

Littell skimmed up. Littell logged stats. Tedrow Senior ran eclectic.

He raised right-wing cash. He might know Guy B. Guy scrounged right-wing funds. Some fat cats greased the hit fund.

Littell skimmed down. Littell logged stats. Littell logged a possible connection.

Guy's backup cop—friend of J. D. Tippit—odds on Maynard D. Moore. Odds on: Mr. Hoover knew it. Mr. Hoover guessed the connection.

Littell skimmed up. Tedrow Senior's CV expanded.

All-Mormon staff. Ties at Nellis AFB. Tight with the Gaming Control Board. One son: a Vegas policeman.

Senior withheld data from Junior. Junior worked the intel squad. Junior kept board files. Junior withheld data from Senior. Senior "assisted" Mr. Hoover. Senior "dispensed propaganda."

Per: Martin Luther King/the Southern Christian Leadership Conference.

Littell skimmed pages. Littell took notes. Howard Hughes loved Mormons. They had "germ-free" blood. Tedrow Senior was Mormon. Tedrow Senior had Mormon connections.

Littell rubbed his eyes. The doorbell rang. He got up and opened the door.

Pete walked in. Pete grabbed the desk chair. Pete sprawled out tall.

Littell shut the door. "How bad?"

Pete said, "Bad. The map looks good, but he won't pop Oswald. He's crazy, but I can't fault him for brains."

Littell rubbed his eyes. "Maynard Moore, right? That's his name."

Pete yawned. "Guy's slipping. He usually plays his names closer than that."

Littell shook his head. "Mr. Hoover made him. He had a file on Tippit. He assumed that Moore had to be somewhere close."

"That's your interpretation, right? Hoover didn't get that specific."

"He never does."

Pete cracked his knuckles. "How scared are you?"

"It comes and goes, and I wouldn't mind some good news."

Pete lit a cigarette. "Rogers made it down to Juarez. The pro got down, but the Border Patrol detained him and ran a passport check. Guy said he's a French national."

Littell said, "Guy's talking too much."

"He's scared. He knows Carlos is thinking, 'If I went with Pete and Ward's crew, none of this shit would have happened.' "

Littell cleaned his glasses. "Where is he?"

"He drove back to New Orleans. His nerves are shot, and he's popping digitalis like a fucking junkie. All this shit is on him, and he knows it."

Littell said, "And?"

Pete cracked a window. Cold air blew in.

"And what?"

"There's more. Guy wouldn't be going back unless he had an excuse to hand Carlos."

Pete flicked his cigarette out. "Jack Ruby knows. He brought one of his flunkies and some women up to the safe house. They saw the targets and guns. Guy's saying we should clip them. I think he'll tell Carlos that, so he can buy his way out of the shit."

Littell coughed. His pulse zoomed. He held his breath.

"We can't take out four people that close to the hit. It's too obvious."

Pete laughed. "Shit, Ward, say it. I've got no balls for clipping civilians, so why should you?"

Littell smiled. "Ruby aside."

Pete shrugged. "Jack's no skin off my ass either way."

"The women, then. That's what we're talking about."

Pete cracked his thumbs. "I'm not negotiating on that. I already warned one of them off, but I couldn't find the other one."

"Give me their names."

"Betty McDonald and Arden something."

Littell touched his tie. Littell scratched his neck. Littell made his hands quash his nerves.

He twitched. He swallowed. He gulped. The room was cold. He shut the window.

"Oswald."

"Yeah. If he goes, this all disappears."

"When are they moving him?"

"Eleven-thirty. If he hasn't named Guy's cutout by then, we can put the skids to all this."

Littell coughed. "I've arranged for a private interview. The ASAC said he hasn't talked, but I want to make sure."

Pete shook his head. "Bullshit. You want to get close to him. You want to run some kind of fucking absolution number on him, so you can do a number on yourself later."

In nomine patris, et filii et spiritus sancti, Amen.

"It's nice to have someone who knows you."

Pete laughed. "I wasn't doubting you. I just want to work this fucking thing out."

Littell said, "Moore. There's no way he—"

"*No.* He knows too much, drinks too much and talks too much. After Oswald goes, *he* goes, and we draw the line at that."

Littell checked his watch. Shit—1:40 a.m.

"He's a policeman. He could get into the basement."

"*No.* He's too crazy. He's working an extradition gig with a Vegas cop, and he gets in the guy's face in the worst possible way. He's not what we want."

Littell rubbed his eyes. "What was the man's name? The cop, I mean."

"Wayne something. Why?"

"Tedrow?"

Pete said, "Yeah, and why do you care? He's got nothing to do with any of this, and the fucking clock is ticking."

Littell checked his watch. Carlos bought it for him. A gold Rolex/pure ostentat—

"Ward, are you in a fucking trance?"

Littell said, "Jack Ruby."

Pete rocked his chair back. The legs squeaked.

Littell said, "He's insane. He's afraid of us. He's afraid of the Outfit. He's got seven brothers and sisters that we can threaten."

Pete smiled. "The cops know he's crazy. He carries a gun. He's been all over the building all weekend, and he's been saying somebody should shoot that Commie. Ten dozen fucking newsmen have heard him."

Littell said, "He's got tax troubles."

"Who told you that?"

"I don't want to say."

A breeze kicked up. The windowpanes creaked.

Pete said, "And?"

"And what?"

"There's more. I want to know why you'll risk it, with a fucking psycho who knows both our names."

Cherchez la femme, Pierre.

"It's a message. It tells everyone who went to that safe house to run."

9

(Dallas, 11/24/63)

Barb walked in. She wore his rain-
coat. The sleeves drooped. The
shoulders sagged. The hem
brushed her feet.

Pete blocked the bathroom. Barb said, "Shit."

Pete checked her ring hand. Pete saw her wedding ring.

She held it up. "I'm not going anywhere. I'm just getting used to it."

Pete carried his ring. It came too small—fucking pygmy-size.

"I'll get used to it when I get mine fitted."

Barb shook her head. "Used to *it*. What *you* did."

Pete snared his ring. Pete tried to squeeze his finger in. Pete jabbed at
the hole.

"Say something nice, all right? Tell me how the late show went."

Barb dumped his coat. "It went fine. The Twist is dead, but Dallas
doesn't know it."

Pete stretched. His shirt gapped. Barb saw his piece.

"You're going out."

"I won't be that long. I'm just wondering where you'll be when I get
back."

"I'm wondering who else knows. I know, so there has to be others."

His headache revived. His headache paved new ground.

"Everyone who knows has a stake. It's what you call an open secret."

Barb said, "I'm scared."

"Don't think about it. I know how these things work."

"You don't know that. There's never been anything *like* this."

Pete said, "It'll be all right."

Barb said, "Bullshit."

. . .

Ward was late. Pete watched the Carousel Club.

He stood two doors down. Jack Ruby shooed cops and whores out. They paired off. They piled in cars. The whores jiggled keys.

Jack closed up the club. Jack cleaned his ears with a pencil. Jack kicked a turd in the street.

Jack went back inside. Jack talked to his dogs. Jack talked very loud.

It was cold. It was windy. Motorcade debris swirled: Matchbooks/confetti/Jack & Jackie signs.

Ward was late. Ward might be with "Arden."

He left Ward's room. He heard the phone ring. Ward made him run. He saw Ward and Arden. They didn't see him. He told Ward the safe-house tale.

He said, "Arden." Ward schizzed. He called Ward on Ruby. Ward played it oblique.

Fuck it—for now.

Jack's dogs yapped. Jack baby-talked Yiddish. The noise carried outside. A Fed sled pulled up. Ward got out. His coat pockets bulged.

He walked up. He unloaded his pockets—rogue-cop show-and-tell.

Brass knucks/a sash cord/a pachuco switchblade.

"I went by the property room at the PD. Nobody saw me."

"You thought it through."

Ward restuffed his pockets. "*If* he doesn't agree."

Pete lit a cigarette. "We'll cut him up and make it look like a heist."

A dog yipped. Ward flinched. Pete blew on his cigarette. The tip flared red.

They walked up. Ward knocked on the door. Pete put on a drawl: "Jack! Hey, Jack, I think I left my wallet!"

The dogs barked. The door opened. There's Jack. He saw them. He said, "Oh." His mouth dropped and held.

Pete flicked his butt in. Jack gagged on it. Jack coughed it out wet.

Pete shut the door. Ward grabbed Jack. Pete shoved him. Pete frisked him. Pete pulled a piece off his belt.

Ward hit him. Jack fell down. Jack curled up and sucked air.

The dogs ran. The dogs crouched by the runway. Ward grabbed the gun. Ward dumped five shells.

He knelt down. Jack saw the gun. Jack saw the one shell. Ward shut the drum. Ward spun it. Ward aimed at Jack's head.

He pulled the trigger. The hammer clicked. Jack sobbed and sucked air. Ward twirled the gun. Ward pulled the trigger. Ward dry-shot Jack's head.

Pete said, "You're going to clip Oswald."

Jack sobbed. Jack covered his ears. Jack shook his head. Pete grabbed his belt. Pete dragged him. Jack kicked out at tables and chairs.

Ward walked over. Pete dumped Jack by the runway. The dogs yapped and growled.

Pete walked to the bar. Pete grabbed a fifth of Schenley's. Pete grabbed some dog treats.

He dumped the treats. The dogs tore in. Ward scoped the jug. Ward was a lush. Ward was on the wagon. Booze turned him to mush.

They pulled chairs up. Jack sobbed. Jack wiped his schnoz. The dogs snarfed the treats. The dogs waddled and wheezed. The dogs crapped out cold by the runway.

Jack sat up. Jack hugged his knees. Jack braced his back on the slats. Pete grabbed a stray glass. Pete dumped ice dregs and poured Schenley's.

Jack studied his shoes. Jack squeezed his Jew star on a chain.

Pete said, "*L'chaim.*"

Jack looked up. Pete waved the glass. Jack shook his head. Ward twirled the gun. Ward cocked the hammer.

Jack grabbed the glass. His hand shook. Pete clamped it down. Jack imbibed. Jack coughed and gasped. Jack held it down.

Ward said, "You've been saying someone should do it all weekend."

Pete said, "You'll do eighteen months tops. You'll get your own fucking motorcade when you get out."

Ward said, "You'll own this town."

Pete said, "He clipped that Tippit guy. Every cop in Dallas will love you."

Ward said, "Your money worries are over as of this moment."

Pete said, "Think about it. A tax-free pension for life."

Jack said, "No." Jack shook his head.

Ward waved the gun. Ward spun the drum. Ward aimed at Jack's head. He pulled the trigger *two times*. He got two dry clicks.

Jack sobbed. Jack prayed—heavy-duty hebe shit.

Pete poured him a refill—three fingers of Schenley's—Jack shook his head. Pete grabbed his neck. Pete cleared his pipes. Pete force-fed him hard.

Jack kept it down. Jack coughed and gasped.

Pete said, "We'll fix up the club and let your sister Eva run it."

Ward said, "Or we'll kill all your brothers and sisters."

Pete said, "She'll make a mint. This place will be a national monument."

Ward said, "Or we'll torch it to the ground."

Pete said, "Are you getting the picture?"

Ward said, "Do you understand your options?"

Pete said, "If you say no, you die. If you say yes, you'll have the world by the balls. If you blow the job, it's '*Shalom,* Jack,' you tried, but we don't appreciate failure, and it's too bad we have to take out your whole fucking family, too."

Jack said, "No."

Pete said, "We'll find a nice home for your dogs. They'll be glad to see you when you get out."

Ward said, "Or we'll kill you."

Pete said, "Your tax troubles will disappear."

Ward said, "Or everyone you love will die."

Jack said, "No." Pete cracked his knuckles. Ward pulled a belt sap—a hose chunk packed with double-aught buck.

Jack stood up. Pete pushed him down. Jack reached for the jug. Pete poured it out. Pete saved a chaser.

Jack said, "No. *No no no no no.*"

Ward sapped him—one rib shot—whap.

Jack balled up. Jack kissed his Jew star. Jack bit his tongue.

Ward grabbed his belt. Ward dragged him. Ward kicked him into his office. Ward kicked the door shut.

Pete laughed. Jack lost a shoe and a tie clip. Ward lost his glasses.

Pete heard thump sounds. Jack screamed. The dogs woke up. Pete popped aspirin and Schenley's. The dogs yapped. The noise got all mixed up.

Pete shut his eyes. Pete rolled his neck. Pete worked his headache—*fuck.*

He smelled smoke. He opened his eyes. Smoke blew out a wall vent. Ash sifted through.

Arden.

Ward got Jack alone. Pete knew why. Do what we want/do what *I* want/don't talk about HER. He torched Jack's files. He torched HER name. He torched Arden WHO?

Jack screamed. The dogs yapped. Smoke blew out the vent. Smoke seeped and pooled.

The door popped open. Smoke whooshed out. Wet ashes flew. Sink sounds. Screams. Loose shot pellets hurled.

Ward walked out. His sap leaked buckshot. The shaft dripped blood. He stumbled. He rubbed his eyes. He stepped on his glasses.

He said, "He'll do it."

10

(Dallas, 11/24/63)

H*angover.*
     The room light hurt. The TV noise hurt. Alka-Seltzer helped. Wayne dosed up and replayed the fight.

He swung. He hit Moore. Moore swung bourbon-blind. Pete got between them. Pete fucking laughed.

Wayne watched TV. Room service was late—SOP for the hotel.

A cop faced a mike. He said we're moving him. Clear a path now.

Willis Beaudine didn't call. Buddy Fritsch did. Buddy had an update. Buddy talked to the border cops.

Wendell Durfee: Still at large.

Wayne dropped *his* plan: I've got a car/I'll drive to McAllen/I'll liaise with the border cops there.

Fritsch said, "Take Moore with you. If you cap that nigger, you'd better have a Texas cop in your pocket."

Wayne argued. Wayne almost said it: My plan is a shuck. Fritsch said, "Take him out. Earn your fucking keep."

Fritsch won. Wayne lost. He stalled. He watched TV. He never called Moore up.

Wayne sipped Alka-Seltzer. Wayne saw cops with Stetsons. The TV picture jumped.

He slapped the box. He tapped the dials. The picture cohered.

Oswald stepped out. Oswald wore handcuffs. Two cops flanked him. They walked through the basement. They faced some reporters. They cleared a path fast.

A man jumped out. Dark suit/fedora. Right arm outstretched. He stepped up. He aimed a gun. He shot near point-blank.

Wayne blinked. Wayne saw it—oh fuck.

Oswald doubled up. Oswald went "Oooh."

The cops blinked. They saw it—oh fuck.

Commotion. Dogpile. The gunman's down. He's prone. He's disarmed. He's pinned flat.

Rerun that. I think I—

The hat. The bulk. The profile. The dark eyes. The fat.

Wayne grabbed the TV. Wayne shook the sides. Wayne focused in tight. Jerky shots/camera jumps/a low zoom.

The bulk grew. The profile blossomed. Someone yelled, "Jack!"

No. Asshole Jack Ruby—the dive club/the dogshit/the—

Someone yelled, "Jack!" A man snared his hat. Cops wrestled him. Cops cuffed him. Cops stood him up. Cops went through his pants.

The picture jumped. Wayne slapped the antenna. The picture went flat. Reruns:

Moore muscles Jack. Jack prowls the PD. Jack knows Pete. Moore knows Pete gooood. Bowers. The thumb. The Kennedy hit—

The picture jumped. The tubes buzzed. The fucking phone rang.

The picture settled. A newsman yelled, "Local nightclub"—

Wayne stood up. Wayne tripped. Wayne grabbed the phone. Wayne snagged the receiver.

"Yeah, this is Tedrow."

"It's Willis Beaudine. Remember, you met me—"

"Yeah, I remember."

"Well, that's good, because Wendell's going for that offer you made. He don't know why you're doing it, but I told him my dog liked you."

The sound died. Jack moved his lips. Cops gave him the big two-cop flank.

Beaudine said, "Man, are you *there?*"

"I'm here."

"Good. Then you be at rest stop number 10, eighty miles south on I-35. Make it three o'clock. Oh, and Wendell wants to know if you've got money."

The cops dwarfed Jack—big men—boots up to six-four.

"Hey, man. Are you *there?*"

"Tell him I've got six thousand dollars."

"Hey, you have to like that!"

Wayne hung up. The TV jumped. Oswald rode a white sheet on a cot.

11

(Dallas, 11/24/63)

He saw it live.

He'd tuned in Channel 4. He squinted to see. He broke his glasses at Jack's club.

He sat in his room. He watched the show. It capped his interview—one hour back.

He sat with Lee Oswald. They talked.

Littell drove I-35. Freeway signs blurred. He hit the slow lane and crawled.

Arden called last night. Oswald died at Parkland. Ruby was under arrest.

Oswald bit his nails. Littell uncuffed him. Oswald rubbed his wrists.

I'm a Marxist. I'm a patsy. I won't elaborate. I'm pro-Fidel. I indict the U.S. I scorn her Cuban misdeeds. I scorn the exiles. I scorn the CIA. National Fruit is evil. The Bay of Pigs was insane.

Littell agreed. Oswald warmed up. Oswald craved perspective. Oswald craved friends.

Littell faltered then. Oswald craved friends. Guy's cutout knew it. Littell shut down. Oswald caught his tone. Oswald threw it back.

Some sound facts. Some nut talk mixed in. You don't love me—so I'll kill you with The Truth.

Littell walked out then. Littell recuffed Oswald. Littell squeezed his hands.

Freeway signs blurred. Signposts popped. Exit posts slithered. Littell saw "Grandview." Littell pulled right. Littell cut down a ramp.

He saw the Chevron sign. He saw the HoJo's.

There—

The shape between them—motel rooms—one long row.

He crossed an access lane. He parked by the HoJo's. He walked by the rooms. He squinted. He saw the "14."

There—the door's ajar. That's Arden on the bed.

Littell walked in. Littell shut the door. Littell bumped a TV set. The juice was off. The box was warm. He smelled cigarettes.

Arden said, "Sit here."

Littell sat down. The bedsprings sagged. Arden moved her legs.

"You look different without your glasses."

"I broke them."

She had her hair up. She wore a green sweater-dress.

Littell turned a lamp on. Arden blinked. Littell bent the lamp down. It shaded the glare.

"What did you do with your things?"

"I rented a storage garage."

"In your own name?"

"You're being disingenuous. You know I'm better than that."

Littell coughed. "You've been watching television."

"Along with the whole country."

"You know some things they don't."

"We've got our version, they've got theirs. Is that what you're saying?"

"*You're* being disingenuous now."

Arden hugged a pillow. "How did they convince him? How do you make someone do something so crazy on live television?"

"He was crazy to start with. And sometimes the stakes are so high that they play in your favor."

Arden shook her head. "I don't want to get more specific."

Littell shook his head. "We don't have to discuss it."

Arden smiled. "I'm wondering why you're going to so much trouble to help me."

"You know why."

"I may ask you to say it."

"I will. If we go forward on this."

" 'This?' Are we going to define *any* of our terms at all?"

Littell coughed—full ashtrays/stale smoke.

"Confirm something for me. You've been in trouble, you've run before, you know how to do it."

Arden nodded. "It's something I'm good at."

"That's good, because I can get you a completely new identity."

Arden crossed her legs. "Is there a disclosure clause in all '*this*'? "

Littell nodded. "We can hold back some secrets."

"That's important. I don't like to lie unless I have to."

"I'm going to Washington for a few days. Then I'll be setting up a base in Las Vegas. You can meet me there."

Arden grabbed her cigarettes. The pack was empty—she tossed it.

"We both know who's behind this. And *I* know they all pass through Vegas."

"I do work for them. It's one reason why you'll be safe with me."

"I'd feel safer in L.A."

Littell smiled. "Mr. Hughes lives there. I'll need to get a house or apartment."

"I'll meet you, then. I'll trust you that far."

Littell checked his watch—1:24 p.m.—Littell grabbed the phone by the bed.

Arden nodded. He pulled the phone to the bathroom. The cord almost snapped. He shut the door. He dialed the Adolphus. The switchboard patched him through.

Pete picked up. "Yes?"

"It's me."

"Yeah, and you're the white man of the week. I wasn't a hundred percent sure that he'd do it."

"What about Moore?"

"He *goes*. I'll tail him and get him alone."

Littell hung up. Littell walked back. Littell dropped the phone on a chair.

He sat on the bed. Arden slid close.

Arden said, "*Say* it."

He squinted. Her freckles jumped. Her smile blurred.

"I've got nothing but the wrong things, and I want to take something good out of this."

"That's not enough."

Littell said, "I want you." Arden touched his leg.

12

(Dallas, 11/24/63)

Reruns:

The thumb. Pete and Moore. Killer Jack and Killer Lee.

Wayne drove I-35. The reruns hit. A soundtrack sputtered:

He calls Moore. He says, "Meet me. I've got a lead on Durfee." He lies. He drops details. Static fries the line and blows the connection.

Moore gets the last word. Moore says, ". . . have us big fun."

The freeway was flat. Flat blacktop/flat empty. Flat sand adjacent. Sand flats and scrub. Jackrabbit bones. Sand grit in circulation.

The soundtrack distorted. He'd fucked up the call. The Jack and Lee Show fucked with him.

A rabbit jumped. It hit the road. It cleared his wheels clean. A wind kicked up. It tossed scrub balls and waxed paper.

There's the sign: Rest Stop #10.

Wayne pulled in. Wayne scoped the parking lot slooooow.

Gravel paving. No cars. Tire tracks on sand adjacent. Flat sand. Drift sand. Scrub balls hip-high.

Goooood cover spots.

A men's room. A ladies' room. Two stucco huts and a crawl space between. The huts fronted sand drifts. Said drifts ran way inland. The wind stirred loose sand.

Wayne parked. Beaudine said 3:00. He told Moore to meet him at 4:00. The current time—2:49.

He pulled his piece. He popped the glove box. He pulled out the money—six cold.

He got out. He walked through the men's room. He checked the stalls gun-first. The wind kicked cellophane through.

He walked out. He hit the ladies' room. Empty stalls/dirty sinks/bugs pooled in Lysol.

He walked out. He hugged the walls. He moved around back. Shitfire—there's Wendell Durfee.

He's got pimp threads. He's got a hair net. He's got a jigaboo conk. He's got a piece—it's a quiff automatic.

Durfee stood by the wall. Durfee ducked sand. It messed up his conk good.

He saw Wayne. He said, "Well, now."

Wayne drew down on him. Durfee raised his hands. Wayne walked up slow. Sand filled his shoes.

Durfee said, "Why you doin' this for me?"

Wayne grabbed his piece. Wayne popped the clip. Wayne tucked it down his pants barrel first.

The wind tore a scrub pile. Durfee's sled got exposed. It's a '51 Merc. It's sand-scraped. It's sunk to the hubs.

Wayne said, "Don't talk to me. I don't want to know you."

Durfee said, "I might need me a tow truck."

Wayne heard gravel crunch—back in the lot. Durfee futzed with his hair net. Durfee heard shit.

"Willis said you had money."

Gravel crunch—*tire* crunch—Durfee missed the sounds dead.

"I'll get it. You wait here."

"Shit. I ain't goin' nowhere without it. You fuckin' Santa Claus, you know that?"

Wayne holstered his piece. Wayne circled back to the lot. Wayne saw Moore's 409.

It's upside his car. It's idling hard. It's throbbing on hi-end shocks. There's Moore. He's at the wheel. He's chomping Red Man.

Wayne stopped. His dick fluttered. Piss leaked out.

He saw something.

A speck—up the freeway—some kind of mirage or a car.

He anchored his legs. He walked up jerky. He leaned on Moore's car.

Moore rolled down his window. "Hey, boy. What's new and note-worthy?"

Wayne leaned in close. Wayne braced on the roof.

"He isn't here. That guy gave me a bad lead."

Moore spat tobacco juice. Moore hit Wayne's shoes.

"Why'd you tell me four o'clock, when you're here before three?"

Wayne shrugged. How should I know? I'm bored with you.

Moore pulled a knife. Moore picked his teeth. Moore sheared pork chop fat. He sprayed juice haphazard. He doused Wayne's shirt.

"He's out back. I reconnoitered a half hour ago. Now, you get your ass back there and kill him."

Wayne saw reruns—in slooooow motion.

"You know Jack Ruby."

Moore picked his teeth. Moore tapped the blade on the dash.

"So what? Everyone knows Jack."

Wayne leaned in the window. "What about Bowers? He saw Kennedy get—"

Moore swung the knife. Moore snagged Wayne's shirt. Moore grabbed Wayne's necktie. They hit heads. Moore swung the knife. His hand hit the door ledge.

Wayne pulled his head back. Wayne pulled his piece. Wayne shot Moore in the head.

Recoil—

It knocked him back. He hit *his* car. He braced and aimed tight. He shot Moore in the head/Moore in the neck/Moore with no face and no chin.

He ripped the seats. He tore up the dash. He blew the windows out. It was loud. It echoed loud. It outblew wind gusts.

Wayne froze. The 409 bounced—reverb off hi-end shocks.

Durfee ran out. Durfee lost his legs. Durfee slid and fell flat. Wayne froze. There's that speck up I-35—it's a car oh fuck.

The car drove up. The car pulled in. The car stopped by Moore's sled. Sand blew. Scrub balls bounced. Gravel scattered.

The speck-car idled. Pete got out. Pete put his hands up.

Wayne aimed at him. Wayne pulled the trigger. The pin clicked— you're empty—you're fucked.

Durfee watched. Durfee tried to run. Durfee stood up and fell flat. Pete walked up to Wayne. Wayne dropped his gun and pulled Durfee's gun. Wayne popped in the clip.

His hand slipped. The gun fell. Pete picked it up.

He said, "Kill him."

Wayne looked at Durfee. Pete said, "Kill him."

Wayne looked at Durfee. Durfee looked at Wayne. Wayne looked at Pete. Pete gave him the gun. Wayne dropped the safety.

Durfee stood up. His legs went. He fell on his ass.

Pete leaned on Moore's car. Pete reached inside. Pete flipped off the key. Wayne leaned in his car. Wayne grabbed the six thousand. Wayne coughed up gravel grit.

Pete said, "Kill him."

Wayne walked up to Durfee. Durfee sobbed. Durfee watched Wayne's hands. He saw a gun. He saw a cash bag. He saw two hands full.

Wayne dropped the bag. Durfee grabbed it. Durfee stood up. Durfee got legs and ran.

Wayne leaned on his knees. Wayne puked his lunch up. Wayne tasted hamburger and sand.

Durfee ran.

He tripped through sand drifts. He got his Merc. He gunned it. He bumped drifts. He plowed them. He made the lot. He made I-35 south.

Pete walked over. Wayne wiped his face. Wayne smeared Maynard Moore's blood.

Pete said, "You picked a good place for it. You picked a good weekend, too."

Wayne leaned on his knees. Wayne dropped the gun. Pete grabbed it up.

"There's an oil dump two miles down. You can ditch the car there."

Wayne straightened up. Pete steadied him. Pete said, "Maybe I'll see you in Vegas."

13

(Dallas, 11/25/63)

Jack's wake blared—epidemic boo-hoo—it cut through the bridal suite walls.

Barb said, "I'm getting the picture. The fix is in."

Pete packed his suitcase. "Some people got Christmas early. They know how things work, and they know what's best for the country."

Barb folded her gowns. "There's a catch. For us, I mean."

Pete tuned her out. He'd just talked to Guy. Guy just talked to Carlos. Carlos loved the Ruby Show. Carlos wanted to clip Maynard Moore.

Guy told Pete that. Pete ad-libbed. Pete said Moore vanished—ka-poof!

Guy spritzed on Moore's Vegas gig. Guy ragged Wayne Junior. Junior knew shit—small fucking world—Wayne Senior greased the hit fund.

Barb said, "The *catch*. Don't tell me there isn't one. And don't tell me those tickets to Vegas aren't part of it."

Pete stashed his piece. "Are you saying that two tickets was being optimistic?"

"No. You know I'll never leave you."

Pete smiled. "There's some fuck-ups I wouldn't have made, if I'd known you better."

Barb smiled. "The catch? *Vegas?* And don't make eyes at me when we have to run for a plane."

Pete shut his suitcase. "The Outfit has plans for Mr. Hughes. Ward's putting some things together."

"It's about staying useful, then."

"Yeah. Stay useful, stay healthy. If I can get them to bend a certain rule, I'd call it a lock."

Barb said, "What rule?"

"Come on, you know what I do."

Barb shook her head. "You're versatile. You run shakedowns and you sell guns and dope. You killed the President of the United States once, but I'd have to call that a one-time opportunity."

Pete laughed. Pete made his sides hurt. Pete leaked some wiiiiild tears. Barb tossed a towel up. Pete wiped his eyes and de-teared.

"You can't move heroin there. It's a set policy, but it's probably the best way I can make the Boys some real money. They might go for it, if I only sell to the spooks in West Vegas. Mr. Hughes hates jigs. He thinks they should all be doped up, like he is. The Boys might decide to humor him."

Barb got This Look. Pete knew the gestalt. *I* fucked JFK. *You* killed him. *My* craaazy life.

She said, "Useful."

"Yeah, that's it."

Barb grabbed her Twist gowns. Barb dropped them out the window. Pete looked out. A kid looked up. The blue gown hit a ledge.

Barb waved. The kid waved back.

"The Twist is dead, but I'll bet you could get me some lounge gigs."

"We'll be useful."

"I'm still scared."

Pete said, "That's the catch."

Part II

EXTORTION

December 1963–October 1964

DOCUMENT INSERT:12/1/63. Internally circulated FBI intelligence report. Marked: "Classified Confidential 2-A: Restricted Agent Access"/"Pertinent Facts & Observations on Major Las Vegas Hotel-Casino Ownerships & Related Topics." Note: Officially logged at Southern Nevada Office, 2/8/63.

The major Las Vegas hotel-casinos are situated in two locales: The downtown (Fremont Street/"Glitter Gulch") area and "The Strip" (Las Vegas Blvd, the city's main north-south artery). The downtown establishments are older, less gaudy & cater to local residents & less affluent tourists who come to gamble, enjoy low-quality entertainment & engage the services of prostitutes. Junket groups (Elks, Kiwanis, Rotary, Shriners, VFW, CYO) are frequent downtown hotel-casino visitors. The downtown establishments are largely owned by "Pioneer" consortiums (e.g., native Nevadans & general non-organized crime groups). Some of the owners have been forced to sell small (5%–8%) interests to organized-crime groups in exchange for continued "Preferential Treatment" (e.g., on-site "protection," a "service" to insure the absence of labor trouble & untoward on-site incidents). Organized-crime associates frequently serve as casino "Pit Bosses" & thus as enforcers and on-site informants for their organized-crime patrons.

The downtown area is jurisdictionally covered by the Las Vegas Police Department (LVPD). The LVPD's jurisdiction adjoins that of the Clark County Sheriff's Department (CCSD). Both agencies work within the other's jurisdiction by mutual consent. The Sheriff's Dept patrols the "Strip" area south of the Sahara Hotel. Like the LVPD, it provides investigatory services for its specific jurisdiction, with an operational mandate inside LVPD, or "City" jurisdiction. The LVPD is similarly allowed to conduct investigations inside Sheriff's Dept, or "County" jurisdiction. It should be noted that both agencies are widely influenced and corrupted by factions of organized crime. This corruption is of the type most identified with "Company Towns" (e.g., casino revenue forms the financial base of Las Vegas & thus influences the political base & law-enforcement policy). Numerous officers within both agencies benefit from organized-crime bestowed "Gratuities" (free hotel stays, free casino gambling chips, the services of prostitutes, "police discounts" at various businesses owned by organized-crime associates) & outright bribery.

The LVPD and Sheriff's Dept enforce organized-crime policies with the implicit consent of the Clark County political hierarchy & by extension the consent of the Nevada State Legislature. (E.g., Negroes are strongly discouraged from entering certain "Strip" hotel-casinos and on-site casino personnel are allowed to see to their expulsion. E.g., crimes against organized-crime-connected casino employees are frequently avenged by LVPD officers, acting on orders from the Casino Operators Council, an organized-crime front group. E.g., LVPD officers and Sheriff's deputies are often used to track down casino card cheats, "discourage" them & run them out of town.)

The best-known hotel-casinos are situated on the "Strip." Many of them have been infiltrated by organized crime, with percentage "Points" divvied up among the overlords of organized-crime cartels. (E.g., the Chicago Crime Cartel controls the Stardust Hotel-Casino & boss Sam "Mo," "Momo," "Mooney" Giancana has an 8% personal interest. Chicago hoodlum John Rosselli (the Chicago Cartel's Las Vegas overseer) has a 3% interest & Chicago Mob enforcer Dominic Michael Montalvo aka "Butch Montrose" has a 1% interest.) (See Addendum File #B-2 for complete list of crime-cartel ownerships & percentage-point estimates.)

Smaller percentage points are traded between organized crime factions as part of an ongoing effort to insure that all factions have a stake in the expanding Las Vegas casino economy. The profit base is thus shared & faction-to-faction rivalry is averted. Thus, organized crime presents a unified face in Las Vegas. The man responsible for developing & maintaining this policy is Morris Barney "Moe" Dalitz (b. 1899), a former Cleveland mobster & organized crime's "Goodwill Ambassador" & Las Vegas "Fix-It Man." Dalitz owns points in the Desert Inn Hotel Casino and is rumored to have points in several others. Dalitz is known as "Mr. Las Vegas," because of his numerous philanthropic endeavors & his convincing non-gangster image. Dalitz founded the Casino Operators Council, dictates their enforcement policies & is largely responsible for the "Clean Town" policy that organized-crime factions believe will help promote tourism & thus increase hotel-casino revenue.

This "Policy" is informally enforced & has the implicit approval of the Las Vegas political machine & the LVPD & Sheriff's Dept. One goal is to enforce ad hoc segregation in the "Strip" hotel-casinos (e.g., admit Negro celebrities or perceived "High Class" Negroes & refuse admittance to all others) & to isolate Negro housing in the slum area of West Las Vegas. (Restrictive real estate covenants are widely observed by Las Vegas–based realtors.) A key "Policy" dictate is the "No Narcotics" rule. This rule applies specifically to heroin. The selling of heroin is forbidden & is punishable by death. The rule is enforced to limit the number of narcotics addicts, specifically those who might support their addiction by means of robbery, burglary, "flim-flam" or other criminal activities that would sully the reputation of Las Vegas & thus discourage tourism. Numerous heroin pushers have been the victims of unsolved homicides & numerous others have disappeared & are presumed to have been killed per the aforementioned policy (see Addendum File #B-3 for partial list). The last homicide occurred on 4/12/60 & there appears to be no heroin traffic in Las Vegas as of this date. It is fair to conclude that the aforementioned deaths have served as a deterrent.

Dalitz is a close associate of Teamster President James Riddle Hoffa (b. 1914) & has secured large loans from the Teamsters' Central States Pension Fund that have covered the cost of hotel-casino improvements. The Fund (estimated assets 1.6 billion dollars) is a "Watering Hole" that organized-crime factions borrow from routinely. Dubious organized-crime-connected "Businessmen" also borrow from the Fund at usurious interest rates that often result in the forfeiture of their businesses. It is rumored that a second set of Pension Fund financial books exists (one that is hidden from government subpoena & thus official audit). These books allegedly list a more accurate accounting of Pension Fund assets & detail the illegal & quasi-legal loans & repayment schedules.

Many of the "Strip" hotel-casinos routinely hide a large portion of their assets. (See the attached IRS-filed table-by-table profit accountings for all craps, roulette, blackjack, poker, loball, keno, fan-tan & baccarat tables, broken down by hotel.) These reported accountings are generally considered to be only 70–80% accurate. (It is very difficult to detect sustained underestimation of taxable income in large cash-base businesses.) Underestimated table profits are estimated to amount to untaxed revenue of over $105,000,000 per year ('62 fiscal estimate). This practice is called the "Skim."

Cash receipts are taken directly from casino counting rooms and dispersed to couriers who messenger the money to pre-arranged spots. Large-denomination bills are substituted for slot-machine coins & daily accountings are fraudulently tallied inside the counting rooms proper. Casino "Skim" is virtually impossible to detect. Most hotel-casino employees subsist on low wages & untaxed cash gratuities & would never report irregularities. This endemic corruption extends to the labor unions who supply the major hotel-casinos with workers.

The Dealers and Croupiers Local #117 is a Chicago Crime Cartel front. Its members are paid a low hourly wage & are given play chips & (presumably stolen) merchandise as bonuses. All chapters of this union are rigidly segregated. The Lounge Entertainers Local #41 is a Detroit Crime Cartel front. Its members are well-paid, but pay weekly kickbacks to crew stewards. This union is nominally integrated. Negro lounge entertainers are "discouraged" from patronizing the hotel-casinos they work in & from fraternizing with white patrons. The four building & building-supply locals who service the "Strip" hotels are Cleveland Crime Cartel fronts & work exclusively with organized-crime-connected contracting firms. The all-female Chambermaids Local #16 is a Florida Crime Cartel front. Many of its members have been suborned into prostitution. The work crews for the above mentioned locals are run by "Ramrods" who report to the Casino Operators Council.

The Kitchen Workers Union (Las Vegas–based only. There are no other chapters) is not organized-crime-connected & is allowed to operate as a sop to the Las Vegas "Pioneer" contingent & the largely Mormon Nevada political machine. The union is run by Wayne Tedrow Sr. (b. 1905), a conservative pamphleteer, real-estate investor & the owner of a bottom-rung or "Grind Joint" casino, the "Land o' Gold." The crew chiefs are all Mormons & the workers (mostly illegal Mexican aliens) are paid substandard wages & are given "bonuses" of dented cans of food & play chips for the Land o' Gold. The workers live in slum hotels in a Mexican enclave on the West-North Las Vegas border. (Note: Tedrow Sr. is rumored to have hidden points in 14 North Las Vegas "Grind Joints" & 6 liquor store/slot machine arcades near Nellis Air Force Base. If true, these ownerships would constitute infractions of the Nevada Gaming Commission charter.)

The Nevada Gaming Commission oversees & regulates the granting of casino licenses and the hiring of casino personnel. The Commission is a "rubber-stamp" panel that does the bidding of the Gaming Control Board and the Clark County Liquor & Control Board. The same five men (the Clark County Sheriff & District Attorney & 3 appointed "Civilian" members) serve on both boards. Thus, the power to approve liquor and casino license applicants for the entire state rests solely in Las Vegas. None of the 5 board

members are overtly organized-crime-connected & it is difficult to
assess the level of collusion the boards engage in, because a majority of the applications they review cloak hidden organized-crime
backing that is difficult to detect. There are no dossiers available on
members of the above organizations. The LVPD Intelligence Unit
keeps detailed files on the Gaming Control & Liquor Board men, but
has consistently refused to grant the FBI & U.S. Attorney's Office
access to them. (As previously stated, the LVPD is strongly orga-
nized-crime-influenced.) The LVPD Intelligence Unit operates city &
countywide & is the sole such unit in Clark County. It is a 2-man
operation. The commanding officer is Lieutenant Byron B. Fritsch
(the adjutant of the LVPD Detective Bureau & strongly connected
to the Casino Operators Council) & the only assigned officer is
Sergeant Wayne Tedrow Jr. (Sgt. Tedrow is the son of the aforementioned Wayne Tedrow Sr. He is considered incorruptible by Las
Vegas Police standards.)

Concluding note: Addendum Files #B-1, 2, 3, 4, 5 require duplicate authorization: Southern Nevada SAC & Deputy Director Tolson.

DOCUMENT INSERT: 12/2/63. Verbatim FBI telephone call tran-
script. Marked: "Recorded at the Director's Request"/"Classified
Confidential 1-A: Director's Eyes Only." Speaking: Director Hoover,
Ward J. Littell.

JEH: Good morning, Mr. Littell.

WJL: Good morning, Sir. And thank you for the carbons.

JEH: Las Vegas is a hellhole. It is unfit for sane habitation,
which may explain its allure to Howard Hughes.

WJL: Yes, Sir.

JEH: Let's talk about Dallas.

WJL: The consensus feels secure, Sir. And the Oswald killing
seems to be a popular denouement.

JEH: Mr. Ruby has gotten four thousand fan letters. He is quite
popular with Jews.

WJL: I'll concede him a certain panache, Sir.

JEH: Will you concede his ability to keep his mouth shut?

WJL: Yes, Sir.

JEH: I agree with you on the consensus. And I want
you to include your thoughts in a detailed report on the events of
that hallowed weekend. I will attribute the report to Dallas agents
and submit it directly to President Johnson.

WJL: I'll begin work immediately, Sir.

JEH: The President will announce a commission to investigate King Jack's death. I will hand-pick the field agents. Your report will provide the President with a snappy preview of their findings.

WJL: Has he formed an opinion, Sir?

JEH: He suspects Mr. Castro or unruly Cuban exiles. In his view, the killing stemmed from King Jack's reckless blunders in the Caribbean.

WJL: It's an informed perspective, Sir.

JEH: I'll concede the point and concede that Lyndon Johnson is no dummy. He has a conveniently dead assassin and a citizenry avenged on national television. What more could he ask for?

WJL: Yes, Sir.

JEH: And he's appropriately fed up with the Cuban boondoggle. He's going to drop it as a national-security issue and concentrate on the situation in Vietnam.

WJL: Yes, Sir.

JEH: Your tone did not escape me, Mr. Littell. I know that you disapprove of American colonialism and consider our God-given mandate to contain global communism as ill-conceived.

WJL: That's true, Sir.

JEH: The attendant irony has not escaped me. A closet leftist as front man for Howard Hughes and his colonialist designs.

WJL: Strange bedfellows, Sir.

JEH: And how would you describe his designs?

WJL: He wants to circumvent anti-trust laws and purchase all the hotel-casinos on the Las Vegas Strip. He won't spend a dime until he settles his stock-divestment suit with TWA and accrues at least 500 million dollars. I think the suit will resolve in three or four years.

JEH: And your job is to pre-colonize Las Vegas?

WJL: Yes, Sir.

JEH: I would like a blunt assessment of Mr. Hughes' mental state.

WJL: Mr. Hughes injects codeine in his arms, legs and penis. He eats only pizza pies and ice cream. He receives frequent transfusions of "germ-free" Mormon blood. His employees routinely refer to him as "the Count," "Count Dracula" and "Drac."

JEH: A vivid assessment.

WJL: He's lucid half the time, Sir. And he's single-mindedly fixed on Las Vegas.

JEH: Bobby's anti-Mob crusade may have repercussions there.

WJL: Do you think he'll remain in the cabinet?

JEH: No. He hates Lyndon Johnson, and Lyndon Johnson more than reciprocates. I think he'll resign his appointment. And his successor may have Las Vegas plans that I will be powerless to curtail.

WJL: Specifically, Sir?

JEH: Bobby had been considering skim operations.

WJL: Mr. Marcello and the others have plans for Mr. Hughes' holdings.

JEH: How could they not? They have a drug-addicted vampire to victimize, and you to help them suck his blood.

WJL: They know that you bear them no rancor, Sir. They'll understand that some of Bobby's plans will be implemented by his successor.

JEH: Yes. And if the Count buys into Las Vegas and cleans up its image, those plans might be abandoned.

WJL: Yes, Sir. The thought had occurred to me.

JEH: I would like to know what the Dark Prince thinks about his brother's death.

WJL: So would I.

JEH: Of course you would. Robert F. Kennedy is both your savior and your bête noire, and I'm hardly the one to indict you as a voyeur.

WJL: Yes, Sir.

JEH: Would a bug-and-tap approach work?

WJL: No, Sir. But I'll talk to my other clients and see what they suggest.

JEH: I need someone with a "fallen liberal" image. I may ask a favor of you.

WJL: Yes, Sir.

JEH: Good day, Mr. Littell.

WJL: Good day, Sir.

14

(Las Vegas, 12/4/63)

They worked him. Two pros: Buddy Fritsch and Captain Bob Gilstrap.

They used the chief's office. They hemmed Wayne in. They deployed the chief's couch.

He'd stalled the meeting. He'd filed a report and filled lies in. He downplayed Moore's vanishing act.

He drove Moore's car to the dump. He stripped the plates. He pulled out Moore's teeth. He dug out his bullets. He stuffed shotgun shells in his mouth. He gas-soaked a rag. He lit it.

Moore's head blew. He fucked up would-be forensics. He dumped the car in a sludge pit. It sunk fast.

The pit steamed. He knew chemistry. Caustics ate flesh and sheet metal.

He mock-chased Wendell D. He called Buddy Fritsch and lied. He said I can't find him. I can't find Maynard Moore.

He leaned on Willis Beaudine. He told him to split Dallas. Beaudine grabbed his dog and skedaddled. He drove by DPD. He pulled some file sheets. He obscured Wendell Durfee's KAs. He buttonholed cops—you seen Maynard Moore?

Fritsch de-Wendellized him. Fritsch pulled the plug. Fritsch called him back home.

They worked him. They hemmed him in. They cracked JFK jokes. JFK groped a nurse and a nun. JFK's last word was "pussy."

Fritsch said, "We read your report."

Gilstrap said, "You must have had some time. I mean, the Kennedy deal and you trading shots with that spook."

Wayne shrugged. Wayne played it frosty. Fritsch lit a cigarette. Gilstrap bummed one.

Fritsch coughed. "You didn't care much for Officer Moore."

Wayne shrugged. "He was dirty. I didn't respect him as a policeman."

Gilstrap lit up. "Dirty, how?"

"He was drunk half the time. He pressed people too hard."

Fritsch said, "By your standards?"

"By the standards of good police work."

Gilstrap smiled. "Those boys do things their own way."

Fritsch smiled. "You can tell a Texan."

Gilstrap said, "But not much."

Fritsch laughed. Gilstrap slapped his knees.

Wayne said, "What *about* Moore? Did he show up?"

Fritsch shook his head. "That question is unworthy of a smart boy like you."

Gilstrap blew smoke rings. "Try this one on. Moore didn't like you, so he went after Durfee himself. Durfee killed him and stole his car."

Fritsch said, "You got a six-foot-four nigger in an easily identifiable hot rod and a tristate APB out. Tell me it's anything else and you're stupid. And tell me the first cop who spots him won't kill him, just so he can brag about it."

Wayne shrugged. "That's what DPD thinks?"

Fritsch smiled. "Them and us. And we're the only two who count."

Wayne shook his head. "You find the half-dozen Dallas cops who aren't in the Klan and ask them what they think of Moore. They'll tell you how dirty he was, how many people he pissed off, and how many suspects you've got."

Gilstrap picked a hangnail. "That's your pride talking, son. You're blaming yourself because Durfee got away and killed a brother officer."

Fritsch stubbed his cigarette. "DPD's working it hard. They wanted to send one of their IA men up to talk to you, but we said no."

Gilstrap said, "They're talking negligence, son. You scuffled with Moore at the Adolphus, so he went out solo and got himself killed."

Wayne kicked a footrest. An ashtray flew.

"He's trash. If he's dead, he deserved it. You can tell those redneck cops I said that."

Fritsch grabbed the ashtray. "Whoa, now."

Gilstrap scooped up butts. "Nobody's blaming you. You proved yourself to my satisfaction."

Fritsch said, "You showed some poor judgment, *and* you showed some stones. You did your reputation in this man's police department a whole lot of good."

Gilstrap smiled. "Tell your daddy the story. Running fire with one baaaad mother humper."

Fritsch winked. "I feel lucky."

Gilstrap said, "I won't tell."

Fritsch grabbed the chief's desk bandit. Gilstrap pulled the handle. Gears spun. Three cherries clicked. Dimes blew out the chute.

Gilstrap caught them. "There's my lunch money."

Fritsch winked. "You mean there's rank. Captains get to steal from lieutenants."

Gilstrap nudged Wayne. "You'll be a captain one day."

Fritsch said, "Could you have done it? Killed him, I mean."

Wayne smiled. "Durfee or Moore?"

Gilstrap whooped. "Wayne Junior's a fireball today."

Fritsch laughed. "Some folks don't think so, but I say he's his daddy's son after all."

Gilstrap stood up. "Tell true, boy. What did you spend that cold six on?"

Wayne grinned. Wayne said, "Liquor and call girls."

Fritsch stood up. "He's got Wayne Senior's blood in his veins."

Gilstrap winked. "We won't tell Lynette."

Wayne stood up. His legs hurt. He had fucking tension cramps. Gilstrap walked out. Gilstrap whistled and jiggled his dimes.

Fritsch said, "Gil likes you."

"He likes my father."

"Don't sell yourself short."

"Did my father tell you to send me to Dallas?"

"No, but he sure liked the idea."

He worked them back—bait-and-switch—diversion. His heartbeat hit 200. His blood pressure soared. "Lone assassin"—shit. I SAW Dallas.

Wayne drove home. Wayne dawdled. Fremont was packed. Rubes waved bingo sheets. Rubes hopped casinos.

Wayne was brain-fucked. Wayne was brain-fucked off Dallas.

Pete says, "Kill him." He can't. He runs PD checks. He gets Pete's name. He queries three intel squads: L.A./New York/Miami.

Pete Bondurant: Ex-cop/ex-CIA/ex–Howard Hughes goon. Current mobbed-up enforcer.

He runs hotel registrations. 11/25: Pete and Frau Pete hit the Stardust. Their suite is comped. Pete's mobbed up. *Chi*-Mob connections implied.

Car traffic was bad. Foot traffic ditto. Rubes lugged highballs and beers.

Tail Pete. Do it discreet. Hire a patrolman. Pay him in Land o' Gold chips.

Wayne circled back. Wayne recruised Fremont. Wayne dodged Lynette and his dinner.

Lynette was running trite. Lynette ran trite lines verbatim. Jack was young. Jack was brave. Jack *realllly* loved Jackie.

Jack and Jackie lost their baby. Circa '62. Lynette fell for them then. He didn't want kids. Lynette did. She got pregnant in '61.

It froze him up. It shut him down. He froze her out. He told her to get an abortion. She said no. He addressed the Latter-day Saints. He prayed for a dead baby.

Lynette caught the gist. Lynette ran to her folks. Lynette mailed off chatty letters. She came home bone skinny. She said she miscarried. He went along with the lie.

Daddy Sproul called him. Daddy waxed revisionist. Daddy dropped details. He said Lynette got scraped in Little Rock. He said she hemorrhaged and almost died.

The marriage survived. Trite shit would tear it for real.

Lynette set up TV trays. LBJ crashed their dinner. He announced some Warren probe.

Wayne killed the sound. LBJ moved his lips. Lynette toyed with her food.

"I thought you'd want to follow it more."

"I had too much stuff going on. And it's not like I had a stake in the man."

"Wayne, you were *there*. It's the kind of thing people tell their grand . . ."

"I told you, I didn't see anything. And we're not in the grandchild business."

Lynette balled her napkin. "You've been nothing but sullen since you got back, and don't tell me it's just Wendell Durfee."

"I'm sorry. That crack was ugly."

Lynette wiped her lips. "You know I gave up on that front."

"Tell me what it is, then."

Lynette turned the TV off. "It's the new sullen you, with that patronizing attitude that all the cops have. You know, 'I've seen things that my schoolteacher wife just wouldn't understand.' "

Wayne jabbed his roast beef. Wayne twanged the fork.

Lynette said, "Don't play with your food."

Wayne sipped Kool-Aid. "You're so goddamn smart in your way."

Lynette smiled. "Don't curse at my table."

"You mean your TV tray."

Lynette grabbed the fork. Lynette mock-stabbed him. Blood juice dripped and pooled.

Wayne flinched. Wayne hit the tray. His glass tipped and doused his food.

Lynette said, "Shit."

Wayne walked to the kitchen. Wayne dumped his tray in the sink. He turned around. He saw Lynette by the stove.

She said, "What happened in Dallas?"

Wayne Senior lived south—Paradise Valley with land and views.

He had fifty acres. He grazed steers. He butchered them for bar-b-que meat. The house was tri-level—redwood and stone—wide decks with wide views.

The carport covered an acre. A runway adjoined it. Wayne Senior flew biplanes. Wayne Senior flew flags: The U.S./the Nevada/the Don't-Tread-on-Me.

Wayne parked. Wayne killed his lights. Wayne skimmed the radio. He caught the McGuire Sisters—three-part harmony.

Janice had a dressing room. It faced the carport. She got bored. She changed clothes. She left her lights on to draw looks.

Wayne settled in. The Sisters crooned. "Sugartime" merged with "Sincerely." Janice walked through the light. Janice wore tennis shorts and a bra.

She posed. She dropped her shorts. She picked up capris. Her panties stretched and slid low.

She put the capris on. She unpinned her hair and combed it back. Her gray streak showed—silver in black—the pink capris clashed.

She pirouetted. Her breasts swayed. The Sisters supplied a soundtrack. The lights dimmed. Wayne blinked. It all went too fast.

He calmed down. He turned the car off. He walked through the house. He went straight back. Wayne Senior always perched outside. The north-deck view magnetized.

It was cold. Leaves strafed the deck. Wayne Senior wore a fat sweater. Wayne leaned on the rail. Wayne killed his view.

"You never get bored with it."

"I appreciate a good vista. I'm like my son that way."

"You never called and asked about Dallas."

"Buddy and Gil briefed me. They were thorough, but I'd still like to hear your version."

Wayne smiled. "In time."

Wayne Senior sipped bourbon. "The crap-game ruckus tickled me. You chasing that colored boy."

"I was brave and stupid. I'm not sure you would have approved."

Wayne Senior twirled his walking stick. "And I'm not sure you want my approval."

Wayne turned around. The Strip beamed. Neon signs pulsed.

"My son rubbed shoulders with history. I wouldn't mind a few details."

Cars left Vegas—the losers' exodus—southbound headlights.

"In time."

"Mr. Hoover saw the autopsy pictures. He said Kennedy had a small pecker."

Wayne heard gunshots north-northeast. Broke gambler blows town. Broke gambler pulls gun. Broke gambler unwinds.

"LBJ told Mr. Hoover a good one. He said, 'Jack was a strange bedfellow long before he entered politics.' "

Wayne turned around. "Don't gloat. It's fucking undignified."

Wayne Senior smiled. "You've got a foul mouth for a Mormon."

"The Mormon Church is a crock of shit, and you know it."

"Then why'd you ask the Saints to kill your baby?"

Wayne grabbed the rail. "I forgot that I told you that."

"You tell me everything—'in time.' "

Wayne dropped his hands. His wedding band slid. He missed meals. He dropped weight. He fretted up Dallas.

"When's your Christmas party?"

Wayne Senior twirled his stick. "Don't divert conversation so abruptly. You tell people what you're afraid of."

"Don't press on Lynette. I know where you're going."

"Then I'll go there. It's a kid marriage that you're bored with, and you know it."

"Like you and my mother?"

"That's right."

"I've heard it before. You're here and you've got what you've got. You're not a cluck selling real estate in Peru, Indiana."

"That's right. Because I knew when to fold my hand with your mother."

Wayne coughed. "You're saying I'll meet my Janice and walk like you did."

Wayne Senior laughed. "Shitfire. Your Janice and my Janice are one and the same."

Wayne blushed. Wayne's ears fucking singed.

"Shitfire. Just when I think I've lost sway with my boy, I light him up like a Christmas tree."

A shotgun blew somewhere. It roused some coyote yells.

Wayne Senior said, "Someone lost money."

Wayne smiled. "He probably lost his stake at one of your joints."

"*One of?* You know I only own one casino."

"The last I heard, you had points in fourteen. And the last time I checked, that was illegal."

Wayne Senior twirled his stick. "There's a trick to lying. Hold to the same line, regardless of who you're with."

"I'll remember that."

"You will. But you'll remember who told you right about the same time."

A flying bug bit Wayne. Wayne swatted it.

"I don't see your point."

"You'll remember that your father told you, and speak some godawful truth out of pure cussedness."

Wayne smiled. Wayne Senior winked. He twirled his stick. He dipped it. He ran his stick repertoire.

"Are you still the only policeman who cares about those beat-up colored whores?"

"That's right."

"Why is that?"

"Pure cussedness."

"That and your spell in Little Rock."

Wayne laughed. "You should have been there. I broke every states' rights law on the books."

Wayne Senior laughed. "Mr. Hoover's going after Martin Luther King. He's got to find himself a 'fallen liberal' first."

"Tell him I'm booked up."

"He told me Vietnam's heating up. I said, 'My son was in the Eighty-Second Airborne. But don't hold your breath for him to re-enlist—he'd rather fight rednecks than Reds.' "

Wayne looked around. Wayne saw a chip bucket. Wayne grabbed some Land o' Gold reds.

"Did you tell Buddy to send me to Dallas?"

"No. But I've always thought a cold money run would do you some good."

Wayne said, "It was enlightening."

"What did you do with the money?"

"Got myself in trouble."

"Was it worth it?"

"I learned a few things."

"Care to tell me?"

Wayne tossed a chip. Wayne Senior pulled his hip piece. He shot the chip. He nailed it. Plastic shards flew.

Wayne walked inside. Wayne detoured by the dressing room. Janice shot him a view.

Bare legs. A dance step. Streaked-hair allure.

15

(Las Vegas, 12/6/63)

Dallas tweaked him. He should have killed Junior. Junior should have killed the spook.

Vegas sparkled—fuck death—should-haves meant shit. Nice breeze/nice sun/nice casinos.

Pete cruised the Strip. Pete logged distractions:

The Tropicana course. Cocktail carts abundant. Drive-ins. Carhops on skates. Uplift abundant.

Pete made two circuits. Shit popped out:

Some nuns hit the Sands. They spot Frank Sinatra. They swoon and piss Frank off. They shvitz up his Sy Devore suit.

Grief by the Dunes:

Two cops grab two spics. The spics bleed very large. The scene vibes busboy brouhaha. Juan fucked Ramon's sister. Ramon had first dibs. Shivs by the low-roller buffet.

Nice mountains. Neon signs. Jap-tourist shutterbugs.

Pete made three circuits. The Strip show wore thin. Pete re-tweaked Dallas.

BE USEFUL: Sacred fucking text. The Hughes deal would take years. Ward said so. Carlos agreed. Carlos said Pete *should* push dope in Vegas—but—the other Boys have to agree.

Ward was *très* smart. The Arden move was *très* dumb. Ward tripped on his dick—at a *très* bad time.

Ward was in D.C. and New Orleans. Jimmy H. wanted him. Carlos beckoned. Carlos wants to snip loose ends. Carlos wants Ward's take. Carlos trusts Ward—but Ward always ridicules slaughter.

Arden saw the hit team. Arden knew Betty Mac. Arden knew Hank Killiam. A *très* safe bet: Carlos wants to clip them. A *très* safe bet: Ward calls it rash.

A bug was spreading. Call it the Mercy Flu. Call it the Me-No-Kill Blues. He should have killed Junior. Junior should have killed the shine.

He watched Junior work. He climbed an adjacent hill. He got a covert view. Junior diced Maynard Moore. Junior cut through his brain pan. Junior pulled slugs. His knife slipped. He ate bone chips. He hacked them out and rocked steady.

He checked Junior out. Three intel squads: L.A./New York/Miami. His guys said Junior checked *him* out.

His contacts hated Junior. They said Wayne Senior was a stud. They said Wayne Junior was a geek.

Junior passed him the mercy bug. Junior let the nigger live. Junior misread his options. The nigger vibed stupe. The nigger vibed homing pigeon. The nigger might home back here.

Pete cruised. Pete checked lounge marquees. Pete got the gestalt.

Name acts. No-name acts. Dick Contino/Art & Dottie Todd/the Girlzapoppin' Revue. Hank Henry/the Vagabonds/Freddy Bell & the Bellboys. The Persian Room/the Sky Room/the Top O' the Strip.

Jack "Jive" Schafer/Gregg Blando/Jody & the Misfits. The Dome of the Sea/the Sultan's Lounge/the Rumpus Room.

Call it: Toilets and carpet joints. Some high-end rooms. Call it for keeps: Find Barb a spot. Find her some nonunion backup. Scotty & the Scabs or the Happy Horseshitters—a fixed rate and a cut.

Pete parked in the Sands lot. Pete hit some casinos—the Bird/the Riv/the DI. He caught a lull. Shit stood out boldfaced.

He played blackjack. He observed:

A pit boss bops on a card cheat. The fuck wears a card-sleeve prosthesis. The fuck shoots cards out his cuffs.

He saw Johnny Rosselli. They schmoozed. They talked up the Hughes deal. Johnny praised Ward Littell—dig the threat implied.

Ward's crucial to our plans. You're muscle—you're not.

Johnny said *ciao.* Two call girls hovered. It vibed three-way.

Pete walked. Pete hit the Sands/the Dunes/the Flamingo. Pete dug the low lights and thick rugs.

Sparks shot off his feet. His socks bipped and buzzed.

He hit bars. He drank club soda. He honed his cave vision. He watched barmen work. Call girls ducked him. He was 6'5"/230. He vibed strongarm cop.

What's *this:*

A barman pours pills—six in a shot glass—a waitress picks up.

He braced the barman. He flashed a toy badge. He growled very gruff.

The barman laughed. His son wore a badge like that. His son ate Cocoa Puffs.

The man oozed style. Pete bought him a drink. The man spritzed on Vegas and dope.

Horse/weed/cocaine—verboten. The fuzz enforced the trifecta. The Mob enforced the No-"H" Law.

They tortured pushers. They killed them. Local hypes copped in L.A. Local hypes rode the Heroin Highway.

Pills were cool: Red devils/yellow jackets/high hoppers. Ditto liquid meth sans spike. Drink it—don't shoot it—fear the spike-phobic fuzz.

The fuzz sanctioned pills. Two Narco units—Sheriff's/LVPD. Pills got pipelined in: T.J. to L.A./L.A. to Vegas. Local quacks consigned pills. They fed barmen and cabbies. They fed pill fiends Vegaswide.

The West LV coons craved white horse. Said coons itched to ride. The No Horse Rule de-horsed them and kept them de-satisfied.

Pete walked. Pete hit the Persian Room. Pete watched Dick Contino rehearse. He knew Dick. Dick played squeeze-box gigs for Sam G. Dick owed the Chicago Cartel. The Boys attached his check. The Boys bought his food. The Boys paid his rent and bought his kids' threads.

Dick pitched a tale of woe—woe is me—lots of woe and no tail. Pete slid him two C's. Dick spritzed the Vegas lounge scene.

The Detroit Boys ran the local. The steward took bribes. He usurped the prime snatch. He suborned them to hook. They worked the Lake Mead cruise boats. Lounge kids kept rough hours. They ate breakfast exclusive. The lounge scene ran on Dexedrine and pancakes.

Pete walked. Pete caught Louis Prima in rehearsal. An old geek chewed his ear off.

Pops booked no-name acts. Pops father-henned the girls if they blew him. Pops told them who to avoid:

Shvartze pimps. "Talent scouts." Cockamamie "producers." Skin-mag men and schmucks with no address.

Pete thanked him. Pops bragged. Pops relived his salad days as a pimp. I ran trim—the best in the west—I scored for the late JFK.

Pete broke three C-notes. Pete glommed sixty five-spots.

He grabbed a scratch pad. He wrote down his phone number sixty fucking times. He hit a liquor store. He bought sixty short dogs. He grabbed his sap and drove to West Vegas.

He cruised in slow. He wore the sap. He held his automatic. He saw:

Dirt streets. Dirt yards. Dirt lots. Shack chateaus abundant.

Tar-paper pads with cinder-block siding. *Beaucoup* churches/one mosque. *ALLAH IS LORD!* signs. Allah signs revised to *JESUS!*

Lots of street activity. Jigs cooking bar-b-que in fifty-gallon drums.

The Wild Goose Bar/the Colony Club/the Sugar Hill Lounge. Streets named for Presidents and letters. Shit cars ubiquitous—ad hoc housing:

Two-tenant Chevys. Bachelor Lincolns. Bring-the-whole-family Fords.

Pete cruised slooooow. Uppity coons flipped him off. They scowled. They chucked beer cans. They dinged his fender skirts.

He stopped at a rib drum. A halfbreed served short ends. A chow line pressed in. They scoped Pete. They snickered. They sneered.

Pete smiled. Pete bowed. Pete bought them lunch.

He tipped the breed fifty. He passed out short dogs and fives. He passed out his phone-number slips.

A silence ensued. Said silence built. Said silence lapsed slooooow.

Say what, big man? Say what, daddy-o?

Pete talked:

Who sells shit? Who's seen Wendell Durfee? Who's hot to buck the No-Horse Law? Shouts overlapped—little gems—some nuggets in rebop & jive.

These busboys sell red devils. They works at the Dunes. Dig on fucking Monarch Cab. Them guys push whites and RDs. Monarch got soul. Monarch work West LV. Monarch go where other cabs won't.

Dig on Curtis and Leroy—they gots plans—they wants to push horse. They baaaaaaaad. They say fuck the rules. They say fuck them wop motherfuckers.

Shouts overlapped—more rebop/more jive. Pete yelled. Pete displayed charisma. Pete restored calm.

He told the breed to call the Wild Goose. He told the spooks to call HIM.

IF you see Wendell Durfee. *IF* Curtis and Leroy move horse.

He pledged a fat reward. He got an ovation: YOU THE FUCKIN' MAN!

He drove to the Wild Goose. Some spooks jogged along. They capered and waved their short dogs.

The Goose was packed. Pete replayed his act. The coons loved it. Pete cut through jive & rebop.

He got no dish on Curtis and Leroy. He got rumors on Wendell D. Wicked Wendell—worse than his rep—a rape-o/a shitbird/a heel. A homing pigeon—Vegas born-and-bred—a Vegas moth to the flame.

Shouts overlapped. Spooks ad-libbed. A spook defamed Wayne Tedrow Senior.

Slumlord Senior stiffed him. Slumlord Senior fucked him. Slumlord Senior raised his rent. The noise got bad. Pete got a headache. Pete dosed it with pork rinds and scotch.

The Senior talk tweaked him—a gem within jive. Junior worked the intel squad. Junior had the gaming board files.

The spook gained steam. The spook digressed off Senior. The spook sparked other spooks. They aired the Spook Agenda *wiiiiide*.

Jim Crow. Civil rights. Real-estate sanctions. Praise for Martin Luther King.

The vibe went bad. The spooks vibed lynch mob. Pete caught bum looks:

WE THE MAN! YOU the ofay exploiter!

Pete walked out. Pete moved fast. Pete caught some elbows.

He hit the sidewalk. A kid buffed his car. He tipped him. He pulled out. A Chevy pulled out on cue.

Pete caught the move. Pete checked his rearview. Pete made the driver:

Young/white/cop haircut. Some kind of kid fuzz.

Pete zigzagged. Pete blew a stop sign. The Chevy stuck tail-close. They hit LV proper. Pete stopped at a light. Pete set the emergency brake.

The Chevy idled. Pete walked back. Pete twirled his belt sap. The kid cop played cool. The kid cop twirled a play chip.

Pete reached in. Pete grabbed it. The kid cop guuuulped.

A red chip—$20—scrip for the Land o' Gold. Shit—Wayne Senior's joint.

Pete laughed. Pete said, "Tell Sergeant Tedrow to call me."

16

(Washington, D.C., 12/9/63)

ID work—old forms and smeared ink. Littell worked. His kitchen table creaked. He knew paper and smudge art. The FBI taught him.

He smudged a birth-certificate form. He baked it on a hot plate. He sliced pen tubes and rolled smears.

The *old* Arden Smith/Coates—now the *new* Jane Fentress.

The apartment was hot. It helped dry forms. Littell rolled ink on a seal-stamp. He stole it from Dallas PD.

Arden was southern. Arden talked southern. Alabama had a lax driver's-license policy. Applicants sent fees in. Birth certificates ditto. Written test forms went out.

They completed them. They mailed them in. They sent in a snapshot. They got their DL return mail.

Littell flew to Alabama—eight days back. Littell researched births and deaths. Jane Fentress was born in Birmingham. Her DOB was 9/4/26. Her DOD was 8/1/29.

He drove to Bessemer. He rented an apartment. He put "Jane Fentress" on the mailbox. Bessemer to Birmingham—twenty-two miles.

Littell switched pens. Littell spread fresh paper. Littell inked vertical lines.

Arden was a bookkeeper. Arden claimed credentials. Arden went to school in DeKalb, Mississippi. Let's upgrade her—Tulane, '49—let's give her an accounting degree.

He was due in New Orleans. He could visit Tulane. He could skim old catalogs. He could learn the academic terrain. He could forge a transcript.

He could solicit Mr. Hoover. Local agents knew Tulane. A man could plant the goods.

Littell lined six sheets—standard college forms. He worked fast. He blotted. He smudged. He smeared.

Arden was safe. He stashed her in Balboa—due south of L.A.

A hotel hideaway—paid for by Hughes Tool. Tool Co. ignored his expenses—per Mr. Hughes' edict.

He swapped notes with Mr. Hughes. They spoke on the phone. They never officially met. He snuck into Drac's lair—one time only—the assassination a.m.

There's Drac:

He's sucking IV blood. He's shooting dope in his dick. He's tall. He's thin. His nails curl back.

Mormons guarded him. Mormons cleaned his spikes. Mormons fed him blood. Mormons swabbed his injection tracks.

Drac stayed in his room. Drac *owned* his room. The hotel endured him—call it squatter's rights—Beverly Hills–style.

Littell spread photos out. Arden—three ways. One passport-DL shot/two keepsakes.

They made love in Balboa. A window blew open. Some kids heard them. The kids laughed. Their dog carried on.

Arden had sharp hips. He was bone-thin. They bumped and scraped and blundered into a fit.

Arden touched up her gray hair. Arden's pulse ran quick. She'd had scarlet fever as a kid. She'd had one abortion.

She was running. He caught her. Her run predated the hit.

Littell studied the photos. Littell studied *her*.

She had one brown eye. She had one hazel eye. Her left breast was smaller than her right. He bought her a cashmere sweater. It stretched snug on one side.

Jimmy Hoffa said, "I'm going *down?* After the fucking coup we just pulled?"

Littell went ssshhh. Hoffa shut up. Littell tossed the room. He checked the lamps. He checked the rugs. He checked under the desk.

"Ward, you worry too much. I got a fucking guard outside my office twenty-four hours a day."

Littell checked the window. Window mounts *worked*. Suction cups could be rigged to glass.

"Ward, Jesus fucking—"

No mounts/no glass plates/no cups.

Hoffa stretched out. Hoffa yawned. Hoffa dipped his chair and dropped his feet on his desk.

Littell sat on the edge. "You'll probably be convicted. The appeal process will buy you at least—"

"That cunt-lapping homo Bobby F-for-Faggot—"

"—but jury tampering is not an offense that falls under Federal sentencing guidelines, which means a discretionary decree, which—"

"—means Bobby F-for-Fuckface Kennedy wins and James R-for-Ridiculous Hoffa goes to the fucking shithouse for five or six fucking years."

Littell smiled. "That's my summary, yes."

Hoffa picked his nose. "There's more. 'That's my summary' is no kind of summary that's worth a fucking shit."

Littell crossed his legs. "You'll stay out on appeals for two or three years. I'm developing a long-range strategy to legitimize Pension Fund money and divert and launder it through foreign sources, which should kick into high gear around the time you get out. I'm meeting the Boys in Vegas next month to discuss it. I can't emphasize how important this may prove to be."

Hoffa picked his teeth. "And in the fucking meantime?"

"In the meantime, we have to worry about those other grand juries that Bobby's impaneled."

Hoffa blew his nose. "That cunt-lapping cocksucker. After what we did to fuck—"

"We need to know what Bobby thinks about the hit. Mr. Hoover wants to know, too."

Hoffa cleaned his ears. Hoffa shined on Littell. He gouged. He went in deep. He jabbed a pen. He prospected for wax.

He said, "Carlos has a lawyer at Justice."

New Orleans was hot. The air hung wet and ripe.

Carlos owned a motel—twelve rooms and one office. Carlos made people wait.

Littell waited. The office smelled—chicory and bug spray. Carlos left a bottle out—Hennessy X.O—Carlos doubted his will to abstain.

He got off the plane. He drove to Tulane. He went through catalogs. He compiled a list of GI Bill classes.

He called Mr. Hoover. He asked his favor. Mr. Hoover agreed. Yes, I'll do it—I'll plant your paper.

The air cooler died. Littell dumped his jacket. Littell undid his tie. Carlos walked in. Carlos slapped the wall unit. Cold air blew high.

"*Come va,* Ward?"

Littell kissed his ring. "*Bene, padrone.*"

Carlos sat on the desk. "You love that shit, and you're not even Italian."

"*Stavo perdiventare un prete, Signor Marcello. Aurei potuto il tuo confessore.*"

Carlos cracked the bottle. "Say the last part in English. Your Italian's better than mine."

Littell smiled. "I could have been your confessor."

Carlos poured two fingers. "You'd be out of a job. I never do anything to piss God off."

Littell smiled. Carlos offered the bottle. Littell shook his head.

Carlos lit a cigar. "So?"

Littell coughed. "We're fine. The commission's a whitewash, and I wrote the narrative brief that they'll work off. It played the way I expected."

"Despite some fuck-ups."

"Guy Banister's. Not Pete's or mine."

Carlos shrugged. "Guy's a capable guy, on the whole."

"I wouldn't say that."

"Of course you wouldn't. You wanted your crew to go in."

Littell coughed. "I don't want to argue the point."

"The fuck you don't. You're a lawyer."

The wall unit died. Carlos slapped it. Cold air blew wide.

Littell said, "The meeting is set for the fourth."

Carlos laughed. "Moe Dalitz is calling it 'the Summit.' "

"That's appropriate. Especially if we still have your vote for Pete's business."

"Pete's *potential* business? Yeah, sure."

"You don't sound too optimistic."

Carlos flicked ash. "Narcotics is a tough sell. Nobody wants to put Vegas in the shitter."

"Vegas *is* the shitter."

"No, Mr. I-Was-Almost-a-Priest, it's your fucking salvation. It's your debt to pay off, and without that debt you'd be in the shitter with your friend Kemper Boyd."

Littell coughed. The smoke was bad. The wall unit swirled it.

Carlos said, "So?"

"So, I have a plan for the Pension Fund books. It's long-range, and it derives from your plans for Mr. Hughes."

"You mean *our* plans."

Littell coughed. "Yes, ours."

Carlos shrugged—I'm bored for now—Carlos held up a file.

"Jimmy said you need a guy next to Bobby."

Littell grabbed the file. Littell skimmed the top page—one Shreveport PD rap sheet/one note.

8/12/54: Doug Eversall drives home. Doug Eversall hits three kids. He's drunk. The kids die. Doug's DA pal buries it.

For *his* pal: Carlos Marcello.

Doug Eversall is a lawyer. Doug Eversall works at Justice. Bobby likes Doug. Bobby hates drunks and loves kids. Bobby doesn't know Doug's a kid-killer.

Carlos said, "You'll like Doug. He's on the wagon, like you."

Littell grabbed his briefcase and stood up. Carlos said, "Not yet."

The smoke was bad. It punched up the booze fumes. Littell almost drooled.

"We got some loose ends, Ward. Ruby bothers me, and I think we should send him a message."

Littell coughed. Here it com—

"Guy said you know the story. You know, all that grief at Jack Zangetty's motel."

Chills now—steam off dry ice.

"I know the story, yes. I know what Guy wants you to do, and I'm against it. It's unnecessary, it's too conspicuous, it's too close to Ruby's arrest."

Carlos shook his head. "They go. Tell Pete to take care of it."

Dizzy—weightless now.

"This is all on Banister. *He* let them go to the safe house. *He* screwed up on Tippit and Oswald. *He's* the drunk who'll be bragging to every right-wing shithead on God's green earth."

Carlos shook his head. Carlos waved four fingers.

"Zangetty, Hank Killiam, that Arden cunt, and Betty McDonald. Tell Pete I don't expect a big delay."

17

The Dallas paper ran it—page 6 news—NO LEADS ON MISSING POLICE-MAN.

Wayne sat in Sills' Tip-Top. Wayne hogged a window booth. He held his gun—locked & cocked—the paper covered it.

The paper loved Maynard Moore. Moore got more ink than Jack Ruby. FAN MAIL FOR ASSASSIN'S SLAYER. CHIEF LAUDS MISSING OFFICER. NEGRO SOUGHT IN BAFFLING DISAPPEARANCE.

Wayne counted down. He had eighteen days in now. The Warren probe/the "Lone Gunman"/no news as good news.

He still worried Dallas. He still skipped meals. He still pissed every six seconds.

Pete walked in. Pete showed up punctual. He saw Wayne. He sat down. He smiled.

He checked Wayne's lap. He peeked and goofed. He saw the paper.

He said, "Aww, come on."

Wayne reholstered. Wayne fumbled his gun. Wayne banged the table. A waitress saw it. Wayne blushed red. Pete cracked his knuckles.

"I watched you clean up. You did a good job, but I wish you'd thought the nigger through."

Wayne felt piss pressure. Wayne clenched up downstairs.

"You're comped at the Stardust. That means the Chicago guys brought you in."

"Keep going."

"You think I owe you for that weekend."

Pete cracked his thumbs. "I want to see your gaming board files."

Wayne said, "No."

Pete grabbed a fork. Pete twirled it. Pete squeezed it and bent it in two. The waitress saw it. The waitress freaked.

She went oooh. She dropped a tray. She made a mess.

"I could go around you. Buddy Fritsch is supposed to be nice."

Wayne looked out the window. Wayne saw a two-car crash.

Pete said, "Fucking tailgaters. I always wrote up guys like—"

"I've got the files stashed, and there's no carbons. It's an old fail-safe policy. If you go to Buddy, I'll have my father intercede. Buddy's afraid of him."

Pete cracked his knuckles. "That's all I get for Dallas?"

"Nothing happened in Dallas. Don't you watch the news?"

Pete walked out. Wayne felt piss pressure. Wayne ran to the can.

18

(Las Vegas, 12/13/63)

ne more headache/one more headache drink/one more lounge.

The Moon Room at the Stardust—low lights and moon maids in tights.

Pete sipped scotch. A moon maid fed him peanuts. Ward left him a message. A desk clerk relayed it. Wait for a Bible code—I'll Western Union it in.

Wayne Junior said no. Nos hurt. Nos fucked with him.

A moon maid dipped by—a faux redhead—dark roots and dark tan. Fuck faux redheads. Real redheads burned.

He got Barb a gig—three days ago—Sam G. pulled strings. Dig it: Barb & the Bail Bondsmen.

Permanent work—4 shows/6 nites—the Sultan's Lounge at the Sahara. Barb was rehearsing. She said the Twist was out. She said the go-go beat was in.

Nigger music. The Swim/the Fish/the Watusi. White stiffs take note.

He shitcanned Barb's ex. He shitcanned his combo. Dick Contino came through. Dick scored Barb a trio—sax/trumpet/drums—three long-term lounge denizens.

Fags. Beefcake types. USDA-certified swish.

Pete cowed them. Pete warned them. Sam G. spread the word: Barb B. was verboten. Approach once and suffer. Approach twice and die.

Barb dug Vegas. Hotel suites and nightlife. No Presidential motorcades.

West LV looked good. West LV looked contained and vice-ready.

Vice zones worked. He hit Pearl in '42. The SPs shut down some roads and cordoned the clap. White horse would work. The niggers craved it. They'd geez up. They'd stay home. They'd soil their own rug.

A moon maid slid by—a faux blonde—dark roots and Miss Clairol. She fed him some peanuts. She dropped off Ward's note.

Pete killed his drink. Pete went up to the suite. Pete got out the Gideon book. The code spanned the whole text—chapter and verse—Exodus to First John.

He worked off a scratch pad—numbers to letters—letters to words. There:

"CM's orders. Elim. 4 from motel/safe house. Call tomorrow night, 10:30 EST. Pay phone in Silver Spring, Md.: BL4-9883."

19

(Silver Spring, 12/14/63)

Perfect:

The off ramp / the road / the train station / the tracks / the platform / the phone.

A freeway adjacent. Off-ramp access. Parking-lot view. Late commuters passing through—milk runs from D.C.

Littell sat in his car. Littell watched the ramp—hold for a powder-blue Ford. Carlos described Eversall. He's a tall guy. He's got one high shoe.

9:26 p.m.

The express blew by. Cars parked and split. The local should stop at 10:00.

Littell studied his script. It stressed Eversall's time in New Orleans. It stressed Lee Oswald's time there. It stressed the '63 racket hearings. It stressed Bobby's star role.

Mob panic ensues. Two months pass. JFK dies. Eversall links the dots. Eversall sees collusion.

Littell checked his watch—9:30 sharp—hold for the man with the high shoe.

A blue Ford pulled in. Littell flashed his lights. Littell strafed the windshield and grille. The Ford braked and stopped. A tall man got out. Said man swayed on a high shoe.

Littell hit his brights. Eversall blinked and tripped. He caught himself. His bad leg buckled. His briefcase balanced him.

Littell killed his brights. Littell popped the passenger door. Eversall limped up—briefcase as ballast—Eversall fell on the seat.

Littell shut the door. Littell hit the roof light. It haloed Eversall.

Littell frisked him.

He grabbed his crotch. He pulled his shirt up. He pulled down his socks. He opened his briefcase. He went through his files. He dropped the script in.

Eversall smelled—sweat and bay rum. His breath reeked of peanuts and gin.

Littell said, "Did Carlos explain?"

Eversall shook his head. His neck muscles bobbed.

"Answer me. I want to hear your voice."

Eversall squirmed. His high shoe hit the dash.

"I never talk to Carlos. I get calls from this Cajun-type guy."

He said it slow. He blinked in time. He blinked and ducked from the light. Littell grabbed his tie. Littell jerked it. Littell pulled him back in the light.

"You're going to wear a wire and talk to Bobby. I want to know what he thinks about the assassination."

Eversall blinked. Eversall st-st-stuttered.

Littell jerked his tie. "I read a piece in the *Post*. Bobby's throwing a Christmas party, and he's inviting some people from Justice."

Eversall blinked. Eversall st-st-stuttered. He tried to talk. He popped *p*'s and *l*'s. He tried to say "Please."

"I've prepared a script. You tell Bobby that you don't like the proximity to the hearings, and you offer to help. If Bobby gets angry, you be that much more persistent."

Eversall blinked. Eversall st-st-stuttered. He tried to talk. He popped *p*'s and *l*'s. He bounced *b*'s for "Bobby."

Littell smelled his piss. Littell saw the stain. Littell rolled the windows down.

He had spare time. The pay phone was close. He cracked all the windows and aired the car out.

Trains rolled in. Women fetched their husbands. A hailstorm hit. It chipped his windshield. He tuned in the radio news.

Mr. Hoover addressed the Boy Scouts. Jack Ruby sulked in his cell. Trouble in Saigon. Bobby Kennedy bereft.

Bobby loved hard. Bobby mourned hard. *He* used to.

Late '58:

He worked the Chicago Office. Bobby worked the McClellan Committee. Kemper Boyd worked *for* Bobby. Kemper Boyd worked *against* him. Mr. Hoover deployed Kemper wide.

Mr. Hoover hated Bobby. Bobby chased the Mob. Mr. Hoover said the Mob did not exist. Bobby humbled Mr. Hoover. Bobby disproved his lie.

Mr. Hoover liked Kemper Boyd. Boyd liked his friend Ward. Boyd got Ward a choice Bureau job:

The Top Hoodlum Program—Mr. Hoover's late retraction—Mr. Hoover's late nod to the Mob. Call it a half-measure. Call it a publicity shuck.

He worked the THP. He fucked up. Mr. Hoover kicked him back to the Red Squad. Boyd stepped up then. Boyd stepped up for Bobby. Boyd offered friend Ward a *real* job.

Covert work—unpaid.

He took the job. He culled anti-Mob data. He leaked it to Boyd. Boyd leaked it to Bobby.

He never met Bobby. Bobby called him the Phantom. Bobby logged a persistent rumor. Bobby passed it on to Kemper Boyd.

The Teamsters kept a *private* set of pension-fund books. The "real" books hid one billion dollars.

He chased the "real" books. He traced them to a man named Jules Schiffrin. He stole the "real" books—late in '60.

Schiffrin discovered the theft. Schiffrin had a heart attack. Schiffrin died that night. Littell hid the books. Said books were coded. Littell decoded one entry fast.

The code rebuked a royal clan. The code proved that Joe Kennedy was mobbed-up tight.

Joe fed the fund. Joe gorged it. Joe invested 49 million dollars. It was laundered. It was lent. It suborned politicians. It financed labor rackets.

The base sum stayed in the fund. The money notched compound interest. The money greeeeeeew.

Joe let it ride. The Teamsters held his assets. Littell did not tell Bobby. Littell did not assault his dad.

He kept the books. He ignored his Red Squad work. He befriended a name leftist. Mr. Hoover found out. Mr. Hoover fired him.

Jack Kennedy was elected. Jack made Bobby his AG. Bobby got Boyd work at Justice.

Boyd interceded. Boyd braced Bobby—employ the Phantom, please.

Mr. Hoover interceded. Mr. Hoover braced Bobby—don't employ Ward J. Littell. He's a drunk. He's a sob sister. He's a Communist.

Bobby kowtowed. Bobby cut the Phantom off. The Phantom kept the "real" books. The Phantom quit booze. The Phantom lawyered freelance. The Phantom cracked the fund-book code.

He tracked a billion dollars. He tracked intakes and transfers. He studied and extrapolated and *knew:*

The funds could be diverted. The funds could be deployed legally.

He hoarded the knowledge. He hid the books. He inked up a duplicate set. He hated Bobby now. He hated Jack K. by extension.

Boyd was fixed on Cuba. Carlos M. ditto. Carlos financed exile groups. The Boys wanted to oust Fidel Castro. The Boys wanted to reclaim their Cuban hotels.

Boyd worked for Bobby. Boyd worked for the CIA. Bobby hated Carlos. Bobby deported Carlos. The Phantom knew deportation law.

Boyd set him up with Carlos. The Phantom became a Mob lawyer. It felt morally and hatefully correct.

Carlos set him up with Jimmy Hoffa. Mr. Hoover reappeared.

Mr. Hoover made nice. Mr. Hoover praised his comeback. Mr. Hoover set him up with Mr. Hughes. Mr. Hoover shared his Bobby-Jack hate.

He worked for Carlos and Jimmy. He planned the Hughes-Vegas deal. Bobby attacked the Mob. Jack dropped the Cuban cause. Jack curtailed the hothead exiles.

Pete and Boyd stole some dope. Things went blooey. The Boys got very mad.

He braced Carlos. He said let's kill Jack. He said let's nullify Bobby. Carlos said yes. Carlos vouched the plan. Carlos brought Pete and Boyd in.

Carlos fucked them. Carlos opted for Guy B. Carlos sent Guy to Dallas.

A late bill came due. Late fees accrued. He had the "real" books. He had the data. He had them unsuspected and clean.

He was wrong. Carlos *knew* he had them. Carlos saw him ascend. Carlos called in the bill due.

Carlos said *you're* going to sell Hughes Las Vegas—and *we're* going to fuck him. *You* know the books. *You* cracked the code. *You* have money plans. *That* money. Plus the *Hughes* money. Equals *our* money—juiced by *your* long-range strategy.

He returned the books. He kept the dupes. His theft was near-open goods. Carlos knew. Carlos told Sam G. Sam told Johnny Rosselli.

Santo knew. Moe Dalitz knew. No one told Jimmy. Jimmy was crazy. Jimmy was shortsighted. Jimmy would kill him.

Littell skimmed newscasts. Littell got crossband blips: LBJ/Kool Menthol/Dr. King and Bobby.

He met Bobby—three days pre-Dallas—he mis-ID'd himself. He said I'm just a lawyer. He said I have a tape. Bobby gave him ten minutes of time.

He played his tape. A hood indicted Joe Kennedy.

For: Pension Fund fraud/collusion/long-term racketeering.

Bobby called his father's bank. The manager confirmed details. Bobby brushed tears back. Bobby raged and grieved. It felt all good then. It felt all hateful now.

The news signed off. A deejay signed on. Mr. Tunes—comin' at ya.

The phone rang.

Littell ran. Littell slid on hailstones. Littell grabbed the receiver.

Pete said, "Junior won't play. The fucking kid stalemated me."

"I'll talk to Sam. We'll make a different app—"

"I'll clip Zangetty and Killiam. That's it. I won't clip the women."

The booth was hot. The windows fogged. The storm produced steam.

"I agree. We'll have to finesse Carlos."

Pete laughed. "Don't shit me. You know it's more than that."

"What are you saying?"

Pete said, "I know about Arden."

DOCUMENT INSERT: 12/19/63. Verbatim telephone call transcript.
Marked: "Recorded at Mr. Hughes' request. Copies to: Permanent
File/Fiscal '63 File/Security File." Speaking: Howard R. Hughes,
Ward J. Littell.

HH: Is that you, Ward?

WJL: It's me.

HH: I had a premonition last night. Do you want to hear
about it?

WJL: Certainly.

HH: I know that tone. Mollify the boss so he'll get back to business.

(WJL laughs.)

HH: Here's my premonition. You're going to tell me that it will
take years to divest my TWA stock, so I should mind my p's and
q's and put the whole thing out of mind.

WJL: Your premonition was accurate.

HH: That's all you have to say? You're letting me off that easy?

WJL: I could describe the legal processes involved in divesting
half a billion dollars' worth of stock and tell you how much you've
impeded the progress by dodging various subpoenas.

HH: You're feeling your oats today. I'm not up to sparring with
you.

WJL: I'm not sparring, Mr. Hughes. I'm observing.

HH: And your latest estimate is?

WJL: We're two years away from a judgment. The appeals
process will extend for at least nine to fourteen months. You
should discuss the details with your other attorneys and move
things along by pre-submitting your depositions.

HH: You're my favorite attorney.

WJL: Thank you.

HH: Only Mormons and FBI men have clean blood.

WJL: I'm not much of an expert on blood, Sir.

HH: I am. You know the law, and I know aerodynamics, blood
and germs.

WJL: We're expert in our separate fields, Sir.

HH: I know business strategy as well. I have the assets to purchase Las Vegas now, but I prefer to wait and make the purchase
with my stock windfall.

WJL: That's a prudent strategy, Sir. But I should point out a few things.

HH: Point, then. I'm listening.

WJL: One, you are not going to purchase the city of Las Vegas or Clark County, Nevada. Two, you are going to attempt to purchase numerous hotel-casinos, the acquisition of which violates numerous state and federal antitrust statutes. Three, you cannot make those purchases now. You would need to deplete the cash flow necessary to operate Hughes Tool to do it, and you have yet to ingratiate yourself with the Nevada State Legislature and the right people in Clark County. Four, that is my job—and it will take time. Five, I want to wait and follow some other hotel-chain developments through the court process and collate the antitrust rulings and precedents.

HH: Jesus, that was some speech. You're a long-winded guy.

WJL: Yes, Sir.

HH: You didn't mention your Mafia pals.

WJL: Sir?

HH: I talked to Mr. Hoover. He said you've got those guys in your pocket. What's that guy's name in New Orleans?

WJL: Carlos Marcello?

HH: Marcello, right. Mr. Hoover said he eats out of your hand. He said, "When the time's right, Littell will jew those dagos down and get you your hotels at rock-bottom prices."

WJL: I'll certainly try.

HH: You'll do better than that.

WJL: I'll try, Sir.

HH: We've got to devise a germ policy.

WJL: Sir?

HH: At my hotels. No germs, no Negroes. Negroes are well-known germ conduits. They'll infect my slot machines.

WJL: I'll look into it, Sir.

HH: My solution is mass sedation. I've been reading chemistry books. Certain narcotic substances possess germ-killing character-istics. We could sedate the Negroes, lower their white-blood count and keep them out of my hotels.

WJL: Mass sedation would require certain sanctions that we might not get.

HH: You're not convinced. I can tell by your voice.

WJL: I'll give it some thought.

HH: Think about this. Lee Oswald was a germ conduit and a

deadly-disease transmitter. He didn't need a rifle. He could have breathed on Kennedy and killed him.

WJL: It's an interesting theory, Sir.

HH: Only Mormons and FBI men have clean blood.

WJL: You've got quite a few Mormons in Nevada. There's a man named Wayne Tedrow Senior that I may approach on your behalf.

HH: I've got some good Mormons here. They set me up with Fred Otash.

WJL: I've heard of him.

HH: He's the "Private Eye to the Stars." He's been running a string of Howard Hughes look-alikes all over L.A., like Pete Bondurant used to. Those subpoena servers follow them around like robots.

WJL: Again, Sir. Dodging subpoenas only prolongs the whole process.

HH: Ward, you're a goddamn killjoy.

(WJL laughs.)

HH: Freddy's Lebanese. Those people have high white-cell counts. I like him, but he's no Pete.

WJL: Pete's working with me in Las Vegas.

HH: Good. Frenchmen have low white-cell counts. I read it in the *National Geographic*.

WJL: He'll be pleased to hear it.

HH: Good. Tell him I said hello, and tell him to procure me some medicine. He'll know what I mean. Tell him my Mormons have been bringing me inferior goods.

WJL: I'll tell him.

HH: Let me make one thing clear before I hang up.

WJL: Sir?

HH: I want to buy Las Vegas.

WJL: You've made yourself clear.

HH: The desert air kills germs.

WJL: Yes, Sir.

20

(Las Vegas, 12/23/63)

The Party—a Vegas perennial—Wayne Senior's Christmas bash.

A fag redid the ranch house. He added ice sculptures and snow-flocked walls. He hired elves and nymphs.

The elves were wetbacks. They slung hors d'oeuvres. They wore mock-rag coats. The nymphs whored at the Dunes. They served cleavage and drinks.

The fag brought a bandstand. The fag added a dance floor. The fag hired a bumfuck quartet.

Barb & the Bail Bondsmen—a singer and three swish ex-cons.

Wayne circulated. The combo bugged him. He popped the trumpet for flim-flam. He popped the sax for stat rape.

The singer compensated—red hair and wild legs.

Lynette circulated. The crowd meshed. Cops and Vegas trash. Mormons and Nellis brass.

Wayne Senior circulated. Janice danced solo. A crowd watched her. Janice shimmied. Janice swayed. Janice dipped looooow.

Wayne Senior walked up. Wayne Senior twirled his walking stick. A Nellis one-star grabbed it.

He cued the combo. Barb tapped a beat. The combo vamped. Barb palmed maracas.

The one-star knelt. The one-star dropped the stick looooooow.

Barb ad-libbed. "Vegas limbo mighty good, lady go down like she should."

Janice spread her legs. Janice rolled her hips. Janice popped looooow. The crowd clapped. The crowd stomped. Barb milked the beat.

Janice went looooow. Janice popped sequins and spangles. Janice popped seams. Her high heels snapped. She kicked off her shoes. She went under and up.

The crowd clapped. Janice bowed looooow. She ripped her dress. Her red panties showed.

Wayne Senior passed her a Salem. The lights went low. The combo vamped "Moonglow." A baby spot blinked. It focused on Janice. It swooped and caught Wayne Senior low.

They linked up. Janice held her cigarette. Smoke blew through the light.

Circle dance.

Wayne Senior smiled. Wayne Senior loved it. Janice mugged and mocked this corny shit.

They swayed. Janice dropped sequins. The spotlight jumped. Wayne saw Lynette. Lynette saw Wayne. Lynette saw Wayne ogle Janice.

He dodged her eyes. He walked outside. He paced the front deck. He smelled marijuana—pot alert below.

Janice toked up for parties. Janice shared with the help. You had zorched valets. You had a hundred cars—now check the runway:

One airplane valet-parked—one guest's Piper Deuce.

Wayne paced. Wayne walked the deck. Wayne fretted Dallas up.

Jack Ruby observed Hanukkah. The paper ran x-clusive pix. Two pages in: HOPE FADES FOR MISSING POLICEMAN.

Wayne watched the party. A glass door killed the noise. Check the wino elves—they're digging on Barb.

Wayne watched her.

Barb moves her lips. Barb bumps her hips. Barb hits the mike stand. Barb scans the room. Barb sees a face and melts.

Wayne hugged the glass. Wayne got an angle. Wayne tracked her eyes.

To Mr. Meltman—Pete Bondurant.

Barb melts. Fucking snowdrifts in August. Big Pete reciprocates.

Wayne cracked the door. Wayne caught the vocal: "I Only Have Eyes for You."

Wayne shut the door. His stomach dropped. He leaned on the glass. He caught a chill and saved his dinner.

Barb blew a kiss. Pete blew one back. Pete stretched and bumped his head on the ceiling.

Pete grinned. Pete went ooops! A man joined him—sunburned and thin—some shitkicker runt.

Wayne grabbed a chair. Wayne kicked up his feet. Wayne rocked off the rail. A match flared below him. Reefer smoke plumed its way up.

It smelled good. It sent him back. He toked once himself. Jump School at Fort Bragg. Let's jump stoned and watch clouds change colors.

The door slid open. Noise spilled out. Wayne smelled Janice—cigarettes and Chanel No. 5.

She walked up. She leaned on him. She pressed his shoulders and back.

Wayne said, "Come on, work."

Janice worked him. Janice dug in. Janice unknotted kinks.

"Something smells sweet down there."

"It smells like a felony roust, if I was inclined."

"Be nice, now. It's Christmas."

"You mean, 'It's Vegas, and the law's for sale.' "

Janice dug in. "I wouldn't be that blunt with a policeman."

Wayne leaned back. "Who's the one-star?"

"That's Brigadier General Clark D. Kinman. He has a powerful crush on yours truly."

"I noticed."

"You notice everything. And I noticed you ogle that singer."

"Did you notice her husband? The big guy?"

Janice worked his spine. "I noticed the airplane he came in, and the ankle holster he's wearing."

Wayne twitched. Janice tickled his neck.

"Did I touch a nerve there?"

Wayne coughed. "Who's the skinny guy?"

Janice laughed. "That's Mr. Chuck Rogers. He described himself as a pilot, a petroleum geologist, and a professional anti-Communist."

"You should introduce him to my father."

"I think they're fast friends already. They were discussing the Cuban cause or some such nonsense."

Wayne rolled his neck. "Who hired that combo?"

"Your father. Buddy Fritsch recommended them."

Wayne turned around. Wayne saw Lynette. Lynette saw him. She tapped the door glass. She flashed her watch. Wayne flashed ten fingers.

Janice said, "Spoilsport." Janice made claws. Janice goofed on draggy Lynette.

Wayne turned on the rail light. Janice walked downstairs. Sequins dropped behind her. The light made them glint.

The valets giggled. *Hola, señora. Gracias por la reefer.*

Wayne fucked with the light.

He swiveled it. He dipped it. He strafed the airplane. He caught a window. He saw shotguns and vests.

The hatch popped open. Pete B. jumped out. Wayne flashed him. Pete waved and winked.

Wayne fretted it. Wayne walked inside and rejoined the party. Midnite hit. Drunks waved mistletoe.

The eggnog was out. Ditto the prewar cognac. Ditto the pre-Castro cigars.

The elves were sloshed. The nymphs were bombed. The Mormons were blotto. The ice sculptures leaked. The manger scene dripped. Baby Jesus was slush. Said Savior played ashtray. His cradle held butts.

Wayne circulated. The Bondsmen packed up. Barb lugged mike stands and drums. Wayne watched her. Lynette watched him.

Wayne Senior held court. Four Mormon elders and chairs tucked in tight. Chuck Rogers sat in. Chuck balanced two bottles. Chuck sucked gin and blueberry schnapps.

Wayne Senior dropped names—Mr. Hoover said this/Dick Nixon said that. The elders laughed. Chuck shared his jugs. Wayne Senior passed him a key.

Chuck palmed it. Chuck stood up. The elders laughed. The elders shared frat-boy looks.

They stood up. They walked down the side hall. Chuck bird-dogged them. They rendezvoused. They all braced the gun-room door.

Chuck unlocked it. The elders piled in. The elders chortled and yukked. Chuck stepped in. The elders snatched his booze. Chuck shut the door fast.

Wayne watched. Wayne grabbed a stray drink. Wayne guzzled it. Vodka and fruit pulp—lipstick on the glass.

The pulp killed the burn. The lipstick tasted sweet. The rush hit him low.

He walked to the gun room. He heard yuks inside. He jerked the door. He popped it.

Movie time.

Chuck ran the projector. Film hit a pull screen. Tight on: Martin Luther King.

He's fat. He's nude. He's ecstatic. He's fucking a white woman hard.

They fucked. They fucked sans sound. They fucked missionary-style. Static hiss and film flecks. Sprocket holes and numbers—FBI code.

Covert work/surveillance film/some lens distortion.

King wore socks. The woman wore nylons. The elders yukked. The projector clicked. Film cut through a slide.

The mattress sagged—plump Reverend King—the woman more so. An ashtray bounced on the bed—butts scattered and flew.

Chuck grabbed a flashlight. Chuck centered the beam. Chuck palmed a 4-by-6 tract.

King thrashed—the camera panned—Trojan rubbers on a nightstand.

Chuck yelled—pipe down now—Chuck read from the tract. "Big Bertha said, 'Maul me, Marty! We shall overcooooooome!' "

Wayne ran up. Chuck saw him. Chuck gawked—what the—

Wayne kicked the projector. The spools flew and rolled. The film hit three walls and went dead. The elders backed up. The elders tripped and banged heads. The elders knocked the screen down.

Wayne grabbed the tract. Chuck backed off. Wayne shoved him and ran out. He cut down the side hall. He grazed the bandstand. He sideswiped some nymphs and elves.

He made the front deck. He grabbed the rail light. He honed it and flashed on the tract.

There—Wayne Senior's print style. The paper stock/the margins/the type.

Text and cartoons. Martin Luther Coon and the plump woman. Fat Jews with fangs.

Martin Luther Coon—priapic.

His dick's a branding iron. It's red hot. The head's a hammer-and-scythe.

Wayne spat on the picture. Wayne ripped it crossways. Wayne shredded it up.

21

(New Mexico, 12/24/63)

Gusts kicked in. The plane dipped resultant.

The sky was black. The air was wet. Ice hit the props. Altus, Oklahoma—due east.

Chuck flew low. Chuck flew radar-proof. Chuck flew minus landing log. No airstrip. No runway. We're heading for Jack's *rural* lodge.

The cockpit was cramped. The cockpit was cold. Pete goosed the heat. He called ahead. He played tourist. He heard that Jack Z. had three guests.

Quail hunters. Praise Jesus—all men.

Chuck knew the lodge. Chuck spent time there. Chuck knew the floor plan. Jack slept in the office. Jack parked his guests close. There'd be three rooms with through doors.

Pete checked the cargo hold:

Flashlights/shotguns/magnums. Kerosene/gunnysacks. Friction tape/rubber gloves/rope. A Polaroid camera/four straitjackets/four honey jars.

It was overkill. Carlos loved wet work. Carlos thought plans up. Carlos popped his rocks secondhand.

Chuck read a hate tract. The dashboard threw light. Pete saw cartoons and FBI text. Hate and smut—a coon named Bayard Rustin—a queer cluster-fuck.

Pete laughed. Chuck said, "Why'd we go to that party? I'm not complaining, now. I met a few kindred souls."

The plane dipped. Pete bumped his head.

"I was letting someone know that I won't go away."

"You want to tell me who and why?"

Pete shook his head. The plane jumped. Pete's knees hit the dash.

Chuck said, "Mr. Tedrow's some kind of American. That's more than I can say for his son."

"Junior's a piece of work. Don't underestimate him."

Chuck popped Dramamine. "Mr. Tedrow knows all the right people. Guy B. said he put some cash into a certain operation."

Pete rubbed his neck. "There *was* no operation. Don't you read the fucking *New York Times?*"

Chuck laughed. "You mean I was dreaming then?"

"Treat it that way. You'll live longer."

"Then I must've dreamed up all those people that Carlos wants to clip."

Pete rubbed his eyes. Fuck—Headache #3,000.

"Then I'll be dreaming when we take out Jack Z., and I'll *really* be dreaming when we find old Hank and those cunts Arden and Bet—"

Pete grabbed his neck. "Nothing happened in Dallas, and nothing's happening now."

3:42 a.m.

They touched down. The ground was glass. Chuck cut the flaps and braked. They spun. They brodied on ice. They did figure eights and stalled in tall grass.

They put their vests on. They grabbed flashlights/shotguns/magnums. They screwed on silencers.

They hiked southeast. Pete paced it out: .32 miles. Low hills. Caves set in sheet rock. Cloud cover and a high moon.

There—the lodge—down on paved land.

Twelve rooms. A horseshoe court. Dirt-road access. No lights. No sounds. Two jeeps upside the office.

They walked up. Chuck stood point. Pete flashed the door. He saw a spring lock. He saw a loose knob. He saw a workable gap.

He pulled his knife. He wedged it in. He snapped the bolt. He walked in. The door creaked. He kept his beam low.

Three steps to the counter—hold for a ledger on a chain.

He walked up blind. Chuck's floor plan worked. He bumped the counter. Eyes left—a side door wide open. Room #1—dark.

His eyes adjusted. He squinted. He caught gray tones in black. He looked through room 1. He squinted. He saw the room #2 door ajar.

Ears left—snores in room 1. Ears front—snores behind the counter.

Pete smelled paper. Pete touched the countertop. Pete brushed the ledger. He flashed the top page. He saw three guests logged in—housed in rooms 1/2/3.

Pete leaned on the counter. Pete pulled his piece. Pete flashed his light and aimed at the snores. There's Jack Zangetty—face-up on a cot—eyes shut and mouth wide for flies.

Pete aimed off the beam. Pete squeezed a shot. Jack's head snapped. Jack's teeth exploded.

The silencer worked—sounds like a cough and a sneeze. One more now—safekeeping.

Pete aimed off the beam. Pete squeezed a shot. Pete nailed Jack's wig. Blood and synthetic hair/a cough and a sneeze.

Impact—the wig flew. Impact—Jack rolled off the cot.

Jack hit a bottle. The bottle fell. The bottle bumped and rolled. *Loud* bumps. *Loud* noise. *Loud* rolls.

Pete killed his light. Pete ducked low. Knee cartilage crunched. Eyes left/ears left/catch the doorway.

There now—a man laughs/a bed squeaks.

"Jack, is that a fresh jug you got?"

Light hues in the doorway—the geek's got white pajamas.

Pete flashed his light. Pete tracked up a white swath. Pete hit the man's eyes. He aimed off the beam. He squeezed a shot. He caught the 10-ring.

Blood and white blotting/a cough and a sneeze.

The man flew. The man hit the door. The man ripped the door loose. Eyes left—there's light—the #2 doorway. Ears left—there's boot thunks and zipper snags.

Pete proned out. Pete aimed. Now—watch the door.

A man opened it. Said man paused. Said man walked through room 1. Said man crouched and aimed a 30.06.

Pete aimed his piece. The man got close. A shotgun went off. Glass shattered—from the *out*side—pellets trashed a *side* window.

Chuck popping rounds. Chuck's special load—poison buckshot.

The man froze. Glass spritzed him. He covered his eyes. He ran blind. He bumped chairs. He coughed glass.

Pete fired. Pete missed. Chuck vaulted the window. He ran up fast. He nudged the man—BOO!—he shot the man in the back.

The man flew. Pete caught shell wads and BBs. Chuck ran south. Chuck blew out door #3.

Pete ran back. Chuck hit the lights. Light hit a man under the bed. He sobbed. His legs stuck out. He wore paisley PJs.

Chuck aimed low. Chuck blew his feet off. The man screamed. Pete shut his eyes.

The wind died. The day sparkled. The cleanup dragged.

They stole the jeeps. They drove the stiffs to the plane. They found a cave and drove the jeeps in. They fucked with some bats. They hit their horns. They evicted them. The bats bumped their windshields. They ran their wipers. They bumped the cocksuckers back.

They dumped kerosene. They torched the jeeps. The fire burned and died. The cave contained the fumes.

They walked to the plane. They wrapped the stiffs in straitjackets. They gunnysacked them. They pried their jaws out. They poured honey in. It lured hungry crabs.

Pete snapped four Polaroids—one per victim—Carlos wanted proof.

They flew low. They hit North Texas. They saw small lakes forever. They dumped three stiffs. Two splashed and sunk. One cracked hard ice.

Chuck skimmed tracts. Chuck flew low. Chuck steered with his knees.

He had a master's degree. He read comic books. He blew JFK's brains out. He lived with his parents. He stuck to his room. He built model planes and sniffed glue.

Chuck skimmed tracts. His lips moved. Pete caught the gist: The KKK klarifies a kontroversy. White men have the biggest dicks!

Pete laughed. Chuck dipped over Lake Lugert. Pete tossed Jack Z. in the drink.

22

(Las Vegas, 1/4/64)

The Summit. The penthouse at the Dunes—one big table.

Decanters. Siphons. Candy and fruit. No cigars—Moe Dalitz was allergic.

Littell swept for bugs first. The Boys watched TV. Morning cartoons—Yogi Bear and Webster Webfoot.

The Boys took sides. Sam and Moe liked Yogi. Johnny R. liked the duck. Carlos liked Yogi's dumb pal.

Santo T. snoozed—fuck this kiddie shit.

No bugs—let's proceed.

Littell chaired the meet. The Boys dressed down—golf shirts and Bermuda shorts.

Carlos sipped brandy. "Here's the opening pitch. Hughes is non compos mental, and he thinks he's got Ward in his pocket. We sell him the hotels and make him keep our inside people. They step up the skim. He don't suspect anything, 'cause we show him some low profit figures before he buys."

Littell shook his head. "His negotiators will audit every tax return filed for every hotel, going back ten years. If you refuse to submit them, they'll try to subpoena them or bribe the right people for copies. And you can't submit doctored returns with low figures, because it will bring down your initial asking prices."

Sam said, "So?"

Littell sipped club soda. "We need the highest possible set purchase prices, with the buyout money dispersed over eighteen months. Our long-term goal is to establish the appearance of legitimately invested money, diverted into legitimate businesses and laundered within them. My plan is—"

Carlos cut in. "The plan—get to it, and lay it out in words we can understand."

Littell smiled. "We have the buyout and skim money. We purchase legitimate businesses with it. The businesses belong to recipients of pension-fund loans. They are the most specifically profitable and cosmetically noncriminal businesses that originated with loans from the 'real' books. Thus, the origin of the money is obscured. Thus, the recipients are prone to extortion and will not protest the forced buyouts. The recipients will continue to run their businesses. Our people will oversee the operations and divert the profits. We funnel the money into foreign hotel-casinos. By 'foreign' I mean Latin-American. By Latin-American I mean countries under military or strongly rightist rule. The casino profits will leave said countries untaxed. They will go into Swiss bank accounts and accrue interest. The ultimate cash withdrawals will be absolutely untraceable."

Carlos smiled. Santo clapped. Johnny said, "It's like Cuba."

Moe said, "It's ten Cubas."

Sam said, "Why stop there?"

Littell grabbed an apple. "For now, it's all long-range and theoretical. We're waiting for Mr. Hughes to dump his TWA stock and secure his seed money."

Santo said, "We're talking about years."

Sam said, "We're talking about patience."

Johnny said, "It's a virtue. I read that somewhere."

Moe said, "We watch the climate south of the border. We find ourselves a dozen Batistas."

Sam said, "Show me a spic you can't bribe."

Santo said, "All they want is a white uniform with gold epaulets."

Sam said, "They're like niggers that way."

Johnny said, "They don't tolerate Commies. You got to give them that."

Carlos grabbed some grapes. "I've got the books stashed. You have to figure that Jimmy'll fall for that jury-tampering thing."

Littell nodded. "That and his other indictments."

Sam winked. "You stole the books, Ward. Now tell us you didn't copy them over."

Johnny laughed. Moe laughed. Santo roared.

Littell smiled. "We should think about the inside people. Mr. Hughes will want to hire Mormons."

Sam cracked his knuckles. "I don't like Mormons. They hate Italians."

Carlos sipped X.O. "Do you blame them?"

Santo said, "Nevada's a Mormon state. It's like New York for the Italians."

Moe said, "You mean the Jews."

Johnny laughed. "It's a serious issue. Hughes will want to pick his own people."

Sam coughed. "We can't back down on that. We've got to keep our people inside."

Littell pared his apple. "We should find our own Mormons. I'll be talking to a man soon. He runs the Kitchen Union."

Moe said, "Wayne Tedrow Senior."

Sam said, "He hates Italians."

Moe said, "He's not wild about Jews."

Santo peeled a cigar. "To me this is bullshit. I want made guys inside."

Johnny said, "I agree."

Moe grabbed the cigar. "Are you trying to kill me?"

Carlos peeled a Mars Bar. "Let's table this for now, all right? We're talking about years down the road."

Littell said, "I agree. Mr. Hughes won't have his money for some time."

Sam peeled a banana. "It's your show, Ward. I know you got more to say."

Littell said, "Four things, actually. Two major, two minor."

Moe rolled his eyes. "So, tell us. Jesus, you have to coax this guy."

Littell smiled. "One, Jimmy knows what Jimmy knows, and Jimmy's volatile. I'm going to do my best to keep him out of jail until we've started to implement our plans for the books."

Carlos smiled. "If Jimmy knew you stole the books, he'd implement you."

Littell rubbed his eyes. "I returned them. Let's leave it at that."

Sam said, "We forgive you."

Johnny said, "You're alive, aren't you?"

Littell coughed. "Bobby Kennedy will probably resign. The new AG might have plans for Vegas, and Mr. Hoover might not be able to curtail them. I'll try to do some favors for him, learn what I can and pass it along."

Sam said, "That cocksucker Bobby."

Moe said, "The bad fucking seed."

Santo said, "That cocksucker used us. He put his faggot brother in the White House at our expense. He fucked us like the pharaohs fucked Jesus."

Johnny said, "The Romans, Santo. The pharaohs fucked Joan of Arc."

Santo said, "Fuck Bobby *and* Joan. They're both faggots."

Moe rolled his eyes. Fuck this goyishe shit.

Littell said, "Mr. Hughes hates Negroes. He wants to keep them out of his hotels, at whatever the cost. I've explained the gentlemen's agreement we've got here, but he wants more."

Santo shrugged. "Everyone hates the shines."

Sam shrugged. "Especially the civil-rights types."

Moe shrugged. "Shvartzes are shvartzes. I don't want Martin Luther King on our doorstep any more than Hughes does, but they'll get their goddamn civil rights sooner or later."

Johnny said, "It's the Reds. They agitate them and get them worked up. You can't reason with an agitated person."

Santo peeled a cigar. "They know they're not wanted. We keep the low-end spooks out and let a few uptown ones in. If King Farouk of the Congo wants to drop a hundred G's at the Sands, I say let him."

Johnny grabbed a peach. "King Farouk's a Mexican."

Santo said, "Good. If he blows all his money, we'll get him a job in the kitchen."

Sam said, "I play golf with Billy Eckstine. He's a wonderful guy."

Johnny said, "He's got white blood."

Moe said, "I play golf with Sammy Davis on a regular basis."

Carlos yawned. Carlos coughed. Carlos cued Littell.

Littell coughed. "Mr. Hughes thinks the local Negroes should be 'sedated.' It's a preposterous idea, but we may be able to turn it to our advantage."

Moe rolled his eyes. "You're the best, Ward. Nobody disputes that. But you tend to beat around the bush."

Littell crossed his legs. "Carlos has tentatively agreed that we should waive our no-narcotics rule and let Pete Bondurant sell to the Negroes here. You all know the precedent. Pete trafficked for Santo's organization in Miami from '60 to '62."

Santo shook his head. "We were funding the exiles then. That was strictly an anti-Castro thing."

Johnny shook his head. "On a one-time-only basis."

Carlos said, "I like the idea. It's a moneymaker, and Pete's a hell of a resource."

Littell said, "Let's keep him busy. We can establish a new cash source and mollify Mr. Hughes at the same time. He doesn't need to know the details. I'll call it a 'Sedation Project.' He'll like the way it sounds and be satisfied. He's like a child in some ways."

Carlos said, "It's a moneymaker. I foresee some big profits."

Sam shook his head. "I foresee ten thousand junkies turning Vegas into a shithole."

Moe shook his head. "I *live* here. I do not want to see a big fucking influx of junkie burglars, junkie heist guys, and junkie rape-os."

Santo shook his head. "Vegas is the Queen City of the West. You don't soil a place like that on purpose."

Johnny shook his head. "You've got a bunch of hopped-up niggers looking for their next fix. You're watching *The Lawrence Welk Show* and some big spook kicks the door in and steals your TV set."

Sam shook his head. "And rapes your wife while he's at it."

Santo shook his head. "You'll send tourism into the shitter."

Moe snatched Santo's cigar. "Carlos, you're outruled on this. You don't shit on your own carpet."

Carlos shrugged. Carlos turned his palms up.

Moe smiled. "You're batting five hundred, Ward. That's a hell of an average in this room. And your long-range plan is a home run."

Sam smiled. "Out of the ballpark."

Santo smiled. "Out of the fucking galaxy."

Johnny smiled. "It's Cuba all over again. With no bearded Commie faggot to fuck things up."

Littell smiled. Littell twitched. Littell almost bit his tongue.

"I want to make sure we get a unanimous license vote from the Gaming Control Board and Liquor Board. Pete tried to get a look at the LVPD intel file and got nowhere."

Santo snatched his cigar back. "We've never been able to buy off the boards. They grant their fucking licenses by whim."

Moe said, "It's the pioneer thing. You know, prejudice. We own this town, but they lump us in with the shvartzes."

Johnny said, "The files are the place to start. We've got to find the weak links and exploit them."

Sam said, "The cops guard that information. Pete B. couldn't shake it loose, so what does that tell you?"

Littell stretched. "Sam, will you have one of your people make an approach? Butch Montrose, maybe?"

Sam smiled. "For you, Ward, the moon."

Littell smiled. "I want to plant support in the state legislature. Mr. Hughes is prepared to make a series of charitable contributions and publicize them throughout Nevada, so do any of you have fav—"

Johnny cut in. "Saint Vincent de Paul."

Sam said, "The K of C."

Santo said, "Saint Francis Hospital. They cut my brother's prostrate out there."

Moe said, "The United Jewish Appeal—and fuck all you dagos."

Dracula supplied lodging—a suite at the DI. Four rooms/golf-course access/open-end lease.

His third place.

He had a place in D.C. He had a place in L.A.—two high-rise apartments. Three homes now. All ready-furnished. All depersonalized.

Littell moved in. Littell dodged golf balls. Littell tore the phones up. Littell bugswept them.

The phones were safe. He rebuilt them. He relaxed and unpacked.

Arden was in L.A. She moved toward him piecemeal. Dallas to Balboa/Balboa to L.A. Vegas scared her. The Boys partied there. She knew the Boys. She wouldn't say how.

She was his "Jane" now. She loved her new name. She loved her revised history.

He finished her transcript. She learned the details. An agent planted the goods. She told him Jane stories—straight off the cuff—she dropped details and recalled them days later.

He memorized them. He caught her subtext:

You made me. Live with your work. Don't challenge my tales. *You'll know me. I'll say who I was.*

Pete knew about Arden. Pete learned in Dallas. He trusted Pete. Pete trusted him. The Boys owned them both.

Carlos told Pete to kill Arden. Pete said, "Okay." Pete won't kill women. That's pure un-okay.

Pete killed Jack Zangetty. Pete flew to New Orleans. Pete briefed Carlos on it. Carlos loved the Polaroids. Carlos said, "Three more."

Pete drove to Dallas. Pete checked around. Pete called Carlos. Pete reported back:

Jack Ruby's nuts. He scratches. He moans. He talks to spirit husks. Hank Killiam split Dallas. Hank booked to Florida. Betty Mac split to parts unknown.

Arden? She vanished—that's all I've got. Carlos said, "Okay—for now."

The Summit succeeded. His plan wowed the Boys. They vetoed the dope plan. Pete logged a No. Pete braced Wayne Junior. Wayne Junior said No. Pete logged two Nos straight.

Doug Eversall called him—on Christmas Eve. Doug said, "I couldn't tape Bobby."

He said, "Keep your tape rig—and brace him again."

Merry Christmas. Don't fall off your high shoe. Don't drop your microphone.

He called Mr. Hoover. He said he had a Bobby source. He said he hotwired him.

He didn't say:

I need to hear Bobby's voice.

23

(Las Vegas, 1/6/64)

The heat ducts blew. The squadroom froze. Fucking igloo time.

Guys split en masse. Wayne worked solo. Wayne cleaned up his desk.

He sifted desk junk. He stacked the Dallas dailies first. He had some Ruby shit. He had bopkes on Moore and Durfee.

Sonny Liston sent a postcard. It rehashed their "good times." Sonny foresaw a Clay fight KO.

He cleaned up one file—the West LV whore jobs/reports and snapshots. Colored whores/bad bruises/smeared lipstick and contusions.

He held the file. He read it. He looked for leads. Nothing popped out. The assigned cop hated Negroes. The assigned cop hated whores. The assigned cop drew dicks in their mouths.

Wayne stacked papers. Wayne cleared his desk. Wayne locked the file up. Wayne typed reports.

The squadroom froze. The ducts blew—brrr-fucking-brrr.

Wayne yawned. Wayne craved sleep. Lynette bugged him incessant. Lynette had one refrain: "What happened in Dallas?"

He dodged her. He split home early. He worked late. He logged lounge time. He nursed beers. He caught Barb B. He nursed this big crush.

He sat near the stage. Pete sat close by. They never talked. They both eyed the redhead.

Call it leverage. Call it a buffer zone—let's stay in touch.

Lynette rode him. Lynette said don't hide from me. Lynette said don't hide with Wayne Senior.

He hid there pre-Dallas. He crushed on Janice pre-Barb. Dallas changed things. He reworked his crush time now.

He watched Barb. He played chicken with Pete concurrent. Janice played supporting crush.

He dodged Wayne Senior now. Christmas tore it. The film and the hate tracts—Wayne Senior's print style.

The oldies were one thing. "Veto Tito!"/"Castrate Castro!"/"Ban the U.N.!" It was fear shit. It was Red Tides. It was no hate overt.

He saw Little Rock. Wayne Senior didn't. The Klan torched a car. The gas cap blew. It put a colored boy's eye out. Some punks raped a colored girl. They wore rubbers. They shoved them in her mouth.

Wayne yawned. Wayne pulled carbons. The fine print blurred.

Buddy Fritsch walked up. "You bored with your work?"

Wayne stretched. "Do you care if blackjack dealers have misdemeanor convictions?"

"No, but the Nevada Gaming Commission does."

Wayne yawned. "If you've got something more interesting, I'll bite."

Fritsch straddled a chair. "I want some fresh leads on the Control Board and Liquor Board men. Everyone but the Sheriff and DA. Submit a report to me before you update your file."

Wayne said, "Why now? I update my files in the summer."

Fritsch pulled a match. His hand jumped. He missed the book. He broke the matchhead.

"Because I told you to. That's all the justifying you get."

"What kind of leads?"

"Anything derogatory. Come on, you've been there. You hold surveillance and see who gets naughty."

Wayne rocked his chair. "I'll finish my work and get on it."

"You'll get on it now."

"Why 'now'?"

Fritsch pulled a match. His hand jumped. He missed the book wide.

"Because you blew your extradition job. Because a cop went off without you and got himself killed. Because you fucked up relations between us and Dallas PD, and because I am determined to get some value out of you before you make more rank and move out of my unit."

"Value" tore it—fuck him sideways.

Wayne pulled his chair up. Wayne leaned in close. Wayne bumped Fritsch's knees hard.

"Do you think I'd kill a man for six thousand dollars and a few pats on the back? For the record, I didn't want to kill him, I couldn't have killed him, I wouldn't have killed him, and that's the best value you'll ever get out of me."

Fritsch blinked. His hands jumped. He popped big spitballs.

It played wrong. Logic 101—E follows D.

Pete wants the files. Pete knows the fail-safe procedure. One cop holds the files. Said cop probes alleged misconduct. Said cop informs the Gaming Commission.

The procedure restricts data. The procedure hinders corrupt cops. The procedure curtails corrupt PDs.

Honest cops rigged the plan—one cop/one file set. Intel cops found protégés. Intel cops passed the job on. The last intel cop died on duty. Wayne Senior pulled strings. Wayne Senior got Wayne the job.

E follows D. Pete's mobbed up. Buddy Fritsch ditto. Buddy knows the files hold *old* data. The last misconduct charge was filed in 1960.

Pete wants *new* dirt. Pete wants *hot* dirt. Pete squeezed Buddy Fritsch. Buddy's pissed at Wayne. Buddy worships Wayne Senior. Buddy knows Wayne *will* do the job.

Wayne kept his files in a bank vault. Per procedure: a safe at the main B of A.

He drove over. A clerk cracked the vault. Wayne cracked the files out. He knew the names already. He skimmed the stats and got refreshed. He wrote down addresses.

Duane Joseph Hinton. Age 46. Building contractor/Mormon. No Mob ties. Drunk/wife beater. 7/59—one accusation logged.

Hinton bribes state legislators. A snitch so states. Hinton buys them whores. Hinton gives them fight tickets. They slip him bid sheets. Thus Hinton underbids. Thus Hinton gets state building jobs.

Said tip—unverified. Case closed—9/59.

Webb Templeton Spurgeon. Age 54. Retired lawyer/Mormon. No Mob ties/no accusations logged.

Eldon Lowell Peavy. Age 46. Owner: the Monarch Cab Company/the Golden Cavern Hotel-Casino.

The Cavern drew low rollers. Monarch Cab was low-end. Cabs drove drunks to grind joints. Cabs perched at the jail. Cabs drove prostitutes. Monarch serviced West LV. Monarch drove Negroes. Monarch got cash up front.

Eldon Peavy was a fag. Eldon Peavy hired ex-cons. Eldon Peavy owned a Reno fruit bar.

Tips logged: 8/60, 9/60, 4/61, 6/61, 10/61, 1/62, 3/62, 8/62. Snitch tips—thus far unverified:

Peavy's drivers pack guns. Peavy's drivers push pills. Peavy runs male prostitutes. Peavy sells choice chicken. Peavy scouts the main-room shows. Peavy recruits dancers to fuck and suck.

They're cute. They're queer. They whore for kicks and amphetamines. They spread for male movie stars.

The last tip: logged 8/62.

Wayne worked Patrol then. Wayne made sergeant. Wayne moved to Intel: 10/8/62. The prior cop logged the tips. Said cop was bribe-proof/mean/lazy.

He crashed a market heist. He took five slugs and fed nine back. He died. He killed two wetbacks en route.

Three board men. Nine tips—unverified. Wayne checked the adjunct forms—they looked kosher.

Peavy registered his ex-cons. Peavy's tax sheets looked clean. Ditto Hinton and Spurgeon.

Wayne locked the files up. The clerk locked the vault. Wayne got some coffee. Wayne killed some time.

He dawdled. He killed more time. He drove to the station. He pulled into the lot. Buddy Fritsch pulled out. It was way weird and un-Fritsch-like.

It was 5:10. Fritsch always booked at 6:00 p.m. Fritsch booked like clockwork.

His wife divorced him—late last year. Said wife split with her dyke lover. Fritsch sulked and mooned. Fritsch grooved a cuckold routine.

He splits work at 6:00. He hits the Elks Lodge. He drinks his dinner and plays bridge.

Wayne drove past the station. Fritsch drove down 1st Street. Wayne watched him go. Fritsch turned east. The Elks Lodge was due *west*.

Wayne U-turned. Wayne laid two cars back. Fritsch hugged the curb lane. Fritsch stopped at Binion's Casino.

A man walked up. Fritsch cracked his window. The man passed an envelope. Wayne jumped lanes. Wayne nailed a view. Wayne nailed an ID:

Butch Montrose. Sam G.'s boy. One piece of shit.

24

Barb did the Wah-Watusi. She sang. She shimmied. She shook. The Bondsmen played loud. Barb missed high notes. She sang for shit. She knew it. She eschewed all airs pertaining to.

The lounge was full. Barb drew men. Call them sad sacks all. Lonely geeks and retirees—plus Wayne Tedrow Junior.

Pete watched.

Barb raised her arms. Barb threw sweat. Barb showed red stubble. It jazzed him. He loved her taste there.

Barb did the Swim. The stage light burned her freckles. Pete watched Barb. Wayne Junior watched Pete. It fucked with his nerves.

His nerves were shot. The Summit came and went. The Boys said no. Ward stated his case. Carlos concurred—let's push Big "H."

They lost the referendum—down by four votes.

He saw Carlos in New Orleans. Carlos saw the Zangetty pix. Carlos said *"Bravissimo."* They schmoozed. They schmoozed Cuba. They launched laments. The CIA shitcanned the Cuban cause. The rank & file Outfit ditto.

Pete still cared. Carlos too. The old crew found *new* work.

John Stanton was in Vietnam. The CIA was there large. Vietnam was Cuba with gooks. Laurent Guéry and Flash Elorde freelanced—right-wing muscle on call. They gigged out of Mexico City. Laurent clipped Reds in Paraguay. Flash clipped Reds in the DR.

Pete and Carlos schmoozed Tiger Kab. Good times in Miami—dope and exile recruitment. Tiger-striped cabs/black-and-gold seats/heroin and *la Causa.*

They schmoozed the hit. Carlos brought it up. Carlos schmoozed new details. Pete keyed on the pro shooter. Chuck said he was French. Carlos had *new* details.

Laurent brought him in. Laurent went Francophile. The pro had frog credentials. He was an ex-Indochine hand. He was an ex-Algerian killer.

He tried to kill Charles de Gaulle. He failed. He hated de Gaulle. He waxed homicidal. Let's kill JFK—JFK french-kissed Charlie in Paris.

Carlos waxed mad—Jack Z.'s body washed up—the Dallas paper ran news. Jack's missing guests got bopkes. Jack was dirty. Jack ran a "hide-out." Jack's death vibed "gangland job."

The wash-up felt like a fuck-up. The wash-up felt like a No. Junior said "No files." The Boys said "No dope."

Carlos said, "March." You know what I want—kill the safe-house crew.

Pete drove to Dallas. Pete fake-searched for Arden. Pete searched for Betty Mac. He tapped out. That was good. He warned Betty. Betty got smart and ran.

He got a lead on Hank Killiam. Hank was now in Florida. Hank read the Dallas paper. The Jack Z. bit scared him.

Pete called Carlos. Pete reported the lead. Pete kissed some wop ass. They schmoozed. Carlos ragged on Guy B.

Guy drank too much. Guy talked too much. Guy loved his blowhard pal Hank Hudspeth. *They* boozed too much. *They* talked too much. *They* bragged to excess.

Pete said, "I'll clip them." Carlos said, "No." Carlos changed the subject. Hey, Pete—where's that hump Maynard Moore?

Pete said a coon killed him. The DPD was pissed. The Klan kontingent issued a kontract.

Carlos laughed. Carlos howled. Carlos oozed delight.

The hit *awed* him.

They did it. They got away clean. The safe-house geeks meant shit. Carlos knew it. The hit was a kick. Let's schmooze it and relive it. Let's kill some geeks for conversation.

Pete sipped a Coke. He quit booze last week. Carlos ragged Guy. Carlos despised drunks.

Barb twirled the mike cord. Barb blew a note. Barb threw perspiration off.

Pete watched Barb. Wayne Junior watched him.

Barb gigged late. Pete went home alone.

He called room service. He stood on the terrace and dug on the Strip. He felt cold air swirl.

The phone rang. He grabbed it.

"Yeah?"

"That Pete? You know, the big guy passin' out his number on the west side?"

"Yeah, this is Pete."

"Well, that's good, 'cause I'm calling 'bout that reward."

Pete said, "I'm listening."

"You should be, 'cause Wendell Durfee's in town, and I heard he bought a gun off a craps dealer. And I also heard that Curtis and Leroy just brought in some hair-o-wine."

DOCUMENT INSERT: 1/7/64. Covert tape-recording transcript. Recorded at Hickory Hill, Virginia. Speaking: Doug Eversall, Robert F. Kennedy.

(Background noise/overlapping voices)

RFK (conversation in progress): Well, if you think it's essen—

DE: If you wouldn't mind, I'd (background noise/overlapping voices) (Incidental noise. Door slam & footsteps)

RFK (conversation in progress): Have been in here. They shed all over the rugs.

DE (coughs): I've got two Airedales.

RFK: They're good dogs. They get along well with children. (Pause: 2.6 seconds) Doug, what is it? You look the way people are telling me I look.

DE: Well.

RFK: Well, what? We're here to set trial dates, remember?

DE (coughs): Well, it's about the President.

RFK: Johnson or my brother?

DE: Your brother. (Pause: 3.2 seconds) It's, well, I don't like the thing with Ruby. (Pause: 1.8 seconds) I don't want to sound out of line, but it bothers me.

RFK: You're saying? (Pause: 2.1 seconds) I know what you're saying. He's got Mob connections. Some reporters have been digging up stories.

DE (coughs): That's the main thing, yes. (Pause: DE coughs) And, well, you know, Oswald allegedly spent some time in New—

RFK: Orleans last summer, and you used to work for the State's Attorney down there.

DE: Well, that's about—

RFK: No, but thanks. (Pause: 4.0 seconds) And you're right about Ruby. He walked in there, he shot him, and he looked relieved as hell that he did it.

DE (coughs): And he's dirty.

RFK (laughs): Cough away from me. I can't afford to lose any more work days.

DE: I'm sorry I brought all this up. You don't need to be reminded.

RFK: Jesus Christ, quit apologizing every two seconds. The sooner people start treating me normally, the better off I'll be.

DE: Sir, I—

RFK: That's a good example. You didn't start calling me "Sir" until my brother died.

DE (coughs): I just want to help. (Pause: 2.7 seconds) It's the time-line that bothers me. The hearings, Valachi's testimony, Ruby. (Pause: 1.4 seconds) I used to prosecute homicides with multiple defendants. I learned to trust time—

RFK: I know what you're saying. (Pause: RFK coughs) Factors converge. The hearings. The raids I ordered. You know, the exile camps. The Mob was supporting the exiles, so they both had motives. (Pause: 11.2 seconds) That's what bothers me. If that's what happened, they killed Jack to get at me. (Pause: 4.8 seconds) If that . . . shit . . . they should have killed . . .

DE (coughs): Bob, I'm sorry.

RFK: Quit apologizing and coughing. I'm susceptible to colds right now.

(DE laughs.)

RFK: You're right about the time-line. It's the order of things that bothers me. (Pause: 1.9 seconds) There's another thing, too.

DE: Sir? I mean—

RFK: One of Hoffa's lawyers approached me a few days before Dallas. It was very strange.

DE: What was his name?

RFK: Littell. (Pause: 1.3 seconds) I made some inquiries. He works for Carlos Marcello. (Pause: 2.3 seconds). Don't say it. Marcello is based in New Orleans.

DE: I'd be willing to contact my sources, and—

RFK: No. It's best for the country this way. No trial, no bullshit.

DE: Well, there's the Commission.

RFK: You're being naive. Hoover and Johnson know what's best for the country, and they spell it "Whitewash." (Pause: 2.6 seconds) They don't care. There's the people who care and the people who don't. They're all part of the same consensus.

DE: I care.

RFK: I know you do. Just don't labor the point. This conversation is starting to embarrass me.

DE: I'm sor—

RFK: Jesus, don't start that again.

(DE laughs.)

RFK: Will you stay on in Justice? If I resign, I mean.

DE: It depends on the new man. (Pause: 2.2 seconds) Are you going to?

RFK: Maybe. I'm just licking my wounds right now. (Pause: 1.6 seconds) Johnson might put me on the ticket. I'd take it if he asked, and some people want me to run for Ken Keating's senate seat in New York.

DE: I'll vote for you. I've got a summer place in Rhinebeck.

(RFK laughs.)

DE: I just wish there were something I could do.

RFK: Well, you made me feel better.

DE: I'm glad.

RFK: And you're right. Something about the time-line feels suspicious.

DE: Yes, that's—

RFK: We can't bring my brother back, but I'll tell you this, though. When the—(footsteps obscure conversation)—right I'll jump on it, and devil take the hindmost.

(Door slam & footsteps. Tape terminates here.)

25

(Los Angeles, 1/9/64)

He bought Jane a wallet. Saks engraved it.

Soft kid. A lowercase "j.f."

Jane fanned the sleeves. "You were right. I showed them my Alabama license, and they gave me a new one right there."

Littell smiled. Jane smiled and posed. She leaned on the window. She jutted a hip out. She blocked off the view.

Littell pulled his chair up. "We'll get you a Social Security card. You'll have all the ID you need."

Jane smiled. "What about a master's degree? You got me the B.A. already."

Littell crossed his legs. "You could go to UCLA and earn one."

"How about this? I could divide my studies between L.A., D.C., and Vegas, just to keep up with my peripatetic lover."

Littell smiled. "Was that a jibe?"

"Just an observation."

"You're getting restless. You're overqualified for a life of leisure."

Jane pirouetted. Jane dipped low and stood on her toes. She was good. She was lithe. She'd studied somewhere.

Littell said, "Some people from the safe house have disappeared. That's good news more than bad."

Jane shrugged. Jane scissored low. Her skirt brushed the floor.

"Where did you learn that?"

Jane said, "Tulane. I audited a dance class, but you won't see it on my transcript."

Littell sat on the floor. Jane scissored up to him.

"I want to find a job. I was a good bookkeeper, even before you improved my credentials."

Littell stroked her feet. Jane wiggled her toes.

"You could find me something at Hughes Aircraft."

Littell shook his head. "Mr. Hughes is very disturbed. I'm working against him on some levels, and I want to keep you out of that side of my life."

Jane grabbed her cigarettes. "Any other ideas?"

"I could get you work with the Teamsters."

Jane shook her head. "No. That's not me."

"Why?"

She lit a cigarette. Her hand shook.

"It's just not. I'll find a job, don't worry."

Littell traced her stocking runs. "You'll do better than that. You'll excel and upstage everyone you work with."

Jane smiled. Littell pinched out her cigarette. He kissed her. He touched her hair. He saw a new gray.

Jane pulled his tie off. "Tell me about the last woman you were with."

Littell cleaned his glasses. "Her name was Helen Agee. She was a friend of my daughter's. I got in trouble with the Bureau and Helen was the first casualty."

"She left you?"

"She ran, yes."

"What kind of trouble were you in?"

"I underestimated Mr. Hoover."

"That's all you'll tell me?"

"Yes."

"What happened to Helen?"

"She's a legal-aid lawyer. The last I heard, my daughter was, too."

Jane kissed him. "We have to be who we decided to be in Dallas."

Littell said, "Yes."

Jane fell asleep. Littell feigned sleep. Littell got up slow.

He walked to his office. He set up his tape rig. He poured some coffee.

He nailed Doug Eversall. He called him yesterday. He threatened him. He crossed the line.

He said don't call Carlos. Don't tell him what Bobby said. Don't rat out Bobby.

He warned him. He said I'm working freelance. Don't fuck me or I'll retaliate. You're a drunk driver/killer. I'll expose you for that. I won't let Carlos hurt Bobby.

Bobby suspected the Boys. That meant Bobby KNEW. Bobby didn't say it flat out. Bobby didn't need to. Bobby sidestepped the pain.

Mea culpa. Cause-and-effect. *My* Mob crusade killed my brother.

Littell spooled the tape—tape copy #2.

He'd doctored a dupe. He pouched it to Mr. Hoover. He retained the small talk. He layered in static. He x'd out Bobby's Mob talk.

Littell hit Play. Bobby talked. His grief showed. His kindness showed through.

Kind Bobby—a chat with his clubfooted friend.

Bobby talked. Bobby paused. Bobby said the name "Littell."

Littell listened. Littell timed the pauses. Bobby faltered. Bobby *KNEW.* Bobby never said it.

Littell listened. Littell *lived* the pauses. The old fear came. It told him this:

You believe in him again.

DOCUMENT INSERT: 1/10/64. Verbatim FBI telephone call tran-
script. Marked: "Recorded at the Director's Request"/"Classified
Confidential 1-A: Director's Eyes Only." Speaking: Director Hoover,
Ward J. Littell.

> JEH: Good morning, Mr. Littell.
>
> WJL: Good morning, Sir.
>
> JEH: Let's get to the tape. The sound quality was very poor.
>
> WJL: Yes, Sir.
>
> JEH: The text was unenlightening. If I wish to discuss Airedale
> dogs with the Dark Prince, I can dial his direct line at will.
>
> WJL: My plant fidgeted, Sir. He moved and caused distortion.
>
> JEH: Will you try again?
>
> WJL: That's impossible, Sir. My plant was lucky to get one audi-
> ence.
>
> JEH: Your plant's voice was familiar. He sounded like a handi-
> capped lawyer the Dark Prince employs.
>
> WJL: You have a fine memory for voices, Sir.
>
> JEH: Yes. And I have a few plants of my own.
>
> WJL: Myself among them.
>
> JEH: I wouldn't call you a "plant," Mr. Littell. You're too gifted
> and diversified.
>
> WJL: Thank you, Sir.
>
> JEH: Do you recall our conversation of December 2nd? I said I
> needed a man with a "fallen liberal" image, and hinted that it
> might be you.
>
> WJL: Yes, Sir. I recall the conversation.
>
> JEH: I'm miffed at Martin Luther King and his egregiously un-
> Christian Southern Christian Leadership Conference. I want to
> further penetrate the group, and you're the perfect "fallen liberal"
> to help me accomplish my goal.
>
> WJL: In what way, Sir?
>
> JEH: I already have a plant within the SCLC. He has established
> his ability to procure dossiers on policemen, organized-crime fig-
> ures and other notables that left-wing Negroes might consider
> adversaries. My plan is to provide him with a dossier on you. The
> dossier will portray you as an ousted Bureau man with leftist ten-
> dencies, ones which you have frankly yet to outgrow.

WJL: You've piqued my interest, Sir.

JEH: Your assignment would be to appear sympathetic to the civil-rights cause, which I know will be no great stretch. You will donate numerous allotments of marked Mob money to the SCLC, in $10,000 increments, over a sustained period of time. My goal is to compromise the SCLC and render them more tractable. Your goal is to convince the SCLC that you have embezzled the money from organized-crime sources, in an effort to assuage your guilt over working for mobsters in the first place. This will also be no great stretch. I'm sure that you can tap the ambivalent aspects of your nature and front a convincing performance. I'm equally sure that you can justify the continued expense to your mobster colleagues, as a proactive means to avoid civil-rights trouble in Las Vegas, which will please them and Mr. Hughes.

WJL: It's a bold plan, Sir.

JEH: It is that.

WJL: I'd appreciate some more details.

JEH: My plant is an ex-Chicago policeman. He possesses chameleon qualities similar to yours. He's ingratiated himself with the SCLC very nicely.

WJL: His name, Sir?

JEH: Lyle Holly. His brother was with the Bureau.

WJL: Dwight Holly. He transferred out, I think.

JEH: That is correct. He's with the Federal Bureau of Narcotics in Nevada now. I think he finds the assignment enervating. A brisk dope trade would be more to his liking.

WJL: And Lyle is—

JEH: Lyle is more impetuous. He drinks more than he should and comes off as a hail-fellow-well-met. The Negroes adore him. He's convinced them that he's the world's most incongruously liberal ex-cop, when in fact that prize goes to you.

WJL: You flatter me, Sir.

JEH: I do anything but.

WJL: Yes, Sir.

JEH: Holly will portray you as a Chicago law-enforcement acquaintance and present the SCLC with documents pertaining to your Bureau expulsion. He will point you to a Negro named Bayard Rustin. Mr. Rustin is a close colleague of Mr. King. He is both a Communist and a homosexual, which marks him as a rara avis by all sane standards. I'll send you a summary on him, and I'll have Lyle Holly call you.

WJL: I'll wait for his call, Sir.

JEH: Do you have other questions?

WJL: On this topic, no. But I would like your permission to contact Wayne Tedrow Senior, on Mr. Hughes' behalf.

JEH: You have it.

WJL: Thank you, Sir.

JEH: Good day, Mr. Littell.

WJL: Good day, Sir.

DOCUMENT INSERT: 1/11/64. "Subversive Persons" summary
report. Marked: "Chronology/Known Facts/Observations/Known
Associates/Memberships in Subversive Organizations." Subject:
RUSTIN, BAYARD TAYLOR (male Negro/DOB: 3/17/12, West
Chester, Pa.). Compiled: 2/8/62.

SUBJECT RUSTIN must be viewed as a cunning subversive with a
significant history of Communist-inspired alliances & as a
pronounced security threat, due to his alliances with perceived
"Mainstream" Negro demagogues, such as MARTIN LUTHER KING
& A. PHILIP RANDOLPH. SUBJECT RUSTIN'S radical Quaker background & his parents' association with the NAACP (National Association for the Advancement of Colored People) point out the
extent of his early radical indoctrination. (See Addendum File
#4189 on RUSTIN, JANIFER & RUSTIN, JULIA DAVIS.)

SUBJECT RUSTIN attended Wilberforce College (a Negro institution) 1932–33. He refused to join the ROTC (Reserve Officers
Training Corps) and led (abetted by numerous Communist sympathizers) a strike to protest the allegedly poor quality of food
served to students. SUBJECT RUSTIN transferred to Cheyney State
Teachers College (Pennsylvania) early in 1934. It is believed that
he communicated with numerous notable Negro subversives while
at the institution. SUBJECT RUSTIN was expelled in 1936. It is
widely assumed that a homosexual incident resulted in his expulsion.

SUBJECT RUSTIN moved to New York City circa 1938–39. He
became a member of the so-called Negro "Intelligentsia," studied
the philosophy of MOHANDAS "MAHATMA" GANDHI & described
himself as a "Committed Trotskyite." SUBJECT RUSTIN (a gifted
musician) fraternized with numerous white & Negro subversives,
including PAUL ROBESON, who have since been identified as mem-

bers of 114 certified Communist-front organizations. (See "Known Associates," Addendum File #4190.)

SUBJECT RUSTIN became a member of the Young Communist League (YCL) at New York City College (NYCC) & was a frequent visitor at a Communist cell on 146th Street. He fraternized with Communist folk singers & led a YCL-inspired campaign to protest segregation in the U.S. Armed Forces. In 1941 SUBJECT RUSTIN became acquainted with Negro labor agitator A. PHILIP RANDOLPH (b. 1889) (see Randolph Files #1408, 1409, 1410). SUBJECT RUSTIN helped to organize the aborted 1941 Negro March on Washington & joined the socialist-pacifist Fellowship of Reconciliation (FOR) & the War Resisters League (WRL). During this time he became a skilled orator and disseminator of Socialist-Communist propaganda.

SUBJECT RUSTIN registered as a conscientious objector with his (Harlem, N.Y.) draft board & was ordered to appear for a physical examination on 11/13/43. SUBJECT RUSTIN sent a letter of refusal (see Addendum Carbon #19) & was apprehended on 1/12/44. He was tried & convicted of violating the Selective Serv. Act (see Addendum File #4191 for trial transcript) & sent'd to 3 yrs in the Federal Penitentiary at Ashland, Ky. SUBJECT RUSTIN led several attempts to desegregate the prison dining hall & was transferred to Lewisburg Penitentiary (Pa). SUBJECT RUSTIN was paroled (6/46) & became a traveling speaker for the FOR. In 1946 & '47 he participated in numerous Communist-inspired attempts (the "Journey of Reconciliation") to desegregate interstate bus lines. In 11/47 SUBJECT RUSTIN joined the "Committee Against Jim Crow in Military Service & Training" & counseled Negro youths to avoid military service (see Addendum File #4192 for list of members & cross-referenced Communist front-group memberships).

SUBJECT RUSTIN traveled extensively in India (1948–'49), returned to the U.S. & served a 22-day jail sentence for his subversive activities in the "Journey of Reconciliation." He spent substantial time (thruout 1950, '51, '52) in Africa & studied insurgent & Negro nationalist movements there. On 1/21/53, SUBJECT RUSTIN was arrested on a morals charge in Pasadena, California (see Addendum File #4193 for arrest rpt. & trial transcript). SUBJECT RUSTIN & 2 white youths were engaged in a homosexual tryst in a parked car. SUBJECT RUSTIN pled guilty & served 60 days in the Los Angeles County Jail. SUBJECT RUSTIN'S homosexuality is well known & is considered to be an embarrassment to the alleged "Mainstream" Negro "Leaders" who utilize his skills as an organizer & orator.

The 1/21/53 incident resulted in SUBJECT RUSTIN'S expulsion from the FOR. SUBJECT RUSTIN moved to New York City and cultivated friendships in the heavily bohemian & leftist-influenced Greenwich Village district. He rejoined the WRL & again traveled to Africa & studied Negro nationalist movements. SUBJECT RUSTIN returned to the U.S. & met STANLEY LEVISON, a Communist-indoctrinated advisor to MARTIN LUTHER KING. (See Files #5961, 5962, 5963, 5965, 5966.) LEVISON introduced SUBJECT RUSTIN to KING. SUBJECT RUSTIN advised KING per the staging of the Montgomery Bus Boycott of 1955–56. (See Central Index for individual files on boycott participants.) SUBJECT RUSTIN then became a trusted advisor to KING & is credited with influencing KING'S Pacifist/Socialist/Communist program of planned disruption & social disorder. SUBJECT RUSTIN drew up a document for the formation of the Southern Christian Leadership Conference (SCLC) & KING adopted it at a (1/10-11/57) church conference in Atlanta. (See Addendum File #4194 & Electronic Surveillance File #0809.) KING was elected leader of the SCLC on 2/14/57 & has remained in power to this (2/8/62) date.

SUBJECT RUSTIN joined the American Forum (classified as a Communist front group in 1947) & planned the SCLC/NAACP "Pilgrimage of Prayer" March on Washington (5/17/57). 30,000 people attended, including numerous Negro celebrities (see Surveillance Films #0704, 0705, 0706, 0708). SUBJECT RUSTIN organized the "Youth March for Integrated Schools" in 10/58. Per this march: associate A. PHILIP RANDOLPH publicly attacked DIRECTOR HOOVER for his comment that the march was a "Communist-inspired promotion." SUBJECT RUSTIN staged a 2nd youth march in 4/59. (See Surveillance Films #0709, 0710, 0711.)

SUBJECT RUSTIN rejected (early 1960) an offer to work full time for the SCLC. He has remained to this date (2/8/62) a vociferous critic of democratic institutions & has continued to support MARTIN LUTHER KING and his socialist designs, serving as an advisor & organizer of SCLC activities. SUBJECT RUSTIN is considered the leader of the SCLC braintrust & the mastermind behind KING'S rise to prominence as a demagogue and fomenter of social unrest. He has strategized & deployed white & Negro demonstrators in the "Sit-In" & "Freedom Ride" demonstrations of 1960–'61

& has retained documented friendships with a total of 94 members of certified Communist fronts (see Known Associate Index #2). In conclusion, <u>SUBJECT RUSTIN</u> must be classified as a Top Priority Internal Security Risk & should be subjected to periodic surveillance & possible mail & trash cover operations. (Note: Addendum files, films & tapes require Level 2 Clearance & Deputy Director Tolson's authorization.)

26

(Las Vegas, 1/12/64)

Tails:

Sitting tails. Moving tails. Three boring tailees. Tail work—five full days in.

Webb Spurgeon lived behind the Tropicana. Webb Spurgeon's pad brushed the golf course. Webb Spurgeon lived bland. Webb Spurgeon stayed home. Webb Spurgeon chauffeured his son.

Wayne watched his front door. Wayne fought the sitting-tail blues.

He yawned. He scratched his ass. He pissed in a milk can. The car smelled. His aim strayed. He sprayed the dash sometimes.

Spurgeon was a yawn. Duane Hinton was a snore. Eldon Peavy was a faggy snooze. The job was shit. Buddy Fritsch wanted dirt. Pete suborned him in. Fritsch met with Butch Montrose—it vibed payoff.

The job was shit. He worked it anyway. He mixed-and-matched. He juggled his tailees.

Hinton stayed home. Hinton drove to his work sites. Peavy logged time at Monarch Cab. The job was shit. Wayne worked it hard. Wayne cranked twenty hours a day.

Lynette bugged him. Lynette torqued him hard. Lynette found his Dallas paper stash. He lied. He said don't bug me. He said it's Moore and Durfee—I'm just tracking the case.

She tripped him up. She nailed his lies. She made him run. He worked his shit tail job. He gauged potential results.

Hide would-be dirt. Fuck Fritsch and Pete—file a fake report. Play ball. File the goods. Hide out at the Sultan's Lounge. Hide from your wife. Hide from Wayne Senior and his fuck film.

Wayne yawned. Wayne stretched. Wayne scratched his balls. Webb

Spurgeon walked out. Webb Spurgeon locked his front door. Webb Spurgeon shagged his Olds 88.

Log it: 2:21 p.m.

Spurgeon drove south. Wayne tailed him. Spurgeon hit I-95. Wayne hit the fast lane. They both drove 50-plus.

Spurgeon signaled. His blinker blinked. He pulled off the freeway. He hit Henderson ramp #1. He drove surface streets. Wayne tailed him semi-tight.

They hit the Mormon Temple. Wayne logged the time: 2:59 p.m.

Spurgeon walked in. Wayne parked catty-corner. Time sitting-tail dragged.

Thirteen minutes. Fourteen/fifteen.

Spurgeon walked out. Wayne logged it: 3:14 p.m.

They backtracked. They hit 95 North. They jumped on two car lengths apart. Wayne hovered back. Wayne slacked his leash. Wayne tailed long-distance.

They drove back to Vegas. They stopped at Jordan High. Weird—Webb Junior went to LeConte.

Spurgeon parked. Wayne parked two slots back. Kids walked by. Spurgeon covered his face.

4:13 p.m.:

A girl walks up. Said girl looks around. Said girl gets in daddy-o's car.

Spurgeon pulled out. Wayne snapped the leash. Wayne tailed him half-tight. The girl bobbed her head down. The car swerved and weaved. The girl bobbed her head up.

She wiped her lips. She fixed her face. She teased her hair up.

They hit 95 South. They cut toward Hoover Dam. They drove through the shitkicker sticks. Traffic thinned. Wayne slacked out the leash.

Spurgeon turned left. Spurgeon hauled up a dirt road. Wayne parked by some scrub pines. Wayne grabbed his binoculars.

He tracked up. He framed shots. He caught a split-rail cabin. The car sliced into the frame. The girl got out. She was sixteen tops. She ran long on hairspray and zits.

Spurgeon got out. The girl jumped on him. They walked inside. Wayne logged the time: 5:09 p.m. Wayne logged stat rape and contributing—two Class B felonies.

Wayne watched the cabin. Wayne watched his watch. He set up his Leica. He fixed the tripod. He slapped on the zoom doohickey.

They fucked for 51 minutes. Wayne shot their exit drape. They kissed long and wet. He got their tongues in tight.

. . .

Wayne parked by Monarch Cab. Wayne logged in at 6:43.

The hut sagged. The roof drooped. Cinder blocks creaked. The lot was dusty. The fleet was old—three-tone Packards exclusive.

Wayne watched the window. Eldon Peavy ran cabs. Eldon Peavy worked a two-way box. Eldon Peavy dealt solitaire.

Drivers bopped through. Wayne made three felons—fruit rollers all. One guy beat Murder One. Said guy shivved a he-she at a drag queen ball. Said guy proved self-defense.

Cabs rolled out. The pistons knocked. The mufflers coughed. The pipes shot fumes. The Monarch logo *gleamed:*

A little man with a big crown. Red dice for teeth.

Wayne yawned. Wayne stretched. Wayne scratched his balls. He was up in North LV. The Bondsmen gigged tonite. Barb wore her blue gown most gigs.

A cab pulled out. Wayne tailed it. Rolling tails revived him. Night tails were cake. Cab tails double so—their roof lights stood out plain.

Wayne sidled close. The cab hauled out Owens. They passed the Paiute graveyard. They hit West LV.

Traffic was brisk. A car cut the cab off. Wayne swerved and hopped lanes. It was windy. It was cold. Tumbleweeds blew stray.

They passed Owens and "H." The bars rocked. The liquor stores rolled. Bottle hounds and out-the-door biz.

There—the cab's braking—upside the Cozy Nook.

The cab stopped. The cab idled. The driver tapped the horn. Wayne idled back. Wayne saw four Negroes walk out.

They saw the cab. They ran up. They flashed money. The driver dispensed packets. The Negroes paid cash. The Negroes unwrapped benny rolls.

They raised flasks. They popped pills. They did dance steps. They shucked and rehit the Nook.

The cab pulled out. Wayne tailed it. The cab hit Lake Mead and "D." There—the cab's braking—upside the Wild Goose.

A curb line stood ready—six Negroes—all with that hophead look. The cab stopped. The driver sold bennies. The Negroes shucked and rehit the Goose.

The cab pulled out. Wayne tailed it. The cab hit the Gerson Park Flats. A man got in. The cab pulled out. Wayne tailed it near-close.

There—the cab's braking—upside Jackson and "E." The driver parked. The driver got out. The driver swished into Skip's Lounge.

The driver wore rouge. The driver wore eye shadow. The driver vibed femme fatale. The driver stayed inside. Wayne clocked his visit: 6.4 minutes flat.

The driver swished out. The driver swished and swung sacks. Said driver lugged *coin* sacks. Said driver fumbled them. Said driver tossed them in the trunk.

Call it: Backroom slots—illegal—Monarch Cab–run.

The cab pulled out. The cab hung a U-ey. Wayne tailed it close-close. There—the cab's braking—upside the Evergreen Project.

The passenger got out. The cab turned north. The headlights strafed parked cars.

There—one parked Cadillac/one white face ducked low. Fuck—it's Pete Bondurant—hunkered down low.

Wayne caught a teaser shot—that and splitsville—poof and adieu.

Wayne tailed the cab. The image stuck—Pete at the wheel. Darktown Pete—say what?—what we gots here?

The cab hauled back to Monarch. Wayne tailed it un-close. Wayne parked in his standard tail spot.

He yawned. He stretched. He pissed in his can. Time dragged. Time crawled. Time meandered.

Wayne watched the window.

Eldon Peavy shagged calls. Eldon Peavy popped pills. Eldon Peavy dealt solitaire.

Drivers clocked in. Drivers lounged. Drivers clocked out. They played cards. They rolled dice. They primped.

Time slogged. Wayne yawned. Wayne stretched. Wayne picked his nose.

A limo pulled up. Whitewalls and fender skirts/mock-leather top. Wayne clocked it: 2:03 a.m.

Peavy walked out. Peavy jumped in the limo. The limo booked south. Wayne tailed it. They hit the Strip. They stopped at the Dunes.

The limo idled doorway-close. Wayne idled three cars back. Three fags walked up. Dig their muscles and teased hair. They vibe chorus-line gash.

They scoped out the limo. They swooned and hopped in. The limo pulled out.

Wayne tailed it. They hit McCarran Field. The limo parked by the gate fence. Wayne parked four cars back.

Peavy got out. Peavy walked. Wayne had a view.

Peavy strolls. Peavy hits the main gate. A flight lands. Tourists get off.

Wayne watched. Wayne yawned. Wayne stretched. Peavy walked back. Two men walked with him. Two men walked close.

Wayne rubbed his eyes. Wayne did a double take. Fuck—it's Rock Hudson and Sal Mineo.

Peavy grins. Peavy snaps a popper. Rock and Sal snort. They grin.

They giggle exultant. They get in the limo. Peavy assists them. Peavy grabs their ass cheeks and hoists.

The limo pulled out. Wayne tailed it. Wayne got tailpipe-close. A window furled down. He saw smoke. He smelled maryjane.

They hit North LV. They hit the Golden Cavern Hotel. The cuties pile out. Rock and Sal weave.

Lynette torched for Big Rock—she'd fucking shit.

Duane Hinton lived off Sahara. Wayne late-logged in: 3:07 a.m.—the late-*late* show.

He parked. He dumped his milk can. He yawned. He stretched. He scratched.

Hinton's pad was new—all prefab—one window glowed. TV test patterns—flags and geometric bands—KLXO.

Wayne watched the window. Time sluiced. Time slithered. Time slid. The pattern popped off. A room light popped on. Hinton walked outside.

Wayne clocked it: 3:41 a.m.

Hinton wore work clothes. Odds on a store run—the Food King ran all night. Hinton shagged his van. Hinton backed out. Hinton turned north.

Late tails ate shit. Wayne hated them—no traffic/no cover.

Wayne stalled. Wayne clocked off two minutes. Wayne ran up lead and leash time. 1:58, 1:59—Go—

He hit the key. He drove north. He made up time. He caught Hinton.

They passed the Food King. Wayne hovered back. Hinton cut west— Fremont to Owens.

They hit traffic. Wayne moved in close. They hit West Vegas. They hit more traffic—pimp cars and jalopies—Negro nite owls on the stroll.

Hinton stopped. There—he's braking—upside Owens and "H."

Upside Woody's Club. Famous for all-nite grease. Renowned for fried everything food.

Hinton parked. Hinton walked in. Wayne parked catty-corner. A bum walked up.

He bowed. He Watusi'd. He groomed the windshield. Wayne hit his wipers. The bum mooned him. Wino spectators cheered.

Wayne rolled down his window. P-U—the air stunk. He smelled puke. He smelled chicken grease. He rolled his window up.

Hinton walked out. Hinton held the door. Hinton squired a whore. She was dark. She was fat. She looked bombed.

They walked to the van. They got in. They drove around the corner. Wayne doused his lights. Wayne tailed them. Wayne hovered close up.

They stopped. They parked. They walked through a vacant lot. Weeds and sagebrush. Tumbleballs. A trailer on blocks.

Wayne hovered and pulled curbside. Wayne parked ten yards back. The whore unlocked the trailer. Hinton stepped in. Hinton fumbled some object.

Maybe a jug. Maybe a camera. Maybe some sex gear.

The whore stepped in. The whore shut the door. A light blipped on and blipped off.

Wayne ran his clock. Two minutes crawled. Hold for some semblance of fuck.

There—2.6 in:

The trailer rocks. The blocks sway. Both parties are fat. The trailer's thin tin.

The shakes stopped. Wayne clocked the fuck: 4.8 minutes.

The light went on. Blips blipped out a window. Blue blips—as in flash-bulbs.

Wayne yawned. Wayne stretched. Wayne scratched his balls. Wayne dumped his piss cup. The trailer rocked—a minute tops—the light went off.

Hinton walked out. Hinton stumbled. Hinton fumbled some object. He cut through the lot. He got his van. He laid some good tread.

Wayne hit his lo-beams. Wayne tailed him. Wayne rubbed his eyes and yawned. The road dipped—dots hit the windshield—say what?/say what?

The car swayed. He swerved. He blew a red light. He hit his brakes. He popped the clutch and stalled the car out.

The van hit a rise. The van vamoosed. Duane Hinton—out of sight.

Wayne hit the key. Wayne punched the gas. Wayne swamped his engine too fast. He clocked two minutes. He hit the key. He kicked the gas slooooooooow.

The engine caught. He yawned and got traction. The whole world sleepytime bluuuured.

Dawn came up. Wayne got in bed dressed. Lynette stirred. Wayne played possum.

She touched him. She felt his clothes. She pulled off his gun.

"Are you having fun? Hiding out from your wife, I mean."

He yawned. He stretched. He banged the headboard.

He said, "Rock Hudson's queer."

Lynette said, "What happened in Dallas?"

. . .

He slept. He got two hours tops. He woke up woozy. Lynette was gone. Nothing happened in Dallas.

He fixed toast. He drank coffee. He went back out. He parked behind Hinton's house. He scoped the backyard.

The alley was packed—construction work next door. His shit car fit right in.

He scoped the driveway. Right there per always—Hinton's van and Deb Hinton's Impala. Clock the tail in: 9:14 a.m.

Wayne watched the house. Wayne yawned and scratched. Wayne pissed out his a.m. coffee. The workers hung drywall—six men with power tools—saws buzzed and jackhammers bit.

10:24:

Deb Hinton walks out. Deb Hinton splits. Deb's Impala knocks and pings.

12:08:

The workers break. They hit their cars. They grab lunch pails and sacks.

2:19:

Duane Hinton walks out.

He walks through the backyard. He lugs some clothes. He wore said clothes last night. He walks to the fence. He feeds the incinerator. He lights a match.

GOD FUCK JESUS CHRIST.

Wayne drove to Owens and "H." Wayne parked by Woody's Club.

He popped his trunk. He grabbed a pry bar. He circled the block—the street was dead—no wits out and about.

He walked through the lot. He knocked on the trailer. He looked around—still no wits out.

He leaned on the pry bar. He snapped the lock. He walked in. He smelled blood. He slammed the door shut.

He tapped the walls. He tripped a switch. He got overhead light.

She was dead. On the floor/stage-one rigor/maggots on call. Contusions/head wounds/shattered cheeks.

Hinton gagged her. Hinton wedged a handball in her mouth.

Ear blood. Socket blood. One eyeball gone. Buckshot on the floor. Buckshot in her blood.

Hinton wore sap gloves. The palm fabric broke. The buckshot flew.

Wayne caught his breath. Wayne tracked blood trails. Wayne read splash marks.

He slid on a rug. He stepped on the eyeball.

Eight assaults. One beating snuff.

He *heard* it. He thought it was fuck #2. It was Murder One. It vibed Manslaughter Two. Hinton was white. Hinton had pull. Hinton killed a *colored* whore.

Wayne drove back. Wayne thought it all through. The gist cohered.

The assault vics pressed charges. They said the assault man took pix. *He* saw flashbulbs pop. *He* knew the MO. He was fried to exhaustion. The gist flew by him.

He fucked up. *He* owed the whore. The cost meant shit.

Wayne parked in the alley. Wayne watched the house. Workmen yelled. Saws buzzed. Jackhammers bit.

Wayne pissed. Wayne missed his can. Wayne sprayed the seat.

Time whizzed. He watched the house. He watched the driveway. Time cranked. Dusk hit. The workmen split.

They grabbed their cars. They cut tracks. They blew horn-honk farewells. Wayne waited. Time labored and lulled.

6:19 p.m.:

The Hintons walk out. They schlep golf bags. Odds on night golf. The range down Sahara.

They take off. They take Deb's Impala. Duane's van stays put.

Wayne clocked down two minutes. Wayne got some nerve up. Wayne got out and stretched.

He walked up. He braced the fence. He vaulted it. He came down hard. He scraped his hands and brushed them off.

He ran to the porch. The door looked weak. The latch wiggled. He shook the door. He forced some slack. He snapped the latch off.

He opened the door. He hit a laundry room. Washer/dryer/clothesline. Window light from inside—and one connecting door.

Wayne stepped inside. Wayne shut the door. Loose floor planks popped up. Wayne stubbed his feet.

He braced the inside door. He jiggled the knob. Bingo—unlocked.

He hit the kitchen. He checked his watch. *Give it twenty minutes tops.*

6:23:

The kitchen drawers—nothing hot—flatware and Green Stamps.

6:27:

The living room—nothing hot—blond wood to excess.

6:31:

The den—nothing hot—skeet guns and bookshelves.

6:34:

Hinton's office—go slow here—it's a logical spot.

File shelves/ledgers/a pegged key ring. No wall safe/one wall pic—Hinton and Lawrence Welk.

6:39:

The bedroom—nothing hot—more blond wood excess. No wall safe/no floor safe/no loose panel strips.

6:46:

The basement—go slow here—it's a logical spot.

Power tools/a workbench/*Playboy* magazines. A closet—locked up. That key ring—remember—keys on a peg.

Wayne ran upstairs. Wayne grabbed the ring. Wayne ran downstairs. Wayne jabbed keys at the lock.

6:52:

Key #9 works. The door pops. The closet unlocks.

He saw one box. That's it, no more. Let's inventory it.

Handcuffs. Handballs. Friction tape. Sap gloves. A Polaroid camera. Six rolls of film. Fourteen snapshots:

Negro whores gagged and stomped—eight certified victims plus six. Plus:

Unused film. One roll. Twelve exposures. Twelve potential shots.

Wayne emptied the box. Wayne cleared floor space. Wayne spread the shit out. Shoot it fast. Put it back. *Display it like you found it.*

He loaded the camera. He shot twelve exposures. They developed and popped out.

Instant prints—Polaroid color.

He grouped Hinton's pix—four separate shots—he got in tight. He got the handball gags. He got the contusions. He got the smashed teeth and the blood.

27

(Las Vegas, 1/14/64)

igger Heaven: Four spooks/four capsules/one spike.

They usurped the carport. They flanked an old Merc. They laid out red devils. They dumped out the goo.

They spritzed it. They cooked it. They fed the spike. They tied up. They geezed. They dipped. They nodded. They swayed.

All riiiiiiiiiiight.

Pete watched. Pete yawned. Pete scratched his ass. Stakeout night #6—the dawn shift—hijinx at five fucking a.m.

He parked at Truman and "J." He lounged low. He dug on the view.

That coon called and tipped him. He said Wendell be back. He said Wendell gots a gun. He said Curtis and Leroy—they baaad. They be pushin' white horse.

Check the carport. Check the Evergreen Project. Dope fiends meet there. Dice fiends too. Wendell the dice fiend soo-preem. Look for Curtis and Leroy—two fat boys—they gots big conk hairdos.

Pete popped aspirin. His headache dipped south. Six nights. Shit surveillance. Headaches and coon food. Grime on his car.

The plan:

Clip Curtis and Leroy. Appease the Boys and play civic booster. Clip Wendell Durfee. Indebt Wayne Junior thus.

You owe me, Wayne. Let's see your files.

Six nights. No luck. Six nights slumming. Six nights lounging low.

Pete watched the carport. Pete yawned. Pete stretched. Pete grew Matterhorn-size hemorrhoids.

The dope fiends swaaayed.

They fumbled Kools. They lit matches. They burned their hands. They lit filter tips.

Pete yawned. Pete dozed. Pete chained cigarettes. Whoa, what's—Two shines cut over "J." Fat boys with big conks—big spray-can hair. Wait—two *more* shines—full-scale shine alert.

They cut over Truman and "K." They met the conk guys. They launched some jive.

One guy schlepped a blanket. One guy schlepped dice. The dice guy schmoozed the conk guys. He called them "Leroy" and "Cur-ti."

The duos teamed up. The duos cruised the carport. The dope guys went oh shit. The conk guys evicted them. The dope guys weaved south. The conk guys threw down the blanket.

Leroy brought breakfast—T-Bird and Tokay. Cur-ti rolled. Green dice twirled. Cur-ti crapped out. Leroy rolled snake eyes.

Pete watched. The jigs whooped. The jigs shucked. The jigs stepped high.

A prowl car drove by. The cops scoped the game. The jigs paid them never-no-mind. Said prowl car split. Said cops yawned—fuck these dumb shines.

Leroy crapped out. Cur-ti exulted. The dice guys drank wine.

A new jig crossed "J." Pete made him quicksville—Wendell (NMI) Durfee.

Check his pimp threads. Check his hair net. Check that gun bulge by his balls.

Durfee joined the game. The jive multiplied. Durfee rolled. Durfee did the Wah-Watusi. Durfee slurped wine.

That prowl car reprised. That prowl car dipped by. The cops looked revitalized. Said car hovered. Said car idled. The radio squawked.

The spooks froze. The spooks went nonchalant. The cops re-revitalized. The spooks went telepathic—we sees de ofay oppressor—the spooks up and ran.

They split up. They hauled. They dispersed cluster-style. They jammed down "J" and "K."

The cops froze. The blanket guys hauled. They dumped their jugs. They moved east. They *hauled.*

The cops unfroze. The cops punched the gas. The cops laid tread and pursued. Durfee ran west. Long legs and low weight. Fat Cur-ti and Leroy pursued.

Pete punched the gas. Pete punched too hard. The pedal slipped. The engine kicked and died.

Pete got out. Pete ran. Durfee ran. Durfee outran his fat pals. The conksters waddled and huffed.

They cut down an alley—trash heaps on gravel—shacks on both sides. Durfee slid. Durfee stumbled. Durfee ripped his pants. Durfee's gun fell out.

Pete slid. Pete stumbled. Pete's belt snapped. Pete's gun fell out.

He gained ground. He stopped. He grabbed Durfee's gun. He lost ground. He gravel-slid.

A siren nudged his ass—loud and full-tilt.

Durfee hopped a fence. The conksters swung over. The prowl car swerved. It fishtailed. It brodied up. It blocked Pete off.

He dropped the gun. He raised his hands. He smiled subservient. The cops got out. The cops pulled saps. The cops raised Ithaca pumps.

They booked him—407 PC.—Clark County Sheriff's.

They dumped him in a sweat room. They cuffed him to a chair. Two dicks worked on him—phone books and verbal shit.

We traced that gun. It's hot. You're a heist man. I found the gun—fuck you.

Bullshit. Why you down here? Tell us your biz.

I crave chitlins. I crave pork rinds. I crave dark trim. Bullshit. Tell us your—

I'm a civil-rights worker. We shall over—

They swung their phone books—fat ones—L.A. directories. You're a heist man. You rob crap games. You tried to rob those coons.

You're wrong—I crave collard greens.

They whopped his ribs. They whopped his knees. They aired it out good. They torqued his cuffs two ratchets up. They let him stew.

His wrists went numb. His arms went numb. He held a class-A piss.

He ran options:

Don't call Littell. Don't call the Boys. Don't look *très* dumb. Don't call Barb—don't scare her.

His back went numb. His chest went numb. He pissed in his pants. He dug in. He dredged some juice. He snapped the cuff chain. He moved his arms and rewired his blood.

The dicks walked back in. They saw the snapped chain. One geek whistled and clapped.

Pete said, "Call Wayne Tedrow. He's on LVPD."

Wayne Junior showed up. The dicks left them alone. Wayne Junior took off his cuffs.

"They said you tried to take down a dice game."

Pete rubbed his wrists. "Do you believe that?"

Wayne Junior frowned—diva with a grievance. Wayne Junior tucked his head up his ass.

Pete stood up. Some blood rewired. His eardrums popped.

"Have they got a seventy-two-hour detention law here?"

"Yeah, release or arraign."

"I'll ride it out, then. I've been there before."

"What do you *want?* You want a favor? You want me to quit coming to your wife's shows?"

Pete jiggled his arms. Some numbness went.

"Durfee's here. He's hanging out with two guys named Curtis and Leroy. I saw them around those shacks on Truman and 'J.' "

Wayne Junior flushed—blood to his brows—blood-circuit overload.

Pete said, "Kill him. I think he came here to kill you."

28

(Washington, D.C., 1/14/64)

White House pickets:

Civil Rights and Ban the Bomb. Young kids on the Left.

They marched. They chanted. Their shouts overlapped. It was cold. They wore overcoats. They wore Cossack hats.

Bayard Rustin was late. Littell waited. Littell sat in Lafayette Park.

Relief pickets chatted. Shop talk swirled. LBJ and Castro. The Goldwater threat.

The groups shared coffee. Lefty girls brought snacks. Littell looked around—no Bayard Rustin yet.

He knew Rustin's face. Mr. Hoover supplied pix. He met the SCLC plant. They talked last night.

Lyle Holly—ex–Chicago PD.

Lyle worked the Red Squad. Lyle studied the Left. Lyle talked Left and *thought* Right. They shared similar credentials. They shared the same disjuncture. Lyle cracked racial jokes. Lyle said he loved Dr. King.

He knew Lyle's brother. They worked the St. Louis Office—'48 to '50.

Dwight H. was Far Right. Dwight worked kovert Klan jobs. Dwight fit *right* in. The Hollys were Hoosiers. The Hollys had Klan ties. Daddy Holly was a Grand Dragon.

They were post-Klan now. They got law degrees and became cops.

Dwight was *post*-FBI. Dwight was *still* Fed. Dwight joined the Narcotics Bureau. Dwight was restless. Dwight jumped jobs. Dwight craved a bold new cop gig: Chief Investigator/U.S. Attorney's Office/Southern Nevada District.

Dwight was hard. Lyle was soft. Lyle oozed Littell-like empathy.

Lyle built the story:

Ward Littell—ex-FBI. He was dismissed. He was disgraced. He was maimed by Mr. Hoover. He's a Mob lawyer now. He's closeted Left. He's close to Mob money.

It was a sound text. Littell conceded it. Lyle laughed. Lyle said Mr. Hoover helped.

The deal was set. He had the money—Carlos and Sam donated it.

He told them straight—it's Mr. Hoover's gig—it's non-Outfit/anti-SCLC. Carlos and Sam loved it. Lyle talked to Bayard Rustin. Lyle gushed:

Ward Littell—my old pal. Ward's kindred. Ward's got cash. Ward's pro-SCLC.

The ban-the-bomb crew walked. A YAF crew appeared. New signs: Bop the Beard and Krucify Khrushchev.

Bayard Rustin walked up.

A tall man—dressed and groomed—more gaunt than his mug shots.

He sat down. He crossed his legs. He cleared bench space.

Littell said, "How did you recognize me?"

Rustin smiled. "You were the only one not involved in the democratic process."

"Lawyers don't wave placards."

Rustin cracked his briefcase. "No, but some make donations."

Littell cracked his briefcase. "There'll be more. But I'll deny it if it ever comes to that."

Rustin took the money. "Deniability. I can appreciate it."

"You have to consider the source. The men I work for are not friends of the civil-rights movement."

"They should be. Italians have been persecuted on occasion."

"They don't see it that way."

"Perhaps that's why they're so successful in their chosen field."

"The persecuted learn to persecute. I understand the logic, but I don't accept it as wisdom."

"And you don't ascribe ruthlessness to all people of that blood?"

"No more than I ascribe stupidity to your people."

Rustin slapped his knees. "Lyle said you were quick."

"He's quick himself."

"He said you go back."

"We met at a Free-the-Rosenbergs rally. It must have been '52."

"Which side were you on?"

Littell laughed. "We were shooting surveillance film from the same building."

Rustin laughed. "I sat that one out. I was never a real Communist, despite Mr. Hoover's protestations."

Littell said, "You are by his logic. You know what that designation codifies, and how it allows him to encapsulate everything that he fears."

Rustin smiled. "Do you hate him?"

"No."

"After what he put you through?"

"I find it hard to hate people who are that true to themselves."

"Have you studied passive resistance?"

"No, but I've witnessed the futility of the alternative."

Rustin laughed. "That's an extraordinary statement for a Mafia lawyer to make."

A wind stirred. Littell shivered.

"I know something about you, Mr. Rustin. You're a gifted and compromised man. I may not have your gifts, but I suspect that I run neck-and-neck in the compromise department."

Rustin bowed. "I apologize. I try not to second-guess people's motives, but I just failed with you."

Littell shook his head. "It doesn't matter. We want the same things."

"Yes, and we both contribute in our own ways."

Littell buttoned his coat. "I admire Dr. King."

"As much as any Catholic can admire a man named Martin Luther?"

Littell laughed. "I admire Martin Luther. I made that compromise when I was more of a man of faith."

"You'll be hearing some bad things about our Martin. Mr. Hoover has been sending out missives. Martin Luther King is the devil with horns. He seduces women and employs Communists."

Littell put his gloves on. "Mr. Hoover has numerous pen pals."

"Yes. In Congress, the clergy, and the newspaper field."

"He believes, Mr. Rustin. That's how he makes them believe."

Rustin stood up. "Why now? Why did you decide to undertake such a risk at this time?"

Littell stood up. "I've been visiting Las Vegas, and I don't like the way things are run there."

Rustin smiled. "Tell those Mormons to loosen the chains."

They shook hands. Rustin walked off. Rustin whistled Chopin.

The park glowed. Mr. Hoover bestows all gifts.

29

(Las Vegas, 1/15/64)

Picture loop:

The dead whore/the eyeball/ Wendell Durfee with fangs.

Pictures and flash dreams. No sleep and rolling blackouts. Two fender-benders at the wheel.

The pictures looped on. Thirty-six hours' worth. Bad rain offset them.

Wayne muscled a Monarch Cab man. Wayne stole some bennies. Wayne called Lynette's school and left a message:

Don't go home—stay with a friend—I'll call back and explain.

He ate bennies. He guzzled coffee. It juiced him. It drained him. It torqued his picture loop.

He staked out Truman and "J." He ran file checks. He glommed mug shots. He got dirt on Leroy Williams and Curtis Swasey.

Pimps. Dice fools. Twelve arrests/two convictions. Vagrants with no known address.

He stayed up—half a day/a night/a full day. He watched the carport. He watched the clubs—the Nook/Woody's/the Goose.

He watched crap games. He scoped bar-b-que lines. He saw wisps. He saw Wendell Durfee. He blinked and vaporized him.

He sat in his car. He watched the alley. It paid off two hours back.

Curtis exits a shack. The rear door flanks the alley. Curtis dumps shit in a trash can. Curtis runs straight back.

He waited. He sat in his car. He watched the alley. Dig this one hour back:

Leroy exits the shack. Leroy dumps shit in a trash can. Leroy runs straight back.

Wayne ran up then. Wayne dumped the can. Wayne saw a plastic sheet. White dust was stuck to it—white powder dregs.

He tasted it. It was Big "H."

He circled the shack. Crimped foil covered the windows. He pulled a piece up. He saw Curtis and Leroy.

That was 5:15 p.m. It was 6:19 now.

Wayne watched the shack. Wayne saw wisps and light. Light cut through rips in the foil.

The rain was bad. Fucking monsoon dimensions. Pictures looped on:

Dallas. Pete and Durfee. Pete says, "Kill him"—this sound loop two days strong.

You should have killed him *then*. He's a homing pigeon. You should have *known*.

KILL HIM. KILL HIM. KILL HIM. KILL HIM. KILL HIM.

The car sat on mud. The roof leaked. Rain seeped in. He owed Pete. Pete's call saved him. Pete's call diverted him.

Fuck Buddy Fritsch—fuck his file job—Hinton pays for the whore.

He detoured once—ten hours back. He drove by the trailer. Said trailer reeked. The whore sat and decomped.

Pictures: The blood peel/the maggots/pellets caked in blood.

Wayne watched the shack. The rain blitzed his view. Time decomped. Time redacted.

The back door opens. A man exits. He walks. He walks *this* way. He gets *close*.

Wayne watched. Wayne popped the passenger door. There—it's Leroy Williams.

He's got no hat. He's got no umbrella. He's got sodden duds.

Leroy walked by. Wayne kicked the door out. It hit Leroy flush. Leroy yelped. Leroy hit the mud. Wayne jumped on out.

Leroy stood up. Wayne pulled his piece and butt-punched him. Leroy fell and grazed the car.

Wayne kicked him in the balls. Leroy yelped. Leroy thrashed. Leroy fell down. He said mothersomething. He pulled a shiv. Wayne slammed the door on his hand.

He mashed his fingers. He pinned them. Leroy screamed and dropped the knife. Wayne popped the wind wing. Wayne reached in and popped the glove box.

He dug around. He grabbed his duct tape. He pulled up a piece. Leroy screamed. The rain ate the noise. Wayne eased off the door.

Leroy flexed his hand. Bones sheared and stuck out. Leroy screamed loud.

Wayne grabbed his conk. Wayne tape-muzzled him. Leroy squirmed. Leroy yelped. Leroy flailed his fucked hand.

Wayne taped him—three circuits—Number 2 duct. He kicked him prone. He cuffed his wrists. He threw him in the backseat.

He got in the front seat. He hit the gas. He swerved through mud and alley trash. The rain got worse. His wipers blew. He drove by feel.

He notched a mile. He saw a sign. He flashed—the auto dump—it's close—it's two clicks downwind.

He drove fifty yards. He cranked a hard right. He braked. He pulled in. He wracked the axle on the pavement.

He hit his brights. He lit the place large: Rain/epidemic rust/a hundred dead cars.

He set the brake. He pulled Leroy up. He ripped up the tape. He ripped off skin and half his mustache.

Leroy yelped. Leroy coughed. Leroy burped bile and blood.

Wayne hit the roof light. "Wendell Durfee. Where is he?"

Leroy blinked. Leroy coughed. Wayne smelled the shit in his pants.

"Where's Wendell Durf—"

"Wendell say he got somethin' to do. He say he be back to get his stuff and leave town. Cur-ti, he say Wendell got bidness."

"What business?"

Leroy shook his head. "I don't know. Wendell's bidness is Wendell's bidness, which ain' my bidness."

Wayne leaned close. Wayne grabbed his hair. Wayne smashed his face on the door. Leroy screamed. Leroy expelled teeth. Wayne crawled over the seat.

He pinned Leroy down. He taped him full-body. He grabbed his cuff chain. He popped the door. He pulled him out. He dragged him to a Buick. He pulled his piece and shot six holes in the trunk.

He dumped Leroy in. He piled on spare tires. He slammed the trunk lid.

He was soaked. His shoes squished. His feet were somewhere else. He saw wisps. He knew they weren't real.

The rain let up. Wayne drove back. Wayne parked in the same alley spot. He got out. He circled the shack. He unpeeled a foil strip.

There's Cur-ti. He's with another guy. The guy's got Cur-ti's face. The guy's Cur-ti's brother.

Cur-ti sat on the floor. Cur-ti jived. Cur-ti crimped bindles. Cur-ti cut dope.

His brother tied off. His brother geezed. His brother untied on Cloud 9. His brother lit a Kool filter-tip.

He burned his fingers. He smiled. Cur-ti giggled. Cur-ti cut dope.

He twirled his knife. He mimed a gutting stroke. He said, "Sheeit. Like a dressed hog, man."

He twirled his knife. He mimed a shaving stroke. He said, "Wendell likes it trimmed. Cuttin' on bitches always been his MO."

He said, "His and hers, man. He lost his gun, so he gets to get in close."

Wayne HEARD it. It clicked in synaptic. Wayne SAW it—instant picture loops.

He ran. He slid. He stumbled. He fell in the mud. He got up and stumble-ran. He got in the car. He stabbed with his key. He missed the keyhole.

He got it in. He turned it. He stripped gears. The wheels spun and kicked the car free.

Lightning hit. Thunder hit. He outran the rain.

He slid through intersections. He ran yellows and reds. He banged railroad tracks. He grazed curbs. He scraped parked cars.

He got home. He brodied on the front lawn. He stumbled out and ran up. The house was dark. The door lock was cracked. His key jammed in the hole.

He kicked the door in. He looked down the hall. He saw the bedroom light. He walked up and looked in.

She was naked.

The sheets were red. She drained red. She soaked through the white.

He spread her. He cinched her. He used Wayne's neckties. He gutted her and shaved her. He trimmed off her patch.

Wayne pulled his gun. Wayne cocked it. Wayne put it in his mouth and pulled the trigger.

The hammer clicked empty. He shot his full six at the dump.

The storm passed through. It dumped power lines. Stoplights were down. People drove crazy.

Wayne drove deliberate. Wayne drove very slow.

He parked by the shack. He grabbed his shotgun. He walked up and kicked the door in.

Cur-ti was packing dope. Cur-ti's brother was watching TV. They saw Wayne. They nodded. They grinned smack-back.

Wayne tried to talk. Wayne's tongue misfired. Cur-ti talked. Cur-ti talked hair-o-wine slow.

"Hey, man. Wendell's gone. You won't see us harboring—"

Wayne raised his shotgun. Wayne swung the butt.

He clipped Cur-ti. He knocked him down. He stepped on his chest. He grabbed six bindles. He stuffed them in his mouth.

Cur-ti gagged. Cur-ti bit plastic. Cur-ti bit at Wayne's hand. Cur-ti ate plastic and dope.

Wayne stepped on his face. The bindles snapped. His teeth snapped. His jaw snapped loose.

Cur-ti thrashed. Cur-ti's legs stiffed. Blood blew out his nose. Cur-ti spasmed and bit at Wayne's shoe.

Wayne goosed the TV. Morey Amsterdam hollered. Dick Van Dyke screamed.

The brother cried. The brother begged. The brother talked in tongues. The brother tongue-talked smacked-out on the floor.

His lips moved. His mouth moved. His lids fluttered. His eyes rolled back.

Wayne hit him.

He broke his teeth. He broke his nose. He broke the gun butt. His lips moved. His mouth moved. His eyeballs clicked up. His eyes showed pure white.

Wayne picked the TV up. Wayne dropped it on his head. The tubes burst and exploded. They burned his face up.

The power lines were rerigged. The streetlights worked fine. Wayne drove to the dump.

He pulled in. He aimed his brights. He strafed the Buick. He got out and opened the trunk.

He untaped Leroy. He said, "Where's Durfee?" Leroy said, "I don't know."

Wayne shot him—five rounds in the face—point-blank triple-aught buck.

He blew his head off. He blew up the trunk. He blew out the undercarriage. He blew the spare tires up.

He walked to his car. Smoke fizzed out the hood. He'd run it dry. The crankcase was shot.

He tossed the shotgun.

He walked home.

He sat by Lynette.

30

(Las Vegas, 1/15/64)

Littell sipped coffee. Wayne Senior sipped scotch.

They stood at his bar—teak and mahogany—game heads mounted above.

Wayne Senior smiled. "I'm surprised you landed in that storm."

"It was touch and go. We had a few rough moments."

"The pilot knew his business, then. He had a planeful of gamblers, who were anxious to get here and lose their money."

Littell said, "I forgot to thank you. It's late, and you saw me on very short notice."

"Mr. Hoover's name opens doors. I won't be coy about it. When Mr. Hoover says 'Jump,' I say 'How high?' "

Littell laughed. "I say the same thing."

Wayne Senior laughed. "You flew in from D.C.?"

"Yes."

"Did you see Mr. Hoover?"

"No. I saw the man he told me to see."

"Can you discuss it?"

"No."

Wayne Senior twirled a walking stick. "Mr. Hoover knows everyone. The people he knows comprise quite a loop."

"The Loop." The Dallas Office file. Maynard Moore—FBI snitch. His handler—Wayne Tedrow Senior.

Littell coughed. "Do you know Guy Banister?"

"Yes, I know Guy. How do you know him?"

"He ran the Chicago Office. I worked there from '51 to '60."

"Have you seen him more recently?"

"No."

"Oh? I thought you might have crossed paths in Texas."

Guy bragged. Guy talked too much. Guy was indiscreet.

"No, I haven't seen Guy since Chicago. We don't have much in common."

Wayne Senior arched one eyebrow—the pose meant oh-you-kid.

Littell leaned on the bar. "Your son works LVPD Intel. He's someone I'd like to know."

"I've shaped my son in more ways than he'd care to admit. He's not altogether ungrateful."

"I've heard he's a fine officer. A phrase comes to mind. 'Incorruptible by Las Vegas Police standards.' "

Wayne Senior lit a cigarette. "Mr. Hoover lets you read his files."

"On occasion."

"He permits me that pleasure, as well."

" 'Pleasure' is a good way to describe it."

Wayne Senior sipped scotch. "I arranged for my son to be sent to Dallas. You never know when you might rub shoulders with history."

Littell sipped coffee. "I'll bet you didn't tell him. A phrase comes to mind. 'Withholds sensitive data from his son.' "

"My son is uncommonly generous to unfortunate people. I've heard you used to be."

Littell coughed. "I have a major client. He wants to move his base to Las Vegas, and he's very partial to Mormons."

Wayne Senior doused his cigarette. Scotch sucked up the ash.

"I know many capable Mormons who would love to work for Mr. Hughes."

"Your son has some files that would help us."

"I won't ask him. I have a pioneer's disdain for Italians, and I'm fully aware that you have other clients beside Mr. Hughes."

Scotch and wet tobacco. Old barroom smells.

Littell moved the tumbler. "What are you saying?"

"That we all trust our own kind. That the Italians will never let Mormons run Mr. Hughes' hotels."

"We're getting ahead of ourselves. He has to purchase the properties first."

"Oh, he will. Because he wants to buy, and your other clients want to sell. I could mention the term 'conflict of interest,' but I won't."

Littell smiled. Littell raised the tumbler—touché.

"Mr. Hoover briefed you well."

"Yes. In both our best interests."

"And his own."

Wayne Senior smiled. "I discussed you with Lyle Holly as well."

"I didn't know you knew him."

"I've known his brother for years."

"I know Dwight. We worked the St. Louis Office together."

Wayne Senior nodded. "He told me. He said you were always ideologically suspect, and your current employment as a Mafia lawyer confirms it."

Littell raised the tumbler. "Touché, but I wouldn't call my employers ideological on any level."

Wayne Senior raised the tumbler. "Touché back at you."

Littell coughed. "Let's see if I can put this together. Dwight's with the Narcotics Bureau here. He used to work mail-fraud assignments for Mr. Hoover. The two of you worked together then."

"That's correct. We go back thirty-some years. His daddy was a daddy to me."

"The Grand Dragon? And a nice Mormon boy like you?"

Wayne Senior grabbed a cocktail glass. Wayne Senior built a Rob Roy.

"The Indiana Klan was never as rowdy as those boys down south. That's *too* rowdy, even for boys like Dwight and me. That's why we worked those mail-fraud assignments."

Littell said, "That's not true. Dwight did it because Mr. Hoover told him to. You did it to play G-man."

Wayne Senior stirred his drink. Littell smelled bitters and Noilly Prat. He salivated. He moved his chair back. Wayne Senior winked.

Shadows creased the bar. A woman crossed the rear deck. Proud features/black hair/gray streak.

Wayne Senior said, "I want to show you a film."

Littell stood up. Littell stretched. Wayne Senior grabbed his drink. They walked down a side hall. The scotch and bitters swirled. Littell wiped his lips.

They stopped at a storage room. Wayne Senior hit the lights. Littell saw a projector and wall screen.

Wayne Senior spooled film. Wayne Senior set the slide. Wayne Senior fed film in. Littell killed the lights. Wayne Senior hit the on switch. Words and numbers hit the screen.

Surveillance code—white-on-black. A date—8/28/63. A location—Washington, D.C.

The words dissolved. Raw footage hit. Speckled black & white film. A bedroom/Martin Luther King/a white woman.

Littell watched.

His legs dipped. He weaved hard. He grabbed at a chair. The skin tones contrasted—black-on-white—stretch marks and plaid sheets.

Littell watched the film. Wayne Senior smiled. Wayne Senior watched him.

All gifts. Mr. Hoover. A gift that he would regret.

31

(Las Vegas, 1/15/64)

The cops kicked him loose. They called around. They got his rep. They got *très* hip. He's mobbed up/he knows the Boys/the Boys dig on him.

Pete walked. Pete paged Barb at work. Pete said I'll be home soon.

He did forty-one hours. He ate jute balls and rice. His head hurt. His wrists hurt. He smelled like Chihuahua shit.

He cabbed to his car. He cabbed Monarch—the Browntown Express. The driver lisped. The driver wore rouge. The driver said he sold guns.

The driver dropped Pete at the carport. Pete's car was trashed/totaled/torched.

No windshield. No hubcaps. No tires. No wheels. The Cadillac Hotel—one wino booked in.

He snored. Bugs bombed him. He cradled Sterno and T-Bird. The car got a paint job—kustom nigger script:

Allah Rules/Death to Ofays/We Love Malcolm X.

Pete laughed. Pete fucking roared. He kicked the grille. He kicked the door panels. He tossed the wino his keys.

A rain hit—light and cold. Pete heard a ruckus close in. He placed it—way close—the shacks off "J" Street.

He walked over. He caught the grief.

Six prowl cars—LVPD and Sheriff's. Two Fed sleds snout-to-snout. Big voodoo upside a jig shack.

Arc lights/crime-scene rope/one ambulance. A cop-jig confluence—large.

Cops inside the crime-scene rope. Jigs outside. Jigs armed with Tokay and fried chicken.

Pete pushed up close. A cop rigged two gurneys. A cop pushed them in the shack. A cop jumped the rope. A cop briefed him. Pete eavesdropped in tight.

A kid called it in. Said kid lives next door. Said kid heard a commotion. A honky do it. Honky got a shotgun. Honky get in his car and ex-cape. Said kid enters the shack then. Said kid sees two stiffs—Curtis and Otis Swasey.

The jigs pressed up. The jigs stretched the crime-scene rope. The jigs Wah-Watusi'd. A cop placed sawhorses. A cop stretched the rope. A cop eased the jigs back.

Jigs eyeballed Pete. Jigs jostled him. White Man—bad juju. White Man—go home. White Man—he kill our kin.

Odds on: Wayne Junior. Odds on: Wendell Durfee—dead and dumped *somewhere*.

The jigs huddled. The jigs mumbled. The jigs pygmy-ized. A jig lobbed a bottle. A jig lobbed a drumstick. A jig lobbed french fries.

Four cops pulled batons. Two cops rolled out the gurneys.

There Curtis—he blue—honky beat his face. There Otis—he crisp— honky torch his face baaaaaad juju.

Pete backed off. Pete caught some elbows. Pete caught some lobbed chicken wings. Pete caught some yam pies.

He walked across "J." He mingled by a cop clique. He leaned on a prowl car. A cop sat in front. Said cop worked a hand mike. Said cop talked loud.

We got another one—shotgun DOA—a coon named Leroy Williams.

Wooooooo! Blew his burrhead cleeean off! The dump guys found him inside this Buick. We got the shotgun.

Call *Leroy* Stiff #3. Wendell—where *you* at?

Pete mingled. The cops ignored him. Cops blocked traffic. Cops stood point. Cops cordoned off "J."

The rain fucking tripled. The clouds let fly. Pete grabbed a stray chicken box. Pete dumped out gizzards. Pete put it on and kept his head dry.

The jigs dispersed. The jigs booked willy-nilly. The jigs ran hellbent.

A Fed car pulled up. A big guy got out. Said guy vibed El Jefe—gray suit and gray Fed hat.

Jefe flashed a badge. Jefe got service. The point guard saluted. A baby Fed bowed. Jefe bootjacked his umbrella.

Pete circled the rope. Pete got in close. Said fuzz ignored him. Fuck you—you're a geek—you've got a chicken-box hat.

Pete stood around. His hat leaked. Chicken grease oiled his hair. The baby Fed brown-nosed the boss Fed—yessir, Mr. Holly.

Mr. Holly was *pissed.* It's *my* case. The vics pushed narcotics. It's *my* crime scene—let's toss the shack.

Mr. Holly stayed dry. The sub-fuzz stayed wet. A sergeant walked up. Said sergeant wore squishy blues.

He talked loud. He pissed off Mr. Holly. He said it's *our* case. *We're* sealing her up. *We'll* bring in Homicide.

Mr. Holly fumed. Mr. Holly fugued out. He kicked a sawhorse. He yelped. He fucked his foot up.

A prowl car pulled up. A cop got out. He gestured wild. He talked wild. Pete heard "car at the dump." Pete heard "Tedrow."

Mr. Holly yelled. The sergeant yelled. A cop raised a bullhorn. Lock her up—let's roll code 3—the Tonopah Dump.

The fuzz dispersed.

They grabbed their cars. They peeled up "J." They fishtailed in mud. They plowed through gravel yards.

One cop stayed behind. Said cop locked the shack.

He stood by the front door. He stood in the monsoon. He smoked cigarettes. The rain doused them. He got two puffs per. He gave up. He ran to his car. He rolled the windows up.

Pete ran. The rain covered him. He kicked up mud. He ran back to the alley. He circled the shack.

No cars. No back-door guard—good. Said door was locked. The windows were tinfoil-patched.

Pete reached up. Pete tore at a foil patch. Pete de-patched a window.

He climbed up. He vaulted in. He saw chalk lines and bloodstains. He saw a burned-up TV-set.

Floor debris—chalk-circled: Bindle scraps/tube glass/fried nigger hair.

Pete tossed the shack. Pete worked *rápidamente.* He grid-scoped. He saw one dresser/one toilet/no shelves.

Two mattresses. Bare walls and floors. No stash-holes inset. A window air-cooler—Frost King brand—matted screens and rusty ducts.

No cord. No plug. No intake valve. Call it dope camouflage.

Pete popped the top. Pete reached in. Pete praised Allah Himself.

White horse—all plastic-wrapped—three bonaroo bricks.

32

(Las Vegas, 1/17/64)

Five cops grilled him.

Wayne sat. They stood. They filled the sweat room.

Buddy Fritsch and Bob Gilstrap. A Sheriff's man. A Fed named Dwight Holly. A Dallas cop named Arthur V. Brown.

The heat went off. Their breath steamed. It fogged the mirror-wall. He sat. They stood. His lawyer stood under a speaker. His lawyer stood outside.

They popped him at home—2:00 a.m.—he was still there with Lynette. Fritsch called Wayne Senior. Wayne Senior came to the jail.

Wayne blew him off. Wayne blew off his lawyer. Dwight Holly knew Wayne Senior. Dwight Holly stressed the friendship thus:

You're not your dad. You killed three men. You fucked my investigation up.

They'd braced him twice. He told the truth. He wised up and called Pete.

Pete knew the scoop. Pete knew a lawyer. His name: Ward Littell.

Wayne met with Littell. Littell quizzed him: Did they tape you? Did they transcribe?

Wayne said no. Littell advised him. Littell said he'd watch the next go. Littell said he'd veto tape and transcription.

The veto worked. The room was cherry—no tape rig/no steno.

Wayne coughed. His breath fogged out.

Fritsch said, "You got a cold? You were sure out in the rain that night."

Holly said, "He was out killing three unarmed men."

Fritsch said, "Come on. He admitted it."

The Sheriff's man coughed. "*I've* got a fucking cold. He wasn't the only one out in the rain."

Gilstrap smiled. "We've cleared up one part of your story. We know you didn't kill Lynette."

Wayne coughed. "Tell me how you know."

"Son, you don't want to know."

Holly said, "Tell him. I want to see how he reacts."

Fritsch said, "The coroner found abrasions and semen. The guy was a secretor. AB-negative blood, which is real rare. We checked Durfee's jail records. That's his blood type."

Holly smiled. "Look, he didn't even blink."

Brown said, "He's a cold one."

The Sheriff's man said, "He wasn't even crying when we found him. He was just staring at the body."

Gilstrap said, "Come on. He was in shock."

Fritsch said, "We're satisfied that Durfee killed her."

The Sheriff's man lit a cigar. "And we're satisfied that Curtis and Otis clued you in to his plan."

Holly straddled a chair. "Someone hipped you to Leroy Williams and the Swasey brothers."

Wayne coughed. "I told you. I have an informant."

"Whose name you refuse to reveal."

"Yes."

"And your intent was to find and apprehend Wendell Durfee."

"Yes."

Brown said, "You wanted to apprehend him, to make up for not doing it in Big D."

"Yes."

"Then, son, here's what bothers me. How did Durfee know that you were the officer sent down to Dallas to extradite him?"

Wayne coughed. "I told you before. I rousted him a few times when I worked Patrol. He knew my face and my name, and he saw me when we exchanged shots in Dallas."

Fritsch said, "I'll buy that."

Gilstrap said, "I will, too."

Brown said, "I won't. I think something happened between you and Durfee. Maybe in Dallas, maybe up here before they sent you down. I don't see him coming all the way up here, presumably to kill you and get his incidental jollies on your wife, unless he had a personal motive."

Tex was good. Tex was better than the Sheriff's man. Pete chased the dice men. The cops chased him. They popped Pete. They filed paper. The Sheriff's man knew shit-all about it.

Brown said, "Your business up here is your business. I wouldn't care about any of this, except for the proximity of a missing Dallas officer named Maynard D. Moore, who you reportedly did not get along with."

Wayne shrugged. "Moore was dirty. If you knew him, you know that's true. I didn't like him, but I only had to work with him for a few days."

"You said 'knew.' You think he's dead, then?"

"That's right. Durfee or one of his asshole Klan buddies killed him."

Gilstrap said, "We've got two APBs out on Durfee. He won't get far."

Brown hovered. "You're saying Officer Moore was in the Ku Klux Klan?"

"That's right."

"I don't like the sound of that accusation. You're defaming the memory of a brother officer."

The Sheriff's man laughed. "This is hilarious. He kills three Negroes and gets on his high horse about the KKK."

Brown coughed. "DPD has been anti-Klan from the get-go."

"Bullshit. You all get your sheets cleaned at the same laundry."

"Boy, you are wearing me thin."

"Don't call me 'boy,' you redneck faggot."

Brown kicked a chair. Fritsch picked it up.

Gilstrap said, "Come on. This line of talk is getting us nowhere."

Holly rocked his chair. "Leroy Williams and the Swasey brothers were moving heroin."

Wayne said, "I know that."

"How?"

"I saw Curtis rolling bindles."

"I've had them under spot surveillance. They were pushing in Henderson and Boulder City, and they were making plans to push in West Vegas."

Wayne coughed. "They wouldn't have lasted two days. The Outfit would have clipped them."

Fritsch rolled his eyes. "He goes from the Klan to the Mob."

Gilstrap rolled his eyes. "You've got the Mob in Vegas like you've got the Klan in Dallas."

Wayne rolled *his* eyes. "Hey, Buddy, who bought you your speedboat? Hey, Bob, who got you that second mortgage?"

Fritsch kicked the wall. Gilstrap kicked a chair. Brown picked it up.

Holly said, "You're not making any friends here."

Wayne said, "I'm not trying to."

Fritsch said, "You've got the sympathy vote."

Gilstrap said, "You've got the chain of events."

The Sheriff's man coughed. "You're trying to apprehend a fugitive cop-killer. You learn that your wife may be jeopardized, so you rush home and find her dead. Your actions from that point on are entirely understandable."

Brown hitched up his pants. "It's your prior relationship with Durfee that I don't understand."

Holly said, "I concur."

Fritsch said, "Look at it our way. We're trying to give the DA a package. We don't want to see an LVPD man go down for three murders."

Gilstrap said, "Let's talk turkey. It's not like you killed three white men."

Brown cracked his knuckles. "Did you kill Maynard Moore?"

"Fuck you."

"Did Wendell Durfee take part in the killing? Is that what all this derives from?"

"Fuck you."

"Did Wendell Durfee witness the killing?"

"Fuck you."

Holly pulled his chair up. Holly bumped Wayne's chair.

"Let's discuss the condition of the shack."

Wayne shrugged. "I only saw the bindles I shoved in Curtis Swasey's mouth. I did not see any other narcotics or narcotics paraphernalia."

Holly smiled. "You anticipated the intent of my question very nicely."

Wayne coughed. "You're a narcotics agent. You want to know if I stole the large quantity of heroin that you think the victims had. You don't care about the murders or my wife."

Holly shook his head. "That's not entirely true. You know I'm friends with your father. I'm sure he cared for Lyn—"

"My father despised Lynette. He doesn't care for anyone. He only respects hard-ons like you. I'm sure he's full of warmth for your days in Indiana and your good times with Mr. Hoover."

Holly leaned in. "Don't turn me into an enemy. You're getting there already."

Wayne stood up. "Fuck you and fuck my father. If I wanted his help, I'd be out now."

Holly stood up. "I think I've got what I need."

Gilstrap shook his head. "You're playing kamikaze, son. And you're bombing your own goddamn friends."

Fritsch shook his head. "You can cross me off that list. We do our best to keep Vegas clean, while you go out and kill three niggers, which is going to bring out every civil-rights chimpanzee in captivity."

Wayne laughed. *"Vegas? Clean?"*

The cops walked out. Wayne took his pulse. It ran 180-plus.

33

(Las Vegas, 1/17/64)

The room was cold. A heat coil blew. It chilled down the jail.

Littell read his notes.

Wayne Junior was good. He diverted Sergeant Brown. He deflected his attack. Pete briefed Littell beforehand. Pete dropped a bomb: Wayne Junior knows about Dallas.

Pete liked Wayne Junior. Pete mourned Lynette. Pete took the blame. Pete stopped there. Pete implied a Dallas snafu.

Littell checked his notes. The smart call: Wayne Junior killed Maynard Moore. The details played schizzy. Wendell Durfee played in somehow.

Wayne Junior had the board files. Littell needed them. Littell might need Wayne Senior. Wayne Senior called him. Wayne Senior made nice. He said I want to help my son. He said I want *him* to ask.

He informed Wayne Junior. Wayne Junior said no. He told Wayne Senior that. It angered him. That was good. He might need Wayne Senior. The "no" knocked him flat.

Wayne Junior was good. Wayne Junior pissed off Dwight Holly. Littell called Lyle Holly. They talked last night. They discussed the Bayard Rustin meet. Lyle said Dwight was mad. The killings fucked with him. Wayne Junior deep-sixed his surveillance.

He chatted Lyle up. He said, "I'm Junior's lawyer." Lyle laughed. Lyle said, "Dwight never liked you."

Littell checked his notes. The room was cold. His breath fogged and steamed. Bob Gilstrap walked in. Dwight Holly followed him. They sat down and kicked back.

Holly stretched. His coat gapped. He wore a blued .45.

"You've aged, Ward. Those scars put some years on you."

"They're hard-earned, Dwight."

"Some men learn the hard way. I hope you have."

Littell smiled. "Let's discuss Wayne Tedrow Junior."

Holly scratched his neck. "He's a punk. He's got all of his daddy's arrogance and none of his charm."

Gilstrap lit a cigarette. "They broke the mold on Senior and him. I've never been able to figure either one of them."

Holly laced his hands. "Something happened with him and Durfee. Where or when, I don't know."

Gilstrap nodded. "That likelihood is what scares me."

A vent thumped. The heat kicked on. Holly hack-coughed.

"The kid mouths off to me and passes his bug on."

Gilstrap said, "You'll survive."

Holly said, "Let's cut the shit. I'm the only one who doesn't want to bury this."

"It's not your agency he hung out to dry."

"Shit, he hung *me* out."

The room warmed up. Holly took his coat off.

"Say something, Ward. You look like the cat who ate the canary."

Littell popped his briefcase. Littell showed the Vegas *Sun.* There's a headline. It runs 40 points. There's a subhead 16:

"POLICEMAN HELD IN TRIPLE SLAYING—CIVIL-RIGHTS PROTESTS FEARED."

"NAACP: 'KILLINGS SPRINGBOARD TO EXPLICATE RACISM IN LAS VEGAS.'"

Gilstrap said, "Shit."

Holly laughed. "Big words and colored bullshit. Give them a dictionary and they think they run the world."

Littell tapped the paper. "I don't see your name, Dwight. Is that a blessing or a curse?"

Holly stood up. "I see where this is going, and if it *does* go there, I'll go to the U.S. Attorney. Civil-rights abridgement and obstruction of justice. I'll look bad, you'll look worse, the kid will do time."

A vent thumped. The heat kicked off. Holly walked out.

Gilstrap said, "The cocksucker means it."

"I don't think so. He goes back too far with Wayne Senior."

"Dwight don't go back, Dwight goes forward. Wayne Senior could squawk and go to Mr. Hoover, who'd most likely pooh-pooh it because, according to my sources, he's got a real soft spot for Dwight."

Littell flipped the paper over. Littell squared the fold. There's the hard news and AP pix: Police dogs/angry Negroes/tear gas.

Gilstrap sighed. "Okay, I'll play."

"Does the DA want to file?"

"Nobody wants that. We're just afraid that we're too far exposed already."

"And?"

"And there's two schools of thought. Bury it and ride out all the Commie bullshit, or file and take our lumps."

Littell drummed the table. "Your department could get hurt very badly."

Gilstrap blew smoke rings. "Mr. Littell, you're leading me. You're playing me and holding back your face cards."

Littell tapped the paper. "Tell me Dallas doesn't scare you. Tell me Junior didn't fuck up there and give Durfee a motive to kill him. Tell me this won't come out in court. Tell me you're convinced that Junior didn't kill Maynard Moore. Tell me you didn't put a bounty on Durfee and pay Junior six thousand dollars to kill him. Tell me you want all this exposed and tell me Junior won't expose it just to flush his life down the toilet."

Gilstrap squeezed his ashtray. "Tell me Dallas PD will just go away."

"Tell me Junior wasn't smart enough to hide the body. Tell me the first cop who spots Durfee won't kill him and eliminate DPD's one potential witness."

Gilstrap slapped the table. "Tell me how we *do* this."

Littell tapped the paper. "I've read the accounts. There's no specified sequence of events. All you have is four killings in one evening."

"That's right."

"The evidence can be reworked to support self-defense. There may be a chance to divert demonstrations."

Gilstrap sighed. "I don't want to owe Wayne Senior."

Littell said, "You won't."

Gilstrap stuck his hand out.

He brewed a plan. He called Pete and told him. Pete said okay. Pete asked one favor.

I want to see Lynette. It's *my* fault. I fucked up in Dallas.

Buddy Fritsch had morgue shots. Littell looked at them. Durfee raped her. Durfee gutted her. Durfee shaved her.

He saw the pix. He studied them. He scared himself. He put Jane's face on Lynette's body.

He sent Pete a morgue pass. Pete said he'd talked to Wayne Junior. Wayne Junior pledged him his files.

Littell called east. Littell pulled strings. Littell buzzed Lyle Holly. He said the snuffs might hurt Dwight—so hear my plan now.

Call Bayard Rustin. Offer this advice: Do not protest the killings—call Ward Littell instead.

Rustin called him. Littell lied. Littell offered a rationale. A Negro man killed a white woman. Three more killings derived. The cop killed in self-defense. It's all certified.

Rustin *got* it—don't build hate—don't martyr an angry white cop. Vegas wasn't Birmingham. Negro junkies weren't four girls in church.

Rustin was savvy. Rustin was gracious. Littell pledged more money. Littell praised Dr. King.

He met Rustin once. He charmed and entrapped him. He *used* him forthwith.

I *believe.* I have horrible debts. I'll try to help more than I hurt.

34

(Las Vegas, 1/19/64)

He saw Lynette.

He saw the flaps. He saw the sheared ribs. He saw where the knife snapped bone. Wayne Junior didn't blame him. Wayne Junior blamed himself.

Pete stood by the freeway. Pete ate gas fumes. Pete had a replacement sled—a boss new Lin*coon*.

A prowl car pulled up. A cop got out. He fed Pete three guns. Three calibers: .38/.45/.357 mag.

Throwdown guns. Taped and initialed: L.W./O.S./C.S.

The cop knew the plan. They had two crime scenes. They had viable blood—good Red Cross stock.

The cop split. Pete drove to Henderson. Pete hit a gun shop. Pete bought ammo.

He loaded the guns. He rigged silencers. He drove back to Vegas.

Wayne Junior was out. He saw him yesterday. The DA dumped his case. They met. They talked. They hit Wayne's bank vault. Wayne dumped his board files and briefed him.

Spurgeon dug jailbait. Peavy was larcenous. Hinton whacked a nigger whore. Three board members—swing votes plus—good news for Count Drac.

Spurgeon vibed easy. Hinton vibed tough sell. Peavy vibed grief. Monarch Cab as Tiger Kab—hold that good thought.

Wayne looked frazzled. His eyes roamed. He strafed jigaboos. They ate lunch and talked.

Neutral shit—Clay versus Liston. Pete liked Liston in two. Wayne said three tops. A shine cleared their table. Wayne fucking seized up.

Pete drove to the car dump. The cop met him there. The dump was closed. The sun was up. A breeze wafted through.

They schmoozed. They jumped the crime-scene rope. Wayne's car was gone. The Buick was cut into scrap.

The cop taped a body—white tape on cement. Pete aimed the .45.

He popped six shots. He nailed a tree. He grabbed the slugs. He gauged trajectories. He dropped the slugs. He chalked them. The cop took pix.

Pete spritzed the body tape. Pete watched the blood dry. The cop took pix.

They drove to the shack. They jumped the crime-scene rope. The cop taped two bodies. The cop spritzed the tape.

Pete shot the .38. Pete popped four rounds. Pete hit the walls and dug the slugs out. The cop bagged them. The cop lab-logged them. The cop took pix.

They drove to the County Morgue. The cop greased the attendant geek. Said geek had three fish. Said fish reposed on three trays.

Leroy had no head. Leroy wore a dashiki. The cop pulled a sap. The cop broke Leroy's right hand. The cop flexed the fingers free.

Pete rolled the fingertips. Pete smudged the magnum. Pete laid two butt spreads.

Curtis was stiff. Otis was stiff. They wore Dodger T-shirts and morgue sheets.

Pete squeezed their hands. Pete broke their fingers. Pete flexed the tips. The cop rolled prints—barrel spreads—the cop rolled the .45 and .38.

The stiffs stunk of morgue rouge and sawdust. Pete coughed and sneezed.

Ward set it up. We'll meet at Wilt's Diner—it's out near Davis Dam.

They showed early. They grabbed a booth. They cleared table space and sipped coffee. Ward propped the bag up. Tabletop center—*très* hard to miss.

Dwight Holly showed. Punctual—2:00 p.m. straight.

He parked his car. He looked through the window glass. He saw them and walked straight in.

Pete made room. Holly sat beside him. Holly eyeballed the bag.

"What's that?"

Pete said, "Christmas."

Holly made the jack-off sign. Holly spread out.

He stretched. He made elbow room. He hard-nudged Pete.

He coughed. "I caught the fucking Tedrow kid's bug."

Ward smiled. "Thanks for coming out."

Holly tugged his cuff links. "Who's the big guy? The Wild Man of Borneo?"

Pete laughed. Pete slapped his knees.

Ward sipped coffee. "Have you spoken to the U.S. Attor—"

"He called me. He said Mr. Hoover told him not to file on the kid. I think Wayne Senior interceded, and I hope you didn't run me out here to gloat."

Ward tapped the bag. "Congratulations."

"For *what?* The investigation your client fucked up?"

"You must have talked to the U.S. Attorney *yesterday.*"

Holly tugged his law-school ring. "You're stringing me, Ward. You're reminding me why I never liked you."

Ward stirred his coffee. "You're the new Chief Investigator for the Southern Nevada Office. Mr. Hoover told me this morning."

Holly tugged his ring. It fell off. It hit the floor. It traveled.

Ward smiled. "We want to make friends in Nevada."

Pete smiled. "You took down Leroy Williams and the Swasey brothers. They were out on bail when Wayne killed them."

Ward tapped the bag. "The reports have been predated. You'll be reading about it."

Pete tapped the bag. "It's a white Christmas."

Holly grabbed the bag. Holly grabbed a steak knife. Holly stabbed one brick. Holly dipped one finger.

He licked it. He tasted it. He got the Big "H" bite.

"You convinced me. But I'm not done with the kid, and I don't care who he's got on his side."

DOCUMENT INSERT: 1/23/64. Las Vegas *Sun* article.

NARCOTICS LINK TO NEGRO KILLINGS REVEALED

At a joint news conference, spokesmen for the Las Vegas Police Department and the Southern Nevada District of the U.S. Attorney's Office announced that Leroy Williams and Otis and Curtis Swasey, the three Negro men killed on the night of January 15th, had been recently arrested by agents of the Federal Bureau of Narcotics and were out on bail at the time of their deaths.

"The three men had been the focus of a long-term investigation," Agent Dwight C. Holly said. "They had been selling large quantities of heroin in nearby cities and were preparing to sell it in Las Vegas. They were apprehended in the early morning hours of January 9th, and three kilos (6½ pounds) of heroin were seized at their residence in West Las Vegas. Williams and the Swasey brothers made bail on the afternoon of January 13th and returned to their residence."

Captain Robert Gilstrap of the LVPD went on to clarify events on the night of January 15th. "Newspaper reporters and local television commentators have assumed that the three men killed that night were killed by LVPD Sergeant Wayne Tedrow Jr. as revenge for the murder of his wife, Lynette, who was raped and killed, presumably by a male Negro named Wendell Durfee," he said. "This is not the case. Durfee was a known associate of Williams and the Swasey brothers, and the brothers paid him to kill Mrs. Tedrow. What has not been revealed until now is that Mrs. Tedrow's death postdated the deaths of Williams and the Swasey brothers and that Sergeant Tedrow, as part of a combined LVPD-Narcotics Bureau operation, had Williams and the Swasey brothers under constant surveillance in an effort to insure that they did not abscond on their bail."

"Sergeant Tedrow heard a ruckus inside their residence, late on the evening of January 15th," Agent Holly said. "He investigated and was fired upon by the Swasey brothers. No shots were heard, because both men fired silencer-fitted pistols. Sergeant Tedrow managed to disable both men and killed them with makeshift weapons he found on the premises. Leroy Williams entered the

residence at that time. Sergeant Tedrow chased him to an automobile dump on Tonopah Highway and exchanged gunfire with
him. Williams died in the process."

Agent Holly and Captain Gilstrap displayed photographic evidence compiled at both death scenes. Mr. Randall J. Merrins of the
U.S. Attorney's Office went on to say that it had been assumed that
Sergeant Tedrow was being kept in custody while possible homicide
charges against him were being discussed and prepared.

"This is not the case," Merrins said. "Sergeant Tedrow was held
for his own safety. We were afraid of reprisals from other
unknown members of the Williams-Swasey dope gang."

Sergeant Tedrow, 29, could not be reached for comment. Mrs.
Tedrow's presumed slayer, Wendell Durfee, was identified by finger-
prints and other physical evidence found in the Tedrow home. Durfee is now the subject of a nationwide all-points bulletin and is also
wanted by Texas authorities for the November 1963 disappearance
of Dallas Police Officer Maynard D. Moore.

Agent Holly's long pursuit of the Swasey brothers and Leroy
Williams was praised by Assistant U.S. Attorney Merrins, who
announced that Holly, 47, will soon take the position of Chief
Investigator for that agency's Southern Nevada Office. Captain
Gilstrap announced that Sergeant Tedrow has been awarded
the LVPD's highest accolade, its "Medal of Valor," for "conspicuous gallantry and bravery in his surveillance and subsequent
deadly confrontation with three armed and dangerous narcotics
pushers."

Mrs. Tedrow is survived by one sister and her parents, Mr. and
Mrs. Herbert D. Sproul, of Little Rock, Arkansas. Her body will be
shipped to Little Rock for interment.

DOCUMENT INSERT: 1/26/64. Las Vegas *Sun* article.

GRAND JURY CLEARS POLICEMAN

The standing Clark County Grand Jury today announced that
no criminal indictments will be filed against Las Vegas Policeman
Wayne Tedrow Jr. for the deaths of three Negro dope pushers.

The Grand Jury heard six hours of testimony from members of
the Las Vegas Police Department, Clark County Sheriff's Department and U.S. Bureau of Narcotics. Members were in unanimous

agreement that Sergeant Tedrow's actions were warranted and justifiable. Grand Jury foreman D. W. Kaltenborn said, "We believe that Sergeant Tedrow acted with great resolve and under all the due guidelines of the laws of the State of Nevada."

A Las Vegas Police Department spokesman attending the grand jury proceedings said that Sergeant Tedrow had resigned from the LVPD that morning. Sergeant Tedrow could not be reached for comment.

DOCUMENT INSERT: 1/27/64. Las Vegas *Sun* article.

NO PROTESTS, NEGRO LEADERS SAY

At a hastily arranged press conference in Washington, D.C., a spokesman for the National Association for the Advancement of Colored People (NAACP) announced that that organization and several other civil-rights groups will not protest the January 15th killings of three Negro men by a white policeman in Las Vegas.

Lawton J. Spofford told assembled reporters, "Our decision is not based upon the recent decree from the Clark County Grand Jury, which exonerated Sergeant Wayne Tedrow Jr. for the deaths of Leroy Williams and Curtis and Otis Swasey. That body is a 'rubber-stamp' implement of the Clark County political establishment and as such has no sway with us. Our decision is based on information we have received from a friendly anonymous source, who told us that Sergeant Tedrow, under great personal duress, acted in a somewhat heedless but recognizably non-malicious manner that did not include racist designs."

The NAACP, along with the Congress of Racial Equality (CORE) and the Southern Christian Leadership Conference (SCLC), had previously announced their intention to stage protests in Las Vegas, in order to "shed light on a horribly segregated city, where Negro citizens live in deplorable circumstances." The killings, Spofford said, "were to have been our point of redress and overall explication."

Other Negro leaders present at the press conference said that they did not rule out the possibility of future civil-rights protests in Las Vegas. "Where there's smoke, there's fire," spokesman Welton D. Holland of CORE said. "We do not expect Las Vegas to change its ways without some notable confrontations."

DOCUMENT INSERT: 2/6/64. Verbatim FBI telephone call transcript. Marked: "Recorded at the Director's Request"/"Classi-fied Confidential 1-A: Director's Eyes Only." Speaking: Director Hoover, Ward J. Littell.

JEH: Good morning, Mr. Littell.

WJL: Good morning, Sir.

JEH: You've been meeting some charming new people and rediscovering old friends. That might be a good place to start.

WJL: "Charming" might describe Mr. Rustin, Sir. "Old friend" would never describe Dwight Holly.

JEH: I could have predicted that response. And I doubt that Lyle Holly will become your lifelong chum.

WJL: We share a wonderful friend in you, Sir.

JEH: You're feeling frisky this morning.

WJL: Yes, Sir.

JEH: Did Mr. Rustin bemoan my efforts against Mr. King and the SCLC?

WJL: He did, Sir.

JEH: And you were properly deplored?

WJL: Cosmetically, Sir, yes.

JEH: I'm sure you were entirely convincing.

WJL: I established a rapport with Mr. Rustin, Sir.

JEH: I'm sure you will sustain it.

WJL: I hope so, Sir.

JEH: Have you spoken to him again?

WJL: Lyle Holly facilitated a second conversation. I utilized Mr. Rustin to forestall some trouble in Las Vegas. It pertained to a client of mine.

JEH: I know elements of the story. We'll discuss it momentarily.

WJL: Yes, Sir.

JEH: Do you still consider it impossible to re-tape the Dark Prince?

WJL: Yes, Sir.

JEH: I would enjoy some glimpses of his private pain.

WJL: I would, too.

JEH: I doubt that. You're a voyeur, not a sadist, and I suspect that you'll never reconcile your old crush on Bobby.

WJL: Yes, Sir.

JEH: Lyndon Johnson finds him difficult to reconcile. Many of his advisors think he should include him on the fall ticket, but he hates the Dark Lad too much to succumb.

WJL: I understand how he feels, Sir.

JEH: Yes, and you disapprove, in your uniquely non-disapproving way.

WJL: I'm not that complex, Sir. Or that compromised in my emotions.

JEH: You delight me, Mr. Littell. I will nominate your last statement for Best Falsehood of 1964.

WJL: I'm honored, Sir.

JEH: Bobby may run for Kenneth Keating's Senate seat in New York.

WJL: If he runs, he'll win.

JEH: Yes. He'll form a coalition of the deluded and morally handicapped and emerge victorious.

WJL: Is he maintaining his work at Justice?

JEH: Not vigorously. He still appears to be shell-shocked. Mr. Katzenbach and Mr. Clark are doing most of his work. I think he'll resign, in a timely fashion.

WJL: Is he monitoring the agents for the Warren Commission?

JEH: I haven't discussed the investigation with him. Of course, he receives summaries of all my field agents' reports.

WJL: Edited summaries, Sir?

JEH: You are frisky today. Impertinent might describe it better.

WJL: I apologize, Sir.

JEH: Don't. I'm enjoying the conversation.

WJL: Yes, Sir.

JEH: Edited summaries, yes. With all contradictory elements deleted to conform to the thesis we first discussed in Dallas.

WJL: I'm happy to hear that.

JEH: Your clients should be, as well.

WJL: Yes, Sir.

JEH: We can't send your plant in again. You're certain?

WJL: Yes, Sir.

JEH: I mourn the missed opportunity. I would like to hear a private assessment of King Jack's death.

WJL: I suspect we'll never know, Sir.

JEH: Lyndon Johnson continues to share his thoughts with me, in his inimitably colorful manner. He has said, quote, It all came out of that pathetic little shithole, Cuba. Maybe it's that cocksucker with the beard or those fucking lowlife exiles, unquote.

WJL: A lively and astute analysis.

JEH: Mr. Johnson has developed a distaste for all things Cuban.

The exile cause has succumbed to factionalism and has scattered to the wind, which pleases him no end.

WJL: I share his delight, Sir. I know many people who were seduced by the cause.

JEH: Yes. Gangsters and a French-Canadian chap with homicidal tendencies.

WJL: Yes, Sir.

JEH: Cuba appeals to hotheads and the morally impaired. It's the cuisine and the sex. Plantains and women who have intercourse with donkeys.

WJL: I have no fondness for the place, Sir.

JEH: Mr. Johnson has developed a fondness for Vietnam. You should inform Mr. Hughes. Some military contracts may be coming his way.

WJL: He'll be delighted to hear that.

JEH: You should inform him that I'll keep you abreast of the Justice Department's plans in Las Vegas.

WJL: I'm delighted to hear that.

JEH: On a need-to-know basis, Mr. Littell. As is the case with all our transactions.

WJL: I understand, Sir. And I neglected to thank you for your help in the Tedrow matter. Dwight Holly was determined to do the boy some harm.

JEH: You deserve an accolade. You bypassed Wayne Senior very effectively.

WJL: Thank you, Sir.

JEH: I understand that he has asked you to lunch.

WJL: Yes, Sir. We haven't scheduled yet.

JEH: He thinks you're weak. I told him that you are a bold and occasionally reckless man who has learned the value of restraint.

WJL: Thank you, Sir.

JEH: Dwight feels quite ambivalent. He got the job he wanted, but he's developed quite a dislike for Wayne Junior. My sources in the U.S. Attorney's Office tell me that he is determined to bypass Senior and do Junior some harm in the long run.

WJL: Despite his friendship with Senior?

JEH: Or because of it. You never know with Dwight. He's quite the provocateur and the rogue, so I indulge him.

WJL: Yes, Sir.

JEH: The same way I indulge you.

WJL: I caught the implication, Sir.

JEH: You dislike Dwight and Wayne Senior, so I'll give you added cause. Their fathers belonged to the same Klan Klavern in Indiana. That said, I should add that it was probably more genteel than the Klan groups currently marauding down south.

WJL: I'm sure they never lynched any Negroes.

JEH: Yes, although I'm certain they would have enjoyed it.

WJL: Yes, Sir.

JEH: Most people have entertained the notion. You must credit their restraint.

WJL: Yes, Sir.

JEH: You might discuss the Indiana Klan with Bayard Rustin. I want you to make another donation.

WJL: I'll bring it up, Sir. I'm sure he'll acknowledge it as a genteel institution.

JEH: You are assuredly frisky today.

WJL: I hope I haven't offended you, Sir.

JEH: Anything but. And I hope I haven't offended you with Junior.

WJL: Sir?

JEH: I had to throw Dwight Holly a bone. He wanted Junior expelled from the LVPD, so I arranged it.

WJL: I assumed that you had, Sir. The newspapers were kind, though. They said he resigned.

JEH: Did you befriend Junior to get at his files? For Mr. Hughes' sake?

WJL: Yes, Sir.

JEH: I'm sure that Senior will enjoy Junior's expulsion. They have an odd relationship.

WJL: Yes, Sir.

JEH: Good day, Mr. Littell. I've enjoyed this conversation.

WJL: Good day, Sir.

35

(Las Vegas, 2/7/64)

The Lincoln gleamed. New paint/ new chrome/new leather.

The car jazzed him. The car distracted him. He kept seeing Lynette. Flaps and sheared ribs. Durfee's knife severed bone.

Pete cruised. Pete tried gadgets. The lighter worked. The heater worked. The seats reclined.

Vegas looked good. Cool air hits mountains and sunshine. Secure-the-Vote Day—one down so far.

He muscled Webb Spurgeon. He explained stat-rape statutes. He detailed consent laws. Spurgeon gulped. Spurgeon kowtowed. Spurgeon pledged votes.

All good so far. One down—two to go.

Pete drove by Monarch Cab. Pete got electrified. Dollar signs boogied and bipped.

Cabs peeled in. Cabs peeled out. Cabs refueled. Drivers ate pills. Drivers drank lunch. Drivers palmed waistband gats.

Monarch Cab. *Maybe:* Tiger Kab redux.

A cash base. A racket hub. Bent personnel. Monarch as Tiger—hold that heady thought.

Pete cruised. Pete meandered. Pete hit West LV. Pete checked out that vacant lot.

There's the trailer. The paint's gone. The shell's cracked. The siding's all scorched.

A kid walked up. Pete jollied him. The kid sermonized.

The trailer smell bad. That be wrong. Somethin' dead be inside. This dude torch it. The stink go. He burn the stink out. No cops come. No fire-men. Somethin' dead *still* be in there.

The kid buzzed off. Pete scoped the trailer. A breeze kicked up. The trailer creaked. Paint chips cracked and blew.

Pete cruised. Pete meandered. Pete drove south. Pete hit Duane Hinton's house.

He parked. He walked up. He knocked on the door. He pulled out Wayne's snapshot.

There's a fat whore bound and gagged. She's sucking a handball.

Hinton opened the door. Pete flashed the photo eye-level.

Hinton plotzed. Pete grabbed his hair. Pete raised one knee. Pete broke his nose up.

Hinton went down. Bones cracked. Cartilage blew.

Pete decreed:

Vote our way. Do not touch whores. Do not hurt whores. Do not kill whores—OR I'LL KILL YOU.

Hinton tried to talk. Hinton gagged. Hinton bit through his tongue.

36

(Little Rock, 2/8/64)

Devoted wife. Schoolteacher. Loving daughter.

The preacher ran on. The casket sat ready. Lakeside Cemetery: cheap burials and segregated plots.

The Sprouls wore black. Janice wore black. Wayne Senior wore blue. The Sprouls stood alone. Wayne stood alone. Daddy Sproul watched him.

Soldier boy. Yankee. She was seventeen. You wooed her. She killed your baby. You made her do it.

Loving spirit. Sacred child. Blessed in Christ's name.

The service was short. The casket was cheap. The plot was low-rent. The Tedrows shipped the body home. The Tedrows lost control.

Lynette despised religion. Lynette loved movie stars and John Kennedy.

A chauffeur stood around. A Negro man. Tall like Wendell Durfee.

The preacher braced Wayne pre-service. The preacher counseled him.

I feel your loss. I know your grief. I *understand*.

Wayne said it: "I'm going to kill Wendell Durfee."

God's will. The ides of fate. Snatched in her prime.

The plots adjoined Central High. He met Lynette there. Soldiers and rednecks. Negro kids scared.

The chauffeur stood around. The chauffeur filed his nails. The chauffeur wore a hair net. He had Durfee hair. He had Durfee skin. He had Durfee's lank frame.

Wayne watched him. Wayne retouched his hair. Wayne retouched his skin. Wayne made him Wendell D.

The preacher prayed. The Sprouls wept. The Tedrows stood calm. The chauffeur buffed his nails.

Wayne watched him.

He burned his face. He smashed his teeth. He fed him Big "H."

37

(Las Vegas, 2/9/64)

The DI count room.

Money—coin bins and hampers stuffed. A swivel spy-camera hooked up.

Your host—Moe Dalitz.

The count men were out. The camera was off. Money sat waist-high. Littell sneezed—the fumes were bad—sting off cash dye and tin.

Moe said, "It's not that complicated. The count guys are in cahoots with the camera guys. The camera goes on the fritz, accidental on purpose, so the count guys can get the skim out and retally it. You don't need a college education."

Mesh hampers—laundry-size. Forty hampers/forty grand per.

Moe dipped in. Moe snagged ten grand—C-notes all.

"Here, for your civil-rights deal. What's their fucking motto, 'We Shall Overcome'?"

Littell grabbed the cash. Littell packed his briefcase.

"The skim interests me."

"You are not alone in that. Certain Federal agencies have been known to be curious."

"Are you looking for couriers?"

Moe said, "No. We use civilians, exclusive. Squarejohns who owe casino markers. They run the skim and pay off their debts at 7½% of the transport."

Littell shot his cuffs. "I was thinking of Mr. Hughes' Mormons, or other trustworthy ones, at a 15% rate."

Moe shook his head. "I don't like to fuck with success, but I'll hear you out anyway."

Littell sneezed. Moe supplied a Kleenex. Littell wiped his nose.

"You're going to sell Mr. Hughes some hotels. He'll want his Mormons or *some* Mormons to run them. You'll want your men, you'll compromise, you'll want to escalate your skim operations."

Moe twirled a dime. "Don't be a cock tease. You've got this tendency to string things out."

Littell hugged his briefcase. "I want to enlist some Mormons, over time, and have them ready by the date you sell Mr. Hughes the hotels. You'd have a pool of potential inside men with skim experience."

"That's not enough inducement to pay 15%."

"At face value, no."

Moe rolled his eyes. "So, lay it out. Jesus Christ, don't make me coax you."

"All right. Mr. Hughes' people travel on Hughes Aircraft charter flights. I could hire some Mormons to work for Mr. Hughes now, and you could ship the skim bulk and avoid airport security risks."

Moe flipped the dime. Moe caught it heads-up.

"At face value, I like it. I'll talk to the other guys."

"I'd like to get started soon."

"Take a breather. Don't wear yourself out."

"I'm sure that's a good tip, but I'd—"

"Here's a better one. Bet Clay over Liston. You'll make a fucking mint."

"Is the fight fixed?"

"No, but Sonny's got some very bad habits."

Littell flew to L.A.

He flew solo. He booked a Hughes plane. The Hughes fleet moored in Burbank. Cessna Twins—six seats each—ample skim space.

The flight ran smooth. No clouds and desert sparkling up.

Moe took the bait. Moe missed the dodge. Moe thought the dodge was pro-Drac. Wrong—the dodge was pro–civil rights.

Call it:

Bagmen. Potential "casino consultants." *Hughes* men. All charter-flight cleared.

He could skim off the skim. He could feed Bayard Rustin. He could blunt Mr. Hoover's damage. Wayne Senior ran Mormon thugs. Wayne Senior knew bagmen types. *He* could coopt them.

The long-term goal: damage abatement.

Mr. Hoover filmed Dr. King. Mr. Hoover tried to entrap him. Mr. Hoover dirt-fed his "correspondents": congressmen/reporters/clergymen.

Mr. Hoover schooled them. Mr. Hoover taught them restraint. Let's collude and leak covert data. Let's leak it smart. Don't leak *strict* bug-and-tap data. Don't jeopardize bug-and-tap mounts.

Mr. Hoover held dirt. Mr. Hoover leaked dirt. Mr. Hoover caused pain. Mr. Hoover hated Dr. King. Mr. Hoover exposed his one weakness:

Sadism. *Sustained.* Inflicted over TIME.

TIME worked two ways. There was TIME to inflict harm. There was TIME to countermand the effects.

The skim plan might work. The skim plan sparked a question: Hughes money—a potential tithe source?

The plane banked. Littell pared an apple. Littell sipped coffee.

Pete had Wayne's files. Pete squeezed Spurgeon and Hinton. Spurgeon fed Pete some dirt. Key legislators and their pet charities—dirt per their philanthropy.

Pete said he bypassed Eldon Peavy. Peavy was cop-sanctioned. Peavy might balk at threats. Pete was disingenuous. Pete's threats *worked*. Pete craved Monarch Cab. Pete was gauging a takeover shot.

The plane dipped low. Burbank showed sunshine and smog.

He'd lunched with Wayne Senior. Wayne Senior praised him—you saved my son.

Junior declined Senior's help. Junior rebuffed his connections. Junior nixed good job offers. Junior nixed work in chemistry. Junior sought his own work. Junior found low-end employment.

The Wild Deuce Casino—night bouncer—6:00 to 2:00 a.m. The Deuce was rough. The Deuce welcomed Negroes. Junior welcomed pain.

Wayne Senior bought Littell's lunch. Wayne Senior made nice. Wayne Senior said ugly things.

Wayne Senior derided the civil-rights movement. Wayne Senior brought up the King film.

Littell smiled. Littell made nice. Littell thought *I will make you all pay.*

Jane said, "I got a job."

The terrace was cold. The view compensated. Littell leaned on the rail.

"Where?"

"Hertz rent-a-car. I'm doing the books for the West L.A. branches."

"Did your Tulane degree help?"

Jane smiled. "It got me the extra thousand a year I asked for."

She used hard vowels. She eschewed slurs. She dropped her southern drawl. She'd reworked her voice and diction—he just noticed it.

She said, "It feels good to rejoin the work force."

Hard *g*'s. Regionless. Pure consonants.

Littell smiled. Littell popped his briefcase. Littell pulled out six sheets.

He landed. He drove to Hughes Tool. He stopped at the bookkeeping pool and stole forms.

Invoices. Bill sheets. All standard paper.

He got in. He got out. He shaped his upcoming lie.

"Would you look at these when you get a chance? I need your advice on a few things."

Jane scanned the sheets. "They're all boilerplate. Cost-outs, overruns, that kind of thing."

Hard *b*'s and *p*'s. Lazy *o*'s deleted.

"I want to discuss embezzling techniques and how to use these forms. There's going to be a buildup in Vietnam, and Mr. Hughes will probably be awarded some contracts. He's afraid of embezzlements, and he asked me to study up."

Jane smiled. "Did you tell him your girlfriend's an embezzler?"

"No. Just that she keeps a good secret."

"God, the way that we live."

Short *a*'s and *e*'s. Crisp inflections.

Jane laughed. "Have you noticed? I gave up my accent."

Jane read in bed. Jane dozed off early. Littell played his tapes.

He got crazy. Two times of late. He ran two crazy risks.

He passed through D.C. He wired Doug Eversall. He squeezed him. He cajoled him. He paid him five G's.

Eversall taped Bobby. Two more times total—two crazy risks. Eversall balked then. Eversall cut Littell off.

That's it. Shove your threats. I refuse to hurt Bobby. You're sick. You're fucked up. Bobby's your sickness.

Littell retreated:

That's it. No more. I promise you. I'll lie to Carlos. I'll say we failed.

Eversall walked then. Eversall tripped. His high shoe buckled and slid. Littell helped him up. Eversall slapped him. Eversall spat in his face.

Littell played the 1/29 tape. Low static/spool hum.

Bobby planned trials. Eversall took notes. Bobby yawned and digressed. His potential Senate run. The VP spot. That "cornpone son-of-a-bitch Lyndon Johnson."

Bobby had a cold. Bobby waxed profane. LBJ was a "dipshit." Dick Nixon was a "numbnuts" with a "kick-me sign." Mr. Hoover was a "psycho fruitcake."

Littell pressed Rewind. The tape reversed. Littell played the 2/5 tape.

Here's Bobby—reverent now.

He toasted Jack. He quoted Housman: "To an Athlete Dying Young." Eversall sniffled. Bobby laughed—"Don't go soft on me."

A new man spoke. Static fizzed his words. Littell heard his garbled "Hoover and King."

Bobby said, "Hoover's scared. He knows King's got balls like J.C."

38

(Las Vegas, 2/10/64)

onarch rocked.

The noon rush / mucho calls / ten cabs out. The hut rocked—Eldon Peavy had guests.

Sonny Liston. Four bad-boy jigs. Conrad & the Congoites or Marvin & the Mau-Maus.

Pete watched.

He dipped his seat. He ran the heat. He did arithmetic. Peavy had twenty cabs. Peavy ran three shifts. Add airport runs and deadheads.

The hut rocked. A driver hawked fur coats. The Mau-Maus mauled them. Sonny fanned a roll. Peavy peeled bills off.

The Congoites capered. They fondled fur. They manhandled mink. They chewed up chinchilla.

Sonny looked bad. The Clay fight boded. Sonny had the odds. Sam G. demurred. Sam liked Clay. Sam said Sonny had habits.

It was cold. Brrr—Vegas winters. Pete shivered and goosed the heat.

Texas was cold. Florida ditto. He just got back from his trip. He didn't find Hank K. He didn't find Wendell Durfee. He traveled alone. He schemed a trifecta.

Plan A: Find and clip Hank. Plan B: Detain Durfee. Plan C: Bring Wayne in to kill him.

No tickee/no washee. No find/go seek.

He got back. He called Ward. He pitched him: I want to buy Monarch Cab. Ward nixed it. Ward said don't bid. Ward said don't extort ownership.

We *need* Peavy. We need his *votes.* Don't scotch his gaming-board status. Sage fucking advice—Ward Littell–style.

Pete skimmed the radio. Pete watched the hut. Peavy quaffed gin. The Mau-Maus quaffed scotch-and-milk. Sonny dumped capsules. Sonny made lines. Sonny sniffed powder up.

Peavy walked out. Sonny strolled with him. The Congoites conga'd. They slurped milk. They grew white goatees. Spooks called scotch-and-milk "pablum."

A stretch pulled up. The crew piled in. The stretch pulled out. Pete tailed it slow.

The stretch hooked west. The stretch stopped quick. There—the Honey Bunny Casino.

Peavy got out. Peavy walked in. Pete idled back. Pete scoped the window.

Peavy hit the chip cage. Peavy bought play chips. The cage man filled a sack. Peavy walked out. Peavy jumped in the stretch. The stretch pulled out fast.

Pete tailed it. It cut west. It stopped mucho quick. There—Sugar Bear Liquor.

Five whores ran out—darkies all—prom gowns and heels.

They piled in the stretch. They huffed hard. The windows fogged up. The stretch wiggled and bounced.

Said whores *worked.*

The axle scraped. The shocks creaked. The undercarriage shimmied. Two hubcaps popped off and rolled.

Pete laughed. Pete fucking roared.

The whores piled out. The whores giggled and wiped their lips. The whores waved sawbucks.

Pete flashed on the dead whore. Pete smelled the torched trailer.

The stretch pulled out. Pete tailed it. They cut west. They hit West Vegas. They went in *waay* deep. There—Monroe High School.

The back gate was down. The bleachers were packed. A banner read: Welcome Champ!

Full house:

Colored kids—two hundred strong—this big schoolday treat.

The stretch parked on the football field. Pete idled by the gate. Pete kicked his seat back.

Sonny got out.

He weaved. He waved the chip sack. He faced the kids and swayed blotto. The kids cheered. The kids chanted "Sonny!" Some geek teachers watched.

The kids yelled. The kids banged their seats. The teachers guuulped. Sonny smiled. Sonny swayed. Sonny said, "Pipe down."

The kids cheered. Sonny swayed. Sonny yelled: "Shut up, you punk motherfuckers!"

The kids shut up. The teachers cringed. Sonny dished inspiration.

Study hard. Learn good. Don't rob no liquor stores. Play to win and go to church. Use Sheik-brand rubbers. Watch me whup Cassius Clay. Watch me kick his punk Muslim ass back to Mecca.

Sonny stopped. Sonny bowed. Sonny pulled a flask. The kids cheered. The teachers clapped demure.

Sonny waved his sack. Sonny grabbed play chips. Sonny tossed them wide.

The kids snatched them. The kids snared them. Kids bumped kids. Kids reached short. Kids fell on kids below.

Sonny tossed chips—big wads—dollar chips all. Kids reached high. Kids toppled. Kids engaged in fistfights.

Sonny raised his flask. Sonny waved bye-bye. Sonny jumped in the stretch.

The stretch pulled out. Pete U-turned and tailed it. Kids shrieked Champ bye-bye!

The stretch hauled. Pete hauled up close. They tore speed limits. They cut east and south. They hit downtown Vegas.

Traffic snarled. The stretch looped Fremont. The stretch braked and stopped.

There—

A parking lot. An army-navy store—Sid the Surplus Sergeant.

The crew piled out. The crew yukked and huddled. The crew piled in the backdoor. The driver waved—adios, Mau-Maus—the stretch vamoosed.

Pete parked. Pete locked his car. Pete dawdled and ambled up. Pete braced the backdoor.

He ambled in. He cut through a storeroom. He pushed through peacoats on racks. He saw crates/cartons/trench tools. He caught a cosmoline stench.

He hit a hallway. He heard sounds. He followed titters and love grunts—aaooooo!

He ambled. He tracked the noise. He crouched and crept. He saw a cracked door and peeked in.

Stag-flick time. A bedsheet screen and a projector. Lez antics—young girls entwined.

The Mau-Maus tittered. Peavy yawned. The girls ran fourteen tops.

Sonny cracked a red devil. Sonny powdered a palm. Sonny sniffed the shit up.

The girls strapped on dildoes. A donkey appeared. El Burro wore *diablo* horns.

Pete walked outside. Pete found a pay phone. Pete called the Stardust book. He placed a bet—forty grand—Clay over Liston.

The Deuce rolled low—nickel slots/bingo/shots-and-beer.

The dealers wore sidearms. The bar served jar brew. The cocktail chicks whored. The Deuce pandered low. You had oldsters and wetbacks. You had more spooks than Ramar of the Jungle.

The lounge supplied a floor view. Pete lounged and sipped club soda. Pete watched the floor show.

A geez pulls his air tube. He's ninety-plus. He smokes a Camel. He hacks blood. He sucks oxygen. Two fruits lock eyes. Said fruits strut green shirts. Green shirts are fruit semaphore.

Two jigs lurk. They're snatch-and-run guys. Dig their gym shorts and sneakers. Wayne walks up. Wayne wears a belt sap. Wayne wears handcuffs.

He taps the jigs. They share a look—woe-is-fuckin'-me.

Wayne slaps them. Wayne kicks them. Wayne grabs their conk napes and shoves them. They get the picture. They evict themselves—We Shall *Not* Overcome.

Pete clapped. Pete whistled. Wayne turned and saw him. He walked up. He swiveled a chair. He nailed a floor view.

Pete said, "I didn't find him. I think he's down in Mexico."

"How hard did you look?"

"Not that hard. I was looking for a guy in Florida, mostly."

Wayne flexed his hands. Knuckle cuts oozed.

"We could teletype the *federales*. They could put out their own APB. We could pay them to hold him for me."

Pete lit a cigarette. "They'd kill him themselves. They'd lure you down there, steal your money, and kill you."

Wayne watched the floor. Pete tracked his eyes. There—one coon/one whore/unruly shit pending—

Wayne stood up. Pete grabbed his belt. Pete yanked him back down.

"Let it go. We're having a conversation."

Wayne shrugged. Wayne looked aggrieved. Wayne looked fucking deprived.

Pete glanced around. "Does your father own this place?"

"No, it's Outfit. Santo Trafficante has points."

Pete blew smoke rings. "I know Santo."

"I'm sure you do. I know who you work for, so I've put that much of Dallas together."

Pete smiled. "Nothing happened in Dallas."

A whore walked by. Wayne drifted. Wayne watched the floor. Pete grabbed his chair. Pete jerked it and centered it. Pete killed the floor view.

"Look at me when I talk to you."

Wayne made fists. His knuckles popped. His knuckles seeped.

Pete said, "Don't use your hands. Use your sap if you have to."

"Like Duane Hint—"

"Can it, all right? I've had dead women up to here."

Wayne coughed. "Durfee's good. That's the part that gets me. He's stayed ahead of everyone since Dallas."

Pete chained cigarettes. "He's not good, he's lucky. He came to Vegas like a dumb bunny, and moves like that will get him dropped."

Wayne shook his head. "He's better than that."

"No, he's not."

"He can give me up for Moore."

"Bullshit. It's his word versus yours and no body."

"He's good. That's the part . . ."

A spook walked by. Wayne eyeballed him. He saw Wayne and blinked.

Pete coughed. "Who owns Sid the Surplus Sergeant?"

Wayne said, "A clown named Eldon Peavy. He named it after some queer buddy of his who died from the syph."

Pete laughed. "He's showing smut films there. Underaged kids, the whole shot. How big a bust is that on his end?"

Wayne shrugged. "The State Code's soft on possession. He'd have to manufacture and sell the films, or coerce and suborn the kids."

Pete smiled. "Ask me why I care."

"I know why. You want to buy out Monarch and relive your fucking Miami adventures."

Pete laughed. "You've been talking to Ward Littell."

"Sure, client to lawyer. I asked him why you take so much shit from me, but he wouldn't give me an answer."

Pete cracked his knuckles. "Bet on Clay. Your boy Sonny needs more time in the gym."

Wayne flexed his hands. "There's a Sheriff's Vice guy named Farlan Moss. He investigates businessmen for people who want to take over their action. He won't fabricate, but if he gets incriminating evidence, he'll turn it over to you and let you use it any way you like. It's an old Vegas strategy."

Pete grabbed a napkin. Pete wrote it down: "Farlan Moss/CCSD."

Wayne twirled his sap. "You've got this weird thing for me."

"I had a kid brother once. Someday I'll tell you the story."

The Bondsmen vamped. Barb grabbed the mike. She curtsied. Her gown hiked. Her nylons stretched.

Pete sat ringside. A geek had Wayne's seat. Wayne worked late now. Wayne caught Barb haphazard.

Ward said he talked to Wayne Senior. Senior ragged on Junior. Ward passed it on.

Junior was a hider. Junior was a watcher. Junior lit flames. Junior torched. Junior lived in his head.

Barb blew a kiss. Pete caught it. Pete covered his heart. He made two T's—their private signal—do "Twilight Time."

Barb caught it. Barb cued the Bondsmen. Barb kicked the tune off.

He missed her for days on. They kept diverse hours and slept diverse shifts. They stashed a cot backstage. They made love between shows.

It worked. *They* worked. It wrecked him. It *scared* him.

Barb watched the news. Barb tracked the Warren thing. Barb nursed Dallas. Barb nursed her link to Jack.

She never said it. He just *knew*. It wasn't sex. It wasn't love. "Awe" said it all. You killed him. The fix held. You killed him and walked.

He played *his* version. "Fear" said it all. You've got her. You could lose her—per Dallas.

You sweat Fear. You ooze Fear. You test the Fear logic. You know you walked because:

It was *that* big. It was *that* audacious. It was *that* wrong.

You test the logic. You fret it. You show fear. You scare people. You pass your fear on. The wrong people find you and knock.

Barb worked "Twilight Time." Barb caressed the low notes.

Wendell Durfee knocked. Lynette paid. Dead women scared him. Lynette as Barb. Lynette as "Jane."

He saw Lynette's body. He had to. The picture stuck. He conjured it. He banished it. He dreamed it and tore the sheets up.

Barb kissed off "Twilight Time." Barb did the Mashed Potato. Barb did the Swim.

The spell died. Her fast tunes deep-sixed it. A waiter schlepped a phone up.

Pete cradled it. "Yeah?"

A man said, "Carlos wants to see you."

"Where?"

"De Ridder, Louisiana."

He flew to Lake Charles. He cabbed to De Ridder. It was wet. It was hot. The heat spawned bugs.

De Ridder was Shit City. Fort Polk stood close. The town lived off Army handouts.

Chicken-fried-steak joints and rib cribs. Beer bars/tattoo parlors/nudie-mag stalls.

Carlos limo'd up. Pete met him. The local crackers watched. *Dumb* crackers—gap-mouthed bug-magnets all.

They drove east. They caught red clay and pine bluffs. They looped the Kisatchee Forest.

Pete raised a screen. Pete cut the driver off. Vents pumped cold air in. Dark tint killed the sun.

Carlos bankrolled a camp—forty Cubans total—would-be killer ops. Carlos said, "Let's see my boys." Carlos said, "Let's talk."

They drove. They talked. They passed Klan klonklaves. Carlos ragged the Klan—they hate Catholics—that means they hate *us*.

Pete nixed him—I'm Huguenot—you fucks fucked my kin.

They talked. They rehashed *la Causa*. Tiger Kab and Pigs. LBJ's big walkoff. Carlos brought a bottle. Pete brought paper cups.

Carlos said, "The Outfit's got zero affection for the Cause. Everyone thinks, 'We shot our wad, we lost the casinos, it's spilled milk under the bridge.'"

They hit a rut. Pete spilled X.O.

"Havana was beautiful. Vegas can't hold a candle."

"Littell's got a foreign-casino plan. Everyone's gaga, as well they fucking should be."

They passed Army trucks. They passed signs. Signs ragged the ACL-*Jew*.

Pete said, "The old crew was good. Laurent Guéry, Flash Elorde."

Carlos nodded. "Good narcotics men and good killers. You never doubted their sincerity."

Pete dabbed his shirt. "John Stanton was a good ops man. You had the Outfit and the Agency together."

"Yeah, like that song. 'For one brief shining moment.'"

Pete crushed his cup. "Stanton's in Indochina?"

"Don't be such a Frenchman. They call it Vietnam now."

Pete lit a cigarette. "There's a cab biz in Vegas. I could turn it into a moneymaker for us. Littell wants me to hold off, because the owner's on the license boards."

Carlos sipped X.O. "Don't work so hard to impress me. You're not Littell, but you're good."

The troops snapped to. Pete paced the line. Pete came to critique and review.

Forty Cubanos—porkers and stringbeans—jail recruits all.

Guy Banister recruited them. Guy knew a cop in John Birch. The cop fudged his jail sheets. The cop freed prospects. Said prospects were pervs. Said prospects were "musicians"—Cugie Cugat manqués.

Pete walked the line. Pete checked guns. M-1s and M-14s—dead bugs chambered in.

Barrel dust. Mildew. Moss rot.

Pete got pissed. Pete got a headache. The head geek paced the line behind him.

An Army stupe—Fort Polk trash—some kiddie kommando. He ran a Klan klique. He ran a still. He sold oat mash. He supplied alcoholic Choctaws.

The troops sucked poodle dick. The camp ditto.

Quonset huts and pup tents—fucking Boy Scout stock. A "Target Range"—scarecrows and tree stumps. An "Ammo Dump"—made from Lego logs.

The troops snapped to. The troops shot a salute. They fumbled their rifles. They fired off-sync. Eight bolts jammed up.

They made some noise. They roused some birds. Birdshit disinterred and fell.

Carlos bowed. Carlos tossed the donation bag. The head geek caught it and bowed.

"Mr. Banister and Mr. Hudspeth will be coming in soon. They're transporting some ordnance."

Carlos lit a cigar. "That my ten grand's paying for?"

"That's correct, sir. They're my chief weapons procurers."

"They're *making money* off my donations?"

"Not in the sense you imply, sir. I'm sure they're not making a personal profit."

Prime "ordnance": One picnic table/one bar-b-que pit.

The geek blew a whistle. The troops hit the range. They fired. They shot low. They missed.

Carlos shrugged. Carlos nursed a grievance. Carlos walked off. The geek shrugged. The geek nursed hurt feelings. The geek walked off.

Pete walked. Pete checked the range. Pete checked the dump. Pete critiqued the stock.

Two machine guns—old 50s—slack triggers/loose belts. Six flame-throwers—cracked feeders/cracked pipes. Two speedboats—pull motors—lawn-mower drive. Sixty-two revolvers—corroded and fucked.

Pete found some oil. Pete found some rags. Pete cleaned some .38s up. The sun felt good. The oil deterred mosquitoes. The "troopers" worked out.

They did push-ups. They wrecked their manicures. They huffed and puffed.

He ran *ace* troops. *He* hit Cuba. *He* scalped mucho Reds. *He* killed Fidelistos. *He* went to Pigs. *He* tried to kill Fidel. They should have won. Jack the K. fucked them. Jack paid. *He* paid. It got all shot to hell.

Pete cleaned guns. He swabbed barrels. He dipped butts. He brushed cylinders. He scoured moss rot.

An old Ford pulled in. The paint job screamed RIGHT-WING NUT!

Dig it:

Crosses. The stars & bars. Inverted swastikas.

A trailer bounced behind the Ford. Gun barrels extruded. The Ford brodied. The Ford slid. The Ford grazed the bar-b-que pit.

The Ford stalled and died. Guy B. got out. Hank Hudspeth helped him up. Guy was cardiac red. Guy survived #3. Carlos said his pump was shot.

Guy looked drunk. Guy looked frail. Guy looked diseased. Hank looked drunk. Hank looked strong. Hank looked dead mean.

Guy lugged out hot dogs. Hank dumped steaks and buns. They looked around. They saw Pete. They puckered up.

Hank whistled. Guy hit his horn. The troops shagged ass up.

Hank dumped briquettes. The head geek filled the pit. Guy gas-spritzed it. They built a fire. They torched hot dogs. The troops swamped the trailer.

They whooped. They yanked guns. They dollied them over—full-drum Thompsons/one hundred plus.

Pete grabbed one. The butt was chipped. The drum was jammed. The balance was off.

Shit knockoffs—Jap stock.

The troops stacked the Tommys. Pete ignored them. The pit whooshed. Bugs bombed the chow.

Guy walked to the limo. Carlos got out. Guy hugged him and chatted him up.

The troops lined up. Hank dispensed plates. Pete grabbed a .38. Pete dry-fired it.

Carlos walked up. Carlos said, "I hate drunks." Pete aimed at Guy. Pete dry-shot him—pop!

"I'll clip him. He knows too much."

"Maybe later. I want to see if we can whip these clowns into shape."

Pete wiped his hands. Carlos palmed the gun.

"I got a lead on Hank Killiam. He's in Pensacola."

Pete said, "I'll go tonight."

Carlos smiled. Carlos aimed at Pete. Carlos dry-shot him—pop!

"Betty McDonald's in the Dallas County Jail. She told a cop that she got warned out of town last November. I'm not saying it was *you,* but . . ."

39

(Las Vegas, 2/13/64)

They blew skeet. They shot custom guns.

They shot off the back deck. They shot custom clays. Janice slung them up. She sat below. She caught some rays. She wore a bikini swimsuit.

Wayne Senior scored persistent. Wayne missed fairly wide. He'd fucked up his hand. He beat up on coloreds. It fucked up his grip.

Janice popped a clay. Wayne fired. Wayne missed.

Wayne Senior reloaded. "You're not holding the stock tight enough."

Wayne flexed his hand. He'd fucked it and *re*-fucked it. It stayed fucked all the time.

"My hand's bothering me. I hurt it at work."

Wayne Senior smiled. "On Negroes or assorted riffraff?"

"You know the answer to that."

"Your employers are exploiting your reputation. That means they're exploiting you."

"Exploitation works both ways. If that sounds familiar, I got it from you."

"I'll repeat myself, then. You're overqualified for random vengeance and work as a casino bouncer."

Wayne flexed his hand. "I'm developing some new tastes. You don't know if you disapprove, or if you should take partial credit."

Wayne Senior winked. "I could help you achieve what you want, in an intelligent fashion. You'd have a good deal of latitude for individual action."

Janice moved her chair. Wayne watched her. Her top chafed. Her nipples swelled.

Wayne said, "No sale."

Wayne Senior lit a cigarette. "I've diversified. You figured that out at Christmas, and you've started coming back for visits again. You should know that I'll be doing some *very* interesting things for Mr. Hoover."

Wayne yelled, "Pull!" Janice tossed a clay. Wayne nailed it. His ears popped. His bad hand throbbed.

"I'm not going to hide under a sheet and rat off mail violators, so that you can sell more hate tracts."

"You've been talking to Ward Littell. You're in a vulnerable state, and men like Littell and Bondurant are starting to look good to you."

The sun hit the deck. Wayne squinted it off.

"They remind me of you."

"I won't take that as a compliment."

"You shouldn't."

"I'll say it once. Don't be seduced by lowlifes and thieves."

"It won't happen. I've resisted you for twenty-nine years."

Janice left for golf. Wayne Senior left for cards. Wayne stayed alone at the ranch.

He set up the gun room. He spooled the film in. He *watched*.

Said film ran high-contrast. Black and white skin/black & white stock.

King shut his eyes. King went ecstatic. King preached in Little Rock. He saw him live in '57.

The woman bit her lips. Lynette always did that. The woman had Barb-style hair.

It hurt. He watched anyway. King thrashed and threw sweat.

The film blurred—lens haze and distortion. The skin tones blurred—King went Wendell Durfee–dark.

It hurt. He watched anyway.

40

(Dallas, 2/13/64)

10:00 p.m.—lights out.

The women's tier. Twelve cells.

One inmate locked up.

Pete walked in. The jailer went ssshh. A Carlos guy bribed him last night.

One cell row. One side wall. Barred-window light.

Pete walked down. His heart thumped. His arms pinged. His pulse misfired. He swilled scotch outside. The jailer supplied it. He shut down. He fueled up. He carved some will out.

He walked. He grabbed at the cell bars. He anchored himself.

There's Betty Mac.

She's on her bunk. She's smoking. She's wearing tight capris.

She saw him. She blinked. I KNOW him. He warned me last—

She screamed. He pulled her up. She bit at his nose. She stabbed him with her cigarette.

She burned his lips. She burned his nose. She burned his neck. He threw her. She hit the bars. He grabbed her neck and pinned her.

He ripped her capris. He tore a leg free. She screamed and dropped her cigarette.

He looped the leg. He looped her neck. He cinched her. He threw her up. He stretched the leg. He looped a crossbar.

She thrashed. She kicked. She swung. She clawed her neck. She broke her nails. She coughed her dentures out.

He remembered that she had a cat.

41

(Las Vegas/Los Angeles/Chicago/
Washington, D.C./Chattanooga,
2/14/64–6/29/64)

He worked. He lived on planes. He compartmentalized.

Legal work: appeals and contracts. Money work: embezzlement and tithes.

He honed his lies. He studied Jane. He learned her lie technique. He juggled his commitments.

3/4/64: Jimmy Hoffa goes down. Chattanooga—the Test Fleet case—twelve bribe-proof jurors.

Littell filed appeals. Teamster lawyers filed writs. The Teamsters passed a resolution: We love Jimmy Hoffa. We stand behind him intact.

Jimmy got eight years Fed time. Trial #2 pends. Chicago—Pension Fund Fraud—a probable conviction.

The "real" books were safe. The Boys had them. The fund-book plan would GO.

Littell wrote briefs. Jimmy's men swooned. Littell wrote more briefs. Littell filed more writs. Littell swamped the courts.

Let's stall. Let's keep Jimmy out. Let's stall and delay—three years and up. Drac will own Vegas then. The Boys will own Drac. The fund-book plan will FLY.

He worked for Drac. He wrote stock briefs. Drac hindered him. Drac dodged subpoenas. PI Fred Otash helped.

Otash ran look-alikes—Howard Hughes clones—subpoena men served *them* thus. Otash was capable. Otash had Pete skills. Otash pulled shakedowns. Otash doped horses. Otash fixed scrapes.

Drac stuck to his coffin. Mormons tended him. Drac sucked blood.

Drac ate Demerol. Drac shot codeine. Drac made phone calls. Drac wrote memos. Drac watched cartoons.

Drac called Littell frequently. Drac monologued:

Stock strategy/stock margins/the germ plague. Quell all microbes! Quell all germs! Place condoms on doorknobs!

Drac craved Las Vegas. Drac bared his fangs. Drac coveted. Drac gloated. Drac sucked blood.

He babied Drac. He coddled Drac. He bared *his* fangs. He bit Drac back. Jane helped.

He coaxed assistance from her. He gleaned her expertise. He loved her. She loved him. He called it true. She lied to live. He lied to live. It might serve to undermine his perception.

They lived in L.A. They flew to D.C. They enjoyed work weekends. He wrote briefs. Jane wrote Hertz reports. They toured D.C. and viewed statues.

He tried to show her the Teamster building. She flushed and balked. She was *too* firm. She played him skewed. She was *mock* indifferent.

He flashed back to L.A.—one recent chat.

He said, "I can get you work with the Teamsters." She said, "No." She was intractable. She came off skewed then.

She knew the Boys. She avoided Vegas. The Boys partied there. They discussed it. Jane was oblique. Jane was *mock* indifferent.

The Teamsters scared her. He knew it. She knew he knew. She lied. She omitted. He reciprocated.

He studied Jane. He indulged conclusions. Her real name *was* Arden. She did come from Mississippi. She did go to school in De Kalb.

He was suspicious. She reciprocated.

She viewed some Hughes bill sheets. She studied them. She explained embezzlement detection. She wondered *why* he cared.

He lied. He *used* her. She helped him bilk Howard Hughes.

He stole vouchers. He forged ledgers. He retallied accounts. He rerouted payments. He billed to a dummy account.

His account—Chicago—the Mercantile Bank.

He laundered the money. He cut checks. He tithed the SCLC. Pseudon-ymous checks—sixty grand so far—more checks en route.

Penance payments. Damage control. Covert ops against the FBI.

He donated Mob money. Mr. Hoover kept tabs. He met Bayard Rustin. He paid him.

Mr. Hoover thought he knew Littell. Mr. Hoover misread his commit-ments. Mr. Hoover spent phone time with Littell. Mr. Hoover misread his loyalty.

Mr. Hoover talked to his correspondents. Mr. Hoover leaked dirt off bug placements. Mr. Hoover attacked Dr. King. Newsmen received invective. They rephrased it. They printed it. They obscured the source.

Mr. Hoover talked. Bayard Rustin talked. Lyle Holly talked. They all talked civil rights.

LBJ pushed his big civil-rights bill. Mr. Hoover loathed it—*but:*

Age 70 bodes. Forced retirement bodes. LBJ says, "*Stay* and strut your stuff."

Mr. Hoover gives thanks. That means quid pro quo. LBJ says, "Now fight my Klan war."

Mr. Hoover agrees. Mr. Hoover complies. The New Klan is outré. Mr. Hoover knows it.

The Old Klan moved hate tracts. The Old Klan burned crosses. The Old Klan severed balls. Castration was a State crime. Mail fraud was Fed.

The Old Klan rigged postage meters. The Old Klan stole stamps. The Old Klan mailed hate tracts. They thus broke Fed laws.

Their mail content was legal. Their mail methods were fraud. The FBI fought the Old Klan. Their mandate was minutiae. Their anti-Klan credentials were soft.

The New Klan was arson. The New Klan was Murder One. The flash point was Mississippi.

Civil-rights kids converge. "Freedom Summer" descends. The Klan sits ready. New klaverns form. Cops join. Diverse klaverns bond tight.

The White Knights. The Royal Knights. Klextors/Kleagles/Kladds/Kludds/Klokards. Klonklaves and Klonvocations.

Church bombings. Mutilation deaths. Three kids in Neshoba County— missing and presumed dead.

LBJ mandates war. Two hundred agents descend. A hundred for Neshoba—three probable victims—thirty-three agents per vic.

Dr. King visits. Bayard Rustin visits. Bayard Rustin briefs Littell. He checks his atlas. De Kalb adjoins Neshoba. Jane's school is there.

Mr. Hoover was torn. The war vexed him. The war offended him. The war brought the FBI praise. Mr. Hoover took credit—reluctantly. The war disrupted him.

It was outré. It was invasive. It pissed off his klavernite plants. They infiltrated klaverns. They snitched off mail fraud. They were shrill. They were racist. They subscribed to Bureau "Guidelines":

"Acceptable Risk" and "Violence Permitted." "Deniable Actions defined."

Mr. Hoover was torn. The war ripped him up. LBJ bruised his racist aesthetic. He'd fight back. He'd fight Dr. King. He'd rack compensation up.

Mr. Hoover called him. They talked and sparred. Mr. Hoover mocked Bobby.

LBJ hated Bobby. LBJ *needed* Bobby. He might make Bobby his Veep choice. Bobby might seek that Senate seat.

He played his Bobby tapes. It was late-night communion. The tapes woke Jane up sometimes. Jane heard voices in her sleep.

He lied. He said you're not dreaming—I'm playing deposition tapes.

Mr. Hoover tracked Bobby's moves—Bobby the lame-duck AG. Bobby *should* step down. Nick Katzenbach *should* succeed.

Fed heat *might* descend then. Fed heat *might* hit Vegas. Mr. Hoover *might* warn him. The Boys *might* say yes—hire those skim men—Wayne Senior *might* provide said.

He lunched with Wayne Senior—once a month—they played at respect. Wayne Senior foresaw Drac's Vegas. Wayne Senior craved his own bite.

Let's confer. Let's place my Mormons near the Count. Let's bite ol' Drac.

Skim runs *might* work. *He* had his own skim plan. He craved yet *another* tithe source.

Money *owned* him. Money *bored* him. He had money alliances. He formed money bonds. He had one nonmoney friend.

Pete left Vegas—mid-February—Pete returned bereft.

Pete flew to Dallas. Pete flew back. Pete returned with burn scars and a cat. Littell bought the Dallas papers. Littell read back-page squibs.

There—PROSTITUTE DIES IN CUSTODY, SUICIDE RULED.

He called Carlos. He played dumb. Carlos brought it up. Carlos laughed. Carlos said she bit her tongue off.

That meant two down. That meant two at large—Hank K. and Arden-Jane.

Littell talked to Pete. They discussed the safe-house hits. They discussed Arden-Jane.

Pete said, "I won't touch her." Pete meant it. Pete looked sad and weak. He got headaches. He'd dropped weight. He worshiped his cat.

Pete wanted Monarch Cab. Pete hired a PI. The PI surveilled Eldon Peavy. Let's stay useful. Let's revive Tiger Kab. Let's help the Boys out.

Pete had money alliances. Pete formed money bonds. Pete had a new cat. Pete had a kid brother. Wayne Junior *et* Pete.

Les frères de sang. Littell, un conseiller des morts.

Everyone's scared. Everyone saw Big D.

42

(Las Vegas, 2/14/64–6/29/64)

HATE.

It moved him. It ran him. It called his shots. He stayed cool with it. He stayed justified.

He never said NIGGER. They weren't all bad. He knew it and stayed justified. He found the bad ones. They *knew* him. Wayne Junior—he *baaaaaaad.*

He worked the Deuce. He threw hurt. He spared his hands and used his sap. He never said NIGGER. He never thought NIGGER. He never condoned the concept.

He worked double shifts. He stayed double-justified. The owner had rules. The pit boss had rules. Rules ruled the Deuce high and wide.

Wayne had rules. Wayne enforced said. Do not paw women. Do not hit women. Treat whores with respect.

He enforced his rules. He bridged race lines. He enforced his Rule of Intent. He predicted rude acts. He preempted them. He employed all due force.

He tracked THEM. He trailed THEM. He prowled West LV. He looked for Wendell Durfee. It was futile. He knew it. The HATE drew him there.

He got FEAR back. Said FEAR made him *stay.*

Wayne Junior—he baaad. He kill black folk. He whip dark boodie.

The Deuce showed the Liston-Clay fight. THEY attended. THEY shucked. THEY cheered.

He perceived intent. He enforced. He preempted. Some Muslims pushed tracts. He ejected them. He abridged their civil rights.

THEY called him "Junior." It fit. It honored his HATE. It distinguished his HATE from Wayne Senior's.

Sonny Liston passed through. Sonny looked Wayne up. Sonny knew Wayne's story. Sonny said, "You did the right thing." Sonny waxed pissed. Cassius Clay kicked his ass. Fuck all that Muslim shit.

They hit the Goose. They got blitzed. They drew a crowd. Sonny said he knew umpteen niggers. Said niggers prowled Niggerland. They'd shake the nigger trees and find Wendell Durfee.

HATE:

He stole play chips. He cruised West LV. He spread said chips around. He called it tip bait. He paid THEM for help to find HIM.

THEY took the chips. THEY *used* him. THEY spit on the chips and broke them.

It was futile. He knew it.

He bought the Dallas papers. He scanned every page. He got no news on Maynard Moore. He got no news on Wendell Durfee.

He read the papers. Sergeant A. V. Brown got sometime ink. Sergeant Brown worked Homicide.

Sergeant Brown knew he killed Maynard Moore. Sergeant Brown had no proof and no body. Sergeant Brown hated him. Ditto Dwight Holly.

Holly tailed him—spot tails/odd nights. Jaunts through West LV—ten minutes per.

Show tails. Overt tails and grudge tails. Fender-to-fender.

Holly tailed him. Holly knew his Darktown biz. Holly was Fed. Holly was cosmetically pro-Negro. The snuffs fucked Holly up. The snuffs fucked Holly up with Wayne Senior.

They went back. They shared laughs in Indiana. They shared their chaste brand of HATE.

HATE lured them places. HATE lured Wayne to the ranch. He prowled the ranch cyclical. He got the urge and savored it. He picked his entry shots.

Janice leaves. Wayne Senior leaves. He watches them go and walks in. He goes to the dressing room. He smells Janice. He touches her things.

He reads Wayne Senior's files. He reads Wayne Senior's tracts.

The Papal Pipeline. Boat Tickets to the Congo—one-way passage on the Titanic.

The tracts went back to '52. The tracts "probed" Little Rock. The tracts "exposed" Emmett Till. The Little Rock kids spread gonorrhea. Emmett Till raped white girls.

It was bullshit. It was chaste and cowardly HATE.

Wayne Senior lied—"I 'diversified' last year." Bullshit—Wayne Senior pushed *long-term* hate.

HATE tracts. HATE comic boox. HATE primers. The HATE alphabet.

Wayne read Wayne Senior's mail file. Mr. Hoover wrote memorandums. Dwight Holly wrote notes. They were long-term pen pals—from 1954 up.

'54 rocked. The Supreme Court banned school segregation. The Ku Klux Klan rocked anew.

Mr. Hoover rocked. Mr. Hoover deployed Dwight Holly. Holly knew Wayne Senior. Mr. Hoover loved Wayne Senior's tracts. Mr. Hoover collected them. Mr. Hoover displayed them. Mr. Hoover rang Wayne Senior up.

They chatted. Mr. Hoover bored in:

You push hate tracts. *Someone* has to. They're harmless and fun. They appeal to the rural right. The rural right is factional. The rural right is dumb.

You have hate credentials. *You* can help me place plants. We place them in Klan groups. Dwight Holly to supervise. They snitch mail fraud. They scotch your tract rivals. They assist the FBI.

Wayne read file notes. Mr. Hoover wrote. Dwight Holly wrote. Klan klowns wrote komedy. They sucked up to Wayne Senior. They yahooed. They described their *koon*tretemps.

The mail file stopped dead—summer '63. No Fed notes/no snitch notes/no kommuniqués: *Why that? Say what?*

Wayne loved the Fed notes. The Fed-speak glowed: "Felony guidelines." "Acceptable acts to sustain informant credibility."

Wayne loved the Klan notes. The text glistened. The Klan-speak glowed.

Wayne Senior suborned rednecks. Wayne Senior koddled them. They lived on Fed money. They bought corn liquor. They pulled "minor assaults."

One note sizzled. Dwight Holly writes—10/8/57.

Holly praised Wayne Senior. Holly enthused: You toughed it out/you retained your kover.

10/6/57. Shaw, Mississippi. Six Kluxers grab a Negro. Said Kluxers employ a dull knife. They sever his balls. They feed their dogs in front of him. Wayne Senior observes.

Wayne read the note. Wayne read it fifty times. The note taught him this:

Wayne Senior fears you. Wayne Senior fears your HATE. It's unmediated. It's unexploitative. It's unrationalized.

Wayne Senior hated petty. Wayne Senior had a rationale. Wayne Senior tried to shape *his* HATE.

Wayne Senior played him a bug tape. Wayne Senior played it over drinks. The date: 5/8/64. The place: Meridian, Mississippi.

Civil-rights workers talked—four Negro males. Said Negroes defamed white girls. Said girls were "liberal cooze." Said girls were "punchboards out for black stick."

Wayne listened. Wayne replayed the tape—thirty-eight times.

Wayne Senior ran a Fed film. Wayne Senior ran it over lunch. The date: 2/19/61. The place: New York City.

A folk club/mixed dancing/dark lips and hickeys.

Wayne watched. Wayne replayed the film—forty-two times.

HATE:

He watched THEM. He found THEM. He nailed THEM in crowds. HATE moved him. HATE rejoined him with Wayne Senior.

They talked. Shit densified. Shit cohered and dispersed. Janice talked to him. Janice studied him. Janice touched him more. She dressed for him. She cut her hair. She wore a Lynette do.

Lynette lost him. She knew it. She knew Dallas cut her loose. He ran from her. He hid out. He carried sex in his head.

Janice and Barb. Snapshots from the ranch. Postcards from the lounge.

His house fucked with him. Wendell Durfee kicked the door in. Lynette died there.

He dumped the bed. He stripped the paint. He peeled the bloodstains. It wasn't enough.

He sold the house. He took a loss. He indulged a spree. He hit the Dunes and shot dice.

He won sixty grand. He rolled all night. He blew the whole stake. Moe Dalitz watched him. Moe bought him morning pancakes.

He moved to Wayne Senior's guest house. He installed a phone. He logged bullshit tips and built a tip file.

He dug his two rooms. He dug on his view. Janice strolled. Janice changed clothes. Janice chipped balls out her window.

He lived in the guest house. He played at the Sultan's Lounge. He met Pete there. They watched Barb and socialized.

Pete introduced him. He blushed. They hit the Sands. They sipped frosty mai tais. They talked. Barb got tipsy and riffed on sex extortion. Barb said, "I worked JFK."

She stopped—looks traveled—looks dispersed wiiiiide. Barb knew about Dallas. The looks said, "We all do."

That was March. Pete and Barb were back from Mexico. Pete and Barb were tan.

They flew to Acapulco. They flew back weird. Pete was thin. Barb was thin. Pete had lip scars. They had a cat—a stripedy tom—they loved his scraggly ass.

Wayne called Ward Littell. Wayne said, "What's up with Pete?" Wayne dropped Pete's "kid brother" line. Ward explained it all:

Pete killed his brother. Pete botched a hit. Pete killed François B. accidental. That was '49. Wayne was fifteen then. Wayne lived in Peru, Indiana.

Pete got phone calls. Pete left Vegas. Wayne met Barb for lunch. They talked. They hashed neutral topics. They eschewed Pete's work. They talked up Barb's sister in Wisconsin. They talked up her Bob's Big Boy franchise. They talked up Barb's lowlife ex.

Barb teased him. Barb saw him with Janice. He copped to his sixteen-year crush.

Pete trusted him. Pete gauged his Barb crush. Pete tagged it kid stuff. Barb was great. Barb made him laugh. Barb pulled his eyes off of THEM.

He pressed Pete—find me *real* work—Pete dodged his requests. He pressed Pete on Dallas—give me more details—Pete dodged his full press.

He said, "Why are you so fucked up and stoked on a cat?"

Pete said, "Shut up." Pete said, "Smile more and hate less."

43

(Dallas/Las Vegas/Acapulco/New Orleans/
Houston/Pensacola/Los Angeles,
2/14/64–6/29/64)

He found the cat. He relocated him. The cat dug Vegas. The cat dug the Stardust Hotel.

The cat dug their suite. The cat dug room-service chow. Barb fucking shit. Who fucking body-snatched you?

You flew off. You flew back. You came home undone. You don't eat right. You don't sleep right. You *shudder*.

He did all that. He chain-smoked too. He gnashed his teeth. He drank himself to sleep. He reran one nightmare:

Saipan, '43. Japs. Roads rigged with slice cords. Jeeps pass by. The cords hit. Heads topple clean.

He got headaches. He popped scotch. He popped aspirin. Bedtime scared him. He read books. He watched TV. He messed with the cat. His arms pinged. He pissed more. His feet got numbed up.

He fought it. He flew to New Orleans. He rigged a slice cord. He staked Carlos out. He thought it through. He ran Yes and No lists. The Nos won in a walk.

Don't do it. The Boys would kill Barb—just for a start.

They'd kill Barb's mother. They'd kill Barb's sister. They'd kill the clan Lindscott worldwide.

He flew back to Vegas. He found a cat-sitter. Barb took a week off. They flew to Acapulco. They got a cliffside suite. They watched spics dive for tourist chump change.

He carved some nerve. He sat Barb down. He told her EVERY-THING.

François and Ruth Mildred Cressmeyer. Each and every paid hit. Betty Mac. The noose on the crossbars. Her nails at her neck.

He spilled facts. He spilled names. He spilled numbers. He spilled details. He spilled new Dallas shit. He spilled on Wendell D. and Lynette.

Barb ran.

She packed her bag. She ran from him. She moved out. He tried to stop her. She grabbed his gun. She aimed at him flush.

He backed off. She ran. He got drunk and studied the cliff. The drop ran six hundred feet.

He ran up. He swayed. He ran up ten times. He ran up sober and drunk. He punked out ten times. He dipped and caught himself. He stopped on pure lack of guts.

He scored some red devils. He slept through whole days. He dungeoned the bedroom up. He ate pills. He slept. He ate pills. He slept. He woke up and thought he was dead.

Barb was there. She said, "I'll stay." He cried and tore the bed up.

Barb shaved him. Barb fed him soup. Barb talked him off pills and cliff drops.

They flew to L.A. He saw Ward Littell. Ward knew about Betty. Carlos had bragged the job up.

They made plans. They schemed precautions. Ward was smart. Ward was good. Ward made an Arden a Jane.

Shit looked all new now. Ward said he understood. Vegas looked new—hard hues and hot weather.

He scored on the Clay fight. He cat-proofed the suite. He banked a six-digit roll. The cat dug the suite. The cat perched. The cat pounced. The cat killed wall mice.

Pete called Farlan Moss. Moss worked Sheriff's Vice. Moss entrapped fruits and whores with panache. Pete hired him. The job: Sift dirt on Monarch Cab and Eldon Peavy.

Moss said he'd do it. Moss promised full disclosure. Moss promised results.

Carlos called Pete. Carlos eschewed Betty talk. Carlos made nice.

"Pete, I hope you swing Monarch. I'd love to buy in for some points."

Pete said, "No." Betty Mac hovered. Carlos said, "Let's wait on Hank K."

Pete said, "Okay." Pete sat and waited. He shitcanned the scotch. His sleep improved. His nightmares lulled off.

He palled with Wayne. He palled with the cat. He spot-checked Monarch. He *drooled*. He called Fred Otash. He called his cop pals. They ran bulletin checks.

Wendell Durfee—where you be? Wendell be *nowhere*.

He got restless. He drove to Big D. Betty Mac hovered and laid down ghost tracks. He checked around. He checked the DPD file. He got no Durfee leads and no sightings.

Carlos called him. Carlos said, "Go. Clip Hank Killiam."

Pete drove to Houston. Pete picked up Chuck Rogers. Chuck lived with his folks. They were dings. They wore Klan sheets to bed.

Pete and Chuck split eastward—Pensacola-bound.

They drove back roads. They dawdled. Chuck talked up Vietnam. John Stanton was there now. The CIA was in deep. Chuck knew a Saigon MP—a cat named Bob Relyea—ex-prison guard/ex-Klan.

Chuck talked to Bob. They enjoyed shortwave chats. Bob extolled Vietnam nonstop. It was *hot.* It was groovy. It was Cuba on Meth.

Chuck talked Cuba—*Viva la Causa!*—Pete ragged the De Ridder "troops." They agreed—fuck Hank Hudspeth and Guy B. in the neck. They drank too much. They talked too much. They sold bad guns.

The South was wild—spring rains and big voodoo.

They drove through Louisiana. They bunked at exile camps. Chuck drilled the troops. Pete cleaned dirty guns.

The troops were substandard. The troops were spic trash. They split Cuba. They migrated. They scrounged right-wing welfare. They lacked balls. They lacked skills. They lacked savoir faire.

Chuck knew all the back roads. Chuck knew rib joints Dixiewide. They cut through Mississippi. They cut through Alabama. They dodged Fed cars. They hit cross burns. Chuck knew sheet boys statewide.

Nice kids—a bit dumb—a bit inbred.

They bunked at Klan kamps. They split at dawn. They passed torched churches. De-churched coons stood by.

Chuck laughed. Chuck waved. Chuck yelled, "Howdy, you-all!"

They hit Pensacola. They staked out Hank K. Hank K. stayed inside. They invaded his pad. They slit his throat. They drove his body around. They dawdled. They cruised to 3:00 a.m. They found a TV-store window.

They tossed Hank in. Hank broke the glass. Hank crashed Zeniths and RCAs.

The Pensacola *Trib*/third column/page 2: BIZARRE SUICIDE. LOCAL MAN DIVES TO DEATH.

Chuck flew to Houston. Pete drove to Vegas. Pete sloughed off Hank K. Hank was male. Hank knew the rules. Hank got no gender relief.

Pete killed time. Pete palled with the cat. Pete palled with Wayne. They caught Barb's gigs. They sat ringside. Wayne dug on Barb. Wayne played it straight. Wayne honored women that way.

6/14/64: Guy Banister dies. It's heart attack #4. Chuck calls. Chuck gloats. Chuck explicates.

Carlos said, "Kill him." Chuck employed excess digitalis.

Chuck laughed. Chuck said, "Don't be hurt. Carlos wanted to give you a rest."

DOCUMENT INSERT: 6/30/64. Confidential Report. From: Farlan
D. Moss. Submitted to: Pete Bondurant. Topic: "Criminal Activities
of Eldon Lowell Peavy (White Male/46), the Monarch Cab Business
& the Golden Cavern Hotel-Casino/with Index of Known Criminal
Associates."

Mr. Bondurant,

As promised, my report & attached rap sheet carbons on Subject Peavy's KAs. As we discussed, please make no copies and
destroy upon reading.

OWNERSHIP & LICENSE/TAX STATUS OF
LEGITIMATELY OWNED BUSINESSES

Subject PEAVY is the sole owner of the Monarch Cab Company
(1st Clark County Licensed 9/1/55), the Golden Cavern Hotel-
Casino (Nevada Gaming Commission licensed 6/8/57), the "Sid
the Surplus Sergeant" Store (business license transferred to Subject PEAVY 12/16/60) & the Cockpit Cocktail Lounge in Reno
(Nevada liquor license #6044/dated 2/12/58). (Note: Said lounge
is a homosexual meeting place.) All of Subject PEAVY's state &
local operating licenses are up-to-date & in good standing, as are
his Federal, state & county (Clark/Washoe) business taxes, personal taxes, property taxes, workers compensation fund taxes &
his registering of ex-convicts in his employ. Subject PEAVY (no
doubt eager to guard his reputation & retain his seats on the
Nevada Gaming Control Board & Clark County Liquor & Control
Board) is a scrupulous record keeper & observer of official business codes.

ILLEGAL ON-SITE ACTIVITIES (PER ABOVE BUSINESSES)

Subject PEAVY's four businesses sustain criminal enterprises &
serve as gathering spots for known criminals & homosexuals. All
four are police-agency protected, which should serve to hinder you
in your takeover strategy. The Cockpit Lounge (protected by

Washoe County Sheriff's Dept.) is a distribution point for homosexual pornography (films & photographs), Mexican-made fetish paraphernalia & amyl nitrite vials pilfered from the Washoe County
Medical Center. Male prostitutes congregate on the premises & the
pay phones are used as contact points for a "Date-A-Boy" service
run by Cockpit bartenders RAYMOND "GAY RAY" BIRNBAUM
(white male/39/see rap sheet index) & GARY DE HAVEN (white
male/28/see index). Subject PEAVY allegedly receives a percentage of all profits accrued from felonious enterprises conducted on
the Cockpit premises.

The "Sid the Surplus Sergeant" Store (521 E. Fremont) serves
as a pick-up point for male prostitutes working out of the Glo-Ann
Motel (604 E. Fremont) and as a contact point for "Chicken
Hawks" (older or married homosexual men who prey on young
boys) attempting to instigate assignations. Losing gamblers & male
UNLV students anxious to earn money congregate in the parking
lot & sleep in their cars there in hope of promoting "dates." The
store manager, SAMMY "SILK" FERRER (white male/44/also a
Monarch cab driver/see rap sheet index), permits said "dates" to
occur in back rooms on the store premises & often surreptitiously
films them thru hidden wall peeks. FERRER compiles film footage,
edits it into pornographic "loops" & sells said "loops" out of the
Hunky Monkey Bar, a notorious establishment catering to "rough
trade" homosexuals. FERRER & Subject PEAVY also screen pornographic films (homosexual & heterosexual content) in back rooms
on the premises. This is a recreational activity for Monarch Cab
personnel & their favored customers. (Note: Actors ROCK HUDSON
& SAL MINEO & ex-heavyweight champ SONNY LISTON are Monarch Cab/Golden Cavern habitues & frequently view films at "Sid
the Surplus Sergeant.")

The Monarch Cab Company & its office/dispatch hut (919
Tilden St., N. Las Vegas) is the hub of Subject PEAVY'S illegal
(albeit protected) enterprises. Subject PEAVY employs 14 full &
part-time drivers, 6 of whom are presumed homosexuals with no
criminal records & no outstanding Nevada State traffic warrants.
The other 8 (all known homosexuals) are:

The prev. ment'd SAMMY "SILK" FERRER; HARVEY D. BRAMS;
JOHN "CHAMP" BEAUCHAMP; WELTON V. ANSHUTZ; SALVATORE
"SATIN SAL" SALDONE; DARYL EHMINTINGER; NATHAN WER-
SHOW & DOMINIC "DONKEY DOM" DELLACROCIO. All 8 drivers
have extensive criminal records, with offenses inc. sodomy, armed

robbery, flim-flam, statutory rape, male prostitution, narcotics possession & dismissed homicide charges (see rap sheet index). DEL-
LACROCIO, BEAUCHAMP, BRAMS & SALDONE also work out of the
Golden Cavern Hotel-Casino as male prostitutes. DELLACROCIO (a
part-time driver & dancer in the "Vegas A Go-Go" show at the New
Frontier Hotel) is also a pornographic film actor. DELLACROCIO
sometimes recruits other chorus dancers to work as male prostitutes.

Monarch Cab maintains & services illegally placed slot
machines in numerous West Las Vegas bars. The operation is over-
seen by MILTON H. (HERMAN) CHARGIN (white male/53/no criminal record), a non-homosexual & former scandal magazine writer
(Lowdown & Whisper magazines), a part-time Monarch Cab dispatcher & Subject PEAVY's on-site "Executive Officer," i.e., the man
who imposes order on Subject PEAVY's crew.

All 14 drivers sell prescription pills (Seconal, Nembutal, Tuinal,
Empirin-Codeine, Dexedrine, Dexamyl, Desoxyn, Biphetamine) supplied to them by Las Vegas-based doctors. (Said doctors are paying
off gambling markers to local hotel-casinos, as part of a reciprocal
agreement between casino pit bosses & Subject PEAVY. See Known
Associates Index for list of doctors & casino personnel.)

The drivers sell largely to Negroes in W. Las Vegas, Mexicans &
Nellis AFB enlisted men in N. Las Vegas, lounge entertainers & Los
Angeles-based homosexual junketeers who use Monarch Cab limou-
sines for airport pick-ups & reside at the Golden Cavern. Again,
this operation is LVPD & CCSD-sanctioned.

The Golden Cavern Hotel-Casino (1289 Saturn St., N. Las Vegas)
is a 35-room/60-table establishment of the "Grind Joint" variety. It
is properly licensed & run & caters to "low-roller" tourists & gamblers. Subject PEAVY & his on-site manager, RICHARD "RAMROD
RICK" RINCON (also a part-time pornographic film actor) retain
six detached bungalows as "Party" or "Orgy Pads" for visiting
homosexuals, who are supplied with male prostitutes, exotic
liquors, take-out food, room projectors, pornographic films & the
prev. ment'd illegal prescription pills, along with amyl nitrite and
marijuana. Numerous movie & TV stars are frequent bungalow
residents, inc. DANNY KAYE, JOHNNIE RAY, LIBERACE, WALTER
PIDGEON, MONTGOMERY CLIFT, DAVE GARROWAY, BURT LAN-
CASTER, LEONARD BERNSTEIN, SAL MINEO, RANDOLPH SCOTT &
ROCK HUDSON. A favored male prostitute of the above is
driver/dancer/pornographic film actor DOMINIC "DONKEY DOM"

DELLACROCIO. The Golden Cavern is well-known in the homosexual underworld & reservations are frequently secured through "Middlemen" who habituate local homosexual bar-tryst spots such as the Klondike, the Hunky Monkey, the Risque Room & the Gay Caballero.

PORNOGRAPHIC FILM BUSINESS OF ELDON PEAVY

Subject PEAVY has placed himself in his greatest business-takeover jeopardy through his funding of and participation in a pornographic film racket with origins in Chula Vista, California (a border town) & Tijuana, Mexico. The racket is implemented by Tijuana policemen who employ & frequently coerce underaged girls to "act" in them, along with male actors (of adult age) & animals used in live Tijuana stage shows. The girls are primarily runaways from California & Arizona & I have identified six of them from viewings of the films & comparisons to photographs on Missing-Persons bulletins. The girls ID'd (MARILU FAYE JEANETTE/14; DONNA RAE DARNELL/16; ROSE SHARON PAOLUCCI/14; DANA LYNN CAFFERTY/13; LUCILLE MARIE SANCHEZ/16 & WANDA CLARICE KASTELMEYER/14) appear in a total of 87 films shot in Tijuana & sold via telephone mail-order by prev. ment'd PEAVY known-associate SAMMY "SILK" FERRER (Note: these are the films shown at the "Sid the Surplus Sergeant" Store).

The films are both hetero & homosexual in content. Prev. ment'd known associate RICHARD "RAMROD RICK" RINCON appears in the homosexual films "Ramrod Man," "Ramrod Boy," "Ramrod King," "Ramrod Stud," "Naughty Ramrod" & "Ramrod Rams It Home." Prev. ment'd KA DOMINIC "DONKEY DOM" DELLACROCIO appears in the homosexual films "Greek Man," "Back-Door Man," "Hung Man," "Big Dick Man," "12-Inch Man," "Moby Dick Man," "Moby Dick's Delight," "Moby Dick Misbehaves," "Moby Dick's Greek Vacation" & "Moby Dick Meets the 69 Boys."

The films are shot on 8-millimeter film stock & shipped to "Sid the Surplus Sergeant" from the main Chula Vista post office. Prev. ment'd KA SAMMY "SILK" FERRER receives & stores the films at his apt. (10478 Arrow Highway, Henderson) & ships them from the Henderson P.O. (See index for list of films, Chula Vista & Henderson ship dates & names & addresses of recipients.)

In conclusion, I believe that ELDON LOWELL PEAVY is indictable on a total of 43 Nevada State, California State, Arizona

State & Federal charges pertaining to his suborning & exploitation of minor children, his transporting of pornographic material & his conspiring to distribute lewd & lascivious products. (See attached mimeograph copies of applicable penal code sections & Fed. statutes.)

Again, please read & destroy.

44

(Neshoba County, 6/30/64)

The AC died. Littell dipped his window.

He drove I-20. He passed Fed cars. He passed camera vans.

Klan kars tailed them. Said kars sported decals. "AYAK" meant "Are You A Klansman?" "AKIA" meant "A Klansman I Am."

He'd called Mr. Hoover. He'd mentioned his trip. Mr. Hoover approved.

"A salutary idea. You can meet with Bayard Rustin and observe 'Freedom Summer' in the flesh. I would be delighted to hear your perceptions, minus your pro-Negro views."

He brought twenty grand. Ten for Bayard Rustin/ten for some Cuban exiles. Pete scored on Clay-Liston. Pete had his own tithe.

It was hot. Bugs bombed the car. Klan kars blew by. Klan klods sneered at him. Klan kooks flipped him off.

He looked Fed. That made him a ten-ring. He brought his gun along—safety first.

Lyle Holly called him in Vegas. Lyle Holly stressed caution. Lyle Holly ragged his planned trip.

Don't do it. You look Fed. The Klan hates you. The whites hate you. The lefties hate your guts.

Littell passed Bogue Chitto Swamp. Littell saw drag-line crews. The kids were dead. Lyle said so. Mr. Hoover said some Choctaws found their car.

It vibed Klan. Mr. Hoover was pissed. We'll martyr the kids now. We'll shit on states' rights.

Littell drove I-15. Littell skimmed the radio. Nut preachers preached. It's a lie. It's a hoax. Them kids are holed up in Jew York.

He'd talked to Moe Dalitz. Moe braced all the Boys. They okayed the Hughes charter plan. That meant more money—another tithe source.

Traffic stalled. Gawkers lined the roadway. Fed cars crawled. News vans crawled. Folks rubbernecked.

State troopers and crackers. Housewives and toddlers in sheets. They flashed hand signals—kall it Klan kode—konfidential konversation.

Littell jumped lanes. Littell veered hard right. There—a cross off the road. A *used* cross—last night's business—gauze on scorched wood.

A crowd gawked the totem. Feds and Negroes. Snow-cone vendors sans sheets.

There's Bayard Rustin—spiffed in a seersucker suit.

Bayard saw him. Bayard waved. Bayard walked over. A man tossed an egg. A man tossed a snow cone. They nailed Bayard flush.

They parked. They viewed a torched church.

The church was razed. The church was molotoved. Tech crews bagged bomb debris.

Littell tithed Bayard. Bayard briefcased the money. Bayard watched the techs.

"Should I be encouraged?"

"As long as you understand that it's Lyndon Johnson's doing."

"Mr. Hoover's been talking a good game."

The sun was way high. Bayard wore egg yolk and slush.

"He wants hate and resentment sustained at what he considers the proper level, and coming down on the Klan gives him a mainstream cachet."

Bayard drummed the dashboard. "Let me ask you a question. Lyle said you have some expertise."

"All right."

"Here's the situation. Martin and Coretta enter their hotel room and want to make sure their friend Edgar hasn't gotten there first. Where do they look for bugs and what do they do when they find them?"

Littell slid his seat back. "They look for small wires with perforated metal tips extending from picture frames and lampshades. They speak innocuously until they determine that there are none, and they do not pull the ones that they find, because it would anger their friend Edgar and cause him to escalate his actions against Dr. King, who is making great strides while Edgar slowly builds a file against him, because Edgar's greatest weakness is implementing institutional sadism at a sedate pace."

Bayard smiled. "Johnson's signing the Civil Rights Bill next week. Martin's going to Washington."

Littell smiled. "That's a case in point."

"Any other advice?"

"Yes. Keep your people out of areas where the Regal and Konsolidated Knights operate. They're full of mail-fraud informants, they're almost as bad as the White Knights, and the FBI will never investigate anything that they do."

Bayard popped the passenger door. The handle burned him.

Littell said, "I'll have more money soon."

The party went late.

He stayed late. He *had* to. The town exiled him. Desk clerks sized him up. Desk clerks saw his suit and gun. Desk clerks said, "No vacancy."

The party was a wake. Guy Banister—*mort*. The camp was gulfside. The Cubans perched on four acres.

Their landlord was Klan. Maynard Moore's Klarion Koalition. They were pro-exile. They spelled "Cuba" with a K. Carlos bankrolled the site. Pete passed through last spring. Pete said the troops needed work.

Littell toured the grounds. Littell dropped off Pete's tithe. Littell chucked his coat and kicked sand.

A bunkhouse. A speedboat. A Klan/exile range. Straw-man targets with cartoon faces: LBJ/Dr. King/Fidel "Beard" Castro.

A gun hut. Stacked flamethrowers. Bazookas and BARs.

The exiles were gracious—he knew Big Pete. The Klan boys were rude—he wore a Fed suit.

The sun went down. The sand dunes launched fleas. The wet air launched mosquitoes.

Bottles traveled. Toasts went up. Klansmen rigged hibachis. They served hot dogs. They overcooked. They flamethrower-broiled.

Littell played wallflower. Guests bopped by. Littell made their reps:

Hank Hudspeth—Guy's pal—kook in mourning. Chuck Rogers clipped Guy. Guy's heart attack was assisted.

Laurent Guéry and Flash Elorde—Pete's right-wing confreres. Mercs/ Dallas backup/late of Pete and Boyd's team.

Laurent was ex-CIA. Laurent clipped Patrice Lumumba. Flash clipped untold Fidelistos.

The Loop. Open secrets. Things you *just knew*.

Laurent dropped hints: *Monsieur Littell, nous savons, n'est-ce pas, ce qui s'est passé à Dallas?*

Littell smiled. Littell shrugged—*Je ne parle pas le français.* Laurent laughed. Laurent praised *"le pro shooter."*

Le pro était un français. Jean Mesplède, qui est maintenant un "merc" à Mexico City.

Littell walked off. Guéry made him nervous. Littell stopped and ate a hot dog. It was bad. It was overcooked. It was flamethrower-broiled.

Littell played wallflower. Littell watched the party. Littell read news magazines. The Civil Rights Bill/the conventions/Bobby's shot at Veep.

The party wore on. Hank Hudspeth blew a tenor sax. The Cubans blew cherry bombs.

Pete loved *la Causa.* The Cause anchored. The Cause justified. The Cause always condoned. They shared a dilemma—penance and tithe. He knew it. Pete didn't.

Littell tried to sleep. The Cubans sang songs. Cherry bombs blew.

De Kalb adjoined Scooba. De Kalb adjoined Neshoba County.

The drive took five hours. The heat sapped his car. De Kalb fit Jane's description.

A main drag. Feed stores. Segregated shade. Whites on the sidewalk/Negroes in the street.

Littell drove through town. Negroes looked down. Whites looked straight through him.

There—the school. Jane's description etched pure.

Bungalows. Walkways. Poplar trees. Pseudo-Quonset huts.

Littell parked. Littell checked his notes. The registrar was Miss Byers—in Bungalow 1.

Littell walked. Littell followed Jane's route. The bungalow fit Jane's description.

One counter. File chutes behind it. One woman—scarves and pince-nez.

The woman saw him. The woman coughed.

"It's a hoax, you want my opinion."

Littell wiped his neck. "Pardon me?"

"Those boys in Neshoba. They're sipping cool ones in Memphis right now."

Littell smiled. "Are you Miss Byers?"

"Yes, I am. And you're an agent with the Federal Bureau of Invasion."

Littell laughed. "I need information on an old student. She would have attended classes in the late '40s."

Miss Byers smiled. "I've been here since this place was chartered in 1944, and in some ways the postwar years were the best we ever saw."

"Why was that?"

"That's because you had those rowdy GI Bill boys, and some girls just as rowdy. We had a girl who became a drug addict and two girls who became traveling prostitutes."

"This girl's name was Arden Smith or Arden Coates."

Miss Byers shook her head. "We've never had an Arden here. It's a pretty name, I would have remembered it. I've been the sole registrar of this institution, and my memory hasn't failed me yet."

Littell checked the chutes. Littell saw year-dated tabs. One chute per year/'44 up.

"Are your student files alphabetized?"

"They certainly are."

"Are student photographs included?"

"Yes, sir. Clipped to the very first page."

"Have you had teachers here named Gersh, Lane, and Harding?"

"Had and have. Teachers who come tend to stay."

"Could I look through the files?"

Miss Byers squinted. "First, you tell me that this big commotion isn't just a hoax."

Littell said, "The boys are dead. The Klan killed them."

Miss Byers blinked. Miss Byers blanched. Miss Byers pushed up the counter. Littell stepped through. Littell pulled the '44 chute.

He checked the first file. He studied the layout. He saw first-page photos and class lists. He saw last-page notes: Job referrals/placements/general postscripts.

Jane knew the school. Jane attended—or knew those who did.

Littell pulled chutes. Littell checked files. He read names. He checked photos. He worked from '44 up. No Ardens/no Jane pix/no Coateses or Smiths.

He read files. He reread files. He went back to '44. He wrote names down. He checked postgrad notes.

Miss Byers watched. Miss Byers kibitzed. Littell jotted names.

Spark points. References. Jane might mention names. Jane dropped names routinely. Jane buttressed her lies. Jane sketched vivid scenes.

Marvin Whitely/'46—a bookkeeper now. Carla Wykoff—a state auditor.

Littell pulled the '47s. Aaron/Abelfit/Aldrich/Balcher/Barrett/Bebb/

Bruvick. Lowly jobs. Prosaic appointments. Construction firms/feed stores/labor stewardships.

Richard Aaron married Meg Bebb. Aldrich stayed in De Kalb. Balcher caught lupus. Barrett worked in Scooba. Bruvick moved to Kansas City. Bruvick joined the AF of L.

Littell checked files. Littell wrote names. Miss Byers kibitzed.

Bobby Cantwell got shingles. The Clunes sisters went chippy. Carl Ennis spread head lice. Gretchen Farr—Satan with bangs. A hophead and worse.

Littell stopped. His knees gave out. His pen ran dry.

Jane built whole worlds. Jane lied past their limits. Jane eclipsed him at lies.

Miss Byers said, "I still think it's a hoax."

45

B ad heat—pure Vegas.

Wayne cranked the AC. Wayne chilled down the room. Wayne clipped an update:

The Dallas *Morning News*—6/29—DPD CONCEDES DEATH OF MISSING PO-LICEMAN.

He filed the clip. He scanned his corkboard. He saw Lynette on a morgue slab. He saw a blow-up of Wendell D.'s prints.

Glossy shots all—plus some FBI pix.

The nude Dr. King. Nude and plump. Nude with a blonde in the sack.

Wayne pulled the drapes. Wayne killed the sun. Wayne killed his Janice view. Janice dressed for the heat now. Janice wore all-day bikinis.

Wayne checked his drawers. Wayne tallied weapons—throwdown shit all. Six shivs/eight pistols/one sawed-off shotgun.

He worked the Deuce. He disarmed punks. He stole their shit. He saved it to plant on Durfee. Janice loved it. Janice called it his hope chest.

He checked his tip file. He'd tallied ninety-one tips. All bullshit/all jive.

Cars pulled up outside. Doors slammed. The carport boomed loud. Your host—Wayne Senior.

Another hate-tract "summit meet." His "biggest and best"—self-described.

Ten meets in ten days. Fund meets and "summits." Tract-distributor drives. Let's fuck civil rights. Let's laud *states'* rights. Let's push more tracts. Mr. Hoover wants speed. Mr. Hoover wants wide distribution.

Wayne Senior told Wayne that. Wayne Senior spieled EVERYTHING. Wayne Senior torqued his HATE.

He held back. *He* observed partial disclosure.

He saw Fed cars. He saw Fed surveillance. Feds perched down the road. Feds watched the meets. Feds checked license plates.

Local Feds—*non*-FBI—Dwight Holly's boys.

Wayne Senior was distracted. Wayne Senior was tract-obsessed. Wayne Senior missed the heat. Wayne Senior talked. Wayne Senior torqued Wayne. Wayne Senior worked to impress.

Wayne Senior knew Ward Littell now. Wayne Senior bragged it up: "Littell needs some help. I might be planting some of my people in the Hughes organization."

Wayne called Littell last week. Wayne warned him: Wayne Senior will fuck you—and Dwight Holly's acting up.

Wayne cleaned his knives. Wayne cleaned his guns. Wayne stacked shotgun shells. Janice walked in. Janice was pool-wet. Janice smelled like Coppertone and chlorine.

Wayne tossed her a towel. "You used to knock."

"When you were a boy, I did."

"Who's he got today?"

"The John Birch people. They want him to change the print style on the fluoridation tracts, to distinguish them from the racier stuff."

Her tan was uneven. Her swimsuit rode low. Some black hair showed.

"You're dripping all over my rug."

Janice toweled off. "Your birthday's coming up."

"I know."

"You'll be thirty."

Wayne smiled. "You want me to say, 'And you'll be forty-three in November.' You want to know if I'm keeping track of those things."

Janice dropped the towel. "Your answer satisfied me."

Wayne said, "I don't forget things. You know that."

"The things that count?"

"Things in general."

Janice scoped out the corkboard. Janice scoped M. L. King.

"He doesn't look like a Communist to me."

"I doubt if he is."

Janice smiled. "He doesn't look like Wendell Durfee, either."

Wayne flinched. Janice said, "I have to go. I've got bridge with Clark Kinman."

The Deuce was dead. Dead occupancy/dead slots/dead tables.

Wayne prowled.

He walked. He perched. He tailed Negroes. He announced his intent and deterred. They ran from him. They ignored him. They played it cooooool.

The shift dragged. *He* dragged. He sat by the teller's cage. He cranked his stool up.

A Negro walks in. He's got a brown bag. He's got a jug. He hits the slots. He drops some dimes. He hits some baaaaad luck.

Forty pulls and no payoffs—righteous baaaad luck.

The guy whips his dick out. The guy urinates. The guy sprays the dime slots. The guy sprays a dykey-ass nun.

Wayne walked over.

The guy laughs. The guy breaks his jug. Glass flies. Wine shvitzes. The nun Hail Marys.

The guy laughs. I gots me a cutter. It gots a paper-bag grip.

He lunged.

Wayne stepped back. Wayne trapped his arm. Wayne snapped his wrist. The guy puked. The guy dropped the cutter.

Wayne kicked him prone. Wayne kicked his teeth in. Wayne knee-dropped him.

46

(Las Vegas, 7/6/64)

Eldon Peavy vibed butch. Eldon Peavy vibed mean queen.

3:10 a.m.

The hut was dead. Peavy worked solo. Pete walked right in. Peavy hinked. Peavy reached. Peavy was *très* slow.

Pete blocked the desk. Pete yanked the drawer out. Pete grabbed the gun.

Peavy regrouped. Peavy showed savoir faire. He dipped his chair. He raised his feet. He stroked Pete's thighs.

"Tall, dark, and vicious. My type to a T."

Pete popped the clip. Pete popped the shells. They bipped and flew.

Peavy smirked. "Want to audition? Kept man or geisha boy, you call it."

Pete said, "Not tonight."

Peavy laughed. "Hey, he speaks."

The desk phone rang. Peavy ignored it. He wiggled his feet. He toe-crawled. He nuzzled Pete's thighs.

Pete lit a cigarette. " 'The film racket is implemented by Tijuana policemen, who employ and frequently coerce underaged girls.' "

Peavy wiggled his toes. "Shit, you had my hopes up. You know that song? 'Someday he'll come along, the man I love.' "

Pete turned out his pockets. Pete pulled out two hundred G's—new K-notes all.

He dropped said money. He grabbed Peavy's feet. He dropped them desk-adjacent.

"We need your Gaming and Liquor Board votes, and you get to keep a 5% interest."

Peavy pulled a comb. Peavy puffed his spitcurl.

"I know shakedowns and legal forceouts intimately, so go to the next step and say you'll blow up my cabs."

Pete shook his head. "If I go to the next step, you lose the 5%."

Peavy flipped Pete off. Pete yukked. Pete showed him three pix.

Rose Paolucci: in church. Rose Paolucci: blowing a bull mastiff. Rose Paolucci with her uncle—John Rosselli.

Peavy smirked—tee-hee-hee—Peavy focused in.

He went pale. He popped sweat. He tossed his dinner. He doused the switchboard. He soaked the phone. He grabbed the money wet.

Pete snagged the Rolodex. Pete grabbed Milt Chargin's card.

They met at Sills' Tip-Top. They talked shit. They noshed pancakes.

Milt was hip. I'm a comic. I gig local. Call me Mort Sahl unchained.

Milt knew Fred Otash. Milt knew Pete's rep. Milt dug the scandal-rag days. Milt knew Moe D. Milt knew Freddy Turentine. Freddy bugged fag pads for *Whisper.*

Pete leveled. Pete said I bought Monarch. Pete said I need your help now.

Milt was glad. Monarch was a fruit bowl. Monarch was a fruit cocktail. You need *some* fruits. The fruit biz rocks. You *don't* need a froufrou aesthetic.

Pete quizzed Milt. Milt leveled.

He eschewed the fruit scene. He eschewed the smut scene. He eschewed the froufrou aesthetic. He said he'd stay on. He made some suggestions.

Peavy owns the Cavern. That homo hut hops. Let's junket the fruits to and fro. Let's be careful. Let's be cool. Let's live with *some* froufrou aesthetics.

They talked shit. They discussed Peavy's gigs. Some to eschew/some to enhance/some to revise.

Pete quizzed Milt. Pete said strut your stuff—play Mr. Vegas insider.

"I'm on the Strip, and I want to get laid for a hundred. Where do I go?"

"Try Louis at the Flamingo. He runs a fuck pad on the premises. You get an around-the-world for a C-note."

"Suppose I want dark stuff?"

"You call Al at the chambermaids' union. It's good trim, if you don't mind shtupping in a mop closet."

"Who do I avoid?"

"Larry, at the Castaways. He runs drag queens in the guise of real women. The rule of thumb is, 'Don't trust what won't disrobe.' "

"Suppose I want a three-way with two lezzies?"

"Go to the Rugburn Room. It's a dyke den by day. Talk to Greta, the barkeep. She'll set you up with two femmes for fifty. She'll take pictures and give you the prints and negatives for an extra twenty. You know, souvenirs."

"Sonny Tufts. What's the story on him?"

"He bites showgirls on the thighs. The girls get rabies shots when they hear he's in town."

"John Ireland?"

"Whip-out man with an eighteen-inch schlong. He goes to nudist retreats and plies his trade. He creates lots of excitement."

"Lenny Bruce?"

"Junkie and snitch for the L.A. County Sheriff's."

"Sammy Davis Jr.?"

"Switch-hitter. He digs tall blonds of both persuasions."

"Natalie Wood?"

"Lez. Currently shacked with a WAC major named Biff."

"Dick Contino?"

"Muff-diver and gamble-o-holic. In hock to the Chicago Cartel."

"The best lounge show in Vegas?"

"Barb & the Bail Bondsmen. You think I don't know which side I butter my bread on?"

"Name me one Mormon fat cat. You know, the 'Mr. Big' type."

"How about Wayne Tedrow Senior? He's a dreck merchant with oodles of gelt. His kid killed three shvoogs and walked on the beef."

"Sonny Liston?"

"Drunk, hophead, whore chaser. Pal of the aforementioned shvoog-killer Wayne Tedrow Junior. Jesus, don't get me going on Sonny."

"Bob Mitchum?"

"Grasshopper."

"Steve Cochran?"

"Rival to John Ireland's crown."

"Jayne Mansfield?"

"Shtupping the world."

"Which local cab company handles the men in the State Legislature?"

"Rapid Cab. The State guys have an account."

"What about the top guys at Nellis?"

"Ditto on Rapid. They've got some good fucking accounts."

"Are they Outfit-connected?"

"No, they're just schmucks who play by the rules."

Pete smiled. Pete bowed. Pete displayed ten grand. Milt spilled his coffee. Milt burned his hands. Milt said, "Craaaaazy."

Pete said, "That's your signing bonus. You're my new intelligence man."

DOCUMENT INSERT: 7/14/64. Verbatim FBI telephone call tran-
script. Marked: "Recorded at the Director's Request"/"Classified
Confidential 1-A: Director's Eyes Only." Speaking: Director Hoover,
Ward J. Littell.

JEH: Good morning, Mr. Littell.

WJL: Good morning, Sir.

JEH: Describe your southern excursion. I receive updates from
my field agents, but I would appreciate a contrasting perspective.

WJL: Mr. Rustin was happy to receive my donation. He
appeared to be pleased about the Civil Rights Bill and praised the
Bureau's presence in Mississippi.

JEH: Did you correct him and say "forced presence"?

WJL: I did, Sir. I stayed in character and credited President
Johnson.

JEH: Lyndon Johnson needs wretched people to love him. He is
quite undiscerning and promiscuous in his need. He reminds me of
King Jack and his lack of discernment with women.

WJL: Yes, Sir.

JEH: I do not share Mr. Johnson's need. I have a pet dog who
fulfills my desire for unconsidered affection.

WJL: Yes, Sir.

JEH: Mr. Johnson and the Dark Prince are determined to make
martyrs of those missing youths. The ill-revered Reverend King
must feel the same way.

WJL: I'm sure he does, Sir. I'm sure he sees the boys as Christian symbols.

JEH: I do not. I cast the State of Mississippi in the martyr's
role. Their sovereignty has been abrogated in the name of dubious
"Rights," and Lyndon Johnson has made me a reluctant accom-
plice.

WJL: I'm sure you'll find ways to make up for it, Sir.

JEH: I will, indeed. You will help me, and you will perform your
own acts of penance in an unfathomable and politically suspect
manner.

WJL: You know me very well, Sir.

JEH: Yes, and I can decipher your inflections and determine
when you wish to change the subject.

WJL: Yes, Sir.

JEH: I'm listening, Mr. Littell. Ask any question or make any statement you wish.

WJL: Thank you, Sir. My first question pertains to Lyle and Dwight Holly.

JEH: Ask your questions. I find preambles boring and taxing.

WJL: Does Lyle share his SCLC intelligence with Dwight?

JEH: I do not know.

WJL: Is Dwight formally investigating Wayne Tedrow, Senior and/or Junior?

JEH: No, although I'm sure he's keeping tabs on them in his uniquely persistent manner, an activity which I would be loath to discourage.

WJL: I may be co-opting several of Wayne Senior's Mormons.

JEH: Into the Hughes organization?

WJL: Yes, Sir.

JEH: Now, or in due time?

WJL: Now.

JEH: Expand your answers, Mr. Littell. I have a lunch date for the Millennium.

WJL: The work I have in mind is potentially risky, especially if the Justice Department should go proactive in Las Vegas.

JEH: I do not dictate Justice Department policy. The FBI is but one cog in a much larger system, as Prince Bobby has pointed out to me on several repugnant occasions.

WJL: Yes, Sir.

JEH: Tell me what you want, Mr. Littell.

WJL: I would like a provisional commitment. If the Mormons incur trouble, you could assess the situation and intercede on their behalf, or use their trouble to put Wayne Senior in your debt.

JEH: Do you want me to offer the Mormons covert protection?

WJL: No, Sir.

JEH: Will you inform Senior and the Mormons of the potential Federal risk?

WJL: The job description carries its own warning. I will not gild the lily beyond that.

JEH: And who will your co-opt strategy benefit?

WJL: Mr. Hughes and my Italian clients.

JEH: Feel free to proceed, then. And feel free to rely on my potential assistance.

WJL: Thank you, Sir.

JEH: Be sure that Mr. Hughes remains convincingly unaccountable.

WJL: Yes, Sir.

JEH: Good day, Mr. Littell.

WJL: Good day, Sir.

47

(Las Vegas, 7/14/64)

Golf bored him. Wayne Senior insisted—I'm playing the DI.

Littell stood by the drink stand. Littell dodged the heat.

Vegas heat scalded. Vegas heat singed.

Some holes ran close. Littell watched the Tedrows play 8. Janice killed Wayne Senior. Janice parred and birdied. Janice drilled shots home.

She moved with grace. She flaunted her gray streak. She moved deft like Jane.

De Kalb scared him. De Kalb taught him:

You welcomed Jane's lies. *You* set up truth points within. *You* rigged the lie game. *You* have no redress.

She trashed his lie aesthetic. She trashed embellishment. She co-opted memories. She furnished her past secondhand.

She lied. She embellished. She codified. He knew her solely through code. He couldn't brace her honestly—he'd exploited her skills. She taught him to embezzle. She helped him bilk Howard Hughes.

The Tedrows played 9. Janice birdied it. Wayne Senior shot bogey. Janice walked to 10. A caddy met her. Wayne Senior waved to Littell.

He drove his cart up. He brodied on grass. The cart awning made some nice shade.

Littell leaned in. Wayne Senior smiled.

"Do you play?"

"No. I've never enjoyed athletics."

"Golf is more of a business activity. Mr. Hughes could buy you less—"

"I want to co-opt three of your men. I can get them courier work now, and casino work when Mr. Hughes settles here."

Wayne Senior twirled his putter. " 'Courier' sounds euphemistic. Are you describing a security operation?"

"Yes, in a sense. The men would fly Hughes charters to various cities."

"Out of McCarran?"

"I was hoping to run them out of Nellis."

"For added security?"

"Yes. You have friends at Nellis, and I'd be remiss if I didn't try to arrange it."

A caddy yelled "Fore!" A ball dinged the cart.

Wayne Senior flinched. "I've got friends in food service and defense purchasing. General Kinman and I are close."

"Would you call him a colleague?"

"Colleague and conduit, yes. He's told me that Vietnam is about to get hot, and he's one who should know."

Littell smiled. "I'm impressed."

Wayne Senior twirled the putter. "You should be. There's going to be a staged naval event next month, which will help LBJ to escalate the war. Mr. Hughes should know that I know people who know things like that."

Littell said, "He'll be impressed."

"He should be."

"Have you considered my off—"

"What will the couriers be transporting?"

"I can't tell you."

"My men will tell me."

"That would be their decision."

"We're talking about accountability, then."

The awning fluttered. Littell blinked. The sun hit his eyes.

"Your men will be paid 10% of the value of each courier shipment. You can work out your cut at your discretion."

Moe agreed to 15. He could pocket and tithe 5.

Wayne Senior squeezed a golf ball. Wayne Senior chewed on a tee.

Skim.

He *knows* it. He won't *say* it. He'll stay clean. He'll risk his men instead.

Janice walked down 11. Her gray streak swirled. She dropped a ball. She set up. She winged a shot. She hit the cart clean.

Littell flinched. Janice laughed and waved.

Wayne Senior said, "I'm interested."

48

(Las Vegas, 7/15/64)

The Deuce was dead.

The dealers yawned. The barman yawned. Stray dogs meandered through. They beat the heat. They scrounged cocktail nuts. They scrounged hugs and pets.

Wayne perched by the bar. Wayne nuzzled a Lab mix. The intercom kicked: "Wayne Tedrow. See the pit boss, please."

Wayne walked over. The Lab tagged along. The pit boss yawned. The Lab pissed on a spittoon.

"You remember that colored guy? Ten, twelve days ago?"

"I remember."

"Well, you should, 'cause you broke a whole lot of bones."

Wayne flexed his hands. "It was a deterrent."

"That's your version, but the NAACP says it was an unprovoked assault, and they allegedly got two witnesses."

"You're saying it's a lawsuit."

The pit boss yawned. "I got to let you go, Wayne. They're asking twenty grand from us and the same from you, and they're hinting they might file on you for some other shit you done."

"Cover yourself. I'll take care of my end."

Wayne Senior loved it. Wayne Senior riffed:

Pay it off—don't call Littell—he's on *their* side.

The deck was hot. The air stung. Fireflies jumped.

Wayne Senior sipped rum. "You disarmed him *and* knee-dropped him. I'm curious about your justification."

"I still think like a policeman. When he broke that bottle, he signaled his intent to hurt me."

Wayne Senior smiled. "You revealed yourself with that answer."

"You're saying I still need a rationale."

"I'm saying you've revised your basis for action. You err on the aggressive side now, which you—"

"Which I rarely did as a cop."

Wayne Senior twirled his stick. "I want to pay off your suit. Will you accept the favor?"

"You can't make me hate them like you do. Will you accept that?"

Wayne Senior flicked a wall switch. Cold air hissed out.

"Am I that predictable a father?"

"In some ways."

"Can you predict my next offer?"

"Sure. It's a job offer. It relates to your quasi-legal union or one of the fourteen casinos you own in violation of Nevada Gaming Commission law."

Cold air swirled. Bugs beat their wings. Bugs evacuated.

"It sounds like you've investigated me."

"I burned my file when I left the PD."

"Your file on your *fath*—"

"You used to run card cheats out of rival casinos. A guy named Boynton and a guy named Sol Durslag, who works for the Clark County Liquor Board. You've got some Nellis guy in your pocket. You're selling pilfered food and liquor to half the hotels on the Strip."

Wayne Senior stretched. "You anticipated my offer. I need someone to run shipments to the hotels."

Wayne counted fireflies. They jumped. They lit up. They fell.

"It's 'yes' to both offers. Don't let it go to your head."

The Rugburn Room:

A hipster hive. Six tables/one stage. A beatnik gestalt.

Milt Chargin employed a duo. They were Miles Davis acolytes. They played bongos and bass sax.

Milt drew a hip crowd. Femme dykes served beer. Sonny Liston showed and dredged some cheers up.

Sonny hugged Wayne. Sonny sat down. Sonny met Barb and Pete. Sonny hugged them. They hugged Sonny. Sonny sized Pete up.

They arm-wrestled. Hipsters bet. Pete won two out of three.

Milt went on. Milt did Lenny Bruce shtick. Lawrence Welk auditions a junkie. Pat Nixon bangs Lester, the priapic shvoog.

The crowd laughed. The crowd toked maryjane. Sonny popped dexies. Pete and Barb declined.

Wayne popped three. Wayne got a hard-on. Wayne scoped Barb sidelong. Wayne grooved on her hair.

Milt did fresh stuff. Milt did "Fucko, the Kids' Show Clown." Milt blew up condoms. Milt tied them off. Milt tossed them high.

The crowd went nuts.

They snared the condoms. They waved cigarettes. They popped them—ka-pow!

Milt did Fidel Castro. Fidel hits a fag bar. Jack Kennedy walks in. Fidel says, "Let's party, muchacho." Jack says, "I'll meet you at the Bay of Pigs, but you've got to shtup Bobby, too."

Pete howled. Barb howled. Wayne roared.

Milt did Sonny shtick.

Sonny kidnaps Cassius Clay. Sonny dumps him in Mississippi. The Klan holds him hostage. Martin Luther King goes down.

Marty wears whiteface. Marty digs being white. It's a bold apostasy. Fuck this negroid shit.

Marty calls God up. God puts J.C. on. J.C.'s a swinger. He's gigging with Judas and the Nail Drivin' Five.

Marty says to J.C., "Listen, daddy-o, I'm having a crisis of faith here, I'm doing this revisionist number. I'm starting to think the white man's got it dicked, he's got all the bread and the white women and the hi-fi shit, and if you can't beat 'em, assimilate and stop all this civil-rights shuck-and-jive."

J.C. sighs. Marty waits. Marty waits a looooong time. Marty waits to hear his life's work affirmed.

J.C. pauses. J.C. laughs. J.C. spiels God's word on high:
NO SHIT, YOU DUMB MOTHERFUCKER!

The crowd cracked up. The room evaporated. Sonny roar-roar-roared.

Milt did LBJ. Milt did James Dean. Jimmy, the mumble-mouthed masochist. Jimmy, the "Human Ashtray."

Milt did Jack Ruby.

Jack's in the slam. Jack's pissed off and hungry. These *farkakte goyim* jailers don't know from good nova lox. Jack needs some food gelt. Jack breaks out and flogs Israel bonds.

Wayne cracked up. The room incinerated. Pete and Barb roar-roar-roar-roared.

They shared looks. They howled. They roared more. Sonny didn't get it. Sonny dug his shtick more.

Pete took Wayne aside. Pete said, "Let's blow up some cabs."

. . .

Rapid Cab was detached. Fourteen cabs/one hut/one lot/one block between.

Pete did the grunt work. Wayne did the chemistry. They worked at Monarch. They worked *très* late.

Pete pumped gas. Pete filled fourteen bottles. Wayne mixed nitrates. Wayne mixed soap flakes. They soaked dunk cords. They soaked feeder cords. They dipped model-kit glue.

Wayne felt giddy. Barb and Dexedrine did it. Barb split from the Rugburn. Barb hugged them. Barb left her scent.

They drove to Rapid. They parked. They cut through the fence. They dollied their shit in.

Fourteen cabs—'61 Fords—snout-to-snout rows. Ground clearance and tank space.

They laid down. They placed the bombs. They looped the cords. They dumped the gas. They soaked a fourteen-car fuse.

Wayne lit the match. Pete dropped it. They ran.

The cabs exploded. Scrap metal flew. The noise hurt. Bursts overlapped.

Wayne ate smoke. Wayne ate fumes. Glass blew across the sky.

49

(Los Angeles, 7/17/64)

Theft tools—paper/pencils/pen. Littell worked. Littell cooked Hughes Tool books. He wrote an invoice. He carbon-copied it. He revised a pay sheet.

Jane was asleep. Jane logged early bedtimes. They devised a routine. They stuck to it. They coded their needs.

Jane needed early sleep. He needed seclusion. Jane sensed his need. Jane deferred to it.

Littell switched pens. Littell blotted ink. He hit snags sometimes. He needed Jane's help. He toughed it out then. He kept Jane out. He embezzled solo.

Littell ran figures. Littell tallied accounts. Jane was edgy tonight. Their dinner was tense.

She said her job bored her. She said her co-workers vexed. He threw her a curveball—the Teamsters need help.

Jane declined. Jane declined too fast. Jane laughed too slow.

He described his trip south. He abridged the text. Jane segued and riffed on De Kalb.

Miss Gersh. Miss Lane. The boy with lupus. Miss Byers mentioned said boy. Jane omitted his name from *her* text.

He asked questions. He *played* her. He played off *his* insider's text. Jane brought up Gretchen Farr. Miss Byers brought her up. Gretchen was "Satan with bangs."

Pilfered memories. Stolen reminiscence. Borrowed anecdotes.

Littell yawned. Littell worked. Littell toughed out an invoice glitch—solo.

He played the radio. He caught the news. Pundits concur—Bobby will run in New York.

Littell rubbed his eyes. Columns blurred. Numbers wiggled.

Wayne Senior sent a list—twelve Mormon thugs—all skim candidates. Littell copied Drac. Drac read the list. Drac told *his* Mormons to pick three "casino consultants."

Littell called Drac. Littell lied:

The men will fly Hughes planes. The men will tour "various cities." They'll meet "made men." They'll "form bonds." They'll "work to procure your hotels."

Drac loved it. Drac loved intrigue. Drac said, "*We're* using *them*." Drac approved the Hughes charters. Wayne Senior cleared the Nellis takeoffs.

Skim clearance—the Air Force and the Mob.

Drac waxed deluded. Drac told his Mormons to sidestep Littell. Ward's *my* boy—*he'll* run the consultants.

Littell waxed bold. Littell ad-libbed. Littell revised his skim plan.

I'll exploit Drac's hubris. I'll write fake reports. I'll ghost-write the so-called "consultants." I'll jolly Drac—"*You're* fucking the Mob—the Mob's not fucking you."

Moe D. waxed grateful. Moe revised the skim end. Moe said, "Take 5% off the top."

Thanks, Moe. Thanks for the tithe cash. I don't have to steal it now.

Made men feed the skim. Mormons fly it. Percentages fly. Cash multiplies. His cash. The Mormons'. Wayne Senior's.

It's a ground builder. It's a pump primer. Let's ford the moat. Let's storm Drac's hotels.

Littell cooked his books. Columns wiggled. Dollar signs blurred.

50

(Las Vegas, 7/18/64–9/8/64)

Rapid Cab—*muerto.*

The torch was impromptu. The torch was unsanctioned. He informed the Boys. He informed them post-torch. He stressed his pure motive.

WE need a cab base. WE need dirt. Let's help Drac. Let's accrue dirt. Let's deploy it.

Carlos clapped. Sam G. clapped. Moe blew kiss bouquets.

Pete braced the Rapid dispatcher. Pete greased him. Pete bought his account book. Pete bought his soul. Pete hired him. Pete resigned his accounts. Pete got nine legislators. Pete got Nellis brass and fat cats galore.

Moe fixed the torch. Moe fixed it with LVPD. Arson cops took bribe cash. Arson cops framed a wino.

Moe fixed the Rapid end. Moe fixed it post-torch. Goons fucked up the owner. Goons relocated him to Dogdick, Delaware.

Pete renamed the biz. Dig it—Tiger Kab refortifies. Tiger Kab resurrects.

He sold the old Packards. He bought twenty Fords. He hired dope-addled "artist" Von Dutch.

Von Dutch ate peyote. Von Dutch painted cabs. Von Dutch laid wiiiild upholstery. He painted tiger stripes. He scrolled kustom script. He fashioned mock-tiger-tuft seats.

Pete bought four limos—high-end wheels—Lincoon Coontinentals. They had hi-fis and recliner seats. They were mobile fuck pads.

He consulted Milt Chargin. He steam-cleaned the hut. He dumped some fruits. He hired some straight guys. He kicked two drag queens out.

He took Milt's advice—keep Nat Wershow—Nat's smart and butch. Keep Champ Beauchamp. Keep Harvey Brams. Keep Donkey Dom—Dom's a fruit magnet—Dom draws fruit biz.

He called his Teamster contact. He signed the crew on. They got pensions. They got health plans. They paid Teamster dues.

Jimmy H. got points. Jimmy was thrilled. The fruits genuflected and swished. They got the clap. They got the syph. The Teamsters now paid for their cures.

Pete hired two jigs—Sonny Liston boys. They were good drivers. They were semi-punch-drunk. They were good Browntown brawn.

Biz was strong. The cash base was strong. No Monarch clients strayed.

Pete ran the hut. Pete worked three shifts. Work drove him. Work drained him. Work killed his bad thoughts.

He lived at the hut. He brought the cat in. The cat chased wall rats. He built a straight john. He kept the fruit john. The straights refused to shit with the fruits.

The straights hated the fruits. The fruits reciprocated. Pete addressed the issue. Pete stressed coexistence. Pete enforced the Law:

No bickering. No fistfights. No factional wars. No sex jive. No queer-straight flirtation.

Both factions kowtowed. Both factions obeyed.

He cut a deal with Johnny R. He got roost rights at the Dunes. He cut a deal with Sam G. He got roost rights at the Sands.

He told the crew: I WANT DIRT.

Quiz hookers. Quiz card dealers. Glom dirt. Glom dirt on celebrity tricks and gamble-o-holics. Accrue dirt. Report dirt to Milt C.

Milt was good. Milt mediated crew complaints. Milt deflected tsuris.

Milt made airport runs. Milt drove famous fruits. Milt drove state legislators. Milt drove them to fuck pads. Milt drove them to dope dens. Milt reported his dirt.

Milt dispersed tip cash. Milt greased bellhops/barkeeps/B-girls. Milt said I WANT DIRT.

Dirt meant leverage. Dirt meant status. Leverage meant juice. Juice for the Boys and Drac Hughes.

Tiger Kab: Dirt Central. The racket hub supreme.

The fruits pulled crimes. The straights pulled crimes. They achieved détente and pulled crimes together. Pete hired drivers off rap sheets. Pete hired drivers off reps. Pete hired bent guys x-clusive.

Pete consolidated. Pete worked two main gigs. Pete worked the pill and slot-machine endeavors.

He dumped the smut gig. He dumped the mule flix. He dumped the T.J. cops. He dumped the smut kids. He leaned on Eldon Peavy. He made him quit making smut.

He hired Farlan Moss. He sent him to T.J. Moss greased the spic cops. Moss shanghaied the kids. Moss sent them home *pronto más.*

Pete stole Peavy's records. Pete logged smut transactions. Pete logged DIRT.

Peavy left town. Pete lost his cab protection. Pete called Sam G. Sam Tigerized and bought points. Sam bought in for 20%.

Sam bought protection—new and improved—Sheriff's *and* LVPD. Co-op deals meant insurance. Insurance meant safety. Safety meant anesthesia.

He shut Betty out. It worked intermittent. He notched minutes and hours and sleep. He did make-work. He did real work. He stretched the time. He cultivated distraction.

He'd get frazzled. He'd get fucked up. Betty jumped him then. It scared him. It relieved him. It said THIS IS REAL.

Betty stuck with him. Dallas faded away.

The Warren thing hits. Lee O. takes the rap. Jack Ruby goes down guilty as charged. Jack stays mute. Jack gets death. Ratfuck Bobby resigns as AG.

Barb dropped the p.m. news. Wayne dropped his Dallas questions. Carlos dropped all the hit talk. Betty took a slug. Arden-Jane dodged one for now.

Jimmy took another slug—pension-fund fraud—two five-year terms concurrent. Jimmy's fucked. Jimmy knows it. Jimmy seeks solace.

His good lawyers helped. His good Teamsters helped. Likewise Ward's fund-book plan.

Tiger was solace plus. Tiger subsumed Betty—intermittent.

Tiger roared. Tiger roamed. Tiger roved West LV. That trailer was still there. That whore decomped within.

Wayne wanted work. Wayne pressed Pete. Pete always said no. Tiger Kab hired spooks. Tiger Kab drove spooks. Wayne was spook-afflicted.

Wayne worked for Wayne *père. Père* tied his apron strings. *Père* had big pull. *Père* foresaw that Gulf of Tonkin thing.

Wayne was wowed—dig my dad—he's a *chingón.*

Wayne Senior pressed Wayne—let's start a snitch-Klan—the Neutered Knights of Natchez or some such fucking shit.

Wayne played along. Pete said: Don't do it—Klans just ain't you.

Wayne Senior bragged to excess. Ward Littell listened. Ward knew Wayne. Ward had pull with him. Ward could cut those strings.

Wayne Senior greased the hit fund. Wayne Senior told Ward. Wayne Senior sent Wayne to Dallas.

Wayne was naive. Wayne didn't know.

Stay naive—you'll live longer. Tiger rules. Ditch the hate and I'll find you a spot. It's elite. It's effete. It helps you shut dead women out.

51

(Las Vegas, 9/10/64)

Canned food and booze. Sauer- kraut and Cointreau—all Air Force stock.

Wayne tossed crates. A swamper stacked them. They worked. They broiled. They hogged the DI dock.

Creamed corn and Smirnoff. Stuffed olives and Pernod. Cheez-Its and Old Crow.

Wayne worked fast. The swamper worked slow. The swamper yak-yakked.

"You know we lost some guys, including our steward. I heard your dad got them work with Howard Hughes. Some lawyer set it up."

Wayne tossed the last crate. The swamper caught it. The swamper peeled his roll and paid up.

He shuffled. He scratched. He played coy. He dragged out the transaction.

Wayne said, "What *is* it?"

"Well, it's sort of personal."

"I'm listening."

"Well . . . you think that Durfee guy's stupid enough to come back here?"

"I don't think he's stupid at all."

Wayne drove to Nellis.

He'd scheduled two loops. A late shot for Twinkies and Jim Beam—all Flamingo stock.

Wayne yawned. Traffic was slow. The job was soporific. The job was a soggy cream puff.

He figured it out. It took him weeks. Wayne Senior *wants* you bored. Wayne Senior has *plans*.

Said plans implied:

Go to Alabama. Stress your reputation. Drop how you avenged Lynette. Start a snitch-Klan. Recruit snitches. Work for the Feds.

He told Pete about it. Pete said, "It's cowardly shit."

He hit Owens. He hit the Nellis gates. He drove straight in. Nellis was beige—beige buildings/beige barracks/beige lawns.

Big barracks. Named for Strip hotels. No goof or satire implied.

His QM contact lived off base. His QM parked on. Wayne had dupe car keys. Wayne left his coin in the car.

He passed the "Sands." He passed the "Dunes." He passed the Officers' Club. He parked. He got out. He saw the QM's Ford.

Two rows up: A '62 Vette.

Red with white side coves. Whitewalls and chrome pipes. Janice's cherried-out car.

Janice left the ranch. Janice left at noon. Janice said she was off to play golf. Boulder/thirty-six holes/Twin Palms Country Club.

Blithe Janice. Golf—shit.

Wayne unlocked the Ford. Wayne rolled down the windows. Wayne scrunched low and tucked himself in.

Cars came. Cars went. He chewed gum. He popped sweat. He stared at the Vette.

Time chugged. Time rescinded. Some instinct said *stick*.

The sun arced. The sun hit the Ford. Wayne broiled. His gum starched and dried out.

There's Janice.

She leaves the O Club. She gets in her Vette. She kicks the key and idles it.

There's Clark Kinman.

He leaves the O Club. He gets in a Dodge. He kicks the key and idles it.

Janice pulls out. Kinman pulls out behind.

Wayne pulled out. Wayne hung back. Cut the leash/cut them some slack.

Wayne hung back. Wayne read his watch dial. Wayne ticked one full minute off.

Now—

He hauled. He closed in. He caught up. Three-car caravan—east-bound—Lake Mead Boulevard.

Janice drove point. Kinman tapped his horn. Kinman goosed her pipes. They *played*. They flirtcd out their windows. They *goofed*.

Wayne hung back. Wayne held two car-lengths down. Wayne sidled one lane over.

They drove east. They logged eight miles. They hit a desert patch. Motel strips and beer bars. Sand and last-chance fill-ups.

Janice signaled. Janice turned right. Kinman signaled. Kinman turned right.

There—The Golden Gorge Motel.

Gold stucco. One-story/one-room row. Twelve connected rooms.

Wayne pulled right. Wayne braked. Wayne stopped. Wayne checked his rearview.

Janice parked in the motel lot. Kinman parked in close.

They got out. They embraced and kissed. They entered room #4. They bypassed the office. They had their own key.

Wayne got butterflies. Wayne locked the car and walked over.

He stood near room #4. He loitered and listened. Janice laughed. Kinman said, "Get that rascal hard."

Wayne scoped the lot. Wayne saw scrub balls and junk cars. Wayne saw Mexican brats.

Thin room walls. Voices *en español*. Bracero cribs. Crop-picker tenants.

Kinman laughed. Janice went "Oooh."

Wayne loitered. Wayne listened. Wayne lurked. Shades went up. Blinds furled. Brown faces bipped out.

He saw something:

Room #5 had no windows. The door had *two* locks.

He held it back. He bypassed Wayne Senior. He ran paper. He checked Clark County deeds. He traced the motel.

Shitfire—Wayne Senior owns it.

It's 6/3/56. Wayne Senior bids and forecloses. The motel's a bargain. The motel's a tax dodge.

Wayne stewed. Pete called the ranch and left messages. Wayne ignored them. Wayne surveilled the motel.

Early p.m. stakeouts. Room #4. Janice and one-star Clark Kinman. Two matinees/three hours per.

He parked down the road. He trained binoculars. He walked by. He listened. He heard Janice sigh.

The Golden Gorge ran twelve units. Beaners camped out in ten. Janice kept her key. It unlocked room #4.

Room #5 had two locks. Room #5 had no windows. Room #5 stayed empty.

The lot buzzed by day. Braceros mingled. Bracero kids yahooed and yelped. Braceros worked hard. Braceros crashed hard. Braceros crashed early.

He popped a burglar once—late in '60. He kept his tool kit. He kept his picklocks.

Room #5 glowed. The door was green. Green like that song:

What's that secret you're keeping?

DOCUMENT INSERT: 9/12/64. Confidential memorandum: Howard Hughes to Ward J. Littell.

Dear Ward,

Bravo on the new casino consultants. My aides have chosen three rough and tumble, no-nonsense men from that list you submitted, and they have assured me that they are devout Mormons with germ-free blood.

Their names are Thomas D. Elwell, Lamar L. Dean and Daryl D. Kleindienst. They have extensive union experience in Las Vegas and, according to my aides, will not be afraid to negotiate and "lock horns" with those Mafia boys that Mr. Hoover tells me you have in your pocket. According to my aides, these men "know the ropes." They did not meet with them in person, but have corresponded with your friend Mr. Tedrow in Las Vegas and have solicited his advice. Mr. Tedrow is well respected in Mormon circles, they tell me, and I confirmed that assessment with Mr. Hoover.

The new men will be traveling hither and yon to advance our Las Vegas plans, so I'm pleased that they are cutting down commercial airline costs by flying Hughes charters. I've sent memos to all the charter crews instructing them to have lots of Fritos, Pepsi-Cola and Rocky Road ice cream on hand, because hard-working men deserve to eat well. Also, thanks for getting charter clearance at Nellis Air Force Base, which cuts down costs as well.

Forewarned is forearmed, Ward. You've convinced me that our Las Vegas approach will take time, and I think this casino consultant plan is a winner. I look forward to receiving your first report.

All best,

H.H.

52

(Las Vegas, 9/12/64)

ayne Senior said, "I know what my men are transporting."

"Oh?"

"Yes, 'Oh.' They've explained the entire procedure."

They sat poolside. Janice stood close. Janice sunned and putted golf balls.

"You knew at our first meeting. It was quite evident."

"An instinct doesn't equal a certainty."

Littell raised one brow. "You're being disingenuous. You knew then, you know now, and you've known at all points in between."

Wayne Senior coughed. "Don't mimic my gestures. You don't have my flair."

Littell grabbed his prop stick. Littell twirled it. Fuck Wayne Senior sideways.

"Tell me what you want. Be direct, and feel free to use the word 'skim.' "

Wayne Senior coughed. "My men have quit the union. They refuse to pay me the percentage I requested."

Littell twirled the stick. "How much do you want?"

"I'd be satisfied with 5%."

Littell twirled the stick. Littell twirled figure-eights. Littell did all Wayne Senior's tricks.

"No."

"No?"

"No."

"Categorically?"

"Yes."

Wayne Senior smiled. "I have to assume that Mr. Hughes doesn't know what his planes are transporting."

Littell studied Janice. She flexed. She putted. She stretched.

"I would advise you not to tell him."

"Why? Because your Italian friends will hurt me?"

"Because I'll tell your son that you sent him to Dallas."

DOCUMENT INSERT: 9/12/64. Dallas *Morning News* article.

REPORTER WRITING JFK BOOK; SAYS HE'LL "BLOW CONSPIRACY WIDE OPEN"

Dallas Times-Herald reporter Jim Koethe has a tale to tell, and he'll tell it to anyone who'll listen.

On Sunday evening, November 24, 1963, Koethe, along with Times-Herald editor Robert Cuthbert and reporter Bill Hunter of the Long Beach (California) Press-Telegram, visited the apartment of Jack Ruby, the convicted killer of presidential assassin Lee Harvey Oswald. The three men spent "two or three hours" talking to Ruby's roommate, novelty salesman George Senator. "I can't reveal what Mr. Senator said," Koethe told this reporter. "But believe you me it was an eye-opener, and it sure got me thinking about some things."

Koethe went on to say that he's done quite a bit of digging into the assassination and is writing a book on the subject. "It's a conspiracy, sure as shooting," he said. "And my book is going to blow it wide open."

Koethe refused to name the people he believes are responsible for the death of President John F. Kennedy and refused to reveal the basic motive and details of the conspiracy. "You'll have to wait for the book," Koethe said. "And believe me, the book will be well worth the wait."

Koethe's friend, reporter Bill Hunter, died in April. Editor Robert Cuthbert declined to be interviewed in depth for this article. "Jim's extracurricular activities are his business," Cuthbert said. "I wish him well with his book, though, because I love a good potboiler. Personally, I think Oswald was the lone assassin, and the Warren Report sure backs me up. Still, I've got to say that Jim Koethe exemplifies the bulldog reporter, so maybe he's on to something."

Koethe, 37, is a colorful local scribe, known for his persistence, assertive behavior and connections within the Dallas Police Department. He is reputed to be a close friend of DPD Officer Maynard D. Moore, who disappeared around the time of the assassination. Asked to comment on Officer Moore's missing status, Koethe said, "Mum's the word. A good reporter doesn't reveal his sources and a good book writer doesn't reveal anything."

I guess we'll have to wait for the book. In the meantime, though, interested parties will have to make do with the 16-volume Warren Report, which for this reporter stands as the authoritative final word.

53

(Las Vegas, 9/13/64)

The cat snared a rat. One chomp—adieu.

The cat prowled the hut. The cat paraded. Harvey Brams crossed himself. Donkey Dom laughed.

Milt grabbed the rat. The cat snarled. Milt dropped the rat in the shitter. The cat nuzzled Pete. The cat clawed the switchboard.

Biz was slow. The 6:00 p.m. blues descended.

Champ B. bopped through. Champ B. juked morale. Champ B. dumped some hijacked Pall Malls.

Pete bought them. Call it PR swag—potential Drac donations. *Hospital* swag—yuk-yuk—lung-ward booty.

Biz picked up. Sonny Liston called. Sonny ordered two cabs. Sonny ordered scotch and red devils.

Pete yawned. Pete stroked the cat. Wayne walked in distracted. Dom checked his basket. Dom eyeball-stroked his bulge.

Pete said, "I've been calling you."

Wayne shrugged. Wayne passed Pete a note. A news clip—two columns. A call came in. Milt plugged it. Pete steered Wayne outside.

Wayne looked frazzled. Pete sized him up. Pete stuck the clip in his pocket.

"Sol Durslag. Ring a bell?"

"Sure. He's a card cheat. He's the treasurer for the Liquor Board, and he used to work for my father."

"Did they fall out?"

"Everybody falls out with—"

"Your father owns the Land o' Gold, right? He's got covert points."

"Right. The Gold and thirteen more."

Pete lit a cigarette. "Milt's been digging up shit. He heard that Dur-slag's been running card counters out of the Gold. I might need his help down the line."

Wayne smiled. "My father used to run him."

"That's what Milt said."

"So you . . ."

"I want you to muscle him. Think about it. You're Wayne Senior's son, and you've got your own reputation."

Wayne said, "Is this a test?"

Pete said, "Yes."

Durslag lived on Torrey. Durslag lived middle-class. Durslag lived in the Sherlock Homes tract.

Said tract was a style clash. Mock Tudors and palm trees. Mock gables and sand lots. Mixed-message *mishegoss*.

It was dark. The house was dark. Clouds draped the moon.

Pete knocked. Pete got no answer. The garage door was up. They lounged inside.

Pete smoked. Pete got a headache. Pete popped aspirin. Wayne yawned. Wayne shadowboxed. Wayne fucked with a gooseneck lamp.

Milt dished on Sol. Milt said Sol was divorced. Good news—no women.

The wait dragged. 1:00 a.m. went south. They loitered. They stretched kinks out. They pissed the walls green.

There—

Headlights/the driveway/incoming beams.

Pete crouched. Wayne crouched. A Caddy pulled in. The beams dimmed. Sol got out. Sol sniffed—

What's that smoke sm—

He ran. Pete tripped him. Wayne threw him up on the hood. Pete grabbed the lamp. Pete whipped the neck down. Pete flashed light on Wayne.

"That's Mr. Tedrow. You used to work for his father."

Sol said, "Fuck you."

Pete flashed him. Sol blinked. Sol rolled off the hood. Wayne grabbed him. Wayne pinned him. Wayne pulled his sap out.

Pete flashed him. Wayne sapped him—tight shots—the ankles/the arms. Sol shut his eyes. Sol bit his lips. Sol squeezed up fists.

Wayne said, "Pull your crew out of the Land o' Gold."

Sol said, "Fuck you."

Wayne sapped him—tight shots—the ankles/the chest.

Sol said, "Fuck you."

Pete said, "Say yes twice. That's all we want."

Sol said, "Fuck you."

Wayne sapped him—tight shots—the ankles/the arms.

Sol said, "Fuck you."

Wayne sapped him. Pete flashed him. The bulb was bright. The bulb was hot. The bulb burned his face.

Wayne raised his sap. Wayne swung it. Pete stopped him short.

"One yes to me, one to Mr. Tedrow. Pull your crew. Do my people some liquor-board favors."

Sol said, "Fuck you."

Pete cued Wayne. Wayne sapped him—tight shots—the arms/the ribs. Sol balled up. Sol rolled. Sol clipped the hood ornament. Sol snapped a wiper blade.

Sol coughed. Sol choked. Sol said, "Fuck you, yes, okay."

Pete pulled the lamp up. The light bounced and fizzed.

"That's two 'yes's,' right?"

Sol opened his eyes. Sol had singed brows. Sol had scorched lids.

"Yeah, two. You think I want this as a steady diet?"

Pete pulled his flask—Old Crow bond—instant headache relief.

Sol grabbed it. Sol drained it. Sol coughed and flushed—Man-o-Manischewitz, that's good!

He winced. He rolled off the hood. He stood straight up. He grabbed the lamp. He bent the neck. He flashed light on Wayne.

"Your father told me some things about you, sonny boy."

Wayne said, "I'm listening."

"I could tell you some things about that sick hump."

Wayne bent the lamp down. The light bounced and fizzed.

"You can tell me. I won't hurt you."

Sol coughed. Sol hacked phlegm—thick and blood-infused.

"He said you had it bad for his wife. Like a little pervert puppy."

Wayne said, "And?"

"And you never had the gumption to act."

Pete watched Wayne. Pete watched his hands. Pete got in close.

Wayne said, "And?"

"And Daddy shouldn't preach, 'cause he's a sick hump as far as his wife is concerned."

Pete watched Wayne. Pete blocked his hands. Pete closed in close.

Wayne said, "And?"

Sol coughed. "*And* Daddy has Mommy screw these guys that he wants to cultivate, *and* Mommy had this unauthorized thing with a colored musician named Wardell Gray, *and* Daddy beat him to death with his cane."

Wayne swayed. Sol laughed. Sol flipped his tie in his face.

"Fuck you. You're a punk. You're a hump like your daddy."

54

(Las Vegas, 9/14/64)

The Golden Gorge—11:00 p.m.

Twelve rooms. Sleepy braceros. Room #5—empty. Room #4—trysted up.

They showed at 9:00. They brought two cars. Kinman brought liquor. Janice brought the key.

Wayne watched. Wayne walked the parking lot. Wayne brought tools. Wayne brought lockpicks and a penlight.

Pervert pup. Hump like your—

The lot was dead. No loungers/no muchachos/no drunks flaked in cars. Room #5—no windows. Room #4—dark.

Wayne braced door 5. Wayne got his tools out. Wayne flashed the locks.

Eleven brown doors. One *green* door as standout. One pervert-pup joke.

Wayne worked the picks. Wayne rotated clockwise and counter. Wayne tapped both locks.

His hands jumped. He dripped sweat. He gored his thumbs. Clockwise/reverse it/go count—

The top lock snapped.

He popped one tumbler. He wiped his hands. He popped one mo—

The bottom lock snapped.

Wayne wiped his hands. Wayne leaned on the door. Wayne rode the door and stepped in.

He shut the door. He flashed the room. It was small. It smelled familiar.

Old smells—*embedded*. Wayne Senior's booze. Wayne Senior's tobacco.

Wayne flashed the floor. Wayne flashed the walls. Wayne got the gestalt.

A chair. A sideboard. One ashtray/one bottle/one glass. One mirror-peek. Room #4 access. A wall speaker/soundproof wall pads/a sound switch.

Wayne sat down. Wayne made the chair—surplus from Peru, Indiana. The peek was dark. Room #4 was dark. Wayne poured a drink.

He downed it. It singed. He rode the burn out. The peek was 3-by-3. The standard cop size—the stock mirror-mount.

Wayne hit the switch. Wayne heard Kinman moan. Wayne heard Janice moan counterpoint.

Janice moaned arch. Janice moaned smut-actress style—Stag Loop 101.

Wayne poured a drink. Wayne downed it. Wayne rode the burn out. Kinman came—ooo-ooo-ooo. Janice came concurrent. Janice came mezzo-falsetto—smut meets the Met.

Wayne heard soft talk. Wayne heard giggles. Wayne heard speaker warp. A light went on. Room #4 flared.

Janice got out of bed. Janice stood up nude. Janice walked to her side of the mirror. She lingered. She posed. She grabbed her cigarettes off a dresser.

Wayne leaned in tight. Janice blurred. Wayne leaned way back to reframe. Kinman said something. Kinman murmured sweet talk. Kinman was oblivious. Kinman knew fuck-all.

Janice rubbed her appendix scar. Janice tossed her hair.

Her breasts swayed. Her hair tousled. She raised steam. She dripped sweat. She smiled. She licked a finger. She wrote "Junior" on the mirror.

55

(Dallas, 9/21/64)

J im Koethe was queer.

He bolstered his crotch. He prowled fag bars. He brought boys home. Home was Oak Cliff—bumfuck Big D. Home was the Oak View Apartments.

Three floors. Outside walkways. All courtyard and streetside views.

Pete hogged a bus bench. Pete watched the pad. Pete carried a treat bag. 1:16 a.m.—fruit alert.

Koethe had a date. Koethe poked his dates for two hours. Pete knew Koethe. Pete knew Koethe's routine.

Wayne read the Dallas papers. Wayne passed a clip on. It pertained to Koethe's "book." It pertained to Koethe's pal Maynard Moore. Pete flew to Dallas. Pete tailed Koethe. Pete played scribe. Pete called Koethe's editor.

The guy ragged Koethe. Koethe was a jack-off. Koethe was Mr. Pipe Dream. Sure—they went to Ruby's crib. Sure—they talked to his roommate. But—the talk was all bullshit. The talk was all jive.

Conspiracy—shit. Read the Warren Report.

The guy was convincing—*but—Jim Koethe knew Maynard Moore.*

A bus pulled up—some late-night express. Pete waved it on.

He killed four days. He tailed Koethe. He grooved Koethe's routine. Koethe loved the Holiday. Koethe loved Vic's Parisian. Koethe loved Gene's Music Room. Koethe sipped sidecars. Koethe prowled the johns. Koethe buzz-bombed young flesh.

Oak Cliff was the shits. Oak Cliff was a ghost zone. Betty Mac/Ruby's pad/the Oswald-Tippit tiff.

Koethe's date walked out. Koethe's date walked bowlegged. He swished by the bench. He checked Pete out. He went uugh and swished away.

Pete put his gloves on. Pete grabbed his treat bag. Koethe lived in 306—one light extant.

Pete took the side stairs. Pete walked up slow. Pete checked the walkways. No outdoor noise/no indoor noise/no visible wits.

He walked over. He braced the door. He tapped the knob. He popped the lock-catch. He opened the door. He walked in. He saw a dark room. He caught sounds and shadows.

Shower noise—down a side hall—off a doorway. Steam and light at that spot.

Pete stood still. Pete strained his eyes. Pete got indoor sight. He saw a living room–office. He saw file drawers. He saw a kitchenette.

Down the hall: A bathroom and bedroom.

Pete dropped his treat bag. Pete crouched. Pete walked down the hall. The shower stopped. Steam whooshed out. Jim Koethe walked through it.

He wore a towel. He turned right. He walked into Pete.

They bumped. Koethe went EEK! Koethe went butch. Koethe snapped to some martial-arts pose.

His towel fell. His equipment dangled. He wore a dick extender. He wore cock rings.

Pete laughed. Pete came in low.

Koethe kicked. Koethe missed. Koethe stumbled and tripped. Pete kicked him. Pete nailed his nards good.

Koethe jackknifed. Koethe re-posed. Koethe tried some karate shit. He flailed. He threw fists. He positioned.

Pete judo-chopped him. Pete nail-raked his face.

Koethe screamed. Pete grabbed his neck. Pete held it and snapped it. Pete felt his hyoid bone shear.

Koethe gurgled. Koethe spasmed. Koethe choked on bile. Pete picked him up. Pete re-snapped his neck. Pete threw him in the shower.

He stood there. He caught his breath. He got a Godzilla-rate headache. He popped the medicine chest. He found some Bayer's. He popped half a tin.

He prowled the pad. He dumped his treat bag. He dropped treats on rugs and chairs: Dildoes/reefers/bun-boy boox/Judy Garland LPs.

His headache dimmed—Godzilla to King Kong. He found some gin. He dosed it more—King Kong to Rodan.

He searched the pad. He tossed the pad. He faked a B&E. He trashed the bedroom. He trashed the kitchen. He searched the file sleeves. He found clips. He found notes. He found a folder marked "Book."

Sixteen pages/typed text. Conspiracy—shit.

Pete skimmed the file. The story wandered. The gist cohered.

Wendell Durfee was a "dumb pimp." He was "too dumb to kill Maynard Moore." Moore had a temp job. Moore had a partner: Wayne Tedrow Junior/LVPD.

Koethe knew Sergeant A. V. Brown. Sergeant Brown said:

"There was bad blood between Moore & Junior. They got in a ruckus at the Adolphus Hotel. Moore allegedly failed to show up for a meeting with Junior. I think Junior killed him, but I've got no proof."

Koethe knew a Fed man. Koethe quoted said Fed:

"Tedrow Senior ran snitch-Klan informants. Maynard Moore reported to him, so I think it's a hell of a coincidence that Moore and Tedrow Junior got assigned together that weekend."

Koethe riffed:

Moore knew J. D. Tippit. They were "Klanned-up." Moore knew Jack Ruby. Moore dug on the Carousel Club.

Koethe riffed *off* Ruby. Koethe quoted a "Secret Source":

"Jack brought some people by this safe house where the hit team was holed up. It might've been North Texas or Oklahoma, and it might've been some kind of motel or a hunting lodge. I think it was Jack and two women and maybe Hank Killiam. I think they saw some things they shouldn't've."

Koethe riffed. Koethe listed Jack Ruby KAs. Starred names: Jack Zangetty/Betty McDonald/Hank Killiam. Koethe listed footnotes—newspaper-sourced:

Jack Zangetty disappears—Xmas '63. Jack washes out of Lake Lugert. Betty McDonald/suicide—2/13/64. Hank Killiam/suicide—3/17/64.

Jim Koethe—verbatim: "Who was the other woman at the safe house?"

Koethe riffs. Koethe thinks the "hit team" disbanded. "They had to leave Dallas. They might have crossed the Mexican border." Koethe secures a "Border-Patrol Source." Said source secures a passport-stop list.

The dates: 11/23–12/2/63.

Koethe works the list. Koethe taps "Secret Sources." Koethe runs 89 names. Koethe nails "a major suspect."

Jean Philippe Mesplède/white male/age 41. Born: Lyon, France. Ex–French Army/ex–OAS trigger.

Mesplède has "right-wing ties." Mesplède has "ties to Cuban exile groups." Mesplède's current address: 1214 Ciudad Juarez/Mexico City.

The pro shooter *was* French. Chuck Rogers said so. Chuck said he walked over the border.

Pete skimmed pages. The text decohered. Koethe's logic went south.

Let's link Oswald and Ruby. Let's link Oswald and Moore. Let's link Lady Bird Johnson. Let's link Karyn Kupcinet.

Pete skimmed pages. Shit decohered. Let's link Dorothy Kilgallen. Let's link Lenny Bruce. Let's link Mort Sahl.

Pete skimmed pages. Shit recohered—FUCK—

There's a mug shot. It's file exhibit A. It's Kansas City PD sourced—3/8/56.

It's Arden-Jane. Arden Elaine *Bruvick* then. Felony bounce—"Receipt of Stolen Goods."

One mug shot. Attached notes. "Confidential" tips:

Jack Ruby's bookkeeper splits Dallas. Her name is Arden *Smith*. She went to the safe house. She saw things she shouldn't. She split Big D. for good.

Koethe worked the name "Arden." Koethe logged tips and tapped sources. This guy knew that guy. That guy knew this. A guy glommed a mug shot. Some guys glommed some tales.

Such as:

Arden went through men. Arden had a husband. Said hubby was a Teamster. Said hubby ran the K.C. local.

Said hubby had accounting skills. Said hubby went to school in Mississippi. Said hubby was anti-Hoffa. Said hubby stole some Teamster funds.

Arden was bent. Arden trucked with whores. Arden was tight with two sisters: Pat and Pam Clunes.

The Arden notes stopped. The "Book" notes stopped. The file dead-ended. Pete felt dizzy. Pete took his pulse—1-fucking-63.

He bagged the file. He checked the drawers. He checked bookshelves and cabinets. No duplicates/no stash of loose clips.

He retossed the crib. He grid-searched it. He re-retossed it. He detossed it quick.

He trashed. He tidied. He worked fast. He worked fastidious.

He tossed the medicine chest. He restacked the shelves. He debuilt and rebuilt the toilet. He tapped the walls. He pulled up rugs. He laid them back straight. He slit-checked the chairs. He slit-checked the sofa. He slit-checked the bed.

No slits. No stash holes. No duplicates extant. No stash of loose clips.

He popped some Bayer's. He chased them with gin. He dredged up some guts. Queers overkilled queers. It was standard cop wisdom. All cops knew it.

He got a knife. He stabbed Jim Koethe ninety-four times.

．　．　．

South—80 miles per hour plus.

He took I-35. He cut through shit suburbs. He smelled like blood and gin. He smelled like Jim Koethe's shampoo.

He passed rest stops. He passed campgrounds. He saw kids' swings and bar-b-que pits. A car laid back—ten car lengths—it spooked him.

He ran tail riffs. He ran no-tail riffs. 4:00 a.m.—one highway/two cars.

His headache rehit. It built and mushroomed. King Kong greets Rodan.

He saw a camp sign. He pulled down a ramp. He saw a grill pit and tables. He nosed up. He killed his lights. He worked in the dark.

He dumped Koethe's file. He filled the pit. He siphoned gas and doused it. He lit a match and got a big whooooosh.

The flames built. The flames leveled off. The heat torqued his headache. It was monster. It was Godzilla-plus. It was the Creature from the Black Lagoon.

Pete ran to his car. Pete swerved up the ramp. Pete hit the highway. Let's ditch Big D. Let's sedate forever. Let's eat secobarbital. Let's geez hair-o-wine.

That car laid back. It's a spaceship. The driver's King Kong. He's got X-ray eyes. He knows you killed Koethe and Betty.

Pete got dizzy. The windshield vaporized. It's a porthole/it's a sieve. The road dropped. It's an inkwell. It's the Black Lagoon.

The Creature bit his head. Pete puked on the wheel.

There's a ramp. It's dropping. There's a sign:

HUBBARD, TEX, POP 4001.

Japs. Slice cords. Betty Mac. Slant eyes/crossbars/capris.

It came. It went. Roads dropped. Roads resurfaced. Ink blots and lagoons.

He came. *He* went. He felt Frankensteined. Sutures and staples. Green walls and white sheets.

Behold the Body Snatchers. Behold Doc Frankenstein:

You're lucky. A man found you. It's been five days now. God must love you—you cracked up near St. Ann's.

Doc had acne scars. Doc had halitosis. Doc had a drawl.

It's been six days. We cut a fat pad from your head—it was benign. I bet you had some darn bad headaches.

Don't worry now—that man in the car called your wife.

They brought him back.

Frankenstein came. Frankenstein went. Nuns fluttered and fussed. Don't hurt me—I'm Protestant French.

Frank destapled him. Nuns shaved him. He dehazed. He saw razors and hands. He rehazed. He saw Japs and Betty.

Hands fed him soup. Hands touched his dick. Hands jabbed tubes in. The haze sputtered. Words filtered through. Decrease his dose—don't addict him.

He dehazed. He saw faces:

Student nuns—the brides of Frankenstein. A slight man—Ivy League threads—John Stanton-like. Memory Lane: Miami/white horse/Outfit-Agency ops.

He squinted. He tried to talk. Nuns went ssshhh.

He rehazed. He dehazed. He dehazed for real. Stanton was real—dig his tan—dig his drip-dry suit.

Pete tried to talk. His throat clogged. He hocked phlegm. His dick burned. He pulled his catheter out.

Stanton smiled. Stanton pulled his chair up.

"Sleeping Beauty awakes."

Pete sat up. Pete stretched his IV taut.

"You were tailing me. You saw me go off the road."

Stanton nodded. "And I called Barb and told her you were safe, but you couldn't have visitors yet."

Pete rubbed his face. "What are you doing here?"

Stanton winked. Stanton popped his briefcase. Stanton pulled out Pete's gun.

"You rest. The doctor said we'll be able to talk tomorrow."

They grabbed a bench. They lugged it outside. Stanton wore a drip-dry. Pete wore a robe.

He felt okay. Headaches—adieu.

He called Barb yesterday. They caught eight days up. Barb was okay. Stanton prepared her. Barb held in tough.

He read the *Times-Herald*. He got the gist. The Koethe snuff came and went. DPD worked it. DPD hassled queers. DPD cut them loose. The case vibed open file. It's a queer job—fuck it.

The *Morning News* ran a piece. They ragged Koethe. They ragged his "wild talk." Koethe was a perennial crank. Koethe was a "conspiracy nut."

He burned Koethe's notes. The Arden dirt went up. He debated. He decided—don't tell Ward Littell.

It was *sketchy* dirt—fill it out first.

A nun walked by—a sweet number—Stanton studied her.

"Jackie Kennedy wore hats like that."

"She wore one to Dallas."

Stanton smiled. "You're a fast study."

"I took Latin in school. I know what 'quid pro quo' means."

The nun smiled. The nun waved and giggled. Stanton was cute. Stanton lived on salads and martinis.

"Did you hear about that reporter who got killed? I heard he was writing a book."

Pete stretched. A head stitch popped loose.

"Let's start over. You were tailing me. You saved my life. I said thank you."

Stanton stretched. His shoulder rig showed.

"We know that some Agency men were *at least* peripheral to the Kennedy thing. We're pleased with the result, we have no desire to dispute the Warren Report, but for deniability's sake, we'd like a rough sketch."

Pete stretched. A stitch popped. Pete rubbed his head. Pete said, "Cuba."

Stanton smiled. "That's not much."

"It says it all. You know who he fucked with, you know who had the money and the means. You saved my life, so I'll be generous. You've met and worked with half the personnel."

The bench was damp. The slats sustained doodles. Stanton drew stars. Stanton wrote "CUBA."

Pete rubbed his head. A stitch unraveled.

"Okay, I'll play."

Stanton drew stars. Stanton put "!" after CUBA.

"Jack broke our hearts. Now Johnson's compounding the hurt."

Pete drew "?" Stanton crossed it out.

"Johnson's quits on the Cause. He thinks it's a loser and he knows it got Jack killed. He's fucked the Agency out of our Cuban ops budget, and some colleagues of mine think it's time to circumvent his policy."

Pete drew "!" Pete drew "$." Stanton crossed his legs. His ankle rig showed.

"I want to bring you to Vietnam. I want you to move Laotian heroin back to the States. I've got a team set up in Saigon. It's all Agency and South Vietnamese Army. You can recruit your own team on both ends. Dope has financed a dozen Vietnamese coups, so let's make it work for the Cause."

Pete shut his eyes. Pete ran newsreels. The French lose Algiers. The French lose Dien Bien Phu.

Et le Cuba sera notre grande revanche.

Stanton said, "You funnel the dope to Las Vegas. I've consulted Carlos on that aspect. He thinks he can get the Outfit to rescind their no-dope rule, if you push exclusively to Negroes. We want you to set up a system, buy off the key cops and limit your street exposure to the last two links on the distribution chain. If the Vegas operation flies, we'll expand to other cities. And 65% of the profits will go to worthy exile groups."

Pete stood up. Pete swayed. Pete threw hooks and jabs and popped stitches.

A nun walked by. She saw Pete. She got spooked. She crossed herself.

C'est un fou.

C'est un diable.

C'est un monstre Protestant.

56

(Las Vegas, 9/30/64)

Break time—4:00 p.m. sharp.

He put his work down. He made coffee. He sat outside his suite. He played the news. He watched the course. Janice played most days.

She'd see him. She'd wave. She'd yell epigrams. She'd say, "You don't like my husband." She'd say, "You work too hard."

Janice played scratch golf. Janice moved lithe. She'd hit shots. Her skirts would hike. Her calves would bunch and stretch.

Littell watched 6. Littell played the news. LBJ barnstormed Virginia. Bobby barnstormed New York.

Janice played 6. Janice outdrove her friends. She saw him. She waved. She yelled.

She said, "My husband fears you." She said, "You need some rest."

Littell laughed. Littell waved. Janice aced a shot.

Jane feared Vegas. The Boys ran the town. Janice *was* Vegas direct. He enjoyed his glimpses. He took them to bed. He put Janice's body on Jane.

The news went off. Janice parred 6 and waved. Littell walked inside. Littell wrote appeal briefs.

Jimmy Hoffa was through. The Boys knew it. Carlos soldiered for Jimmy. Carlos dunned donations. Carlos built a Help Jimmy Fund. It was futile. It was hopeless. Their bribe roll had crapped out.

Littell put his brief down. Littell grabbed his bankbooks. Littell ran figures and totaled his tithes.

Glad tidings:

The bagmen aced Wayne Senior. The bagmen stole his skim fees. The bagmen were duplicitous. The bagmen were good. The bagmen were Mormon-rowdy.

He directed them. He ran the skim. He wrote fictive reports. He lied to Drac. He embezzled Drac. He sucked Drac's blood.

The bagmen bagged. The bagmen moved six hundred grand—two weeks' worth of skim. He took his 5%. He fed his Chicago account. He opened accounts in Silver Spring and D.C. He used fake ID. He laundered the cash. He tithed the SCLC.

He wrote tithe checks. Five grand per. He wrote them under pseudonyms. He print-wiped the envelopes.

Drac and the Boys meet Dr. King—We Shall Overcome.

His desk phone rang. He grabbed it.

"Yes?"

Static hiss—long distance. A garbled Pete: "Ward, it's me."

The hiss built. The line buzzed. The hiss leveled flat.

"Where are you?"

"I'm in Mexico City. I'm losing the fucking connection, and I need a favor."

"Name it."

"I need Wayne to cut the apron strings and come to work for me."

Littell said, "With pleasure."

57

(Las Vegas, 9/30/64)

Janice fucked Clark Kinman. Wayne watched.

She left the lights on. She knew he was there. She rode Kinman. She showed her backside.

Wayne braced the mirror. Wayne sipped Wayne Senior's scotch. It was her sixth show. It was his sixth hide-and-see.

He surveilled the motel. Janice fucked every night. Wayne Senior caught her most times. The gigs were synced. Ditto the arrivals.

Kinman shows at 9:00. Janice shows at 9:10. Wayne Senior shows at 9:40. Kinman comes to fuck. Janice comes to act. Kinman co-stars unasked.

She fucked in the dark for Wayne Senior. She fucked in the light for Wayne.

He thought it out.

She saw him at Nellis. She *knew* him. She *knew* he'd break in. He'd log Wayne Senior's routine. He'd seize on his off nights and LOOK.

Janice bent back. Her hair flew. Wayne saw her face topsy-turvy. The speaker popped. Kinman moaned. Kinman said dumb sex things.

Janice bent up. Janice raised her hips. Wayne saw Kinman inside her.

Sol Durslag checked out. The Vegas *Sun* ran the story. May '55— Wardell Gray/tenor sax. Beaten dead/body dumped/sand dune/DOA. No suspects—case closed.

Janice bent back. Her hair dropped. Wayne saw her eyes upside down.

Kinman moaned per I'm-coming. Kinman said dumb sex things. Janice grabbed a pillow. Janice muzzled him.

His toes curled. His knees contracted. His feet clenched. Janice rolled clear and free.

Kinman dumped the pillow. Kinman smiled and scratched his balls. Kinman tapped his Saint Chris on a chain.

They talked. Their lips moved. The speaker fuzzed sighs.

Kinman kissed his Saint Chris. "I always wear this for protection. Sometimes I think you're likely to kill me."

Janice sat up. Janice faced the mirror-wall.

Kinman said, "Wayne Senior should take better care of you. Shit, I think we've gone sixteen days straight."

Janice winked. Janice said, "You're the best."

"Tell true. Is he good?"

"No, but he's got qualities."

"You mean money."

"Not exactly."

"He's got to have something, or you'd've found yourself a steady before me."

Janice winked. "I've sent out invitations, but nobody knocked on my door."

"Some boys don't know how to read signs."

"Some boys need to look first."

"Shit, if your hubby could see you now."

Janice raised her voice. Janice talked overt slow.

"I had a thing with a musician once. Wayne Senior found out."

"What did he do?"

"He killed him."

"Are you ribbing me?"

"Absolutely not."

Kinman kissed his Saint Chris. "You'll be the ruin of me. Shit, and I thought Junior was the only killer in the family."

Janice got up. Janice walked to the mirror.

She primped. She fogged the glass. She licked a finger. She drew arrows and hearts.

A dust storm kicked through. Hot winds kicked sand and sagebrush.

Wayne drove to the ranch. Wayne walked to the guest house. Wayne saw a stray car en route.

There's Ward Littell.

He ducked the wind. He blocked Wayne's door. He looked sandblown and storm-fucked.

He said, "Your father sent you to Dallas."

DOCUMENT INSERT: 10/1/64. Covert Intelligence Dossier. From: John Stanton. To: Pete Bondurant. Marked: "Hand-Courier Only/Destroy Upon Reading."

P.B.,

I'm hoping this gets to you in time. It's really no more than a highlighted summary & I've edited out the extraneous details. I'm routing it through the Mexico City Station to meet that deadline you requested. Note: Data culled from Interpol files in Paris & Marseilles. Agency copy file #M-64889/Langley.

Per: MESPLEDE, JEAN PHILIPPE, W.M., 8/19/22. LKA: 1214 Ciudad Juarez, Mexico City.

1941-'45: Conflicting accts. MESPLEDE (an alleged anti-Semite) was either a Nazi collaborator or a member of the Armed French Resistance in Lyon. Conflicting accts: MESPLEDE turned over Jews to the SS/MESPLEDE assassinated Nazis at a health retreat in the Arbois. Note: One Interpol wag concluded that he did a little of both.

1946-'47: Whereabouts unknown.

1948-'50: Mercenary work in Paraguay. The Asuncion Ops Station has a 41-page file. MESPLEDE infiltrated leftist student groups at the behest of the Paraguayan Association of Police Chiefs. MESPLEDE (Spanish fluent) assassinated 63 suspected Communist sympathizers per association guidelines.

1951-'55: French Army service (Indochina—now Vietnam—& Algeria). MESPLEDE served as a paratrooper, saw action at Dien Bien Phu & allegedly became bitter over the French defeat & withdrawal. Reports (unconfirmed) <u>have him moving opium base & hashish to his next duty station in Algiers.</u> In Algiers, MESPLEDE transferred to an occupation unit & taught torture techniques to members of a mercenary police unit employed by wealthy French colonialists. MESPLEDE (a committed anti-Communist) allegedly executed 44 Algerian nationalists suspected of Communist ties & gained a reputation as a superb wet arts specialist.

1956-'59: Whereabouts largely unknown. MESPLEDE is believed to have traveled extensively in the U.S. during this time. The Atlanta (Ga) PD has a 10/58 file note on him. MESPLEDE was suspected of taking part in the bombing of a synagogue targeted by neo-Nazis. The New Orleans PD has a 2/9/59 file note. MES-

PLEDE was suspected of 16 armed robberies in N.O., Metairie, Baton Rouge & Shreveport. Note: unconfirmed rpts. state that MESPLEDE traveled in Organized Crime circles during this interval.

1960–'61: Mercenary work in the Belgian Congo. MESPLEDE (a known associate of our KA LAURENT GUERY) served as an enforcer for Belgian landowners & worked with an Agency liaison in the anti-Lumumba incursion. MESPLEDE & GUERY engineered the capture & execution of 491 leftist rebels in Katanga Province. The landowners gave MESPLEDE carte blanche & told him to implement a deterrent measure to scare would-be rebels. MESPLEDE and GUERY herded the rebels into a gully & killed them with flamethrowers.

1962–'63: At large in France. MESPLEDE (who lost land holdings when DeGaulle granted Algerian independence) allegedly joined the French OAS & took part in the 3/62 & 8/63 assassination attempts on DeGaulle. MESPLEDE resurrected in Mexico City (9/63) & has allegedly been in touch with our KAs GUERY & FLASH ELORDE. MESPLEDE is known to be committed to the anti-Castro cause & as previously stated, is determinedly anti-Communist, Spanish fluent & has both probable narcotics experience & military experience in the Southeast Asian Theatre. All in all, I think we can use him.

I'm heading back to Saigon. Pouch all future communications through my P.O. box at Arlington. We'll use drops & cutout couriers from here on in. Remember: We're Stage 1 Covert, like our Tiger ops in Miami. You know the old drill: Read, memorize & burn.

Thumbs up on MESPLEDE, if you think he fits in. You can recruit the rest of the team on your own autonomy. Per MESPLEDE: Watch out. His curriculum vitae is a bit scary.

For the Cause,

J.S.

58

(Mexico City, 10/2/64)

 Mex brought coffee. Said Mex kissed ass. Big teeth/big bows/ big compliance.

Pete lounged. Pete noshed rolls. Pete taped his piece under the table. The trigger sat flush. The silencer worked. The barrel faced the opposite seat.

Pete sipped coffee. Pete rubbed his head. Mexico City—*nyet.*

It's a skunk zone. It's rife with dog turds. Give me pre-Castro Havana.

He looked for Flash and Laurent. He tapped out. He dropped a note. Mesplède dropped a note back:

Let's talk—I've heard about you.

He killed time. He called Barb every day. He called the K.C. Local. He dropped names. He asked questions—per Arden Elaine Bruvick.

The gist: She was Frau Danny Bruvick. Danny ran Local 602—'53–'56. Danny stole Teamster money. Danny split. Jimmy H. decreed a hit. Danny vanished. Arden stayed in K.C.

Jimmy pulled strings. The KCPD popped Arden. Arden bailed out fast. Arden split K.C.

Pete knew a KCPD guy. Pete called him. He ran Arden's bail stats. He called Pete back.

Arden bailed out—3/10/56. The T&C Corp bailed her. Carlos M. owned T&C. T&C was his tax front.

A frayed cord. A teaser. Carlos says, "Clip Arden." His front corp bails her.

Get more. Learn more. Don't warn Littell *yet.* The cord felt thin. The cord could fray. The cord could strip.

A man walked in. He was fat. He wore glasses. His hands were smudged black. Odds on: French Para tattoos.

Para pit dogs—*très* French—fangs and parachutes.

Pete stood up. The man saw him. The man grabbed a front table.

Pete ad-libbed:

He crouched. He untaped his gun. He reholstered and walked over. He bowed to the man. They shook hands. The pit dogs had red eyes.

They sat down. Mesplède said, "You know Chuck Rogers."

"Chuck's a piece of work."

"He lives with his parents. A man more than forty years old."

He sounded *sud-Midi*. He looked *marseillais*. He dressed *très fasciste*—all-black ensemble.

Pete said, "He's a committed man."

"Yes. You can forgive his more outlandish beliefs."

"He's got a sense of humor about them."

"The Ku Klux Klan disgusts me. I enjoy Negro jazz."

"I like Cuban music."

"I like Cuban food and Cuban women."

"Fidel Castro should die."

"Yes. He is a *cochon* and a *pédé*."

"I saw Pigs. I ran troops out of the Blessington campsite."

Mesplède nodded. "Chuck told me. You shot *communistes* out an airplane window."

Pete laughed. Pete mimed gunshots. Mesplède lit a Gauloise. Mesplède offered one.

Pete lit up. Pete coughed—it was rolled muskrat shit.

"What else did Chuck tell you?"

"That you were a committed man."

"That's all?"

"He also said that you, *qu'est-ce que c'est?*, 'snipped links.' "

Pete smiled. Pete showed his pix. There's Jack Z. trussed up. There's Hank the K. dumped.

Mesplède tapped them. "Unfortunate men. They saw things they should not."

Pete coughed. Pete blew smoke rings.

Mesplède coughed. "Chuck said the blond woman killed herself in jail."

"That's right."

"You did not take her picture?"

"No."

"Then Arden is the only one left."

Pete shook his head. "She's unfindable."

"No one is that."

"She has to be."

Mesplède chained cigarettes. "I saw her once before, in New Orleans. She was with one of Carlos Marcello's men."

"She's unfindable. Leave it at that."

Mesplède shrugged. Mesplède dropped his hands. There's the click. There's the slide. There's the hammer back.

Pete smiled. Pete bowed. Pete showed his gun. Mesplède smiled. Mesplède bowed. Mesplède showed *his* gun.

Pete grabbed a napkin. Pete draped the table. Pete covered the guns.

Mesplède said, "Your note mentioned work."

Pete cracked his knuckles. "Heroin. We move it from Laos to Saigon and funnel it to the States. It's Agency-adjunct and completely unsanctioned. All the profits go to the Cause."

"Our colleagues?"

"We work under a man named John Stanton. I've run dope and exiles for him. We bring in Laurent Guéry, Flash Elorde, and an ex-cop to do the chemical work."

A whore walked by. Said whore looked down. Mesplède flashed his tattoos. He flexed his hands. The dogs snapped. The dogs grew big *chorizos*.

The whore crossed herself. The whore buzzed off—*gringos malo y feo!*

Mesplède said, "I am interested. I am devoted to the cause of a free Cuba."

"Mort à Fidel Castro. Vive l'entente franco-américaine."

Mesplède grabbed a fork. Mesplède cleaned his nails.

"Chuck described you as 'soft on women.' I will concede the unfindability of Arden if you further prove your loyalty to the Cause."

"How?"

"Hank Hudspeth has defrauded the Cause. He has sold faulty weaponry to exile groups and has diverted the good merchandise to the Klan."

Pete said, "I'll take care of it."

Mesplède flexed his hands. The dogs went priapic.

"I would appreciate a memento."

The setup worked—let's talk guns—my money/your stuff.

Pete called from Houston. Hank was eager. He said catch you a plane. I got a bunker near Polk.

Pete flew to De Ridder. Pete rented a car. Pete hit a Safeway. Pete bought a cooler. Pete bought dry ice.

He hit the local PO. He bought a box. He air-mail-stamped it. He wrote Jean Mesplède's address on top.

He hit a gun shop. He bought a Buck knife. He hit a camera store. He bought a Polaroid. He bought some film.

He drove north. He took back roads. He cut through the Kisatchee Forest. It was hot—80 at dusk.

Hank met him. Hank was eager—I got the stuff!

The bunker was a mine shaft. Part gun hut/part igloo. Ten steps below ground.

Hank walked ahead. Hank hit the top step. Pete pulled his piece and shot him in the back.

Hank tumbled. Pete shot him again. Pete blew his ribs out.

He turned him over. He prepped his camera. He snapped a close-up. The bunker was hot—paved walls in tight.

Pete pulled his knife. Pete stretched Hank's hair. Pete cut side to side.

He notched the blade. He hit the bone. He sheared over and up. He stepped on Hank's head. He jerked hard. He pulled his scalp up.

He wiped it off. He dry-iced it. He boxed it. His hands shook—first-timer shakes—he'd scalped a hundred Reds.

He wiped his hands. He inscribed the snapshot. He wrote "Viva la Causa!" on the back.

59

(Las Vegas, 10/4/64)

Janice was in. Wayne Senior was out. Wayne paced his room. Wayne groomed and primped.

He saw Pete at Tiger. They talked an hour back. Pete worked on him. Pete hit him up.

You're a chemist. Let's go to Vietnam. *You'll* cook heroin. *We'll* work covert ops.

He said yes. It felt logical. It felt wholly right.

Wayne shaved. Wayne combed his hair. Wayne dabbed a razor cut. Ward slammed him—four nights back—Ward fucked him way up.

He tracked Ward's logic. He improvised. Wayne Senior ran snitches. Wayne Senior thus ran Maynard Moore. Thus he was in on the hit.

Ward left blank spots. Wayne improvised. Wayne Senior dumped his late snitch files. Wayne Senior ran Maynard Moore *then*.

Wayne brushed his hair. His hand jerked. He dropped the brush. It hit the floor and shattered.

Wayne walked outside. It was windy. It was hot. It was dark.

There—her room/her light.

Wayne walked inside. The hi-fi was on. Cool jazz or some such shit—matched horns discordant.

He turned it off. He tracked the light. He walked over. Janice was changing clothes. Janice saw him—bam—like that.

She dropped her robe. She kicked off her golf cleats. She pulled off her bra and golf shift.

He walked up. He touched her. She pulled his shirt off. She pulled down his pants.

He grabbed her. He tried to kiss her. She slid away. She knelt down. She put his cock in her mouth.

He got hard. He leaked. He got close. He grabbed her hair and pulled her mouth away.

She stepped back. She pulled off his pants. She tripped on his shoes. She sat on the floor. She balled up a skirt. She tucked it under her.

He got down. He ratched his knees. He spread her legs. He kissed her thighs. He kissed her hair and put his tongue in.

She trembled. She made funny sounds. He tasted her. He tasted her outside. He tasted her in.

She trembled. She made scared sounds. She grabbed his hair. She hurt him. She pulled his head up.

He jammed her knees out. He spread her full. She pulled him in. She squeezed a fit. She shut her eyes.

He squeezed her brows. He forced them back open. He put his face down. He keyed on her eyes. He saw green flecks he never saw before.

They moved. They got the fit. They found the sync. They held each other's faces. They locked their eyes in.

He got close. He conjured shit up and held back. Janice buckled. Janice spasmed. Janice clamped her legs.

Wayne sweated. Wayne doused her eyes. She blinked it off. She kept her eyes locked.

A door opened. A door shut. A shadow crossed the light.

Janice buckled. Janice started to cry. Wayne got close. Wayne let go. Wayne shut his eyes.

Janice wiped off her tears. Janice kissed her fingers. Janice put them in his mouth.

They got in bed. They shut their eyes. They left the door open. They left the light on.

House sounds kicked in. Wayne heard Wayne Senior whistle. Wayne smelled Wayne Senior's smoke.

He opened his eyes. His kissed Janice. She trembled. She kept her eyes shut.

Wayne got up. Wayne got dressed. Wayne walked to the bar. Bam— there's Wayne Senior.

Wayne grabbed his stick. Wayne twirled it. Wayne did Daddy's stock tricks.

Wayne said, "You shouldn't have sent me to Dallas."

Part III

SUBVERSION

October 1964–July 1965

DOCUMENT INSERT: 10/16/64. Pouch communiqué. To: Pete Bondurant. From: John Stanton. Marked: "Hand Pouch Deliver Only"/
"Destroy Upon Reading."

P.B.,
Here's the summary you requested. As always, please read and
burn.

First off, there's a consensus among Agency analysts: we're in
Vietnam to stay. You know how far the trouble goes back—with the
Japanese, the Chinese and the French. Our interest dates to '45. It
was shaped by our commitment to France and our desire to keep
Western Europe out of the Red Bloc, and was spurred by China
going Red. Vietnam is a key chunk of real estate. We'll lose our
foothold in Southeast Asia if it goes Red. In fact, we'll risk losing
the entire region.

Much of the current situation derives from the Viet Minh defeat
of the French forces at Dien Bien Phu in March, '54. This led to
Geneva accords and the partitioning of what is now "North" and
"South" Vietnam, along the 17th parallel. The Communists withdrew from the south and the French from the north. A nationwide
election was called for the summer of '56.

We installed our man Ngo Dinh Diem in the south. Diem was a
Catholic who was pro-US, anti-Buddhist, anti-French colonialist and
anti-Communist. Agency operatives rigged a referendum that
allowed Diem to succeed Premier Bao Dai. (It wasn't subtle. Our
people got Diem more votes than the actual number of voters.)

Diem renounced the '56 Geneva Accord elections. He said the
presence of the Viet Minh insured that the elections could not be
"absolutely free." The election deadline approached. The U.S.
backed Diem's refusal to participate. Diem initiated "security measures" against the Viet Minh in the south. Suspected Viet Minh or
Viet Minh sympathizers were tortured and tried by local province
officials appointed by Diem. This approach was successful, and
Diem managed to smash 90% of the Viet Minh cells in the Mekong
Delta. During this time Diem's publicists coined the pejorative term
"Vietnam Cong San" or "Vietnamese Communist."

The election deadline passed. The Soviets and Red Chinese did
not press for a political settlement. Early in '57, the Soviets proposed a permanent partition and a U.N. sanctioning of North and

South Vietnam as separate states. The U.S. was unwilling to recognize a Communist state and rebuffed the initiative.

Diem built a base in the south. He appointed his brothers and other relatives to positions of power and in fact turned South Vietnam into a narrowly ruled, albeit stridently anti-Communist, oligarchy. Diem's brothers and relatives built up their individual fiefdoms. They were rigidly Catholic and anti-Buddhist. Diem's brother Can was a virtual warlord. His brother Ngo Dinh Nhu ran an anti-Viet Cong intelligence network with CIA funds.

Diem balked at land reforms and allied himself with wealthy landowning families in the Mekong Delta. He created the Khu Tru Mat, i.e., farm communities to buffer peasants from Viet Cong sympathizers and cells. Peasants were uprooted from their native villages and forced to build the communities without pay. Government troops often pilfered their pigs, rice and chicken.

Diem's actions created a demand for reform. Diem closed opposition newspapers, accused journalists, students and intellectuals of Communist ties and arrested them. At this time, the U.S. had a billion dollars invested in South Vietnam. Diem (dubbed "a puppet who pulls his own strings") knew that we needed his regime as a strategic port against the spread of Communism. He spent the bulk of his U.S.-donated money on military and police build-up, to quash Viet Cong raids below the 17th parallel and quash domestic plots against him.

In November '60, a military coup against Diem failed. Diem-loyalist troops fought the troops of South Vietnamese Army Colonel Vuong Van Dong. Diem rebuffed the coup, but his actions earned him many enemies among the Saigon and Mekong Delta elite. In the north, this internal dissent emboldened Ho Chi Minh. He embarked on a terror campaign in the south and in December '60 announced the formation of a new insurgent group: the National Liberation Movement. Ho contended that he did not violate the Geneva Accord by sending troops into the south. This was, of course, a lie. Red troops had been steadily infiltrating the south along the "Ho Chi Minh Trail" since '59.

Shortly after his inauguration, John Kennedy read a Pentagon analysis of the deteriorating Vietnamese situation. The analysis urged that aid to Diem be increased. Kennedy increased the number of in-country "advisors" to 3,000. The advisors were really military personnel, in violation of the Geneva Accord. Kennedy issued a foreign-aid order which served to increase the size of the

South Vietnamese Army (the ARVN, or Army of the Republic of
South Vietnam) by 20,000 men, to a total of 170,000.

Diem resented the presence of the U.S. "advisors." Then large
Viet Cong units began attacking ARVN posts. At that juncture,
Diem told the advisors that he wanted to form a bilateral defense
pact between the U.S. and South Vietnam.

Kennedy sent General Maxwell Taylor to Saigon. Taylor
reported back and reconfirmed the strategic importance of a stand
against the Viet Cong. He called for more advisors, along with heli-
copters and pilot-support for the ARVN. Taylor requested 8,000
troops. The Joint Chiefs and Secretary of Defense McNamara
requested 200,000. Kennedy compromised and sent more financial
aid to Diem.

Diem initiated the "Strategic Hamlet" program early in '62. He
detained peasants in armed stockades in an effort to thwart their
susceptibility to the Viet Cong. In reality, the program supplied the
Viet Cong with converts. In February '62, Diem survived another
coup. Two ARVN pilots attacked the presidential palace with
napalm, bombs and machine-gun fire. Diem, his brother Nhu and
Madame Nhu survived.

Ngo Dinh Nhu had become an embarrassment. He was an
opium addict prone to bouts of paranoia. Madame Nhu had convinced Diem to sponsor edicts abolishing divorce, contraceptives,
abortion, boxing matches, beauty contests and opium dens. These
edicts spawned great resentment. The U.S. advisors noted a new
groundswell of anger against the Diem regime.

Anti-Diem sentiment was building within the ARVN command.
Diem's Can Lao (the South Vietnamese Secret Police) stepped up its
arrests and torture of suspected Buddhist dissidents. Four Buddhist monks publicly incinerated themselves in protest. Madame
Nhu praised the suicides and created more resentment. Kennedy
and the new Vietnamese ambassador, Henry Cabot Lodge,
concluded that the Diem regime was becoming an embarrassing
liability, and that Ngo Dinh Nhu and Madame Nhu were the heart
of the problem. Covertly, Agency operatives were told to sniff out
discontent within the ARVN high command and discuss the viability of a coup.

It was determined that numerous plots already existed, in various states of readiness. Diem sensed the existing ARVN discontent
and ordered a show of force against Buddhists and Buddhist sympathizers in Saigon and Hue. It was Diem's intention to turn the

Buddhists against the ARVN and exploit the situation to his advantage. On 8/21/63, Diem troops attacked Buddhist temples in Saigon, Hue and other cities. Hundreds of monks and nuns were killed, injured and arrested. Riots and protests against the Diem regime followed.

The Agency learned of Diem's machinations in the ensuing weeks. Kennedy and his advisors were furious and still convinced that Ngo Dinh Nhu was the problem. Diem was instructed to get rid of Nhu. Agency operatives were told to contact potential coup leaders should he refuse, and to pledge our post-coup support.

Ambassador Lodge met with Diem. He became convinced that Diem would never drop Nhu. Lodge informed his Agency contacts. They contacted plotters within the ARVN high command. Lodge, Kennedy, McNamara and the Joint Chiefs met. They discussed the cutoff of financial aid to the Diem regime.

The cutoff was announced. The plotters proceeded. Chief among them were General Tran Van Don, General Le Van Kim and General Duong Van Minh, aka "Big Minh." Agency operatives met with General Don and General Minh and promised them continued U.S. financial aid and support. Kennedy determined that his administration would remain convincingly unaccountable and that the coup would publicly present itself as an all-Vietnamese affair.

The coup was planned and postponed throughout the early fall. Kennedy's advisors included pro-coup and anti-coup factions. The anti-coup faction argued that the autonomous nature of the coup might lead to another "Bay of Pigs fiasco."

Internal bickering diverted the plotters. The generals argued over which position of power they would assume in post-coup Saigon. The coup was finally scheduled for 11/1/63. It was implemented that afternoon.

Madame Nhu was in the U.S. Premier Diem and Ngo Dinh Nhu hid in the basement of the presidential palace. Insurgent units captured the palace, the guard barracks and the police station. Diem and Nhu were apprehended and given "safe passage" in an armored personnel carrier. The carrier stopped at a railroad crossing. Diem and Nhu were shot and stabbed to death.

A 12-man "Military Revolutionary Council" took over and then succumbed to internal squabbles. Concurrent with this, riots swept the south and steady streams of Viet Cong infiltrated from the north. ARVN troops deserted in large numbers. Concurrent with this, Kennedy was assassinated. Lyndon Johnson and his advisors reevaluated the ambiguously defined Vietnamese policy of the

Kennedy administration and decided to expand our financial-military commitment.

General Nguyen Khanh toppled the "Military Revolutionary Council" on 1/28/64. ("Bloodless" describes it best. The other generals abdicated and returned to their military fiefdoms.) Concurrently, the Viet Cong stepped up its southern incursion, defeating the ARVN in several encounters and staging a series of terrorist attacks in Saigon, including the bombing of a movie theater, where three Americans were killed. Throughout early '64, the Viet Cong forces doubled to 170,000 (mostly recruited in the south) with a commensurate improvement in their ordnance: Red Chinese and Soviet-supplied AK-47s, mortars and rocket launchers.

Secretary McNamara visited Vietnam in March and toured the south in a propaganda effort to bolster Premier Khanh. McNamara returned to Washington. He proposed and secured President Johnson's approval of an "action memorandum." The memorandum called for increased financial aid, to provide the ARVN with more aircraft and other ordnance. Premier Khanh was allowed to stage cross-border raids against Communist strongholds in Laos and to study the feasibility of possible incursions into Cambodia to interdict Viet Cong supply routes. Pentagon specialists started pinpointing North Vietnamese targets for U.S. bombing raids.

Ambassador Lodge resigned to pursue a career in domestic politics. President Johnson appointed General William C. Westmoreland as Commander of the U.S. Military Advisory Group (MACV) in Vietnam. Westmoreland remains committed to a greatly expanded American presence. There is now a formidable U.S. contingent in the south, among them servicemen, accountants, doctors, mechanics and sundry others involved in dispensing the $500,000,000 that Johnson has pledged in fiscal '64 aid. Much of the U.S. donated food, weaponry, medicine, gasoline and fertilizer has ended up on the black market. The U.S. presence in South Vietnam is rapidly becoming the foundation of the South Vietnamese economy.

Johnson has approved a covert plan called "OPLAN 34-A," which calls for larger incursions north of the 17th parallel, an expanded propaganda effort and covert ops to intercept Communist ships delivering material to the Viet Cong in the south. The Gulf of Tonkin incident (8/1–8/3/64, wherein two U.S. destroyers were fired upon by Communist seacraft and returned said fire) was largely a staged and improvised event that Johnson capitalized upon to get congressional sanction for planned bombing raids. The 64 bombing sorties that followed were limited to one day, so as to not give the appearance of overreaction to the Gulf of Tonkin provocation.

As of this (10/16/64) date, there are just under 25,000 "advisors" in Vietnam, and the bulk of them are, in fact, combat troops. These troops are Army Special Forces, Airborne Rangers and support personnel. President Johnson has committed to a covert escalation plan which will allow him to introduce an additional 125,000 troops by next summer. Expected North Vietnamese provocations will help him push this troop commitment through Congress. The plan will allow for a large deployment of marines in the winter and spring of '65, and a large influx of army infantry in the summer. Johnson is also committed to sustained bombing raids into North Vietnam. The raids will begin in the late winter-early spring of '65. Again, Agency analysts believe that Johnson will commit to Vietnam for the long haul. The consensus is that he sees Vietnam as a way to establish his anti-Communist credentials to their fullest advantage and use them to counterbalance any political dissension he creates with his liberal domestic reforms.

This overall escalation should serve to cloak our in-country activities. Opium and its derivatives have fueled the Vietnamese economy going back to its early French-colonial days. Intelligence units of the French Army ran the opium trade and managed most of the opium dens in Saigon and Cholon from '51 to '54. The opium traffic has financed dozens of coups and coup attempts, and the late Ngo Dinh Nhu was planning to circumvent Premier Diem's anti-opium edict at the time of his death. Since the 11/1/63 coup, 1,800 opium dens have reopened in Saigon and 2,500 in the heavily Chinese enclave of Cholon (Cholon is 2.5 miles up the Ben Nghe Channel from Central Saigon). Premier Khanh has established a hands-off policy toward the dens, which will serve us well. It should be noted that Khanh is extremely malleable and beholden to our presence in South Vietnam. He loves American money and will not risk offending even adjunct Agency personnel such as our cadre. He is not a "puppet who pulls his own strings." I doubt if he'll last long, and I doubt that his successor(s) will give us any trouble.

The crop source for our potential merchandise is situated in Laos, near the Vietnamese border. The fields near Ba Na Key are rich in the limestone soil component that poppy bulbs thrive on, and dozens of large-scale farms are situated there. Ba Na Key is close to the North Vietnamese border, which invalidates it for our purposes. A strip of acreage further south, near Saravan, is limestone-rich and accessible to the South Vietnamese border. Several poppy camps are situated near Saravan. They are run by Laotian "Warlords" who employ "Armies" of overseers, who work "Cliques" of Laotian/Vietnamese "Slaves," who harvest the bulbs. I've been grooming an English-speaking Laotian named Tran Lao Dinh, and my plan is to have you and Tran purchase or somehow co-opt the services of the Laotian warlords.

The standard procedure is to refine the poppy sap into a morphine-base that can be further refined into heroin. My goal would be to accomplish that at the farm(s) and ship the base to your chemist's lab in Saigon. We could fly it or move it by PT boat, which would require a pilot-navigator familiar with Vietnamese waterways. The standard way to move morphine-base out of Vietnam is via freighter to Europe and China. That's counterproductive in our case. We need your chemist to refine it in-country, in order to reduce the bulk size and render it easier to ship to Las Vegas. Please think of a way we can courier the finished product stateside, and limit our exposure on both ends.

Some closing thoughts.

Remember, I'm in this with six other agents, and we're Stage-1 Covert, with no Agency sanction. You'll meet the other men on a need-to-know basis. You're the operations boss and I'm the personnel runner. I know you're anxious to start funneling money to the Cause, but we're going to accrue large operating expenses in-country and out, and I want to make sure we're cash fluid first. The Agency has a front-company in Australia that will trade Vietnamese piastres for U.S. dollars, and we may be able to utilize a Swiss bank-account system for the laundering of our ultimate profits.

Let me stress this now. No morphine-base or fully refined merchandise should be allowed to slip into the hands of the U.S. military—for accountability's sake—or into the hands of ARVN personnel. Most ARVNs are highly corruptible and cannot be trusted around saleable narcotics.

I think you'll like my end of the cadre. I've co-opted an Army 1st Lt. named Preston Chaffee. He's a language whiz, Airborne-certified and an all-around good scout. He's my projected liaison to the ARVNs, the Saigon politicos and Premier Khanh.

I need to assess your projected plans and vet your chosen personnel. Can you pouch me, Vegas to Arlington?

For the Cause,

J.S.

J.S.,

I read your summary. Vietnam sounds like my kind of place. Here's my personnel:

1 - Wayne Tedrow Jr. U.S. Army, '54–'58 (82nd Airborne Division). Former Las Vegas policeman. Chemistry degree/Brigham Young University/'59.

Tedrow's solid. He's proficient with small arms & larger weaponry. He'll do a solid job on the chemical side. He told me he studied "opiate balances" & "narcotic component theory" in college. His plan is to find human "test pilots" or "guinea pigs" to test maximum dosage levels on, such as junkies or opium addicts with opiate tolerances. That way he can take the refining process to the final level in Saigon & ship street-ready merchandise back to Vegas.

Tedrow's father is a big wheel in Nevada. Tedrow's <u>very</u> estranged from him, but the old man has connections at Nellis AFB that we may be able to use. More on this later.

2, 3 - Laurent Guery & Flash Elorde.

You know them from our Miami days. They've been merc'ing out of Mexico City since late '63 & they're anxious to find a permanent duty station. They're devoted to the Cause & will fit in on the cultivation, enforcement & distribution ends. Both men have ties to gulf coast-based exiles that we'll be able to utilize.

4 - Jean Philippe Mesplede.

You sent me his dossier, so I won't repeat his stats. I met him in Mexico City & liked him. He's French-English fluent & knows some Vietnamese dialect from his '53–'54 tour. He's got in-country narcotics experience, along with some exile ties & is solidly committed to the Cause.

5 - Chuck Rogers.

Another old Tiger ops grad. You know his stats: pilot, wet-arts, shortwave radio skills. Deep exile ties & connections on the southern gun circuit. A valuable all-around guy. He wants to distribute hate leaflets and broadcast short-wave tirades in-country, & I'll humor him on that until it gets out of hand.

6 - Bob Relyea.

I don't know him & I'm hiring him off Rogers' recommendation. (They've been shortwave buddies for years. Rogers vouches for him & he's already in-country.)

Relyea's a Staff Sgt. with the MP Brigade in Saigon. He was formerly a prison guard in Missouri & has strong right-wing ties in the south. He's allegedly a great sharpshooter & all-around weapons man.

Per my plan:

I want to get into Laos quick & have Tran Lao Dinh negotiate with the "warlords" for their poppy farms. I want to bribe the right ARVN men & other Saigon officials to procure us the right level of protection. Then I'll have Rogers fix up a small 2-engine aircraft & fly circuits from Laos to Saigon. He'll conduit the morphine-base to Tedrow's lab & double as an enforcer at the slave farm(s).

Per the stateside conduit:

I'd like to ship via Agency-courier flights to Nellis. I've got a well-placed lawyer friend who may be able to pull strings & get us clearance there. Then we'll distribute out of Tiger Kab, to (expendable) Negro pushers who'll push exclusively in West Vegas. Rogers, Guery & Elorde will funnel the final profits to exile groups on the gulf.

The team is solid. I'm confident that they'll work well together. Let's stay focused on the Cuban end of things.

Viva la Causa!

P.B.

DOCUMENT INSERT: 10/29/64. Pouch communiqué. To: Pete Bondurant. From: John Stanton. Marked: "Hand Pouch Deliver Only"/ "Destroy Upon Reading."

P.B.,

I like your personnel and plan, per one proviso.

You'll need cargo-manifest cover to land at Nellis, and it must be convincing. What do you advise?

J.S.

DOCUMENT INSERT: 10/31/64. Pouch communiqué. To: John Stanton. From: Pete Bondurant. Marked: "Hand Pouch Deliver Only"/ "Destroy Upon Reading."

J.S.,

Per your last pouch:

Howard Hughes (my old boss & my lawyer friend's current boss) wants to curry favor with politicians & military personnel in Nevada & already has Hughes Aircraft-Tool Co charter clearance at Nellis. My lawyer friend will try to convince H.H. to purchase ARVN-surplus ordnance to donate to the Nevada National Guard, as a PR ploy. This will expand his ground clearance & allow us to hide our merchandise in with the ordnance & fly it straight to Nellis & Vegas.

What do you think?

P.B.

DOCUMENT INSERT: 11/1/64. Pouch communiqué. To: Pete Bondurant. From: John Stanton. Marked: "Hand Pouch Deliver Only"/ "Destroy Upon Reading."

P.B.,

Contact your lawyer friend and try to implement ASAP. I approve your selected personnel, and I'll have Lt. Chaffee approach and detach Sgt. Relyea from his regular duties. See you in Saigon: 11/3/64.

J.S.

DOCUMENT INSERT: 11/2/64. Verbatim FBI telephone call transcript. Marked: "Recorded at the Director's Request"/"Classified Confidential 1-A: Director's Eyes Only." Speaking: Director Hoover, Ward J. Littell.

JEH: Good morning, Mr. Littell.

WJL: Good morning, Sir.

JEH: The election bodes. Prince Bobby's probable victory must hearten you.

WJL: It does, Sir.

JEH: The Dark Prince has plundered New York State with great verve. I liken it to the Visigoths storming Rome.

WJL: It's a vivid comparison, Sir.

JEH: Lyndon Johnson was Bobby's reluctant henchman. He told me, quote, Edgar, I hate that little rabbit-faced cocksucker, and it galls me to hustle him votes.

WJL: President Johnson has verve of his own.

JEH: Yes, and much of it is directed toward the passage of dubious legislation. I view the words "Great Society" as fresh lyrics to "The Internationale."

WJL: It's a deft analogy, Sir.

JEH: Lyndon Johnson will deplete his prestige on the home-front and recoup it in Vietnam. History will judge him as a tall man with big ears who needed wretched people to love him.

WJL: Said with verve, Sir.

JEH: Lyndon Johnson appreciates the verve of one Martin Lucifer King. I've been sending him motel-room tapes. Lucifer performs with equal verve in bed and at barricades.

WJL: Dr. King wears many hats, Sir.

JEH: Yes, and he also wears garishly patterned Fruit-of-the-Loom briefs.

WJL: You're maintaining a close surveillance, Sir.

JEH: Yes, and I have Lyle Holly to direct me to Lucifer's favored tryst-spots. I talk to Lyle on a near-daily basis, and he tells me that Bayard Rustin is very much taken with you and your allegedly pilfered organized-crime donations.

WJL: Mr. Rustin finds me sincere, Sir.

JEH: Because you are.

WJL: I work at verve, Sir.

JEH: You succeed.

WJL: Thank you, Sir.

JEH: I detect a shift in tone. Do you wish to ask a question?

WJL: Yes, Sir.

JEH: Ask, Mr. Littell. You know I find preambles taxing.

WJL: Do you know when you'll leak word of my donations?

JEH: When I sense that my missives on Lucifer's Communist ties and sex life have reached their cumulative peak.

WJL: That's a sound strategy, Sir.

JEH: It's an inspired strategy. It's inimical to your recent gambit with Wayne Senior.

WJL: Is he peeved at me, Sir?

JEH: Yes, but he won't tell me why.

WJL: I set up a deal for him. He facilitated some charter flights out of Nellis and wanted a higher percentage. His Mormons have cut him out of his existing one.

JEH: Percentage of what?

WJL: The casino skim his Mormons were moving.

JEH: I am as delighted by that bit of data as Wayne Senior is vexed.

WJL: I'm always pleased to amuse you, Sir.

JEH: Wayne Senior has been in a thoroughly vexed state lately. He's rebuffed all my inquiries about his son.

WJL: I'm going to raise his percentage, Sir. That should improve his mood.

JEH: Why? What do you need from him?

WJL: I need to expand my Nellis clearance.

JEH: To include?

WJL: Flights from Vietnam.

JEH: Data coheres in odd fashions. You're my second postcard from Vietnam this morning.

WJL: Sir?

JEH: Dwight Holly called. He told me that Wayne Tedrow Junior and Pete Bondurant were recently granted Vietnamese travel visas.

WJL: That is odd, Sir.

JEH: Yes, and you are being oddly and blithely disingenuous, so I'll change the subject. How are Count Dracula's colonization plans proceeding?

WJL: Very well, Sir. Pete Bondurant has purchased a taxi stand and is using it to accrue intelligence for Mr. Hughes. The drivers have picked up dirt on several Nevada state legislators.

JEH: It's ingenious. Cab drivers are night-riding denizens of the first order. They view wretched foibles from a gutter perspective.

WJL: I thought you'd appreciate it, Sir. And while we're on the topic of—

JEH: Don't lead me. Ask your favor while I'm still pixilated and bemused.

WJL: I'd like to initiate a standing-bug operation in Vegas. I want to bug the hotel rooms the legislators stay in most frequently. I'll bring in Fred Turentine to help me with the installation, and I'd like local agents to do the retrievals and forward copies to me.

JEH: Do it. I'll assign two agents from the Las Vegas Office.

WJL: Thank you, Sir.

JEH: Thank yourself. You charmed me out of a bad mood.

WJL: I'm glad, Sir.

JEH: What would Tedrow Junior and Le Grand Pierre be doing in Vietnam?

WJL: I couldn't begin to guess.

JEH: Good day, Mr. Littell.

WJL: Good day, Sir.

60

(Saigon, 11/3/64)

D ig it:
         Rickshaw bikes and sand-
bags. Gun nests and frangipani
trees. Grenade nets and gooks.

Saigon at high noon—Brave New Fucking World.

It's big. It's tricultural. It's hot. It's noisy. It stinks.

The limo crawled. The limo bucked rickshaws. They bumped. They slid. They locked à la *Ben-Hur*.

White buildings. Pagodas. Propaganda signs: VIGILANCE IS FREEDOM/TREASON HAILS NORTH!

The limo crawled. The shocks creaked. The wheels slid. The cooler fan died.

Mesplède smoked. Chuck smoked. Flash smoked. The driver sold them black-market Kools. Guéry smoked a Cohiba. Chaffee smoked a Mecundo. They smoked pro-Fidel.

Wayne moaned. Wayne got green-gilled. Pete got queasy. Pete read native tongue:

A BAS LES VIET-CONG! HO CHI MINH, LE DIABLE COMMUNISTE!

Qu'est-ce que c'est, toute cette merde?

The limo crawled. They hit Tu Do Street—the Gook Sunset Strip.

Big trees and big shops. Big hotels and big traffic. Big noise *en gook*.

Pete yawned. Pete stretched. They flew nineteen hours in. Stanton set their rooms up. Hotel Catinat upcoming—sleep most ricky-tick.

The driver rode his horn. The driver clipped a rickshaw. Mesplède sniffed the air and nailed scents.

Nuoc mam—fish sauce—goat bar-b-que. Machine-gun oil/frangipani blossoms/goat shit.

Stanton said, "You'll lay up for two days, then fly to Dak Sut. You'll cross into Laos and meet Tran Lao Dinh. An ARVN rifle squad will walk point for you. Two Hueys will meet you and fly you to a dope camp near Saravan. You'll negotiate right there."

Buddhist monks jaywalked. Traffic stalled up. Pete yawned. Pete stretched. Pete elbowed more room.

Milt C. ran Tiger now. Milt ran liaison gigs. Milt ran adjunct ops:

Ward Littell to bug hotel suites. Milt to bribe hotel clerks. Milt to schmooze them. Milt to tell them: place state legislators within.

Pete's bigggg decree:

Restrict the Tiger crew. Restrict all pill ops. Rat rival pill crews. Rat said crews to Agent Dwight Holly.

Trash the Vegas pill trade. Dry up West Vegas. Deprive hopheads. Tempt taste buds. Prepare hopheads for Big "H."

Chaffee waved his ditty bag. Chaffee offered gifts. Shrunken heads— *certified*—all VC *très bien*.

Wayne tossed his out. Flash kissed his. Guéry named his "Fidel."

Pete yawned. Pete popped Dramamine. The Arden bit bugged him. It bugged him incessant. It bugged him nonstop.

He factored Carlos in. 3/56: Carlos bails Arden/Arden splits K.C.

New Orleans—'59—Mesplède sees Arden. Arden has a date. He's a Carlos man/he's a wop. 11/63: Arden visits the safe house. Carlos thus orders her clipped.

He factored Carlos in. He held back. He never told Ward. He called Fred Otash. He said call around.

Run Arden. Call your contacts. Glom me some leads. Check Arden out. Check out her ex—one Danny Bruvick.

Flash kissed his shrunken head. Flash applied some tongue. Chaffee laughed. Mesplède named his head "de Gaulle."

Chuck waved his head. Wayne grabbed it. Wayne threw it out.

Chuck said, "There's times I think we hired the wrong Tedrow."

No sleep—his head wouldn't stop.

The room was okay—*comme ci/comme ça*—likewise the Tu Do Street view.

The bed sagged. The grenade-screen creaked. The AC sputtered. Fumes cut through—*nuoc mam* sauce—*ce n'est pas bon*.

Street noise carried up. Choppers buzzed the roof.

Pete gave up. Pete oiled his piece. Pete put out his bedside pix. Barb/the cat snarling/Barb with the cat.

Stanton set up an outing—1900 hours—Saigon by night. We'll check out the natives. We'll dig the night view.

Pete sat on the terrace. Pete dug the *now* view. Pete saw ARVN cliques. Pete saw gook cops.

Chaffee called them "White Mice." Mesplède called GIs "Con Van My."

The skyline clashed—tin roofs and spires—M-60 machine guns.

He loved war zones. He saw Pearl Harbor. He saw Okinawa. He saw Saipan. He saw Pigs. He avenged Pigs. He scalped Reds *beaucoup.*

Dusk hit. The roof crews rejoiced. They arced their guns. They shot tracer rounds. They made fireworks.

The new cadre was gooooood. The new cadre was #1. Cadre with a "K" now.

Stanton liked the guys. Stanton said Bob Relyea was a "Head Man." He killed VC. He chopped their heads off. He sold them to clinics.

Flash named his head "Khrushchev." Stanton named his head "Ho." Chuck named his head "JFK."

They rendezvoused. They grabbed a stretch limo.

Bob Relyea showed up. Chuck hugged him. They laughed. They shared spit. They talked Klan.

The limo sagged—nine riders plus weight.

The kadre packed sidearms. The driver packed grenades. Relyea packed a 30.06.

They swung off Tu Do. They hit side streets. The limo flew flags: The MACV/the ARVN/the skull & bones.

Rickshaws clogged traffic. The driver rode his horn. The gooks ignored it. The driver yelled, "*Di, di!*"

Mesplède popped the sunroof. Mesplède popped a clip up. The noise was bad. The shells blew down. Flash caught them hot. The gooks heard the noise. The gooks pulled over. The gooks ducked low and booked.

The driver punched it. Mesplède flexed his tattoos. Two pit bulls grew boners. Two parachutes flew.

"You must announce your intent to these people. They understand only force."

Reylea fanned playing cards—all ace-of-spades.

"They understand force and superstition. These cards, for instance. You drop one on a dead VC and scare off potential converts."

Chaffee said, "Affirmative on that. I like the Viets, but they're primitive as hell. They talk to shadows and dead chickens."

Flash chewed a shell. "Where the GIs? I only count four men so far."

Stanton said, "They tend to wear civvies. They stand out because they're white or colored, and they don't like to compound things by wearing uniforms."

Flash shrugged. *Qué pasa* "compound"?

Pete lit a cigarette. "A six-figure troop commitment by summer. That means breathing room."

Flash shrugged. *Qué pasa* "commitment"? Guéry shrugged. *Qu'est-ce que c'est?*

Pete laughed. Stanton laughed. Relyea cut cards. He fanned cards. He flipped cards. He pulled cards off Wayne's shirt.

"Chuck and me got distribution plans. I been sending tracts to inmates throughout the Missouri prison system, which was my pre–U.S. Army employer. I been sending them stuck inside these Voice of America pamphlets, which means the inmates get a soft version of the truth and the real thing."

Chuck lit a cigarette. "Aerial drops are the best. You fly low and bombard the troops."

Relyea shook his head. "Negative on that. You waste good tracts on the nigger EM."

Chuck winked. "Wayne's daddy's a tract man. He throws a good party, too."

Wayne stared at Chuck. Wayne cracked his thumbs.

Chuck said, "Wayne's a Martin Luther Coon fan. He's seen all his films."

Wayne stared. Chuck stared back. The stretch swerved. Chuck blinked first. Wayne blinked last.

The stretch swayed. The driver dodged a pig. Pete looked out. Pete looked up.

He saw tracer rounds. Tracers as firefly flares.

They cruised Khanh Hoi. They scoped the clubs. They hit the Duc Quynh.

It was small. It was dark. It was French. Banquettes/mood lights/jukebox. They got a booth. They ordered wine. They ate bouillabaisse.

Wayne sulked. Pete watched him.

Ward snipped his daddy cord. Hey, Wayne, dig this: Daddy bought you Dallas. Wayne took it hard. Wayne held his mud. Wayne waxed sullen resultant.

The food rocked—garlic and squid—*chow indigène.* Bar girls performed.

They peeled to pasties. They lip-synced tunes. They sang some Barb cover songs.

Chuck got drunk. Bob got drunk. They talked Klan shit resultant. Flash got drunk. Guéry got drunk. They talked patois.

Chaffee got drunk. Chaffee waved shrunken heads. Chaffee spooked the girls off resultant.

Stanton sipped martinis. Wayne sipped vichy. Mesplède smoked a Gauloise a minute. Pete heard bombs. Pete gauged directions.

Small bombs—two clicks over—reverb off water.

Chaffee called it—White Mice and VC. Gadfly stuff—pipe bombs *pas beaucoup.*

The club filled up. Stag GIs cruised stag nurses.

They hobnobbed. They danced. They hogged the jukebox. They played Vietrock—Ricky Nelson in gook—"Herro, Maly Roo."

Two niggers showed up. They vibed jungle stud. They vibed plantation buck.

They hit on white nurses. They sparked rapport. They sat with them. They danced with them. They danced sloooow.

Wayne seized up. Wayne watched them. Wayne gripped the table.

They danced. They did the Stroll. They did the Watusi. Wayne watched them. Chuck caught it. Chuck signaled Bob.

They watched Wayne. Pete watched Wayne. Wayne watched the niggers dance. They worked their hips. They lit cigarettes. They fed the nurses puffs.

Wayne gripped the table. Wayne tore a plank loose. The stew pot fell. Fishheads flew.

Pete said, "Let's walk."

They hit the docks. They met Stanton's ARVNs. Two *trung uys*—junior grade—first-lieutenant gooks.

The lab was close. They walked over. The ARVNs walked point. Tracers popped. Red light tinged the water.

There—

The building's white brick. It's smeared with gook graffiti. One night-club/one dope den/one floor per each. *Three* floors—with lab space on top.

They walked in. They scoped out the Go-Go. There's a bar. There's a bandstand. There's a shrunken-head motif.

Shrunken-head wall mounts. Shrunken-head ashtrays. Shrunken-head candlesticks.

More B-girls. More ARVNs. More GIs. More musk and more Ricky Nelson. More "Herro, Maly Roo."

They walked upstairs. The ARVNs chaperoned them. There's the dope den.

Floor pallets/wood planks recumbent/dope beds boocoo. Piss troughs and shit buckets. Four walls as fart envelopes.

O-heads boocoo. O-heads in orbit. Slants and some round-eyes. One jigaboo.

They walked through. They pallet-hopped. They dodged fumes. Pete held his nose. Scents sizzled and mixed.

Sweat/smoke/fart residue.

The ARVNs wiggled flashlights—you rook rook rook:

See the dope skin. See the dope eyes. See the Jockey shorts de rigueur.

Chaffee said, "The Americans are ex-Army. They got discharged and stuck around. The colored guy pimps slant girls out of the Go-Go."

The ARVNs flashed the spook's pallet. Said spook flew dee-luxe. Dig his silk pillow. Dig his down bed and silk sheets.

Pete sneezed. Flash coughed. Stanton squashed a turd. Chuck laughed. Guéry kicked a pallet. Guéry dislodged a gook.

Mesplède laughed. Bob laughed. Wayne watched the spook.

They walked. They hit the back door. They took side stairs up. There's the lab—dig it!

Stoves. Vats. Oil drums. Beakers/kettles/pans. Shelves. Mustard jars with taped labels.

Stanton said, "I got everything Wayne asked for."

Chaffee sneezed. "It's quality stuff. I got most of it in Hong Kong."

Coffee filters. Lime sacks. Suction pumps and extraction tubes.

Pete said, "We cook it bulk and ship it that way. Wayne and I work the in-country and Vegas ends. We follow the courier flights to Nellis and go from there."

Chuck lit a cigarette. "Ward Littell's got to get clearance, which as I understand it means he's got to brown-nose Wayne Senior."

Wayne shook his head. "He doesn't need to. There's a one-star named Kinman who can do it."

The room smelled. Caustic agents settling in. Lime dust boocoo.

Pete sneezed. "I'll call Ward and tell him."

Wayne checked the shelves. Wayne read labels:

Chloroform. Ammonia. Sulfate salts. Muriatic Acid. Hydrochloric Acid. Acetic anhydride.

He cracked jars. He smelled compounds. He touched the powder stock.

"I want to refine to the maximum viable dosage strength here. We finalize the quality here and tell the distribution guys in Vegas not to cut it any further."

Stanton smiled. "You've got your test pilots one floor down."

Chaffee smiled. "They've got opiate tolerances you can work off."

Mesplède smiled. "Inject them with a caffeine compound first. It will serve to open their capillaries and secure you a more accurate reading."

Pete cracked a window. Tracers rounds flew. Dig the streetside procession:

Slants in robes—baldies all—loud chants in sync.

Yawns went around. Looks went around. Fuck this—we're jet-fucked and fucked from no sleep.

Stanton locked the lab. Chaffee greased the ARVNs. You guard the lab/you stay all night—ten dollars U.S.

Everyone yawned. Everyone was fried. Everyone dog-yawned and stretched.

They walked downstairs. They cut through the den. They cut through the Go-Go. The Go-Go rocked anew.

More round-eyes. More GIs. Some U.S. embassy types.

The spook pimp was up. The spook pimp was de-O'd and revived.

He bossed his whores around. He made his whores strip. He made his whores hop on three tables.

They linked up. They performed table tricks. They French-kissed and went 69.

Wayne weaved. Pete steadied him. A Buddhist monk walked in.

His robe dripped. He looked stupefied. His robe reeked of gas. He bowed. He squatted. He lit a match. He gook-cooked with gas.

He whooshed. He flared. Flames hit the ceiling. The lez shows dispersed. The monk burned. The fire spread. Some clubhoppers screeched.

The barman stretched a fizz cord. The barman spritzed club soda. The barman sprayed the monk.

61

(Las Vegas, 11/4/64)

Bugwork.

Littell twisted wires. Littell hung microphones. Fred Turentine hung feeder cords.

They laid cords. They taped wires. They perforated wall mounts. They spackled wall plates.

The Riviera—bug job #9. A big suite—three rooms in. Bugwork—Vegas-wide. Bribed access—four hotels in.

Moe Dalitz bribed managers. Milt Chargin bribed clerks. Mr. Hoover bribed the Vegas SAC. Said SAC pledged agents. Said SAC pledged speed. Said SAC pledged copied tapes.

Tapes to Mr. Hoover. Tapes to Ward Littell.

Turentine looped wires. Littell ran the TV. The news ran on. They caught LBJ's landslide. They caught Bobby's Senate sweep.

Turentine picked his nose. "I hate spackle mounts. The fucking paste stings."

LBJ praised the voters. Ken Keating conceded. Bobby hugged his kids.

"I guess I'm lucky to get the work. It's not like the scandal-rag days. Freddy Otash had me wire every fucking toilet in L.A."

Goldwater conceded. Hubert Humphrey smiled. LBJ hugged his kids.

Turentine flicked snot. "Freddy's scuffling. Pete's got him running leads on some woman. Her husband screwed Jimmy H. on a deal."

Littell killed the sound. Humphrey went mute. LBJ moved his lips.

"Who has the old scandal-rag morgue files? Would Freddy know?"

Turentine hooked wires. "You mean the *hot* dirt? The unprintable shit that never got published?"

"That's right."

"Why do you—"

"The information could help us. The rags always kept stringers in Vegas."

Turentine popped a neck zit. "If you're willing to pay, Freddy'd be willing to look."

"Call him, will you? Tell him I'll pay double his day rate and expenses."

Turentine nodded. Turentine popped a chin zit. Littell goosed the TV. LBJ praised Bobby. Bobby praised LBJ. Bobby praised the Great Society.

Littell miked a nightstand. Littell miked a couch leg. Littell miked a lamp.

Morgue dirt was old. Morgue dirt was still ripe. Morgue dirt might help Mr. Hughes. They needed dirt. Dirt incurred debt. Let's call Moe D. Let's call Milt C. Let's bug more rooms yet.

Grind joints next—bedroom mounts—Milt to retrieve. Let's bug Vegas. Let's cull dirt. Let's extort.

Littell miked a chair. Turentine flipped channels. There's Mr. Hoover in the flesh.

He said, "King." He said, "Communist sympathizer." He looked old. He looked weak.

The news ran late. Bobby's segments ran long.

Littell went "home." Littell called room service. Littell ate dinner and watched TV.

Home-*suite*-home. Room service and valets.

He missed Jane. He pressed her to come for Thanksgiving. She agreed. It scared her. The Boys owned the town.

She told lies. It disturbed him in L.A. He missed her and wanted her here.

Bobby praised LBJ. Bobby praised his programs. Bobby praised Dr. King.

He played his Bobby tapes. He played them most nights. Sometimes Jane overheard. He punted. He lied. He described depositions.

Lies:

Bayard Rustin pressed him—meet Dr. King—Bayard proposed a dinner. He declined. He *lied*. He stressed nonexistent engagements. He *lied*. He never said "distance."

Distance balanced his risk. Distance balanced his commitment. He subverted King. He aided King. He worked for a balance.

Personal moments would kill it. Affection would blitz respect. Compartments would burn. The risk would grow exponential.

Bobby promised legislation. Bobby promised hard work. Bobby did not mention organized crime. Bobby did not mention Jack.

He *knew* Bobby. Bobby *knew* the Boys killed Jack. Bobby on tape: "When the time's right I'll jump on it, and devil take the hindmost."

Don't. Please. Don't risk your safety. Don't risk yourself.

Littell flipped channels. Littell saw LBJ. Littell saw Blatz beer and Vietnam. U.S. advisors. More troops pledged. Buddhist monks on fire.

Pete called him this morning. Pete pitched a plan: Call Drac/*work* Drac/help me work *this* new plan.

He agreed. He called Drac and snowed him. Drac agreed to Pete's "plan." Pete dropped the name Clark Kinman. Bypass Wayne Senior through him.

He called Kinman. He pitched a meet. He deciphered the gist of Pete's "plan."

Heroin/Vietnam. "Ordnance"/hidden dope/cosmetic donations.

It meant one thing. The Boys waived the no-dope rule. The Boys never told him.

Pete sounded happy. Pete came off engaged. Pete built airtight compartments. There's Betty Mac. There's heroin. There's the partition.

Littell flipped channels. Bobby waved. Bobby hugged his kids.

Kinman served drinks. Littell sipped club soda. Kinman sipped scotch himself.

"I know about you. You brought the Hughes charter deal to Wayne Senior."

The den was stuffy. The den was GI. Airplane models and airplane wall plaques.

Littell smiled. "I hope your compensation sufficed."

Kinman sipped scotch. "I'm an officer in the United States Air Force. I'm not going to tell a perfect stranger if, where, or how I was compensated, if in fact I was."

Littell twirled his coaster. "You could call Wayne Senior for a reference."

"We're not on good terms. He told me he doesn't like you, which refers you pretty good these days."

A door slammed upstairs. Music kicked on. A female voice hummed along.

Littell stirred his drink. "Do you know who I work for?"

"I was informed that it was Howard Hughes, who folks say has designs on Las Vegas. I figured he was good for the town, which is why I facilitated the charter deal."

"For which you were or were not compensated."

The music dipped. Footsteps tapped downstairs. A woman hummed along.

Kinman smiled. "I've got a friend here. That means you've got five minutes to state your case and skedaddle."

Littell toed his briefcase. "Mr. Hughes wants to donate U.S.-supplied Vietnamese Army surplus to the Air National Guard. He wants to publicize the donations and credit you with inspiring the gift. All he requires is expanded ground clearance for periodic courier flights from Saigon."

Kinman chewed ice. "With no contraband checks?"

"He would appreciate that courtesy, yes."

" 'That courtesy' will cost $5,000 per month, in cash, nonrefundable."

Littell popped his briefcase. Littell dumped forty grand. Drac gave him fifty. He kept and tithed ten.

Kinman whooped. Janice Tedrow walked in.

She limped. She swung a cane. She rubbed a scar on her lips.

62

(Dak Sut, 11/7/64)

Heat. Bugs. Bullshit.

Dak Sut featured peasants. Dak Sut featured clay-mud. Dak Sut featured thirty-three huts.

ARVNs called peasants *que lam*. Chaffee called ARVNs "Marvin." Pete called them "Marv." Chuck called them "Marv." Bob Relyea called them "Sahib."

Wayne itched. Wayne slapped bugs. Wayne scoped Dak Sut. He saw pigs. He saw rice bins. He saw the Dak Poko River.

A bridge. Brown water. Thick jungle ahead.

They flew up. Three Marvs came along. Chaffee hired a Huey. The pilot slurped wine. Chuck and Bob tossed hate tracts out.

Wayne itched. Wayne slapped bugs. Wayne wore fatigues and a .45. Wayne packed a 12-gauge pump.

GI gear—kadre kustomized. Dum-dums and beehive rounds—steel darts encased.

Laos was close. The Marvs knew the way. The Marvs had *their* guide—some ex-Cong stashed in a hut.

Tran Dinh camped near Saravan. Tran Dinh had men. Tran Dinh had two Hueys prepped. They'd fly to Joe Warlord's camp. They'd "negotiate."

Wayne itched. Wayne slapped bugs. Wayne scoped Dak Sut. Peasants hovered. Mesplède dispensed Kools. Pete hit hut 16. Pete hauled the Cong out.

Chuck deshackled him. Bob rigged a collar. The Marvs leashed him up. *Nice* collar—poodle-sized and spiked.

Chuck fucked with the leash. Chuck laid some slack in. Chuck cinched the Cong up.

Wayne walked over. The Cong wore black pj's. The Cong wore torture cuts.

Chuck said, "Bow wow."

Bob sang "Walkin' the Dog."

They moved out.

They walked single-file. They crossed the Dak Poko. They hit the province hut. The Marvs greased the hut boss—five bucks U.S. The hut boss swooned.

They hit Laos. They walked foot trails. Hills and brush cover. Krazy Glue clay.

The Cong walked ahead. Chuck snapped his leash. Chuck named him "Fido." Fido tugged. Fido walked barefoot. Fido stretched his leash.

Wayne walked rear point. My craaaazy life—Army Airborne to *this*.

He killed time in Saigon. He read his chemistry texts. He hit the USO. He ordered the Vegas and Dallas papers. He moved into the lab. He stored his Durfee file.

He filed tips. He summarized tips. He ate at the Go-Go. He dug on the weird food. He offered the owner some help.

The fried monk caused damage. The fried monk burned beams. The fried monk scorched the paint job.

Wayne repainted. Wayne redrilled beams. The pimp hung around. Wayne watched him. Wayne learned his stats:

Maurice Hardell/aka Bongo/ex-QM PFC. Stockade time and a pervert DD.

He watched Bongo. He watched the kadre men. The kadre men watched him. They knew *his* stats. They dug on them. Chuck spieled them out.

He got *their* stats. Pete supplied them:

Guéry hated Reds. Mesplède hated Reds. They killed Congo rebels. They killed Algerians. Chuck hated Reds. Chuck was ex-CIA. Chuck killed Fidelistos.

Flash hated Reds. Flash killed Reds. Flash used to pimp girls in Havana. Flash split Cuba. Flash hit the U.S. Flash robbed liquor stores.

Flash knew Guéry. Flash met Pete. Flash met John Stanton. Chuck knew Bob. Bob pushed hate tracts. Bob mailed hate tracts to prisons.

Chaffee was a blueblood. Chaffee went Army. Stanton was a blueblood. Stanton went to Yale. Stanton knew Chaffee's dad. Stanton owned

United Fruit stock. The Beard kicked UF out of Cuba. The Beard fucked with their stock.

Cuba drove them. Cuba drove Pete. Cuba drove the dope plan. Cuba drove Viet ops. Something said Cuba drove Dallas.

They talked:

Guéry and Mesplède/Chuck and Pete/Flash Elorde. They spoke English. They stopped. They spoke Spanish and French. They said "Dallas" trilingual.

Dallas—a noun—a city in Texas. Dallas—the break point for *him*.

He waited since childhood. He notched a fast fuck. He dropped his Dallas punchline. He fucked Janice. He jeopardized her. They both wanted out from Wayne Senior. They fucked to burn their lives down.

He bought the Vegas papers. He checked the missing persons logs and obits. Wayne Senior killed Wardell Gray. Wayne Senior did not kill Janice.

He cut them off. He left them. He walked. He ignored them. He thought about Bongo. He thought about Wendell D.

The kadre trudged. The trail swerved. Bush hemmed them in. Chaffee read his compass. They held northwest.

They crossed clearings. They spread out. They flanked. Wayne switched positions. Wayne took Fido's leash.

Fido walked fast—good dog—most ricky-tick.

Wayne walked fast. Fido tugged. Wayne caught up and ran abreast. Fido went darty. Wayne tracked his eyes. Fido lurched. Fido weaved.

Marv One yelled, "*Chuyen gi vay?*"

Marv Two yelled, "*Chuyen, chuyen?*"

Fido yelled, "*Khong co chuyen gi het.*"

They hit a clearing. They reflanked. Fido tugged left. Fido squatted. Fido dropped his pants.

Wayne saw a turd drop. Wayne saw a tree stump. Wayne saw an X. Fido grabbed something. Fido threw something. Something blew up.

Fuck—smoke/shrapnel/gunfire.

Chaffee caught metal scraps. Chaffee went down. Two Marvs caught it tight. An arm flew. A foot flew. Stumps spattered.

Wayne proned out. Wayne rolled. Wayne pulled his .45. Pete proned out. Chuck proned out. Marv Three fired wide.

Pete fired. Chuck fired. Fido tugged his leash. Wayne dug in. Wayne pulled the leash. Wayne reeled him in.

He's close—there's his neck/there's his eyes.

Wayne aimed. Wayne popped four shots off. Fido's teeth shattered. Fido's neck blew.

Wayne heard yells. Wayne saw three VC.

They charged. They aimed carbines. They got kadre klose. Pete stood up. Chuck stood up. Mesplède waved *come on*.

Bob stood up. Bob aimed his pump. Bob shot low. A beehive blew—darts blew—darts on fire.

The spread cohered. The spread hit. The spread severed legs. Three trunk sections detached and fell.

Pete fired. Chuck fired. Mesplède fired tight. They popped full clips—.45 ACPs—they ten-ringed head shots.

Wayne walked over. Wayne kicked a loose leg. Wayne saw a Ho Chi Minh tattoo. Wayne saw needle marks.

Pete said no burials. Chuck said no evidence. Mesplède said guts lured wild pigs.

Bob disemboweled the Marvs. Pete disemboweled Chaffee. Bob disemboweled the VC. Wayne flipped a coin. Marv Three called heads. Wayne got tails—tough luck.

He disemboweled Fido. He thought of Maynard Moore. He smelled the rest stop near Dallas.

They walked away. Chuck left hate tracts. Bob left an ace of spades.

They walked.

They lost Chaffee's compass. They tracked off the sun. Dusk hit. They tracked off starlight.

A haze hit. The stars died. The foot trail bisected. They veered instinct-right. Ursa Minor broke through. They resighted and cut back.

They walked. They used flashlights. They hit undergrowth. Thick shit—leaves and roots.

They kicked through it. A haze hit. The stars died. They cut back. They fried their flashlights. They walked in the dark.

They saw lights. Marv Three called it:

Two clicks over—village—*que lam beaucoup*. I go now. I get village help. I bring guide back.

Pete said go. Marv Three walked. They waited. Nobody talked. Nobody smoked. Wayne clocked off forty-six minutes.

Marv Three walked back. Marv Three brought Fido Two. An old guy—the papa-san type—Ho beard and tire-tread shoes.

Chuck leashed him up. Chuck named him "Rover." Chuck fed him cigarettes. Rover had good wind. Rover walked fast. Rover leaped limbs and brush piles.

They hit a clearing. They flanked wide. They aimed in a 360 arc. A flare popped at ten o'clock—pink light streaked and poofed.

They cut loose. They blew beehives. Darts disinterred.

Somebody yelled, "Friend!"

Somebody yelled, "Tran Dinh!"

Tran had a campsite. Pete called it Tran's Fontainebleau.

One acre. Weeds and mulched dirt. Bug nets and grenade nets. Brushed-steel lean-tos.

They slept hard. They slept late. Tran's men cooked brunch.

Tran scrounged off Stanton. Stanton scrounged the Army. Stanton scrounged pancake batter. Stanton scrounged pork rinds and Spam.

Tran had six slaves—all ARVN rejects. Tran vibed Baby Caesar. Tran vibed diva.

The slaves served chow. Flapjacks flambé—torched in T-bird wine.

Chuck loved it. Pete went yum-yum. Bob gagged. Mesplède gagged. Marv Three scarfed it up. Wayne took a bite. Wayne gagged. Wayne fed Tran's pet snake.

Tran spoke English. Tran spoke French. Tran ran the drill:

Two Hueys come. We go then. We co-opt poppy farms. We "negotiate."

Pete took Tran aside. Wayne watched the tête-à-tête. Wayne heard "improvisation." Pete grinned. Tran grinned. Tran went tee-hee. Wayne caught the gist—"negotiate," *shit*.

Chuck issued ammo. Chuck issued rules: We all carry birdshot—beehives verboten.

Wayne dumped his ammo. Wayne reloaded. Wayne thought it through:

Short-range loads. "Improvisation." Pete knows/Tran knows/Chuck knows. They *all* know—but *you*.

Tran gave a speech. Tran indicted the Cong. Tran indicted the French. Tran excluded Pete and Mesplède. Tran indicted Ho Chi Minh. Tran indicted Ngo Dinh Diem. Tran indicted gnarly Charlie de Gaulle.

Tran eulogized Preston Chaffee. Tran indicted the Beard. Tran extolled boss-man LBJ. Tran yelled. Tran coughed. Tran chewed an hour up and went hoarse.

Wayne heard chopper thumps. Wayne saw the Hueys.

They closed in. They hovered. They landed and perched. The doors popped. The pilot Marvs motioned them up.

Tran said a prayer. Tran issued bullet-proof vests. Wayne looked at Pete. Pete smiled and winked.

▪ ▪ ▪

They did staggered takeoffs. Bob took Flight #1. Bob packed a 7-65 sniper-scope.

Pete clocked off ten minutes. Flight #2 readied. Tran yelled, "All aboard!"

They climbed in. Wayne grabbed a door spot. Chuck rode the door gun. Pete got a back seat. Mesplède stuck close. Tran stuck by the Pilot Marv and Marv Three.

The Pilot Marv goosed it. The rotors whipped. They climbed. They leveled. They held.

3K level—check that green—green valleys/green hills/green brush.

Wayne looked down. Wayne saw soil rows and hollows. Wayne caught the gray tint.

Sweet soil. Good alkalines—low pH all. Poppy food. Dope slaves burn trees. Ash feeds the soil.

Calcium and potassium. High phosphate counts. Spring burns and fall plantings. Beans and corn for interim crops.

They passed Saravan. Wayne saw tin roofs and spires. Wayne saw stick figures and grids. Saravan came and went fast. The ground regreened.

Chuck got airsick. Chuck puked in a bag. Wayne looked away and looked down.

There—

Dope fields/row furrows/coolie-hat slaves.

Pete grabbed the Pilot Marv's headset. He listened. He laughed. He held three fingers up. Tran laughed. Chuck laughed. Mesplède laughed. Marv Three went bang-bang.

Wayne got the gist:

Bob's up in chopper 1. Bob's got a rifle. Bob's popping outland guards. Bob's toppled three.

The Pilot Marv banked. Wayne saw huts. Wayne saw a landing strip. He pulled his .45. He checked the clip. He jacked a round in.

The Pilot Marv leveled. The Pilot Marv rotored down.

There—

A barracks. A slave jail. A volleyball court. A welcome line—Li'l Tojo plus six. Little Laotians/fatigues and jump boots/World War II Nazi lids.

Pete laughed. Chuck pointed *way* east—check the brush/catch that glint.

Wayne looked over. Wayne caught the glint. There's Bob. There's chopper 1 perched. That glint's off a hog machine gun.

The Pilot Marv touched down. The Pilot Marv cut the props. Tojo saluted. Tojo's goons snapped to.

Tran jumped out. Pete jumped out. Chuck jumped out and tripped. The Pilot Marv jumped out. Marv Three steadied him.

Mesplède jumped out. Mesplède tripped. Wayne jumped and caught him. The ground dipped. There's seven kadre men—up against Tojo plus six.

Tran hugged Tojo. Tran played MC. Tran dropped kadre bios—all last names *di di*.

Tojo was "Dong." The Tojoettes blurred—Dinh/Minh/whoever. They all laughed. They all hugged. They all bumped sidearms and hips.

Wayne looked around. Jail slaves loitered close. They wore loincloths. They sucked pipes. It was O-head servitude.

Wayne saw Tojoette volleyball—four goons per team/a thirty-goon barracks hard right.

Wayne coughed. His vest fit tight. His breath butterflied. Tran reached in the Huey. Tran grabbed their pumps. The Tojoettes bristled uptight.

Tran passed the pumps out—all kadre/one per. Dong smiled. Dong said, "You carry guns. That all right. Guns number-one A-OK."

Tran smiled. Tran talked Viet. Dong talked Viet back. Marv Three translated—all pidgin-gook:

We get nice tour. We have lunch then. All A-OK.

Dong whistled. Dong gestured. Dong dispatched a Tojoette. He ran off. He hit the barracks. He ran back. He schlepped six M-1s.

Dong bowed. Dong issued guns—all Tojoettes/one per. Dong smiled. Dong talked Viet. Marv Three translated—all pidgin-gook:

Trust A-OK. Parity better. Lunch and peace accord.

Dong bowed. Tran bowed. Dong went you first. The kadre hiked out. The Tojoettes hiked close behind. Dong and Tran hiked back.

They cut through the dope fields—poppy stalks 4-ever—grids/rows/grid paths. Slaves raked soil. Slaves dropped seeds. Slaves trimmed stalks back.

They wore coolie hats. They wore shackles. They wore floral BVDs. They walked weird. They shuffled. Their shackles gouged bone.

It was *good* soil. It looked limestone sweet. It vibed low pH.

They hiked. The sun arced. The Tojoettes lagged behind. The Tojoettes breathed curry fumes. Wayne smelled it. Wayne gauged it—just ten feet back.

The Tojoettes had M-1s. The Tojoettes had bolt-throw rifles—one shot per throw. The Tojoettes had .38s. They were flap-holstered—slow-draw style.

Not here—not now—they won't try.

Wayne looked sideways. Pete caught it. Pete winked. Wayne read, "Your call, kid."

They had bullet-proof vests. *They* had better weapons. The Tojoettes had Nazi lids.

Wayne gulped air. Wayne stretched his vest tight. Wayne smelled fish stew.

There's the lunch hut. It's all bamboo. Four frond-and-stalk walls. Wide doorway opened up.

Wayne looked sideways. Wayne winked. Pete winked back. Wayne walked ahead. Wayne hit the hut. Wayne doorway-lounged.

The kadre caught up. Wayne bowed. Wayne went you first. The guys shook their heads. The guys aped gook manners. The guys went *you* first.

Wayne shook his head. Wayne bowed. Wayne went *you* first. The guys laughed. The guys shucked. The guys jived.

The Tojoettes caught up. The guys bowed. The guys went you first. The Tojoettes shrugged. The Tojoettes went fuck it. The Tojoettes walked straight in.

The guys blocked the door. The guys aimed. The guys jammed their backs point-blank.

Wayne shot his .45. Pete shot his pump. Bullets and bird pellets flew. The noise got four-walled—back shots/powder burns/muzzle roar.

Chuck shot. Marv Three shot—full magazines. Mesplède tripped. Mesplède shot. Rounds ricocheted.

Pete got dinged. Pete went down. Pete's vest bullet-flared. Wayne got dinged. Wayne went down. Wayne's vest popped and flamed.

Pete rolled. Wayne rolled. Dirt ate the vest flames. Recoil and reverb. Ricochets ricky-tick.

Wayne saw blood spatter. Wayne saw big stew pots. Wayne saw blood in fish stew.

He heard hog-fire—way off—Bob R. at three-o'clock high. He rolled. He pulled his vest off. He ditched his shirt.

There's Dong.

He's running. Tran's chasing him. Tran's got his hair. Tran's got him down. Tran's got a knife. Tran's waving his head.

Wayne shut his eyes. Somebody jerked him. Somebody pulled him up hard.

He opened his eyes. Pete said, "You passed."

63

(Saigon, 11/11/64)

Stanton said, "You fucked up."

The Go-Go was dead. That bar-b-que'd monk deterred trade.

Pete lit a cigarette. "I didn't feel like negotiating. Tran was up for it, so we ad-libbed."

"'Ad-lib' doesn't cut it. I went to Yale with Preston Chaffee's father, and now he won't be able to bury his son."

Pete blew smoke rings. "Toast a monk and ship him in a body bag. He won't know the difference."

Stanton slapped the table. Stanton kicked a chair. It roused Bongo. It roused two whores.

They twirled their stools. They looked over. They looked back.

"A fuck-up is a fuck-up and money is money, and now I'm going to have to pay some Can Lao guys to go up to Laos to guard the fields *you* stole and replace the guards *you* kill—"

Pete slapped the table. Pete kicked a chair.

"Tran had some napalm. Chuck and Bob Relyea flew over and dropped it last night. They waxed the barracks and the ops huts at both of the camps next to Dong's. They spared the refineries and the jails, so you tell me what the fucking upshot of all that is."

Stanton crossed his legs. "You're saying . . ."

"I'm saying we now own *the only three poppy farms* south of Ba Na Key. I'm saying we've got viable slaves at all three locations. I'm saying Tran knows some Chinese chemists we can bring in to work the morphine base and get it ready for Wayne. I'm saying all three camps are fucking physically connected, with forest, mountain, and river cover, and all I need from you is some warm bodies to run the slaves and work under the Laotian end of the kadre."

Stanton sighed. "Warm bodies cost money."

"The Marvins work cheap. Bob said they fucking desert a hundred a day."

"You're missing the point. Money is money, and we're stage-1 covert. I'm accountable to other Agency sources, and now I'm going to have to tell them that the cost of your escapade is coming out of the 45% profit nut that we've earmarked for the Cause."

Pete shook his head. "The Cause gets 65. You told me that."

Stanton shook his head. "There's too many hands out. The ARVN boss heard about your little adventure and upped the rent on every transport vehicle and live body he lets us have."

Pete kicked a chair. It hit the bar. It reroused the whores. They twirled their fingers. They touched their heads. They mimed he claaaazy.

Stanton smiled. "Let's hear some good news."

Pete smiled. "We took ten kilos of morphine base out of Laos. Wayne's doing tests now."

"You shouldn't have risked him on that raid. He's the only heroin chemist we've got."

"I needed to see what he had. It won't happen ag—"

"What else? Did you talk to Litt—"

"Heads up on that. Dracula gave him a hundred grand for the ordnance. It's coming in on the pouch flight at noon."

Stanton smiled. "That means . . ."

"Right, he swung Nellis. Five G's a month, cheap for what it gets us."

Stanton coughed. "Have you got a source?"

"Bob does. Some breed in Bao Loc. He's got some U.S. shit captured back from the Cong."

"Don't skimp. Let's make Hughes and the Air Force look good."

"You don't have to tell me that."

"I'm not so sure."

"*Be sure.* We're in this for the same reason."

Stanton leaned in. "We're *here* now. We're *not in Cuba.* When the buildup starts next year, we'll have a lot more cover to work in."

Pete looked around. The whores went you claaaazy.

"You're right. And I've been in worse places."

Bao Loc was north. 94 clicks. They limo'ed up.

Mesplède booked a stretch. Chuck and Flash reclined. The pouch flight landed early. Drac delivered. Ward delivered Drac.

Old bills—C-notes—one hundred K in all.

Pete reclined. Pete dug on the countryside.

He'd called Ward. They'd talked—Saigon to Vegas. Ward ragged him. Ward ragged on narcotics.

Flash *back*—ten months—Ward *loves* dope then. Ward lauds dope at the Summit.

Dope made money. Dope pleased Drac. Dope sedated jigs.

Flash *up*—Ward is pissed—Ward has *ideals*.

Dope is bad. Dope is crass. Dope means risk. Don't disrupt my fund-book plan. Don't disrupt Drac's incursion.

Ward was Ward. Ward got pissed easy. Ward lugged a Jesus cross in his sewer.

He told Ward to visit Barb. He told Ward to watch Tiger. Check the hut/tail the cabs/vet my no-pill policy.

Pete yawned. The stretch hauled. The wheels kicked mud. Mesplède ran the radio. Chuck and Flash gawked. Dig the rivers. Dig the inlets. Dig the sampans. Dig the kute and komely gook quail.

Chuck loved Laos. Mesplède said napalm glowed. Tran said he saw a white tiger. We own it now—the Bolaven Plateau.

Three poppy farms. The Set River. Big tiger tracks.

Guéry was there now. Tran was there now. Tran ran a shorthanded crew. Six goons for three camps—slaves thus on hiatus.

The slaves survived the bombing. The old goons fried. The refineries stood untorched. Tran knew potential chemists. Tran knew potential Marv guards. Tran knew geography.

Tran say you smart. You raid Bolaven. You no raid Ba Na Key. Ba Na Key north—closed to VC—tribe farms *boocoo*. Hmong tribes. Tough. No slaves there—Hmong work *en famille*. They fight. They no hide. They no run ricky-tick.

The radio blared—discordant shit—Mesplède loved nigger jazz. The highway veered. They hit Tran Phu Street. Bao Loc—2 km.

They cut right. They passed silk looms. They passed rubber farms. They crossed the Seoi Tua Ha River. They passed beggar squads.

Mesplède tossed some chump change. The beggars descended. The beggars scratched and clawed. They passed a province hut. They passed tea farms. They passed gook priests on mopeds.

There's Bob. There's the ARVN's dump.

Dig it:

ARVN guards. K-9 Korps. Gun stacks under dropcloths—open for biz.

They pulled in. They got out. Bob saw them. Bob walked a breed up.

"This is François. He's half French, and I think he likes boys, which don't discredit all the fine shit he's got for sale."

François wore pink pj's. François wore hair curlers. François wore Chanel No. 5.

Chuck vamped him. "Hey, sweetcakes, have we met before? Did you take my ticket at Grauman's Chinese?"

François said, "Fuck you. You cheap Charlie. American Punk No. 10."

Chuck howled. Flash yukked. Mesplède roared. Pete took Bob aside.

"What have we got?"

"We got .50-caliber HMGs, MMGs up the wazoo, M-132 flamethrowers with replacement parts, .45-caliber SMGs with 30-round magazines, a fucking shitload of M-14s and 34 M-79 grenade launchers."

Pete looked over. Pete saw six pallets—fat under dropcloths.

"You figure six planeloads?"

"I figure six *big* planeloads, 'cause each stack has two stacks behind it, and we got to string out the flights to keep Wayne's shit going in."

Pete lit a cigarette. "Run down the quality."

"It's just below Army standard, which is what we want, 'cause then it qualifies as surplus, which means it won't draw no suspicion when it goes through Nellis."

Pete walked over. Pete pulled dropcloths. Pete smelled cosmoline. Wood crates/nailed planks/stencil-mark designations.

Bob walked over. "It goes to Nellis, right? Some EM unload it and drive to an Agency drop."

"Right. They won't know that they're transporting covert, so we've got to hide the shit in with some stuff they won't want to pilfer."

Bob scratched his balls. "Flamethrower parts. I got to say there ain't much demand for them in Lost Wages."

Pete nodded. Pete whistled. Pete cued Mesplède. Mesplède grabbed François and bartered in.

Pete signaled—six loads/six payments.

Mesplède bartered. François bartered. Mesplède bartered back. They talked polyglot—French-Viet—diphthongs and shouts.

Pete walked up. Pete listened. He got the *bonnes affaires*. He got the *tham tham*s. He got the Lyonnaise slang.

François rolled his eyes. François stamped his feet. François steamed up his pajamas. Mesplède rolled his eyes. Mesplède balled his fists. Mesplède smoked three Gauloises.

François went hoarse. Mesplède went hoarse. They coughed. They slapped backs. They bowed.

François said, "Okay, big daddy-o."

■ ■ ■

They drove back. They talked shit. They cut through Bien Hoa. The Cong hit ten days back—mortars predawn.

The stretch got close. They saw the mess. They saw flags at half-mast.

They cut back. They laughed. They slugged Bacardi. They told tales—Paraguay to Pigs—they goofed on CIA gaffes.

It's '62. Let's pluck the Beard. Let's shave him impotent. Let's dope the water. Let's spook the spics. Let's stage a visit from Christ.

They laughed. They drank. They vowed to free Cuba. They stopped and hit the Go-Go.

There's Wayne.

He's alone—per usual. He's pissed—per always. He's watching Bongo and his whores.

64

(Las Vegas, 11/22/64)

One year.

He knew it. Jane knew it.

They never *said* it.

Littell drove to Tiger Kab.

Littell played the radio. Radio pundits assessed. One fool stressed Jackie. One fool stressed the kids. One fool stressed innocence lost.

Jane drove to Vegas. Jane holed up. Jane stayed in his suite. They called it "Thanksgiving." The date hit. They never factored it in.

The papers rehashed it. The TV rehashed it. It rehashed all day. He left early. Jane kissed him. Jane turned on the TV. He returned late. Jane kissed him. Jane turned off the TV.

They talked. They skirted it. They discussed prosaics. Jane was mad. He'd coaxed her to Vegas. He'd coaxed her for IT.

He said he had business. He kissed Jane and walked out. He heard Jane turn on the TV.

Littell killed the radio. Littell cruised by Tiger Kab. Littell perched across the street.

He parked. He watched the hut. He saw Barb B. There's Barb in lounge garb—heels put her over six feet.

Milt Chargin ran shtick. Barb laughed. Barb palmed a package. Barb grabbed an outgoing cab. Tiger stripes—Miami West—all roads to Cuba.

Littell watched the hut. Drivers walked through—fey minions of tolerant Pete. Pete collected strays. Pete ignored their faults. Pete courted diversion. Pete said he clocked Betty's visits. Pete said he clocked Betty gone.

Two hours tops—don't kill what you can't suppress.

Littell watched the hut. A cab pulled out. Littell tailed it. The cab drove west. Littell stuck close. They hit West LV.

The cab stopped—Monroe and "J"—two men got in. The cab pulled out. Littell stuck close. They hit Tonopah Highway.

The cab stopped. The men got out. The men hit the Moulin Rouge. The cab pulled out. Littell stuck close. They drove straight back to Tiger.

Memo to Pete: No pill sales/no inferred betrayal.

Littell yawned. Littell went queasy. He skipped his dinner. Jane cooked prime rib. She'd cooked all day. She'd watched TV concurrent.

He lied his dinner off. He walked out. He invented "business."

Littell skimmed the radio. Littell caught Jack's Greatest Hits: "Ask not" and "*Ich bin.*" The passed torch and more.

He killed the sound. He drove to the Sahara. The lounge was packed. He stood ringside. He caught Barb's closer.

Barb sang "Sugar Shack." Barb blew the crescendo. She saw him. She waved. She said, "Oops."

She was bad. She knew it. She goofed on it. She played off it. She ragged her shelf life as a chick.

Men loved her. She goofed on her height. She played off it and went knock-kneed. She was a con. She played to the men who knew it.

The Bondsmen bowed. Barb jumped off stage. A heel jammed. She teetered. Littell caught her. He felt her pulse. He smelled her soap. He felt her perspiration.

They walked to the bar. They got a booth. Littell faced the TV.

Barb lit a cigarette. "Pete's idea, right? Look in on me."

"Partially."

"Partially, how?"

"I'm killing time. I thought I'd kill it with you."

Barb smiled. "I'm not complaining. I've got forty minutes."

The TV blipped. Jack's Greatest Hits revived. Paris with Jackie. Touch football games. Romps with his kids.

Barb looked over. Barb saw the TV. Barb looked straight back at Littell.

"You can't run from it."

Littell smiled. "Some of us try."

"Do you think about it?"

"It comes and goes."

"I'm all right until something reminds me. Then it gets scary."

Littell checked the screen. Jack and Bobby laughed. A waitress showed. Barb shooed her off.

"Pete never talks about it."

"We're useful. He knows it comes down to that."

Barb chained cigarettes. "Wayne knows. I figured it out."

"Did you brace him?"

"No, I just put it together."

Littell smiled. "He's in love with you."

Barb smiled. "In a tolerable way."

"We're useful. Tell yourself that the next time something reminds you."

Barb stubbed her cigarette. Barb burned her hand. She flinched and cradled it. She said, "Shit."

Littell checked her eyes. Littell saw pinholes—nerves off amphetamines.

Barb lit a cigarette. Littell checked the TV. Jack laughed. Jack worked That Old Jack Magic.

Barb said, "Jane knows."

Littell flinched. "You've never met her. And Pete wouldn't have—"

"He didn't. I heard you two being oblique and put it together."

Littell shook his head. "She's back at the hotel. She's teething on it right now."

"Do you talk about it?"

"We talk *around* it."

"Is she scared?"

"Yes, because she knows who did it, and there's no way she can be useful."

Barb smiled. Barb wrote "useful" in the air.

"I got a letter from Pete. He said it's going well."

"Do you know what he's doing there?"

"Yes."

"Do you approve?"

Barb shook her head. "I like the useful part, and I don't think about the other."

"Like the notion of plundering one nation in order to liberate another?"

Barb squeezed his hands. "*Stop it.* Remember what *you* do and who you're talking to."

Littell laughed. "Don't say you just want him to be happy."

Barb laughed. "To a free Cuba, then."

Janice Tedrow walked in. Littell saw her. Littell watched her. Barb watched him watch.

Janice saw him. Janice waved. Janice grabbed a side booth. She ordered a drink. She faced the TV. She watched Jack and Bobby.

Barb said, "You're blushing."

"No, I'm not. I'm fifty-one years old."

"You're *blushing*. I'm a redhead, and I know a blush when I see one."

Littell laughed. Barb pulled his sleeve up. Barb checked his watch.

"I have to go."

"I'll tell Pete you're okay."

"Tell him 'I'm useful.' "

"He knows that already."

Barb smiled. Barb walked. Barb went knock-kneed. Men stirred. Men watched her. Littell watched the TV.

There's Bobby with Jackie. There's Jack in the Senate. There's old Honey Fitz.

Littell got hungry. Littell ordered dinner—the prime rib he'd missed. The waitress was Jack-struck. The waitress perched by the TV.

Littell ate. Littell watched Janice. Janice watched the TV.

She sipped toddies. She chained cigarettes. She twirled her cane. She didn't *know*. Wayne Senior wouldn't tell her. He knew him well enough to say.

She looked over. She saw him watching. She got up. She maneuvered with her cane.

She cocked one hip. She stabbed her cane. She limped *con brio*. Littell pulled a chair out. Janice grabbed Barb's cigarettes.

"That redhead played my Christmas party last year."

"She's an entertainer, yes."

Janice lit a cigarette. "You're not sleeping with her. I could tell that."

Littell smiled. Littell twirled her cane.

Janice laughed. "Stop it. You're reminding me of someone."

Littell squeezed his napkin. "He used his stick on you."

Janice twirled her cane. "It was part of the divorce settlement. One million with no beating, two million with."

Littell sipped coffee. "You're volunteering more than I asked for."

"You hate him like I do. I thought you might like to know."

"Did he find out about General Kinman?"

Janice laughed. "Clark didn't bother him. The young man in question did."

"Was he worth it?"

"*It* was worth it. If I didn't do something drastic, I would have stayed with him forever."

Littell smiled. "I thought you had a life sentence there."

"Seventeen years was plenty. I loved his money and some of his style, but it wasn't enough anymore."

Littell spun the cane. "The young man?"

"The young man is a former client of yours, and he's currently abetting the war effort in Vietnam."

Littell dropped the cane. Janice snatched it up.

"You didn't know?"

"No."

"Are you shocked?"

"I'm hard to shock and easy to amuse sometimes."

Janice squeezed his hands. "And you've got old scars on your face that remind me of this temporary harelip of mine."

"Wayne's mentor put them there. He's my best friend now."

"He's the redhead's husband. Wayne told me."

Littell leaned back. "You're not playing golf. I've been looking for you."

"I'm retrieving my swing. I'm not going to walk eighteen holes with a cane."

"I enjoyed watching you play. I scheduled my breaks around it."

Janice smiled. "I've leased a cottage on the Sands course. Your view inspired me."

"I'm flattered. And you're right, the view makes all the difference."

Janice stood up. "It's off the first hole. The one with the blue shutters."

Littell stood up. Janice winked and walked away. She waved. She dropped her cane and left it there. She limped *molto con brio.*

He caught Barb's tenner. He stood ringside. He killed time. He ducked Jane's bedtime. He schemed up a trip.

I'll fly to L.A. You drive back. I'll meet you.

He drove home. The lights were on. Jane was still up. The TV was on. A newsman mourned Jack at great length.

Littell turned it off. "I have to fly to L.A. tomorrow. I'll be leaving early."

Jane spun her ashtray. "It's abrupt, and we're coming up on Thanksgiving."

"You should have come next week. It would have been better all around."

"You wanted me here, so I came. Now you're leaving."

Littell nodded. "I know, and I'm sorry."

"You wanted to see if I'd come. You were testing me. You broke a rule that we set for ourselves, and now I'm stuck in this suite."

Littell shook his head. "You could take a walk. You could get a golf lesson. You could read instead of watch TV for sixteen goddamn hours."

Jane threw her ashtray. It hit the TV.

"Given the date, how could you expect me to do anything else?"

"Given the date, we could have talked about it. Given the date, we could have stretched the rules. Given the date, you could have given up some of your goddamn secrets."

Jane threw a cup. It hit the TV.

"You carry a gun. You carry briefcases full of money. You fly around the country to see gangsters, you listen to tapes of Robert Kennedy when you think I'm sleeping, and *I've* got secrets?"

They slept solo.

He scooped up her butts. He packed a bag. He packed his briefcase. He packed three suits. He packed appeal briefs and money—ten grand in cash.

He made up the couch. He stretched out. He tried to sleep. He thought about Janice. He thought about Barb. He thought about Jane.

He tried to sleep. He thought about Barb. He thought about Janice.

He got up. He cleaned his gun. He read magazines. *Harper's* ran a piece—Mr. Hoover misbehaves.

He gave a speech. He fomented. He attacked Dr. King. He disrupted. He appalled. He stirred hate.

Littell turned the light off. Littell tried to sleep.

He counted sheep. He counted money. Skim cuts and embezzlements—civil-rights tithes.

He tried to sleep. He thought about Jane. He counted her lies. He lost count. He ricocheted.

Barb goes knock-kneed. Janice waves her cane. Janice smiles. Janice limps. Janice drops her cane.

He got up. He got dressed. He drove to McCarran. He saw a sign for Kool Menthol—all swimsuits and sun.

He turned around. He drove back. He drove to the Sands. He parked. He primped in his rearview mirror.

He walked by the golf course. He found the cottage and knocked. Janice opened up.

She saw him. She smiled. She plucked her curlers out.

65

(Saigon, 11/28/64)

White Horse—grad research. Wayne mixed morph clay and ammonia. Wayne ran three hot plates. Wayne boiled three kilos. Shit filtered out.

Wayne dumped the ammonia. Wayne cleaned the beakers. Wayne dried the bricks.

Call it: Test batch #8.

He blew twenty bricks. He filtered wrong. He fucked the process. He learned. He added steps. He sluiced out organic waste.

Pete postponed the ship date. Pete let him learn.

Wayne boiled water. Wayne gauged it. Roger—182F.

He dumped it. He poured acetic anhydride. He filled three vats. He boiled it. He *got* it.

Roger—182F.

He measured base. He chopped it. He added it. He got the mix. He got the look. He got the smell—vinegar and prune.

He sniffed it. His nose burned. It looked good—good bonds—good reaction mix.

Call it batch #9—diacetyl morphine/impure.

Wayne sneezed. Wayne rubbed his eyes. Wayne scratched his nose.

He lived at the lab. He worked at the lab. He sniffed caustic agents. He built allergies. The kadre bunked away. He dodged them. He dodged Chuck and Bob.

They bugged him. They said go Klan. They said hate spooks. They said hate like we do.

His hate was his hate. They didn't KNOW.

He lived at the lab. He slept all day. He worked all night. Day noise bugged him. He heard mopeds and chants outside. He heard slogan gobbledygook.

He slept through it. He set his clock—tracer rounds at six.

Night noise unbugged him. He heard jukebox clang downstairs. He heard music up his vents.

He did dope work. He built shelves. He filed newspapers. He crossfiled his clips. The Dallas rag and Vegas rag—a week old here.

The Dallas rag flaunted the birthday. The Dallas rag flaunted old stuff. Sidebars and *more* birthdays—"unrelated" stuff.

Where's Maynard Moore? Where's that Wendell Durfee?

Wayne checked batch #9. There—the right smell/the right burn/the right mass. Precipitants—visible—nondiacetyl mass.

Wayne worked alone. Wayne worked kadre-adjunct. The kadre was in Laos. The kadre was overworked.

Their bomb raid killed camp guards. They needed new guards. Stanton told Pete to hire some Marvs. On-duty Marvs ran expensive. Tran hired deserters—Marvs *and* VC.

Forty-two guards/eighteen Marvs/twenty-four Congs.

They worked hard. They worked cheap. They shrieked their views: Ho versus Khanh/North versus South/Mao versus LBJ.

Pete got pissed. Pete chartered laws. Pete segregated guard crews. Pete pouched notes down—Saravan to Saigon—on CIA flights boocoo.

Pete praised the kadre. Pete praised Tran. Pete passed a rumor on: The Premier P.R.-prone. The Premier order "review."

Many dope dens exist now. Many GIs come here soon—troop buildup boocoo. Dope dens big. Dope dens *bad.* My den policy need review.

Stanton didn't buy it. Stanton knew said Premier. Said Premier was a puppet. Money pulled his strings. Said Premier *taxed* his dope dens boocoo.

West Vegas stood ready. Milt Chargin told Pete. Pete pouched word to Wayne. Milt ratted pill crews. Milt snitched to Dwight Holly. Holly told the apropos Feds. West LV stood dry. The funnel stood ready. Wayne pledged the goods:

Heroin—grade 4—ready by 1/9/65.

Wayne checked the clock. Wayne checked the vats. He measured sodium carbonate. He measured chloroform. He filled three tubes.

He locked the lab. He walked downstairs. The den was dark. The den was full. A Chinaman sold cubes. A Chinaman cleaned pipes. A Chinaman hosed stray turds.

Wayne blocked his nose. Wayne walked flashlight-first.

He walked bed rows. He stubbed pallets. He kicked piss bowls. O-heads stirred. O-heads cringed. O-heads kicked out.

He strafed their eyes. He strafed their arms. He strafed their needle tracks. Arm tracks/leg tracks/dick tracks/*old* tracks/*test* tracks.

The air reeked of smoke and piss. The light scattered rats. Wayne walked. Wayne carried tape. Wayne marked eight pallet slats.

He flashed eyes. He flashed arms. He flashed a corpse. Rats had it. Rats gnawed on the crotch. Rats lapped shit water. Rats surfed the floor.

Wayne walked. Wayne checked Bongo's bed.

Bongo snored. Bongo slept with two whores. Bongo had down pillows and silk pallet slats.

Wayne flashed Bongo's eyes. Bongo slept on. Wayne made him Wendell Durfee.

It worked. It happened. It cohered. He did it—he made white horse.

He cooked all day. He filtered. He worked carbonates. He purified. He refined. He mixed charcoal and alcohol.

He hit #3—6% pure.

He walked downstairs. He selected three O-heads. He packed their pipes full. They smoked #3. They puked. They launched. They hit orbit.

He walked back up. He mixed ether. He mixed hydrochloric acid. He dissolved #3. He laced it. He mixed hydro *and* ether.

He worked all night. He waited. He watched tracer rounds. He filtered. He dried. He got precipitant flakes and got *it:*

Heroin—#4—96% pure.

He mixed sugar base. He diluted it. He cut it. He prepped eight syringes. He prepped eight swabs. He prepped eight good shots.

He yawned. He crapped out. He slept nine hours straight.

Two Marvs assisted. Two Marvs marched them in. They smelled. They outstunk his ammonia. They outfumed his carbonates.

Wayne cracked a window. Wayne measured their pupils. The Marvs jabbered in Anglo-gook:

Cleanup come—buildup come—cleanup do much good.

Wayne cooked up eight shots. Wayne fed eight spikes.

Two heads ran. Four heads grinned. Two heads pumped their veins. The Marvs grabbed the runners. The Marvs pumped their veins.

Wayne tied them off. Wayne geezed them. They seized up. They shook. Wayne flashed their eyes. Their pupils contracted. Their pupils pinned.

They nodded. They weaved. They upchucked and hurled. They doused the sink. They rubberized. They zombified.

They plopped down prone. They nodded out. The Marvs grabbed the last six. The Marvs prepped them good.

They swabbed their arms. They tied them off. They pumped out their veins. Wayne geezed them six across.

They seized up. They shook. They doused the sink. They heroinized.

The Marvs cheered. The Marvs jabbered in Anglo-gook.

Dignitaries come—that mean much money—cleanup much good.

The O-heads weaved. The O-heads bumped. The O-heads swacked and swerved. Blastoff and orbit—Big "H" *très* boocoo.

Wayne greased the Marvs. Wayne paid ten bucks U.S. The Marvs hauled the O-heads out. The lab smelled. Wayne Lysoled the sink. Wayne wiped his needles blood-free.

"If there's more of that, I'll fly."

Wayne turned around—whazzat?—Wayne dropped a needle tray.

There's Bongo. He's in bikini briefs. He's in fruit boots.

"What kind of reading can you get off little slopes like that? You need a big guy like me to gauge the fuckin' quality of your shit."

Wayne gulped a tad. Wayne checked vat dregs and spoons. Wayne saw one dose tops.

He strained it. He siphoned it. He cooked it.

Bongo said, "You always starin' at me. Then you gets to meet me formally, and you gots nothin' to say."

Wayne grabbed a tourniquet. Wayne fed a spike.

"There's this rumor goin' around that you killed these three brothers, but I don't believe it. You more the voyeur type to me."

Wayne grabbed his arms. Wayne pumped his veins. Wayne primed a fat blue.

"Cat got your tongue? You a fuckin' deaf-mute or somethin'?"

Wayne tied him off. Wayne geezed him.

Bongo seized. Bongo shook. Bongo upchucked and hurled. He doused the floor. He doused Wayne's shoes. He grinned. He weaved. He danced.

He did the Swim. He did the Wah-Watusi. He lurched. He grabbed at shelves. He stumbled out.

Wayne heard tracers. Wayne cracked his windows. There's the arc. There's the rush. There's the pink glow.

Wayne cracked the vents. Music flew up. There's "Night Train"— Sonny Liston's song.

Bongo walked back in. Bongo brought two whores. They held him. They propped him up.

He said, "Yours, baby. Around the world, free."

Wayne shook his head. One whore said, "He crazy." One whore said, "He queer."

66

(Saravan, 11/30/64)

Mail run—Aéroport de Saravan. Mail flew in. Mail hit Saigon. Mail hit Ops South. Marvs snatched kadre mail. Marvs called up the kampsite. Marvs pouched it up.

The airstrip reeked. Goats grazed adjacent. One runway/one hut.

Pete waited. Pete jeeped in. Pete brought two guards. Pete brought an ex-Cong kontingent.

The ex-Congs mingled. The ex-Congs disdained the ex-Marvs. The ex-Marvs mingled. The ex-Marvs disdained the ex-Congs.

Pete feared riots. Pete stole their guns. Pete issued rubber-bullet pumps. Pete neutered the guards. Pete pampered the slaves. They got fresh food and water. They got fresh chains.

Tran sacked a village. Tran killed VC. Tran stole their swag. Tran got canned goods and penicillin. Tran got methamphetamine.

The slaves were soft. The slaves were weak. Harvest time was near. Pete stole their "O." Pete fed them soup. Pete fed them franks and beans.

The slaves were sick—fevers and flu—Pete fed them penicillin. The slaves lacked will. The slaves lacked oomph. Pete fed them methamphetamine.

They worked triple shifts. They soared. The fields sparkled. The bulb yield soared. Tran hired six chink chemists. Said chinks cooked M-base. The refineries soared.

Wayne worked the base. Wayne pledged white horse. Wayne's production skills soared.

The mail plane touched down. Goats scattered. The pilot tossed mail sacks. Marvs deplaned fast. Pete's Congs shagged the pouch.

They ran it over. Pete pulled the letters. Pete read them through.

Ward wrote. Ward said he checked Tiger. Ward said Tiger looked good. Nellis looked good. Kinman looked good. Kinman pledged help. Airmen to unload crates/airmen to lug crates/airmen to drive crates to the Agency drop.

Ward said he saw Barb. Barb was lonely. Barb was good.

Wayne wrote. Wayne said we're on go: 1/9/65.

Fred Otash wrote. Fred had no Arden dope. Fred had no dope on D. Bruvick. Queries out/will continue/will update as told.

Barb wrote. Barb wrote vignettes. Her thoughts jumped. Her handwriting jerked.

I'm up. I'm down. I sleep odd hours.

"Not *our* odd hours. Not where we met & made love going & coming to bed."

She saw Ward. "He's hot for Wayne's stepmom." The cat missed him. "He sleeps on your pillow now."

She hung out at Tiger. "Milt kills me. He auditions all his shticks."

"Donkey Dom drives me to work. He wonders why he can't keep boyfriends, esp. considering his 'equipment.' I said, 'Maybe it's because you're a male prostitute.'"

The cat bit a maid. The cat clawed a couch. The cat bit her drummer.

"I miss you . . . I miss you . . . I get crazy when you're gone because you're the only one who knows what I do & so I go up & down & get a little crazy pretending I'm talking to you & wondering where I'll be in 5 yrs., when my regulars trade me in for a newer model & I'm not so useful. Have you ever thought about that?"

Pete read the letter. Pete smeared the ink. He smelled Barb. He felt Barb. "Up & down" fucked him up.

The camp soared. Pete jeeped through. Pete toured.

Kall it one kamp now. Straight acres—marked by fence posts and huts.

Forested borders. Clay underbrush. Bulb rows/furrows/walkways. Refinery huts and guard huts. Slave jails and ops huts.

Magic beasts roamed the forest. White tigers prowled boocoo.

Pete dug cats. Pete dug tigers. Pete dug nifty names. Pete konkokted "Tiger Kamp."

Flash sketched for kicks. Flash dug on tigers. Flash tigerized the huts. Flash painted tiger fangs and tiger stripes.

Pete cruised the walkways. Pete cruised the bulb rows. Pete watched.

Slaves raked. Slaves tilled. Slaves pulled rickshaws. Shackle lines—twelve slaves per—slaves fueled by meth.

Slaves worked. Slaves paused too long. Guards popped rubber rounds.

Laurent waved. Flash waved. Mesplède waved. Laurent urged speed—*di thi di*—Mesplède flexed his tattoos.

Pete counted stalks. Pete multiplied: bulbs per stalk/yield per bulb/sap-to-M-base. Stalks blew by. Pete blew the count. Pete mismultiplied.

He hit Ops North. The Congs took his jeep. He walked in. He saw Chuck and Bob. He saw their canned smorgasbord:

Chili and kraut. Franks and beans. Tokay/T-Bird/white port.

Chuck said, "We're losing Bob."

Pete grabbed a chair. "Why?"

"It's not like we're losing him altogether, it's more like he's relocating to help out a kindred soul."

Bob sipped T-Bird. "Chuck set me up with Wayne's daddy, unbe-fucking-knownst to Wayne, of course. His people offered me a chance to take over a snitch-Klan in Mississippi when the Army cuts me loose."

Chuck sipped Tokay. "The Feds are bankrolling his klavern. That means official sanction and discretionary leeway as to how much rowdy shit he can pull."

Pete cracked his knuckles. "It's bullshit. You'd give up our thing for the chance to torch a few churches?"

Chuck noshed beans. "Pete's got these gaps in his political education. He don't think much past Cuba."

Bob belched. "I like the discretionary part and the leadership part. I get to recruit my own Kluxers, pull my own shit and get me some mail-fraud indictments that can't be traced back to me."

Chuck snarfed franks. "How far can you go?"

"That's the $64,000 Question, so I gotta assume that 'discretionary' means according to the guidelines my handler sets up, along with shit he don't know about. Wayne Senior said I'm supposed to start with a show of force, you know, to establish my rep, which suits me just fine."

Pete lit a cigarette. "Don't let Wayne know that you're in touch with his father, and don't talk that Klan shit in front of him. He's off the deep end on niggers, and that kind of talk scares him."

Chuck laughed. "Why? He's a coon killer."

Pete laughed. "He's afraid he'll start liking your crazy shit too much."

Chuck snarfed chili. "Statements like that are politically suspect. I think you been spending too much time with Victor Charlie."

Rain hit. Bob shut the window.

"Here's why all this don't mean goodbye to the kadre. One, Mississippi runs down to the Gulf Coast. Two, you got lots of Cubans down there.

Three, I could work liaison with Chuck, funnel our profits into guns, and shoot them down to the Gulf."

Pete said, "I like it. *If* you can get a hands-off policy going with the cops and Feds down there."

Thunder hit. Chuck cracked the window. Pete looked out. Slaves whooped. Slaves danced. Slaves did the Methedrine Mambo.

Chuck said, "This fucking 'cleanup' intrigues me. You got troops coming in, and Stanton says Khanh wants Saigon to look like Disneyland for all the fucking journalists and hotshots."

Slaves shook their chains. Slaves did the Shackle Shimmy-Shake.

Bob said, "I want to build up a roll for Mississippi. Maybe I can sell some surplus shit to the troops coming in."

Pete turned around. "No one sells to our troops. I'll kill anyone who does."

Chuck laughed. "Pete's got that World War II thing. *Semper fi,* Boss."

Bob laughed. "He *dinky dau.* He get too sentimental."

Pete pulled his piece. Pete dumped three rounds. Pete spun the chamber. Chuck laughed. Bob made the jack-off sign.

Pete aimed. Pete pulled the trigger. He shot Bob three times. The hammer clicked three times. He hit three blank chambers.

Bob screamed. Bob puked. Bob hurled franks and beans.

DOCUMENT INSERT: 11/30/64. Verbatim FBI telephone call tran-
script. Marked: "Recorded at the Director's Request"/"Classified
Confidential 1-A: Director's Eyes Only." Speaking: Director Hoover,
Ward J. Littell.

JEH: Good afternoon, Mr. Littell.

WJL: Good afternoon, Sir.

JEH: Let's discuss Southeast Asia.

WJL: I'm afraid I'm not informed on the topic, Sir.

JEH: I was informed that Pierre Bondurant and Wayne Tedrow
Junior have gone on covert contract status with a stellar spy
agency. Little birdies tell me things, and I would be remiss not to
share them with you.

WJL: I was aware of that, Sir.

JEH: They are stationed in Vietnam, no less.

WJL: Yes, Sir.

JEH: Would you care to expand your answers?

WJL: I'd rather not be too specific. I think you know enough
about Pete's past dealings and Wayne Junior's chemistry
background to be able to extrapolate.

JEH: I am extrapolating at warp speed. I must conclude that
our Italian friends have revised their fatuously conceived "Clean-
Town Policy" in Las Vegas.

WJL: Yes, but the distribution will be rigorously localized.

JEH: I see a salutary convergence. The distribution will accom-
modate Count Dracula's prejudices and facilitate our Italian
friends' desire to bilk him.

WJL: It's an astute observation, Sir.

JEH: Our friends must bristle at the thought of Jimmy Hoffa's
forthcoming doom.

WJL: They know he's finished, Sir. They know the appeals
process will terminate within two years.

JEH: The attendant irony has not escaped me. A gaudy homicide served to neutralize the Dark Prince, yet the Dark Prince toppled his bete noire in the end.

WJL: I have often considered that irony, Sir.

JEH: The Prince is now a senator-elect. Have you considered
how he'll fare?

WJL: I haven't given it much thought.

JEH: A barefaced lie, Mr. Littell, and wholly unworthy of you.

WJL: I'll concede, Sir.

JEH: Do you think he will sponsor anti-organized crime legislation?

WJL: I would hope not.

JEH: Do you think he will attack organized crime from the Senate floor?

WJL: I would hope not.

JEH: Do you think he learned an enduring lesson from that gaudy homicide?

WJL: I would hope so.

JEH: I will not comment on your complex relationship with Robert F. Kennedy.

WJL: Your comments to date are most eloquent, Sir.

JEH: Let's jump from the frying pan to the fire. I'm meeting with Martin Lucifer King tomorrow.

WJL: The purpose of the meeting, Sir?

JEH: Lucifer requested it. He wants to discuss my attacks in the press. Lyle Holly has informed me that Lucifer has correctly added two and two and has determined that I've run black-bag operations against him, which must vex him as well.

WJL: How did he learn? Do you suspect a leak?

JEH: No. I publicly referred to information that Lucifer disseminated in private and betrayed bug and tap placements in that manner. Those references were, of course, deliberate.

WJL: I concluded that, Sir.

JEH: Lucifer, Rustin and the others now shut their mouths in hotel rooms. Lucifer has confined his sexual antics to beds outside my electronic range.

WJL: You're implying a larger design here, Sir.

JEH: You are correct. I am going to drastically upscale my operations against Lucifer and the SCLC. You are to stop donating organized-crime money to the organization, but to continue to meet with Bayard Rustin. You will continue to portray yourself as an ardent supporter whose Mob pilfering source has run dry. You will wear wires to your meetings with Rustin. You will wheedle him into suggesting meetings. You will exploit his homosexuality and susceptibility to sincere and politically unstable men.

WJL: Yes, Sir.

JEH: This endeavor will be Stage-1 Covert. I have dubbed it

OPERATION BLACK RABBIT. The title bows to the sex drive, prowess and heedlessly puerile demeanor of our long-eared friends. You will receive copies of most memoranda, because you are a deft extrapolator of complex data. Code names have been assigned to the key personnel. You will use them in place of real names. They derive from the rabbit motif and hint at the inherent psyches of the subjects.

WJL: You've whetted my appetite, Sir.

JEH: Martin Luther King will be RED RABBIT. Bayard Rustin will be PINK RABBIT. Lyle Holly will be WHITE RABBIT. You will be most appropriately known as CRUSADER RABBIT.

WJL: It's a witty touch, Sir.

JEH: I want you to learn what King has planned in the south. Your data will supplant Lyle Holly's. I'm going to launch a White-Hate Cointelpro in Louisiana, Alabama and Mississippi, and I want information to complement that incursion.

WJL: You've targeted the Klan, Sir? For mail-fraud indictments?

JEH: I've targeted the most violent, inept, felony-prone and altogether outlandish Klan groups in that three-state vector. God will punish them for lynchings and castrations, should He lapse on the side of compassion and find them unjustified. I will punish them for Federal Mail Fraud.

WJL: You've divided the punishment well, Sir.

JEH: The Cointelpro will begin in June, '65. Your old chum Wayne Senior has recruited a man to form his own splinter Klan. The man will return from Army service and begin his assignment in May.

WJL: Will Wayne Senior run—

JEH: Wayne Senior will be code-named FATHER RABBIT. The Klan runner will be named WILD RABBIT. I have withdrawn the funding for all of Wayne Senior's long-standing informant Klans, with his approval. I want to consolidate my anti-Klan broadside under the banner of WILD RABBIT's stalwart group, the Regal Knights of the KKK.

WJL: The name packs a punch, Sir.

JEH: You're being egregiously flip, Mr. Littell. I know you are delighted, and I know you disapprove as well. Do not underline the latter.

WJL: I apologize, Sir.

JEH: To continue. Both operations will be run by Dwight Holly,

who will be code-named BLUE RABBIT. Dwight has resigned from
the U.S. Attorney's Office and has transferred back to the Bureau. I
chose him because he is a brilliant operative. He is also Lyle
Holly's brother, and Lyle knows the SCLC better than any white
man alive.

WJL: I'm confused, Sir. I thought Dwight was estranged from
Wayne Senior.

JEH: Estrangement comes and goes. Dwight and Wayne Senior
have reconciled. The Negroes that Wayne Junior killed were simply
a temporary roadblock. Wayne Senior is estranged from Wayne
Junior now, in the manner of the patriarchy worldwide.

WJL: Will I need to deal with Wayne Sen—

JEH: Not directly. You trumped him on your courier arrange-
ment, and he's sustained a simmering grudge.

WJL: Dwight Holly has never been a friend to me, Sir.

JEH: Dwight acknowledges your gifts, however reluctantly. You
saved him face on the dead-Negro front, which indebted him to
you. That said, I must observe that Dwight Chalfont Holly hates
indebtedness and was having you spot-tailed by agents of the U.S.
Attorney's Office, as part of an ill-conceived plan to build a derogatory profile against you. He considered you a dangerous presence
in Nevada.

WJL: Given Dwight's nature, that's a compliment.

JEH: It pained him to pull the tails. He gives up very badly. You
share that trait.

WJL: Thank you, Sir.

JEH: Thank me with hard work on OPERATION BLACK RAB-
BIT.

WJL: I will, Sir. In the meantime, would you like me to pull any
of the bugs you've placed against the SCLC?

JEH: No. They might get careless and talk.

WJL: That's true, Sir.

JEH: Lucifer has been awarded the Nobel Peace Prize. It infuri-
ates me as much as I'm sure it moves you.

WJL: I'm moved, yes.

JEH: Those three words define your value to me.

WJL: Yes, Sir.

JEH: Learn your rabbit codes.

WJL: I will, Sir.

JEH: Good afternoon, Mr. Littell.

WJL: Good afternoon, Sir.

DOCUMENT INSERT: 12/2/64. Washington *Post* article.

HOOVER MEETS WITH KING; AIDES DESCRIBE "TENSE CONFRONTATION"

Washington, D.C., December 1.

FBI Director J. Edgar Hoover and Assistant Director Cartha DeLoach today met with Dr. Martin Luther King, Jr. and his aides Ralph Abernathy and Walter Fauntroy. The meeting took place in Hoover's office at FBI Headquarters.

A range of topics were discussed, including the alleged presence of Communists and Communist sympathizers within the civil-rights movement and the FBI's handling of police brutality charges levied by Negroes and civil-rights workers in the south. King clarified recent statements he had made pertaining to the conduct of FBI agents in Mississippi and their alleged fraternizing with local law-enforcement officials. Hoover countered with a recitation of recent FBI successes in Mississippi and Alabama.

It was expected that rumors of FBI bugs and wiretaps, allegedly deployed against King and the Southern Christian Leadership Conference, would be discussed. "This was not the case," Dr. Abernathy said. "The dialogue was increasingly subsumed by Mr. Hoover's monologues against Communists and his repeated contention that 'in due time' attitudes and practices in the south would change."

"Mr. Hoover encouraged Dr. King to 'get out the Negro vote,'" Mr. Fauntroy said. "He did not offer a substantive pledge of support for civil-rights workers in great peril at this very moment."

Both aides described the meeting, which lasted one hour, as "tense." Following the meeting, King met with reporters and stated he believed that he and Mr. Hoover had reached "new levels of understanding."

Hoover declined to comment. Assistant Director DeLoach issued a press release that covered the topics discussed.

DOCUMENT INSERT: 12/11/64. Los Angeles *Times* article.

KING ACCEPTS PEACE PRIZE; EXPRESSES "ABIDING FAITH" IN U.S.

Oslo University. Oslo, Norway, December 10.

With Norwegian royalty and members of the Norwegian Parliament in attendance, the Reverend Martin Luther King, Jr. stepped on stage to receive the Nobel Peace Prize.

The chairman of the Norwegian Parliament introduced Dr. King as "an undaunted champion of peace, the first person in the western world to have shown us that a struggle can be waged without violence."

Dr. King, visibly moved by the introduction, climbed on stage to accept the award. He said that he considered it "a profound recognition that nonviolence is the answer to the crucial political and moral question of our time, the need for man to overcome violence and oppression without resorting to violence and oppression."

Speaking into glaring television lights and a sea of rapt faces, Dr. King continued. "I refuse to accept the belief that man is mere flotsam and jetsam in the river of life which surrounds him," he said. "I refuse to accept the view that mankind is so tragically bound to the starless midnight of racism and war that the bright daylight of peace and brotherhood can never become a reality."

Citing the "tortuous road which has led from Montgomery, Alabama to Oslo," Dr. King said that the Nobel Prize was really for the "millions of Negroes on whose behalf he stood here today."

"Their names will never make Who's Who," Dr. King said. "Yet when the years have rolled past and when the blazing light of truth is focused on this marvelous age in which we live, men and women will know and children will be taught that we have a finer land, a better people, a more noble civilization, because these humble children of God were willing to suffer for righteousness' sake."

Thunderous applause greeted Dr. King's address. Hundreds of students, carrying torches, surrounded a large Christmas tree and greeted Dr. King and his entourage as they departed.

DOCUMENT INSERT: 12/16/64. Internal memorandum. Marked: "Stage-1 Covert"/"Director's Eyes Only"/"Destroy After Reading." To: Director Hoover. From: SA Dwight Holly.

Sir,

Per our phone conversation:

I agree. In light of your recent meeting with SUBJECT KING, you should suspend all public attacks and derogatory references to him, which should serve to deepen the cover needed to mount the SCLC and WHITE-HATE arms of OPERATION BLACK RABBIT. I agree further that no memorandums should be filed by any participant and/or circulant, that a strict read-and-burn policy should be observed and that all telephone communiqués should be patched through Bureau scramblers.

Per said participants/targets and our stated objectives:

1 - BLUE RABBIT (the undersigned/SA D. C. Holly). To oversee and coordinate both operational arms and direct the activities of:

2 - WHITE RABBIT (Lyle D. Holly). Our plant within SCLC. Conduit for data pertaining to SCLC policy and exploitable personal data on TARGETS KING and RUSTIN.

3 - CRUSADER RABBIT (Ward J. Littell). Cosmetically vouched civil-rights sympathizer. Has donated $180,000 in cosmetically proffered organized-crime funds, allegedly pilfered from organized-crime sources. Our plant, charged to tape and extract incriminating, embarrassing and compromising data from TARGET RUSTIN.

4 - FATHER RABBIT (Wayne Tedrow Senior). Conservative pamphleteer, covert handler of FBI informants and long-term KKK mail-fraud operative. Our liaison to the WHITE-HATE arm of OPERATION BLACK RABBIT. Liaison to our newly recruited Klan runner. Charged to provide said runner with lists of his hate pamphlet subscribers, including those within the Oklahoma & Missouri state prison systems, and to aid said runner in his Klan recruiting.

5 - WILD RABBIT (U.S. Army Staff Sgt. Bob D. Relyea). Said Klan runner, currently on duty with Military Police Battalion 618 in Saigon, Vietnam, and on loan-out to (Stage-1 Covert) CIA operation in Laos. (Note: Sgt. Relyea refuses to reveal the details of his current assignment and will not divulge the names of his CIA handler or ops colleagues. I did not pursue this inquiry. Sgt. Relyea is observing Stage-1 sanctions and secrecy waivers, and this speaks well of his ability to honor such.)

Sgt. Relyea is an experienced hate pamphleteer and a former Missouri State prison guard with pre-existing segregationist contacts throughout the midwest and south. He continues to mail hate pamphlets of his own design throughout the Missouri prison system. Sgt. Relyea will be discharged from the Army 5/65 and will terminate his CIA ops at that time. We can expect him to begin work on OPERATION BLACK RABBIT in early 6/65.

Per targets RED RABBIT (Martin Luther King) and PINK RABBIT (Bayard Rustin) and our objectives.

Said objectives:

1 - To discredit RED RABBIT and PINK RABBIT and undermine their subversively socialistic designs.

2 - Via the accumulating and disseminating of incriminating

and/or embarrassing data pertaining to their Communist associations, hypocritical moral behavior and sexual degeneracy.

3 - To precisely orchestrate the release of said data, in order to reveal the socialistic underpinnings of the entire civil-rights movement.

4 - To create distrust within the civil-rights movement.

5 - To engender distrust and resentment against RED RABBIT within the Negro community and undercut the recent non-Negro cache that RED RABBIT has engineered.

6 - To reveal the Socialist-Communist designs of RED RABBIT, the SCLC and the civil-rights movement and influence an effective political backlash.

7 - To assail RED RABBIT's obviously disturbed and deteriorated psyche with an anonymous mail campaign.

8 - To implement the WHITE-HATE arm of OPERATION BLACK RABBIT concurrent with 1-7, in order to buttress the FBI's anti-Klan, anti-racist credentials and rebuff anti-FBI sentiment disseminated by civil-rights provocateurs and members of the liberal-socialist press.

In addition, I urge:

9 - SCLC MAIL COVERS. The intercepting, reading, logging and resending of all U.S. and foreign mail sent to the main and regional SCLC Offices.

10 - SCLC TRASH COVERS. The examination, logging & evidentiary seizure of all garbage and discard material dumped in trash bins at all SCLC Offices.

11 - An anonymous letter, to be written from a Negro perspective and sent to RED RABBIT's home in Atlanta.

The letter will begin "King, look into your heart" and will recount what a "grim farce" the Nobel Peace Prize and RED RABBIT's other recent accolades are held to be within the mainstream Negro community. The letter will subtly urge RED RABBIT to commit suicide rather than risk further disfavor within the Negro community, and will include bug-tap excerpts, pertaining to RED RABBIT's promiscuity, to buttress your deliberate public statements and convince RED RABBIT that those statements are widely received and accepted by mainstream Negroes.

In closing:

Our bugs and wiretaps remain in place, although they are severely compromised. Per our last phone call, I agree with your assessment. OPERATION BLACK RABBIT must launch and sustain at Stage-1 Covert status. RED RABBIT has reached an unbearably high level of public acceptance that only our most diligent and secretive efforts will be able to dislodge.

Respectfully,

D.C.H.

DOCUMENT INSERT: 12/21/64. Pouch communiqué. To: John Stanton. From: Pete Bondurant. Marked: "Hand Pouch Deliver Only"/ "Destroy Upon Reading."

J.S.,

Wayne hit paydirt. We're on go for 1/9/65, & after final distribution, I'm predicting a net profit of $320,000. That makes the kadre's profit nut (45%) about $150,000. Right now I'm working out the details, but the plan is unchanged.

Laurent, Chuck and Flash will purchase weapons on the right-wing circuit in Texas & the south & will funnel them to exiles on the Gulf. That's the essential plan, with one proviso.

We've both been the coastal harassment route, and running missions out of South Florida & the Gulf got us nowhere. I think our exiles should take advantage of being Cuban & should conduit the weapons to anti-Castro groups inside Cuba. I'm emphatic about this.

What do you think? Please reply ASAP.

P.B.

DOCUMENT INSERT: 12/26/64. Pouch communiqué. To: Pete Bondurant. From John Stanton. Marked: "Hand Pouch Deliver Only"/ "Destroy Upon Reading."

P.B.,

I approve the general outline of your plan and agree that our ultimate goal should be to provide on-island dissidents with the weapons our net profits secure. That said, I should again point out that you're jumping the gun on the Cuban end of things. Make no specific profit distribution plans until our in-country costs can be assessed, with all monies flagged for laundering through appropriate Agency fronts. We do not want our Cuban "contributions" to be traceable back to our Las Vegas business.

To close:

The Saigon cleanup will be implemented soon. A Can Lao contin-

gent will secure the area around Khanh Hoi, but I have been
assured that the lab will not be touched. Have Tedrow secure the
lab and be off the premises by the a.m. of 1/8/65.

Por la Causa,

J.S.

DOCUMENT INSERT: 1/6/65. Body-wire transcript. Marked: "Route
to: Director/Blue Rabbit/White Rabbit/Father Rabbit/Live Tape
Destroyed/Read & Burn."

Location: Washington, D.C. (Lafayette Park). Date:
1/4/65/0842 hrs. Speaking: CRUSADER RABBIT/PINK RABBIT.

CR (conversation in progress): What I (static/ambient noise)
read in the press. Dr. King sounded encour—

PR (laughing): With Martin, nonviolence extends to the absence
of invective (pause/2.1 seconds). No, Hoover was rude and
intractable. Martin said he was shaking.

CR: No progress, then?

PR: None. He did not affirm or deny the existence of the bugs
and the taps. (Static/2.8 seconds.) Didn't really press it. He's so
goddamn Christlike at times.

CR: Dr. King was wise not to rile him.

PR: You're right, Ward. You have a hateful lunatic in his declin-
ing years and a hugely important figure in his ascent. You have to
believe that people will see through to the gist of that.

CR: Never condescend or underest (ambient noise/2.9 seconds)
abilities.

PR: That was reinforced for Martin soon after.

CR: How—

PR (interrupting): Martin received a letter, and regretfully
Coretta saw it first. It was allegedly written by a Negro man, who
urged Martin to kill himself. There were (static/3.3 seconds) refer-
ences, and I won't comment on their veracity, to philanderings that
Martin (static/1.6 seconds) may or may not have committed.
Coretta was (pause/0.9 seconds) well, she was devastated.

CR: Jesus Christ.

PR: That about says it.

(Static/ambient noise/9.3 seconds.)

PR (conversation in progress): No saint, but I never fully
grasped the man's evil nature until that moment. (Pause/4.1 sec-

onds/PR laughs) Why so glum, Ward? Really, you're looking positively spectral.

CR: I can't give you any more money, Bayard. It's getting too risky on my end. (Static/0.8 seconds) later, but not for the foreseeable future.

PR: You needn't (pause/2.2 seconds). Stop with the glum looks, child. You've done the cause a world of good, and I for one hope you'll stay in touch.

CR: I want to. You know how I feel.

PR: I do indeed. I enjoy our talks, and I rely on your perceptions of the FBI mindset.

CR: I'll continue to offer them. And I'm always passing through D.C.

PR: I'm always good for a drink or a cup of coffee.

CR (static/3.4 seconds/conversation in progress): Dr. King have planned?

PR: We've got a big push coming up in Selma, Alabama. We're making plans to reprise "Freedom Summer" in Mississippi, and we've targeted Eastern Louisiana in June.

CR: You've got a strong Klan presence there. The Baton Rouge Office has a substantial file.

PR: Bogalusa's a simmering hotbed of our pointy-headed friends. We're going to mount voter registration drives and vex them out of their sheets.

CR (laughing/ambient noise/20 seconds): Anticipate resistance?

PR: Yes, but Martin was encouraged by the FBI's presence in Mississippi last summer, and he's convinced that the evil Mr. Hoover will work for the safety of our people, however reluctant—
(Sustained static/tape ends here.)

DOCUMENT INSERT: 1/7/65. Courier message: Saravan, Laos, to Saigon, South Vietnam.

To: Wayne Tedrow Junior. From: Pete Bondurant. Marked: "Hand Pouch Deliver."

W.T.,
Be ready to follow first shipment stateside a.m. of 1/9/65. Be off lab premises by 1/8. Urgent! Respond today!
P.B.

DOCUMENT INSERT: 1/8/65. Courier message: Saravan, Laos, to Saigon, South Vietnam.

To: Wayne Tedrow Junior. From: Pete Bondurant. Marked: "Hand Pouch Deliver."

W.T.,

Board up lab & vacate immediately! Urgent! Respond immediately!

P.B.

67

(Saigon, 1/9/65)

Let's stay. Let's get close. Let's *watch.*

The lab was secure. He pouched Chuck last night: I'll meet Pete/Tan Son Nhut Airport/flight 29. I packed the shit. I hid it—check the box marked "Flamethrower Parts."

Let's linger. Let's get close. Let's watch the "Cleanup."

The Can Lao hit last night. The Can Lao precleaned. They stink-bombed the Go-Go. They ran out the patrons. They ran out the whores. They locked up the dope den. They secured the O-heads. Said O-heads dozed on.

Wayne checked his watch—6:14 a.m.—Wayne checked his window.

Marvs draped flags. Marvs unfurled banners. Marvs muscled vendors out. Marvs stole their cash. Marvs dumped their stalls. Marvs cued hose crews up.

The crews aimed. The crews fired. Water smashed walls and stalls. Water squashed fruit. Water launched debris and scoured graffiti. Vendors flew—flyweights—hose confetti.

The Marvs raised banners. There's LBJ. Dig his big schnoz and Smile of Love. There's Premier Khanh. He's got big teeth. Dig his Big Smirk of Love.

A vendor flew. Water tossed him. Water tossed rickshaw bikes.

"You a watchin' motherfucker."

Wayne gulped a tad. Wayne turned around. Wayne saw Bongo.

In his tight fruit briefs. In his pointy fruit boots. With a chubby whore.

"You know what I like about you? It's that 'meek-shall-inherit-the-earth' thing. You like to watch, but you never say a motherfuckin' word."

The whore wore skivvies. The whore wore thigh hickeys. The whore wore cigarette burns.

"You like her? I call her 'Ashtray.' You don't need to reach for one when she's around."

Wayne shut the window. Bongo hoisted his balls. Bongo pumped up his veins.

"I figured I'd trade you for a taste. I get to geez, you get to watch Ashtray french me."

Wayne smiled. Wayne gulped a tad. Wayne unlocked his closet.

He prepped water. He prepped a spike. He prepped a spoon. He prepped horse. He cooked it. He siphoned it in.

Bongo laughed. Ashtray giggled. Wayne blocked their view. He siphoned in ammonia. He siphoned in rat poison. He siphoned in strychnine.

Bongo said, "You slow, you know that?"

Wayne turned around. Bongo looped a tourniquet. Bongo tied off a vein.

Wayne saw it. Wayne tapped it. Wayne jabbed it. Wayne pushed the plunger in sloooooow.

There now—how's that?

Bongo lurched. Bongo jumped. Bongo sprayed piss and shit. Bongo fell down and spasmed and thrashed.

Wayne stepped back. Wayne watched. Ashtray stepped up close.

Bongo coughed foam. Bongo coughed blood. Bongo bit his tongue off. Wayne stepped up. Wayne stepped on his head. Wayne cracked his skull.

Ashtray held her nose. Ashtray crossed herself. Ashtray kicked Bongo in the balls. Wayne grabbed him. Wayne dragged him. Wayne dropped him down the air vent.

Ashtray said, "Bongo cheap Charlie. Bongo number ten."

Wayne saw Leroy and Cur-ti. Wayne saw Wendell Durfee.

More cleanup—his and theirs.

Wayne cleaned the lab. Wayne watched the outside show. Marvs hosed monks. Marvs hosed walls. Marvs abridged graffiti.

The vent shook. Rats bopped through. Rats found Bongo. Rats ate him.

10:05 a.m.—flight time soon.

Theeeeere—

Voices and clumps now—two clicks downstairs. There—it's coming— you knew it would.

Wayne walked down. Wayne stood on the landing. Wayne found a shadow patch.

There—ten Can Lao goons. Two five-man teams paired off. They've got flashlights and silencered magnums. They've got hoses/flamethrowers/sacks.

They dispersed. They walked the pallet rows. They shot faces in tight.

It went soft—silencers—head shots in light.

They flashed. They shot. They dumped shells and reloaded. Heads snapped inside halos. Heads cracked pallet slats.

Opium—*hush now anesthesia*—in slow and tight.

Wayne watched. Wayne saw faces alight. B-girls and Ashtray. Uncle Ho–types.

The goons finished up. The goons regrouped in the doorway. The goons stood way back.

A goon aimed a toaster. Said goon strafed low. Said goon cooked body rows tight.

Three sweeps out and back. Flame levels in tight.

The goon turned the toaster off. A goon strafed a hose. Said goon sprayed water down tight.

Flames sputtered. Bodies flared. Pallets cracked.

Wayne watched. The goons regrouped. The goons walked and dispersed.

They took their pants off. They kicked through hose water. They lugged gunnysacks. They poured out quicklime. They perfumed bodies. They flour-dipped flesh.

DOCUMENT INSERT: 2/8/65. Internal memorandum. Topic: OPER-
ATION BLACK RABBIT. To: DIRECTOR. From: BLUE RABBIT.
Marked: "Stage-1 Covert"/"Eyes Only"/"Read and Burn."

Sir,

My first summary report on OBR.

1 - CRUSADER RABBIT met PINK RABBIT on two occasions in
Washington, D.C. (1/6/65, 1/19/65) and forwarded his tapes to
me. Per Stage-1 Covert guidelines, I personally transcribed the
tapes and destroyed the live tape copies. Tape #1 and Tape #2
transcripts are included (Addendum #A) with this memorandum.
Per guidelines, please read and burn.

2 - Although there were numerous moments of poor sound
quality, I feel confident in my assessment of the tapes. It is obvious
that the effeminate and witty PINK RABBIT is much taken with
the wit, beautifully feigned sincerity and ardently expressed ideals
of CRUSADER RABBIT. You were farsighted in your instinct to
match them up. PINK RABBIT accepted CRUSADER RABBIT's
stated withdrawal of "pilfered" organized-crime monies with mag-
nanimity and both men expressed a desire to "keep in touch." That
desire, expressed on Tape #1, was confirmed by the second meeting of PINK RABBIT and CRUSADER RABBIT, recorded on Tape #2.

3 - CRUSADER RABBIT deftly questioned PINK RABBIT on both
tapes. (See transcripts.) To date, however, PINK RABBIT has
revealed only information already revealed by our "in-house"
SCLC source, WHITE RABBIT. The broad outline includes:

3-A: Planned agitation in Selma, Alabama (picketing, boycotts,
voter-registration drives);

3-B: A (6/65) projected school desegregation drive in Chicago;

3-C: Early plans (but no compelling specifics) regarding SCLC
participation in a second "Freedom Summer" campaign of agitation
in Mississippi;

3-D: Planned agitation in and around Bogalusa, Louisiana, to
commence in 6/65.

4 - I've reviewed the recent tapes retrieved from our remaining
hotel-room bug-posts. RED RABBIT, PINK RABBIT and other SCLC
members have stayed in said rooms on a total of 14 occasions
from 1/1/65 to 2/4/65. No salient information was gleaned. The
innocuous conversations and frequent whispers indicate that the

subjects suspected the presence of electronic surveillance. Said bugs will remain in place.

5 - WHITE RABBIT reports that RED RABBIT, PINK RABBIT and other SCLC members have discussed the anonymous "suicide letter" sent to RED RABBIT and concluded that it derived from an FBI source. WHITE RABBIT further reports that RED RABBIT and PINK RABBIT have verbally attacked you on numerous recent occasions, much in the manner that PINK RABBIT attacked you on Tape Transcript #1. WHITE RABBIT stated that RED RABBIT was "very upset" by the letter, especially the "crippling effect" it had on his wife.

6 - Per MAIL COVERS. To date, assigned agents have intercepted, logged and remailed numerous letters of support, along with large and small donations to the SCLC, many of them sent by notable leftist-sympathizers, members of Communist front groups and movie stars, among them Danny Kaye, Burt Lancaster, Walter Pidgeon, Burl Ives, Spencer Tracy, Rock Hudson, Natalie Wood and numerous folk singers of lesser repute. (See Addendum List #B for details. Per guidelines, please read and burn.)

7 - Per TRASH COVERS. To date, assigned agents have collected and logged large quantities of discarded left-wing periodicals and risqué magazines with photographs of nude white women, along with innocuous and non-itemized trash. (See Addendum List #C for inventory.) (Note: An Addendum List #B inventory log will soon be compiled & stored per Stage-1 Covert guidelines. It will be used to facilitate, should you so direct, an SCLC BANK ACCOUNT COVER, to determine if the above-noted contributions were banked legally, which should help us gauge the viability of an IRS cross-check of the SCLC's federal and state tax returns.)

In conclusion:

All COVERS to proceed as directed. A summary report on the WHITE-HATE arm of OPERATION BLACK RABBIT to follow.

Respectfully,
BLUE RABBIT

DOCUMENT INSERT: 2/20/65. Internal memorandum. Topic: WHITE-HATE/OPERATION BLACK RABBIT. To: DIRECTOR. From: BLUE RABBIT. Marked: "Stage-1 Covert"/"Eyes Only"/"Read and Burn."

Sir,

My first summary report on the WHITE-HATE arm of OBR.

1 - I have compiled, with the help of FATHER RABBIT's aides, a list of potentially dissident Klansmen now at loose ends since FATHER RABBIT dissolved his previously funded informant Klan groups in 12/64. (See Addendum #A for list of said Klansmen.) (Note: Per Stage-1 guidelines, please read and burn said addendum. I have retained an original copy, per guidelines.)

Also, FATHER RABBIT has supplied (see Addendum #B/read & burn) a 14,000 name list of white male hate-pamphlet subscribers in Louisiana and Mississippi, all devotees of specific segregationist/anti-Negro tract series distributed by FATHER RABBIT's organization. A criminal records cross-check of these subscribers has yielded the names of 921 men with misdemeanor and felony arrests and memberships in extreme right-wing organizations.

2 - My plan would be to have FATHER RABBIT solicit these men by mail, under an "anonymous patriot" letterhead, and refer them by mail to WILD RABBIT, upon his (5/65) release from the U.S. Army. WILD RABBIT would assess the mail he has received, contact the most promising prospects and build the nucleus of his new Klan group on that basis. He will establish boundaries as to what and what not his recruits can do, and gather information on their previous hate-group associations. WILD RABBIT will also define their future informant duties.

3 - CRUSADER RABBIT and WHITE RABBIT have mentioned the proposed "Second Freedom Summer" agitation campaign in Mississippi and planned (6/65) agitation in and around Bogalusa, Louisiana. WILD RABBIT wants to exploit these situations, and I believe that if he delivers a properly restrained but somehow flamboyant show of force in that region at that time, he will be able to mobilize a sizable number of recruits resultant. To further induce subservience in his recruits, WILD RABBIT will supply them with low-quality rifles and sidearms purchased by his friend CHARLES "CHUCK" ROGERS (white male/age 43), a covert CIA contract employee currently serving with WILD RABBIT in Vietnam. ROGERS has extensive gun connections among rightist Cuban exile groups in the Gulf Coast region.

4 - WILD RABBIT has also established a "Hate-Leaflet Mail Ministry" among convicts and ex-convicts he knew while working as a Missouri state prison guard, and plans to recruit from the "eager beaver" parolees who contact him upon their release. I believe that this is also a viable recruiting approach.

In conclusion:

I believe that we are theoretically operational as of this (2/20/65) date. Please respond as your schedule allows.

Respectfully,

BLUE RABBIT

DOCUMENT INSERT: 3/1/65. Internal memorandum. Topic: OPERATION BLACK RABBIT/2/20/65 MEMO. To: BLUE RABBIT. From: DIRECTOR. Marked: "Stage-1 Covert"/"Eyes Only"/"Read and Burn."

BLUE RABBIT,

Consider the proposed measures described in your 2/20/65 memo approved in full. Cold funds to follow. You may share information on a need-to-know basis with FATHER RABBIT and WHITE RABBIT. Given his suspect ideology, do not share any WHITE-HATE information or in any way contact CRUSADER RABBIT, unless so directed.

DOCUMENT INSERT: 3/8/65. Pouch communiqué. To: John Stanton. From: Pete Bondurant. Marked: "Hand Pouch Deliver Only"/"Destroy Upon Reading."

J.S.,

We're operational on both ends now. Here's the summary you asked for.

It's all running smooth. A) - Milt Chargin greased cops working the Records Divisions of the Vegas PD & Clark County Sheriff's & got a list of all the previously busted colored junkies in West Vegas.

B) - I recruited 4 expendable colored pushers to work the bottom-rung distribution in West LV. They've got menial casino jobs & were happy to get the gigs. I gave them copies of the prev. ment'd junkie list & had them supply the junkies with free pops taken from our 1st stateside shipment of 1/9/65. The "free samples" got them anxious for more. I told my 4 guys to push "free tastes" on anybody who asked, colored only. They got a lot of tak-ers & we got a lot of steady "Clients" (Milt C.'s word, not mine).

C) - I lean on the 4 guys periodically & up to now I'm convinced that they (1) haven't stolen kadre merchandise; (2) haven't sold to non-Negro clients; (3) haven't snitched off kadre or Tiger Kab personnel; (4) haven't bragged to their lowlife pals & implicated kadre or Tiger Kab personnel & will not (5) do so if they get popped, which is unlikely, because (6) Milt has greased the LVPD & Sheriff's Narco squads & has secured a hands-off policy, & if any 1 of the 4 is popped, the plan is to bail them out & clip them before they talk too much.

So, (7), everything is buffered. Tiger drivers deliver the mer-chandise to drop points & the pushers pick it up, distribute it & funnel the money back the same way. The drivers are all solid pros & will not talk if busted. On his one stateside run, Wayne periodi-cally spot-tailed the pushers & determined that they weren't skim-ming or fucking up other ways. Wayne's got an evil reputation on the west side & it keeps the pushers on a tight leash.

D) - As you know, Wayne's made one rotation from Saigon & sent the 2nd shipment (4 lbs) stateside on 3/2/65. Rogers, Relyea, Mesplede, Guery & Elorde remain in Laos & oversee the M-base production at Tiger Kamp (while you & the other guys who con-cocted this whole thing roam around S.E. Asia pulling your clan-destine shit). The production level at Tiger Kamp remains high & the January-February harvest beat the chemists' estimates. Tran's methedrine ran out (mixed blessing—it killed 3 slaves) & we had a slow week (late Feb.) while the slaves smoked heavy amounts of "O" & rode out withdrawals. We've got to burn the fields in April to prepare the soil for the fall planting, but we've got enough back-stock of M-base to see us through to the next harvest, because the 3 refineries were overstocked when we raided & consolidated last November. So far, my rubber-bullet policy is working, because the ex-ARVNs & ex-Congs continue to feud. Mesplede is staging weekly Cong-ARVN boxing matches (slave cornermen & referees) which helps blow off steam & boosts morale.

E) - You were right about the "cleanup." The Can Lao took out the den below the lab (& supposedly 600 others) but now that the initial troop arrival bullshit is over, things are back to normal. None of Chuck's Saravan-to-Saigon merchandise flights have been messed with at either end & Customs has not checked any of his cargoes. The den below the lab & the Go-Go have reopened & Wayne still tests dosage levels on the resident heads. Tran said

Khanh's stopped making anti-dope statements & everyone in Saigon seems distracted by the troops coming in & the way the war is flaring up. You were right, it feels like the buildup is giving us added operational cover.

F) - The pipeline's running A-OK. So far, no Customs checks & glitches flying out of Tan Son Nhut & no trouble at Nellis. My friend Littell surveilled the 1/9/65 shipment from Nellis to the Agency drop-off point thru to the final "donation" point at the Nevada Guard Armory. Milt C. has been transporting the merchandise from the drop-point to Tiger Kab. It's a foolproof system & the Guard is thrilled with Mr. Hughes' "donations."

G) - Some unexpected expenses came up on Milt's end, but aside from that, we're $182,000 up from our Vegas profits on the 1/9 batch & 3/2 batch so far. I'm ready to rotate Chuck, Laurent & Flash stateside & have them scout exile camps, assess the troops & get going on an arms conduit to the ones they choose. Bob Relyea leaves the Army to work for the Feds in May, & he'll be situated near the Gulf. He'll utilize his gun connections & assist Chuck, Laurent & Flash in funneling to the exiles.

That's it. I'm anxious to move on the Cuban end. Let's put all this caution & budgetary constraint shit aside & get going.

Viva la Causa!

P.B.

68

(Las Vegas, Los Angeles, Miami, Washington, D.C.,
Chicago, Selma, 3/21/65–6/15/65)

Penance. Tithe. Counterthrust.

He obeyed Mr. Hoover. He taped Bayard Rustin. He rabbitized. He performed new betrayals—RABBIT ops—Mr. Hoover's counter tithes.

He traveled for work. He worked for Drac and Jimmy. He worked for Drac and the Boys. He flew D.C. to Miami. He flew Chicago to L.A.

He cruised banks. He set up new accounts. He used fake ID. He dumped cash. He cut checks. He tithed the SCLC.

Counter ops:

Skim fees. Embezzlement. Let's declaw BLACK RABBIT.

He drained Drac. He took small bites—little rabbit nips. It worked. The skim plan worked. Counter cash accrued.

He worked.

He worked for Jimmy Hoffa. He filed briefs. He fought two convictions. He dunned the Boys. He bagged two mill for Jimmy's Hope Chest.

New hope. Nonhope. No hope. There were no bribable jurors. There were no bribable courts.

Mr. Hoover had pull. Mr. Hoover liked Jimmy. Mr. Hoover could help. Don't brace him or beg him. Don't incur more indebtedness—yet.

He worked for Drac. He filed briefs. He bought time. He needed twelve months—sixteen tops.

Let Drac dump his stock then. Let Drac get his stash. Let Drac inject Las Vegas.

Fred Otash worked.

Fred Otash culled. Fred Otash sifted. Fred Otash scandalized. Let's raid files. Let's find dirt. Let's utilize.

The files existed: *Confidential/Rave/Whisper/Lowdown* and *Hush-Hush.* The files existed. The files eluded. The files dirtified.

Bugs dirtified.

Littell hung Vegas bugs. Fred Turentine assisted. They bugged hotel rooms. They trapped dirt. They trapped legislators.

Three so far—three cheaters/three whorehounds/three drunks.

Feds manned the bug posts—two agents for three months. Mr. Hoover got bored. It was dirt insufficient. Call it a dirt deficit.

Mr. Hoover pulled the Feds. Fred filled in for them. Fred dirtified. Fred stored dirt. Fred aged dirt. Fred saved dirt for Pete.

Three legislators and one Pete. Compliance guaranteed. We've got the board votes. We've got YOU now. Pledge your support.

Watch us abridge antitrust laws. Watch our Vegas spree. Watch hotel profits plunge. Watch skim ops soar. Watch Littell invest skim money.

We've got the "real" books. We've got the goods. We've got the buyout stats. We co-opt businesses. We funnel cash. We build foreign casinos.

The Boys hoard. The Boys divert. The Boys avoid obstructions—*usually.*

Sam G. was obstructed now. It was recent news. Sam was in jail in Chicago. A grand jury subpoenaed him. Bobby paneled it. Bobby was AG then.

Sam refused to testify. Sam took the Fifth. The judge cited him.

Contempt of Court—Cook County Jail—for the grand-jury term. One year—jail to spring '66.

The judge ragged on Sam. The judge aped Bobby. Bobby ragged Sam in '57. Bobby was Senate counsel then. Bobby was a senator now.

He played his Bobby tapes. He toured the Senate. He prowled the gallery. He watched Bobby. He read the Senate Record. He tracked Bobby's words through.

Bobby debunks bills. Bobby lauds bills. Bobby never mentions the Boys. Bobby presses for civil rights. Bobby lauds Dr. King.

Littell taped Bayard Rustin. Bayard praised King. Littell met Bayard sans tape. Bayard waxed sad that day. Bayard showed him the letter.

"King, look into your heart."

"King, like all frauds, your end is approaching."

"You are a colossal fraud, and an evil, vicious one at that."

"King, there is only one thing left for you to do."

They met in Lafayette Park. Bayard showed him the letter. He read it. He went queasy. He walked.

He met Bayard one more time. Lafayette Park again. They talked sans tape. It sparked him. It scared him.

Tails.

Dwight Holly had him tailed. Mr. Hoover said so. *Vegas* tails—pre-RABBIT.

Holly was BLUE RABBIT. Holly ran BLACK RABBIT. Holly hated him. Spot tails meant checks. Spot tails meant notes. Spot tails meant data accrued.

He met Jane in Vegas—that one bad time—potential tails were out. He met Janice—their first time—potential tails were out.

Holly pulled the tails. Holly pulled them pre-RABBIT. Mr. Hoover said so. Holly ran RABBIT. Holly had juice. Holly could tail-reinstate.

He met Bayard. They had two meets sans tape. He ran tail checks. None were visible. None were obvious. None were probable or certified.

Bayard said, "Come to Selma. You'll see history."

He did it.

He flew down. He used fake ID. He forged a press card. He ducked the marchers. He ducked the cops. He joined a press crew.

He watched. He fretted tails. He saw Bloody Sunday.

Highway 80. The Edmund Pettus Bridge. Sheriff Clark's posse—horses and patrol cars with rebel bumper-flags.

Clark braced the marchers. Clark said disperse in two minutes. The posse charged one minute in. They charged with tear gas and billy clubs. They charged with bullwhips and barbed-wire saps.

The posse hit the marchers. The posse cut through them. The posse mowed them down. He watched. He hid behind cameras. He saw saps rip noses. He saw whips sever ears.

He hid. Meek CRUSADER RABBIT. Unworthy of brave RED and PINK.

He flew back to Vegas. He thought about tails. He thought about Mr. Hoover. Mr. Hoover pledged memos—RABBIT details—Mr. Hoover sent none.

Let's extrapolate. Let's grow some fear.

Mr. Hoover is busy. He's deep in BLACK RABBIT. BLUE RABBIT counsels him. BLUE hates CRUSADER. BLUE hoards memorandums. BLUE restricts their flow.

Or:

Mr. Hoover has plans. They're draconian. They supersede suicide letters. Why disturb CRUSADER? Why risk his specious reproach?

Don't tweak him with knowledge. Don't risk his betrayal. Don't test his silly ideals.

Or:

BLUE has a puppet—WILD RABBIT on strings—WILD RABBIT works alone. WILD runs Klansmen. WILD might run autonomous. WILD might run outright rogue.

Mr. Hoover knows it. BLUE knows it—so why tell CRUSADER that?

Need-to-know. Read-and-burn. Compartments. Sealed access. Love-and-hide.

He had Jane. Jane survived her Vegas trip. Jane never went back. They went back to their rules. They resealed their compartments. They hid in L.A.

They ignored their fight. They revived their game. He lied. She lied. They codified. Their code said we aired it. Their code said it hurt. Their code said we survived Dallas.

Jane knew he taped Bobby. Jane knew he bilked Howard Hughes. Jane knew the Boys. Jane knew the Life. Jane feared the Teamsters for real.

Compartments. Sealed access. Love-and-lie. The love worked. The lies hurt. The seal cracked.

He traveled. He sealed off Vegas. He compartmentalized. He met Barb. He joined her fan club. He sat ringside.

They were prom dates. Admiration and earnest chats. Chaste drinks and her show.

Pete rotated through—Vietnam to Vegas—they all socialized. Barb rotated with him. Her eyes went from pinholed to bright.

Pills. Her secret. Her Pete's-gone-rotation delight.

All men loved her. He told Pete. Pete said he knew that. Barb grew. Barb changed while he watched her. Barb changed her ridiculous lounge act.

She put out more knock-knees. She put out more ad-libs and goofs. I'm six feet tall. I can't sing. I know terrible things.

He loved her. He loved her more than Janice and Jane.

Janice was Vegas. Jane was L.A. He rotated through. Compartments: candor and lies/separate disclosures.

Janice spilled her secrets. Janice *never* lied. She bragged about sex. She proved her points. She flaunted her prowess.

She talked too much. She enticed men. She lived for the thrill. She thought she controlled men. Her stories disproved it. She confused prowess with heart.

She divorced Wayne Senior. She ditched his name. She went back to "Lukens." She earned her two million. She paid with cramps. She paid with a limp.

She fought back. She played golf. She broke par as a gimp. She never cried. She never whined. She never complained.

They met at her cottage. They made love. They talked.

Janice *talked.* He listened.

She fucked a Negro man. Wayne Senior found out and killed him. She fucked Clark Kinman. Wayne Senior watched. She fucked bellboys on dares and bets.

She fucked Wayne Junior. She paid.

She talked too much. She drank too much. She limped through A-club tennis. She was pure will unconsidered. She was inimical to Jane.

Janice talked. Janice digressed. Janice discussed Wayne Senior. He was bad. He was cruel. He'd do ANYTHING.

Janice talked. Janice scared him. Wayne Senior was FATHER RABBIT.

69

(Las Vegas, Miami, Port Sulphur, Saigon,
Saravan, Dac To, Dak Sut, Muang Kao,
3/21–6/15/65)

Rotation:
East to west—V to V—Viet-
nam to Vegas.
He flew west—rotation 1—
Barb met his plane. She sparkled. She beamed. She refuted that letter.

The letter bugged him. Jerky words and the lines "up & down." He
thought about pills—lounge-popcorn uppers and reds to come down.

No/*nyet/nein. Noi* in Viet. Barb radiated. Barb fucking glowed.

They glowed three years in. They glowed with crazy shit concurrent.
Barb got better. Barb got stronger. Barb got X-ray eyes.

She saw through show people. She saw through the Life. The Life was
rigged. The men took the risks. The men had the fun. The men conspired.
The men served causes. The women served tea.

Barb said it: "I peaked early. I extorted JFK." Barb said it: "You've got
Cuba. I've got the Sultan's Lounge."

She didn't nag him. She didn't play shrew. She just said she'd changed.

They hashed it out. He sensed cabin fever. Vegas hemmed her in. He
sold dope batch #1. He bought two tickets east.

They booked to Miami. They took the cat. They booked a suite at the
Doral. The cat leveled it.

He clawed the drapes. He shit on chairs. He killed terrace birds. He
bootjacked their room-service food.

They caught Dino. They caught Shecky Green. They got ringside seats.
They slept late and made love.

They talked. He laid out Vietnam. He lied. He downplayed the killing.
He downplayed the slaves.

Barb pressed him. Barb tripped him up. Barb nailed his lies. He said fuck it. He cut loose. He disclosed.

Barb said, "All that for *Cuba?*"

They got some rays. They ran into Jimmy H. They went out for stone crabs. Jimmy fumed. Jimmy fugued. Jimmy ran nonstop boo-hoo.

His legal woes. Sam G. in stir. His ripe hemorrhoids.

Pete bored in. Pete pumped him. Pete worked his mood. Pete pumped angles. Pete pumped oblique.

It's Kansas City. It's '56. Danny Bruvick fucks you.

Jimmy cut loose—six fucks!/six cocksuckers!/six Arden cunts! Jimmy dished on Arden. Jimmy tossed a bomb:

Arden Bruvick—that cunt—she was Jules Schiffrin's ex.

Pete said, "Excuse me." Pete walked to the john. Pete found a throne. Pete sat down. Pete hashed it all through.

Jules Schiffrin—Mob money man—dead in '60. The "real" fund books—Schiffrin's property. Arden Bruvick: *book*keeper.

It's '56. It's K.C. Danny Bruvick splits. Jimmy fugues out. Cops bust Arden. The T&C Corp bails her. Carlos M. owns T&C.

Cut to:

'59—New Orleans—J.P. Mesplède passes through. Mesplède sees Arden—with some Carlos goon.

Cut to:

1960—Wisconsin—Ward Littell steals the books. Schiffrin heart-attacks and drops dead.

Cut to:

Fall '63. Carlos taps Ward. Carlos says this:

You got the books. Jimmy don't know it. The Boys and I do. We know you. We *own* you. You'll sell Drac our hotels. You'll *work* the books. You'll dredge up data. You'll funnel skim through.

Cut to:

Dallas—hit time—Arden meets Ward. She works for Jack Ruby. She keeps *his* books. She's seen the safe house. She's seen the targets. She's seen the crew.

Ward falls for Arden. Carlos wants her dead. Ward makes Arden "Jane." Ward hides "Jane." Ward brews fund-book schemes.

So:

Did Carlos find Arden? Did Carlos pledge mercy? IF YOU SPY ON LITTELL? Arden was a bookkeeper. Arden knew Schiffrin. Arden *lived* with Littell.

Sound logic, but:

He saw Ward with "Jane." They were *real*. He *knew* it.

It scared him. He teethed on it. He riffed: *Real* deals with women could be undercut—and thus shot to shit.

Barb saw him pump Jimmy. Barb gauged his john run. Barb got halfway hip. He filled her in. He abridged it. He omitted Carlos. He omitted Big D.

Barb loved it. Barb loved secrets. Barb held them tough. They discussed it. He told her—I'll probe up more stuff.

He called Fred Otash. Otash weighed in. Otash said I'm on it—don't sweat. I'll buy *more* cops. I'll put out *more* search fees. My cops will check files and call back.

They schmoozed. Otash had news. Otash said Ward hired him. Ward craved dirt. Ward bought a dirt search—let's find the old scandal-rag files.

Pete riffed on his Arden search. Pete said don't tell Ward—don't clue Ward in. Otash played ball. Otash had Arden pix already. Otash *knew* Arden was Jane.

Pete teethed on it. Pete sifted it. Pete lived with it. Pete ran rotations.

Vegas was good—100%. White horse hits. The word expands. Clients accrue: Sniffers/tasters/junkies/skin-popper geeks.

The street pushers worked. The street pushers proselytized. They wore flash threads. They drove jig rigs. They glorified "H." They glamorized it. They accessorized it. They Tupperwared it.

They cruised the projects. They drew crowds. They sniffed powdered milk and bopped strong. They debunked that addiction jive.

They wore pendants. They wore processed hair. They carried mock-gold guns. They lied. They said spooks ran the biz. They denied that the White Man existed.

Wayne tailed them. It scared them. They knew Wayne's rep. Wayne Junior be baaaaaaaaaaaad. Wayne Junior kill our kin.

Profits accrued. Milt totaled them. Milt praised the horse epidemic. It was restricted. It was contained. No whites need apply.

A dope punk moved in. Said punk brought ambition. Said punk sniffed the air. Said punk sniffed the wrong vibration:

Horse is cool—let's sell some—the Mob don't mind.

Pete dispatched his niggers. Said niggers grabbed said punk.

Santo T. had a shark named Batista. He lived in Santo's pool. He ate burgers. He ate steak. He ate pizza.

The niggers dropped the punk in the pool. Batista ate him live.

White horse stayed west. Junkies stayed home. Junkies eschewed white Vegas. Tiger Kabs prowled west. Tiger orbs glowed.

So far:

No new pushers. No pending fuzz heat. No unbribed narcs making noise.

Tiger Kab was hip. Sonny Liston tigerized. Sonny ate at the hut. Sonny drank at the hut. Sonny went on local TV.

Sonny did ads. Sonny proselytized:

"Tiger Kab packs a knockout punch." "Tiger Kab kicks Cassius Clay's patootie."

Fag drivers drove. Straight drivers drove. Pete enforced faction détente. Fag drivers sold boys. Fag celebs bought boys. Fag drivers drove fags to hotels.

Fag clerks minced. Fag clerks smirked. Fag clerks supplied rooms. Said rooms: Bugged/tapped/extortionized.

Fag drivers drove fags. Fag drivers turned tricks. Donkey Dom tricked with Sal Mineo. Donkey Dom tricked with Rock Hudson.

Sonny said it:

"Tiger prowls 24 hours! If you don't swing, don't ring!"

Tiger Kab swung in Vegas. Tiger Kamp rocked Laos hard.

Pete rotated. Pete left Vegas. Pete cut the Barb cord. Wayne rotated. Stanton worked in Saigon. Laurent and Chuck worked in Laos.

Pete detached Flash—4/65—strict orders: Hit the Gulf. Hit exile camps. Scout for good troops.

Pete detached Mesplède—4/65—strict orders: Hit the U.S. Hit the South. Scout gun dealers out.

Bob Relyea left Laos—5/65—Bob Relyea hit Mississippi. Bob was Fed now. Bob did snitch work. It was klandestine.

Chuck to follow Bob. Chuck to hit Houston. Chuck to scout guns. Chuck to scout Gulf-close—close to Mississippi. Close to Mesplède and pal Bob.

Chuck snickered to Bob. Bob snickered to Chuck. They snickered contrapuntal. They snickered through Bob's big farewell.

They implied mischief. They indulged wordplay. They inferred klownery. Birmingham, Alabama. Really BOMBingham. Bogalusa—tee-hee—BOMBalusa.

Bob split for Fed work. Chuck changed roommates. Chuck bunked with Laurent Guéry now. Chuck bugged him. Chuck hassled him. Chuck harangued him:

With Klan klaptrap. With klownish klaims. With klaims of krossburns to kome.

Rotations all—Dallas to Vegas—Dallas to Vietnam. Grad-school hijinx and reunions.

Chuck shot. Chuck shot from the knoll. Mesplède shot Oswald's gun. Flash and Laurent stood in Boyd's team. They got scuttled pre-hit.

Rotations—Saigon to the Gulf—the Gulf to Cuba. Flash is Cuban. Flash is dark. Flash could get in.

The plan:

Flash goes in. Flash charts resistance. Flash finds good men. Flash smuggles them out. Flash boats them in. Flash feeds Guéry and Mesplède.

They've got a shack. It's Gulf-close. They've got electrodes. They torture the men. They test their balls. They ensure their loyalty.

Rotations—Cuba to the Gulf—the Gulf to Vietnam. *Biggggggggg* U.S. troop numbers.

Stanton logged said numbers. Stanton logged provocations. Stanton vibed a long war.

The Cong hits Pleiku. Eight Yankees die. LBJ reacts. Air strikes: Operation Flaming Dart.

The Cong hits Qui Nhon. Twenty-one Yankees die. LBJ reacts. More air strikes: Flaming Dart II.

U.S. troops arrive—"advisors"—two Marine battalions. More air strikes: Operation Rolling Thunder.

Two battalions arrive—logistical troops—20,000 men. They get deployed. They get dispersed. They get detached to Marv units.

Firefights. Dead Yanks. Incoming rotations. Buildups—incremental—40,000 men per.

Troops hit Saigon. Troops R&R. Troop numbers swell. Long war good. Kadre like it. Buildup most boocoo.

Wayne lived in Saigon. Wayne lived in his lab. Wayne said *his* fucking world swelled. More people. More noise. More songs up his vents. More Marvs. More O-heads. More whores.

More cover. More white horse. More money.

Stanton laundered profits. Stanton fed Pete. Pete fed Mesplède. Mesplède bought righteous *guns.*

.50-calibers/Ithacas/BARs/antitank guns.

Flash found a troop site. It was Gulf-close and gooood. It was near Port Sulphur, Louisiana. It housed sixty troopers—Cubano shitkickers all.

Mesplède dropped some guns off. The shitkickers roared. Pete rotated through. Pete dug on the troops. Pete dug their maneuvers.

The troopers were hard-ons. The troopers were *très* hard. The troopers were *très sanguinaire.*

Pete rotated. Pete hit Saigon. Pete met Stanton's CIA crew. Six men plus Stanton—all Cubafied.

They talked Cuba. They talked ops. They talked polygraph tests. They'd be mandatory and random. They'd go kadre-wide. Let's ID and whack traitors. Let's uproot thieves. Let's assure loyalty.

Stanton flew to Laos. Stanton brought his poly machine. Pete tested. Pete tested clean. Tran tested. Tran tested clean.

Stanton stayed for a visit. Stanton watched the spring burn.

Guards unshackled slaves. Slaves piled brush. Guards formed a fire brigade. They stacked the piles. They positioned them—one per stalk row.

Slaves filled drums with propane gas. Guards dipped torches. Guards whooped. Guards lit torches. Guards torched brush.

The fields burned. The sky flared. The fields burned all night. Guards cheered. Slaves cheered. Tiger Kamp cinderized.

Ash blew. Ash settled. Ash nourished kamp-wide.

Stanton loved it. Stanton stayed. Stanton stayed for the Clay-Liston fight. Chuck rigged a hookup—closed-circuit shit—a feed off MACV in Saigon.

Sonny lost. The fight vibed nonclimax. Sportswriter stupes yelled, "Fix!"

Pete laughed. Fuck it—Pete *knew:*

Sonny was old. Sonny was slow. Sonny was tigerfried.

70

(Las Vegas, Saigon, Saravan, Bao Loc,
3/21/65–6/15/65)

Let's escalate. Let's *watch*.

Khanh is in. Khanh is out. Premier Ky kreams Premier Khanh. Don't blink—koups and kreamouts kome kwick.

"Escalate"—a verb—LBJ's word: "To increase, enlarge or intensify."

The war escalated. Wayne watched.

More troops came in. More troops got pledged. Provocation meant response. More Marines came in. More Marines got pledged. More Airborne came in. More Airborne got pledged in response.

More dead:

More bomb attacks in mid-Saigon. More mid-range dead. The Brinks Hotel/the embassy—more Yankee dead.

More VC. More night patrols. More sabotage.

Pleiku—much aircraft blow—nice U.S. fleet. VC attack—most bold and sincere. VC use pole-and-satchel bombs—homemade/*très* VC. TNT/palm leaves/bamboo.

Many planes blow. *One* VC die.

Provocation meant response. Response meant bomb runs. More pilots. More troops. More artillery.

Stanton ran numbers. Provocation meets response—thus fervor meets weight. Stanton predicted two hundred K troops—in by '66.

Big numbers. Big ordnance. Big weight.

Wayne watched. Wayne dug it. Wayne missed the point. Vietnam was a shithole. The Cong couldn't lose. The Cong lived to die.

A Cong walked in the Go-Go. Said Cong wore Cong drag—black pj's deluxe. A spec-4 shot him. A chest bomb blew. Oops—Cong booby-trapped.

Six dead—all U.S.—Cong reigns six-to-one.

Stanton loved the war. Pete loved the war. Stanton and Pete loved Cuba. Cuba was a shithole. Cuba was Saigon with sand.

The kadre loved the war. The kadre kame for Kuba. Wayne came to watch.

He stayed in Saigon. He cooked dope. He watched. GIs hit the Go-Go. GIs bought whores. GIs fucked whores on floor planks.

He watched.

The O-heads decomped. Quicklime ate bone. Marvs made fertilizer. Marvs sold it discount.

He watched.

The Cong burned pylons. Saigon went dark. Pilots dropped psyche-delic-tint flares.

He watched. He worked. He lived in Saigon. He cabbed to Bao Loc. He bought weapons. Said weapons were dope cover. Said weapons were donation stock.

He jeeped up and back. He tailed patrols. His standard procedure was *watch*.

4/8/65—near Dinh Quan. Rice field firefight—jarheads and VC.

A road mine popped. Wayne's jeep flew. The windshield blew up. The driver ate glass. The driver died. Wayne crouched by his stiff.

Bushes—off the road. They're moving now. They're bush-wrapped VC.

They charged. The jarheads proned out. Fair fight/no cover.

Wayne rolled free. Wayne pulled his piece. Wayne shot three VC. His shots dinged. He hit tin vests—fucking trashcan lids.

The VC fired. The jarheads fired. The jarheads aimed high and low. They shot feet. They shot legs. They shot faces. They hit vest-free zones.

The VC went down. Rounds dinged off the jeep. A medic went down with one in the neck. Wayne rolled and fired free.

He hit six VC. He notched all head shots. He double-killed.

The jarheads stood up. A jarhead tripped a punji stick. Spikes slammed him—knees to nipples—punctures and rips.

Wayne rolled to the medic. Wayne grabbed his Syrettes—pure mor-phine cc's.

He rolled to the jarhead. He shot up the jarhead. The jarhead con-vulsed. The jarhead hurled chunks of his spleen.

Wayne had white horse—one spike in his pocket—one short test dose.

He found a vein. He geezed the man. The man gasped. The man smiled. The man nodded out.

Wayne timed his death. He went out in sixteen seconds. He went out wispy and numb.

Pete was World War II. Pete had a rule: Don't sell to GIs. It was naive. It negated the real rule: provocation meets response.

"Our Boys" would fight the war. "Our Boys" would look for outs. "Our Boys" would find Big "H."

Stanton had terms: "the Agency's War" and "the Personal Commitment."

He killed Bongo. He committed. He joined the war then. He squashed a bug. It felt right. It felt impersonal. He killed Bongo. He dumped Bongo. He took his own pulse. Sixty-two beats a minute—no malice/no stress.

Rats ate Bongo. Some Marvs found his bones. A rumor spread: Chemist do it—chemist kill pimp.

Whores braced Wayne. They said be our pimp—we love you. He said no. He saw that colored whore. He saw her trailer.

The rumor spread. Chuck heard it. Chuck told Bob. Bob braced him. Bob said come south and join my Klan—we'll fuck niggers up.

Wayne said no. Bob dropped hints: I work for your dad. Wayne said no. Bob laughed. Wayne said he might come to WATCH.

He watched in Saigon. He watched in Bao Loc. He watched in Vegas. He watched the pushers. He tailed the pushers. He ensured subservience.

He watched West LV. He watched the bars. He watched that trailer. Junkies used it now. Junkies geezed within. They ignored the soot. They ignored the smell. They ignored the whore's bones.

He watched West LV. He asked around. He trawled for Wendell Durfee. The locals ignored him. The locals misled him. The locals spit on his shoes.

He logged tips. He paid rewards. He logged futile data. He hit the bars. He logged fear. He brought Sonny Liston along.

Sonny quaffed J&B. Sonny popped pills. Sonny ran riffs: Wendell Durfee went Muslim—Muhammad speaks—it gots to be!

Wendell runs a mosque. Wendell knows Cassius Clay. Wendell knew the late Malcolm X.

Storm the Nigger Mosques. Climb the Nigger Grapevine. Comb the Nigger Underworld. Patch the Nigger Switchboard. Punch the Nigger Teletype—and track that nigger down!

Sonny peeled his nigger eyes. Sonny filed his nigger claws. Sonny tapped his nigger intuition. Sonny logged tips. Sonny dished out rewards. Sonny pledged results.

Pete said Durfee was dead. DPD killed him unpublicized. They killed him for Maynard Moore.

Wayne said no—you're wrong. Wayne logged tips and WATCHED.

He logged lounge time. He watched Barb. He took side seats. He looked backstage. He got candid shots.

The Bondsmen smoked weed there. Barb popped pills. Barb popped Johnnie Black. Her eyes showed it. Her pulse showed it. She cleaned up for Pete's rotations.

He watched. He saw things everywhere. He felt invisible.

He logged lounge time. He caught Barb's gigs. He saw Janice and Ward Littell. They sat close. They held hands. They brushed knees.

He saw them. They never saw him. Sonny had a theory: Only niggers see you.

71

(Las Vegas, 6/18/65)

Janice hit balls.

She chipped off her porch. Said porch as golf range—tee/putting strip/net.

It was hot. Janice wore a middy blouse and shorts. Littell watched her concentrate. Littell watched her hit.

Janice teed balls. Janice hit shots. Janice stretched the net. She swiveled. Her blouse gapped. Her beating scars flexed.

She said, "I saw Wayne Senior at the DI. He was making a phone call."

Littell smiled. "Why are you telling me this?"

"Because you hate him, and you're curious about the men I've slept with."

Littell sipped coffee. "I hope I haven't been prying."

"That's impossible with me. You know how I love to divulge."

"I do know. It's something that separates—"

"Me from Jane, I know."

Littell smiled. "Tell me what you heard."

Janice teed a ball. "He was in the casino, and he was using one of those courtesy phones. He didn't see me behind him."

"And?"

"And he was talking to a man named Chuck. He was talking about the bad reception from Vietnam, and he was cracking jokes about Bogalusa and 'Bombalusa.' "

Littell stirred his coffee. "That's it?"

"That and the way he was gloating, with that Indiana drawl of his."

Hold it. Stop right—

Littell stirred his coffee. Littell thought it through. Bogalusa was East Louisiana. Bogalusa was Klan kountry.

Vote drives—right now—fronted by SCLC. BLACK RABBIT on go. Wayne Senior as FATHER RABBIT.

Hold it. Stop right—

You're CRUSADER RABBIT. Bayard Rustin's PINK. You taped PINK. PINK told you about Bogalusa. You told Mr. Hoover.

Mr. Hoover knows. Mr. Hoover never calls. Mr. Hoover pledges memos. Mr. Hoover sends none.

Janice built a martini. "Is there room for two in that trance of yours, or should I leave you alone?"

Littell coughed. "Do you have any idea who Chuck is?"

"Well, I'd say he's that little man who flew a plane to Wayne Senior's Christmas party, and showed up with your caveman friend Pete."

Hold it. Stop right—

Chuck Rogers: Pilot/killer/racist nut/Dallas shooter. Vietnam and Pete's gig—covert CIA.

FATHER RABBIT runs WILD RABBIT. WILD RABBIT is Army. WILD RAB-BIT serves "overseas." Mr. Hoover talked rabbits. Mr. Hoover talked dates. WILD RABBIT to leave the Army—5/65. WILD RABBIT to go Klan then.

"Ward, am I going to have to do a striptease to pull you out of that trance?"

He worried it. He tested it. He dreamed RABBITS. He carried it with him. He brought it home. He slept with it.

BOMBalusa. BOMBingham: September '63. A bomb blows at 16th Street Baptist Church. Four Negro girls die.

He woke up. He made coffee. He built rationales:

Don't call Mr. Hoover. Don't raise an alarm. Don't call Pete. Don't men-tion Chuck. Don't breach need-to-know. Don't call Bayard. Don't probe Bogalusa. Don't sound his alarm.

Don't call BLUE RABBIT. Don't call WHITE RABBIT. Don't rouse the Holly boys. They hate Negroes. They love Mr. Hoover.

Wayne Senior's FATHER RABBIT. FATHER knows Chuck. FATHER runs WILD RABBIT. WILD RABBIT runs a klavern. The Feds fund it and impose rules:

"Operational guidelines." "Violence to sustain informant credibility." BOMBingham/BOMBalusa/BOMB—

Littell grabbed the phone. Littell called Barb. Littell ran a riff:

Laos. Pete's dope clique. Is Chuck Rogers in?

Barb said, "Yes."

Littell hung up. Littell called the switchboard. Littell braced an operator: Get me U.S. Customs—the passport office—New Orleans.

The operator ran it. Littell got the number. Littell dialed direct.

A man picked up. "Customs, Agent Bryce."

"My name's Ward Littell. I'm ex-FBI, with reserve credentials. I was hoping you'd do me a favor."

"Well, sure, if I can."

Littell grabbed a pen. "I need you to check your recently collated entries for flights from Laos and Vietnam. I'm looking for commercial or military landings at Customs-manned facilities in your jurisdiction, and I need the names on the passport-check lists."

Bryce coughed. "Can you hold? I doubt if we've had more than three or four of those, tops."

Littell said, "I'll hold."

Bryce hit a button. The connection fuzzed. Static hit the line. Littell held. Littell checked his watch. Littell counted rabbits.

BLUE RABBIT/WILD RABBIT/RED RABBIT. Three minutes/forty-two sec—

Bryce picked up. "Sir? We've only got one. I—"

"Can you give—"

"One ordnance flight. Saigon to the Air National Guard facility near Houston. The crew plus one passenger, a man named Charles Rogers."

72

(Saravan, 6/19/65)

Poly test—pure impromptu—John Stanton dropped in.

He cleared the hut. He rolled graph sheets. He rigged the machine. He fired the needle. He fired the pulse clip. He fired the dials.

Pete rigged a chair. Laurent Guéry sat down. Stanton rigged the blood-pressure cuff.

Stanton clamped the cuff. Pete looped the chest cord. Stanton pumped the cuff. Stanton read the dial:

Normal stats—110/80.

A wind stirred. Dope seeds blew. Pete shut the window.

Stanton grabbed a chair. Stanton pulse-clipped Guéry. Pete grabbed a chair. Pete watched the needle.

Stanton said, "Do you drink water?"

Guéry said, "Yes."

The needle bumped. The needle slid. The needle flatlined. Stanton read the cuff and clip:

Okay—normal signs.

Stanton said, "Are you a citizen of the Republic of France?"

Guéry said, "Yes."

The needle bumped. The needle slid. The needle flatlined. Stanton read the cuff and clip:

Okay—normal signs.

Pete stretched. Pete yawned—fuck this pro-forma jive.

Stanton said, "Are you a committed anti-Communist?"

Guéry said, "Yes."

Flatline.

Stanton said, "Are you pro–Viet Cong?"

Guéry said, "No."

Flatline.

Stanton said, "Have you ever stolen from the kadre?"

Guéry said, "No."

The needle dipped two inches. The needle laid swerve lines. Stanton pumped the cuff. Stanton read the dial.

Not okay—140/110—*non*-normal signs.

Guéry squirmed. Pete eyeballed him. Pete read his signs: Chills/goose bumps/sweat.

Stanton said, "Have you ever stolen from kadre-adjunct personnel?"

Guéry said, "No."

The needle dipped three inches. The needle laid swerve lines.

Stanton hit the intercom switch. Stanton talked gook: "*Quon, Minh. Mau len. Di, thi, di.*"

Two gooks ran in—one Marv and one Cong doubletime. Guéry squirmed. Pete read signs: Wet hands/wet armpits/crotch leaking sweat.

Stanton nodded. The gooks flanked Guéry. The gooks pulled batons.

Stanton said, "Do you have knowledge of such thefts?"

Guéry said, "No."

The needle dipped six inches. The needle laid swerve lines.

Stanton said, "Do you have knowledge that Pete Bondurant perpetrated such thefts?"

Guéry said, "No."

Needle bump. Flatline.

Stanton said, "Do you have knowledge that Jean Philippe Mesplède perpetrated such thefts?"

Guéry said, "No."

Needle bump. Flatline.

Stanton said, "Do you have knowledge that Wayne Tedrow Junior perpetrated such thefts?"

Guéry said, "No."

Needle bump. Flatline.

Stanton said, "Do you have knowledge that Chuck Rogers perpetrated such thefts?"

Guéry said, "No."

The needle dipped eight inches. The needle laid swerve lines.

Guéry squirmed. Stanton cued the gooks. They grabbed ropes. They looped them. They tied Guéry to the chair.

Stanton pulled his piece. Stanton cocked it. Pete grabbed the field phone. Pete patched the lab.

Chuck was gone. Chuck split to Saigon. Chuck split four days back.

Chuck bunked with Guéry now. Chuck hassled Guéry. Chuck drove Guéry nuts.

Pete got a dial tone. Pete got line fuzz. Pete got a click.

Wayne picked up. "Yeah?"

"It's me. Have you seen Chuck?"

"No. Was he supposed—"

"He was supposed to go through Bao Loc and Saigon and pick up some guns."

"I haven't seen him at all. He always comes by the Go-Go when he's—"

Pete hung up. Stanton cued him—go check the hooch.

Pete ran over. Pete popped the door. Pete tripped on the mat. He caught himself. He eyeball-walked. He quadrant-scanned.

Four walls/two fart sacks/two nightstands/two lockers/one shitter/one sink.

Pete dumped the nightstands. Pete combed debris. Toothpaste/rubbers/stroke books/hate tracts/*Ring* magazines.

Two passports—both Guéry's—CIA/French.

Pete dumped the lockers. Pete combed debris. Hate tracts/bug spray/beaver pix/gun oil/*Swank* magazines.

No Chuck passports. No Chuck ID.

Pete grabbed the field phone. Pete patched Saigon direct. He got Ops South. They repatched him. He got Tan Son Nhut. They repatched him. He got static. He got Customs.

He got a gook. He spoke French. The gook spoke strict Viet. The gook repatched him. He got static. He got a white man.

"Customs, Agent Lierz."

"This is Sergeant Peters, CID. I'm checking on a civilian who might've cleared Customs within the past four days."

Lierz coughed. The line coughed. Static brizzed.

"You got a name?"

"Rogers. First name Charles."

Lierz coughed. "I've got my log here. Hold on . . . Rice, Ridgeway, Rippert . . . yeah, Rogers. He flew out four days ago. He showed manifest docs, loaded explosive material and caught a transport to the National Guard strip in Houston, Tex—"

Pete hung up. Pete *got* it: Thefts/fake docs/explosives.

Guéry screamed. Pete heard it loud. It carried from forty yards up.

He ran back. He smelled smoke and piss. He cracked the door and *saw* it.

There's Guéry.

He's tied up. He's pantless. He's scared. Stanton's got the hot box. Stanton's got the switch. Stanton's got the clamps on his balls.

The gooks watched. The gooks smoked bootjack Kools. The gooks slurped gook wine.

Stanton said, "What did Chuck Rogers steal?"

Guéry shook his head. Stanton hit the switch. Stanton tossed volts. Guéry buckled and screamed.

Stanton said, "If the theft is kadre-adjunct and you didn't participate or report it, I'd be inclined to go easy."

Guéry shook his head. Stanton hit the switch. Stanton tossed volts. Guéry buckled and screamed.

Stanton said, "Where's Rogers now? What did he steal and who did he steal it from?"

Guéry shook his head. Stanton hit the switch. Stanton tossed volts. Guéry buckled and screamed.

Pete *got* it—for real now.

Chuck and Guéry worked Dallas. Stanton's got no clue. Guéry won't talk. Guéry won't rat Chuck for *anything*.

Stanton said, "Is Rogers in-country? Did he fly back to the States?"

Guéry shook his head. Stanton hit the switch. Stanton tossed volts. Guéry buckled and screamed.

The gooks laughed—he claaazy—he *dinky dau*.

Stanton hit the switch. Stanton tossed volts. Guéry buckled. Guéry screamed. Guéry yelled, "*Assez!*"

Stanton cued the gooks. The gooks pulled the clamps. The gooks untied Guéry. The gooks sprayed his balls with baby oil. The gooks fed him gook wine.

He slurped it. He stood up. He teetered. He fell back in his chair.

Stanton leaned in. "If I said it hurt me more than it hurt you, I'd be a fucking liar."

Pete sneezed—the hut smelled—fried ball hair and sweat.

Guéry said, "The ammo dump . . . Bao Loc . . . Chuck, *qu'est-ce que c'est,* burglarized bomb material . . . from François."

Stanton shook his head. "Did he tell you what he had in mind?"

Pete leaned in. "Chuck flew to the States. If you let me talk to him alone, I'll get the rest of it."

Stanton nodded. Stanton stood up. Stanton cued the gooks—*venez, venez.*

They walked out together. Pete grabbed the bottle. Guéry snatched it. Guéry drained it. Guéry hitched his pants up.

"I will never have children now."

"It's not like you want them."

"No. The world has become too communistic."

"I think I know why you held back."

Guéry wiped his nose. "I did not betray the kadre."

"I know you didn't."

Guéry rubbed his balls. "Chuck . . . *qu'est-ce* . . . received a letter from his parents. I think they are not sane."

Pete lit two cigarettes. Guéry snatched one.

"Chuck lives at their house. They said they found his . . . *journal?*"

"Journal, right."

"Which described our operation in Dallas . . . for which . . . they demanded an explanation . . . which . . . Chuck said he would fly home and . . . *qu'est-ce* . . . take care of it."

Pete kicked a doorpost. "He stole bomb ordnance for *that?*"

Guéry coughed. "No. For something else. He would not tell me."

Pete walked outside. Slaves double-timed past him. Guards popped rubber rounds.

Stanton straddled a fence rail. "How bad?"

Pete shrugged. "You tell me. Laurent said it's a family grudge, and Chuck flew out with explosives."

Stanton chewed a hangnail. "There's a courier flight leaving for Fort Sam Houston. You and Wayne go find him and kill him."

73

(Houston, 6/21/65)

Gulf heat:
Low clouds and thick air.
Air as bug propellant.
And bug catalyst. And bug haven. And bug launching pad. Bug *heat*—80 at 2:12 a.m.

The freeway was dead. Bugs bipped off the car. Pete drove. Wayne read maps.

Chez Chuck was on Driscoll. Chez Chuck was close. Chez Chuck was near Rice U.

Wayne yawned. Pete yawned. They yawned contrapuntal. They flew eighteen hours—Saigon to Houston—they plowed six time zones.

They flew transport. They sat on crates. They ate canned corn exclusive. Stanton set a car up—a '61 Ford—there at Fort Sam.

Bum wheels altogether. No muffler. No fucking Air King.

Stanton knew some of it. Pete said so. Pete said he withheld the key shit. Maybe Chuck's here. Maybe Chuck's not. Maybe Chuck's in Bogalusa.

With Bob Relyea—kadre-ex—kurrent Klan klown. Bob ran a snitch-Klan. Wayne Senior ran Bob. That meant *he* could WATCH.

They ditched the freeway. They took side streets. They ran their high beams. Houston was the shits—brick cribs and bug lights abundant.

Stanton shot them filework: stats per Chez Chuck. Chuck's dad and mom were Fred and Edwina. They had a '53 Olds.

Texas plates: DXL-841.

They hit Kirby Street. They hit Richmond. They turned hard right. There—Driscoll—1780/1800/1808.

1815 was glazed brick. No palace/no slum. Two floors and no lights extant.

Pete parked. Wayne grabbed two flashlights. They got out. They circled the house. They flashed the windows. They flashed the doors.

Bugs stirred. Owls stirred. Wasps bombed a nest.

Wayne flashed the back porch. Pete flashed a hedge. Wayne caught a glint—light on steel—Pete threw his beam down.

Wayne reached in. Wayne grabbed and pulled. Wayne sliced two fingers up.

There—

One Texas license plate—stuffed in a hedge. Bingo on DXL-841.

Pete said, "He changed plates on the Olds."

Wayne sucked his fingers. "Let's go in. We might find something."

Pete flashed the back door. Wayne walked up and looked. Okay: One lock/flat bolt/wide keyhole.

Pete cupped his light. Wayne pulled his picks and jabbed at the hole. Two missed. One hit. One slid in deep.

He twisted it. He turned it. He popped the bolt. They popped the door and walked in.

They flashed the floor. They flashed a stairwell. Wayne smelled mold. Wayne smelled baked beans.

They turned left. They hit a hall. They hit a kitchen. Wayne felt trapped heat. Moonlight sieved through venetian blinds.

Pete pulled the blinds. Wayne hit the lights. There:

Sink water—dark pink—carving knives afloat. Baked beans and fruit flies on mold. Hair in a colander. Dots on the floor. Dots by the fridge.

Pete opened it. Wayne smelled it. They *saw* it:

The severed legs. The diced hips. Mom's head in the vegetable bin.

74

(Bogalusa, 6/21/65)

Phone work:
Room 6—the Glow Motel—direct calls out. Outside noise as direct counterpoint.

Shouts. Rebel yells. Nigger! Nigger! Nigger! We Shall Overcome!

We're in BOMBalusa now. We remember BOMBingham.

He slept with the riddle. He lived with it. He ran.

To: Marches and pray-ins and cross burns. To: Beatings and hecklings and shouts.

He assumed a Fed presence. He laid cover tracks. He called Carlos. He set up a meet. He flew through New Orleans.

BLUE RABBIT might be here. Add BLUE's Brother WHITE. Add Hoover confidants. Add local Feds.

He laid tracks. I was close. *It* was close. I had to see. I'm CRUSADER RABBIT. I'm a fool for civil rights.

Littell checked his phone book. Littell ran motels. He called the Texas DMV this morning. He got Chuck Rogers' stats.

Houston/Driscoll Street/one Oldsmobile. Texas plates: DXL-841.

He got the stats. He got the room. He called motels. Forty-two local—dull phone-book stats.

He played Fed. He dropped his stats. He checked registrations. He made 19 calls. He got all nos. He hit Clerk 20.

"You the second police type who called 'bout that Olds. Only this other guy didn't give me no DXL number, he said it'd have hot Texas plates."

He brainstormed the response. He ran RABBITS. FATHER RABBIT's Wayne Senior. FATHER knows Chuck. FATHER runs WILD RABBIT. WILD RABBIT's close. WILD RABBIT's Klan.

There's BLUE RABBIT. He's Fed. Who *else* wants Chuck?

He called motels. He hit 28. He got nil results. The outside noise got bad—these loud Nigger! shouts.

Littell worked. Littell called motels. Littell got nil results. Motel 29. Motel 30. Motel 31-2-3.

Motel 34: "You're the second guy askin' about that Rogers an' that car, but I ain't seen him or it."

The Moonbeam Motel/the Lark Motel/the Anchor Motel—nil results. The Dixie/the Bayou/the Rebel's Rest:

"Office. May I help you?"

"This is Special Agent Brown, FBI."

The guy laughed. "You come to curtail these agitators?"

"No, sir. It's about something else."

"That's too bad, because—"

"I'm looking for a white man driving a 1953 Oldsmobile with Texas license plates."

The man laughed. "Then you're one lucky member of the Federal Bureau of Integration, 'cause he checked into room 5 yesterday."

"What? Repeat th—"

"I got it right here. Charles Jones, Houston, Texas. '53 Olds sedan, PDL-902. By my lights, he's a mean motherhumper. Probably gargles with antifreeze and flosses with razor blades."

Traffic crawled. The disruption ratched it up.

Sidewalk marches. Hecklers. TV crews out. Signs and countersigns. Shriekers with good lungs. Nonparticipants out for yuks.

Freedom Now!/Jim Crow Must Go!/Nigger Go Home! We shaaaall overcome! in re-run shouts.

Littell drove his rental car. Traffic slogged. Littell parked and walked. Egg crews roamed. White kids chucked eggs. They chucked at Negroes. They nailed perceived Feds.

Littell walked. Littell dodged eggs. Eggs hit marchers. Eggs hit picket signs.

Egg crews walked. Egg trucks roamed. Egg men trucked ammo. Eggs flew. Eggs hit doors. Eggs hit awnings and cars.

The marchers wore slickers. The slickers dripped yolk. The slickers dripped cracked shells. Cops stood around. Cops dodged eggs. Cops sucked Nehi and Coke.

Littell walked. Eggs creased him. Littell looked *all*-Fed.

He cut left. He walked two blocks. He passed two egg huts. Egg crews formed. Egg crews armed. Egg trucks loaded up.

He saw it—right there—the Rebel's Rest.

One floor. Ten rooms. All street-view units. Rebel flag and rebel sign—neon Johnny Reb.

Parking slots/outdoor walkway/the office detached.

Littell palmed a credit card. Littell cut straight over. Littell saw room 5.

He knocked. He got no answer. No car in front/no people/no Olds 88.

He faced the street. He braced the door. He worked backwards. There now—by touch:

The jamb. The bolt. Wedge the card and slide it through fast.

He did it. The door popped. He fell backwards inside. He locked the door behind him. He hit the lights. He checked the room out.

One bed. One bathroom. One closet. One overnight bag on the floor.

He tossed the bag. He saw clothes and a razor. He saw hate tracts. He checked the closet. He checked the shelf. He saw a box of fuses—half full.

He saw a Mossberg pump. He saw a .45. He saw a .357 mag.

He grabbed the pump. He dumped the shells. He grabbed the .45. He popped the hot round. He popped the clip.

He grabbed the mag. He popped the cylinder. He dumped the shells. He pulled the rug up.

He hid the ammo. He shut the closet door. He killed the room lights. He sat down. He pulled his piece. He cocked the hammer.

He leaned on the bed. He faced the door. He counted rabbits full-out.

He dozed. He cramped up. He heard chants outside. Two words—say two blocks out.

"Freedom" and "nigger"—two words overlapped.

The sun arced—light cut through window shades—shades going black.

Littell dozed. Littell stirred. Littell heard siren bursts. Short bursts—per stalled traffic.

He got up. He walked outside. Tenants mingled. Tenants rebel-yelled.

A man laughed. A man went "Ka-pow!"

A man said, "A nigger church just went ka-blooey."

Littell ran.

He cut left. He ran two blocks. He passed the egg huts. His coat flapped. His piece showed. Some egg men perked up.

They chucked eggs. They hit him. They dosed his pants. They grazed his head.

He hit the main drag. He cut right. He pushed through pickets. He ate eggs. He ate picket signs.

He slid. He hit eggshells. He tripped. A redneck kicked him. A marcher kicked him for kicks.

Horns. Sirens. Shouts—street blockade dead ahead. Egg trucks and egg men. An ambulance stalled and bucked.

Rednecks ran over. Marchers ran over. Fat cops ran up slow. They hit the blockade. They yelled. They shoved.

The blockade held. Pushing and shoving. Horns/sirens/shouts.

Littell got up. Littell dripped eggshells. Littell ran over fast. The cops saw him. Looks traveled—check Johnny Fed.

Littell pulled his badge. Littell pulled his gun. The cops smirked. The egg men smirked. The marchers stepped back.

Louder now: Yahoos and nigger yells. Horns/sirens/shouts.

Littell grabbed an egg man. Said egg man smirked. Littell smashed his face on his truck. He hit the door. He hit the ground. His false teeth popped out and cracked.

The egg men stepped back. The cops stepped back. The cops bumped the marchers. The cops brushed picket signs.

Littell cracked the door. Littell jerked the brake. The truck rolled. The truck hit a light pole. The ambulance swerved and cut through.

Littell stepped back. Eggs hit his glasses. Tobacco juice hit his shoes.

Gutted:

Scorched timber/wet timber/wet dirt. Two dead—a boy and his dad.

The bomb hit a 4:00 p.m. service. The bomb made a floorboard blast. It reached up. Pews shattered. Wood sheared.

Littell mingled.

He saw the meat wagons. He saw the dead. He saw a boy with no toes. He saw fire trucks. He saw TV trucks. He saw some Klan youth.

They kliqued up. They klanvoked. They klowned for kamera krews.

Littell mingled.

He drew stares. He smelled like egg. He dripped shells and yolk.

Some marchers showed. Some Feds showed. The marchers consoled the victims. Folks bled and wept.

Medics hauled gurneys. Medics hauled vics. Meat wagons hauled Code 3.

Littell tailed them. Littell watched them unload. Folks limped. Folks hobbled. That boy held his toes.

The clinic was old. The clinic was unkempt. A sign read Colored Only.

Littell watched. The Feds watched Littell. Nurses pushed IV stands. A woman fell. The toe boy convulsed.

Littell drove to a liquor store. Littell bought a pint of good scotch.

75

(Bogalusa, 6/21/65)

Radio rock:

Hatenanny stuff. "Who Needs Niggers?" and "Ship Those Niggers Back." Katchy. Kool kombos. Kall-ins on K-L-A-N.

Pete dipped his seat. Wayne watched the door. Door 5—the Rebel's Rest Motel.

Chuck was out. Pete was right. Chuck shagged to Bogalusa. Chuck diced his folks. Chuck stole their car. Chuck shagged his ass here.

They tossed the house. They found body parts. They found no hit notes. They drove east. They called motels. They found Chuck.

They drove fast. They drove fried. No sleep since Saigon. They stopped in Beaumont. They scored bennies. They revitalized.

Pete told Wayne the hit story. Pete spieled full disclosure.

He named names. He dropped details. He spieled perspective. He blew Wayne's mind. He framed Wayne's own Dallas tale.

Wayne talked up Wayne Senior. Wayne Senior fed the hit fund. Wayne Senior ran snitch-Klans. Wayne Senior ran Bob Relyea now.

Pete said it: Wayne Senior runs *YOU.*

Radio rock: Odis Cochran/the Coon Hunters/Rambunctious Roy.

Wayne flipped the dial. Wayne caught a newscast.

". . . leaky pipe explosion at a Negro church outside Bogalusa, which civil-rights agitators have called a 'bomb blast.' A spokesman for the Federal Bureau of Integration said that early evidence points to a faulty gas main."

Pete turned it off. "That's the Feds. They got to the radio people."

Wayne popped two bennies. "They know it's Bob."

Pete sipped RC. Bennies parched him bad.

"They've got a hunch, and they want to cover their bets. They didn't tell him to do it, they didn't want him to do it, but he figured he could get away with it, and if they made him for it, they'd let him slide and warn him not to do it again."

Wayne watched the doors. Night-lights bipped above them. Doorways glowed blue.

"You think Bob's with Chuck?"

Pete cracked his knuckles. "I hope not. I don't want to kill a Federal employee who's hooked up with your dad."

Wayne grabbed the RC. "I don't like the chronology. Chuck gets the letter, Chuck flies home and clips his parents. He's *probably* got the journal, and he *might've* told Bob about the hit."

Pete cracked his thumbs. "We'll ask him about that."

Wayne sipped RC. An Olds pulled up. Pete made the plates: PDL-902.

Chuck got out. Chuck picked his teeth and swaggered. Chuck entered room #5.

Wayne said, "He's alone."

Pete popped two bennies. Wayne grabbed their guns. Pete tapped the silencers. They pulled up their shirttails. They stuffed the guns down. They covered the grips.

They walked over. The room-row rocked—shitkicker tunes and full tenancy.

Wayne tried the door. It was locked. Pete shouldered it. The jamb cracked. The lock split. They rode the door in. There's this shit room—but where's Ch—

Chuck exits a closet. Chuck has two guns. Chuck aims and fires. Two hammers click. Chuck fucking plotzes. Chuck fucking *shits*.

Pete charged him. Pete grabbed him. Pete threw him down. Wayne shut the door. Wayne tossed his cuffs. Pete snagged them.

Chuck crawled. Chuck tried to run. Pete grabbed his hair. Pete banged his head on the floor.

Wayne cuffed him. Pete picked him up. Pete threw him into a wall. He hit hard. He made dents. He hit the floor.

Wayne knelt down. "Did you tell Bob about Dallas?"

Chuck dribbled blood. "I told your daddy you're a punk motherfucker."

"Did you and Bob bomb that church?"

Chuck dribbled bile. "Ask Daddy Rabbit. Tell him Wild Rabbit's his boy."

Pete grabbed a hot plate. Pete plugged it in. Pete sparked the coils.

Wayne said, "Where's the notes your parents found?"

Chuck pissed his pants. "Wild Rabbit says fuck you. Father Rabbit says he's your daddy."

Pete dropped the hot plate. It hit coil side down. It singed up Chuck's hair.

Chuck screeched. The coil sizzled. Chuck yelled, "All right!"

Wayne grabbed the hot plate. Wayne grabbed a pillow. Wayne fluffed out Chuck's hair.

Chuck dribbled blood. Chuck dribbled bile. Chuck rubbed his head on the floor.

"I . . . didn't . . . tell Bob. I . . . I burned them notes."

Pete cued Wayne. Wayne cranked the radio. Wayne reprised Rambunctious Roy:

". . . White Man's wise to Martin Luther Coon. Eatin' watermelon in the month of June. Big teeth chompin' sweet potato pie—"

Wayne pulled his piece. Pete pulled his piece. Chuck said, "No, *please*."

The door creaked. The jamb snapped and sheared. Ward Littell walked in.

He was egg-spattered. He was blotto. He was non compos something. He put out booze breath.

Pete said, "Fuck."

Wayne said, "Jesus Christ."

Ward turned the music off. Ward walked up to Chuck. Chuck shit his pants. Chuck dribbled teeth.

Ward said, "Wild Rabbit."

Chuck coughed. Chuck dribbled teeth.

"Wild Rabbit's got the Federal pedig—"

Ward pulled his piece. Ward shot Chuck's eyes out.

Part IV

COERCION

July 1965–November 1966

DOCUMENT INSERT: 7/2/65. Internal memorandum. To: Director. From: BLUE RABBIT. Topic: OPERATION BLACK RABBIT. Marked: "Stage-1 Covert"/"Eyes Only"/"Read and Burn."

Sir,
Per the church bombing and related actions in Bogalusa, Louisiana.

Locally assigned agents have completed their internal investigation. They have reported to me orally, have filed no official reports and have confirmed the official judgment of the Bogalusa Police Department: that the "accidental explosion" was caused by a leaky pipe main. That judgment should stand as the authoritative verdict on this matter. It is crucial to the continued success of the WHITE-HATE arm of OPERATION BLACK RABBIT.

I've spoken to WILD RABBIT. His denials of complicity in the bombing were not convincing. I warned him that church bombings were outside his operating parameters and that no such incidents should happen again. WILD RABBIT seemed cowed and did not protest the reprimand. It should be noted that his arms bore odd bruises and that in fact he seemed to have sustained a recent beating.

WILD RABBIT refused to comment on his bruises and overall beaten appearance. I queried him on the possible presence of his known Vietnam associate Charles Rogers per the time of the church incident, and WILD RABBIT became visibly upset. It should be noted: The dismembered bodies of Rogers' elderly parents were found in their Houston, Texas, home on 6/23, and Rogers (who cannot be located) is the leading suspect in this double homicide. I checked Vietnamese-U.S. passport records for the two weeks preceding the assumed date-of-death, learned that Rogers flew from Saigon to Houston on 6/15 and that the cargo on his flight included bomb material. It is my belief that Rogers supplied the explosives for the bombing and that WILD RABBIT assisted him in this unsanctioned provocation.

It should also be noted that local agents spotted CRUSADER RABBIT at the Negro hospital shortly after the bombing. He was visibly distraught and of unkempt appearance. I checked region-wide flight and car-rental records and learned that CRUSADER RABBIT flew from Las Vegas to New Orleans and drove to

Bogalusa. I consider it likely that he met his client Carlos Marcello in New Orleans and took advantage of its proximity to
Bogalusa.

I view CRUSADER RABBIT's trip to Bogalusa as fully in character, and it does not surprise me that he wished to view the planned
civil-rights agitation in person. Please respond per CRUSADER
RABBIT.

Respectfully,
BLUE RABBIT

DOCUMENT INSERT: 7/6/65. Internal memorandum. To: BLUE
RABBIT. From: Director. Topic: OPERATION BLACK RABBIT.
Marked: "Stage-1 Covert"/"Eyes Only"/"Read and Burn."

BLUE RABBIT,
Take all measures to see that the accidental explosion verdict is
sustained in the Bogalusa case. Allow WILD RABBIT to claim credit
for the "Bombing" and thus gain credibility for his new Klan unit.
Continue to discourage WILD RABBIT from committing acts of violence outside his operating parameters.

I agree: CRUSADER RABBIT's presence in Bogalusa was
entirely in character, albeit marginally disturbing. CRUSADER
RABBIT is a close associate of Pete Bondurant, who is a close associate of Charles Rogers.

The confluence troubles me. Have Los Angeles and Nevada-
based agents tail CRUSADER RABBIT at irregular intervals. Initiate trash and mail covers at his Los Angeles and Las Vegas
residences.

DOCUMENT INSERT: 7/8/65. Internal memorandum. To: Director.
From: BLUE RABBIT. Topic: OPERATION BLACK RABBIT. Marked:
"Stage-1 Covert"/"Eyes Only"/"Read and Burn."

Sir,
I've talked to WHITE RABBIT. He told me he'll be taking a Las
Vegas vacation soon. Should I have him meet with CRUSADER
RABBIT and judiciously assess his state of mind?

Respectfully,
BLUE RABBIT

DOCUMENT INSERT: 7/10/65. Internal memorandum. To: BLUE
RABBIT. From: Director. Topic: OPÉRATION BLACK RABBIT.
Marked: "Stage-1 Covert"/"Eyes Only"/"Read and Burn."

   BLUE RABBIT,
   Yes. Have WHITE RABBIT contact CRUSADER RABBIT during
his stay in Las Vegas.

76

(Port Sulphur, 7/14/65)

Prospects: Gaspar Fuentes/Miguel Díaz Arredondo. Cubano/anti-Beard/allegedly pro-*Tigre*.

Flash boated to Cuba. Flash found them. Flash boated them out. Flash praised their skills. Flash praised their pidgin English. Flash praised their balls.

The venue: a cinder-block shack/10-by-10/a heat sponge. Two electric chairs—straps and hoods—bought from Angola Pen. A dynamo/two chair feeds/two polys.

Flash strapped Fuentes. Laurent G. strapped Arredondo. Wayne and Mesplède watched.

Shots popped outside. Troopers hit targets. Tiger South—Kamp with a "K." Exiles in residence—sixty strong—kadre-adjunct/kadre-armed/ kadre-fed.

Flash rigged the needles. Laurent pumped the cuffs. Wayne watched. Wayne drifted off.

We're in Port Sulphur. Go north a bit—you'll hit Bogalusa.

Littell shoots Chuck. Littell's drunk. Littell vows sobriety. Pete consoles him: I'll dump Chuck and brace WILD RABBIT. Wild Bob's Fed now. He's Wayne Senior's boy.

Flash ran the polys. Laurent ran the quiz: Do you drink water? Is your shirt blue? Do you hate Fidel Castro?

Needle dip—short—no lies.

Port Sulphur—stone's throw to Bogalusa.

They drove Chuck around. They found a swamp. They dumped Chuck in. Gators ate him. Wayne and Pete watched.

Wayne toured the hospital. Wayne saw the bomb damage. Wayne saw a boy minus toes.

Pictures. Add-on shots. Let's augment your Bongo pix. Let's augment Wendell D. Pictures: The icebox/Chuck's parents/those big gator teeth.

Flash ran the polys. Laurent ran the quiz: Are you a spy? Do you serve the Cuban militia?

Needle dip—short—no lies.

Wayne drifted. Wayne yawned. The stateside runs bored him. He missed Saigon. He missed the lab. He missed the war and the threat.

Are you anti-*Communisto?* Are you pro-*Tigre?* Will you serve *El Gato* supreme?

Needle dip—short—no lies.

Flash smiled. Laurent smiled. Mesplède up and cheered.

They unstrapped the prospects. They hugged them. Fuentes hugged Wayne. Fuentes oozed Brylcreem. Arredondo hugged Wayne. Arredondo oozed VO5.

Looks traveled. Hey—it's lunchtime—let's cook by electric chair.

They scrounged. They ad-libbed. Flash scrounged hot dogs. Laurent scrounged corned beef.

They packed them in. They stuffed the hoods. They pulled the switches. Sparks popped. The meat fried. The hoods dripped fat.

The meat cooked uneven. The concept rocked. The reality stunk.

Mesplède supplied mustard. Flash supplied buns.

77

(Las Vegas, 7/16/65)

Candles—a full forty-five.

Pete blew them out. One puff did it. Barb cut the cake.

"Make a wish, and don't mention Cuba."

Pete laughed. "I already did."

"So tell."

"No. You jinx it that way."

Barb cranked the AC. Barb chilled down the suite.

"Did it involve Cuba?"

"I'm not saying."

"Vietnam?"

Pete licked icing. "Vietnam's no Cuba."

Barb scratched the cat. "Tell me why. It's your birthday, so I'll indulge you."

Pete sipped coffee. "It's too big, too fucked up, and too mechanized. You've got choppers with belly lights that can flash a one-mile-square patch of jungle. You've got carpet bombing and napalm. You've got gooks with no fucking charm and a bunch of shifty little cocksuckers in black pajamas who've lived guerrilla warfare for fifty fucking years."

Barb lit a cigarette. "Cuba's got more pizzazz. It fits your imperialist aesthetic."

Pete laughed. "You've been talking to Ward."

"You mean I stole his vocabulary."

Pete cracked his knuckles. The cat humped his knees.

"Flash smuggled two guys in. They were heisting casinos and killing croupiers. In Havana, that takes balls."

"Killing unarmed men?"

Pete laughed. "Militia guys work the casinos."

Barb laughed. "Distinction noted."

Pete kissed her. "Nobody disapproves like you. It's one of the ten thousand reasons why we work."

Barb pried the cat off. Barb squeezed his knees.

"Ward said you've let me grow up."

Pete smiled. "Ward gets to you. You think you know him, then he pulls out one more stop."

"For instance?"

"He cares about people who can't do him any good, but he's not a sucker about it."

"For example?"

"He got wind of some Klan shit. He pulled a stunt that nobody else would have pulled."

Barb smiled. "Including you?"

Pete nodded. "I helped him out on the back end. I braced a kadre guy and laid down some rules."

Barb stretched. The cat clawed her skirt.

"I had lunch with Ward. He was worried. He saw Jane going through his papers."

Pete stood up. Pete spilled his coffee.

Fuck—

"The ARVN boss man's getting ready to bomb Hanoi. He's talking to his financial advisor, One Lump Sum, and his Secretary of Fruitness, Come San Chin. They're in this chink restaurant in Saigon. Come San Chin's snarfing a big bowl of cream-of-some-young-guy."

Pete yukked. Pete watched the building.

He flew to L.A. He brought Milt C. for chuckles. He shagged a rental car.

He *felt* it: Jane's bent. She's a plant. Carlos placed her with Ward.

He called Fred Otash. He quizzed him—what have *you* got? Otash spieled a tip per Danny Bruvick—Arden-Jane's ex.

Danny's a boat man. Danny's got a pseudonym. Danny runs a charter biz—"somewhere in Alabama."

Carlos lived in New Orleans. Alabama was close.

Pete watched the building. Milt picked his nose. Ward was in Chicago. Sam G. called him in. Arden-Jane was upstairs.

"The Rat Pack tours Vietnam. Frank's glomming all the slant-eyed trim. Dino's bombed out of his gourd. He's so blotto that he blunders behind the Viet Cong lines. This little slant comes up to him. Dino says, 'Take me to your leader.' The slant says, 'Ky, Mao, or Ho Chi Minh?' Dino says, 'We'll dance later. Right now, take me to your leader.' "

Pete yukked. Pete watched the building.

Milt bummed a cigarette. "Freddy T. sent me a tape. Three legislators and six hookers jungled up at the Dunes."

Pete stretched. Pete watched the building.

Milt blew smoke rings. "I'm doing some more TV ads with Sonny. 'Tiger Kab, the Vegas champ. Call now or I'll kick your patootie.' "

Pete yukked. Pete watched the building. Milt ditched his shoes. Milt aired out his feet.

"We've got some deadbeats. I do not see the wisdom of consigning white horse on credit."

"I'll take care of it."

Milt yukked. "Let's use Sonny. Dig, he loves fur coats, he's always buying them for his bitches, and Donkey Dom just clipped a fur shop in Reno. Dig, Sonny can do our collections, and we can pay him off in fur."

Pete yukked—Milt, you slay me. Pete saw Jane walk out.

The doorman smiled. The doorman shagged her car. She got in. She pulled out. She drove west.

Pete kicked the engine. Pete pulled out. Pete tailed her. They took Wilshire west. They took Bundy south. They took Pico west toward the beach.

Pete laid back. Jane jumped lanes. Jane pulled right. Jane signaled. Jane turned.

There: the B. of A.—West L.A. branch.

She pulled up. She locked the car. She walked in.

Milt scoped her. "Nice pins. I could dig her love in a semi-large way."

Pete lit a cigarette. Milt bummed one.

"So, who is she? You call me at 5:00 a.m. You say, 'Let's go to L.A.,' you don't explain yourself. I'm starting to think you just brought me along for the laughs."

Jane walked out. Jane lugged a coin sack. Jane walked to the parking-lot phone.

She dialed "0." She fed the slots. She talked. She listened. She cupped the receiver. The call dragged on. She jiggled coins. She refed the slots.

Pete watched her. Pete timed her: five minutes/six/eight.

Milt yawned. "I'm digging on the intrigue. It's not like she hasn't got a phone at her crib."

Ten minutes/twelve/fourteen.

She hung up. She walked to her car. She got in and pulled out.

Pete tailed her. They took Pico east. They drove six miles plus. They took La Brea north.

They crossed Wilshire. They crossed 3rd. They took Beverly east. They took Rossmore north.

There—she pulls left. She signals. She turns. She's upside the Algiers—a white-brick/mock-mosque motel.

She parked. She got out. She palmed a folder. The joint had big windows. Dig the see-thru surveillance.

She walked inside. She stopped a clerk. She passed him the folder.

Milt said, "I smell tsuris. Carlos has points in that joint."

Pete said, "I know."

He weighed it. He diced it. He fucking julienned it. Carlos had points. Carlos had *control* points. Carlos hired the crew.

They flew home. Milt buzzed off. Pete hit Tiger Kab. He rehearsed his shtick. He built some lies. He called PC Bell.

A clerk picked up. "Police Information. Who's requesting?"

Pete coughed. "Sergeant Peters, LAPD. I need the connect on a pay-phone call."

"Time, location, and origin number, please."

Pete grabbed a pen. "1:16 p.m. today. No origin number, but it's the pay phone outside the Bank of America at 14229 West Pico, Los Angeles."

The clerk coughed. "Please hold for that information."

Pete held. Pete watched the lot. Donkey Dom shot dice. Donkey Dom ogled boys. Donkey Dom adjusted his basket.

The line buzzed. The clerk coughed.

"That call was long-distance. The connect was a charter-boat slip in Bon Secour, Alabama."

78

(Chicago, 7/19/65)

S am kvetched.

Per the jail food. Per the jail lice. Per his jail hemorrhoids.

Sam talked loud. The attorney room buzzed. The lice had feet. The lice had wings. The lice had fangs like Godzilla.

Littell stretched. His chair squeaked. The seat itched—lice like Godzilla.

Sam said, "I found a bug in my corn flakes this morning. He had a wingspan like a P-38. I attribute all this shit to the cocksucker who impaneled this cocksucking grand jury, that well-known cocksucker Robert F. Kennedy."

Littell tapped his pen. "You'll be out in ten months. The jury term expires."

Sam scratched his arms. "I'll be dead in six months. You can't go up against lice that big and survive."

Littell laughed. Sam scratched his legs.

"It's all Bobby's fault. If the cocksucker ever runs for President, he will rue the fucking day, and that is no shit, Dick Tracy."

Littell shook his head. "He'll never try to hurt you again. He has a different agenda now."

Sam scratched his neck. "Right. He's in bed with the nigger agitators, which don't mean his hard-on for us has subsided."

A bug cruised the table. Sam smashed it.

"One for the home team. Breed no more, you cocksucker."

Littell cleared his throat. "We're on schedule in Vegas. We've got the board votes and the legislators. Mr. Hughes should get his money sometime next year."

Sam scratched his feet. "Too bad Jimmy won't be around to see it."

"I may be able to keep him out until after we get in."

Sam sneezed. "So he celebrates en route to Leavenworth. We keester Howard Hughes, and Jimmy packs his pj's for the pen."

"That's about it, yes."

Sam sneezed. "I don't like that look in your eyes. It says, 'I got some momentous shit for you, even though *you* called *me* in.'"

Littell cleaned his glasses. "I've talked to the others. They have an idea that they think you should consider."

Sam rolled his eyes. "Then *tell* me. You've got this tendency to coax things and lay out these big preambles."

Littell leaned in. "They think you're through in Chicago. They think you're a sitting duck for the Feds and the State AG. They think you should move to Mexico and run your personal operations from there. They think you should start making Latin-American connections, to aid us in our foreign casino strategy, which will begin sometime after we sell Mr. Hughes the hotels."

Sam scratched his neck. Sam scratched his arms. Sam scratched his balls. A bug leaped. Sam caught it. Sam smashed it.

"Okay, I'll play. I know when over's over, and I know the future when I see it."

Littell smiled. Sam rocked his chair back.

"You still got that look. You should unload before I start itching again."

Littell squared his necktie. "I want to oversee the buyouts for the pension-book plan, assist in the foreign casino negotiations, and retire. I'm going to ask Carlos formally, but I wanted to get your blessing first."

Sam smiled. Sam stood up. Sam played street mime. He sprayed holy water. He gave Holy Communion. He ran the Stations of the Cross.

"You've got it. *If* you help us out on one last thing."

"Tell me. I'll do it."

Sam straddled his chair. "We got hurt on the '60 election. I bought Jack West Virginia and Illinois, and he sicced his cocksucking kid brother on us. Now, Johnson's okay, but he's soft on the niggers, and he might not run in '68. The thing is, we're prepared to be very generous to the right candidate, if he pardons Jimmy and helps us out on some other fronts, and we want *you* to work it out."

Littell inhaled. Littell exhaled. Littell went dead faint.

"Jesus Christ."

Sam scratched his hands. "We want Mr. Hughes to put up 25% of our contribution. We want our guy to agree to a hands-off policy on the Teamsters. We want him to slow down any Fed shit aimed at the Outfit. We want no foreign-policy grief aimed at the countries where we plant our casinos, right- or left-wing."

Littell inhaled. Littell exhaled. Littell went faint-faint.

"When?"

"The '68 primaries. Around that time. You know, the conventions."

A bug jumped. Sam caught it. Sam smashed it.

"Breed no more, you fuck."

Charts: Profit flow/overhead/debits.

Littell read charts. Littell studied charts. Littell took notes. He worked on the terrace. The view distracted him. He loved Lake Michigan.

The Drake Hotel—two-bedroom suite—on Sam Giancana.

Littell read charts. Fund-book stats jumped. Money lent/money invested/money repaid.

Business targets. Fund-financed. Potential takeover prey. Let's extort said businesses. Let's build foreign casinos. Let's buy a President. Let's shape policy. Let's reverse 1960. Let's spread our bets. Let's cover all odds. Let's subvert left-wing nations.

That was odd—the Outfit leaned right—the Outfit bribed right per said leaning.

Chicago broiled. Wind scoured the lake. Littell ditched his charts. Littell studied briefs.

Appeal briefs—let's keep Jimmy out. Stock briefs—let's get Drac in. It was shit work. It was repetitive. It was post-dead.

He got up. He stretched. He watched Lake Shore Drive. He saw car lights as streamers.

He went by his banks yesterday. He withdrew tithe money. He cut tithe checks. He mailed them. He worried a phone call.

He called Bayard Rustin. He lied off Bogalusa. He did it to protect himself. He did it to protect Pete and Wayne.

He'd read the papers. He saw the news. The church blew "accidental." No one linked Chuck. No one linked WILD RABBIT.

He called Bayard. He dittoed the news. He said a gas main blew. He cited fake sources. Bayard expressed gratitude. Bayard expressed belief. *He* lied. *He* lied deftly. *He* acted late.

The church blew. His late fees accrued—fees for *his* dead and maimed.

He saw the maimed. Some Feds saw him. Said Feds might inform Mr.

Hoover. He got drunk. He killed Chuck. He got sober. He still wanted it. He still tasted it. Liquor signs glowed.

He killed Chuck. He slept twelve hours. He woke up to this: End it. Leave the Life. Cut and run when you can.

Sam said yes. Sam gave his blessing. Sam had stipulations. Carlos might say yes. Carlos might have stipulations.

Tithes/stipulations/election years.

He served Mr. Hoover. They colluded. It spawned BLACK RABBIT. It spawned WILD RABBIT. It spawned dead and maimed. He killed Chuck. Pete braced WILD RABBIT. It was catch-up penance. It was wholly insufficient.

The lake glowed. Cruise boats cruised. He saw bow lights. He saw dance bands. He saw women.

Jane was war now. Jane outflanked him. Jane *knew* him before he *knew* her. She knew he stole. She knew he bagged money. She knew he played covert tapes.

She went through his papers. He caught her at it. They retreated. They quashed talk. They quashed confrontations.

Jane had plans. He *knew* it. She might want to hurt him. She might want to use him. She might want to know him more.

It scared him. It moved him. It made him want her more.

A boat drew close. A band played. A blue dress twirled. Janice wore dresses like that.

She was still bawdy. It was still good. She still served up stories and sex.

She dished Wayne Senior. The details scared him. Wayne Senior was FATHER RABBIT. Janice dished him. Janice loathed him. Janice still felt his hold.

The boat cruised by. The blue dress vanished. Littell called the Sands. Janice was out. Littell called the DI. Littell checked his messages.

One message: Call Lyle Holly—he's at the Riv. Shit—WHITE RABBIT wants you.

Littell got the number. Littell put the call off. Littell prepped a tape. Littell grabbed a spool.

Sam scared him. Sam waxed profane. Bobby/cocksucker/rue the fucking day.

Littell prepped his tape-rig. Littell memory-laned.

Chicago, 1960—the Phantom loves Bobby. Chicago, 1965—Bobby lives on tape.

79

(Las Vegas, 7/20/65)

Tiger teemed.

Scribes pressed Sonny—give us quotes—rag that punk Cassius X. Sonny ignored them. Sonny quaffed Chivas. Sonny pawed mink coats.

Donkey Dom stole them. Donkey Dom sold them. Donkey Dom name-dropped. I pop fur shops/I bone Rock Hudson/I poke Sal Mineo.

His bun boy sulked. His bun boy griped hypocritical. His bun boy pimped drag queens full-time.

Wayne watched. Barb watched.

Dom shagged calls. His bun boy buzzed drivers. They juked the noon rush. Sonny bought mink mittens. Sonny bought mink jockstraps. Sonny bought mink earmuffs.

A scribe said, "Are those furs hot?"

Sonny said, "Your mama's hot. I'm your daddy."

A scribe said, "Why don't you join the civil-rights movement?"

Sonny said, "'Cause I ain't got no dog-proof ass."

The scribes yukked. Wayne yukked. Barb walked out to the lot. She popped pills. She chased them. She chugged flat 7-Up.

Wayne walked out. Wayne braced her in close.

"Pete's rotating back. You start flying the second he's gone."

Barb stepped back. "Think about what *you* do, and tell me you disapprove then."

Wayne stepped close. "Look who we sell to."

"Look at *me*. Do I look like one of the junkie whores you've created?"

"I'm looking. I'm seeing lines you didn't have a year ago."

Barb laughed. "I've earned them. I've got fifteen years in the Life."

Wayne stepped back. "You're dodging me.."

"No. I'm just saying I've been around longer, and I know how things work better than you."

"Tell Pete that. He won't buy it, but tell him anyway."

Barb stepped close. "You're hooked, not me. You're hooked on the Life, and you still don't know how it works."

Wayne stepped close. They bumped knees. Wayne smelled Barb's soap.

"You're just pissed that there's no place in it for you."

Barb stepped back. "You're going to do things that you won't be able to live with."

"Maybe I have already."

"It gets worse. And you'll do worse things, just to prove you can take it."

Test run:

Four collections. Four junkie deadbeats. Sonny's collection debut.

Said junkies annexed a church basement. Said junkies had squatters' rights. Their pastor skin-popped Demerol. Said junkies geezed up in church.

Wayne drove. Sonny cleaned his nails with a switchblade. Sonny sipped scotch. West LV sizzled. Folks soaked in kiddie pools. Folks lived in air-cooled cars.

Wayne said, "I killed a colored guy in Saigon."

Sonny said, "I killed a white guy in St. Louis."

There's the church. It's dilapidated. It's sandblasted. It's neon-signed. Dig the prayer hands and crosses. Dig the Jesus rolling dice.

They parked. They walked back to the basement door. They picked the lock. They walked in.

They saw four junkies. They're crapped out on car seats—scavenged off old Cadillacs. They saw spoons and matchbooks. They saw spikes and tube ties. They saw bindles and white dregs.

There's a hi-fi. There's some LPs. It's all gospel wax.

The junkies reposed—one per seat—the land of Naugahyde Nod. They saw Sonny. They saw Wayne. They snickered. They giggled. They sighed.

Wayne said, "Go."

Sonny whistled. Sonny stomped. Sonny stormed Naugahyde Nod.

"You motherfuckers have got ten seconds to quit fucking with this house of worship and pay up what you owe."

One junkie giggled. One junkie scratched. One junkie chuckled. One junkie yawned.

Wayne turned on the hi-fi. Wayne flipped a disc. Wayne laid the needle down. It was loud shit. It was ecstatic—Crawdaddy's Christian Chorale.

Wayne said, "Go."

Sonny kicked the car seats. Sonny dumped the junkies. Sonny threw the junkies down. They squirmed. They squealed. They evacuated Naugahyde Nod.

Sonny kicked them. Sonny picked them up. Sonny dropped them. Sonny grabbed the car seats. Sonny aimed. Sonny dropped them on their heads.

They squealed. They screeched. They howled and bled.

Sonny slapped them. Sonny picked their pockets. Sonny tossed pocket trash. One guy turned his pockets out. One guy ran pleas.

Sonny picked him up. Sonny dropped him. Sonny kicked him. Sonny bent down. Sonny caught his pleas.

Sonny stood up. Sonny smiled. Sonny signaled Wayne. Crawdaddy crescendoed. Wayne pulled the plug and walked up.

Sonny smiled. "As of spring, Wendell Durfee was running a string of wetback whores in Bakersfield, California."

80

(Bon Secour, 7/22/65)

Boats:

Charter jobs. Teak hulls and big motors. Forty slips / thirty bare / thirty boats out.

Pete strolled dockside. Pete scoped slip 19. There's the *Ebbtide*. It runs fifty feet. Dig those high gunwales.

Nice shit. Mounted poles and cargo space. Spiffy brass fittings.

A guy worked on deck. He was mid-size. He ran mid-forties. He had a bum leg. He had a bad limp.

It was hot. The air dripped. Clouds densified. Mobile Bay—Shitsville—bait shacks and congestion.

Pete strolled deckside. Pete scoped slip 19.

He traced Jane's call. He flew in. He ran checks. "Dave Burgess" owned the *Ebbtide*. "Dave Burgess" chartered out. "Dave Burgess" knew guys in New Orleans. Add 2 and 2. Add D.B. "Dave Burgess" was Danny Bruvick.

The T&C Corp owned the *Ebbtide*. Carlos owned T&C. Carlos *was* New Orleans.

He bribed a cop. He checked phone sheets. He ran phone checks. "Burgess" was good. "Burgess" used pay phones—right off the dock.

"Burgess" called Carlos. "Burgess" called Carlos frequent. "Burgess" called Carlos four times last month.

Pete walked slip 19. "Burgess" scrubbed fishhooks. Pete stepped on deck. "Burgess" looked up.

He tweaked a bit. He perked a bit. His antennae twitched.

That speargun—*watch*.

"Burgess" reached for it. "Burgess" grabbed. "Burgess" nailed the grip. Pete aimed. Pete kicked out. Pete nailed the grip.

The speargun skittered. "Burgess" said, "Shit."

Pete walked up. Pete grabbed the speargun. Pete popped the spear out to sea.

"Burgess" said, "Fuck."

Pete pulled his shirt up. Pete showed his piece.

"You're thinking 'Jimmy Hoffa sent this guy,' and you're wrong."

"Burgess" sucked a thumbnail. "Burgess" flexed his hand. Pete checked the boat out. The boat enticed. The boat seduced.

Nice: Steel hull/grappling posts/fittings. *Nice:* Hardwood from the Philippines.

"Burgess" flexed his wrist. "She's an old rum-runner. She's got all the—"

Pete pulled his shirt up. Pete showed his piece. Pete pointed below-deck. "Burgess" stood up. "Burgess" sighed. "Burgess" squared his bum leg and limped.

He wore shorts. Dig his scars. Dig his bullet-pocked knee.

He crossed the deck. He passed the wheelhouse. He took back stairs down. Pete tailed him. Pete scoped details.

Two wheel stands/control posts/full instruments. Teak walls/hall space/rear cabins. Rear engines/rear storage/rear cargo traps.

Pete walked ahead. Pete saw an office: two chairs/one desk/one booze shelf.

He pulled "Burgess" in. He grabbed a chair. He pushed "Burgess" down. He tucked "Burgess" in. He poured a libation.

The boat swayed. Pete sloshed Cutty. "Burgess" grabbed it. "Burgess" drained it. "Burgess" liquor-flushed.

Pete poured a refill. Pete poured big. "Burgess" refueled. "Burgess" sucked Cutty up.

Pete cocked his piece. "You're Danny Bruvick. I'm Pete Bondurant, and we've got some friends in common."

Bruvick burped. Bruvick flushed. Bruvick vibed lush.

Pete twirled his piece. "I want the whole story of you, 'Arden,' and Carlos Marcello. I want to know why Arden is shacked up with Ward Littell."

Bruvick eyed the bottle. Pete poured him a pop. Bruvick refueled. The boat dipped. Bruvick doused his lap.

"You shouldn't let me drink too much. I might get courageous."

Pete shook his head. Pete pulled his silencer. Pete tapped his piece. Bruvick gulped. Bruvick pulled beads out. Bruvick rosaried.

Pete shot the Cutty. Pete shot the Gilbey's. Pete shot the Jack D. Bottles spritzed. Teakwood cracked. Soft-points tore holes.

The room shook—sonic booms—the boat aftershocked.

Bruvick spazzed out. Bruvick squeezed his beads. Bruvick grabbed his ears.

Pete pulled his hands down. "Start with Arden. Give me her real name and lay out some perspective."

Bruvick sneezed. Gunpowder tickled noses. Gun cordite stung.

"Her real name's Arden Breen. Her old man was a labor agitator. You know, a Commie type."

Pete cracked his knuckles. "Keep going."

Bruvick tossed his hair. Glass shards flew.

"Her mother died. She got rheumatic fever. The old man raised Arden. He was a drunk and a whore chaser. He had a different name for every day of the week, and he raised Arden in whorehouses and union halls, meaning *bad* union halls, meaning the old man talked Red, but cut management deals every chance he got, which was—"

"Arden. Get back to her."

Bruvick rubbed his knees. "She quit school early, but she always had a head for figures. She met these two whores who went to the bookkeeping school I went to in Mississippi and picked up some skills from them. She kept some whorehouse and union hall books, you know, gigs her old man got her. She'd work these classier houses and spy on the johns. She'd pump them for stock tips and shit like that. She was good at anything involving numbers and ledgers. You know, money calculations."

Pete cracked his thumbs. "Get to it. You're working up to something."

Bruvick rubbed his bad knee. Scar tissue pulsed.

"She started working in some classier houses. She met this money guy Jules Schiffrin. He was tied in with—"

"I know who he was."

"Okay, so she started tricking with him regular. He *kept* her, you know, and she met lots of people in the Life, and she helped him with these so-called 'real' pension-fund books that he was working on."

Pete cracked his wrists. "Keep going."

Bruvick rubbed his knee. "Her old man got killed in '52. He screwed Jimmy H. on a management deal, so Jimmy had him clipped. Arden didn't care. She hated the old man for his goddamn hypocrisy and the shitty way he raised her."

The boat pitched. Pete grabbed the desk.

"Arden and Schiffrin. Spill on that."

"Spill *what?* She learned what she could from him and broke it off."

"And?"

"And she started hooking freelance, and got a thing going with Carlos. I met her in '55. We had mutual friends in those whores who went to school with me. I was working the K.C. local. We got married and cooked up some plans."

"Like 'Let's embezzle Jimmy.' "

Bruvick lit a cigarette. "I admit it wasn't the smartest—"

"You got caught. Jimmy put a contract out."

"Right. Some guys cornered me and shot me. I got away, but I almost lost my leg, and the fucking contract's still out."

Pete lit a cigarette. "Jimmy had the K.C. cops run Arden in. Carlos bailed her out and hid you. He didn't fuck with Jimmy's contract, because he wanted a wedge on you."

Bruvick nodded. Bruvick scoped the booze shelf.

"You're a hump. You wasted my liquor."

Pete smiled. Pete aimed. Pete cocked his piece. Pete shot Bruvick's chair.

The legs sheared. The chair crashed. Wood shattered. Bruvick tumbled. Bruvick yelped. Bruvick rosaried.

Pete blew smoke rings. "Carlos set up your charter business. What happened to Arden then?"

The boat pitched. Bruvick dropped his beads.

"She didn't trust Carlos. She didn't want to owe him, so she split to Europe. We worked out a pay-phone thing and kept in touch that way."

Pete coughed. "She came back to the States. She couldn't give up the Life."

"Right. She landed in Dallas. She got in trouble there, like late in '63. She wouldn't say what happened."

Pete flicked his cigarette. Pete nailed Bruvick flush.

"Come on, Danny. Don't make me get ugly."

Bruvick stood up. His knee went. He stumbled. He braced the wall. He slid back and sat.

He rubbed his knee. He snuffed Pete's cigarette.

"That's straight. She wouldn't tell me what happened. All I know is she hooked up with Littell, then around that time Carlos found her. He said we'd both be safe if she watchdogged Littell, but he still refused to square us with Jimmy."

Solid. Confirmed. Two-front blackmail. Jimmy's contract/the safehouse snafu. Arden—that first name unique.

Carlos *knows* Arden. Carlos makes her *name*. Carlos distrusts Littell. Carlos finds Arden. Carlos plants Arden. Arden spies on Littell.

It vibed solid—90%—it vibed incomplete.

Pete said, "I don't want Littell to get hurt."

Bruvick stood up. His bad knee held.

"I don't think Arden does, either. She's playing out some weird thing with him."

He called Carlos. He got Frau M. He left a message:

I braced D.B.—Danny the boat man—tell Carlos that. Tell him I'll be by. Say I'd love to chat.

He drove to New Orleans. He stopped in libraries. He studied books en route.

Boats:

Galleys/bridges/radar/trawl decks/scuppers/masts.

He studied the nomenclature. He studied engine stats. He studied maps. Pine Island/Cape Sabel/Key West. Pit stops—Cuba due south.

He detoured. He cruised by Port Sulphur. He saw Tiger Kamp South. He saw the troops. He saw Flash and Laurent. He met Fuentes and Arredondo. They talked night raids. They talked scalp runs. They talked insurgency.

Wayne was in Saigon—one fast rotation—one scheduled run back. Wayne loves to WATCH. Wayne wants to GO. Wayne wants to SEE Cuba up close.

Flash had a plan. I'll do a speedboat run. I'll drop Fuentes and Arredondo. Fast—off the north shore—Varcadero Beach.

They reinfiltrate. They build drop zones. They recruit internal. They speedboat back. They funnel arms. They bounce off the Keys. They pull a boat hitch. They lug guns. They fly fast and low. They shuttle. They duck radar—six runs a week.

Pete said no. Pete said why: It's high mileage/it wastes two men/it's low capacity.

Flash said, "*Que?*"

Laurent said, "*Quoi?*"

Fuentes said, "*Que pasa?*"

Pete talked hold nets. Pete talked gunwales. Pete talked fuel efficiency. Pete talked *boats.*

Carlos said, "Sure, she's my watchdog. Tell me Ward don't play angles, then tell me I don't need one."

Galatoire's was dead. They hogged a prime table. Carlos dipped his cigar. Mecundo meets anisette.

"Ward's fund-book thing is a fucking extravaganza, and Arden is a brilliant fucking bookkeeper. I'm protecting my franchise, and Ward gets some good cooze in the process."

Pete lit a cigarette. "He's in love with her. I don't want him to get hurt."

Carlos winked. "I don't want *you* to get hurt. We go back like Ward and me go back. Some guys would have been miffed at what you did to Danny B., but I am not one of them."

Pete smiled. "I copped to it, didn't I? I called you."

"That is correct. You did the wrong thing and covered your bets."

"I just don't want—"

"He won't be. They're good for each other. I know Arden, and Arden knows she can't shit me. Arden tells me Ward's not scheming against me, so I believe her. I've always had this feeling that Ward was skimming Howard Hughes, but Arden says it's not so, so I believe her."

Pete burped. Pete undid his belt—rich Creole food.

"Give me the warning. Let's get it over with."

Carlos burped. Carlos undid his belt—rich Creole food.

"Don't tell Ward about this. Don't make me peeved at you."

"*This*"—still solid—still incomplete.

A waiter cruised by. Pete nixed a comped brandy.

Carlos belched. "What's this about 'ideas'?"

Pete cleared some plates. Pete laid his map out. Pete swamped the table.

"Speedboat runs waste man-hours. You can't move ordnance in bulk. I want to refit and camouflage Bruvick's boat and run it out of Bon Secour. I want to move guns in quantity and pull terror missions."

Carlos checked the map. Carlos lit his cigar. Carlos burned a big hole in Cuba.

81

(Las Vegas, 8/7/65)

Lyle Holly: Dwight Holly built small. BLUE to WHITE RABBIT. A Hoosier/a loudmouth/a fraud.

They met at the DI. They sat in the lounge. Lyle was blunt. Lyle was coarse. Lyle was buzzed at noon.

Lyle said, "I think I'm schizophrenic. I work for the SCLC, I work for Mr. Hoover. I'm on Black Rabbit one minute, voting-rights drives the next. Dwight says I'm psychically unhinged."

Littell sipped coffee. Littell smelled Lyle's scotch.

"Did Mr. Hoover send you in to spy on me?"

Lyle slapped his knees. "Dwight suggested it. He knew I was coming to Vegas, so what the hell."

"Is there anything you'd like me to reveal?"

"Shit, no. I'll tell Dwight that the Ward I saw is the same Ward I allegedly knew back in Chicago, except now he's just as schizo as I am, and for all the same reasons."

Littell laughed. Sammy Davis Jr. walked by. Lyle stared at him.

"Look at that. He's ugly, he's got one eye, and he's colored *and* Jewish. I heard he gets lots of white pussy."

Littell smiled. Lyle waved to Sammy. Sammy waved back.

Lyle sipped Johnnie Red. "Marty gives this speech in New York. He's got a captive audience of liberal Jews with deep pockets. He starts attacking the Vietnam War and pissing all the hebes off with words like 'genocide.' He's going outside his civil-rights bailiwick and biting the hand that feeds him."

Pete was in Laos. Wayne was in Saigon. The war hid them there. He called Carlos. Carlos talked up Pete. Carlos said they'd just schemed plans for Cuba.

Littell said let me retire. Carlos said okay. Carlos dittoed Sam's consent. Carlos talked up the '68 election.

Lyle sipped scotch. Peter Lawford walked by. Lyle stared at him.

"He used to pimp for Jack Kennedy. That makes us comrades-in-arms. I get Marty all his white snatch, and sometimes I dig up young meat for Bayard Rustin. Mr. Hoover's got a photo of Bayard with a dick in his mouth. He made a dupe for President Johnson."

Littell smiled. Lyle hailed a waitress. Lyle shagged a quick refill.

"Dwight said they blew that church up with C-4 explosive. Bayard told me it really *was* a leaky gas main, which makes me think *you* told him."

Littell sipped coffee. "I told him, yes."

Lyle sipped scotch. "Crusader Rabbit's a white man. I'll tell Dwight that."

Littell smiled. Lyle grinned. Lyle pulled out a checkbook.

"I feel lucky. You think you can cash a check into play chips for me?"

"How much?"

"Two grand."

Littell smiled. "Put my initials and 'suite 108' on the check. Tell the cashier I'm a permanent resident."

Lyle smiled. Lyle wrote the check. Lyle got up and walked—half-steady.

Littell watched.

Lyle weaved. Lyle slurped scotch. Lyle trekked the casino. Lyle braced the teller's cage. Lyle passed the check. Lyle got his chips.

Littell watched. Littell let some thoughts stir—CRUSADER RABBIT/White Man/gas main.

Lyle braced a roulette stand. Lyle stacked his chips. Red chips—hundreds—two G's. The wheelman bowed. The wheelman twirled. The wheel spun. The wheel stopped. The wheelman raked chips.

Lyle slapped his forehead. Lyle moved his lips. Littell watched. Littell read his lips. Lyle said, "Oh, shit."

Schizo/comrades/young meat.

Lyle might keep *private* files. Said files might indict. Said files might indict BLACK RABBIT.

Lyle looked around. Lyle saw Littell. Lyle waved his checkbook. Littell waved and nodded.

Lyle walked to the cage. Lyle grabbed the grate. Lyle wrote a check. Lyle fumbled chips.

Their waitress walked by. Littell stopped her.

"My friend's on the floor. Bring him a triple Johnnie Walker."

She nodded. She smiled. Littell gave her ten bucks. She walked to the bar. She poured the drink. She trekked the floor. She hit the roulette stands. She saw Lyle and fueled him.

Lyle guzzled scotch. Lyle stacked his chips. Red chips—hundreds—big stacks.

The wheelman bowed. The wheelman twirled. The wheel spun. The wheel stopped. The wheelman raked chips.

Lyle slapped his forehead. Lyle moved his lips. Littell watched. Littell read his lips. Lyle said, "Oh, shit."

Littell walked over. Littell passed the waitress. Littell slid her ten bucks. She nodded. She *got it.* She smirked.

Lyle walked up. Lyle killed his drink. Lyle chewed the ice.

"I'm down, but I'm not licked, and I've got resources."

"You were always resourceful, Lyle."

Lyle laughed. Lyle swayed half-blotto. Lyle burped.

"You're patronizing me. It's that saintly quality that Dwight hates about you."

Littell laughed. "I'm no saint."

"No, you're not. Martin Luther Coon's the only saint I know, and I've got some hair-curling shit on him."

The waitress swooped by. Lyle grabbed his refill.

"Hair-curling. Or hair-*kinking,* in his case."

Work him—slow now—ease in.

"You mean Mr. Hoover has shit."

Lyle swirled scotch. "He's got his, I've got mine. I've got a big stash at my place in L.A. Mine's better, 'cause I've got daily access to Saintly Marty himself."

Tweak him—slow now—ease in.

"Nobody has better intelligence than Mr. Hoover."

"Shit, I do. I'm saving it for my next contract powwow. I tell my handler, 'You want the goods, you raise my pay—no tickee, no washee.' "

Sammy Davis walked by. Lyle bumped into him. Sammy swerved. Sammy goofed—cat, you are blitzed!

Lyle swerved. Lyle slugged scotch. Lyle pinched a zit on his chin.

"White chicks dig him. He must be hung."

Fumes glowed. Mash and smoke—86 proof. Littell salivated. Littell stepped away.

Lyle pulled two checkbooks—both embossed—"L.H." and "SCLC." He kissed them. He slung them. He drew them quick-draw style. He twirled them and aimed.

"I've got a lucky feeling, which means I just might have to float a loan from the civil-rights movement."

Littell smiled. Lyle weaved. Lyle settled. Lyle walked off blitzed. Littell watched.

Lyle braced the cage. Lyle showed a checkbook—blue for SCLC. Lyle wrote a check. Lyle kissed said check. Lyle fumbled chips.

Reds—ten stacks—five G's.

Slow now—ease in—this is for real.

Littell walked to the phone stand. Littell grabbed a booth. He picked up. The line clicked active. He got service quick.

"Desert Inn. How may I help you?"

"It's Littell, suite 108. I need an outside line to Washington, D.C."

"The number, please."

"EX4-2881."

"Please hold. I'll connect you."

The line buzzed—long-distance coming—static popped and clicked. Littell looked around. Littell saw Lyle. Lyle's at a crap table. Lyle's stacking chips.

The shooter rolls. Lyle slaps his forehead. Lyle says, "Oh, shit."

Static clicked. The call clicked in. Mr. Hoover said, "Yes?"

Littell said, "It's me."

"Yes? And the purpose of this unsolicited contact?"

"White Rabbit suggested a meeting. He arrived at the Desert Inn drunk. He's running up a casino debt with SCLC money."

The line fuzzed. Littell cleared the cord. Littell slapped the receiver. There's Lyle. Lyle's at the cage. Lyle's ecstatic. Lyle's got more chips.

Reds—high stacks—maybe ten G's.

The line fuzzed. The line popped. The line cleared.

Mr. Hoover said, "Cut off his credit and get him out of Las Vegas immediately."

The line fuzzed. The call faded. Littell heard hang-up clicks. There's Lyle. Lyle's at a crap table. Lyle's in a crowd. Lyle's stacking chips.

Sammy Davis bows. Sammy Davis prays. Sammy Davis rolls the dice. The crowd cheers. Lyle cheers. Sammy Davis genuflects.

Littell walked over. Littell pushed his way in.

Lyle crowded Sammy. Lyle played Sammy's foil. Sammy goofed on the white freak. He winked at a blonde. He flicked lice off his coat. He went ick.

Red chips down—pass-line bets—all Lyle's money. Good money— Lyle's up twenty G's.

Sammy gets the dice. Sammy holds them out. Lyle blows wet kisses. Sammy goofs on Lyle—he's a Rat Pack reject—the crowd genuflects.

Sammy rolls. Sammy hits 7. Lyle hits forty G's. The crowd cheers. Lyle hugs Sammy. Sammy grabs the dice.

Lyle blows on them. Lyle drools on them. Lyle genuflects. Sammy pulls a handkerchief. Sammy makes entertainment. Sammy wipes said dice.

Sammy rolls. Sammy hits 7. Lyle hits eighty G's. The crowd cheers. Lyle hugs Sammy. Lyle snuffs his cigarette.

Sammy grabs the dice. Lyle shoves up close. Sammy steps way back. The blonde horns in. Sammy grabs her. Sammy rubs the dice on her dress.

The crowd laughs. Lyle says something. Littell caught "coon" or "kike."

Sammy rolls. Sammy makes 9. Sammy craps dead out. Sammy shrugs—life's a crapshoot, baby. The crowd claps and laughs.

The dealer raked in—all Lyle's chips—big ten grand stacks.

Lyle killed his drink. Lyle dropped his glass. Lyle sucked cracked ice. The crowd dispersed. Sammy walked. The blonde chased his back.

Lyle walked. Lyle staggered. Lyle lurched. Lyle navigated. Lyle tried handholds. Lyle grabbed at slot-machine racks.

He lurched. He made the cage. Littell cut in sidelong. Littell mimed *cut him off*. Lyle bumped the window. The cashier shook his head. Lyle kicked a slot machine rack.

Littell grabbed him. Littell steered him. Littell walked him half-slack. Lyle went limp. Lyle tried to talk. Lyle blathered mumbo-jumbo.

They crossed the floor. They got outside. They made the parking lot. Hot skies—blowtorch time—dry Vegas heat.

Lyle passed out. Littell hauled him—dead weight.

He picked his coat pockets. He checked his billfold. He got his address and car stats: Merc coupe/'61/CAL-HH-492.

Littell looked around. Littell saw the car. Littell lugged Lyle Holly slack. Lyle was small—one-forty tops—slack weight but light.

He made the car. He rolled down the windows. He rolled Lyle in and made him comfy. He pushed the seat back.

L.A.—five hours tops.

Lyle would sleep in his car. Lyle would rouse. Lyle would rouse in the DI lot. Lyle gambled compulsive. Lyle knew the drill:

First they vet you. Then you lose. Then they check your money.

Lyle lost his own coin. Lyle lost the SCLC's. The DI calls fast. The SCLC stops payment. Lyle lives in D.C. Lyle lives in L.A. Casino collectors move. Said collectors hit L.A. first.

Said collectors break laws routinely. Said collectors seize assets. Said collectors kick ass.

Littell drove. His car overheated. Littell drove I-10 west.

He gauged time. He knew booze regimens. He knew pass-outs and wake-ups. He knew pass-out stats.

Three hours—four tops. Lyle wakes up/Where am I?/Oh fuck.

The desert torched. Heat rays jumped. The heat gauge swerved. Littell made Baker. The heat ebbed. Littell made San Berdoo.

He made Redlands. He made Pomona. He made L.A. He drove one-handed. He read street maps. He logged a route.

Lyle lived on North Ivar. It was downscale Hollywood—a cul-de-sac chute.

He ditched the freeway. He took side streets. He looped through Hollywood. There—North Ivar/2200.

Small houses. Sun-scorched awnings. Drab pastel paint. 7:10/summer dusk/quiet.

A cul-de-sac. An end-of-block barrier: a fence and a cliff.

Littell cruised slow. Littell read curb plates. Littell read numbers. Lyle's house—there:

2209. Brown lawn. Peach paint weather-stripped.

He parked two doors down. He got out and popped his trunk. He grabbed a crowbar. He walked up. He looked around. He saw no eyeball wits.

Hardwood door/strong jambs/good fittings.

He worked the crowbar. He tapped the jamb. He leaned hard. He made slack. He wedged his blade in.

He pushed. He shoved. He applied. Wood cracked. Wood splintered. Wood sheared.

He regripped. He rewedged. He snapped the bolt. He popped the door. He stepped inside and shut himself in.

He brushed the walls. He tripped switches. He got lights.

WHITE RABBIT's den:

Dusty and musty. Beaten-down bachelorized.

Living room. Kitchen. Side doors. Gag wall prints—dogs at card games and dogs in black tie. Faux-leather couches. Faux-leather ottomans. Faux-leather chairs.

Littell prowled. Littell checked the kitchen. Littell checked the bedroom and den.

Old fixtures. Cold cuts and liquor. Ratty drawers and cupboards. Undusted shelves.

More prints—dogs at stag nights and dogs ogling chicks.

One desk. One file drawer. Please: No wall panels or safes.

Now: *Trash it first.*

Littell put gloves on. Littell grid-worked. Littell trashed systematic.

He dumped drawers. He scattered clothes. He stripped the bed. He found a German Luger. He found Nazi flags. He found Nazi hats. He bagged them in a pillowcase. They played burglar swag.

He found a Nazi dagger. He found Krugerrands. He found a Jap knife. He bagged them in a loose sheet. They played burglar swag.

He popped the fridge. He dumped the cold cuts. He dumped the booze. He swung the crowbar. He ripped up the couches. He sliced up the chairs.

He dumped the kitchen cabinet. He found a Mauser pistol. He found a Nazi knife. He bagged them in a paper bag. They played burglar swag.

He swung the crowbar. He ripped up floorboards. He tore up wall beams.

Now: the desk and file drawer.

He walked back. He tried them. They were unlocked.

He went through them. He bagged bills. He bagged letters. There: one file extant.

It was folder-sealed. It was doodled up. Lyle drew Nazi maidens and shivs.

It was marked. It was circled: "Marty."

He drove south. He got out of Hollywood. He found a trash bin. He dumped Lyle's swag.

Don't go home—Jane's there—find a motel.

He cruised south. He found a place on Pico. He booked a one-night room. He locked himself in. He skimmed Lyle's bills. He read Lyle's letters.

Bland: Phone bills/gas bills/second-mortgage strife. Flyers from gun shows/notes from ex-wives.

Slow now—here's "Marty."

He opened the folder. He saw typed notes—sixteen pages single-spaced.

He skimmed through. He got the gist. Dr. King plans. Dr. King plots. Dr. King *schemes*.

The intro—WHITE RABBIT verbatim:

"The following points detail MLK's overall designs between now (3/8/65) and the '68 Pres'l election. MLK has discussed the following topics in high-level SCLC staff meetings, has forbidden staff members to announce them publicly or discuss them outside staff meetings and has rebuffed all criticism that points out one obvious fact: The breadth of his socialistic agenda will divert his energies, deplete SCLC resources and undermine the credibility of the civil-rights movement. It will enrage the American status quo, perhaps cost him congressional and presidential support and will earn him the enmity of his 'limousine liberal' supporters. The true danger of his plans is that they may well serve to fuel and unite a coalition of hard-core Communists, Communist sympathizers, far-left intellectuals, disaffected college students and Negroes susceptible to inflammatory rhetoric and prone to violent action."

MLK on Vietnam:

"Genocide cloaked as anti-Communist consent. An evil war of attrition."

MLK plans speeches. MLK plans boycotts. MLK plans dissent.

MLK on slums:

"The economic perpetuation of Negro poverty. The bedrock of de facto segregation. 20th-century slavery, euphemized by politicians of all stripes and creeds. A cancerous social reality and a condition which mandates a massive redistribution of assets and wealth."

MLK plans speeches. MLK plans boycotts. MLK plans rent strikes.

MLK on poverty:

"The Negro will not be truly free until his God-given rights to coexist with whites are supplanted by economic entitlements which make him the financial equal of whites."

MLK plans speeches. MLK plans dissent. "Poor People's Unions." "Poor People's Marches." Poor people hooked on dissent.

MLK on inclusion:

"We can only topple the apple cart of the American power structure and commandeer and equitably redistribute its resources through the creation of a new consensus, a new coalition of the disenfranchised, which will not tolerate men living in luxury while other men live in wretchedness and filth."

MLK plans speeches. MLK plans workshops. MLK plans dissent.

Summits. Workshops. Brain pools. Coalitions. War protesters. Pacifists. Leftist pamphleteers. Vote drives. Reapportionment. Resultant mainstream clout.

WHITE RABBIT cited concepts. WHITE RABBIT ran timetables. WHITE RABBIT quoted dates.

MLK prophesied. MLK decried Vietnam:

"It will escalate into the most murderous misadventure of the American 20th century. It will divide, rip asunder and produce skeptics and people of conscience in epic numbers. They will form the nucleus of the consensus that will burn America as we know it to the ground."

Timetables. Fund drives. Operating costs assessed. Vote potentials. District boundaries. Registration stats. Tallies. Figures. Prognostications.

It's huge. It's grand. It's magnificent. It's insane. It's megalomaniacal.

Littell rubbed his eyes. Littell fought double-vision. Littell dribbled sweat.

Sweet and blessed Christ—

Mr. Hoover would cringe. Mr. Hoover would gasp. Mr. Hoover would FIGHT.

Littell cranked a window. Littell looked out. Littell saw freeway ramps. The cars looked new. The taillights streamed. The signposts blurred bright.

He lit a match. He burned the file. He flushed the ashes down the sink. He prayed for Martin Luther King.

His words stuck.

He savored them. He replayed them. He said them in Dr. King's voice.

He surveilled Lyle's house. He parked adjacent. No Merc extant/no collectors/no movement. Say Lyle dozed late—give him time—time the collectors' approach.

North Ivar was dead. Windows glowed black & white. The glass bounced TV shadows. He shut his eyes. He dipped his seat. He waited. He yawned. He stretched.

Headlights—

They passed his car. They swiveled. They strafed Lyle's house. There—the blue Merc.

Lyle parked in his driveway. Lyle got out and walked up. Lyle saw the door crashed and trashed.

He ran inside. He hit lights. He screeched.

Littell shut his eyes.

He heard crash sounds. He heard toss sounds. He heard oh no yells. He opened his eyes. He checked his watch. He timed Lyle *seeing* things.

More toss sounds. More crash sounds—no yells or screams.

Lyle ran out. Littell clocked it: 3.6 minutes.

Lyle stumbled. Lyle looked woozy. Lyle looked unkempt. Lyle got in his car. Lyle pulled out. Lyle hit reverse and floored it.

He gunned it. He smoked tread. He smashed the barrier fence. The car flew. The car upended and flipped.

Littell heard the crash. Littell heard the tank blow. Littell saw the flames.

DOCUMENT INSERT: 8/11/65. Internal telephone call transcript. (OPERATION BLACK RABBIT addendum.) Marked: "Recorded at the Director's Request"/"Classified Confidential 1-A"/"Director's Eyes Only." Speaking: Director, BLUE RABBIT.

DIR: Good morning.

BR: Good morning, Sir.

DIR: I was saddened by the news on your brother. You have my condolences.

BR: Thank you, Sir.

DIR: He was a valued colleague. That makes the circumstances surrounding his death all the more troubling.

BR: I won't apologize for him, Sir. He indulged occasional binges and behaved accordingly.

DIR: The suicide aspect troubles me. A neighbor saw him back his car off that hillside, which confirmed the LAPD's findings and the coroner's verdict.

BR: He was impetuous, Sir. He'd been married four times.

DIR: Yes, in the manner of one Mickey Rooney.

BR: Sir, did you—

DIR: I've reviewed the LAPD's paperwork and I've spoken to the Las Vegas SAC. WHITE RABBIT's house had been thoroughly ransacked. A neighbor told officers that WHITE RABBIT's souvenir gun collection had been stolen, along with the contents of his desk and file cabinets. Agents questioned the collection crew at the Desert Inn. A man admitted that he broke into WHITE RABBIT's house, two days after the suicide, and that it had already been ransacked, which is undisputedly a lie. The LAPD officers who responded to the suicide call said that they found the door open and that they viewed the ransacked state of the living room.

BR: It fits, Sir. My brother had run up casino debts before, although never to such a large amount.

DIR: Did WHITE RABBIT keep a private file on the dealings of the SCLC?

BR: I don't know, Sir. He adhered to a need-to-know policy with me on most security matters.

DIR: CRUSADER RABBIT's proximity to the incident bothers me.

BR: It bothers me as well, Sir.

DIR: Was he being spot-tailed during the time preceding WHITE RABBIT's binge?

BR: No, Sir. We had already set WHITE RABBIT up to meet him, and I didn't want complications. Nevada agents had been rotating on and off of him, though.

DIR: CRUSADER RABBIT keeps popping up. He hops from catastrophe to catastrophe with rabbitlike aplomb.

BR: Yes, Sir.

DIR: He appears in Bogalusa. Voila, WILD RABBIT's friend Charles Rogers disappears. He appears in Las Vegas. Voila, he views the prelude to WHITE RABBIT's suicide.

BR: You know my distaste for CRUSADER RABBIT, Sir. That said, I should add that he did call and warn you.

DIR: Yes, and I spoke to him yesterday. He told me that he helped WHITE RABBIT outside, and that WHITE RABBIT simply passed out in his car. His story sounded plausible, and the assigned agents have not been able to crack it. They tell me that he did terminate WHITE RABBIT's casino credit, which further buttresses his credibility.

BR: He may have somehow capitalized on the incident, Sir. I seriously doubt that he provoked it.

DIR: I'm keeping an open mind for the moment. CRUSADER RABBIT is capable of outlandish provocations.

BR: Yes, Sir.

DIR: To digress. Tell me how WILD RABBIT is behaving.

BR: He's doing well, Sir. He's building up his Klan unit nicely, chiefly on the basis of FATHER RABBIT's recruitments. He's debriefed a number of recruits with mail-fraud information on rival klaverns and paramilitary groups. The Bogalusa incident appears to have chastened him, and he seems to be adhering to his operational parameters.

DIR: WILD RABBIT is an obstreperous bunny who has endured very obvious reprimands.

BR: That's my assessment, Sir. But I don't know who the reprimander is, and the Rogers angle eludes me.

DIR: The chain of events is seductive. Rogers kills his parents and disappears. A Negro church explodes 800 miles east.

BR: I only like riddles I can solve, Sir.

DIR: I had the Houston SAC run a passport check. Pete Bondurant and Wayne Tedrow Junior arrived in Houston shortly after Rogers. I think they killed him, but their motive flummoxes me.

BR: Again, Sir. CRUSADER RABBIT and his proximity.

DIR: Yes, an additional vexation.

BR: Sir, do you—

DIR: RED RABBIT will seek to attend WHITE RABBIT's funeral. Will you allow it?

BR: Yes, Sir.

DIR: May I ask why?

BR: My reason may sound flip, Sir.

DIR: Indulge yourself. Walk on the wild side.

BR: My brother enjoyed RED RABBIT, Sir. He knew him for what he was and liked him anyway. He can come and give a big oration and repeat his "I Have a Dream" speech for all I care. Lyle only made 46, so I'm prone to humor his memory.

DIR: The fraternal bond deconstructed. Bravo, Dwight.

BR: Thank you, Sir.

DIR: Has it occurred to you that CRUSADER and WHITE RAB-BIT share certain characteristics and a common moral void?

BR: It has, Sir.

DIR: Is your hatred for RED RABBIT escalating?

BR: It is, Sir. It was my hope that we could escalate BLACK RABBIT and recoup our loss.

DIR: In due time. For now I want to wait and assess an adjunct plan.

BR: Covert ops?

DIR: No, a formal shakedown.

BR: Run by field agents?

DIR: No, run by one Pierre Bondurant, known in unpolite circles as "Mr. Extortion" and "The Shakedown King."

BR: He's a rough piece of work.

DIR: He's close to CRUSADER RABBIT. We might learn a few things.

BR: Yes, Sir.

DIR: Good day, Dwight. And, again, my condolences.

BR: Good day, Sir.

82

(New Hebron, 8/12/65)

NIGGER.

He never thought it. He never said it. It was ugly. It was stupid. It made you THEM.

Wayne took back roads. Wayne saw shit shacks and crop rows. Wayne saw THEM.

They tilled dirt. They hauled brush. They dished slop. Wayne watched. Wayne made them Bongo. Wayne made them Wendell D.

Wicked Wendell—last seen in Bakersfield—redneck California. Work first/Bakersfield *soon*/New Hebron now.

New Hebron was redneck. New Hebron was small. New Hebron was *très* Mississippi. Bob Relyea gigged there. Bob ran Wild Rabbit's hutch. Bob ran his Klan kompound.

Bob had kadre guns. Wayne had kadre money. Kall it: Kadre meets Klan.

Wayne drove slow. Wayne watched THEM. He felt bifurcated. He felt travel-fucked.

He'd rotated west. He split Saigon. He had three weeks in. He cooked horse. He packaged horse. He followed horse west.

Pete was in Laos. Ditto Mesplède. Mesplède just rotated in. They ran Tiger Kamp. They ran slaves. They cooked base.

Pete got antsy there. Pete got bored. Pete bought a bomb raid. Pete bought some Marv pilots. Said pilots napalmed Ba Na Key.

They deforested. They depilatoried. They defoliated. They torched a dope camp. They torched a dope field. They spared the camp lab. They cued in Tran Lao Dinh. Tran sacked the lab. Tran stole M-base and equipment. Tran fed it to Tiger Kamp.

Laurent was in Bon Secour, Alabama. Ditto Flash E. Pete nailed a boat there. Flash knew boats. Laurent knew carpentry.

One charter boat—one overhaul—one war boat boocoo.

Pete's plan: You view the guns. You pay Bob. You route said guns—New Hebron to Tiger South. *You* drive to Bon Secour then. *You* play backup. *You* jam this clown Danny Bruvick.

Loops. Rotations. Travel fucks.

Flash was travel-fucked. Flash looped through Cuba. Flash dipped in via speedboat. Flash dropped Fuentes and Arredondo. They stayed there. Flash looped on back. Flash looped to Bon Secour.

Soon:

Arms run #1. The *Ebbtide* revamped—the new *Tiger Klaw* boocoo.

Wayne cut east. Wayne hit dirt roads. Wayne saw paper mills and compost burning. Wayne saw Bob's "farm."

One shack—Bob's "Führer Barn." One gun range adjacent. Klan klowns kluster. Klan klowns klique. Klan klowns klip targets.

Wayne pulled in. Wayne parked. Wayne smelled cordite and horse shit. Wayne walked in the barn. Cold air hit him—the "Führer Igloo."

He shut the door. He laughed. He sneezed.

Rebel-flag drapes. Rebel-flag rugs. Rebel-flag furniture. Tracts on a table—Wayne Senior's script—"Red Racemixers"/"Spook *Coon*fidential."

Ammo on a couch/sheets on a table/hoods on a stool. Dry-cleaned and folded. All cellophaned.

Wayne laughed. Wayne sneezed. The door popped open. Bob Rabbit walked in. Bob wore fatigues. Bob wore jump boots. Bob detached his Klan hood.

Wayne laughed. Bob shut the door. Bob refroze the igloo.

"It ain't *GQ,* but it works."

Wayne tapped his pockets. "I brought the money."

"Your daddy says hi. He always asks about you."

"Let's see the guns."

"Let's jaw first. 'Hey, Bob, how's the hammer hangin'?' 'Long and strong, Wayne, how about you?' "

Wayne smiled. Pete whomped on Bob. Pete boxed his rabbit ears. Pete avenged Ward Littell.

"Let's see the guns."

Bob packed his nose. Bob jammed in Red Man snuff.

"The niggers are rioting in L.A. I told my boys, 'It'd take some napalm and two hundred Wayne Juniors to stop that thing.' "

Wayne sneezed—cold air and snuff.

"Cut the shit and show me the guns."

"Let's jaw first. We discuss the nigger problem, and I show you my correspondence file from the Missouri State Pen."

Wayne said, "You're wearing me thin."

Bob rubbed his nose. "I got letters from Jimmy Ray and Loyal G. Binns. They're both good haters and pliable as shit. I think they'll join up when they get—"

Wayne walked. Wayne bumped Bob deliberate. Wayne walked to the kitchen.

A TV was on. Negroes cavorted. Negroes threw rocks. Negroes stole liquor. The sound was off. Said Negroes yelled. Their teeth glowed bright.

Bob walked in. Bob bumped Wayne deliberate. Bob popped an unplugged meat freezer.

Guns: M-14s/pumps/bazookas.

Bob pinched a nostril. Bob blew excess snuff.

"I got all the requisite ammo and eight M-132 Zippos out at the range. Some guys heisted a National Guard post in Arkansas. My contact knows them, so we got first dibs. I figure you got plenty of shit for Tiger South and your Cuban run."

"How much?"

"Thirty-five, which is a yard-sale fucking price, if you want my opinion."

Wayne grabbed a pump. Wayne checked the slide. Burn marks/no maker code.

"It's been dipped. There's no serial numbers."

"They're all that way. The guys didn't want the shit to be traced back to the heist."

Wayne grabbed an M-14. Wayne grabbed a bazooka.

"It's good ordnance. It looks too good to be Guard issue."

"Don't complain. We got a fucking bargain."

Wayne grabbed an M-14. Wayne checked the barrel lug.

"Pete wanted the serial numbers to show. It's a terror tactic. If the stuff gets captured, the Castro guys will know it's U.S. donation stock."

Bob shrugged. "It's not like you got it at Sears, with the fucking price tag attached and the lifetime warranty."

Wayne peeled K-notes—all krisp and klean/all logged and laundered.

Bob laughed. "You don't try to break one of those at your local Tastee Freez."

Wayne tapped the TV. Wayne got some sound. Guns popped. Sirens hummed. Negroes frolicked.

. . .

Boat work:

Laurent rigged the gun nests. Flash scraped the hull. They lugged tools. They dropped tools. They dripped sweat.

They devolved the *Ebbtide*. They refaced the *Ebbtide*. They re-Cubafied.

They draped nets. They smeared sails. They scraped teakwood. They camouflaged. They built a mock-Cuban boat.

Flash gripped a sander. Flash scuffed the bridge. Flash scraped mahogany. Danny Bruvick watched. Danny Bruvick moaned. Danny Bruvick sipped Cutty Sark.

Wayne watched. Wayne prickled. Wayne yawned. He drove sixteen hours. He loop-the-looped. He scoured ol' Dixie.

He split New Hebron. He popped bennies. He drove to Port Sulphur. He hit Tiger South. He dropped the guns. He drove to Bon Secour.

Flash had orders—direct from Pete.

Pete don't trust Danny. Danny's got this ex. She's shacked with Ward Littell. We brace Danny—me and Laurent—*Jefe* Carlos too. We read Danny Tiger Law. You kowtow to Tiger Kode. You kart us to Kuba.

Danny's a punk. Danny's a souse. Danny might call his ex and boo-hoo. Your job—don't let him.

Dusk hit. Flash rigged work lights. Laurent Cubafied. Wayne sipped beer. Wayne studied maps.

Sexy Cuba and Bakersfield—bumfuck California.

Boat work:

Laurent climbed masts. Laurent stitched sails. Flash tuned the engines. Danny Bruvick watched. Danny Bruvick watched blotto.

Wayne walked to slip 18. Wayne watched long-distance. Flash had new orders—direct from Pete.

The ex is named Arden. Danny's pussy-whipped. Danny might call her and sing the blues. Your job—don't let him. It pertains to Carlos—some weird gig—thus mum's the word.

Flash hauled fuel cans. Laurent soldered drums. Wayne watched. Bennies parched him dry. Wayne sipped apple juice.

A stretch pulled up and idled. A chauffeur popped the back door. Carlos got out. He's the stock *padrone*. He's got the stock sharkskin suit.

He walked slip 19. Laurent snapped to attention. Bruvick rosaried. Flash snapped to. Carlos bowed. Carlos hugged Laurent.

Bruvick snapped to. Carlos ignored him. Carlos walked below deck. Flash walked down. Laurent walked down. Bruvick limped down slow.

The boat pitched and settled. Wayne heard screams.

He found a slip light. He read his maps. The boat pitched. He heard thumps. He heard whimper-screams.

Flash walked up. Laurent walked up. Carlos swaggered à la Il Duce. They walked down slip 19. They wiped their hands on paper towels. They bagged the stretch limo.

The limo pulled out. Wayne watched the boat. Wayne checked his watch and ticked seconds.

There—

Bruvick comes topside. Bruvick limps. Bruvick deboats. He counts change. He hits the dock. He hits the pay phones.

Wayne ran over. Bruvick saw him. Bruvick said, "Fuck."

Wayne saw the hurt:

Loose teeth and fat ears. Puffed lips and abrasions.

Bon voyage.

They fueled up. They stocked transfer guns. They stocked their personal shit: Browning pumps and Berettas. Scalp knives and suppressors. One Zippo choked for big flames.

Tiger Klaw—kool kamouflaged. Guns port. Guns starboard. Six gunwale slits. Tommys below-deck—hooked to swivel tricks.

They shoved off—6:00 a.m.—south by southeast. Bruvick navigated. Laurent read maps. Flash read comic books. Wayne read street maps. Wayne studied Bakersfield. Truck farms and wetbacks. Stoop crops and Wendell Durfee.

They bucked waves. They made time. It was hot. They got spray wet. They caught glare off the sea.

They wore Coppertone. The boat pitched. They ate Dramamine. Bruvick got the sweats and shakes—forced sobriety.

Flash hid his booze. Flash said Pete loathed Bruvick. Flash said it was private shit—per Ward Littell.

Flash read compass stats. Flash read maps. Flash ran the script:

We rendezvous offshore—near Varcadero Beach. We meet our men. We grapple boats. They get the guns. We get carte blanche. We're upside the beach. We're close to a Militia post—one barracks with Beards.

Flash was happy. Flash was homicidal. Flash waxed cautionary. Flash said:

Watch for boat robbers—they kill fishermen—they got little skiffs. They steal fish. They steal boats. They sport Fidel beards.

Laurent was happy. Laurent was homicidal. Laurent pumiced his scalp knife.

Dusk hit. They made Snipe Key. They refueled. They ran their sails. They recamouflaged.

Bruvick begged for booze. Flash shackled him up. They walked off-boat. They found a crab shack. They ate crab claws and Dexedrine.

Wayne got buzzed. Flash went pop-eyed. Laurent ratched his teeth. They brought Bruvick dinner. They deshackled him. They brought him one *cerveza*. Bruvick siphoned it.

They shoved off. They ran south-southeast. They plowed currents. The boat pitched. Clouds hid the moon.

Bruvick steered. Bruvick sweated. Bruvick rosaried. Flash fucked with him. Flash issued threats. Flash mocked his rosaries.

They applied lampblack. Their hands jumped—wiiild Dexedrine. They went blackface. Laurent was tall. Laurent looked like Wendell Durfee.

Flash ran compass stats. They hit Cuban waters.

Wayne walked the bow. Wayne caught spray. Wayne ran his Bausch & Lombs. Waves jumped. Fish jumped. A flare popped and streaked. Wayne saw *the* boat. Wayne saw a boat in retreat.

Due right—four hundred yards—speck in retreat.

Flash popped a flare. The sky whooshed. Bruvick cut the boat near. There: *Their* boat/the meet.

The boats bumped. Flash tossed a grappling hook. Flash hooked a deck ledge clean. Wayne saw Fuentes and Arredondo.

They tossed their hooks. They jumped bows. They flew. Laurent grabbed them. They dogpiled. They rolled.

Wayne said, "The other boat? *La boata? Qué es esto?*"

Fuentes stood up. "Militia. They . . . *qué es* . . . checked us out?"

Arredondo stood up. "*Los putos de Fidel.* They smell our fish."

Wayne smelled fish. Wayne scoped the boat. Wayne saw their camouflage: Fish poles/fish guts/fish heads.

Flash ran up. Flash hugged the guys. Flash went effusive. Spanish flowed—"*chinga*" for "fuck." "*Puta roja*" for "whore red."

Wayne lugged weapons—plastic-wrapped/tape-sealed/heavy.

He double-timed. He hit the cargo holds. He ran the galley steps. He funneled. He made eight trips. He ran the swamp line.

He tossed. Flash tossed. Fuentes caught. Arredondo caught and stacked. Little guys—strong—good catchers.

Bruvick watched. Bruvick scratched a neck rash. Bruvick rosaried. Fuentes degrappled. Fuentes waved. Arredondo shoved their boat off.

Laurent grabbed Bruvick. Flash mummyized. He cuffed him. He taped him. He made him King Tut. He taped his mouth. He taped his legs. He mast-pole mummified.

Laurent rigged a raft. Wayne dropped anchor. Flash said, "Let's kill Communists."

They took Berettas. They took knives. They took Browning pumps. They took a plastic-wrapped Zippo. They took a raft. They oared in. They surfed swells and ate grit.

Two miles of black sea. Three miles to beach lights. There now: One barracks and one sentry hut.

Off the beach. Off loose sand. Off dirt access ruts.

They flanked. They oared left. Breakers slammed them. Wayne and Flash puked.

They cut through it. A current hit. They pulled left. They scraped sand. They capsized. They rolled.

They dragged the raft up to high sand. They scoped out the hut. Twelve-by-twelve/four men in it/forty yards up.

Beside it: The barracks/one doorway/one floor.

They shared binoculars. They honed the lens. They nailed snapshots. One open door. Two bed-rows. 2:00 a.m./thirty men/bunks and bug nets.

Flash hand-talked. Flash said hut first. We go with silencer pops.

They checked their Berettas. They unwrapped the Zip. They bug-crawled three abreast. Laurent lugged the Zip.

Wayne wheezed. Wayne ate sand. Wayne jittered. They got close—six yards out—Wayne saw whole faces.

The Militia guys sat. The Militia guys smoked. Wayne saw four carbines stacked.

Flash lip-synced numbers—shoot prone on three.

One—they aimed prone. Two—they triggered up. They fired on three—synced silencer plops.

They hit strong. They hit main mass. They hit heads and chests. They double-tapped. They aimed up. They shot fast. They hit groins. They hit backs. They hit necks.

Two fucks fell. Two chairs toppled. Two fucks scree-screeched. Two mouths gapped. Two mouths flapped soundless—wave-noise suppressed.

Flash rolled up. Flash got close. Flash shot main mass. The bodies jerked. The bodies sponged lead.

Flash signaled. The barracks—NOW.

Laurent lit the Zippo. The cherry top flared. They crawled up. They got close. There's the target. There's the door.

Laurent stood up. Laurent braced the doorway. Laurent Zippo-ized. He strafed the beds. He strafed the bug nets. He strafed *putos Red*.

Commies burned. Commies screamed. Commies rolled out of fart-sacks. Commies tangled up bug nets and ran.

Laurent burned bed sheets. Laurent burned walls. Laurent burned men in skivvies and pajamas. Commies ran. Commies fell. Commies crashed windows out.

The barracks burned. Commies ran—Reds on fire.

They ran out the back door. They ran to the beach. They fell in the sand. They ran and hit water.

Waves doused them. Waves deflamed them. Waves sucked them in. Waves boiled. The barracks burned. Ammo ignited.

Laurent chased fireballs. Laurent strafed wet sand. Laurent cooked salt water.

Flash walked to the hut. Flash dragged two dead men out. Flash dumped them and pissed on their heads.

Wayne walked up. Wayne got stage fright. Do it. Show them. Show *Pete*.

He pulled his knife. He picked a scalp. He dug the blade in.

Bakersfield—travel-fucked. Dusty streets/dusty skies/dusty air. The San Joaquin Valley—wall-to-wall dust—farm dirt and glare.

He was travel-fucked. He jumped Cuba to Snipe Key. He jumped Snipe Key to Bon Secour. He jumped Bon Secour to New Orleans. He took three flights west. He got bad sleep. He went off Dexedrine.

He called Saigon. Mesplède patched him to Pete. He praised the run. He praised the guns. He ragged Bob's number-dips.

Pete was pissed. Pete ragged Bob. *Stamp* the numbers—*scare* the Beard—flaunt U.S. Code.

Wayne called Barb. It was tense. Tense off that fight. Barb had news. Barb had a pending gig—adjunct-USO.

We're doing Saigon. We're doing Da Nang. Please lure Pete to the show. He said sure. He said I'll be back. He said I'll be travel-fucked.

Wayne cruised Bakersfield. Wayne read his maps. He flew in. He glommed a rental car. He cruised straight back out.

Mextown ran east. The truck farms ran east. You had beer bars/trailers/motels. You had dust. You had dust bugs. You had Mex cribs galore.

He hit the bars. He sipped beer. He coaxed information. Barmen talked. Barmen travelogued.

Wetback whores? *Shit.* Wetbacks *are* whores.

They jump borders. They steal jobs. They work cheap. They over-breed. They live to fuck. They whelp like chihuahuas. They pick crops.

They get paid—they fuck *real* whores then. Wetback pimps pimp wetback whores—the payday proliFUCKation.

They swarm motels. They production-fuck. They proliFUCKate. Check the Sun-Glo. Check the Vista—check the whole scene. Payday's tomorrow—the wets proFUCKate—you'll dig the scene.

Wayne dropped the name "Wendell Durfee." Wayne dredged up some shrugs.

Who's that? Some jigaboo?

That's right—he's colored. He's quite loud and tall.

Sheeeit—

Wetbacks hate jigs. Crop men hate jigs. That jig better haul.

Payday:

Wayne cruised truck farms. Wayne loitered. Wayne watched.

Wets pick cabbage. Wets yank weeds. Wets fill garbage drums. Sirens blow. The wets yell. The wets drop hoes and run.

They hit pay trucks. They line up. They shag cash and run—families/*hombres/muchachos*.

Some clique up. Some walk off. Some liiiiinger. *Hombres todos*—men with shit-eater grins.

Trucks pull up. *Hombres* greet *hombres*. *Hombres* dispense: Jar brew/rubbers/French ticklers/T-Bird/white port/nude Polaroids. Beaver pix of Mexi-whores—let's proFUCKate.

Wayne walked over. *Hombres* cringed. Wayne vibed *Migra* fuzz. Wayne mollified. Wayne spoke pidgin-Mex. Wayne coaxed info.

Dig:

The truck men pimped. They signed johns up early—supply meets demand. Go to the Sun-Glo and Vista. See the Fuckathon.

Wets scoped the beaver pix. Wets signed up. Wayne flashed Wendell Durfee pix and got nada. Shit—we ain't seen him/we don't know him/we hate *negritos.*

Wayne split. Wayne braced more truck pimps. Wayne got more nada. He regrouped. He read his maps. He crossed the tracks and cruised Darktown. *De facto* segregation—wets north/coloreds south.

He yawned. He fought sleep-fuckification. He slept too long last night. He slept fourteen hours. He logged some bad dreams.

Barb rags him—don't pop pills—he rags Barb back. Don't you do it—you'll age bad—I love you.

Bongo co-starred. Bongo convulsed. Bongo snitched Wendell Durfee. Wendell's in Cuba. He's got the cold six thousand. He's got a Castro beard.

Wayne cruised Darktown. Wayne hit pool halls. Wayne hit lounge spots. He vibed cop. He vibed grief. He wore his gun out.

Cops saw him. Cops waved. Cops vibed brother cop. He braced coloreds. He flashed his Wendell pix. He got huh?s. He got indignation.

You dig Watts? It could happen *here*. It could happen NOW.

He worked through it. He worked all day. He wore Darktown out. Nobody knew Wicked Wendell. Nobody knew jackshit.

Dusk hit. He drove to the Sun-Glo. He caught the Fuckathon.

Ten rooms/ten whores/ten parking-lot lines. Wets twenty-deep and pimps with stopwatches—you fuck off *my* clock.

Snack stands—all jerry-rigged/all run by *mamacitas*. They served beans. They served *cerveza*. They served *carnitas*.

It was hot. Fried pork spattered. Jalopy pipes popped.

Doors opened. Doors shut. Wayne got snapshots: Nude girls and wide-leg poses. Soiled sheets trashed up.

The lines moved fast—six minutes per fuck. Cops stood around. Pimps greased them—a dollar a fuck.

The cops ate *carnitas*. The cops worked the line. The cops sold boot-jack penicillin. Wayne stood in line. Wayne drew stares. Wayne showed *his* snapshots.

Que? No se. Negrito muy feo.

Wayne braced a mama-san. Wayne waved fifty bucks. He pidgin-talked. He told her—beer on the house.

She smiled. She shagged Lucky Lagers. She served the wets. She served the pimps. She served the cops.

She praised Wayne—*gringo muy bueno.*

Wayne got applause. Wets pumped his hands. Pimps waved sombreros. He re-showed his pix. They went around. They toured all the fuck-istos. The pix circuited. The pix got pawed. The pix came back.

A cop nudged Wayne. "I ran that smoke out of town three months ago. He was trying to pimp white girls, which didn't sit right with me."

Wayne goose bumped. The cop tapped his teeth.

"I heard he was tight with a smoke named King Arthur. I think he owns a queer bar in Fresno."

The Playpen Lounge was a storefront. The Playpen Lounge sat off skid row.

Wayne drove to Fresno. Wayne polled street creeps. Wayne found it. The creeps spieled lore—the Pen's a pus-pit—all fear the King!

He's this mean swish. He's Haiti-bred. He's pure calypso. He sports a crown. He's a he-she. He's a hermaphrodite.

Wayne walked in. The decor clashed—Camelot meets Liberace.

Velvet walls. Purple drapes. Nail-studded armor. A bar and wall booths—pink Naugahyde.

A jukebox cranked. Mel Tormé crooned. The natives stirred. Wayne drew looks. Wayne drew ooh-la-las.

Colored trade—queens and jockers.

There's the King. He's got a booth. He's got his crown. He's got the pedigree: Knife scars/mashed ears/pipe-wound regalia.

Wayne walked over. Wayne sat down. King Arthur sipped a frappé.

"You're too haughty to be Fresno PD, and you're too butch to be anything but a cop."

The jukebox vibrated. Wayne reached back. Wayne grabbed and yanked the cord.

"My money. Your information."

The King tapped his crown. It was kid-pageant issue—rhinestones on tin.

"I just consulted my thinking cap. It said, 'Policemen demand, they don't pay.' "

The King lisped. The King trilled. The King sashayed. Two fags swished by. One tittered. One waved.

Wayne said, "I *was* a cop."

"Oh, pshaw, you silly savage. You didn't have to say that."

Wayne pulled out his money. Wayne fanned his money. Wayne flashed a table lamp down.

"Wendell Durfee. I heard you know him."

The King tapped his crown. "I'm getting a vision . . . yes . . . there it is . . . you're that Vegas cop who lost his poor wife to Wendell."

The jukebox popped. Kay Starr popped on. Wayne reached back and popped the cord. A fag grabbed his hand. A fag scratched his palm. A fag giggled lewd.

Wayne pulled his arm back. The fags giggled. The fags withdrew. They swished off. They vamped Wayne. They blew kisses.

Wayne wiped his hand. The King laughed. The King went oh, pshaw.

"I had a brief encounter with Wendell, several months ago. I bought a string of girls from him."

"And?"

"And the Bakersfield fuzz discouraged me from procuring in their jurisdiction."

"And?"

"And Wendell was looking for a *nom de pimp* with irresistible panache. I suggested the name Cassius Cool, which he adopted."

Wayne tapped the money. "Keep going. I know there's more."

The King tapped his crown. "I'm getting a vision . . . yes . . . you killed three unarmed Negro men in Las Vegas . . . and . . . yes . . . Wendell made your wife climax before he killed her."

Wayne pulled his piece. Wayne raised it. Wayne cocked it. Wayne heard echoes. Wayne heard hammers click.

He looked around. He checked the bar. He saw fags. He saw guns. He saw suicide.

He holstered up. The King grabbed his money.

"Wendell enticed some crackers into a rigged dice game and was firmly advised to leave Bakersfield. I heard he lit out for L.A."

Wayne looked around. Wayne saw fags with guns. Wayne saw mean faces.

The King laughed. "Grow up, child. You can't kill *all* the niggers."

83

(Saigon, 8/20/65)

Pete said, "Wayne took some scalps."

Cocktail hour. Drinks at the Catinat. Grenade nets and gook brass galore.

Stanton snarfed pâté. "Cuban or Negro American?"

Pete smiled. "He's back. I'll tell him you asked."

"Tell him I was pleased to learn that he's diversified."

The bar was packed. MACV guys hobnobbed. Trilingual talk flowed.

Pete lit a cigarette. "The Relyea thing pissed me off. I want to move recognizable U.S.-sourced guns."

Stanton smeared toast. "You've made that clear. That said, I should state that Bob's done a bang-up job so far."

"He has, but he's deep off in all that Klan shit, which could draw heat any fucking second. You want my opinion? We should rotate Laurent back to Laos to work Tiger Kamp, and keep Mesplède in the States permanently to shag guns. He's got good connections, he's willing, and he's fucking capable."

Stanton shook his head. "One, Bob's got better connections, and he's got enough FBI cover to divert any trouble he might create. Two, you brought that Bruvick guy in, which lit a fire under Carlos, who is now all aflutter for the Cause, in a way he hasn't been since '62. He's *active* now, he's the *only* committed Outfit man, and I'm sure he's got gun sources. Three, Laurent's tight with Carlos, which is why I want him full-time stateside, instead of Mesplède. He's the best man to work with Carlos and funnel our weaponry."

Pete rolled his eyes. "Carlos is a *Mob* executive. The only gun contacts he's got are other exile groups with shit ordnance of their own. He won't be able to shag stuff as good as that Relyea batch, and how many fucking armory heists can we count on?"

A siren blew. The room froze. The gook brass drew guns. The siren died. The all-clear blew. The gook brass stashed their guns.

Stanton sipped wine. "We're covered as is. You and Wayne rotate, because you're the A-level personnel and you know the in-country and Vegas ends of the business. When Wayne's caught up at the lab, he's free to work Vegas and the funnel, and you—"

"John, Jesus Christ, will you—"

"No, let me finish. We lost Chuck, *c'est la guerre,* but Tran and Mesplède are more than enough to run Tiger Kamp. We keep Mesplède in-country, and we leave Flash and Laurent in Port Sulphur and Bon Secour. In other words, we're *covered,* and I don't want you second-guessing a perfectly operational system."

The siren blew. The all-clear blew. The AC died. A waiter cracked doors. A waiter cracked windows. A waiter rigged bomb nets.

Pete checked his watch. "I'm meeting Wayne. He's got a lead on some donation shit in Da Nang."

Hot air settled in. Waiters pulled fan cords.

"How many scalps did he take?"

"Four."

"Do you think he enjoyed it?"

Pete smiled. "With Wayne you never know."

Stanton smiled. "Will you allow me some sort of concession before you go?"

Pete stood up. The ceiling loomed. Pete dodged fan blades.

"Your shit's operational. It's just not as passionate as my shit."

They flew up. MACV ran Hueys—milk flights from Tan Son Nhut.

They sat on the back slats. Some admin pogues flew along. Dig it—let's catch this show in Da Nang.

Wayne yawned. Wayne just rotated in. Wayne was travel-fucked.

The flight overbooked. The kiddie brass partied. They made noise. They matched coins. They twirled their .45s.

The rotors whipped. The doors shook. The radio screeched. Pete and Wayne huddled. Pete and Wayne talked loud.

Agreed: Bob Relyea bites. Agreed: He's Wayne Senior's punk rabbit. Agreed: He shags good guns. Agreed: D. Bruvick's sly and yellow.

Carlos warned Bruvick. Carlos said don't call Arden—don't rat our Cuban runs. Bruvick fudged and tried to call. Wayne interdicted.

Agreed: Let's oust him. Agreed: Let's find a new boat man.

They agreed. Pete hedged somewhat. Pete said Carlos wants Bruvick. Bruvick's his inside man. Carlos distrusts everyone. Carlos plants informants.

Ergo: Bruvick makes Cuban runs. Bruvick calls Carlos. Bruvick informs on *us*.

Wayne *got* it. Wayne digressed. Bruvick's ex Arden—now with Ward Littell. She's a spy. She watches Ward. She reports to Carlos.

Right—you got it—and that's *all* you get.

Wayne said okay. Pete riffed on Carlos—the Graduate Course.

He runs people. He eats people. He's tight with John Stanton. He's greedy. He'll press John—feed me dope points. John will bow. *We'll* bow too. We owe Carlos that. Carlos braced the other Boys. They waived Outfit laws. They let us white-dust West Vegas.

Agreed: We owe Big Carlos. Agreed: We owe Blueblood John.

The flight bumped. The gun doors shook. The pogues ate Dramamine.

Agreed: Tiger ops—overhead stratospheric—the lab/Tiger Kamp/Tiger South. Bribes to ARVNs/bribes to Can Lao boss-man "Mr. Kao"/bribes to Tran Lao Dinh.

Transport bribes. Nellis AFB bribes. Cop bribes: Sheriff's and LVPD. Ops costs: in-country and out. Ops costs transcontinental.

We ship white horse—big poundage—we dust West LV. Profits soar. Jigs love white horse. Profits dip non sequitur. Because of the fucking Watts Riot—live on fucking TV.

Jigs see the riot. Jigs exult. Monkey see/monkey do. They roam West LV. They chuck some spears. They burn some shacks. We suspend kadre business. We retrieve Tiger Kabs. Cops quell the riot. Jigs go to jail. Profits de-escalate.

Agreed: Biz is down now—we're in bear-market turf. Agreed: We'll expand—and we'll re-escalate. We'll hire more pushers—expendable jigs—we'll bull-market reintegrate.

The Huey cruised low. They saw firefights. They saw villages sacked. Wayne talked expansion—let's *re*-dust West Vegas. Let's *pre*-dust black L.A.

Pete laughed—the Boys won't vouch it—you fucking *know* that.

Know *shit*. Durfee might be there. I fucking know *that*.

Da Nang: Hot sun and hot sea winds. Spritzy sea spray.

Their gun contact no-showed. Pete got pissed. Wayne pitched diversion: Let's hit that USO show.

They rickshawed in. Their coolie pulled weight. Their coolie ran chop-

chop. They raced some shavetails. Said shavetails were bombed. The rickshaw race rocked.

Pete ate Dramamine. Wayne ate salt pills. They hit access roads. They hit the naval base. They hit the bleacher setup.

The coolies saw it. The coolies braked hard. Four wheels brodied. Four wheels slid and locked.

Dead heat.

Pete laughed. Wayne laughed. The shavetails went green and up-chucked.

The show was free. A crowd filed in. Pete and Wayne lined up. It was hot-plate hot.

The stage was ground-level. The bleachers ran sixty rows up. Onstage: Hip Herbie & Ho—low-rent topical yuks.

Ho was a puppet. Hip Herbie held him. Hip Herbie held a hand mike. Hip Herbie ventriloquized. Hip Herbie moved his lips. Hip Herbie vibed hophead or souse.

They found seats. They got cramped arm- and legroom. They sat ten bleacher rows up.

Stage speakers tossed sound. Ho tossed a tantrum: "GIs scare me! Me most scared! You kill Cong ricky-tick!"

It was hot. The sun torched down. Pete got queased up. The crowd yukked halfhearted. Ho wore red devil horns. Ho wore red diapers.

Hip Herbie said, "What have you got against Uncle Sam, anyway?"

Ho said, "I come to U.S.! They no let me in Disneyland!"

The crowd yukked distracted. Ho blathered: "I get revenge! I plant land mines! I kill Donald Duck!"

The crowd yukked nonplussed. A stage geek signaled Hip Herbie—wrap this shit up.

Ho raged: "Me try sit-ins! Me try pray-ins! Me shoot Donald Duck!"

The stage geek cued a sound geek. A sax vamped low. Hip Herbie got the bum's rush.

He bowed. Ho leaked sawdust. A curtain dropped. The crowd clapped lackluster—fuck that puppet and lush.

The sax scaled up sequential. The curtain rose. Pete saw loooooong legs furl up.

No. It can't be. Please, yes. Slow now, in sync: The curtain and sax—both scaling up.

There—not no, it's yes.

Pete saw her legs. Pete saw *her*. Pete caught her kiss standing up. Wayne smiled. The Bondsmen clicked in. Barb launched Viet rock.

Whistles/wolf calls/cheers—

Barb danced. Barb shimmied. Barb kicked a shoe off. The shoe sailed high. Guys grabbed and reached. Pete reached higher up.

It's close. It's—

His chest popped. His wind died. His left arm blew up.

It's close. It's high-heeled and spangled. It's green and—

His left arm died. His left wrist torqued. His left hand blew up.

He grabbed right. He caught the shoe. He kissed it. He fell down. He squeezed the shoe. Barb blurred white white.

84

(Washington, D.C., 9/4/65)

Riot. Revolt. Insurrection.

NBC ran replays. TV pundits assessed.

Littell watched.

Negroes threw Molotovs. Negroes threw bricks. Negroes sacked liquor stores. Chief Parker blamed hoodlums. Bobby urged reforms. Dr. King urged dissent.

Dr. King digressed. Dr. King stressed other riots. Dr. King stressed Vegas West.

Replays: Negroes throw Molotovs/Negroes throw bricks/Negroes sack liquor stores.

Littell watched replays. Littell replayed vintage Drac:

"We've got to sedate those animals, Ward. We don't want them *that* agitated *that* close to my hotels."

Don't say it: "Pete's selling sedation, sir, but it doesn't appear to be working right now."

Ditto Pete. Barb called him last week. Barb said Pete had a heart attack.

It was bad. Pete was stable now. The old Pete was fucked. Barb came on strong. Barb begged him:

Pull strings. Brace Carlos. Make Pete retire. Bring him home. Make him stay. Do this for me.

Littell said he'd try. Littell called Da Nang. Littell talked to Pete. Pete was hoarse. Pete was tired. Pete sounded weak.

Littell called Carlos. Carlos said it's up to Pete.

Littell killed the TV. Littell eyed his news pic. He'd clipped it. He'd saved it. He'd laminated it.

The Washington *Post:* "KING ATTENDS AIDE'S FUNERAL." Aide Lyle Holly—dead per suicide—FBI plant WHITE RABBIT.

King's RED RABBIT. Bayard Rustin's PINK. Brother Dwight Holly's BLUE. They all stand close. RED and PINK mourn. BLUE RABBIT smirks.

He clipped the shot. He studied it. He built some rage. He watched riot footage. He watched replays. He built more rage.

He traveled for work. He left Vegas. He drove to L.A. He saw a tail. He ignored it. He built more rage.

He knew:

Mr. Hoover doubts you. BLUE RABBIT doubts you. Said doubts plague BLACK RABBIT. WHITE RABBIT dies. You view the prelude. You spark apprehension. Mr. Hoover calls. You dissemble. He probes.

Call it a spot tail. You've seen none since. Logic meets rage.

You *were* spot-tailed pre–BLACK RABBIT. Mr. Hoover told you. Mr. Hoover pulled said tails. Mr. Hoover reinstated them—post–Lyle suicide.

Ergo:

He did not suspect you *then.* He does suspect you *now.*

He worked. He traveled—Vegas to L.A. He saw no tails en route. He saw Janice in Vegas. He saw Jane in L.A. He saw no tails at either venue.

Jane scared him. Jane *knew* him. Mr. Hoover knew about Jane. Agents planted her fake transcript. Agents gave her Tulane.

He checked for tails. He checked daily. He saw none. He replayed riot footage. He replayed Dr. King's words. He replayed Lyle's file near-verbatim.

He built a plan. He decreed escalation. He flew to D.C. He did some Teamster work. He stopped by the SCLC. He logged no tails en route.

He talked to Bayard Rustin. Bayard took a call. He excused himself. He found Lyle's old cubbyhole. He worked fast. He deployed his briefcase. He went through boxed items. He stole Lyle's typewriter. He stole Lyle's memo stack.

The office mourned Lyle. They didn't know Lyle was WHITE RABBIT.

Lyle gambled. Lyle stiffed you. You lost no respect. Lyle betrayed you. Lyle died. Now Lyle resurrects and repents.

Littell made coffee. Littell studied Lyle's memos. Littell traced the name Lyle D. Holly.

He practiced. He got it. He prepped Lyle's portable. He rolled in an envelope. He typed all caps:

"TO BE SENT IN THE CASE OF MY DEATH."

He unrolled the envelope. He rolled in a carbon sheet and paper. He squared off the SCLC letterhead.

Lyle Holly confessed.

To booze binges. To gambling. To passing bad checks. To betrayal—FBI-funded—at J. Edgar Hoover's behest.

Count 1: Mr. Hoover is crazy. He hates Dr. King. I joined his hate campaign.

Count 2: I joined the SCLC. I hoodwinked Dr. King. I hoodwinked key staff.

Count 3: I rose within the movement. I wrote policy briefs. I logged secrets shared.

Count 4: I leaked secret data. I supplied the Feds. I said tap here. I said bug there.

Addendum 1: A tap and bug list. *Certified* taps and bugs—known to Littell. Said bugs and taps—*likely* known to Lyle Holly.

Count 5: I logged Dr. King's indiscretions. I told Mr. Hoover. He penned a "suicide note." It was mailed to Dr. King. It urged him to take his own life.

Count 6: Mr. Hoover's hate grows. Mr. Hoover's hate deepens. Mr. Hoover's campaign will ascend.

Littell stopped. Littell thought it all through. Littell reassessed.

No—don't snitch BLACK RABBIT. Don't snitch BLUE RABBIT. Don't snitch WILD RABBIT's snitch-Klan. Don't exceed credibility. Don't indict yourself. Don't reveal what Lyle might not know.

Count 7: I have done great harm. I despair for Dr. King. I indulge thoughts of *my* suicide. This letter remains sealed. Staff members will find it. They will send it if I die.

Littell unrolled the document. Littell signed it Lyle D. Holly.

He rolled in an envelope. He typed an address: Chairman/House Judiciary Committee. He rolled out the envelope. He rolled in an envelope. He typed an address: Senator Robert F. Kennedy/Senate Office Building.

It was risky. Bobby ran Justice—'61–'64. Bobby ran Mr. Hoover. Mr. Hoover ran autonomous. Mr. Hoover ran his hate campaign under Bobby's flag. Bobby might thus feel guilty. Bobby might thus feel shame.

Trust Bobby. Trust the risk. Hit the SCLC. Drop the letters. Get the meter stamp.

Wait—then read the papers. Wait—then watch TV.

Bobby might report the leak. *You* could contact him. *You* could resurrect anonymously.

85

(Da Nang, 9/10/65)

Sickbay—pills / drips / IVs. Pete's world now—Pete the Zonked and Weak.

Wayne pulled a chair up. Pete laid in bed. Barb fluffed his pillow.

"I talked to Ward. He said he's dying to test his pull with the gaming boards. He thinks he can get you a license for a grind joint."

Pete yawned. Pete rolled his eyes. That meant Fuck You.

A nurse walked in. She took Pete's pulse. She checked Pete's eyes. She ran Pete's blood pressure. She logged it in.

Wayne checked the board. Wayne saw normal stats. The nurse split. Barb fluffed Pete's pillow.

"We could run the place together. Ward says it's a revolutionary concept. You with a legitimate source of income."

Pete yawned. Pete rolled his eyes. That meant Fuck You. His weight was down. His skin was slack. His bones jutted out.

He fell off that bleacher. Wayne caught him. Pete gripped Barb's shoe. Barb jumped off the stage. A guy caught her. Two medics showed.

One guy resuscitated. One guy grabbed at the shoe. Pete kicked him. Pete bit him. Pete kept the shoe.

Barb said, "I quit smoking. If you can't do it, I can't either."

She looked frazzled. She looked fried. She looked fragged. Call it a pill run—grief-justified.

Pete said, "I want a cheeseburger and a carton of Camels."

His voice held—good timbre/good wind.

Wayne laughed. Barb kissed Pete. Pete goosed her and went goo-goo eyed. She blew kisses. She walked out. She pulled the door shut.

Wayne straddled his chair. "Ward will make you buy a place. For Barb's sake, if nothing else."

Pete yawned. "She can run it. I'm too busy as it is."

Wayne smiled. "You're dying to talk business. If that's the case, I'm listening."

Pete cranked the bed up. "You're running things until I get out of here. That means in-country and stateside."

"All right."

"We've got a backlog of shit at the lab, so we're freed up there. I want Mesplède and Tran to run Tiger Kamp. I want you, Laurent, and Flash to handle the conduit and oversee the Cuban runs, and I want you to back Milt up at Tiger Kab."

Wayne nodded. Wayne leaned on the bedrail.

Pete said, "I got a pouch from Bob. He's got two truckloads of bazookas and high explosives pilfered out of Fort Polk. It's a big haul, and it might take two boat runs. You take care of the Cuban transport, but in that case and in all future fucking cases, don't go near the weaponry transactions and let Laurent and Flash drive the shit from New Hebron to Bon Secour. Bob's got FBI cover, so I want him to stand as our most expendable guy. Laurent and Flash drive the guns, so they're less expendable than Bob and a shitload more expendable than you. *You* stay safe, and *you* watch Danny Bruvick, who I do not trust worth a fucking shit."

Wayne clapped. "Your wind is back."

Pete checked the stat board. "Not bad. I'll be out of here soon."

Wayne stretched. "I talked to Tran. He said some slaves escaped with some M-base. They're ex-VC, and Tran thinks they hooked up with some VC guys running a lab near Ba Na Key. He thinks they plan to cook up some shit and distribute it to our troops in the south, to demoralize them."

Pete kicked the bedpost. The stat board fell.

"Have Mesplède interrogate the rest of the slaves. We might learn something that way."

Wayne stood up. "Get some rest, boss. You look tired."

Pete smiled. Pete grabbed Wayne's chair. Pete snapped the back slats. Wayne clapped.

Pete said, "Rest, shit."

Barb danced. Barb obliged horny sailors. They swarmed her. They cut in. They swarmed three per song.

Canned songs/all staples/service club stock. "Sugar Shack"/surf shit/the Watusi.

Wayne watched. Barb's hair bounced. Wayne saw new grays in the red. "Surf City" tapped out. Sailors clapped. Barb walked on back.

Wayne pulled her chair out. She sat down. She lit a match.

"I want a cigarette."

Wayne plucked those new grays. Barb made an uggh face. Wayne sheared a few reds.

"You'll get over it."

Barb lit the grays. They poofed and burned up.

"I should go home. If I stay, I'll start seeing things I don't like."

"Like our business?"

"Like the boy three wards down with no arms. Like the boy who got lost and got napalmed by his own guys."

Wayne shrugged. "It goes with the job."

"Tell Pete that. Tell him, 'The next one might kill you, if the war doesn't get you first.' "

Wayne plucked a gray. "Come on. He's better than that."

Barb lit a match. Barb lit the hair. Barb watched it burn.

"Get him out. You and Ward know the guys who can make it happen."

"They won't go for it. Pete's in hock, and you know why."

"Dallas?"

"That and the fact that he's too good to let go."

A sailor bopped by. Barb signed his napkin. Barb signed his jumper sleeve.

She lit a match. "I miss the cat. Vietnam gets me mushy for Vegas."

Wayne checked her hair. Perfect—all red now.

"You'll be home in three days."

"I'll kiss the ground, believe me."

"Come on. It's not that bad."

Barb snuffed the match. "I saw a boy who lost his equipment. He was joking with a nurse about the Army buying him a new one. The second she walked out, he started to cry."

Wayne shrugged. Barb tossed the match. It hit him. It stung. Barb walked. Sailors watched her. Barb walked to the john.

"Sugar Shack" kicked on. Time warp—that song on Jack Ruby's juke-box.

Barb walked out. A sailor braced her. He was colored. He was tall. He looked like Wendell D.

Barb danced with him. They danced semi-slow. They shared some contact.

Wayne watched.

They danced nice. They danced hip. They danced by the table. Barb was loose. Barb was cool. Barb wore white dust on her nose.

DOCUMENT INSERT: 9/16/65. Verbatim FBI telephone call tran-
script. (OPERATION BLACK RABBIT Addendum.) Marked:
"Recorded at the Director's Request"/"Classified Confidential 1-A:
Director's Eyes Only." Speaking: Director, BLUE RABBIT.

DIR: Good morning.

BR: Good morning, Sir.

DIR: Let's discuss WILD RABBIT's work in Mississippi. The oxy-
moronic phrase "Redneck Intelligence Network" comes to mind.

BR: WILD RABBIT has been doing well, Sir. Our stipends have
allowed him to recruit and secure intelligence, and FATHER RABBIT
has supplied him with funds as well. He told me that he's donating
a portion of his hate-tract profits to WILD RABBIT's incursion.

DIR: And the well-funded WILD RABBIT is achieving results?

BR: He is, Sir. His Regal Knights have been infiltrating other
hate groups and supplying WILD RABBIT with information. I think
we'll have some mail-fraud indictments before too long.

DIR: FATHER RABBIT's donations are in part self-serving. He
aids WILD RABBIT's cause and depletes the resources of his hate-
tract rivals.

BR: Yes, Sir.

DIR: Is WILD RABBIT remaining tractable?

BR: He is, although I've learned that he's running weaponry to
Pete Bondurant's narcotics cadre. As I understand it, he secures
the weapons from armory heists and army base pilfering, which is
odd, because I haven't been able to find any recently filed reports
on such incidents, anywhere in the south.

DIR: Yes, odd does describe it. That said, do you think WILD
RABBIT will retain an acceptable level of deniability pertaining to
his gun-running activities?

BR: I do, Sir. But should I tell him to stop?

DIR: No. I like his connection to Bondurant. Remember, we'll be
approaching Le Grand Pierre when we move BLACK RABBIT into
the shakedown phase.

BR: I heard that he had a heart attack last month.

DIR: A pity. And the prognosis?

BR: I think it's guardedly positive, Sir.

DIR: Good. We'll let him recover and then add some stress to his
overtaxed arteries.

BR: Yes, Sir.

DIR: Let's discuss CRUSADER RABBIT. Have you accrued any substantive data?

BR: Yes and no, Sir. We've gotten nothing off the spot tails and the trash and mail covers, and I'm convinced that he's too technically skilled to bug and tap. He's retained his friendship with PINK RABBIT and visits him in D.C., which is hardly incriminating, since you urged him to do so.

DIR: Your tone betrays you. You're tantalizing me. Shall I hazard a guess?

BR: Please do, Sir.

DIR: Your revelations pertain to CRUSADER's women.

BR: That's correct, Sir.

DIR: Expand your answers, please. I have a lunch date in the year 2000.

BR: CRUSADER has been seeing Janice Lukens, FATHER RABBIT's ex-wife, in Las—

DIR: We know that. Pray continue.

BR: He lives with a woman in Los Angeles. Her alleged name is Jane Fentress.

DR: "Alleged" is correct. I helped to establish her identity two years ago. A New Orleans agent planted her college transcript.

BR: There's much more to her, Sir. I think she could serve as our wedge if we need to disrupt CRUSADER.

DIR: Expand your thoughts. The millennium bodes.

BR: I had her spot-tailed. My man took a set of prints off a glass she left at a restaurant. We ran them and got her real name, Arden Louise Breen, B-R-E-E-N, married name Bruvick, B-R-U-V-I-C-K.

DIR: Continue.

BR: Her father was a left-wing unionist. The Teamsters killed him in '52, and it's still a St. Louis PD unsolved. Allegedly, the woman held no grudge against the Teamsters, allegedly because her father forced her to become a call-house prostitute. She absconded on a KCPD receiving stolen goods warrant in '56, at the same time her husband embezzled some money from a Kansas City Teamster local and disappeared.

DIR: Continue.

BR: Here's the ripe part. Carlos Marcello's front corporation bailed her out on the Kansas City bounce. She disappeared then, she's got a bookkeeping background, and she's rumored to have had a long-term affair with that old Mob hand Jules Schiffrin.

DIR: Boffo news, Dwight. Well worth your vexing preambles.

BR: Thank you, Sir.

DIR: I think your tale boils down to one salient truth. Carlos Marcello does not trust CRUSADER RABBIT.

BR: I came to that conclusion, Sir.

DIR: Pull the tails, along with the trash and mail covers. If we need to get at CRUSADER, we'll go through the woman.

BR: Yes, Sir.

DIR: Good day, Dwight.

BR: Good day, Sir.

86

(Saravan, 9/22/65)

Torture:
Six slaves strapped down. Six Cong-symps wired. Six hot seats / six juice buttons / six testicle feeds.

Mesplède worked the juice box. Mesplède ran the juice. Mesplède asked the questions. Mesplède talked franglogook.

Pete watched. Pete chewed Nicorette gum. It was wet and hot—rainstorm boocoo. The hut sponged heat. The hut stored heat. The hut was a hot-plate boocoo.

Mesplède talked gook. Mesplède talked threat. Mesplède talked fast. His words slurred—gobblede*GOOK*.

Pete knew the gist. Pete wrote the script. Pete read six faces.

Slaves escape. All pro-Cong. Who let them? I no know!—all six say it—I know no who!

It droned on—you tell me!—no no! Pete watched. Pete chewed gum. Pete read eyes.

Mesplède lit a Gauloise. Pete cued him. Mesplède hit the buttons. Juice flooowed.

Testicle ticklers—black box to balls—nonlethal volts. Gooks tingle. Gooks absorb. Gooks yell boocoo.

Mesplède cut the juice. Mesplède pidgin-gooked: Congs run! Steal M-base! Tell what you know!

The gooks buzzed. The gooks squirmed. The gooks afterglowed. Talk now! You tell me! Tell what you know! Six gooks jabbered—this gook ensemble—we no know who!

One gook squeals. One gook yips. One gook salivates. Loincloths to ankles/grounded gonads/feed plugs to feet. One gook squirms. One gook prays. One gook urinates.

Pete cued Mesplède. Mesplède hit the buttons. Juice flooowed.

The gooks buckle. The gooks absorb. The gooks gyrate. The gooks scream. The gooks thrash and pop veins.

Pete cogitated. Pete chewed gum. Pete brainstormed eyes shut.

Tran tells Wayne—slaves escape—steal M-base boocoo. They cook it. They dump it. Fuck up our GIs boocoo.

But:

You don't dump Big "H." You *sell* it.

And:

Wayne rotates home. Wayne's lab is empty. Rival dope cooks could sneak in. Said cooks could utilize. Said cooks could appropriate.

Surveille the lab—do it soon—before *you* rotate.

Mesplède coughed. "Has that chewing gum put you in a trance, Pierre?"

Pete opened his eyes. "One of them has to know something. Ask them *why* the guys ran, and turn up the juice if they shit you."

Mesplède smiled. Mesplède coughed. Mesplède pidgin-gooked. He talked fast. He blurred inflections. He fastballed his words.

Gooks listen. Good absorb. Gooks say: No No No No—

Mesplède hit the buttons. Juice flowed. *Near*-lethal volts. The gooks screamed. Their nuts flushed. Their nuts swelled.

Mesplède cuts the juice. Gooks absorb pain. Gook 5 talks ricky-tick. Mesplède smiles. Mesplède absorbs. Mesplède translates.

"He said he woke up and saw Tran pull them out of the hut. Tran . . . *qu'est-ce* . . . forced them to run, and he heard shots a few minutes later."

Pete spit his gum out. "Cut them loose. Give them some extra beans for dinner."

Mesplède said, "I appreciate compassion."

The hills hurt.

He breathed hard. He walked slow. He trailed back. Mesplède walked fast. Two guards flanked him.

They cut through camp. They pushed through brush. They dodged biter snakes. The rain held. Brush slapped them. Pete gobbled breath.

He took pills. They thinned his blood. They scrubbed his veins. They sapped him. They fucked him up. They held him back.

He ran. He caught up. He gobbled breath.

They kicked through mud. The mud had weight. The weight hurt his chest. They walked two miles. They hit downslopes. His chest weight slacked off.

Pete heard grunts and oinks. Pete saw a mud pit. Pete smelled human decomp. Pete saw wild pigs root.

There:

Said mud pit. A buffet. Said pigs and boned flesh.

Pete jumped in. The pigs scattered. The mud was deep. The mud had weight. Pete bobbed for flesh.

He rooted. He flailed. He found an arm. He found a leg. He found a head. He shook off mud. He pulled off skin. He peeled off scalp flaps.

He saw a hole. It was bullet-sized. He gripped the jaws. He cracked the skull back.

Good breath. Good strength. Good outpatient stats.

A bullet dropped. Pete caught it. It was butterflied and smashed. It was a soft-point magnum. It was Tran Lao Dinh's brand.

Tran tried charm. Tran tried shit. Tran tried shuck-and-jive. Mesplède hooked him up. Mesplède hooked dual clamps—gonads and head.

The rain held. Monsoon stats—mud 4-ever.

Pete chewed gum. Pete cracked the door. Pete stirred outside air.

"Your shit's not working. Give up the details and tell us who you're in with, and I'll see what John Stanton says."

Tran said, "You know me, boss. I no work with Victor Charles."

Pete hit the switch. Juice flowed. Tran buckled. Tran clenched.

The clamps sparked. His hair sparked. His nuts spasmed. He bit his lips. He bit his tongue. He cracked his false teeth.

Pete said, "That demoralize-the-GIs story you told Wayne was bullshit. Admit it and go from there."

Tran licked his lips. "Victor Charles, boss. You don't underestimate."

Pete hit the switch. Juice flowed. Tran buckled. Tran clenched.

His bladder blew. The clamps sparked. His head twitched. His dentures flew.

Mesplède said, "*Il est plus que dinky dau, il est carrément fou.*"

Pete kicked the dentures. They hit the doorway and popped out. They hit the mud monsoon. Tran flashed his gums. Pete saw old scars—Cong torture tattoos.

"I'll double up next time. You don't want that. You won't—"

"Okay okay okay. I kill slaves and sell base to ARVN."

Pete spit his gum out. "That's a start."

Tran worked his chair back. Tran flipped Pete off—*le bird boocoo.*

"You French fuck number ten. You *carrément fou.*"

Pete popped more gum. "You're in with somebody. Tell me who."

Tran flipped Pete off. The wop stiff-arm—*il bah-fungoo.*

"Fuck the frogs. You number ten. You run at Dien Bien Phu."

Pete worked his gum. "Tell me who's running you. We'll have a drink and discuss it."

Tran wiggled. Tran worked his chair back. Tran flipped Pete off—up and rotated—you twirl boocoo.

"You French *cochon.* You fuck fat men."

Pete worked his gum. Pete blew a bubble. It popped ka-poo.

"Who's running you? You're not in this all by yourself."

Tran worked his chair back. Tran spread his legs. Tran humped his hips boocoo.

"I run your wife. I eat red pussy 'cause you homo—"

Pete hit the switch. Pete *locked* the switch. Tran buckled. Tran humped his hips. Tran worked his chair back boocoo.

He slid it. He squared it. He made the doorway. Mesplède jumped. Pete tripped.

Tran flipped them off. Tran dumped his chair. Tran went BONZAI! He hit the rain. He hit the mud. He electrified.

87

(Los Angeles, 9/28/65)

ormons:
Mormon lawyers. Mormon aides. Mormon worker drones. Drac's Mormons—Latter-day Saints.

It was their summit. It was their turf. It was their hotel call. They stormed the Statler. They booked a suite. They brought their own refreshments. Their names blurred. Littell called them all "sir."

He was distracted. Fred O. just called him. Fred O. found the scandal-rag files. They're yours for ten G's. I want them/I'll meet you/they're mine.

The summit kicked off. Six Mormons hogged one table. A Mormon prepped a tape rig. A Mormon looped a tape in. A Mormon pressed Play.

Drac speaks:

"Good morning, gentlemen. I trust that you have clean air in your conference room, along with appropriate snacks such as Fritos corn chips and Slim Jim beef jerky. As you know, the purpose of this meeting is to establish ballpark price estimates for the hotel-casinos I wish to purchase, and to devise strategies to circumvent recent so-called civil-rights laws, which are in fact civil-wrongs laws, which will prove detrimental to the American free-enterprise system. It is my intention to cunningly and willfully abrogate these laws, retain segregated work crews and discourage Negroes from habituating my casinos, with exceptions to be made for stellar Negroes such as Wilma Rudolph, the so-called fastest woman alive, and the multi-talented Sammy Davis Jr. Before I turn the meeting over to my Las Vegas point man, Ward J. Littell, I should inform you that I have been studying the tax code for the state of California and have determined that it is in fact unconstitutional. It is my intention to avoid paying

California state income tax for the upcoming fiscal year of 1966. I may decide to remain mobile until the time that I establish permanent residence in Las Vegas. I may travel by train, avoid undue stays in all fifty states and thus avoid paying state income tax in toto."

The off switch clicked. The tape died. The Mormons stirred. The Mormons checked the credenza.

Salty Fritos. Congealed cheez dip. Tasty Slim Jims.

Littell coughed. Littell dispensed graph sheets. Price projections/per twelve hotels. Gaming projections/per twelve casinos.

Doctored paper. Revised and cooked. Your chef—Moe Dalitz.

The Mormons read. The Mormons skimmed columns. The Mormons cleared their throats. The Mormons took notes.

A Mormon coughed. "The purchase prices are high by 20%."

Moe set the prices. Carlos consulted. Santo T. helped.

Littell coughed. "I think the prices are reasonable."

A Mormon said, "We'll need tax returns. We'll need to calibrate off reported profits, not estimates."

A Mormon said, "That part doesn't bother me. We're dealing with organized-crime proprietors, to one degree or another. You have to believe that they report low."

A Mormon said, "We can subpoena their tax returns from the IRS. That way they can't submit fakes."

Wrong. Mr. Hoover will act. Mr. Hoover will quash selectively. Mr. Hoover will pick what you see.

No oldies. No pre-64s. *Good* '64s/the Boys report high/the Boys bait-and-switch.

A Mormon said, "Mr. Hughes is adamant on the Negro issue."

A Mormon said, "Wayne Senior can help us out there. He segregates his work crews, and he knows his way around those new laws."

Littell stabbed his pencil. Littell hit his notepad. Littell broke the tip.

"Your suggestion offends me. It's unsavory and altogether repugnant."

The Mormons stared at him. Littell stared straight back.

Fred Otash was big. Fred Otash was gruff. Fred Otash was Lebanese. He lived in restaurants. He loved Dino's Lodge and the Luau. Clients found him there.

He doped race horses. He fixed fights. He brokered abortions. He traced fugitives. He pulled shakedowns. He sold smut pix. He knew things. He found things out. He charged high fees.

Littell hit the Luau. Otash was splitsville. Littell hit Dino's. Littell hit paydirt—there's Freddy O. in his booth.

He's in nubby silk shorts. He's in a hula shirt. He's got a tan. He's spearing calamari. He's skimming racing forms. He's sipping cold chablis.

Littell walked over. Littell sat down. Littell dropped the cash on the table.

Otash kicked a lettuce box. "It's all there. I photocopied the choice stuff, in case you were wondering."

"I thought you might."

"I found a snapshot of Rock Hudson browning a Filipino jockey. I sent a dupe to Mr. Hoover."

"That was thoughtful."

Otash laughed. "You're droll, Ward, but you're not my cup of tea. I've never understood your allure to Pete B."

Littell smiled. "Try shared history."

Otash poked a squid. "Like Dallas '63?"

"Does the whole world know?"

"Just some guys who don't care."

Littell kicked the box. "I should go."

"Go, then. And beware the ides of fucking September."

"Would you care to explain?"

"You'll see soon enough."

Jane was out. Littell lugged the box in. Littell checked the papers first. Three subscribed dailies: L.A. *Times*/New York *Times*/Washington *Post*.

He skimmed the front sections. He skimmed the B-sheets. No word—nineteen days in.

The letters went out—mea culpa/Lyle Holly—postmarked SCLC. One to the House Committee/one to Bobby.

Littell skimmed the C-sheets. Littell skimmed the D. Nothing—no word yet.

He dumped the papers. He cleared some desk space. He dumped the lettuce box.

Files and carbon sheets. Photos and tip sheets. Unpublished smears—full pieces. The gamut—*Confidential* to *Whisper/Lowdown* to *Hush-Hush*.

He stacked piles. He skimmed sheets. He read fast. He rolled in dirt.

Dipsomania. Nymphomania. Kleptomania. Pedophilia. Coprophilia. Scopophilia. Flagellation. Masturbation. Miscegenation.

Lenny Bruce rats Sammy Davis. Sammy swings bilateral/Sammy sniffs cocaine. Danny Thomas hits sepia sinspots. Bob Mitchum dips his dick in Dilaudid and fucks all nite.

Sonny Liston killed a white man. Bing Crosby knocked up Dinah Shore.

Dinah got twin Binglets scraped at a clap clinic in Cleveland. Lassie has K-9 psychosis. Lassie bites kids at Lick Pier.

Paydirt: Two casino front men/one date-a-boy.

They rendezvous at the Rugburn Room. They trick at the Dunes. They party with peyote and poppers. The front men work the date-a-boy. He sustains damage and hemorrhages. The front men check the register. The front men look for doctors. The front men hit suite 302.

The doc's a drunk. The doc's a hophead. The doc's got King Kong on his back. The doc soaks his tools in vodka. The doc operates. The date-a-boy dies. The doc dips back to Des Moines. A desk clerk calls *Confidential.*

One hit. One bite for Drac. One blackmail wedge.

Littell clipped pages. Littell scanned carbons. Littell skimmed tip sheets. Payoffs/bribes/slush funds/dope cures/nut bins/car wrecks.

Johnnie Ray. Sal Mineo. Ad*lay* Stevenson. Toilet stalls/glory holes/gonorr—

No. Wait. Ides of Sept—

Hush-Hush-10/57/unpublished. The title: RED LINK TO RACKETS.

Arden Breen Bruvick. Her Commie dad—killed in '52. "Who Iced Daddy Breen? Temperamental Teamsters? Arden or Hubby Dan?"

Arden's a party girl. Arden's a call girl. Arden fled grief in K.C. Dan B.'s a lamster. He's on the run. He split K.C.

Arden's a femme fatale. Arden has Mob ties. Arden knows "Shifty" Jules Schiffrin.

A clipped photo/a caption/a date:

8/12/54—RED PARTY GIRL PARTIES WITH RANDY RACKETEER.

There's Arden. She's young. She's dancing with Carlos Marcello.

Littell trembled. Littell got the shakes. Littell got instant DTs.

He palsied. His hands jerked. He ripped the photo. He dropped the tip sheets.

He *saw* things:

Cords stuck to walls. Cords stuck to lamps. Cords off the TV.

He *heard* things:

Tap sounds. Phone buzz. Line clicks.

His chair slid. He fell. He saw wall cords. He saw bug mounts. He saw wisps. He got up. He stumbled. He braced the walls. He saw shapes. He saw flecks. He saw wisps.

88

(Las Vegas, 9/28/65)

The cat abused him. He loved it. He lived for his shit.

The cat clawed his pants. The cat snagged his socks. The cat dropped turds on his shirts. He loved it. Shit on me more now. I live for your shit.

The AC dipped. Pete slapped the wall unit. The cat clawed his shirt.

Biz was slow. The p.m. lull dragged. Pete shagged calls. His drivers smoked outside.

New rules: The Tiger Kab Manifesto.

Don't smoke near me. Don't eat near me. Don't snarf fat-rich food. Don't tempt me with taste treats—let me get back.

I've got more wind now. I've got more spunk. I've got more pizzazz. I dumped the pills. They fucked with me. I let the cat do that.

Don't smoke. Don't eat bad food—the docs said that.

Okay—I'll play.

Don't worry. Don't work hard. Don't pull rotations—fuck you on *that*.

Tran iced himself. He worried it. He worked it. He hired some Marvs. They surveilled the lab. They reported:

Some Can Lao snuck in. They let chemists in. Said chemists brought M-base boocoo. Said chemists cooked white horse. Said chemists used Wayne's shit.

Pete braced Stanton. Stanton was sheepish. Stanton said: "I was going to tell you—*after* you got well."

Pete said TELL ME NOW. Stanton said the new regime's tough. You know that. No fuck with Can Lao cat Mr. Kao. He's tough. He's greedy. He's savvy. He's cooking "H" in our lab—on Wayne's rotations. He's shipping "H" to China. He's routing "H" west. He's got a French clientele.

Pete blew up. Pete kicked walls. Pete strained arteries. Stanton smiled. Stanton jollied him. Stanton popped a ledger book.

Said book held figures. Said figures said: Mr. Kao *bought* his lab time. Mr. Kao paid big coin. The kadre made money.

Stanton reasoned. Stanton explicated. Stanton mollified. He said Kao's pro-U.S. and pro-kadre. He said Kao won't sell dope to GIs.

Pete reasoned. Stanton reasoned. They rehashed Tran's suicide.

Tran killed the slaves. Tran stole the M-base. Mr. Kao bought Tran's base ricky-tick. Tran fears Kao. Tran won't snitch Kao. Tran electrifies.

Stanton said he'd brace Kao. Stanton said he'd say this: We're your friends. Don't use us. Don't fuck us. Don't sell dope to GIs.

Pete was relieved. Pete rotated west. Pete relieved his arteries. Wayne was stateside now. Wayne was in Bon Secour. Wayne dipped south per gun-run rotations.

Pete called him. Pete spilled on Tran. Pete spilled on Can Lao Kao.

Wayne went nuts. Wayne loved his lab/Wayne loved his dope/Wayne loved his chemistry. Pete calmed him down. Pete yelled and cursed. Pete strained his arteries.

Donkey Dom swished in. The cat hissed. The cat hated fags. The cat hated wops.

Dom hissed back. Pete laughed. The phone rang.

Pete picked up. "Tiger."

"It's Otash. I'm in L.A., and I don't need a cab."

Pete stroked the cat. "What is it? Did you find anything?"

"Yeah, I did. The trouble is, I won't fuck one client in favor of another, which means I found those files for Littell, which contained some racy shit on his girlfriend and Carlos M., so I'm telling *you,* because you're paying me for some version of the same—"

Pete hung up. Pete plugged the switchboard. Pete dialed Bon Secour direct. He got dial tones. He got rings. Ward *knows* now. Ward will—

"Charthouse Motel."

"Wayne Tedrow. He's in room—"

Dial tones/clicks/rings—

Wayne picked up. "Yeah?"

"It's me. I want—"

"Jesus, calm down. You'll have another—"

"Lock up Bruvick. Make him call Ward at 10:00 p.m. L.A. time."

Wayne said, "What *is* this?"

Pete said, "I'm not sure."

89

(Los Angeles, 9/28/65)

Trashed: the living room/the bedrooms/the kitchen.

He saw wisps. He saw cords. They weren't there. He trashed the phones. He looked for taps. They weren't there. He trashed the TV. He looked for bugs. They weren't there.

He trashed his study. He trashed Jane's den. They were cord and bug-free. He walked to a liquor store. He bought Chivas Regal. He walked it on back.

He opened it. He smelled it. He dumped it out.

He rebuilt the phones. He reread the story. Arden Breen Bruvick/Carlos and Jane.

He clipped the piece. He cropped the pic. He taped them inside the front door. He taped them at Jane's eye-level.

Jane was late. Jane was due—Arden Breen Bruvick Smith Coates.

Littell grabbed a chair. Littell sat outside. The terrace view enticed. West L.A./count the lights/gauge that long drop.

There's the key. It's her. It's Arden Breen Bruv—

The lock clicked. The door slammed. There's the pause. There's the gasp.

She dropped her keys. She scraped a match. She's scheming. She's lighting up. She needs hand props.

Littell heard her foot scuffs. High heels tapped hardwood. Littell smelled her smoke.

There—she's behind you.

"It's not what you're thinking. There's an explanation for all of it."

His neck went warm. He felt her breath. He stared at the lights. He hid from her face.

"Carlos protected you before Dallas. I protected you after. You went back to Carlos and started spying on me."

Jane traced his shoulders. Jane traced his neck. She probed. She worked his kinks. Geisha/spy/whore.

"Carlos found me *after* Dallas. He knew I had to be the Arden at the safe house. He lied to Pete and pretended that he didn't know who I was."

She probed. She worked his neck. Call girl/liar/whore.

"Carlos was hiding my husband. He said he'd hand us up to Jimmy Hoffa if I didn't report back on you. I'd had a thing with Jules Schiffrin, and Carlos told me about your Teamster-book plan."

Her hands *worked*. Her voice *worked*. Concubine/whore.

"But I loved you, and I loved our life, and I loved what you'd done for me."

She traced his neck. She kissed his neck. Mob slattern/whore.

"Yes, I went through your things. But I didn't tell Carlos that you were stealing from Howard Hughes, or that you were sending money to the SCLC, or that you sleep with Janice Tedrow when you're not sleeping with me, or that you hoard these pathetic mementos of Robert Kennedy."

Littell rubbed his eyes. Streetlights blurred. Littell gauged the drop.

"You've got a file. You're too good not to have one."

Jane dropped her hands. Jane went through her purse. Jane dropped a key in his lap.

"The Encino B. of A. You can have it. That's how much it means to me now."

Littell squeezed the key. Jane kissed his neck.

"I loved my father. That rumor that I hated him was nonsense. Danny and I didn't kill him. Jimmy Hoffa did."

Littell rubbed his eyes. Jane leaned in. Jane rubbed her tears on his neck.

"This all goes back to Jimmy and the Outfit. I was going to complete my commitment to Carlos and go to the FBI. I was going to give them everything I had on every Outfit man I knew, and try to cut a deal to save you."

Littell rubbed his eyes. Littell rubbed his neck. Traitor/spy/whore.

He stood up. He turned around. He *saw* Jane. He made fists. Her eyes were wet. Her cheeks were wet. She'd trashed her makeup.

The phone rang. He stared at Jane. Jane stared hard back. The phone rang. He stared. He saw:

New gray hairs. New face lines. Neck veins on a roar.

The phone rang. He stared. He saw: One hip cocked/those cheekbones/her pulse on a roar.

The phone rang. Jane broke the stare. Jane walked and got it. She said, "Hello." She trembled—pulse on a roar.

He followed her. He stared at her. He saw her neck veins and cheek veins. He saw her pulse on a roar.

She turned away. She cupped the receiver. He walked around her. He grabbed the hall phone.

He heard a man. He heard "run." He heard "blown with Littell." He heard the man falter. He heard Jane get strong.

She said, "Run." She said, "Hush now." She said, "Carlos *will* care."

She hung up. The line-click boomed. Littell dropped his phone.

He walked over. He saw her eyes start to dry. He saw her pulse ebb off that roar.

"Were we ever real?"

"I think we loved risk more than we ever loved each other."

"You were always an Arden. You were never really a Jane."

DOCUMENT INSERT: 10/2/65. Atlanta *Constitution* headline:

FBI RAIDS MISSISSIPPI HATE-MAIL RING

DOCUMENT INSERT: 10/11/65. Miami *Herald* subhead:

GRAND JURY INDICTS KLAN LEADERS FOR
MAIL-FRAUD AND INTERSTATE COMMERCE VIOLATIONS

DOCUMENT INSERT: 10/20/65. Jackson *Sentinel* headline and
subhead:

NEO-NAZI LEADERS INDICTED
MEMBERS BLAST "FBI POGROM"

DOCUMENT INSERT: 10/26/65. Mobile *Daily Journal* headline and
subhead:

MYSTERY AT BON SECOUR
POPULAR CHARTER SKIPPER AND BOAT DISAPPEAR

DOCUMENT INSERT: 10/31/65. San Francisco *Chronicle* headline
and subhead:

VIETNAMESE TROOP COUNT AT 240,000
KING CALLS FOR PROTESTS TO INFLUENCE NEGOTIATED SETTLEMENT

DOCUMENT INSERT: 11/4/65. Mobile *Daily Journal* headline and
subhead:

BON SECOUR SKIPPER'S BOAT FOUND IN FLORIDA KEYS
MYSTERY DEEPENS: SKIPPER NOT ON BOARD

DOCUMENT INSERT: 11/8/65. Los Angeles *Times* subhead:

RFK SAYS NO PREZ'L BID IN '68

DOCUMENT INSERT: 11/18/65. Chicago *Tribune* headline and subhead:

U.S. ATTORNEY CITES "BRILLIANT WORK" IN FBI HATE WAR
RECORD NUMBER OF MAIL-FRAUD INDICTMENTS

DOCUMENT INSERT: 11/20/65. Milwaukee *Sentinel* headline:

KING ANNOUNCES "ANTI-SLUM CAMPAIGN" IN CHICAGO

DOCUMENT INSERT: 11/26/65. Washington *Post* headline and subhead:

HOOVER ATTACKS KING AT AMERICAN LEGION RALLY
CALLS CIVIL-RIGHTS LEADER "DEMAGOGUE"

DOCUMENT INSERT: 11/30/65. Washington *Post* headline and subhead:

CRITICS DENOUNCE HOOVER ATTACK
ANTI-KING STATEMENTS CALLED "SHRILL"
AND "HYSTERICAL"

DOCUMENT INSERT: 12/5/65. Seattle *Post-Intelligencer* headline and subhead:

HOUSE COMMITTEE INVESTIGATING "ILLEGAL" BUGS
AND WIRETAPS
CIVIL-RIGHTS LEADERS CALL "FOUL"

DOCUMENT INSERT: 12/14/65. Los Angeles *Herald-Express* headline and subhead:

HOWARD HUGHES AND TWA:

BILLIONAIRE RECLUSE AGREES TO DIVEST STOCK

DOCUMENT INSERT: 12/15/65. Denver *Post-Dispatch* subhead:

HOFFA CONVICTION APPEALS FILED
WITH SUPREME COURT

DOCUMENT INSERT: 12/18/65. Chicago *Sun-Times* subhead:

KING REVEALS DETAILS OF "ANTI-SLUM CAMPAIGN"

DOCUMENT INSERT: 12/20/65. New York *Times* subhead:

"CITIZENS FOR RFK" GROUP ANNOUNCES EXPLORATION
OF '68 CANDIDACY

DOCUMENT INSERT: 12/21/65. Chicago *Tribune* headline and sub-head:

GIANCANA STILL IN JAIL
REFUSES TO TESTIFY BEFORE GRAND JURY

DOCUMENT INSERT: 1/8/66. Washington *Post* subhead:

JUDICIARY COMMITTEE TELLS HOOVER:
REMOVE ALL BUGS AND WIRETAPS NOT VETTED BY AG

DOCUMENT INSERT: 1/14/66. Mobile *Daily Journal* headline and subhead:

MYSTERY CONTINUES:
WHERE IS POPULAR BON SECOUR SKIPPER?

DOCUMENT INSERT: 1/18/66. Mobile *Daily Journal* headline and subhead:

MYSTERY DEEPENS:
DOES SKIPPER'S DISAPPEARANCE LINK TO '56 CHARGES
AND LONG-MISSING WIFE?

DOCUMENT INSERT: 1/19/66. Atlanta *Constitution* headline:

MAIL FRAUD INDICTMENTS CONTINUE

DOCUMENT INSERT: 1/26/66. Chicago *Tribune* headline and subhead:

BOLD WORDS FROM REV. KING:
"THE PRIMARY OBJECTIVE OF THE CHICAGO FREEDOM MOVEMENT
WILL BE TO BRING ABOUT THE UNCONDITIONAL SURRENDER OF FORCES
DEDICATED TO THE CREATION AND MAINTENANCE OF SLUMS"

DOCUMENT INSERT: 1/31/66. Denver *Post-Dispatch* headline and subhead:

JURY-TAMPERING CONVICTION UPHELD
HOFFA FACES JAIL TIME

DOCUMENT INSERT: 2/8/66. Los Angeles *Herald-Express* headline and subhead:

FOES DENOUNCE HOOVER
FBI BOSS CATCHES HEAT FOR ATTACKS ON KING

DOCUMENT INSERT: 2/20/66. Miami *Herald* subhead:

RFK STUMPS FOR NEGOTIATED VIET SETTLEMENT
ECHOES DR. KING'S PLEAS

DOCUMENT INSERT: 3/3/66. Los Angeles *Times* headline and sub-head:

HUGHES DIVESTS TWA STOCK

6.5 MILLION SHARES NET $546,000,000

DOCUMENT INSERT: 3/29/66. Internal memorandum. To: BLUE RABBIT. From: Director. Topic: OPERATION BLACK RABBIT. Marked: "Stage-1 Covert"/"Eyes Only"/"Read and Burn."

BLUE RABBIT,

Pull all SCLC bugs and wiretaps immediately. Implement at Stage-1 Priority. It is imperative that this be accomplished before the Judiciary Committee begins a formal inquiry.

Initiate the first stage of OPERATION BLACK RABBIT/ADJUNCT. Pick a target and assess the health of P. Bondurant, henceforth to be known as BIG RABBIT.

90

(Vietnam, Laos, Los Angeles, Las Vegas, Bon Secour, Bay St. Louis,
Cuban Waters, 4/1/66–10/30/66)

Ghosts: Arden-Jane and Danny Bruvick.

Wayne watchdogged Danny. Danny called Arden-Jane. Arden-Jane left Ward Littell. Wayne stuck with Danny. Wayne wet-nursed Danny. Wayne worked to save Ward Littell.

Pete said guard Danny. Pete said release him. Pete said cut him two days' slack. Call Carlos then. Say Danny booked. Cite parts unknown.

He did it. He stayed with Danny. Danny boozed. Danny reminisced.

Danny loves Arden. Arden loves Ward. Arden loves Danny half-baked. Arden works for Carlos. Arden spies on Ward. Part-time spy/full-time lover/long-distance wife.

Wayne *got* it:

Danny was weak. Arden was strong. Arden hooked him on the Life. It all pertained to Teamster shit—embezzlement and flight.

Wayne waited. Danny waited. Arden came by. She chain-smoked. She den-mothered. She fussed.

She knew it was over. She said it: "I'm tired of running—and Ward knows that."

Wayne left the boat. Danny cast sail. Wayne killed two days. Wayne called Carlos up.

He said Danny split. He said Danny took *Tiger Klaw*. Coward Danny—scared of scalp runs/scared for his life.

Carlos yelled. Carlos fumed. Carlos made vicious threats. Wayne tracked newspapers. Wayne logged updates.

Tiger Klaw drifts. *Tiger Klaw* runs aground. Danny and Jane are nowhere. Carlos stays mum. Carlos stays clueless. Carlos does not brace Pete. Carlos does not brace Wayne.

Pete clued Ward to Arden. Pete bucked Carlos. Arden ran to Danny. They ran to their death. They held in strong. They did not rat Pete and Wayne. Pete and Wayne would have heard otherwise.

Pete loves Ward. Ward loves Jane the ghost. Pete knows they're dead. Pete never says it. Dead women fuck him up.

Pete loves Barb. Pete rotates home. Pete stays off rotation. Barb lured him home. Ward licensed him in.

Pete bought the Golden Cavern. Pete bought his own hotel-casino. Eldon Peavy had syph. Eldon Peavy sold cheap. Eldon Peavy dumped his fruit bowl.

The Cavern welcomed fruits. The Cavern housed fruits. The Cavern rejoined Tiger Kab. Fruit drivers drove fruit tenants. Fred T. bugged the rooms. Fruit moths were drawn to the flame.

Dirt accrued: Fruit dirt/hip dirt/pol dirt/fruit celebs/fruit hipsters/ fruit politicos.

Pete installed "Swinger Suites." Fred bugged the walls. Pete drew non-fruit biz. State legislators/junket groups/Shriners on toots.

Pete accrued dirt. Pete accrued straight dirt and fruit dirt. The word spread—the Cavern's hip—dig the straight-fruit détente.

Biz boomed. Pete stored dirt and made money. Pete reprised health-wise. Pete looked good now. Pete restored his bad pump.

He stopped smoking. He dumped weight. He chewed gum incessant. He worked incessant. He ran the dope biz. He ran Tiger Kab. He ran the Cavern. He refurbished the lounge. He shot Barb a permanent gig.

Milt C. gigged with her. Milt did topical shtick. Milt had a puppet. Said puppet was a hairy ape. Milt called him Junkie Monkey. Junkie Monkey ragged celebs. Junkie Monkey ragged fruits. Junkie Monkey perved on Barb B.

Barb drew biz. Milt drew biz. Pete made *more* money.

Sonny Liston loved the Cavern. Sonny moved in. Sonny hid from his wife and helped Pete.

Sonny roamed the casino. Sonny made dope collections. Sonny mus-cled deadbeats. Wayne ran with Sonny. *They* made dope collections. Their reps drew heat.

Their reps clashed. They were salt-and-pepper. They were black-black and white-white. They prowled West LV. They talked Wendell Durfee. Sonny ran riffs. Sonny ran theories. Sonny dug that nom de pimp:

Cassius Cool—the ex–Wendell Durfee. I calls him Cassius X.

Wayne rotated. Wayne ran Saigon to Vegas. Wayne ran due west.

He cruised L.A. He stalked Wendell Durfee. He prowled Watts. He drew hate vibes. Call them riot aftershocks.

He hit pimp bars. He polled pimps. He polled whores. He got zero results. He palmed cops. He bought jail checks. He logged rumors. He got zero results. He prowled south. He tooled main drags. He watched faces. He got zero results.

He braced street creeps. He passed out cards. He logged jive. He got pushed. He got shoved. He got spit on. L.A. was L.A. He had no rep.

He rotated east. He rotated south. He did kadre biz. He cooked dope in Saigon. He ran dope in Vegas. He ran guns through Mississippi.

Profits were up. Kadre kosts accrued konkurrent. Guns moved south. They lost *Tiger Klaw.* They lost Skipper Bruvick. They bought a new boat. They armored it. They bought a new skipper. Dick Wenzel—seaborne merc—tight with Laurent Guéry.

Tiger Klaw II. Out of Bay St. Louis, Mississippi.

Wenzel made Cuban runs. Wenzel brought Laurent. Wenzel brought Flash and Wayne. Wenzel was good. Wenzel was bold. Wenzel had boulder-size balls.

The runs went gooooood. No glitches/no bullshit/no surprise attacks. They probed the coast. They grappled up. They met Fuentes and Arredondo.

They dispensed weaponry. They fed insurgents. The funnel moved inland. The coast fed the hills. The kadre fed fuel to *la Causa.*

The kadre was kautious. Pete said trust no one. Pete decreed poly tests. Laurent ran said tests. Laurent ran the Port Sulphur hot seats. Wayne tested clean. Flash tested clean. Ditto Fuentes and Arredondo.

The Cuban runs worked. Mucho runs with no glitches and shit. Bob worked. Laurent worked. They shagged guns. They hid their sources. They said they hit the Minutemen. They said they hit John Birch. They said they tapped Army QMs.

Bob played it close. Bob cited need-to-know laws and source restrictions. Bob shagged good guns. Bob made concessions.

His sources feared tracebacks. His sources dipped their guns. His sources burned serial numbers. Pete hated it. Pete craved confiscation. Let's tell the Beard that it's *us.*

Bob shagged *good* guns. Bob shagged *dipped* guns. Pete went along with it.

The funnel ran to Cuba. The funnel ran back. The funnel ran information. Fuentes reported. Arredondo assisted.

Dig it: Skirmishes/village raids/running fire. Varaguay/Las Tunas/

Puerto Guinico. Insurgents hit. Insurgents kill. Insurgents die. Insurgents find replacements.

Good, but:

No major battles *yet.* No major progress discernible. No kadre guns thus decisive.

Wayne loved the Cuba runs. Wayne ate Dexedrine. Wayne notched seven run-notches. Dick Wenzel played skipper. Pete made two runs. Flash and Laurent made seven.

They got close. They dropped guns off. They shot inland. They torched huts. They scalped Fidelistos. They saved the scalps. They dry-cured them. They burned on their initials. They tallied them. They nailed them up. They served as boat decorations.

Wayne had sixteen scalps. Flash had twelve scalps. Laurent and Pete had nine each. Pete craved more. Pete craved escalation.

The war escalated. Their crops escalated. White horse escalated konkurrent. Mesplède ran Tiger Kamp solo. Mesplède brought in reinforcements.

Chuck was dead. Tran was dead. Pete was stateside. Laurent was stateside. Flash was stateside. Wayne was on rotation. Mesplède needed help. Mesplède bought more Marvs. Mesplède bought some Can Lao goons. They backstopped him. They ran the slaves. They surveilled the chemists.

Wayne knew the Tran story. Pete told him late. Pete said it's all kool. Mr. Kao's boys *rent* the lab. They work there on *your* rotations. It's kosher. Goons guard *your* lab. Said goons pay tribute to Stanton.

The war escalated. Big troop stats swelled through '66. Kao escalated. Kao pushed horse in France. Kao pushed horse in Saigon.

To slants only. No round-eyes. No GI biz.

Kao formed a dope squad. It was all Can Lao and all klandestine. They swarmed Saigon. They trashed "O" dens. They made them horse pads.

They ran said pads. They sold horse. They kept said pads klean. They scrubbed floors and swabbed spikes.

Kao had his fiefdom. Kao had export and Saigon. The kadre had Vegas.

They shared lab space. They shared vats. They shared guinea pigs. Junkies swarmed the Go-Go. Junkies geezed upstairs. Kao's chemists *used* them. They brewed new formulas. They tested dosages. They notched fatalities.

Wayne rotated east. Wayne saw the war grow. Wayne saw horse grow konkurrent. Wayne rotated west. Wayne saw the war grow—every night on TV.

Barb saw the war. Barb loathed the war. Barb watched the war on TV. There's Barb. She's in Da Nang. She scores this white powder.

She toured Da Nang. She saw the maimed. She saw Pete fucked up. She dug pills. She craved more. She found it. She found horse. She sniffed horse. She disproved Pete's assertion: *We* control horse/*we* contain horse/all whites verboten.

Barb flew home. Barb brought hospital snapshots. Barb watched the war on TV.

She had Pete full-time. She loved it. Pete loves the war. Barb hates the war. Barb sparks *their* war for real.

She ragged the war. She talked antiwar shit. She rode horseback.

She took tastes. It went up her nose. It went there under Pete's eyes. She scored horse. She disproved Pete. She disproved containment.

Small tastes. No arc up to skin pops. No mainline spikes.

Wayne knew she did it. Pete didn't. Wayne looked at her closer. Wayne loved her long-distance. Wayne lived to WATCH.

He watched in Vegas. He watched in L.A. He watched in Vietnam. The war escalated. The war was the Life uncontained.

Pete was wrong. We couldn't win. We couldn't force containment. Pete was wrong. White horse would reign. White horse would smash containment. Barb proved him wrong. GIs would follow her. White horse would reign uncontained.

Wayne watched the war. Wayne read body counts. Wayne prowled dope galleries. Wayne logged rumors.

More troops were pledged. That meant more bomb runs. That meant more ground expansion.

Mr. Kao expanded. Mr. Kao bombed Ba Na Key. Dope fields burned. Mr. Kao's Laotian rivals de-expanded.

Stanton said Kao's kool. Kao won't fuck us. We're localized. We're self-contained. We're fine in West Vegas.

Wayne and Pete knew otherwise. Wayne and Pete knew this:

We're *too* localized/we're *too* contained/we're hamstrung in West Vegas.

Wayne pressed Pete. Wayne pressed the case. Let's press Stanton. Let's press Carlos. Let's tell them this: Let's push white horse in L.A.

Pete said, "Don't shuck me." Pete said, "It's about Wendell Durfee." Pete knew him. Pete knew his shit. Pete knew his dreams.

Bongo/King Arthur/Cassius Cool/black faces/white backdrops/white sheets. Cur-ti and Leroy. Otis Swasey. The dead whore/her trailer/the ball in her teeth.

The dreams reran. The dreams dredged Wayne Senior. It was dream clockwork. Dream and wake. Father Rabbit's there on your pillow.

The dreams recycled. The dreams reran. The dreams ran in rotation.

Rotate east—see Bongo—you killed him there. Rotate west—see

black faces—you found them there. Rotate south—see new faces—they lynch that type there.

White sheets. Klan sheets. Bob Relyea—Wild Rabbit.

Bob tweaked him. Bob told him: Your daddy loves you. He misses you. He told me so. He digs on you. He's Daddy Rabbit. He's hip. He's cool. He funds my Klan. We fight mail fraud. We help Mr. Hoover.

We hate smart. We contain. We consolidate. We fuck the bad haters. We spread the good hate.

Dreams. Reruns. Rotations.

Sleep on planes—crash time zones—see faces. Hate smart. Consolidate. Hail Father Rabbit!

The dreams reran. The concept held. The gist accrued: He needs you. He sees you. He *wants* you.

91

(Las Vegas, Bay St. Louis, Cuban Waters, 4/1/66–10/30/66)

ars:
The real war. The TV war. Barb's running fire.
They watch the news. He comments. He says we'll win. Barb says we shouldn't. Barb says we can't and we won't.

He says I've *been* there. He says I *know*. *She* says *I've* been there. She says *I* know. They escalate. They debate control. They debate containment. TV wars—parlor shit—sniper attacks.

It raged. It escalated. It stopped. Barb nuked him. Barb won.

She said, "Nobody's controlling the war, and *you* don't control the dope traffic, because *I* met a doctor in Da Nang, and *he* sends *me* little tastes, and I boot them when I get bored to death or afraid that you'll fall off a fucking boat in the fucking Cuban sea."

He flipped out. He threw shit. He taxed out his heart. He tossed chairs. He broke windows. He chucked the TV out. One hoist—two hundred pounds airborne. One badass heart-patient trick.

The TV flew. The TV dropped fourteen stories. The TV dive-bombed a blue Ford.

He raged. His veins throbbed. His pump swelled. He crashed. He dive-bombed the couch. Barb talked up a truce.

I'm no junkie. I sniff it. I taste it. I never shoot up. I hate your work. I hate the war—it covers you.

He tried to fight. He gobbled air. His pump puttered and slogged. Barb held his hands. Barb held the cat. Barb talked *très* slow.

I hate your work. I hate the Life. I hate Vegas now. We'll ride it out. We'll survive it. We'll win.

They made up. He got calm. He got some back-end wind. They made love. They wrecked the couch. The cat refereed.

Shit got said. Shit got aired. Shit went *un*said. No vows of abstinence/no vows to stop/no vows to change.

Truce.

They split the Stardust. They moved into the Cavern. They bought a new TV. Barb watched the war. Barb sulked and judged. He worked the biz. He ran dope. He ran guns.

Barb worked the Cavern. Barb wore go-go gowns. Barb showed off skin-plus. Dig it: No pinholes/no bruises/no tracks.

Truce.

They lived. They made love. He traveled. Barb flew then. He knew it. Barb flew White Powder Air.

They lived the truce. He nailed the Shit Clause:

Barb was right—the war was fucked—we couldn't win. Barb was right—they had big love—they'd stick and win. Barb was wrong—white horse had teeth—white horse bit to win.

White flag/ceasefire/truce.

He conceded points. He owed Barb. He brought her to Dallas. The truce held. The clause held. The ink ran.

You've got Barb. Jane is dead. Ward knows it. Ward said it once. Ward said Jane left me. Ward stopped short then.

Ward knew Jane's backstory. That scandal file told him. Ward could fill in the rest. Arden runs to Danny. They set sail. Gulf waters entice. They're tapped and tired—long years of flight.

Ward lost a woman. Carlos lost a boat. Carlos lost a spy. Carlos lost Danny. Carlos *killed* Danny. Carlos dropped *la Causa* flat.

The new boat bored him. The boat runs bored him. It was gadfly shit. The runs bored Pete. The runs vexed Pete. The runs stressed his pump.

Coast prowls and gun transfers—too easy. Raft runs and scalp hunts—light counts.

It's 1/66. Pete gets frustrated. Pete sends Flash in. Flash is Cuban. Flash is dark. Flash fits right in.

Flash tours Cuba. Flash meets Fuentes and Arredondo. They hit the hills. They tour kampsites. They see kadre gun-stocks.

Big kampsites. Big personnel. Big inventories stocked.

They lead a raid. They run sixty men. They blitz a Militia camp. They flank in. They lob shells. They pop bazookas. They run in under cover. They flank wide. They throw Zippo flames.

They killed eighty men. They lost three men. They shaved beards boocoo. Pete loved it. Pete revived behind it. Pete dropped pump weight boocoo.

Weight was weight. Shit was shit. Work was work. The docs said don't smoke. He did it. The docs said eat light. He did it. The docs said work light. He said Fuck You.

He worked the dope biz. He worked Tiger Kab. He worked the Cavern. The Cavern pandered. The Cavern rocked.

Hipsters loved it. Hipsters dug Milt C. and Junkie Monkey. Horn dogs loved it. Horn dogs drooled for Barb B. Sonny Liston loved it. Fruits loved it. Fruits swished in and Liberace'd.

Wayne Senior came by. Wayne Senior waxed nice. Need some help? Call if so—I know grind-joint casinos. Pete waxed nice. Pete said sure—I'll do that.

Wayne Senior came back. Wayne Senior lost money. Wayne Senior talked.

Life's cruel. Life's odd. Ward Littell's with my ex. How's my son? I know he's tough now. I know he works for you.

Pete waxed nice. Pete waxed bland. Pete waxed noncommittal. Wayne Senior talked. Wayne Senior talked truce. Wayne Senior said I miss my son—I know he's been wiiiiiild places.

Wayne Senior waxed anxious. The word was out—Drac's on his way. Drac the bloodsucker. Drac the Mob puppet. Drac the greedy centipede.

The prelude ran long. Pete worked it for three years. Pete notched some gooood benefits.

You're forty-six years old. You're a killer. You're a frog arriviste. You're rich. You're worth two million legit.

Pas mal, mais je m'en fous.

Preludes and fringe benefits. Money and debits. Barb and white horse. Barb and ennui. Barb and Vietnam.

They played a game. He got her nude. He got in tight. He checked her arms. He checked her veins. He checked her toes. He tickled her all over. He checked for needle tracks.

None.

It's contained. I control it. I taste little drops.

He checked her ankles. He tickled her. He traced her veins. She touched him. She pulled him in.

The game helped. The game hurt. The game took him back:

It's hot. His heart rips. He leaps for her shoe.

92

(Los Angeles, Las Vegas, Washington, D.C., Boston, New Orleans, Chicago, Mexico City, 4/1/66–10/30/66)

ourner. Lover bereft. She died. She left a file. She left a legacy. He tracked her southbound. He ran logic.

Logic:

Otash sees the scandal files. Otash spots Carlos and Jane. Otash calls Pete. Pete doubts Jane. Pete's doubts *pre*-exist. Jane runs. Jane finds Danny Bruvick.

He called airlines. He checked flights. He found the name Arden Breen. She flew to Mobile, Alabama. She flew to Bon Secour.

Logic:

Pete had Gulf ties. Pete ran guns. Pete gigged from Bon Secour. Pete interceded. Pete bucked Carlos. Pete made Jane run.

Carlos found Danny. Carlos found him with Jane.

That was theory logic. It was buttressed by facts. It was shaped by news clips.

She was dead. He mourned her. He worked with Carlos. They both kept mute. Carlos said nothing. Pete stayed mute. They both misread it. They both called it this way: Ward doesn't know what we know.

I know. I did the logic. I dream the gist.

Carlos kills flamboyant. His teams pack power tools. Carlos kills slow. Chainsaws/shears/drills. Lathe chisels and fungo bats.

He dreamed it. He heard it. He saw it. He slept with it. He lived it. He didn't drink. He didn't seek numbness. He didn't anesthetize. He worked. He maneuvered. He hidey-hole stashed.

He hit the bank. He grabbed Jane's file. He studied it: six folders/typed notes/comprehensive.

Jane *knew* him. The file *nailed* him.

She predicted his embezzlements. She tracked his travels. She surmised his bank accounts. She critiqued his technique. She guessed at amounts. She assumed his guilt tithes.

She prowled his papers. She linked facts. She extrapolated lucidly. She prowled his trash. She studied said trash. She corroborated spectacularly.

She nailed his target businesses. She estimated profits. She ballparked skim flow. She predicted overhead. She guessed launder fees. She calibrated foreign currencies.

He devised the fund-book plan. *She* ran up to speed.

She tracked his travels. She tallied phone calls. She tracked his lies and omissions.

She nailed it:

The Hughes incursion. The full trust breach. The Boys sell Drac Las Vegas.

Casino profits/cash-flow charts/skim currency/front men/hidden points/rigged prices.

She took common knowledge—Hughes wants Las Vegas—she tracked back inductively.

The text jumped. The file nailed Jules Schiffrin. Jane knew Jules. Jules revealed things unwittingly. Jane extrapolated. Jane thus ascribed:

Jules builds the pension fund. Jules builds dummy books. Jules builds the "real" book scam.

Details. Facts. Guesses. Assertions. Astonishing—all *new* text—things *he* didn't know.

The text jumped. The file nailed Jimmy Hoffa.

Jimmy killed Arden's father. Eyewits spieled facts off-the-cuff. Jimmy cut management deals. Jimmy ordered beatings. Jimmy ordered hits.

Jane was smart. Jane *allegedly* hated her father. Jane lied. Jane drew heat off Jimmy. The file was Jane's revenge: long-standing/long-planned.

The text jumped. The file nailed the Boys.

Carlos/Sam G./John Rosselli/Santo/Moe Dalitz/hoods in K.C.

Details. Facts. Rumors. Assertions.

Per: Hits/botched hits/extortion. Judges bought/juries bought/cops purchased wide. Rackets developed/rackets ditched/rackets reborn and revised.

Astonishing. Incendiary. Densely inclusive.

Jane builds a testament. Jane grows weary then. Jane gets tweaked and runs.

Jane holds the file. Jane forfeits it. Jane pays off her Dallas debt. Jane pays him for two years as "Jane."

Her testament. *His* now. *His* safeguard. Tell Carlos. Tell *all* the Boys: I've served you. I'm tired. Please let *me* run.

He picked a bank in Westwood. He rented a stash vault. He stashed the file. He mourned Jane.

He dreamed. He saw icepicks and drills deployed. He prayed. He tallied his dead from Big D on up.

He stole. He bilked Howard Hughes. He tithed the SCLC. He mourned. His grief transmogrified. His hurt grew into HATE.

Carlos killed Jane. His hate bypassed him. His hate bypassed all the Boys. His hate dispersed and coalesced. His hate found Mr. Hoover.

He *watched* him.

Mr. Hoover spoke in D.C. Mr. Hoover wooed the American Legion. He watched. He stood at the back of the hall.

The hall roared. Mr. Hoover sailed clichés. Mr. Hoover attacked Dr. King. Mr. Hoover looked old. Mr. Hoover looked frail. Mr. Hoover spewed HATE.

Littell watched.

Mr. Hoover ceded irony. Mr. Hoover ceded taste. Mr. Hoover relinquished control. Mr. Hoover spewed HATE. It was unassailable/unvanquishable/unmediated.

Littell gauged it.

Mr. Hoover was old. The world outgrew him. He outlived his reign of control. *His* hate dispersed. *His* hate coalesced. *His* hate found Dr. King.

Littell gauged *his own* hate.

He lived by hubris. He overcommitted. He outflanked *his* sphere of control. His hate dispersed. His hate condensed. His hate scattergunned. He outgrew his world. He retained his ideals. He outgrew his love of intrigue. His hate dispersed and coalesced. His hate found John Edgar Hoover.

He acted on it. He acted passively. Wait. Do nothing yet. Let Mr. Hoover HATE.

Let the world rock. Let Dr. King meld with Bobby. They have bold designs. They despise the war. They may collaborate.

Dr. King planned revolt. Lyle Holly detailed it. Littell destroyed Lyle's notes. Let Dr. King live the notes. Let Dr. King act *non*passively.

Peace broadsides. Voter drives. Antislum campaigns. Revolt in its early stages—planned through '68.

Wait. Do nothing yourself. Let Mr. Hoover HATE.

His hate burns. His hate shows. His hate discredits him. Dr. King plans. Dr. King schemes. Dr. King's status grows.

Don't push *too* hard. Don't push *too* fast. Don't strain credibility. Let the world rock at its own pace. Let some things go.

LBJ fights his foreign war. Mr. Hoover approves. LBJ pushes civil rights. Mr. Hoover fumes silently. Mr. Hoover spews hate.

LBJ might assess him. Edgar—you're moribund. You've got to go.

The war will extend. The war will divide. The war might derail LBJ. Bobby might run in '68. Dr. King might downscale his agenda. Bobby might endorse it.

He watched Bobby. He read the Senate Record. He tallied Bobby's votes. Bobby was smart. Bobby never said "The Boys." Bobby hated circumspectly.

Hate strong. Hate brave. Don't hate like Mr. Hoover.

Mr. Hoover called him. The phone rang in mid-July. Mr. Hoover stirred some fear.

The spot tails were gone. He *knew* it. He was safe per Chuck Rogers. He was safe per Lyle H.

Still—Mr. Hoover stirred fear.

He was brusque. He was rude. Howard Hughes and Las Vegas—update me on that.

Littell said Drac's crazy. Drac fears state taxes. Drac's booked a whole railroad train. Drac trained to Boston. Drac brought his Mormons. Drac booked a floor at the Ritz.

Drac wants hotels. I've braced the *registered* owners. It's pro forma. The Boys have the points. The Boys will rig the fees.

Mr. Hoover laughed. Mr. Hoover schemed. Mr. Hoover promised a no-skim-bust policy. Let's not stir enmity. Why stir publicity? Why sully the Count and his kingdom?

Littell digressed. Littell said Drac has a plan. He'll hit Vegas in late November.

The red tape will clear. He'll have his cash. He'll storm the DI then. He's booked a floor. He'll bring his slaves. They'll bring his blood and dope.

Mr. Hoover laughed. Mr. Hoover probed:

I pulled some bugs. I pulled some taps. A House Committee made me. I got a tip: Lyle Holly braced Bobby. Lyle sent him a posthumous "confession."

Littell feigned shock: Not Lyle H.! Not our WHITE RABBIT!

Mr. Hoover probed. Mr. Hoover ranted. Mr. Hoover steamed. He disdained WHITE and CRUSADER. He dissected their "twin moral voids." He blasphemed WHITE the betrayer.

Littell assessed the rant. Littell concluded: He doesn't suspect me/he buys the "confession"/he buys the "betrayal" that way.

Mr. Hoover digressed. Mr. Hoover attacked Dr. King. His HATE showed. His HATE beamed. His HATE crescendoed.

Littell said let me help. You know I have documents. They detail my "Mob donations."

Mr. Hoover said no. Mr. Hoover said it's too little. Mr. Hoover said it's much too late.

Littell heard hate. Littell heard resolve. Littell knew this: He's got new plans. He'll escalate.

Mr. Hoover signed off. Mr. Hoover omitted:

Mail-fraud news. News per one arm of BLACK RABBIT. A big success/gloat-worthy. A telling omission.

Littell translated said omission. Littell knew this:

He's got new plans. He'll escalate.

Wait. Do nothing. Let his hate show. Let his hate self-indict.

The Boys had plans. It's time for relocation—Sam G. leaves custody.

Littell drove him home. Sam packed his bags. They flew to Mexico City. Sam bought knickknacks. Sam bought a house. Sam discussed his schemes.

We buy the '68 election. We throw it to *our* candidate. He takes our cash. He bows. He obeys. He pardons Jimmy Hoffa. He lets us expand. He ignores our colonizations.

We move south. We colonize. We plant our casinos. Let us thrive—don't fuck with said colonies—right- *or* left-wing.

Memo: *We* buy the candidate. *We* buy the bulk of him. Drac supplies 25%. We collude. Drac gets perks—time will determine which or what.

Jimmy's through. He's dead on appeals. He'll be jailed next spring. Let him stew. Buy a candidate. Elect him.

Said candidate waits. Said candidate pardons Jimmy. We get one pardon. We get one colony policy—per nations right- *or* left-wing.

Cuba was left-wing. They couldn't plant casinos there. Their plant targets were all *right*-wing. Think back. Go back three years—fall '63.

The hit plan's on. The Boys are mad. The Boys want their Cuban casinos. They tried to kill Castro. They indulged covert ops. They failed.

Sam enlists Santo. Santo lures Johnny Rosselli. They brace the Beard. They make nice—*please* return our casinos. The Beard says no. They clip Jack. The world rocks and sways.

Then to now—plans crass and audacious.

Like the war—Big Pete's preferred misalliance.

He met Barb for lunch. They met once a week. They discussed it. Barb hated the war. Barb felt new love for Bobby. Barb assailed Pete.

Barb talked political. Barb talked lounge gossip and segued. Barb said "exploitation." Barb said "mass murder" and "genocide."

Barb was moody. Barb took pills. Barb anesthetized. They discussed Pete's business. They discussed Pete's compartments.

Barb temporized. Barb straddled fences. Barb compartmentalized: I love Pete/I hate Pete's business/I hate Pete's war.

He loved her. Wayne loved her. She knew it. All men loved her. He told her. She knew it.

She said I like it. She said I hate it. She said I outgrew it late.

She knew Jane left him. She didn't know details. She teased him per Janice. He told her flat-out. He played it blunt—Janice was diversion.

Janice was sex. Janice was style. Janice was will bravura.

Wayne Senior beat her. Janice still limped. Janice still got cramps. Janice still shot scratch golf. Janice still played A-club tennis.

She charged the net. She limped. She cramped. She slammed shots. She made points. She won by attrition.

She rebuffed Mormon goons. Said goons were putting feelers out. Wayne Senior misses Wayne Junior.

She replied one way. Her words were Get Fucked. It was her one response verbatim.

He liked her. He loved Barb. He loved Jane.

Barb got dreamy looks. She hid from Pete then. He envied her looks. He envied her sedation.

DOCUMENT INSERT: 10/30/66. Internal memorandum. Topic:
OPERATION BLACK RABBIT. To: BLUE RABBIT. From: Director.
Marked: "Stage-1 Covert"/"Eyes Only"/"Read and Burn."

BLUE RABBIT,

I have been digesting my July phone call to CRUSADER RABBIT
for some time. I could not read his response to my mention of
WHITE RABBIT's alleged confession, and perceived his mental
state to be problematic.

WHITE RABBIT was, of course, your brother. I have given your
repeated assertions that his confession was fabricated considerable
thought. You have stated that CRUSADER RABBIT is the only one
in our purview capable of such a fabrication, and I cannot in any
way dispute that assessment.

CRUSADER RABBIT troubles me. As you have noted, his para-
mour, Arden Breen/Jane Fentress, disappeared last October and
has presumably been killed by members of organized crime. I suspect that her absence and assuredly grisly fate have contributed
to CRUSADER RABBIT's funk. You have often characterized CRU-
SADER RABBIT as a "wimp," but I would add that his propensity
for kamikaze action marks him as the world's most dangerous
wimp.

All told, I think we should reinstate our spot-surveillance of
CRUSADER RABBIT and reinstate our Trash and Mail Covers.
These actions will supplant our decision to exclude him from all
aspects of OPERATION BLACK RABBIT.

Per the "Shakedown" adjunct:

I veto your recommendation that we target RED RABBIT. RED
RABBIT will simply be too wary of entrapment.

The target will be PINK RABBIT. His heedless pursuit of homosexual encounters marks him as more suitable and vulnerable.

BIG RABBIT seems to have recovered from his heart attack.
Contact him by 12/1/66.

DOCUMENT INSERT: 11/2/66. Miami *Herald* headline:

KING DECRIES "IMPERIALISTIC" WAR IN VIETNAM

DOCUMENT INSERT: 11/4/66. Denver *Post-Dispatch* headline and subhead:

HOFFA WITH MARCH PRISON DATE
APPEAL LAWYERS GLUM

DOCUMENT INSERT: 11/12/66. Atlanta *Constitution* subhead:

WAR A "MORAL OUTRAGE," KING DECLARES IN SPEECH

DOCUMENT INSERT: 11/16/66. Los Angeles *Examiner* subhead:

NO '68 PREZ'L PLANS, RFK TELLS PRESS

DOCUMENT INSERT: 11/17/66. San Francisco *Chronicle* subhead:

"DRAFT KENNEDY" MOVEMENT GROWING DESPITE
SENATOR'S STATED RELUCTANCE

DOCUMENT INSERT: 11/18/66. Chicago *Sun-Times* headline and subhead:

KING SPEAKS TO DRAFT RESISTANCE WORKSHOP
HOOVER CALLS CIVIL-RIGHTS LEADER
"COMMUNIST PAWN"

DOCUMENT INSERT: 11/23/66. Washington *Post* subhead:

BACKLASH ON HOOVER FOR ANTI-KING REMARKS

DOCUMENT INSERT: 11/24/66. Boston *Globe* subhead:

HOWARD HUGHES' BIZARRE CROSS-COUNTRY TRAIN RIDE

DOCUMENT INSERT: 11/25/66. Las Vegas *Sun* headline and sub-head:

HUGHES TRAIN EN ROUTE

WHAT DOES BILLIONAIRE RECLUSE BODE FOR LAS VEGAS?

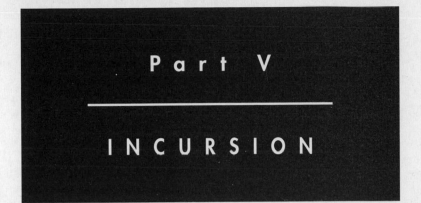

Part V

INCURSION

(November 27, 1966–March 18, 1968)

93

(Las Vegas, 11/27/66)

He's coming.

He's Mr. Big. He's Howard Hughes. He's the Count of Las Vegas.

Littell watched.

He joined newsmen. He joined camera crews. He joined Joe Vegas. Word leaked. The Count's coming. The train station—11:00 p.m.

He's coming. Check track 14. Behold the Drac Express.

The platform rocked. Newsmen cliqued up. Grips wheeled arc lights. Camera guys lugged film.

Littell watched.

He'd braced Drac's Mormons. They talked renovation. They said they'd hit the DI. They said they'd Draculized. They germ-proofed the penthouse. They lugged freezers in. They stocked snacks and treats.

Snow cones/pizza/candy bars. Demerol/codeine/Dilaudid.

They said we launch soon. We negotiate and bargain. We *buy* the DI. The Boys said *we* launch soon. *We* bargain and set the price.

It's large. Drac will balk. Drac will pout. Drac will pay. Drac will stump for a Mormon hegemony. Drac will shout: Mormons must run my casino!

The Boys will renavigate. The Boys will plot. The Boys will decree: Littell must brace Wayne Tedrow Senior.

They'll talk. *They'll* bargain. Small talk will run cruel. Wayne Senior will tweak him on Janice.

The platform shook. The rails shook. A train whistle blew.

He's coming.

A cop van pulled up. Cops got out. Cops hauled equipment. A cop pushed a gurney. A cop wheeled a tent. A cop slung oxygen cans.

Cops shoved newsmen. Cops shoved citizens. Cops pulled cameras back. Newsmen pushed. Newsmen jockeyed. Newsmen shoved back.

Train lights coming—that whistle full blast.

Littell stood tiptoed. A kid jostled him. Littell stepped back. Littell got perspective.

Sparks flew. The train braked. The train stopped and sat. The crowd shoved. Flashbulbs popped. The crowd scattered.

They hit the train. They cupped their eyes. They peeped window slats. Doors cranked open—up and back—the crowd tailed the cop with the gurney.

Littell laughed. Littell knew Drac strategy. Littell knew diversions.

Look:

There's gurney 2. There's tent 2. They're *all* the way back.

Mormons stepped out. Mormons signaled. Mormons dropped a ramp. Mormons formed a cordon. Mormons pushed a wheelchair. Mormons wheeled Drac.

He's tall. He's thin. He's wearing a Kleenex-box hat.

94

(Las Vegas, 11/27/66)

H*e's coming.*

He's off the train. He's in the car. He's got this dumb hat.

Wayne walked the DI. The floor buzzed electric. Ghouls circulated. Wayne logged rumors.

He's overdue. He's due soon. He's due *now*. He's got plane-crash scars. He's got skin disease. He's got neck bolts like Frankenstein.

Ghouls positioned. Ghouls vultured. Ghouls swarmed the casino. Ghouls stood on chairs. Ghouls slung cameras. Ghouls perched with autograph books.

Ghouls swarmed outside. Wayne saw Barb there. Glass walls provided views. Barb saw Wayne. Barb waved. Wayne waved back.

Ghouls prowled. Hotel fuzz prowled. Somebody yelled, "Limos!" Somebody yelled, "*Him!*"

Ghouls whooped. Ghouls dispersed. Ghouls ran outside. Wayne checked the glass walls. Wayne caught a view.

He saw cops. He saw limos. He saw a mock Howard Hughes. He made him. He *popped* him—back in '62.

He hosted a kid's show. He flashed his dick. He groped prepubescents. Cops called him "Chester the Molester."

Ghouls jumped him. Chester posed for pix magnanimous. Chester signed autographs. A limo eased by. A window went down. Wayne caught a blip: White hair/dead eyes/dumb hat.

Somebody yelled, "He's a fake!" The ghouls up and ran. The ghouls chased the limo.

Barb walked inside. Wayne saw her. Wayne detoured up.

"Aren't you working tonight?"

Barb laughed. "I could ask you the same thing."

Wayne smiled. "I was thinking of Pete and Ward, and how this whole thing started."

Barb yawned. "Tell me over coffee, all right?"

A ghoul ran by. They dodged him. They walked to the bar. They grabbed seats and faced the casino.

A waitress showed. Barb cued her. She brought coffee fast. The floor was slow. Chester shot craps. Ghouls meandered through.

Barb sipped coffee. "It's been months, and I still want a cigarette."

"Not like Pete does."

Chester rolled. Chester crapped out. Chester blew money.

Barb watched him. "There's these secrets that people know."

"Not *everyone*."

Barb unrolled her napkin. Barb twirled her spoon.

"To start, there's a certain city in Texas. Then there's the plans the Outfit has for Mr. Hughes."

Wayne smiled. "Tell me some secrets I don't know."

"For instance?"

"Come on. Pete has half the rooms in Vegas bugged."

Barb twirled her knife. "All right. Donkey Dom's shacked at the Cavern. He's four nights in with Sal Mineo, and they haven't left the suite. Bellboys are bringing them poppers and K-Y. Pete's wondering how long it can last."

Wayne laughed. Wayne checked the floor. Chester rolled. Chester made his point. Chester made money.

Barb smiled. Barb walked. Barb hit the john. Ghouls swarmed Chester. Chester-Hughes magnetized.

Chester sponged love. Chester bowed magnanimous. Chester posed for pix.

Barb walked back. Barb walked unsteady. She sat down. Her lids dipped. Her eyes went smack-back.

She smiled. She twirled her knife. Wayne slapped her. She gripped the knife. She stabbed down. She missed Wayne's hands.

Wayne slapped her. Barb stabbed down. The blade hit the table. It stuck. It twanged. The knife held.

Barb touched her cheek. Barb rubbed her eyes. Barb shot some tears.

Wayne grabbed her hands. Wayne bent her arms. Wayne jerked her head low.

"You're strung out. You're sticking shit up your nose and fucking over Pete every time you do it. You think you're high and mighty because you hate the war and Pete's business, but it's just a bullshit excuse, because you're a no-talent lounge chick with a dope habit and limited fucking—"

Barb jerked her hands. Barb grabbed the knife. Wayne slapped her. She dropped the knife. She rubbed her cheek. She wiped her eyes.

Wayne touched her hair. "I love you. I'm not going to let you fuck yourself over without a fight."

Barb stood up. Barb wiped her eyes. Barb walked off smack-back unsteady.

Floorshow:

Chester performed. Crowds cliqued up—all drunks and geeks. Chester posed. Chester huckstered Las Vegas. Chester ran airplane crash riffs.

Newsmen bopped by. Newsmen yukked. Fuck you—you're that kids-show freak.

Wayne watched. Wayne scoped the floor.

He sipped bourbon. He sulked. He sniffed Barb's napkin. He smelled her hand cream. He smelled her bath oil.

Chester signed autographs. Chester riffed on Jane Russell's breasts. Chester eyed little kids.

Wayne sipped bourbon. His thoughts raced. He saw Janice walk by. She still limped. She still strutted. Her gray streak still glowed.

She walked the floor. She fed baby slots. She blew money. She nailed a jackpot. She scooped coins. She tithed a slot-machine bum.

The bum groveled. The bum gave thanks. The bum wore mismatched shoes. The bum braced a baby slot. The bum yanked the arm. The bum blew his dole.

He shrugged. He regrouped. He panhandled. He hit up Chester. Chester said, "Fuck you."

Janice limped. Janice strolled. Janice left Wayne's view. She's out the back door now—dig that golf-course view.

She's heading to Ward's suite. It's a late-night rendezvous.

Wayne sniffed the napkin. Wayne smelled Barb. Wayne got a Janice jolt. His thoughts raced. He vibed rendezvous.

He drove straight out. The road dipped. He drove eighty-proof. He walked straight in. He grabbed a jug off the bar. He walked straight through.

There's the deck. There's Wayne Senior. He's close to old now. He's sixty-plus. He's old as brand-new.

He's got the same grin. He's got the same chair. He's got the same view.

"You drink from the bottle now. Two years away gets me that."

Wayne grabbed a footstool. "You make it sound like it's the only thing I've learned."

"Not hardly. I get reports, so I know there's more."

Wayne smiled. "You've been putting out feelers."

"You've been rejecting them."

"I guess the time wasn't right."

Wayne Senior smiled. "Howard Hughes and my son the same evening. Be still, my heart."

The stool sat low. Wayne looked straight up.

"Don't labor it. It's just a coincidence."

"No, it's a confluence. Bondurant precipitates Hughes. Hughes means that Ward Littell will be begging favors soon."

Wayne heard gunshots due north. Call it cop familiar. Broke gambler blows town. Broke gambler unwinds.

"Ward doesn't beg. You should know that."

"You're leading me, son. You're trying to get me to praise your ex-lawyer."

Wayne shook his head. "I'm just trying to steer the conversation."

Wayne Senior toed the footstool. Wayne Senior toed Wayne's knee.

"Shitfire. What's a father-son reunion without a few blunt questions?"

Wayne stood up. Wayne stretched. Wayne kicked the stool.

"How's the hate business?"

"Shitfire. You're more of a hater than I ever was."

"Come on, answer the question."

"All right. I've relinquished my hate-tract business, in order to serve the cause of changing times at a higher level."

Wayne smiled. "I see Mr. Hoover's hand."

"You see twenty-twenty, which tells me the years have not dulled your—"

"Come on, *tell* me."

Wayne Senior twirled his cane. "I've been working with your old chums Bob Relyea and Dwight Holly. We've derailed some of the most outlandish overhaters in the whole of Dixie."

Wayne slugged bourbon. Wayne sucked dregs. Wayne killed the jug.

"Keep going. I like the 'overhaters' part."

Wayne Senior smiled. "You should. There's hating smart and hating dumb, and you've never learned the difference."

Wayne smiled. "Maybe I've been waiting for you to explain it."

Wayne Senior lit a cigarette—gold-filigreed.

"I fully believe that coloreds should be allowed to vote and have equal rights, which will serve to increase their collective intelligence and inure them to demagogues like Martin Luther King and Robert Kennedy. Your pharmaceutical endeavor gives them the sedation that most of them want and insulates them from the fatuous rhetoric of our era. My policemen friends tell me that colored crime in white Las Vegas has not increased appreciably since your operation began, and your operation serves to isolate coloreds on their side of town, where they would much rather be anyway."

Wayne stretched. Wayne looked north. Wayne checked the Strip view.

Wayne Senior blew smoke rings. "You're looking pensive. I was gearing up for a smart answer."

"I'm all out."

"I got you at the right time, then."

"In a sense, yeah."

"Tell me about Vietnam."

Wayne shrugged. "It's futile bullshit."

"Yes, but you love it."

Wayne grabbed the cane. Wayne twirled it. Wayne did dips. Wayne did spins. Wayne did curlicues.

Wayne Senior snatched it. "Look at me, son. Look at me while I say this one thing."

Look: you've got *his* face. Look: you've got *his* eyes.

Wayne Senior dropped the cane. Wayne Senior grabbed his hands. Wayne Senior squeezed them way tight.

"I'm sorry for Dallas, son. It's the one thing in this life I am truly sorry for."

Look—he *means* it—those eyes getting wet.

Wayne smiled. "There's times when I think I was born there."

"Are you grateful?"

Wayne torqued his hands free. Wayne shook some blood in. Wayne cracked his thumbs.

"Don't press me. Don't make me regret coming out."

Wayne Senior stubbed his cigarette. The ashtray jumped. His hand shook.

"Have you killed Wendell Durfee?"

"I haven't found him."

"Do you know—"

"I think he's in L.A."

"I know some LAPD men. They could issue a covert APB."

Wayne shook his head. "This is mine. Don't press me."

Gunshots popped—ten o'clock/northwest.

Wayne said, "I'm sorry for Janice."

Wayne Senior laughed. Wayne Senior howled. Wayne Senior roared shitfire.

"My son fucks my wife and tells me he's sorry. Excuse me for laughing and saying I don't care, but I always loved him more."

Look—wet eyes and laugh lines—he *means* it.

A breeze stirred. Cold air whipped. Wayne prickled.

Wayne Senior coughed. "Will you entertain an offer?"

"I'll listen."

"Dwight Holly's going to be running some very sophisticated civil-rights ops. You'd be a perfect backup man."

Wayne smiled. "Dwight hates me. You know that."

"Dwight's a smart hater. He knows how you hate, and I'm sure he knows how useful you could be."

Wayne cracked his thumbs. "I only hate the bad ones. I'm not some Klan fuck who gets his rocks off bombing churches."

Wayne Senior stood up. "You could run high-level ops. You know how the world works and how to keep things stable. You could get all this risky business out of your system, hitch your star to the right people and do some very exciting things."

Wayne shut his eyes. Wayne ran signs: *Hate/Love/Work*.

"You're waxing pensive, son. You've got your daddy's nose for opportunity."

Wayne said, "Don't press me. You'll fuck it all up."

95

(Las Vegas, 11/28/66)

The cat prowled. The bed was his turf.

He clawed the headboard. He clawed the sheets. He clawed Pete's pillow. Pete woke up. Pete kissed Barb. Pete saw this big bruise.

He sacked out early. Barb sacked out late. He missed her coming in.

He touched her hair. He kissed the bruise. The doorbell rang—Barb slept through it.

Shit—7:40 a.m.

Pete got up. Pete put a robe on. Pete walked out and popped the door. Shit—it's Fred Turentine.

Frizzy-haired Freddy—fucked-up and frazzled. In *his* robe. In fuzzy slippers. In fucking shock.

With a tape rig. With a tape. With the jit-jit-jit-jitters.

Pete pulled him inside. Pete grabbed his gear. Pete shut the door. Fred got his sea legs. Fred quashed his shit-shakes and jitters.

"I was at the listening post. I was running last night's tapes off the swinger suites. I heard this grief with Dom and Sal Mineo."

Hold on. What's—

Pete cleared chair space. Pete laid the gear out. Pete plugged the rig in. Pete looped the tape.

He hit the volume. He hit Play. He heard static hiss. He heard timed beeps—no voice to activate.

There—Sal's voice/the on-click/we activate.

"Dom . . . hey . . . you hump, that's my wall—"

Dom: ". . . not what you . . . just looking . . . that phone numb—"

Sal: "You hump. You fucking sissy cocksucker."

Dom: "*You're* the cocksucker. You suck my big *braciol'* every chance you get, you fucking has-been cock—"

Crash sounds/breath sounds/clatters. Kitchen noise/drawer noise/ glass shatters.

Clatters. *Knife* pings. "Sal no no no." Yelps/gurgles/choked breath.

Silence. Timed beeps. Static. Sobs. Drag sounds. Clatters.

Sal: "Please please please. God please please please."

Sobs. Heaves. Breath and prayers—this papal shit: "O my God I am heartily sorry for having offended Thee. I detest all my sins because I dread the loss of—"

Pete got prickles. His balls contracted. His neck hair stood up. He hit Stop. He grabbed his pass keys. He grabbed his piece.

He walked outside. He checked the lot. He scoped the bungalow suites. 8:00 a.m./cars parked/all quiet.

Sal flew to Vegas. Dom drove to their tryst. Dom always drove to his shack jobs.

Dom's T-Bird: Gone.

Pete walked over. Easy now—there's the fuck pad. Easy now—jiggle the door.

He did it. The lock held stiff. He pulled his keys. He unlocked the door. He walked in. He saw:

Pink carpets—deep shag—blood-spritzed. Pizza boxes. Beer cans. Pizza crusts on plates. Dumped chairs. Dumped tables. White walls with red marks scrubbed pink.

Pete shut the door. Pete hit the kitchen. Pete checked the sink.

Ajax. Sponge. Clogged drain meat. *Organ* meat—hair-clotted—wop skintone meat.

Queers killed butch. Queers killed operatic. Queers killed *buon gusto*.

Pete checked the bathroom.

No shower curtain/knives in the toilet/knives in the sink. Floor dots— loose bristles—bath mats scrubbed pink.

A thumbprint on a wall. Print-points still visible. Print whorls scrubbed red into pink.

Pete walked the suite. Pete nailed the damage. Pete got the gist. Pete locked up. Pete walked back. Pete unlocked his suite.

There's Fred T.

He's slugging Jack Daniel's. He's noshing corn chips. He's fine now. He's *de*shocked. He's blitzed.

Fred laughed. Fred dribbled Black Jack. Fred spewed corn chips.

"I see potential in this. Sal's an Academy Award nominee."

Pete pulled drawers. Pete grabbed his Polaroid. Pete snatched film and loaded it in.

Fred said, "I hope he saved Dom's pecker. I could use a transplant."

Barb was up. Pete heard her. Pete heard her fluff sheets.

Fred said, "I never liked Dom. He had the arrogance that always complements a big dick."

Pete grabbed him. Pete pinned his wrists.

"Talk to Barb. Keep her here while I take some pictures."

"Pete . . . Jesus . . . come on . . . I'm on your side."

Pete torqued his wrists. "Keep your mouth shut while I work this. I don't want any shit coming back to the Cavern."

"Pete, Pete, Pete. You know me. You know I am the Pharaoh's own fucking sphinx."

Pete let him go. Pete walked out. Pete jogged through the lot. Pete rehit the suite.

He unlocked it. He stepped in. He shot pix. Polaroids—twelve color prints.

He got the thumbprint. He got the bloodstains. He got the meat. He got the pink rugs. He got the knives. He got the spritz.

Pete shot twelve photos. The camera developed them. The camera made sounds. The camera cranked wet prints.

He grid-searched. He reloaded. He shot more pix:

Dom's thumb—drain-trapped—stuck between grates. A dildo/a hash pipe/hash dregs.

He dried the prints. He spread them out on a sofa. He grabbed the phone. He dialed L.A. direct.

Three rings—*be there*—

"This is Otash."

"It's Pete, Freddy."

Otash laughed. "I thought you were pissed at me. The Littell thing, remember?"

Pete coughed. His chest bipped. His pulse raced.

"I'm the forgiving type."

Otash yukked. "You're a lying frog fuck, but I'll let it go for old times' sake."

Pete coughed. His chest bipped. His pulse raced.

"Do you know Sal Mineo?"

"Yeah, I know Sal. I pulled him out of some grief with some high-school quiff."

"He's in the shit again. It's a two-man job, and I'll explain when I see you."

Otash whistled. "He's in Vegas?"

"I think he's driving back to L.A."

"Money?"

"We'll muscle him and work something out."

"When?"

"I'll catch a noon flight."

"My office, then. And bring some coin in case Sal craps out."

Pete hung up. The door jiggled. Lock tumblers clicked. Barb walked in. Pete said, "Shit."

Barb looked around. Barb saw things. Barb caught the drift. She toed a rug stain. She bent down. She pinched fiber tufts. She sniffed her fingers. She made a face. She said, "Shit."

Pete watched her. Barb rubbed her cheek. She looked around. She saw the wall stains. She saw the pix.

She studied them. She eyeball-cruised all twenty-four. She looked at Pete.

"Sal or Dom? Fred wouldn't say."

Pete stood up. His pulse raced. He grabbed a chair. He steadied in. He checked out Barb's cheek.

"What happened to your face?"

Barb winced. "Wayne did a good job of getting my attention."

Pete gripped the chair. Pete dug his hands in. Pete ripped fabric free.

Barb said, "I asked for it. I've asked for it from you, but Wayne cares about me in a different way, and he sees things you don't."

Pete threw the chair. It hit a wall. It gouged pink bloodstains.

"You're mine. Nobody's got the right to care for you, and nobody's seen things in you that I didn't see first."

Barb looked at Pete. Barb scoped the wall stains behind him. Barb closed her eyes. Barb ran. Barb ran straight past Pete.

Otash said, "Dom's in the trunk. I'll lay you six to one."

Car surveillance—Fred O.'s car—the seats pushed way back. Fred O.'s farts and Fred O.'s cologne.

They lounged. They scoped Dom's T-Bird. They scoped Sal's apartment house.

Pete said, "You're on. I say he dumped him in the desert."

Otash lit a cigarette. Smoke billowed. Pete caught the backdraft.

Barb ran. He let her. She'd run straight back. Wayne hit her. Wayne loved her. Wayne's fucking cork snapped. Wayne loved weird. Wayne was fucked up. Wayne was woman-fucked. Wayne gets muscled soon. Wayne gets lectured soon. Wayne's cork gets desnapped.

Pete yawned. Pete stretched. Pete craved Fred O.'s cigarettes.

He scrubbed the suite. He wiped the walls. He burned the rugs. He called Dom's bun boy. He played dumb. He said where's Dom at? The geek said, "Huh?" The geek didn't know. The geek knew shit from Shinola.

He talked to his bellboys. They never saw Sal. Dom signed all the room-service chits. Dom booked the suite. That was good. That played their way.

Otash said, "Sal's on the skids. What kind of movie star lives in a fucking apartment?"

Pete scoped the street. We're in West Hollywood—the fucking Swish Alps.

"You mean what kind of coin can he have?"

Otash picked his nose. "Yeah, after he spends it all on fruit hustlers and dope."

Pete cracked his knuckles. "He's got a gold Rolex."

"That'll do for a start."

The sky went dark. Rain hit. Otash rolled his window up.

"You want to hear my one concern? That he's out spilling his guts to some faggot priest or the queens at the Gold Cup."

Pete cracked his thumbs. "He's out drinking. I'll give you that."

"Dom's in the trunk. I can smell his rancid ass from here."

"The desert. A hundred says so."

"You're on."

Pete peeled off a C-note. A car pulled up. Pete made the paint job—Sal's '64 Ford.

Sal parked. Sal got out. Sal walked inside. Pete cued Otash—we roll on ten.

They ticked down. They ticked slow. They hit ten. They got out. They hauled. They ran up. They made the front door. They made the main hallway.

There's Sal. He's at *his* door. He's got his mail. He's got his key.

He saw them. He dropped his mail. He fumbled his key. They ran up. Pete frisked him. Otash grabbed his key.

He popped the door. He shoved Sal in. Pete grabbed a chair. Pete shoved Sal down. Otash pried his watch off.

"This and half your pay for your next picture. Cheap for what it gets you."

Brash Sal: "This is a gag, right? The Friars Club sent you."

Pete said, "You know what it is."

Bold Sal: "Yeah. It's a fraternity stunt. You and Freddy joined Chi Alpha Omega."

Otash buffed the Rolex. "Think back, *paisan.* You'll put it together."

Wise Sal: "I get it. I split the Cavern and didn't pay the bill. You're the collection agency."

Otash said, "The Cavern. That's a start."

Cool Sal: "I get it now. I made a bit of a mess. You want a damage deposit."

Pete said, "He's getting warm."

Otash said, "He'll be hot in two seconds."

Calm Sal: "You guys make a good team. The beefcake Abbott and Costello."

Pete sighed. "The time is upon us."

Otash sighed. "Yeah, just when I started digging on the repartee."

Smart Sal: "That's a big word, Freddy. You must have learned it in goon school."

Pete said, "The trunk or the desert?"

Otash said, "We've got a bet. I say he's outside right now."

Pete said, "The desert, right? You pulled off outside Vegas."

Otash said, "There's always Griffith Park. You've got all those hills and caves."

Pete said, "I saw one of Dom's movies. That thing had to be a yard long."

Brave Sal: "Hills, yards, shit. You're talking Sanskrit."

Pete hummed "The Man I Love." Otash flopped a limp wrist.

Sharp Sal: "I didn't think you guys were that way. Jesus, that's a revelation."

Pete sighed. Otash sighed. Pete picked Sal up. Pete slapped him. Pete dropped him.

Sal spit a tooth out. Said tooth hit Pete's coat. Otash slapped Sal. Otash wore signet rings. Otash laid cuts.

Sal wiped his face. Sal blew his nose. Sal made a mess.

Pete said, "This can all go away. I work the Vegas end, Freddy watchdogs you here. I don't want bad publicity at the Cavern, you don't want a manslaughter bounce."

Sal wiped his nose. Otash supplied a hankie. Pete pulled his photos. Pete tossed them. Pete hit Sal's lap.

Dig that disarray. Dig that drain hair. Dig that blood. Dig that severed thumb.

Sal dabbed his cuts. Sal checked the pix. Sal went gray-green.

"You know, I really liked him. He was bad, but he had this sweet side."

Otash rubbed his knuckles. Otash wiped his rings.

"Us or the fuzz?"

Sal said, "You."

Otash said, "Where is he?"

Sal said, "In the trunk."

Otash drew a dollar sign. Pete paid off—the trunk/six to one.

...

He flew home. The ride bumped. He worried Barb and Wayne.

Barb sniffed white horse. Wayne knew it. Wayne grieved. Wayne loves Barb. Wayne eschews women. Wayne's a watcher. Wayne's a martyr. Wayne's woman-fucked.

Warn Wayne. Tell Barb soft: *I know you—just me.*

The plane landed. Vegas glowed radioactive. Pete cabbed to the Cavern. Pete unlocked the suite.

The cat jumped him. He picked him up. He kissed him. He saw the note.

It's flat on the wall. It's taped high. It's his eye-level.

Pete,

    I'm leaving you for a while to sort some things out. I'm not hiding; I'll be staying at my sister's house in Sparta. I need to get away from Vegas and figure out a way to be with you as long as you're doing the things that you do. You're not the only one who knows me, but you're the only one I love.

Barb

Pete tore the note up. Pete kicked walls and shelves. Pete hugged the cat. Pete let the cat claw his shirt.

96

(Las Vegas, 11/29/66)

Moe Dalitz said, "Look."

Littell checked the window. Littell saw nuts below. Ten floors down. Nuts with cameras. Nuts with kids in tow.

Moe said, "They think Hughes sleeps in a coffin. They figure he'll wake up at dusk and sign autographs in his cape."

Littell laughed. Littell went ssshhh. Hush now—biz-in-progress.

Ten yards up. Two tables—Mormons meet front men.

Moe grinned. "It's my fucking hotel and my fucking king-size conference room. I'm supposed to whisper in my own joint?"

A Mormon glanced over. Moe smiled and waved.

"Goyishe shitheels. Mormons are roughly synonymous with the Ku Klux Klan."

Littell smiled. Littell steered Moe. They walked ten yards. They bypassed three tables.

"Would you like an update?"

Moe rolled his eyes. "Tell me. Use words of one syllable only."

"Short and sweet, then. I think we'll get our price. They're discussing undistributed profits tax now."

Moe smiled. Moe steered Littell. They walked ten yards. They bypassed three tables.

"I know you don't like him, but that well-known goyishe shitheel Wayne Tedrow Senior is essential to our plans. We need his union, and we need to keep his ex-buddies and Mormons in general running skim on those charter flights. Now, we've got the papers and TV bribed to do this

'Hughes is cleaning out Mob influence in Vegas' number, which makes me think we should recruit some *more* clean Mormon skim guys, because Hughes will insist on hiring Mormons to work the key fucking managerial positions, and I do not want any old-line skim people hanging around looking conspicuous when we can have some well-scrubbed shitheel Mormons, *especially* since the skim ante is about to go way up."

Littell brainstormed. Littell checked the window. He saw nut swarms. He saw newsmen. He saw clowns with snack carts.

"The publicity heat will be going up, too."

Moe lit a cigarette. Moe popped digitalis.

"Tell me what you're thinking. Go to two syllables if you have to."

Littell brainstormed—one quick brain draft. Propose it/convince Moe/refine the draft. Gift Mr. Hoover/earn a gift reciprocal/earn back to BLACK RABBIT.

Moe rolled his eyes. "A trance you're in. Like the Vegas sun finally got to your head."

Littell coughed. "Are you still buffered from your old-line skim people?"

"The ones we replaced? The ones we shitcanned for the Mormons?"

"Right."

Moe rolled his eyes. "We always buffer. It's how we survive."

Littell smiled. "Let's give some of them up to the Feds, as soon as Mr. Hughes takes over a few hotels. It will buttress our publicity campaign, it will make Mr. Hoover happy, it will tie the Feds here up in litigation."

Moe dropped his cigarette. Moe singed deep-pile carpet. Moe toed the butt flat.

"I like it. I like all deals that fuck disenfranchised personnel."

"I'll call Mr. Hoover."

"You do that. You say hi and give him our best regards, in your best lawyer way."

Voices boomed eight tables up—tax rates/tax incentives. Moe smiled. Moe steered Littell. They walked eight yards. They bypassed two tables.

"I know you been through this with Carlos and Sam, but I want you to hear it from my perspective, which is we do not want a fucking repeat of the 1960 election. We want to back a strong guy who'll come down hard on all this agitation and civil unrest and stand firm in Vietnam, as well as leave us the fuck alone. Now, per the aforementioned goyishe shitheel Wayne Tedrow Senior, let me say this. We've heard that he's no longer schlepping hate pamphlets, that he's cleaned up the seedier aspects of his act, and that him and his Mormons are getting tight with that well-known political retread Richard M. Nixon, who has always hated the Reds a good deal more than he's hated the so-called Mafia. We want you to talk to Wayne Senior and get an indication as to whether Nixon will run, and if he says yes, you know what we want and what we're willing to pay."

Voices boomed ten tables up—tax nuts/tax credits.

Littell coughed. "I'll call him when I get a—"

"You call him in the vicinity of the next five minutes. You meet him and lay it out. You get him to plant the seed with the Nixon people, and you tell him *you'll* be the guy to sit down with Nixon, if and when that shifty cocksucker runs."

Littell said, "Jesus Christ."

Moe said, "Your goyishe savior. A presidential cat in his own right."

Voices boomed ten tables up—Negro hygiene/Negro sedation.

The T-Bird—hole 10.

Play crawled. Duffers hacked. Oldsters bumped carts. Littell sipped club soda. Littell watched hole 9.

Women dumped shots. Women blew putts. Women sprayed sand. Ball beaters all—no Janice types.

He called Wayne Senior. He made the meet. He called Mr. Hoover. He got an aide. He promised news. He promised hard data. Mr. Hoover was out. The aide said he'd find him. The aide called back. The aide said:

Mr. Hoover's busy. Talk to SA Dwight Holly—he's in Vegas now.

Littell agreed. Littell assessed.

Mr. Hoover loves Dwight. Dwight's *his* assessor. Dwight will see you and assess. Work Dwight/work said assessment/work back to BLACK RABBIT.

A breeze strafed through. Golfers blew shots. Putts blew way wide. Littell brainstormed. Littell watched hole 9.

Work Wayne Senior. Glean data. His union broke laws. His union ignored civil-rights codes. Glean said data. Leak it to Bobby. Maybe now/maybe later/maybe '68.

He'd be free. He'd be "retired." Bobby might run for Prez. Funnel the leaks/buffer the leaks/cloak the source disclosure.

Littell watched hole 9. Wayne Senior played up.

He dumped his approach. He hit the trap. He chipped out wide. He three-putted. He laughed. He left his golf pals.

He walked over brisk. Littell arranged a lawn chair.

"Hello, Ward."

"Mr. Tedrow."

Wayne Senior leaned on the chair. "Things run dense with you. Every word has its meaning."

"I'll state my case briefly. I'll have you back on the tee in five minutes."

Wayne Senior smirked. Wayne Senior grinned aw-shucks.

"I thought we might work at a thaw. We could commiserate over a cer-tain woman and go from there."

Littell shook his head. "I don't kiss and tell."

"That's a shame, because Janice certainly does."

A ball shanked close. Wayne Senior ducked.

Littell said, "My people will be needing some men to work at Mr. Hughes' hotels, along with some new couriers. I'd like to go through your union files and look for prospects."

Wayne Senior twirled his putter. "*I'll* pick the men. The last time we did business, my men quit the union and I lost my percentage."

Littell smiled. "I reinstated it."

"You reinstated it reluctantly, and you're the last man on God's green earth that I'd let in my files. Dwight Holly thinks you're a bad man to trust with information, and I would guess that Mr. Hoover concurs."

Littell cleaned his glasses. Wayne Senior blurred.

"I was told that you've become friends with Richard Nixon."

"Dick and I are getting close, yes."

"Do you think he'll run in '68?"

"I'm sure he will. He'd prefer to run against Johnson or Humphrey, but he'll buck the younger Kennedy if he has to."

Littell smiled. "He'll lose."

Wayne Senior smiled. "He'll *win*. Bobby isn't Jack by a long shot."

A ball rolled up. Littell grabbed it.

"If Mr. Nixon runs, I'll ask you to arrange a meeting with me. I'll state my clients' requests, gauge his response, and take it from there. If Mr. Nixon agrees to honor the requests, he'll be compensated."

Wayne Senior said, "How much?"

Littell said, "Twenty-five million."

97

(New Hebron, 11/30/66)

Klantics:
    Klan klowns hauled guns. Klan klowns oiled guns. Klan klowns klipped koupons.

They sat around. They worked inside. They ducked a hailstorm outside. The Führer Bunker—ripe with farts and gun residue.

Wayne lounged. Bob Relyea dipped numbers. Bob Relyea bitched.

"My fucking contacts are getting lazy. They want to burn the serial codes as part of the deal, that's fine with me, even though Pete don't like it. But doing the job myself is another fucking thing."

Wayne watched. Wayne yawned. Bob dabbed M-14s. Bob dabbed pumps. Bob dabbed bazookas. He wore rubber gloves. He swiped a brush. He smeared caustic goo.

Wayne watched. The goo ate numbers—three-zero codes.

Bob said, "My contacts boosted some Army trucks near Memphis. There's this little town called White Haven, where all the caucasoids moved to to get away from the spooks. Half the town's Army EM."

Wayne sneezed. The caustics stung. Wayne lounged and drifted. Wayne Senior/job deals/"Hate Smart."

Bob said, "What do you call a monkey sitting in a tree with three niggers? You call him the Branch Manager."

The Klan klods howled. Bob booted snuff. Bob dipped M-14s. Pete kalled the kompound. Pete found Wayne an hour back. Pete reworked Wayne's rotation.

Don't surveille the gun run. Don't boat to Cuba. Fly to Vegas/meet Sonny/muscle a deadbeat.

Bob packed guns. Flash was due—kadre on kall. The karavan—New Hebron to Bay St. Louis.

Wayne stood up. Wayne toured the hate hut. Dig the wall-mounted shivs. Dig the Rebel drapes. Dig the wall photos: George Wallace/Ross Barnett/Orval Faubus.

Dig the group shots. There's the Regal Knights. There's a jail pic—three cons in the "Thunderbolt Legion."

Said cons wore jail garb. Said cons grinned. Said cons signed their names: Claude Dineen/Loyal Binns/Jimmy E. Ray.

Bob said, "Hey, Wayne. You ever talk to your daddy?"

He drove north. He flew Memphis to Vegas. He thought about Janice. He thought about Barb. He thought about Wayne Senior.

Janice aged strong. Good genes and will meet carnal desires. Barb aged fast. Bad habits and will meet fucked-up desires. Wayne Senior looked old. Wayne Senior looked good. Wayne Senior had hate-smart desires.

Janice limped. She'd fuck harder now. She'd outgun her handicap. She'd compensate.

The plane touched down. Wayne got off bleary—1:10 a.m.

He walked down the ramp. He trailed some nuns. He dodged skycaps with dollies.

There's Pete. He's by the gate. He's perched by some bag carts. He's *smoking*.

Wayne hitched up his garment bag. Wayne walked over bleary.

"Put that fucking cigarette—"

Pete pushed a bag cart. It hit Wayne's knees. It capsized him. It knocked him flat. Pete ran over. Pete stepped on his chest.

"Here's the warning. I don't care what you feel for Barb or what you think she's doing to herself. Hit her again and I'll kill you."

Wayne saw starbursts. Wayne saw sky. Wayne saw Pete's shoe. He sucked air. He ate jet fumes. He got breath.

"I was telling her something you won't, and I fucking did it to help you."

Pete flicked his cigarette. Pete burned Wayne's neck. Pete dropped a note on his chest.

"Take care of it. You and Sonny. Barb's gone, so we'll pretend this never happened."

A nun walked by. Said nun shot a look—you pagans stop that!

Pete walked off. Wayne sat up. Wayne got more breath. Two punks strolled by. They saw Wayne recumbent. They giggled it up.

Wayne stood up. Wayne dodged skycaps and bag carts. Wayne hit a phone booth.

He dropped coins. He dialed. He got a buzz tone. He got three rings. He got *Him*.

"Who's calling at this ungodly hour?"

Wayne said, "I want that job."

98

(Las Vegas, 12/1/66)

Onstage: Milt C. and Junkie Monkey.

Milt said, "What's all this tsuris with Howard Hughes?"

Junkie Monkey said, "I heard he's a swish. He moved in to get next to Liberace."

The crowd yocked. The crowd roared.

Milt said, "Come on. I heard he was shtupping Ava Gardner."

Junkie Monkey said, "*I'm* shtupping Ava. She traded up from Sammy Davis. Sammy's on the golf course. This square comes up to him and says, 'What's your handicap?' Sammy says, 'I'm a one-eyed shvartze Jew. Nobody will sell me a house in a nice neighborhood. I'm trying to effect a peace accord between Israel and the Congo. I've got no place to hang my Sy Devore beanie.'"

The crowd yocked. Milt moved his lips. Milt puppet-talked bad. Pete watched. Pete smoked. Pete mourned Barb.

She was three days gone. She didn't call. She didn't write. *He* didn't call. *He* didn't write. He braced Wayne instead.

It was bullshit. Wayne was right. He knew it. Barb split. He exploited it. He indulged. He smoked. He ate burgers. He worked the Fuck-It Diet. He boozed. He caught Milt. He caught Barb's crew. The Bondsmen sans Barb—Shit City.

The lounge was packed. Young stuff mostly. Milt drew hip kids.

Junkie Monkey said, "Frank Sinatra saved my life. His goons were stomping me in the Sands parking lot. Frank said, 'That's enough, boys.'"

The crowd yocked. Pete smoked. A geek tapped his arm. Pete turned around. Pete saw Dwight Holly.

They hit Pete's office. They stood by the wet bar. They crowded each other. They stood in tight.

Pete said, "It's been a while."

"Yeah, as in '64. Your boy Wayne killed three shines."

Pete lit a cigarette. "And you made out."

Dwight shrugged. "Wayne fucked me up, but you and Littell set it straight. Now, ask me if I came to say thanks."

Pete poured a scotch. "You were in town, so you thought you'd drop by."

"Not quite. I'm in town to see Littell, which I'd prefer you keep to yourself."

Pete sipped scotch. Dwight tapped his chest.

"How's your ticker?"

"It's fine."

"You shouldn't be smoking."

"You shouldn't be jerking my chain."

Dwight laughed. Dwight poured a scotch.

"How'd you like to help me entrap a Commie sympathizer?"

"You and Mr. Hoover?"

"I won't say yes or no to that. Silence implies consent, so draw your own conclusions."

Pete said, "Lay it out. The money first."

Dwight swirled scotch. "Twenty grand for you. Ten each for your bait, your backup, and your bug man."

Pete laughed. "Ward's a good bug man."

"Ward's a prince of a bug man, but I'd prefer Freddy Turentine, and I'd prefer that Ward be kept in the dark about this."

Pete grabbed an ashtray. Pete stubbed his cigarette.

"Give me one good reason why I should fuck Ward over to help you."

Dwight undid his necktie. "One, all this shit is tangential to Ward. Two, it's a high-line gig that you won't be able to resist. Three, you're in the Life for life, you'll fuck up sooner or later, and Mr. Hoover will intercede for you, no questions asked."

Pete sipped scotch. Pete rolled his neck. Pete tapped his head on the wall.

"Who?"

"Bayard Rustin, male Negro, age fifty-four. Civil-rights agitator with a yen for young white boys. He's horny, he's impetuous, he's as Red as they get."

Pete tapped his head. "When?"

"Next month, in L.A. There's an SCLC fund-raiser at the Beverly Hilton."

"That's cutting it close."

Dwight shrugged. "The bait's the only holdup. Do you think you—"

"I've got the bait. He's young, he's queer, he's attractive. He's got some potential cop shit hanging over him, which—"

"Which Mr. Hoover will frost out, no questions asked."

Pete tapped his head. Pete tapped it hard. Pete sparked a headache.

"I want Fred Otash on backup."

"Agreed."

"Plus Freddy Turentine and ten grand for expenses."

"Agreed."

Pete's stomach growled. The scotch fucked with it. Pete thought Cheeseburger.

Dwight smiled. "You bit fast. I thought I'd have to work you."

"My wife left me. I've got time to kill."

Otash said, "Sal scores tonight. I'll lay you six to one."

Car surveillance—Fred O.'s car—the seats pushed way back. Fred O.'s farts and Fred O.'s cologne.

They watched the street. They watched Sal's car. They watched the Klondike Bar. Pete lit a cigarette. Pete had gas. Pete snarfed two cheese-burgers late.

"Of course he'll score. He's a half-assed movie star."

He flew straight out. He called Otash. He briefed him. They checked Sal's pad. Sal was gone. They checked Sal's known haunts: The 4-Star/the Rumpus Room/Biff's Bayou.

Shit—no Sal car/no Sal.

They checked the Gold Cup. They checked Arthur J's. They checked the Klondike—8th and LaBrea.

Tilt—

Pete said, "You're sure he won't rabbit?"

"On *Dom?* Sure I'm sure."

"Tell me why."

"Because I'm his new daddy. Because I'm the guy he has coffee with every morning. Because I'm the guy who dumped Dom and his fucking car down a lime pit in the fucking Angeles Forest."

Pete chained cigarettes. "The Vegas end's good. No cops so far."

"Dom was a fly-by-night. You think his pimp boyfriend will file a missing-persons report?"

Sal walked out. Sal had a date. Sal hung on some hunky young quiff.

Otash hit the horn. Pete hit the lights. Sal blinked. Sal saw the car. Sal stalled the quiff and walked over.

Pete rolled his window down. Sal leaned on the ledge.

"Shit. It's a life sentence with you guys."

Pete flashed a snapshot reminder. Streetlight hit Donkey Dom's thumb. Sal blinked. Sal gulped. Sal vibed sick.

Pete said, "You like dark stuff, right? You get the urge once in a while."

Sal weaved a hand—dark meat/*comme ci comme ça.*

Otash said, "We're fixing you up."

Pete said, "He's a nice guy. You'll thank us."

Otash said, "He's cute. He looks like Billy Eckstine."

Pete said, "He's a Communist."

99

(Las Vegas, 12/2/66)

Tour time:

The DI sub-penthouse. Big Drac's sub-lair. Littell as tour guide. Dwight Holly as tourist.

Look:

There's the blood pumps. There's the drips. There's the freezers. There's the candy. There's the pizza. There's the ice cream. There's the codeine. There's the meth. There's the Dilaudid.

Dwight loves it. Dwight yuks. Dwight offends Mormons. Said Mormons scowl at said Fed.

Big Drac's incursion—now one week in.

The legislature waives anti-trust laws. The legislature delivers—go, Drac!

Buy the DI. Buy the Frontier. Buy the Sands. Buy big! Buy *laissez-faire!* Buy the Castaways. Gorge yourself. Buy the Silver Slipper.

Littell cracked windows. Dwight looked out. Dwight saw nuts with signs: "We love H.H.!"/"Wave to us!"/"Hughes in '68!"

Dwight laughed. Dwight tapped his watch—real business now.

They walked. They trekked hallways. They bagged a storeroom. File boxes hemmed them in.

Littell pulled his list out. Moe prepped it last night.

"Skim couriers. Easy litigations by any and all standards."

Dwight faked a yawn. "Expendable, buffered, non-Mormon couriers that divert heat from Dracula and ingratiate you with Mr. Hoover."

Littell bowed. "I won't dispute it."

"Why should you? You know we're grateful, and you know we'll prosecute."

Littell creased the list. Dwight grabbed it. Dwight dropped it in his briefcase.

"I figured you'd try to softsoap me about Lyle. The 'you lost a brother, I lost a friend' routine."

Littell coughed. "It was fifteen months ago. I didn't think it was fresh on your mind."

Dwight squared his necktie. "Lyle was doubling. He leaked some anti-Bureau shit to the House Judiciary Committee and Bobby Kennedy. Mr. Hoover had to pull a few bugs."

Littell went slack-jawed. I don't believe it! Littell made big eyes.

Dwight said, "Lyle, the closet liberal. It took some getting used to."

"I could have helped you."

Dwight laughed. "Yeah, you wrote the book."

"Not completely. You know I'd rather scheme against liberals than be one."

Dwight shook his head. "You *are* one. It's this fucked-up Catholic thing you've got going. You love high-level ops, you love the great unwashed, you're like the fucking Pope ashamed that his church makes money."

Littell roared—Blue Rabbit—*mon Dieu!*

"You flatter me, Dwight. I'm not that complex."

"Yeah, you are. It's why Mr. Hoover enjoys you. You're Bayard Rustin to his Marty King."

Littell smiled. "Bayard has his own ambiguities."

"Bayard's a piece of work. I ran surveillance on him in '60. He poured Pepsi-Cola on his Cheerios."

Littell smiled. "He's King's voice of reason. King's been pushing on too broad a front, and Bayard's been trying to restrain him."

Dwight shrugged. "King's a bullet. It's his time, and he knows it. Mr. Hoover's getting old, and he's letting his hatred show in the worst possible ways. King orates and pulls his Mahatma Gandhi shit, and Mr. Hoover plays in. He's afraid that King will team up with Bobby the K., which as fears go has its merits."

Blue Rabbit shows insight. Blue Rabbit shows balls. Blue Rabbit doubts Mr. Hoover.

"Is there anything I can do?"

Dwight tugged his necktie. "On the King front, zero. Mr. Hoover thinks you were too close to Lyle's death and that Bogalusa bombing."

Littell shrugged—*moi?*—how *could* he.

Dwight smirked. "You want back in. You got cut out of BLACK RABBIT, and it's galling you."

Littell smirked. "I'm wondering why Mr. Hoover had you pick up the list, when I could have airtelled it."

"No, you're not. You know he sent me to gauge your line of shit and decode your dissembling."

Littell sighed—how *passé*—you *know* me.

"I miss the game. Tell him that for a fucked-up liberal, I'm on his side."

Dwight winked. "I was talking to him this morning. I proposed a job for you, pending my assessment."

"Which is?"

"That you're a fucked-up liberal who disapproves of bugs and wire-taps, but loves to install them anyway. That you wouldn't mind bugging sixteen Mob joints for us, just so you can stay in the game."

Littell tingled. "Quid pro quo?"

"Sure. You plant the wires. You get out. We don't tell you where the listening posts are. You deny Bureau complicity if you get caught, and you win points with Mr. Hoover."

Littell said, "I'll do it."

The door blew open. Smells blew in: burnt pizza/spilled blood/ice cream.

DOCUMENT INSERT: 12/3/66. Verbatim FBI telephone call tran-
script. (OPERATION BLACK RABBIT Addendum.) Marked:
"Recorded at the Director's Request"/"Classified Confidential 1-A:
Director's Eyes Only." Speaking: Director, BLUE RABBIT.

DIR: Good morning.

BR: Good morning, Sir.

DIR: Start with Le Grand Pierre, henceforth to be known as BIG
RABBIT.

BR: He's in, Sir. Along with Fred Otash and Freddy Turentine.

DIR: Has he recruited his bait?

BR: He has, Sir. He'll be using a homosexual actor named Sal
Mineo.

DIR: I'm delighted. Young Mineo was boffo in *Exodus* and *The
Gene Krupa Story*.

BR: He's a talented youth, Sir.

DIR: He is talented and given to Greek profligacy. He has
indulged numerous liaisons with male movie stars, among them
James Dean, the "Human Ashtray."

BR: BIG RABBIT has chosen well, Sir.

DIR: To continue.

BR: BIG RABBIT has a wedge on Mineo, which he declines to
reveal. He wants him protected if he's arrested by an outside
agency. I think BIG RABBIT is buying himself protection, too.

DIR: He's buying, we're selling. I would be delighted to protect
BIG RABBIT and young Mineo.

BR: I gave BIG RABBIT a fact sheet for Mineo to memorize. We
want him to be able to convince PINK RABBIT that he's a civil-
rights zealot.

DIR: That will be no great stretch. Actors are morally decen-
tered and psychically unhinged. They cling to their scripts of the
moment with great verve. It fills their voids of emptiness and
allots them the will to exist.

BR: Yes, Sir.

DIR: To continue. Describe your meeting with CRUSADER RAB-
BIT.

BR: To start, I'll finally have to concede that he's just as gifted
as you've always contended. That said, I don't know how trustworthy he is, or isn't, for that matter. He seemed sincerely shocked

when I mentioned my brother's alleged leaks to Bobby Kennedy
and the Judiciary Committee, but he may have calculated his
response in advance.

DIR: Do you remain convinced that your brother did not write
that "Confession"?

BR: More than ever, Sir. Although now I'm starting to think
that it was not CRUSADER RABBIT. I think there's a fair chance
that it could have been someone within the SCLC, who had a private investigator or someone of that ilk sweep and find the bugs
and taps, and then decide to capitalize on my brother's death and
send in the "Confession."

DIR: I will concede the possibility.

BR: I think your basic assessment of CRUSADER RABBIT is
valid, Sir. He lives for intrigue, he'll betray his moral convictions
for the chance to do high-level ops, and he's trustworthy and
exploitable within a limited sphere.

DIR: Did you offer him the chance to install the bugs?

BR: I did, Sir. He accepted immediately.

DIR: I thought he would.

BR: I'm glad you approved my proposal, Sir. Public opinion has
turned against electronic surveillance, and we need organized-
crime wires in place.

DIR: I would amend your statement. We need covertly planted,
deniable bugs monitored by handpicked agents in place.

BR: Yes, Sir.

DIR: How did you describe the assignment?

BR: I said sixteen cities, Stage-2 Covert. I mentioned Mike
Lyman's Restaurant in Los Angeles, Lombardo's in San Francisco,
the Grapevine Tavern in St. Louis, and a few others.

DIR: Did you mention the stately El Encanto Hotel in Santa Barbara?

BR: I did, Sir.

DIR: How did CRUSADER react?

BR: He didn't. He obviously has no idea that Bobby Kennedy
keeps a suite there.

DIR: The attendant irony delights me. CRUSADER RABBIT bugs
Prince Bobby's hotel digs. He's convinced the suite belongs to a
prince of organized crime.

BR: It's a pisser, Sir.

DIR: CRUSADER RABBIT is an entrenched Bobbyphile. You're
sure that he has no knowledge of Bobby's suite?

BR: I'm certain, Sir. I've got the manager in my pocket. He told me that Bobby's policy is never to reveal that he stays there. He'll let CRUSADER in to do his work, and he'll make sure that Bobby's personal belongings are temporarily removed.

DIR: Salutary.

BR: Thank you, Sir.

DIR: We need access to Bobby. I'm convinced that he'll form an unholy alliance with RED RABBIT.

BR: We're covered on the Bobby front, Sir.

DIR: As we'll be on PINK front, assuming that young Mineo is convincingly fetching.

BR: He will be, Sir. We hired queer to entrap queer, which should pay off in the end.

DIR: I want a duplicate copy of the film. Have it processed the morning after the fund-raiser.

BR: Yes, Sir.

DIR: Make two copies. I'll give Lyndon Johnson one for his birthday.

BR: Yes, Sir.

DIR: Good day, Dwight. Go with God.

BR: Good day, Sir.

100

(Las Vegas, 12/5/66)

ayne picked the lock.

He worked two picks. He tweaked the bolt. He jiggled hard right. Deadbeat patrol/ room 6/Desert Dawn Motel.

Sonny said, "Motherfucker's got two last names. Sirhan Sirhan."

The door popped. They stepped inside. Wayne toed the door shut. Check the four-wall dump-site.

Soiled bed. No rugs. Horse-race posters/jockey silks/racing forms stacked.

Sonny said, "Motherfucker's a track nut."

The room smelled. Scents mingled. Spilled vodka and stale chink. Stale cheese spread and cigarettes.

Wayne checked the dresser. Wayne pulled drawers. Wayne sifted junk. Acne swabs/booze empties/cigarette butts.

Sonny said, "Motherfucker's a pack rat."

Wayne pulled drawers. Wayne perused. Wayne sifted junk. Racing forms and tip logs. Scratch sheets and hate tracts.

Cheap-paper tracts. *Non*–Wayne Senior stock. Text and cartoons— anti-Jew stuff.

Dollar-sign skullcaps. Bloody prayer shawls. Fangs dripping pus. "The Zionist Pig Order"/"The Vampire Jew"/"The Jewish Cancer Machine." Jews with claw hands. Jews with pig feet. Jews with scimitar dicks.

Wayne skimmed text. Said text waxed repetitious. The Jews fucked the Arabs. The Arabs vowed payback.

Sonny said, "Motherfucker don't like the hebes."

The text rambled. Typos reigned. Longhand margin notes crawled. "Kill Kill Kill!"/"Death to Israel!"/"Zionist Pig-Suckers Must Die!"

Sonny said, "Motherfucker's got a grievance."

Wayne dropped the tracts. Wayne shut the drawers. Wayne kicked a chair back.

"We'll give him two hours. He owes Pete a grand and change."

Sonny chewed a toothpick. "Barb split on Pete. Frankly, I seen it coming."

"Maybe I got to her."

"Maybe Pete's evil ways did. Maybe she said, 'Quit selling hair-o-wine to Sonny's fellow niggers or I'll leave your white ass, you honky motherfucker.'"

Wayne laughed. "Let's call her and ask."

"*You* call. You the motherfucker who's in love with her and too motherfucking scared to say boo."

Wayne laughed. Wayne chewed his nails. Wayne tore a nail back.

The Pete thing hurt. Pete bruised his balls. Pete trimmed his balls back. He was wrong. Pete was right. He knew it.

He called Wayne Senior. They talked. Wayne Senior pledged Work. "Good work"/"in time"/"soon." He might take it. He might not. He owed Pete rotations: Saigon/Mississippi/the funnel.

Sonny said, "Let's go to L.A. We'll find Wendell Durfee and shoot his black ass."

Wayne laughed. Wayne chewed his nails. Wayne tore hangnails back.

Sonny said, "Let's kill some street nigger and say it's Wendell. It'll put the fucking quietus on all that shit you carrying around."

Wayne smiled. The door jiggled—whazzat?

The door stuck. The door popped. A doofus walked in. A young guy/all swarthy/thick rat's-nest hair.

He saw them. He trembled. He crap-your-pants cringed.

Sonny said, "Ahab the A-rab. Where's your camel, motherfucker?"

Wayne shut the door. "You owe the Golden Cavern eleven-sixty. Fork up or Brother Liston will hurt you."

The doofus cringed. *Don't hurt me.* His shirttail hiked up. Wayne saw a belt piece. Wayne snatched it fast. Wayne dumped the clip.

Sonny said, "How come you got two last names?"

Sirhan gestured. His hands moved mile-a-minute. He made geek semaphore.

"Forgive me . . . I take falls . . . race horses . . . many headaches . . . I forget I lose money if I don't take medicine."

Sonny said, "I don't like you. You starting to look like Cassius Clay."

Sirhan spieled some Arab shit. Sirhan spieled singsong. Sonny threw a left. Sonny hit the wall. Sonny tore plaster.

Wayne twirled the gun. "Brother Liston knocked out Floyd Patterson and Cleveland 'Big Cat' Williams."

Sonny threw a right. Sonny hit the wall. Sonny tore plaster. Sirhan moaned. Sirhan exhorted Allah. Sirhan dumped his pockets fast.

Booty: ChapStick/pen/car keys. C-notes/fives/dimes.

Wayne grabbed the money. Sonny said, "What you got against the kikes?"

Wayne hit the Cavern. Wayne unlocked his room. Wayne saw a letter on the dresser.

He opened the envelope. He smelled Barb straight off.

Wayne,

I'm sorry for that night & I hope it didn't cause any trouble between you & Pete. I told him you were justified, but he didn't get it. I should have told him that I tried to stab you, which might have told him how far down I'd sunk & how much sense you made.

I'm a coward for not writing directly to Pete, but I'm going to invite him to Sparta for Christmas, to see if we can work things out. I hate his business & I hate his war & I'd be an even bigger coward if I didn't say so.

I miss Pete, I miss the cat & I miss you. I'm working at my sister's Bob's Big Boy & avoiding the bad habits I picked up in Vegas. I'm starting to wonder what a 35-year-old ex-shakedown girl-lounge bunny does with the rest of her life.

Barb

Wayne reread the letter. Wayne caught subscents. There's the Ponds and lavender soap. He kissed the letter. He locked up his room. He walked to the lounge.

There's Pete.

He's drinking. He's smoking. The cat's on his lap. He's watching the Bondsmen—Barb's combo sans Barb.

Wayne shagged a waiter. Wayne passed him the letter. Wayne tipped him five bucks. Wayne pointed to Pete. The guy understood.

The guy walked over. The guy dropped the letter. Pete tore at the envelope.

He read the letter. He wiped his eyes. The cat clawed his shirt.

DOCUMENT INSERT: 12/6/66. Las Vegas *Sun* headline and subhead:

HOWARD HUGHES IN VEGAS!
EXCLUSIVE PIX OF HERMIT'S LAIR!

DOCUMENT INSERT: 12/7/66. Las Vegas *Sun* headline and subhead:

NO CLUES IN DISAPPEARANCE OF DANCER-CAB DRIVER
FRIENDS APPEAL TO POTENTIAL WITNESSES

DOCUMENT INSERT: 12/8/66. Las Vegas *Sun* headline and subhead:

HUGHES SPOKESMAN SAYS:
BILLIONAIRE HERMIT TO "NURTURE"—NOT "MONOPOLIZE" HOTEL SCENE

DOCUMENT INSERT: 12/10/66. Las Vegas *Sun* headline and subhead:

FBI ARRESTS SKIM BAGMEN
HUGHES SPOKESMAN PRAISES DIRECTOR HOOVER

DOCUMENT INSERT: 12/11/66. Chicago *Tribune* headline and subhead:

MORE MAIL-FRAUD RAIDS IN SOUTH
22 INDICTMENTS PENDING

DOCUMENT INSERT: 12/14/66. Chicago *Sun-Times* headline and subhead:

KING ATTACKS FBI'S SOUTHERN MANDATE
"KLAN TERROR—NOT MAIL-FRAUD—SHOULD BE PRIORITY"

DOCUMENT INSERT: 12/15/66. Los Angeles *Times* subhead:

KING INDICTS "GENOCIDAL" WAR IN VIETNAM

DOCUMENT INSERT: 12/18/66. Denver *Post-Dispatch* subhead:

RFK DENIES RUMORS OF PREZ'L BID

DOCUMENT INSERT: 12/20/66. Boston *Globe* headline:

NIXON NON-COMMITTAL ON '68 WHITE HOUSE PLANS

DOCUMENT INSERT: 12/21/66. Washington *Post* headline and sub-head:

SCATHING INDICTMENT:
FOREIGN JOURNALISTS ATTACK LBJ FOR
CIVIL-RIGHTS-VIETNAM "DICHOTOMY"

DOCUMENT INSERT: 12/22/66. San Francisco *Chronicle* headline and subhead:

HOOVER ATTACKS KING IN CONGRESSIONAL RECORD
CALLS CIVIL-RIGHTS LEADER "DANGEROUS TYRANT"

DOCUMENT INSERT: 12/23/66. Las Vegas *Sun* headline and sub-head:

HUGHES NEGOTIATORS SWARM STRIP
HOTEL PURCHASES LOOM

DOCUMENT INSERT: 12/26/66. Washington *Post* headline and sub-head:

DOMESTIC STUDY GROUP VOICES OPINION:
J. EDGAR HOOVER "OUTMODED"

<u>DOCUMENT INSERT</u>: 1/2/67. Los Angeles *Examiner* subhead:

CIVIL-RIGHTS FUND-RAISER
TO DRAW STELLAR CROWD

<u>DOCUMENT INSERT</u>: 1/3/67. Dallas *Morning News* headline:

JACK RUBY—DEAD OF CANCER

101

(Beverly Hills, 1/3/67)

igns:

> Mau-Mau shit. Peace doves.
> Nigger hands clasped.
> Said signs blitzed walls. Said

walls ran high. The ballroom soared up. Said ballroom welcomed oreos—race-mixer deelites.

There's celebs and pols. There's spook matrons. There's Marty the K. There's Burl Ives. There's Banana Boat Belafonte.

Pete watched. Pete smoked. His tux fit tight. Otash watched. Otash smoked. His tux fit right.

Ballroom accoutrements—dais and lectern. Ballroom seats and ballroom fare. Steam trays leaking steam—chicken à la coon deelite.

Cops mingled. Their cheap suits stood out. Waiters roamed. Waiters schlepped trays. Waiters flogged deelites.

Pete worked the Fuck-It Diet. Pete noshed meatballs. Pete noshed pâté. Pete noshed pygmy deelites.

There's Mayor Sam Yorty. There's Governor Pat Brown. There's Bayard Rustin—he's tall and thin—dig that tartan tux. There's Sal Mineo—he's hovering—dig that swish lollapalooza.

There's Rita Hayworth. Who let *her* in? She vibes dipsomaniac.

Otash said, "Has it occurred to you that we stand out here?"

Pete lit a cigarette. "Once or twice."

"Rita looks soused. I had a two-second thing with her, about ten years ago. Redheads tend to age bad, Barb excepted."

Pete watched Rita. Rita saw Otash. Rita went ugh and stepped back.

He flew to Sparta. He spent Christmas. He shacked up with his wife. They made love. They fought. Barb ragged his "war enterprise."

Barb quit sniffing "H." Barb quit popping pills. Barb glowed non-Rita-like. Barb goosed his pulse. Barb wrung him out. Barb told him straight: I hate dope. I hate lounge work. I hate Vegas. I won't back down. I won't go back.

He regrouped. He compromised. He punted. He said I'll work in Milwaukee. I'll push white horse there. We'll live in Sparta full-time.

Barb howled. Barb said never.

They talked. They fought. They made love. He regrouped. He repunted. He recompromised. He said I'll split Vietnam. I'll dump Tiger Kamp on John Stanton. John to run it/Wayne to rotate/Mesplède to assist.

Barb tweaked him. Barb said you *love* Wayne. Barb said he hit me. Okay—he *knows* you—you win.

They talked truce. They notched points. They nailed details. He said I'll stay in Vegas. I'll run Tiger Kab and the Cavern. I won't touch the dope. I'll just surveille shipments in.

I have to—the heat's up—Drac brought publicity. I'll work in Vegas and rotate to you in Sparta.

Barb bought the plan. Said plan stressed Vietnam. Said plan stressed his exclusion.

They made love. They sealed the pact. They fucking snowmobiled. Fucking Sparta, Wisconsin—Lutherans and trees.

Pete scoped the ballroom. Pete watched the floor. Sal M. looked over. Sal M. looked away.

Dom's bun boy filed missing-persons. LVPD worked the case. It got some ink. Cops checked out the Cavern. Pete bribed them. They dumped the case resultant.

Otash watchdogged Sal. Sal learned his script. It was simple shit: I just *loooove* civil rights! Otash worked with Dwight Holly. They redid Sal's pad. They ripped out a closet. They hung 1-way glass and rigged a camera. Said camera faced Sal's bed.

Fred T. assisted. Fred T. bugged lamps. Fred T. bugged walls. Fred T. bugged mattress springs.

Pete scoped the ballroom. Pete watched the floor. Celebs hobnobbed. Celebs sucked up to King.

Otash said, "You see the paper? Jack Ruby died."

"I saw it."

"You guys went back. Sam G.'s dropped a few hints."

Sal looked over. Pete cued him—*go in strong now.*

Sal shagged a waiter. Sal cadged a drink. Sal chugalugged. Sal flushed bright. Sal mingled. Sal walked.

Fruit Alert—Bayard Rustin—fruit fly at ten o'clock high. Bayard's got backscratchers—Burl Ives plus two—Sal's moving in tight.

Sal sees Bayard. Bayard sees Sal. Two smiles and wet lips aflutter. Strings swell. "Strangers in the Night." "Some Enchanted Evening."

Burl's pissed. Who's *this* punk? *I'm* old-line Left. Sal said hi. Sal drifted off. Bayard eye-tracked his ass.

Otash said, "Contact."

A bell rang. It's chow time. Hold for pygmy banquet fare.

Cliques dispersed. The guests hit the tables. Sal eye-tracked Bayard. Sal sat nearby.

Bayard saw him. Bayard wrote a napkin note. Pat Brown passed it down. Sal read it. Sal blushed. Sal passed a note back.

Pete said, "Liftoff."

They killed time.

They walked next door. They hit Trader Vic's. They quaffed mai-tais. They noshed rumaki sticks.

Cops passed through. Cops dished updates.

Dinner's done. King's talking. King's dripping foam at the mouth. He's Red. He's a puppet. I know it. The peaceniks love him. It burns me. My son's in Vietnam.

A TV kicked on. The barman flipped channels. The barman shut off the sound. There's war news on three channels. There's choppers and tanks. There's Commie King on two more.

Pete checked his watch. It was 10:16. Hold for fruit flies on high. Otash wolfed a puu-puu platter. His cummerbund swelled.

10:28:

Sal walks in. Sal sits down. Sal ignores them.

10:29:

Bayard walks in. Bayard sits down. Bayard greets Sal: Child, how *are* you! I'm *such* a fan!

Otash got up. Pete got up. Pete grabbed a shrimp spear for the road.

Setup:

They hit Sal's pad. They aired out the closet. They prepped the camera. They loaded film. They waited. They sat still.

The closet was hot. They popped sweat. They stripped to socks and shorts.

They sat still. They killed the lights. Their watch dials ran fluorescent. 11:18. 11:29. 11:42.

Poof—doorway light. Off the bedroom—stage right.

Pete squared the camera. Otash rolled film. More light/bedroom fix-tures/beams overhead.

Sal walked in. Bayard squeezed in tight. They laughed. They touched. They brushed hips. Bayard kissed Sal. Otash went ugh. Sal kissed Bayard back.

Pete squared the camera. Pete nailed the bed. Pete got Ground Zero in mid-shot.

Sal said, "Martin gives a good speech, but you're handsom—"

Sal stopped. Sal stopped what the—

His voice fluttered. His voice echo-chambered. His voice woofered. His voice tweetered. His voice bounced high and wide.

FUCK—

Overfeed. Overamp. Microph—

Bayard tweaked. Bayard hinked. Bayard looked around fast. Bayard yodeled. Bayard yelled, "Hell-o!" Bayard got echoes back.

Sal grabbed his neck. Sal blitzed a kiss. Sal squeezed his ass. Bayard shoved him. Sal hit the bed. A mattress-mike snapped.

It hit the floor. It bounced. It rolled. It stopped.

Pete said, "Shit."

Otash said, "Fuck."

Bayard yelled—"Hell-o, J. Edgar!"—Bayard got echoes back.

Sal grabbed a pillow. Sal hid his face. Sal nellied out. Sal kicked his legs nonstop.

Bayard looked around. Bayard saw the mirror. Bayard ran up.

He hit the glass.

He gouged his hands.

He tore his hands up.

102

(Silver Spring, 1/6/67)

Bank work:
      The B. of A. South of D.C.
      Tithe tunnel 3.
      Littell wrote a deposit slip.
Littell wrote a withdrawal slip. Littell scrawled an envelope.

Seven grand—one Drac-pilfered deposit. Five grand—one tithe withdrawn. A donation from "Richard D. Wilkins"—tithe pseudonym 3.

Littell got in line. Littell saw a teller. Littell showed his slips and bankbook. The teller smiled. The teller ran his paperwork. The teller metered his check.

He checked his book balance. He creased the check. He sealed the envelope. He walked outside. He dodged snowdrifts. He found a mail chute.

He dropped the letter. He checked for tails. Standard procedure now.

Negative. No tails extant. He *knew* it.

He stood outside. It felt good. The cold air revived him. He was tired. He'd been running—all-Bureau ops.

He toured sixteen cities. He did sixteen bug jobs. He bugged sixteen Mob meeting spots. He worked solo. Fred T. was booked. Fred T. had work with Fred O. He had off-time himself. It was Drac-approved. Drac's Mormons filled his spot.

Said Mormons haggled in Vegas. They said sell us the DI. They said sell us more hotels.

He flew loops. He did bug jobs. He called Moe D. Moe was jazzed. Moe said we'll bilk Drac—I *know* it.

He flew circuits. Chicago/K.C./Milwaukee. St. Louis/Santa Barbara/L.A. He nursed plans. He hit L.A. He acted.

He went through Jane's file. He sifted dirt. He culled dirt on second-line hoods—all East Coast men.

It was prime Arden data. It detailed hijacks and Mob hits. It was non-tangential. It was non-fund-book-related. It was not related to: Carlos/Sam G./John Rosselli/Santo/Jimmy/et al.

He typed out the facts. He wrote succinct. He print-wiped the paper. He flew back out. He traveled. He bugged more meet spots. He hit Frisco/Phoenix/Philly. He hit D.C. and New York.

He stayed in Manhattan. He booked a hotel room. He used a pseudonym. He altered his appearance. He cosmeticized.

He bought a beard. It was dark blond and gray. It was superb quality. It covered his scars. It reshaped his face. It aged him ten years.

He met Bobby once. He met Bobby three days pre-Dallas. Bobby would remember him. Bobby knew his look.

He bought work clothes. He bought contact lenses. He surveilled Bobby's billet: The UN Towers/old brick/off 1st Avenue.

He braced the doorman. The doorman knew Bobby. The doorman said Bobby rotates. Bobby runs south to D.C. Bobby runs back to New York.

Littell watched. Littell waited. Bobby showed two days in. Bobby brought a young aide north.

A thin boy. Dark hair and glasses. Said boy looked bright. Said boy adored Bobby. Said boy's adulation glowed.

They walked the East Side. Constituents waved. The boy rebuffed hecklers and creeps. Littell tailed them. Littell got close. Littell heard Bobby speak.

The boy had a car. Littell got the plate stats. Littell ran them through the DMV. He got Paul Michael Horvitz/age 23/address in D.C.

Littell called Horvitz. Littell dropped hints. Littell said he had information. Horvitz bit. They arranged a meet—on for tonight in D.C.

Tellers walked out. A guard locked the bank. Snow fell. It felt cold. It warmed him.

He prepped. He worked up mannerisms. He culled a new wardrobe. He dredged up a drawl.

One tweed suit. One soft chambray shirt. Beard/lisp/fey posture.

He showed early. He named the spot: Eddie Chang's Kowloon. The lighting was murky. Said lighting would camouflage.

He got a booth. He sprawled invertebrate. He ordered tea. He watched the door. He checked his watch.

There's Paul.

It's 8:01. He's punctual. He's youthful and sincere. Littell geared up—be aged/be fey.

Paul glanced around. Paul saw couples. Paul saw one solo act. He walked back. He sat down. Littell poured him tea straight off.

"Thanks for coming on such short notice."

"Well, your call intrigued me."

"I was hoping it would. Young men like you get all sorts of dubious overtures, but this is certainly not one of them."

Paul dumped his overcoat. Paul untied his scarf.

"Senator Kennedy gets the overtures, not me."

Littell smiled. "That's not what I meant, son."

"I got your meaning, but I chose to ignore it."

Littell sprawled. Littell drummed the table.

"You look like Andrew Goodman, that poor boy who died in Mississippi."

"I knew Andy at the COFO School. I almost went down myself."

"I'm glad you didn't."

"Are you from there?"

"I'm from De Kalb. It's a smidge between Scooba and Electric Mills."

Paul sipped tea. "You're some sort of lobbyist, right? You knew you couldn't get to the senator, so you thought you'd find yourself an ambitious young aide."

Littell bowed—courtly/*très* South.

"I know that ambitious young men will risk looking foolish and go out on a snowy night on the off-chance that something is real."

Paul smiled. "And you're 'real.' "

"My documents are wholly real, and one thorough reading will convince you and Senator Kennedy of their authenticity."

Paul lit a cigarette. "And yours?"

"I claim no authenticity, and would prefer that my documents speak for themselves."

"And your documents pertain to?"

"My documents pertain to misdeeds perpetrated by members of organized crime. I will supplant the initial batch with subsequent parcels and deliver them to you in discreet bunches, so that you and/or Senator Kennedy can investigate the allegations at your leisure and your discretion. My only requirement is that there be no public disclosure pertaining to any information I give you until late 1968 or early 1969."

Paul twirled his ashtray. "Do you think Senator Kennedy will be President or President-elect then?"

Littell smiled. "From your mouth to God's ears, although I was thinking more of where I'll be then."

Wall vents popped. The heat came on. Littell broke a sweat.

"Do you think he'll run?"

Paul said, "I don't know."

"Does he remain committed to the fight against organized crime?"

"Yes. It's very much on his mind, but he feels uncomfortable going public with it."

Littell popped sweat. His tweeds broiled. His faux beard slipped. He splayed his hands. He cupped his chin. It played effete. It stopped the slip.

"You can depend on my loyalty, but I would prefer to remain anonymous in all our transactions."

Paul stuck his hand out. Littell passed the notes.

DOCUMENT INSERT: 1/8/67. Verbatim FBI telephone call
transcript (OPERATION BLACK RABBIT Addendum.) Marked:
"Recorded at the Director's Request"/"Classified Confidential 1-A:
Director's Eyes Only." Speaking: Director, BLUE RABBIT.

DIR: Good afternoon.

BR: Good afternoon, Sir.

DIR: I read your memo. You attribute the failure of a Stage-2
operation to faulty condensor plugs.

BR: It was a technical failure, Sir. I would not blame Fred Otash
or BIG RABBIT.

DIR: The blameworthy one is thus Fred Turentine, the reptilian
"Bug Man to the Stars," a lowly minion of Otash and BIG RABBIT.

BR: Yes, Sir.

DIR: I gain no succor from foisting blame on a hired hand. I
gain only dyspeptic fury.

BR: Yes, Sir.

DIR: Give me some good news to allay my agitation.

BR: Otash was very good on the post-op. He leaned on Mineo
and warned him to keep quiet. I would strongly suggest that PINK
RABBIT will not risk personal ridicule or bad publicity for the
SCLC by going public with word on the shakedown.

DIR: I was looking forward to the film. Bayard and Sal, O bird
thou never wert.

BR: Yes, Sir.

DIR: Let's discuss CRUSADER RABBIT.

BR: He did a superb job on the installations, Sir.

DIR: Did you have him spot-tailed?

BR: On three occasions, Sir. He's tail-savvy, but my men managed to sustain surveillance.

DIR: Expand your answers. I have a lunch date in the year
2010.

BR: CRUSADER RABBIT was not spotted doing anything
remotely suspicious.

DIR: Besides installing illegal bug-mounts at our behest.

BR: Including Bobby Kennedy's place in Santa Barbara, Sir.

DIR: Thrillingly ironic. CRUSADER bugs his savior and my bete
noire. Unwitting complicity of a high order.

BR: Yes, Sir.

DIR: How long will it take to recruit men to man the listening posts?

BR: A while, Sir. We've got sixteen locations.

DIR: To continue. Update me on WILD RABBIT.

BR: He's doing well, Sir. You've seen the results. We keep getting mail-fraud indict—

DIR: I know what we keep getting. I know that we do not come close to getting anything remotely resembling satisfaction in the matter of one Martin Luther King, aka RED RABBIT, aka the Minstrel Antichrist. Our attempts to dislodge him and subsume his prestige have consumed tens of thousands of man-hours and have garnered nil results. He has turned us into dung beetles and rare, indigenous African birds who peck through elephant shit, and I am woefully sick and tired of waiting for him to discredit himself.

BR: Yes, Sir.

DIR: You're a rock, Dwight. I can always count on you to say "Yes, Sir."

BR: I would like to seek more radical means to nullify RED RABBIT. Do I have your permission to bring in a trusted friend and explore the possibilities?

DIR: Yes.

BR: Thank you, Sir.

DIR: Good day, Dwight.

BR: Good day, Sir.

DOCUMENT INSERT: 1/14/67. Telephone call transcript. Taped by: BLUE RABBIT. Marked: "FBI-Scrambled"/"Stage-1 Covert"/ "Destroy Without Reading in the Event of My Death." Speaking: BLUE RABBIT, FATHER RABBIT.

BR: Senior, how are you? How's the connection?

FR: I'm hearing some clicks.

BR: That's my scrambler. The beeps mean we're tap-proof.

FR: We should be talking in person.

BR: I'm down in Mississippi. I can't get away.

FR: You're sure it's—

BR: It's fine. Jesus, don't go cuntish on me.

FR: I won't. It's just that—

BR: It's just that you think he's got superhuman powers, and he doesn't. He can't read minds and he can't tap scrambled frequencies.

FR: Well, still . . .

BR: Still, shit. He's not God, so quit acting like he is.

FR: He's something similar.

BR: I'll buy that.

FR: Did he—

BR: He said yes.

FR: Do you think he knows what we're planning?

BR: No, but he'll be glad to see it happen, and if he thinks it's us, he'll make sure the investigation obfuscates.

FR: That's good news.

BR: No shit, Sherlock.

FR: People hate him. King, I mean.

BR: Those that don't love him, yeah.

FR: What about the bug—

BR: We're A-OK on that front. I talked him into letting me wire sixteen spots. He'll read the transcripts, hear the hate building and get his rocks off.

FR: There's a scapegoat aspect here.

BR: That is correct. Guinea hoods hate coloreds and civil-rights fucks, and they love to talk about it. Hoover hears the hate, the whole thing starts feeling inevitable, pow, then it happens. The whole Mob-hate thing serves to muddy the waters and gets him thinking that it's too big to mess with.

FR: Like Jack Kennedy.

BR: Exactly. It's coming, it's inevitable, it's accomplished and it's good for business. The nation mourns and hates the clown we give them.

FR: You know the metaphysic.

BR: We all went to school on Jack.

FR: How long will it take to get the bugs in place?

BR: About six weeks. You want the punch line? I had Ward Littell do the mounts.

FR: Dwight, Jesus.

BR: I had my reasons. One, he's the best bug man around. Two, we may need him somewhere down the line. Three, I needed to throw him a bone to keep him in the game.

FR: Shitfire. Any game with Littell in it is a game to fix from the get-go.

BR: I threw Hoover a bone. He hates Bobby K. almost as much

as he hates King, and he shares all his dirt with LBJ. I had Littell bug one of Bobby's hotel suites.

FR: I'm getting chills, Dwight. You keep dropping the "Mister" off "Hoover."

BR: Because I trust scrambler technology.

FR: It's more than that.

BR: Okay, it's because he's slipping. Why mince words? King's the one guy he wanted to break the most, and King's the one guy he can't break. Here's another punch line for you. Lyle liked King. He worked against him and admired him anyway, and I'm starting to feel the same way. That grandiose cocksucker is a jigaboo for the ages.

FR: I've heard everything now.

BR: No, you haven't. Try this. Hoover's a hophead.

FR: Dwight, come—

BR: That Dr. Feelgood guy flies down from New York every day, on the Bureau's time-card. He gives Hoover a pop of liquid methamphetamine mixed with B-complex vitamins and male hormones. The old boy fades about 1:00 p.m. and perks up like a dog in heat around 2:00.

FR: Jesus.

BR: He's not God or Jesus. He's slipping, but he's still good. We've got to be careful around him.

FR: We need to start thinking about a fall guy.

BR: I want to bring in Fred Otash and Bob Relyea to help us look. I've gotten tight with Otash, he's solid, and he's got juice on the coast. Bob's your rabbit, so you know the score there. That hump knows every expendable race-baiter in the south.

FR: I've got an idea. It might help to facilitate things.

BR: I'm listening.

FR: We should do some hate-mail intercepts on King and the SCLC, to see if we can find a guy who's sent them letters. I know the Bureau's doing mail covers, so I think we should bring in a man to go through the covered mail, photograph it and return it to the covering agent, on the sly.

BR: It's a good idea, if we can find a man we can trust.

FR: My son.

BR: Shit. Don't give me that.

FR: I'm serious.

BR: I thought you and the kid were estranged. He was moving dope with Pete Bondurant, and you two were on the outs.

FR: We've reconciled.

BR: Shit.

FR: You know how he hates coloreds. He'd be perfect for the job.

BR: Shit. He's too volatile. You recall that little run-in I had with him?

FR: He's changed, Dwight. He's a brilliant kid, and he'd be perfect for the job.

BR: I'll buy brilliant. I bought him his first chemistry set in 1944.

FR: I remember. You said he'd figure out how to split the atom.

BR: You've reconciled, you trust him, I concede he'd be good. That said, we don't want him to know what we're building up to.

FR: We'll muddy things. We'll have him cull mail on King, plus one liberal and one conservative politician. He'll think I'm just building my intelligence base.

BR: Shit.

FR: He'll be good. He's the right man for—

BR: I want a wedge. I'll bring him in, as long as we've got something on him. I know he's your son, but I'm still going to insist.

FR: Let's see if we can hand him Wendell Durfee. He's allegedly in L.A., which means I could put my LAPD contacts on him covert. You know what Wayne will do if he finds him.

BR: Yeah. And I could make like I still hate him and squeeze him with that.

FR: It might work. Shitfire, it will work.

BR: Durfee's a long shot. He might take time and we might tap out on him.

FR: I know.

BR: We need to bring in our mail guy within the next six weeks.

FR: I'll bring Wayne in. We'll work on Durfee in the meantime.

BR: That fucks up the wedge aspect.

FR: Not in the long run.

BR: What are you saying?

FR: We don't need a wedge for his mail work. We've got to have one in place when I tell him he'll be there for D-Day.

BR: Jesus Christ.

FR: My son doesn't know it, but he's been waiting his whole life for this.

BR: In your words, "Shitfire."

FR: That about says it.

BR: I've got to go. I want to get some coffee and think this all through.

FR: It's going to happen.
BR: You're damn fucking right it is.

DOCUMENT INSERT: 1/26/67. Las Vegas *Sun* headline:

HUGHES-DESERT INN NEGOTIATIONS CONTINUE

DOCUMENT INSERT: 2/4/67. Denver *Post-Dispatch* subhead:

FEDERAL INDICTMENTS ON CASINO SKIM-COURIERS

DOCUMENT INSERT: 2/14/67. Las Vegas *Sun* headline and subhead:

WHERE'S DOM DELLACROCIO?
VEGAS POLICE BAFFLED

DOCUMENT INSERT: 2/22/67. Chicago *Tribune* subhead:

KING PREDICTS "VIOLENT SUMMER" IF NEGROES DO NOT GET "FULL JUSTICE"

DOCUMENT INSERT: 3/6/67. Denver *Post-Dispatch* subhead:

SKIM COURIERS PLEAD GUILTY

DOCUMENT INSERT: 3/6/67. Las Vegas *Sun* subhead:

HUGHES SPOKESMEN CITE SKIM PLEAS
AND PLEDGE TO WORK FOR "CLEAN LAS VEGAS"

DOCUMENT INSERT: 3/7/67. Los Angeles *Times* headline and subhead:

HOFFA ENTERS PRISON
58-MONTH SENTENCE LOOMS

DOCUMENT INSERT: 3/27/67. Las Vegas *Sun* headline:

HUGHES-DESERT INN DEAL FINALIZED

DOCUMENT INSERT: 4/2/67. San Francisco *Chronicle* subhead:

KING ATTACKS "RACIST" WAR IN VIETNAM

DOCUMENT INSERT: 4/4/67. Bug-extract transcript. Marked: "Confidential"/"Stage-1 Covert"/"Eyes Only": Director, SA D. C. Holly.
    Location: Office/Mike Lyman's Restaurant/Los Angeles/listening-post-accessed. Speaking: Unidentified Males #1 & #2, presumed organized-crime associates. (Conversation 2.6 minutes in progress.)

UM #1: . . . under Truman and Ike you had order. You had Hoover, who bore us no ill fucking will. Fucking Bobby and Jack changed all that.
    UM #2: LBJ's got schizophilia. He don't take no shit from the Reds in Vietnam, but he sucks up to that King like he's his long lost soul brother. The policy guys back east see this correlation. King comes to Harlem, gives these speeches and gets all the pygmies hopped up. They quit playing the numbers, our policy banks take it in the shorts, and the fucking pygmies get agitated and start feeling their oats.
    UM #1: I see the correlation. They quit betting policy, their minds wander. They start thinking about Communism and raping white women.
    UM #2: King likes white women. I heard he's a pig for it.
    UM #1: All the niggers want it. It's the fruit of the forbidden fucking tree.
    (Non-applicable conversation follows.)

DOCUMENT INSERT: 4/12/67. Bug-extract transcript. Marked: "Confidential"/"Stage-1 Covert"/"Eyes Only": Director, SA D. C. Holly.
    Location: Rec room/St. Agnes Social Club/Philadelphia/listening-post-accessed. Speaking: Steven "Steve the Skeev" DeSan-

tis & Ralph Michael Lauria, organized-crime associates. (Conversation 9.3 minutes in progress.)

SDS: . . . Ralphie, Ralphie, Ralphie, you can't talk to them. You can't reason with them like they're regular people.

RML: This is not news to me. I have been a landlord for many fucking years.

SDS: You're a slumlord, Ralphie. Do not try to shit a well-known shitter like me.

RML: You're talking like that nigger fuck King, which is just the point I wanted to make. I run to my buildings on the first, the welfare checks are out and it's payday for the few shvoogies who work. Now, one old nigger lady shows me Time Magazine with King on the cover and says, "I don't gots to pay no rent 'cause the Reverend Dr. Martin Luther King Junior says you a slumlord who is exploiting me." This fuck two doors down demands his civil rights, which he fucking describes as "I don't have to pay no rent until all my peoples is free."

SDS: They're way out of line. As a fucking race, I mean.

RML: That King's got them hopped up. You got a whole race of overstimulated people.

SDS: Someone should clip that hump King. They should slip him a poison watermelon.

RML: We should join the Ku Klux Klan.

SDS: You're too fat to wear a sheet.

RML: Fuck you. I'll join anyway.

SDS: Forget it. They don't take Italians.

RML: Why? We're white.

(Non-applicable conversation follows.)

DOCUMENT INSERT: 4/21/67. Listening-post report. Marked: "Confidential"/"Stage-1 Covert"/"Eyes Only": Director, SA D. C. Holly.

Location: Suite 301/El Encanto Hotel/Santa Barbara/listening-post-accessed.

Sirs,

During the 1st monitoring period (4/2/67–4/20/67), Subject RFK was not in residence at the target location. Subject RFK rents the suite on a yearly basis & it remains empty during his absences. The (voice-activated) mounts have thus far picked up only the non-applicable conversations of El Encanto caretakers & other employees. Per orders, the listening post will continue to be manned full-time.

Respectfully,
SA C. W. Brundage

DOCUMENT INSERT: 5/9/67. Bug-extract transcript. Marked: "Confidential"/"Stage-1 Covert"/"Eyes Only": Director, SA D. C. Holly.

Location: Card room/Grapevine Tavern/St. Louis/listening-post-accessed. Speaking: Unidentified males #1 & #2, presumed organized-crime associates. (Conversation 1.9 minutes in progress.)

UM #1: . . . Klan's willing to stand up and be counted, which means you've got to call them our shock troops.

UM #2: I'm for segregation, don't get me wrong.

UM #1: St. Louis is a good example. One, it's hillbilly. Two, it's got lots of Catholics. I ain't ashamed to say I'm a hillbilly, you're sure as hell an Italian and a Catholic, we work together good 'cause you so-called Mafia guys are white men who worship Jesus just like me, which means we hate alike, too, so you got to concede that the Klan's got some answers, and if they put their anti-Catholic shit aside you'd be the first to make some big donations.

UM #2: That is true. I sub-contract to you because you okies, no offense, think and hate like we do.

UM #1: If Nigger King walked in here right now, I'd kill him.

UM #2: I'd fight you for the right. King and Bobby Kennedy, those are the shitbirds I hate. Bobby fucked and fucked and fucked and fucked and fucked and fucked the Outfit until we had no place left to bleed. King's doing the same thing right now. He'll fuck this country in the keester and fuck us and fuck us and fuck us and fuck and fuck us and fuck us while the other boogies overbreed and turn this country into a welfare-state shithole.

UM #1: I'm 3rd-generation Klan. There, I said it, and you ain't shocked. You may take your orders from Rome, but I don't care. You're a white man, just like me.

UM #2: Fuck you. I take my orders from a fat dago with a pinkie ring.

(Non-applicable conversation follows.)

DOCUMENT INSERT: 5/28/67. Bug-extract transcript. Marked: "Confidential"/"Stage-1 Covert"/"Eyes Only": Director, SA D. C. Holly.

    Location: Card room/Grapevine Tavern/St. Louis/listening-post-accessed. Speaking: Norbert Donald Kling & Rowland Mark DeJohn, paroled felons (Armed Robbery/Bunco/GTA) & presumed organized-crime associates. (Conversation 3.9 minutes in progress.)

    NDK: . . . like a kitty, I mean.

    RMDJ: I get it. Guys pitch in, you watch the kitty grow.

    NDK: We don't pitch in. Guys with real coin do, until you got a big enough pot to attract a guy who can do it.

    RMDJ: Right. It's a bounty. The word goes out that it's there, you do the job, you prove you did it, you collect.

    NDK: Right. You attract a pro, and he gets away with it. It's not like Oswald, you know, with Kennedy.

    RMDJ: Oswald was a Commie and a psycho. He wanted to get caught.

    NDK: Right. And people loved Kennedy.

    RMDJ: Well, some people. Personally, I hated the son-of-a-bitch.

    NDK: You know what I'm saying. With King you got a nigger that everyone hates. The only white people who don't hate him are some Jews and pinkos, but every other white person knows that integration will put this country in the toilet, so you get rid of Public Nuisance Number One and nip that eventuality in the bud.

    RMDJ: He's dead, the country rejoices.

    NDK: You put the word out. That's the thing.

    RMDJ: Yeah, the bounty.

    NDK: We ain't got the scratch, but there's guys around here who do.

    RMDJ: He's begging for it.

    NDK: That's the part I like. You beg for it, you get it.

    (Non-applicable conversation follows.)

DOCUMENT INSERT: 6/14/67. Hate-mail extract. Compiled by: FATHER RABBIT. Sealed and marked: "Destroy Without Reading in the Event of My Death."

Mail sender: Anonymous. Postmark: Pasadena, California.
Recipient: Senator Robert F. Kennedy. From page 1 (of 19):

DEAR SENATOR KENNEDY,
I KNOW THAT YOU & THE ZIONIST WORLDWIDE PIG ORDER
HAVE PUT THE PUS IN THE JEWISH CANCER MACHINE AND
GAVE ME HEADACHES, NOT FALLS FROM HORSES AS DR'S
BELIEVE. YOU SAY THAT ALLAH DRIVES AN IMPALA BUT I KNOW
THAT THE JEWISH CONTROL APPARATUS CONTROLS
AUTOMOBILE PRODUCTION IN DETROIT AND BEVERLY HILLS.
YOU ARE A PUS PUPPET IN THE CONTROL OF THE JEWISH VAM-
PIRE AND MUST STOP EMITTING HEADACHES IN THE NAME OF
THE CHIEF RABBI OF LODZ AND MIAMI BEACH AND THE PROTO-
COLS OF THE LEARNED ELDERS OF ZION.

DOCUMENT INSERT: 7/5/67. Hate-mail extract. Compiled by:
FATHER RABBIT. Sealed and marked: "Destroy Without Reading in
the Event of My Death."
Mail sender: Anonymous. Postmark: St. Louis, Missouri. Recipient: Dr. M. L. King. From page 1 (of 1):

Dear Nigger,
You better fear the ides of July and June;
There's going to be a bounty on you, Coon;
You're a traitor and a Commie and an evil ape;
All you do is lie, steal and rape;
But the White Man's wise to your evil ways;
The bounty means you'd better pray and count your days;
You can't dodge bullets like Superman;
You can't run away from the White Man's Plan;
When you get this letter you better hide;
Because you can't escape the White Man's fearless tide.

Signed,
U.W.M.A. (United White Men of America)

DOCUMENT INSERT: 7/21/67. Hate-mail extract. Compiled by:
FATHER RABBIT. Sealed and marked: "Destroy Without Reading in
the Event of My Death."

Mail sender: Anonymous. Postmark: Pasadena, California. Recipient: Senator Robert F. Kennedy. From page 2 (of 16):

[And] YOU HAVE BETRAYED THE ARAB PEOPLE AND STOLEN OUR LAND OF MILK AND HONEY TO MILK PUS FROM THE WORLDWIDE ZIONIST PIG ORDER AND THE JEWISH CANCER MACHINE. BAYER ASPIRIN AND BUFFERIN AND ST. JUDE'S HOSPITAL CANNOT STOP MY HEADACHES FROM THE PUS INFLICTED BY THE JEWISH VAMPIRE AND CANNOT HEAR ME SAY RFK MUST DIE RFK MUST DIE RFK MUST DIE RFK MUST DIE RFK MUST DIE RFK MUST DIE RFK MUST DIE RFK MUST DIE!!!!!!!!!!!

DOCUMENT INSERT: 7/23/67. Boston *Globe* headline and subhead:

RIOTS SWEEP CITY
ARSON, LOOTING, REIGN

DOCUMENT INSERT: 7/29/67. Detroit *Free Press* headline and subhead:

RIOTS ROCK DETROIT
DEATHS AND DAMAGE MOUNT

DOCUMENT INSERT: 7/30/67. Boston *Globe* headline and subhead:

KING TO PRESS:
RIOTS "MANIFESTATIONS OF WHITE RACISM"

DOCUMENT INSERT: 8/2/67. Washington *Post* subhead:

RIOT DAMAGE MOUNTS; POLICE CALL DISTRICT "COMBAT ZONE"

DOCUMENT INSERT: 8/5/67. Los Angeles *Times* headline and subhead:

KING ON RIOTS:
"THE FRUIT OF WHITE INJUSTICE"

DOCUMENT INSERT: 8/6/67. Telephone call transcript. Taped by:
BLUE RABBIT. Marked: "FBI-Scrambled"/"Stage-1 Covert"/
"Destroy Without Reading in the Event of My Death." Speaking:
BLUE RABBIT, FATHER RABBIT.

BR: Senior, hi.

FR: How are you, Dwight? It's been a while.

BR: Don't mind the clicks. My scrambler's on the fritz.

FR: I don't mind. I'd rather talk than mess with pouches.

BR: Have you been watching the news? The natives are restless.

FR: King predicted it.

BR: No, he promised it, and now he's gloating.

FR: He's making enemies. There's times I think we might not
get there first.

BR: There's times I agree. The Outfit hates him, and every
cracker in captivity has got his tits in a twist. You should hear my
listening-post tapes.

FR: Shitfire, I'd like to.

BR: There's a joint in St. Louis. A dump called the Grapevine.
Outfit guys and sub-lease hoods frequent it. They've been talking
up a fifty-grand bounty. It's starting to feel like a giant wet dream
out there in the spiritus mundi.

FR: You slay me. "Wet Dream" and "Spiritus Mundi" in the
same sentence.

BR: I'm a chameleon. I'm like Ward Littell that way. I alter my
vocabulary to suit the company I'm with.

FR: At least you know it. I can't say Littell's that much in control of his effects.

BR: He is and he isn't.

FR: For instance?

BR: For instance, he watches for tails everywhere he goes. Mr.
Hoover's been running spots on him off and on for years, and he
knows it. He catches 90% and misses 10. He's probably got just
enough hubris to think he's batting a hundred.

FR: Hubris. I like it.

BR: You should. I picked it up at Yale Law.

FR: Boola, boola.

BR: Tell me about the intercepts. By my lights, your son should
be twelve weeks in.

FR: More like eight. You know how he travels for Bondurant. It
took him months to set up his system.

BR: Tell me about it.

FR: He rented a place in D.C. He's pulling mail off King, Barry Goldwater, and Bobby Kennedy. The Bureau's running normal intercepts, and all their mail comes addressed to the SCLC head-quarters and the Senate Office Building. There's a four-agent team running a mail drop at 16th and "D." The night shift goes home at 11:00, so Wayne lets himself in at 1:00, pulls the mail, copies it and returns it at 5:00. He shuttles down from New York when he rotates in from Saigon.

BR: How does he get in?

FR: He made a mold of the door lock and had duplicate keys made.

BR: And he picks up at irregular intervals?

FR: Right. All synced to his rotations. He print-dusts the mail he picks up, since those hate-mail guys never put their return addresses on the envel—

BR: It's redundant. The mail teams dust the incomings. Every-thing's been wiped by the time he sees it.

FR: Shitfire. My boy's a chemist. He sprays the pages with some goop called ninhydrin and brings up partial prints all the time. He said he's working out his technique, and one of these days he'll be able to bring up completes.

BR: Okay. He's good. You've convinced me.

FR: And he's careful.

BR: He'd better be. We do not want it known that outside eyes saw that mail.

FR: I told you. He's care—

BR: What about prospects?

FR: None so far. All he's got are a bunch of lunatics who sound like they're one step ahead of the net.

BR: Bob's got a prospect. We might not need Wayne's help on that end.

FR: Bob should have told me. Shitfire, I'm his runner.

BR: You're his Daddy Rabbit. There's things he won't tell you for just that reason.

FR: All right. You tell me.

BR: The guy escaped from the Missouri State Pen in April. Bob knew him when he worked as a guard there. They were jungled up in Bob's right-wing foolishness.

FR: That's all you've got?

BR: Bob's pouching me a memo. I'll forward it to you.

FR: Shit, Dwight. You know I've got a veto on this.

BR: Yeah, you do, and we won't use the guy unless we both agree that he's perfect.

FR: Come on. You owe me more—

BR: He's on the lam. He was afraid to stay at Bob's compound, so he split to Canada. Bob's got a line on him. If we agree that he's the guy, I'll send Fred Otash up to work him.

FR: Hands-on? I thought we'd bring in some cutouts.

BR: I made Freddy lose 60 pounds. He was tall and heavy, now he's tall and thin.

FR: He looks different.

BR: Completely. He's Lebanese, he speaks Spanish, we can pass him off as some kind of beaner. Bob said the prospect is malleable. Freddy eats up that kind of guy.

FR: You like the guy.

BR: He's a strong prospect. Read the memo and let me know what you think.

FR: Shit. This is taking time.

BR: All good things do.

FR: Someone might beat us to it.

BR: If they do, they do.

FR: What's Mr. Hoover been—

BR: He's afraid that Marty and Bobby will team up. It's all he talks about. BLACK RABBIT's been up in the air since the shakedown flopped. Hoover knows I'm "exploring more radical means," but he hasn't asked me a single question about it since I made the proposal.

FR: That means he knows what you're planning.

BR: Maybe, maybe not. Second-guessing the old poof gets us nowhere.

FR: Dwight, Jesus.

BR: Come on. Remember what I told you? He can't read minds and he can't patch scrambled calls.

FR: Still.

BR: What about Durfee? Have your LAPD guys turned up anything?

FR: Nothing. They've got covert bulletins out, but they haven't got a single goddamn bite.

BR: First we've got to find him. Then we've got to rig it so Wayne doesn't know that we're handing him up.

FR: That's easy. We stiff a call through Sonny Liston, who's allegedly got people out looking for Durfee, not that that impresses—

BR: I want that wedge. I'm not bringing Wayne any closer without one.

FR: I owe him Durfee. I have a debt to repay to him, and Durfee will settle it.

BR: I'll put my sources on him. Between yours and mine, we might hit.

FR: Let's try. I owe Wayne that.

BR: I'm glad I never had any kids. They end up killing unarmed Negroes and pushing heroin.

FR: The Gospel According to Dwight Chalfont Holly.

BR: Enough. Let's discuss ops money.

FR: I'm in for two hundred cold. You know that.

BR: Otash wants fifty cold.

FR: I'm sure he's worth it.

BR: Bob's putting in a hundred.

FR: Shitfire. He hasn't got that kind of money.

BR: Are you sitting down?

FR: Yes. Why—

BR: I was down in New Hebron. I saw Bob dipping the numbers off some flamethrowers he was getting ready to route to the Gulf. They had triple-zero prefixes, which I just happened to know designates CIA-disbursement lots. I asked Bob about it. He lied, which was the wrong thing to do under the circumstances.

FR: You're talking Swahili, Dwight. I've got no idea where this is going.

BR: I leaned on Bob. He gave it up.

FR: Gave what up?

BR: His Cuban gun-running gig is nothing but a shuck. Carlos Marcello and that CIA guy John Stanton cooked it up. The guns have been going to Castro sources inside Cuba, with Marcello's best wishes. The Outfit's been sucking up to Castro, so he'll help them implement some plan they've got to plant casinos in Latin American countries. Castro's got juice with leftist insurgents in the countries the Outfit's looking at, and he's sending them the guns that Bob and the other guys smuggle in. That way, if the lefties implement takeovers in their countries, they'll let the Outfit in. If they don't take over, the Outfit will grease the right-wing guys still in power.

FR: I'm seeing visions, Dwight. I'm seeing all the Latter-day Saints.

BR: It gets better.

FR: It couldn't. And you don't need to warn me not to tell Wayne, because we both know this would drive the boy insane.

BR: The Outfit's covered on both ends. Castro's sacrificed X-number of Militia troops to the venture, because Bondurant, Wayne and their guys have been boating in and taking scalps with impunity. Castro's making money, it's worth a few Soldiers of the Revolution in the long run, it all goes to fuel the Commie agenda in Latin America.

FR: Dwight, I'm flabber—

BR: Stanton and the other CIA guys involved have been kicking back Bondurant's dope profits to an Agency source. He's been supplying Bob with CIA disbursement weaponry, which fucking Bob has been passing off as ordnance stolen from armory heists and Army pilferings. Stanton and Marcello have diverted millions in profit overflow, and they've paid Bob and these guys Laurent Guery and Flash Elorde percentage cuts to work the scam from the beginning. Only Bondurant, your son, and some guy named Mesplede think the whole thing is for real. They're the stupes and the true believers.

FR: My lord. All the Saints and the Angel Moroni.

BR: Bob's socked away a hundred cold. He'll kick it into our operation, if we let him shoot or play back-up to our fall guy.

FR: I wouldn't deny him. Not after a story like that.

BR: He's in, then. He kept all that covert for years, so I think we can trust him.

FR: We've got to keep this quiet. If Bondurant or my son find out, it all hits the—

BR: I've got Bob's balls. He won't talk to anyone else.

FR: Dwight, I should . . .

BR: Yeah, go. Have a drink and talk to your saints.

FR: Visions, Dwight. I mean it.

BR: I almost went into civil law. Can you believe it?

DOCUMENT INSERT: 8/12/67. Pouch communiqué. To: FATHER RABBIT. From: BLUE RABBIT. Marked: "Eyes Only"/"Read and Burn."

FATHER,

Here's Bob's memo. His facts & observations are based on his personal relationship with the PROSPECT & on files he stole from

the Missouri State Prison System. I cleaned up his grammar &
spelling & included some perceptions. READ, BURN & pouch me
your response.

The PROSPECT:

Ray, James Earl/white male/5'10"/160/DOB 3-16-28/Alton,
Illinois/1 of 10 children.

PROSPECT grew up in rural Illinois & Missouri. Father was
career petty larcenist. PROSPECT first arrested (1942) at age 14
(theft). Became frequenter of traveling carnivals & houses of prostitution. Became friendly with older man (German immigrant) who
was pro-Hitler & member of German-American Bund. PROSPECT
began to develop anti-Negro attitude at this time.

PROSPECT enlisted in U.S. Army (2/19/46) & requested Germany as duty station. Attended basic training at Camp Crowder,
Missouri & assigned (as truck driver) to Q.M. Corps in occupied
Germany (7/46). Later assigned as driver to MP battalion in Bre-
merhaven. Trafficked in black market cigarettes, frequented prostitutes & was treated for syphilis & gonorrhea. Began drinking
heavily & taking Benzedrine. Transferred to Infantry Battalion,
Frankfurt (4/48) & requested immediate discharge.

Request was denied. PROSPECT charged with being drunk in
quarters (10/48) & held in post stockade. PROSPECT escaped, was
recaptured & sentenced to 3 months hard labor. Returned to the
U.S. (12/48) & given "general discharge." Spent time at family's
home in Alton, Illinois. Hitchhiked to Los Angeles (9/49), arrested
for burglary (12/9/49), sentenced to 8 months county jail time,
released early for good behavior (3/50).

PROSPECT traveled east. Arrested for vagrancy (Marion, Iowa,
4/18/50), released 5/8/50. Arrested for vagrancy (Alton, Ill.,
7/26/51), released 9/51. Arrested for armed robbery (taxicab
hijack, Chicago, 5/6/52, shot while attempting escape).

PROSPECT received two-year sentence. Served time at Joliet &
Pontiac facilities. Established reputation as prison "Loner" & habit-
ual user of home-brew alcohol & amphetamines. Paroled 3/12/54.

PROSPECT arrested for burglary (Alton, Ill., 8/28/54). Bailed
out & absconded before trial date. Traveled east with criminal com-
panion & shared political views (e.g., all Negroes were inferior &
should be killed). Arrested (robbery of post office, Kellerville, Ill.)
3/55. Sentenced to 36 mos. Federal prison. Received at Leavenworth Penitentiary, 7/7/55. Paroled 5/58.

PROSPECT's parole jurisdiction transferred to St. Louis (family members lived there). In 7 & 8/59, PROSPECT & 2 accomplices went on supermarket robbery spree (St. Louis & Alton, Ill.). PROSPECT arrested 10/10/59. Attempted jail escape 12/15/59. Sentenced to 20 yrs. Missouri State Penitentiary. Received at Jefferson City Facility, 3/17/60.

Jeff City reputedly the toughest & most harshly run prison in the U.S. White & Negro inmates largely segregated. White inmates mostly of "Hillbilly" lineage & vocal per their hatred of Negroes. Facility had informal chapters of KKK, National States Rights Party, National Renaissance Party & Thunderbolt Legion.

PROSPECT worked in dry cleaning plant & unsuccessfully attempted escape in 10/61. PROSPECT bootlegged prison bakery goods & amphetamines, habitually injected amphetamines & frequently indulged anti-Negro tirades when "high." PROSPECT also sold & rented contraband pornographic magazines & joined informal meetings of extreme right-wing groups (attended by both convicts & guards) & often discussed his desire to "kill niggers" & "Martin Luther Coon."

PROSPECT also discussed desire to move to segregated African countries, become a "Merc" & "kill niggers." BR contends that PROSPECT was especially vituperative, even by white convict standards.

PROSPECT openly fantasized that a "White Businessman's Association" had a $100,000 bounty out on King. This is enticing when considering recent "bounty-talk" picked up via bug at Grapevine Tavern in St. Louis. BR contends that "Bounty" concept strongly plays into PROSPECT's "get-rich-quick mentality."

PROSPECT denied parole in '64. Attempted escape 3/11/66. Escaped 4/23/67 (hiding in an outbound bread truck).

PROSPECT stated to BR:

That he walked hill roads to Kansas City, did "odd jobs & built up a stake," bussed to Chicago & got dishwasher's job at restaurant in Winnetka. PROSPECT visited family members & childhood haunts in Alton, Quincy & East St. Louis & determined that no intensive manhunt was being conducted. PROSPECT robbed liquor store in East St. Louis (6/29/67) & stole $4,100.

PROSPECT traveled south & spent week at BR's compound (7/5–7/12/67). Grocery store near New Hebron robbed (7/8/67). BR believes PROSPECT was perpetrator. PROSPECT & BR discussed "politics" & PROSPECT apparently was not afraid that BR would report his fugitive status. PROSPECT "kept to himself," drank &

took amphetamines, ignored BR's Klansmen, talked to BR exclusively & frequently stated his desire to "kill niggers," "collect nigger bounties," "hire on as a merc & kill niggers in the Nigger Congo" & "live in a white man's paradise like Rhodesia."

PROSPECT left compound (7/13/67), told BR he was driving to Canada & would call & reestablish contact. PROSPECT called 7/17/67 & gave BR phone # in Montreal.

Summation:

BR characterizes the PROSPECT as moody, acquiescent, limitedly self-sufficient and cunning, socially clumsy, easily led by stronger personalities and easily manipulated on the level of his political beliefs. His frequently stated desire to "kill niggers" and his "bounty" fixation are encouraging and serve to underline the possibility that he may require minimal sheep-dipping. The PROSPECT may be willing to shoot himself and we may be able to manipulate him into and/or control the context he shoots in.

I think he's the one. Let me know if you agree.

To digress:

I had a long conversation with Mr. Hoover yesterday. I expressed concern about the degree to which his anti-King incursions had already become public knowledge. I mentioned his statements about King, the SCLC's bug and wiretap accusations and reports on the letter which was sent to King and urged him to commit suicide, which has been detailed in several left-wing periodicals. I told him that to further protect the WHITE-HATE and anti-King arms of OPERATION BLACK RABBIT and any escalations that might arise from them, a cosmeticized, largely downscaled anti-King file should be created and stored in the FBI Archives, where it would remain and stand ready for scrutiny in the event of congressional subpoena or subpoena for civil lawsuit.

Mr. Hoover understood that this mock-file would serve to obfuscate the rowdier aspects of OBR, protect Bureau prestige and buttress the validity of his earlier, less vindictive digs at King and the SCLC. He charged me to create file entries, combine them with file entries pertaining to events within public knowledge and whip them into an overall package.

I will undertake and accomplish this over the next several months. This mock-file will, of course, serve to obfuscate our independent escalations. I'm code-naming the file OPERATION ZORRO, a reference to the fictional do-gooder with the black mask.

I'm open to suggestions per the mock-file entries. Let me know if you have any. I would strongly advise you to burn all your

OPERATION BLACK RABBIT memoranda at this time, along with this memo.

DOCUMENT INSERT: 8/14/67. Pouch communiqué. To: BLUE RAB-BIT. From: FATHER RABBIT. Marked: "Eyes Only"/"Read and Burn."

BLUE,

Per PROSPECT: I enthusiastically endorse. Has he contacted BR from his Montreal location? If so, have Otash establish contact.

Per OPERATION ZORRO: I endorse the concept and laud your farsightedness. I'll burn my BLACK RABBIT paperwork.

I'm assuming there's no word on Wendell Durfee. Can you have your people step up their search?

DOCUMENT INSERT: 8/16/67. Pouch communiqué. To: FATHER RABBIT. From: BLUE RABBIT. Marked: "EYES ONLY"/"READ AND BURN."

FATHER,

The PROSPECT contacted BR. Otash contacted the PROSPECT in Montreal & advises: He will sever contact until he successfully suborns or recruits.

Per Wendell Durfee: My people are still looking. They've brought in three more men.

READ THIS & BURN.

DOCUMENT INSERT: 8/22/67. Bug-extract transcript. Marked: "Confidential"/"Stage-1 Covert"/"Eyes Only": Director, SA D. C. Holly.

Location: Card room/Fritzie's Heidelberg Restaurant/Milwau-kee/listening-post-accessed. Speaking: Unidentified males #1, #2 & #3, presumed organized-crime associates. (Conversation 5.6 min-utes in progress.)

UM #1: (And) he will rue the day he comes here and agitates, because the day he marches in the Saint-Whoever Parade is the day all the white folks put their goddamn internecine and intra-mural differences aside and unite.

UM #2: They think they're white. That's what kills me.

UM #3: I saw a nigger march in the St. Patrick's Parade. He had this sign that said, "Kiss Me, I'm Irish."

UM #2: King puts them up to it. They get a toe in our world, then a foot, then an ankle.

UM #1: It's their peckers I'm worried about. Most of them bucks got ones the size of a bratwurst.

UM #2: I was talking to Phil. You know him? "Phil the Pill." He runs semis out of St. Louis.

UM #3: I know him. Phil the Pill. He eats co-pilots like they're popcorn.

UM #2: Phil says there's a contract out. You know, a bounty. Like Steve McQueen in "Wanted Dead or Alive."

UM #1: I heard that story. You clip that nigger, you make 50 grand. It's a story I don't believe for one second.

UM #3: That's right. Some cracker clips King, he comes to the Grapevine and says, "Pay me." Everybody says, "Why? It was just a fucking rumor, and the nigger's dead, anyway."

(Non-applicable conversation follows.)

DOCUMENT INSERT: 9/1/67. Listening-post report. Marked: "Confidential"/"Stage-1 Covert"/"Eyes Only": Director, SA D. C. Holly.

Location: Suite 301/El Encanto Hotel/Santa Barbara/listening-post-accessed.

Sirs,

As per the last 9 monitoring periods (4/2/67 to date), Subject RFK was not in residence at the target location. Subject RFK rents the suite on a yearly basis & it remains empty during his absences. The (voice-activated) mounts have thus far picked up only the non-applicable conversations of El Encanto caretakers & other employees. Per orders, the listening post will continue to be manned full-time.

Respectfully,
SA C. W. Brundage

DOCUMENT INSERT: 9/9/67. Bug-extract transcript. Marked: "Confidential"/"Stage-1 Covert"/"Eyes Only": Director, SA D. C. Holly.

Location: Banquet room/Sal's Trattoria Restaurant/New York City/listening-post-accessed. Speaking: Robert "Fat Bob" Paolucci & Carmine Paolucci, organized-crime associates. (Conversation 31.8 minutes in progress.)

RP: You are seeing the fall of civilization as we know it.

CP: It's just a phase. It's like the Twist and the Hula Hoop. Right now, the shvoogs want their civil rights, so they burn a few buildings and make some woop-dee-doo. You want to stop all this riot bullshit? Give every shvoog in the country an air-conditioner and some Thunderbird Wine and let them ride out the heat in style.

RP: It's more than the heat that gets them agitated. It's that King and his soul brother Bobby Kennedy. They get them seeing things that ain't there. They give them an excuse that they can pin their shitty fucking lives on, like "the white man fucked you, so what's his is yours." You get ten million fucking people thinking like that, and maybe one in ten acts, so you got a million angry niggers out for white scalps like fucking Cochise and Pocahontas.

CP: Yeah. I see what you mean.

RP: Someone should clip King and Bobby. You would save a million white lives, minimum.

CP: I dig you. You save lives in the long run.

RP: You clip those cocksuckers. You do it and save the world as we know it.

(Non-applicable conversation follows.)

DOCUMENT INSERT: 9/16/67. Bug-extract transcript. Marked: "Confidential"/"Stage-1 Covert"/"Eyes Only": Director, SA D. C. Holly.

Location: Card room/Grapevine Tavern/St. Louis/listening-post-accessed. Speaking: Unidentified Males #1 & #2, presumed organized-crime associates. (Conversation 17.4 minutes in progress).

UM #1: He saw it. My brother, I mean. He's in the National Guard.

UM #2: But that's Detroit. You got a higher ratio of spooks to whites there.

UM #1: Don't tell me it can't happen and won't happen everywhere else. Don't tell me it won't happen, because it will. You trace everywhere Martin Luther Coon goes and you see pins in the map that mark dead white people.

UM #2: That's true. You got Watts, you got Detroit, you got D.C. You got riots in our nation's capital.

UM #1: You also got the bounty. I realize that it's something like half real—

UM #2: Yeah, at best, because—

UM #1: Because it don't matter as long as Joe Patriot thinks it's real and does the job.

UM #2: Pow. He does the job. That's the goddamn thing.

UM #1: You got to believe there's more bounties out there. Myth or not, it just takes one guy to believe.

UM #2: Coon's a dead man. It's—what's that word?

UM #1: Inevitable?

UM #2: Yeah, right.

UM #1: We outnumber the niggers. Like 20 to 1. That's why I think it'll happen.

(Non-applicable conversation follows.)

DOCUMENT INSERT: 9/21/67. Las Vegas *Sun* headline and subhead:

HUGHES BUYS SANDS
PAYS $23,000,000 FOR HOTEL-CASINO

DOCUMENT INSERT: 9/23/67. Las Vegas *Sun* headline and subhead:

HUGHES ON ROLL
BILLIONAIRE RECLUSE EYES CASTAWAYS AND FRONTIER

DOCUMENT INSERT: 9/26/67. Las Vegas *Sun* headline and subhead:

LAS VEGANS PRAISE HUGHES:
HE'S KING O' THE STRIP!

DOCUMENT INSERT: 9/28/67. Los Angeles *Examiner* subhead:

KING ESCALATES ATTACKS ON "IMPERIALIST" WAR

DOCUMENT INSERT: 9/30/67. St. Louis *Globe-Democrat* subhead:

RFK ECHOES KING: DECRIES WAR IN SPEECH

DOCUMENT INSERT: 10/1/67. San Francisco *Chronicle* subhead:

RFK MUM ON PREZ'L PLANS

DOCUMENT INSERT: 10/2/67. Los Angeles *Times* headline and subhead:

NIXON TO PRESS:
KEEPING '68 OPTIONS OPEN

DOCUMENT INSERT: 10/3/67. Washington *Star* subhead:

SOURCES CITE LBJ'S "CONSTERNATION":
PREZ PUZZLED OVER KING'S BROADSIDES AGAINST WAR

DOCUMENT INSERT: 10/4/67. FBI field report. Marked: "Confidential"/"Eyes Only": Director, SA D. C. Holly.

Sirs,
Per spot-tail Subject Ward J. Littell.
Subject Littell continues to divide his work time between Los Angeles, Las Vegas, and Washington, D.C. He is currently working on the Las Vegas end of negotiations for the purchase of the Castaways Hotel and on the Washington end of conferences pertaining to appeals on the behalf of Teamster President James R. Hoffa. Subject Littell also continues to be intimately involved with Janice Tedrow Lukens. I have concluded, along with the other assigned agents, that Subject Littell assumes the presence of sporadically

initiated tails and thus drives different workday routes in order to thwart them. That said, I should also state that Subject Littell has not been seen engaging in any sort of activity that might be deemed suspicious.

Spot-tails to be continued on the ordered basis.

Respectfully,
SA T. V. Houghton

DOCUMENT INSERT: 10/9/67. Hate-mail extract. Compiled by: FATHER RABBIT. Sealed and marked: "Destroy Without Reading in the Event of My Death."

Mail sender: Anonymous. Postmark: St. Louis, Missouri. Recipient: Dr. M. L. King. From page 1 (of 1):

Here's another ditty for you, Coon;
The Bounty Man's going to get your black ass soon;
Fear the NSRP, John Birch and the Klan;
Fear the wrath of the righteous All-White Man;
Better get your shroud and wait for Judgment Day;
The White Man says you've outlived your stay;
Grab your pickaninnies, your wine and your dope;
Grab your watermelons and don't you mope;
Better head for Africa lickety-split;
The White Man's going to tar your hide in shit;
When that happens all the white folks will go hooray!
And say we killed that nigger who outlived his stay!

DOCUMENT INSERT: 10/30/67. Hate-mail extract. Compiled by: FATHER RABBIT. Sealed and marked: "Destroy Without Reading in the Event of My Death."

Mail sender: Anonymous. Postmark: Pasadena, California. Recipient: Senator Robert F. Kennedy. From page 8 (of 8):

THE WORLDWIDE JEWISH PIG ORDER HAS CHRISTENED YOU WITH THE BLESSING OF THE RAPIST POPE AND THE LEARNED ELDERS OF ZION WHO HAVE CAST A SPELL OF PUS OVER THE CHILDREN WHO DARED TO FIGHT THE JEW INFIDEL IN THE NAME OF THE ARAB DIASPORA. YOUR UGLY MOTHER KNOWS

YOU ARE THE SPAWN OF THE HEBREW COCKSEED AND THE RABID GOAT. THE JEWISH CANCER MACHINE FEARS THE HEADACHE DOCTOR. HE SMOKES MARLBORO CIGARETTES NOT GEFILTE FISH. HE SAYS RFK MUST DIE! RFK MUST DIE! RFK MUST DIE! RFK MUST DIE!!!!!!!

103

(Las Vegas, Los Angeles, Washington, D.C.,
New Orleans, Mexico City, 11/4/67–12/3/67)

Dominoes: the DI/the Sands/the Castaways. On tap: The Frontier.

Ten pins: Non-Mormon skim men snitched to the Feds. Old skim hands in custody.

Littell planned. Littell sowed. The Boys reaped. Bribes/PR/extortion. Blackmail/philanthropy.

It took four years. Drac owns Las Vegas now. It's Drac's kingdom complete.

Three units down. More up. Eight pending. Drac buys Vegas. Drac owns Vegas—cosmetically.

The Boys exult. The Boys praise Littell. The Boys co-opt Wayne Senior. Wayne Senior deploys. Wayne Senior recruits:

Mormons for the DI. Mormons for the Castaways. Mormons for the Sands. Mormon floor men/Hughes-vetted/legit. Mormon *skim* men/*non*-vetted/*non*-legit.

More hotels on tap. More Mormon hires pending. Drac gets the inked deeds. Drac gets the glory. The Boys get the money.

Littell braced the Boys. The Boys agreed: Let's suspend the skim. Let Drac move in. Let the ink dry. Let the shouts subside.

Skim then. Rig the vacuums. Put the hose to Drac.

Littell said we're ready. I've pegged sixty-one businesses. They're pension-fund-indebted. They're subornable. They're cake. We revive the skim. We suborn said businesses. We divert profits and plant foreign casinos.

It looked good on paper. It *was* good for him. It upped his retirement stakes.

Retire me. I'm stretched thin. I'm *scared*. Drac scared him. Drac talked PR. Drac talked financial disclosure.

I'll buff my image. I'll audit my books. I'll publish clean stats. *Don't* do it. *I've* pilfered. Don't disclose *my* tithe stats.

Retire me. I'm stretched thin. My love life's a mess. I dream about Jane. I make love to Janice.

Janice found work. Janice bought a golf shop. She sold golfwear at the Sands Hotel. She built a rep.

She did trick shots at her indoor range. She built a rep. She ragged herself like Barb did. She built a rep. She performed. She drew customers. She made money.

She still limped. She still cramped. She still spasmed up. She drank less now. She clowned less. She tattled less. She laid off the Tedrows. She'd outgrown their spell.

He slept with Janice. Jane shared the bed. Jane bludgeoned/Jane shotgunned/Jane bled.

Retire me. I'm stretched thin. It hurts to sleep. My hate life's a mess.

He worked with Wayne Senior. They haggled business points. Wayne Senior talked Image.

Shitfire—looks *count*. Screw hate tracts—*I* know Dick Nixon.

Wayne Senior talked Image. Wayne Senior talked change. Wayne Senior did not talk BLACK RABBIT. Wayne Senior performed. Wayne Senior delivered.

He saw Nixon. He passed the word. He said Dick *will* run. He said Dick wants that sitdown. He said Dick wants your cash.

Littell called Drac. Drac agreed. Drac said he'd pay that percentage. Littell called the Boys. The Boys whooped and crowed.

Dick likes money. Dick will grant "favors." Wayne Senior says so. He'll run. He'll gain ground. He'll win primaries. He'll get the nomination. He'll meet with Littell.

Retire me. I'm stretched thin. I hate Wayne Senior. I hate Tricky Dick. I love Bobby. I love Bobby's kid.

He passed through D.C. He met Paul Horvitz. He culled Jane's file. He retyped her notes. He snitched second-line mobsters to Bobby.

He met Paul four times. He delivered four parcels. Paul was wowed. Paul cited Bobby. Bobby was very impressed. They held the data. They verified facts. They withheld disclosure.

Paul said our deal holds. We'll hold your dirt—until late '68. Paul said Bobby might run. LBJ might retire. Let's await '68.

He met Paul. He played southern poof. He deployed a fake beard and drawl. They talked politics. He weaved lies. He described his life in Mississippi.

School in De Kalb. Liberal values. Southern gentility. The Klan drove him out. He moved north. Displaced aristocracy.

Paul heard his tales. Paul endured dinner dates. He's lonely. He's old. He loves Bobby.

Retire me. I'm stretched thin. I indulge fantasies.

He traveled. He worked. He tithed the SCLC. He ran tail checks. He caught tails. He diversionaried.

He calculated. He tail-scanned. He nailed the rotation: Spot tails/one day on/nine days off. He confirmed the nine to one ratio. He tail-checked accordingly.

Paranoia: valid and justified. Nine days free. One day restricted. Act accordingly.

Mr. Hoover never called. Ditto BLUE RABBIT. He did the bug jobs. Agents directed him. BLUE RABBIT disappeared. He got no pouches. He got no attaboys. He got no thank-yous. He got no welcome back. He got no tix to BLACK RABBIT.

It scared him. It said they've upscaled BLACK RABBIT. It said they're doing bad things.

He met Bayard Rustin once a month. They had lunch in D.C. Bayard said he almost got blackmailed—child, what a scene!

Bayard ran it down. Bayard described mirrors and mike plants. Bayard described a fruit squeeze. It felt like Freddy Otash. It could be Pete B.

Pete was bereft then. Barb had left him. Pete sulked accordingly. Littell tracked the date Bayard gave him. Littell tracked probability.

He was bugging Mob spots then. He braced Freddy T. Freddy declined work. Freddy *had* work. Freddy said Fred O. gigs me.

Don't ask Pete. He might say yes. He might say I pulled that queer squeeze.

Retire me. I'm stretched thin. My friends frighten me.

He met Bayard. Bayard talked. Bayard said Martin scares me. He's making plans. They're his boldest yet. He'll make more enemies.

Rent strikes/boycotts/poor people's unions/poor people's marches/ poor people's heresies.

Littell heard it. Littell remembered—it's Lyle Holly's prophecy.

Bayard was scared. Martin was crazed. Martin breathed enmity. His plans would shock. His plans would divide. His plans would stir enmity. His plans would trash his triumphs. His plans would spark backlash. His plans would build heresy.

Littell *saw* it:

It's Martin Luther/1532. It's Europe aflame. There's the Pope. He's Mr. Hoover. His old world's aflame.

Retire me. I want to watch. I want to watch passively.

Jimmy Hoffa's in jail. I'll file his appeals. Retire me. I travel to excess. I country-hop. Please retire me.

He flew south. He hit Mexico City. He made four trips and met with Sam G. They talked colonization. Sam talked travel spree.

Sam toured Central America. Sam toured the Caribbean. Sam brought interpreters and money. Sam talked to dictators. Sam talked to puppet thugs. Sam talked to rebel fiends.

Sam did gruntwork. Sam did groundwork. Sam laid seeds. Sam said I love your cause. I support it and pledge fraternity. Here's some money. There'll be more. You'll hear from me.

Sam spread seed money. Sam seeded all ideologies. Plant seeds—sow revolt and repression—casino ideology.

Retire me. I get airsick. Casino smoke sickens me. Retire Pete. He's tired too. His work sickens me. I disapprove—I've got no right—it's hypocrisy.

Pete sold dope. Pete ran his cab stand. Pete ran his hotel-casino. Pete had Cuba. Pete had Vietnam. Pete had two-front lunacy. Pete missed Vietnam. Pete missed Barb more. Barb made him stay home. Pete curtailed his lunacy.

Pete stayed home. Pete travel-spreed. Pete went to Barb's turf. Pete went to smalltown Wisconsin.

Pete called him. Barb called him. He got two versions. Vegas to Sparta—Pete leaves expectant—Pete returns whipped.

Pete worked his scams. Pete praised the war. Pete indulged habits. Barb slung hash. Barb reviled the war. Barb eschewed habits.

Love as stasis. Two takes. His-and-hers.

Retire Pete. Upgrade Wayne—*le fils de* Pete.

Pete had nightmares. Pete described them. Betty Mac/the crossbars/the noose. Pete had real pictures. *He* didn't. That made it worse.

There's Jane Fentress—Arden Breen/Bruvick/Smith/Coates. She's dead by knife/dead by cudgel/dead by steel sap.

The pictures varied. One soundtrack held in. Mr. Hoover's letter—addressed to Dr. King.

"What a grim farce." "One way out." "A liability."

Retire me. I'll try to live idle. I might not succeed.

104

(Vietnam, Las Vegas, Los Angeles, Bay St. Louis, Cuban Waters,
11/4/67–12/3/67)

ore:
Troop infusions. Troop movements. Troops dead.
More:

Bomb raids. Ground raids. Resistance.

Resistance in-country. Resistance at home. Resistance worldwide. The war was MORE. The biz was LESS. Wayne knew it.

Less:

Territory. Profit growth. Potential.

The kadre shared lab space. The Can Lao co-opted. Why do it? The Can Lao shipped to Europe. The kadre shipped to Vegas. Note the dichotomy.

The kadre did good biz. The Can Lao did great biz. Note the discrepancy. The war defined MORE. The biz defined LESS. Note the inconsistency.

Their turf was restricted. West Vegas was sapped. They had no growth room. Pete pouched Stanton. Pete pouched once a month. Pete said let us GROW.

Out of Vegas. Into L.A. Into Frisco.

We've got Tiger Kamp. We've got poppy slaves. We've got dope fields boocoo. We can GROW. We can earn MORE. The Cause will GROW.

Stanton said no. Stanton insisted. Wayne read his tone. Said tone was hinky. Said tone was quasi-weird. Pete wants MORE. Stanton wants LESS. Note the entropy.

Wayne wanted MORE. Wayne rotated east. Wayne saw more incessant. More troops smoking weed. More troops popping pills. More troops scared incessant.

Big "H" killed fear. They'd find it. Wayne knew.

The war thrilled him. The war rocked. The war grew. The "Cause" bored him. The "Cause" vexed. The "Cause" entropied.

Log it: Cuban runs/forty-plus/no at-sea resistance. It was boring now. It was impotent. It was quasi-weird.

The Cause was flypaper. Pete was a fly. Pete was stuck on 1960. Laurent was a fly. Flash was a fly. They buzzed Cuba persistent.

They talked stale shit. They talked coups and Reds. They talked domino jive. Bob talked stale shit. Bob talked race and Reds. Bob talked domino jive.

Bob vibed hinky. Bob vibed it weeks running. Bob vibed quasi-weird. Bob vibed anxious. Bob vibed scared. Bob vibed jazzed.

Bob vibed stuck. Cuba is flypaper. Cuba is quicksand. Cuba is glue.

Vegas is quicksand. Barb knows it. Barb extricates. Pete knows it. Pete stays.

Pete hit Wayne. Wayne took it. Pete apologized. Pete was frayed. Barb was in exile. The biz was exiled.

Pete wants MORE. Pete's frustrated. Stanton's entrenched. Pete's stuck. Pete's impeded. Pete's fuse might fry.

Pete and Barb cut a truce. Said truce was a travel ban—Vietnam *nyet*. Pete was stuck. Pete was truce-restricted. Pete talked truce overrides.

I'll fly to Saigon. I'll brace Stanton. I'll demand MORE.

And Stanton will wink. And Stanton will smile. And Stanton will mollify.

The war was MORE. The biz was LESS. Wayne Senior was MORE plus. They were equals now. Friends of sorts. Friends with non-Pete dimensions.

Pete seeks MORE. Pete seeks more dope turf and money. Wayne Senior seeks MORE. Wayne Senior dumps his hate biz. Wayne Senior disdains more money. Pete finds frustration. Wayne Senior finds Dick Nixon.

Pete hobnobs with pushers. Pete schleps cab calls. Pete walks flypaper. Wayne Senior plays golf. Wayne Senior shoots skeet. Wayne Senior drinks with Dick Nixon.

He worked for them. They were inimical types. They ran real to putative father. He loved both their women. He lived sans women. Wendell D. and Lynette made that fly. He head-tripped women. He head-tripped Barb mostly. He head-tripped Barb until then.

He hit her. She grabbed a knife. She ran from him and Pete. She grabbed the war. She sifted shit through.

Pete. Pete's gigs. The Life.

She kicked dope. She kicked the Life. She ran smug now. She jumped off flypaper. Her shit cohered. She lost her allure. He loved her more. He liked her less. His torch fizzled.

He head-tripped Janice. It ran twenty years now. He fucked her for payback on Dallas. He extricated. She paid.

She still limped. She still cramped. Her breath still spasmed. He saw her in Vegas. He saw her with Ward and solo. She saw him watching sometimes. She always smiled. She always waved. She always blew kisses.

It took him back. Old glimpses in windows. Peeks through cracked doors.

She was forty-six now. He was thirty-three. Her hips cocked funny. She had limp side-effects. He wondered how far her legs spread.

Relight the torch. Dig the glow. Groove on the cause-and-effect. She's real again. She's in your head—because you're back with Wayne Senior.

Grunt work. Hate-mail duty. Let's study hate. Let's see how it works. Let's see what it says.

Wayne Senior said I'm storing intelligence. I'm skimming data off the FBI. I'm polling resentment. I'm taking its pulse. It's academic for now.

Wayne Senior spoke lofty. Wayne Senior spoke abstract. Wayne Senior spoke with forked tongue.

Wayne knew:

He's teaching you. Read the hate. Don't hate fatuously.

He rotated. He ran Saigon to D.C. He pulled intercepts. He did sneak-ins. He bagged mail. He mimeographed. He print-dusted. He got zero. He ran ninhydrin tests. He got loop whirls and partials. He learned the Hate Alphabet.

He did re-sneaks. He replaced the mail. He savored the Hate Alphabet.

A for Anger. F for Fear. I for Idiocy. D for Dumb. R for Ridiculous. J for Justification.

Coloreds mock order. Coloreds foist chaos. Coloreds breed lunacy. The haters knew it. Wayne Senior knew it. *He* knew it. The haters lived to hate. That was wrong. *That* was lunacy. The haters lived disordered lives. The haters thrived on chaos. The haters mimed the hatees.

S for Stupid. R for Resentful. W for Weak.

He learned his lessons. He took Wayne Senior's Hate Course. He searched for Wendell Durfee.

He rotated south. He made Cuban runs. He rotated west to L.A. He prowled Compton. He prowled Willowbrook. He prowled Watts.

He watched Negroes. Negroes watched him. He stayed cool. He stayed calm. He knew his ABCs. Wendell was nowhere. Wendell, where you be? I hate you. I'll kill you. Hate won't hinder me.

Hate smart—like Wayne Senior. P for Poised. B for Brave. C for Collected.

He did intercepts. He culled hate. He caught lunacy.

Weird:

He muscled a deadbeat. It was late '66. The clown was named Sirhan Sirhan. Sirhan had hate tracts. RFK got some hate notes. They were margin scrawled the same way.

All cap letters/headaches and pus/"Jewish Cancer Machine." Sirhan drools. Sirhan hates stupid. Sirhan foists lunacy.

Don't do it. It's counterproductive. It's dumb. It's insanity.

Hate smart. Like Wayne Senior. Like me.

105

(Las Vegas, Sparta, Bay St. Louis, Cuban Waters, 11/4/67–12/3/67)

You're homeless.

You're a Vegas transient. You're embargoed at home. You're a fucking refugee.

It's jail. It's Skid Row. It mocks rotation. It's Splitsville. It's mock-divorce. It's past separation.

Barb split. Pete traveled—all-love rotations. Pete flew back alone—non-love rotations. The trips trashed him. The trips taught him. The trips made him see: You hate Vegas now. Without Barb it's shit. You're Joe Vegas Refugee.

He had the trifecta. It was all Vegas-bred—Tiger/the dope biz/the Cavern. He couldn't split. The Boys held his lease. It was sealed and marked "Dallas."

He loved the trifecta. He hated the venue. They all intertwined.

Stateless.

He met Barb. She slung plates. No high heels/no spangles. Her sister worked her. Her sister lubed her—gooooood profit perks. Barb B.—ex-lounge queen. Waitress/restaurateur.

He couldn't have her. He couldn't have her on his terms. He couldn't have her at *his* location.

He hubbed in Vegas. He flew to Mississippi. He hated it. Dumb crackers and dumb niggers. Bugs and sand fleas.

He made boat runs. He got seasick. His pulse raced. He snarfed Dramamine. The runs bored him. Stealth and scalps and nothing more. No good resistance.

He was a transient. He was travel-screwed. He was a rotation refugee.

You want things. You can't have things. You can't give things up. You've got habits. You don't need them. You can't give them up.

Cigarettes. Pizza pie and pecan pie. Stiff drinks and steak.

He hid his habits in Sparta. Barb never saw. He flew out. He depurified. He binged on rotations.

Transient. Glutton. Exile. Exiled on boat runs/exiled down south/ exiled in Vegas.

Drac's town now—Drac's town cosmetic.

He knew Drac. They went back. They met in '53. He worked for Drac. He scored Drac dope. He scored Drac his women. Drac was a glutton then. Drac was a glutton still.

He cruised the DI. He bribed a Mormon for a look-see. He bought a looooong look.

Drac dozed. Drac wore drip cords. Drac got a transfusion. Mormon blood/hormone-laced/pure. Drac was gaunt. Drac was svelte. Drac was chic. Drac wore a Kotex-box hat and Kleenex-box slippers.

Drac was on dope. Barb was off dope. Pete pushed dope non-boocoo. Pete was hamstrung. Pete was profit-screwed. Pete was a dope refugee.

He begged Stanton. He said *let me expand.* Stanton always refused. He pouched Stanton. He pleaded and begged. Stanton always refused. Stanton always cited Carlos. Stanton always cited the Boys.

They don't want it. Live with it. It stands as their call. He lived with it. He hated it. He felt refugized.

He got ideas.

I'll fly to Saigon. I'll brace Stanton. I'll break the truce. I'll tell Barb to stamp my visa. I'll make her unleash my gonads.

I'll tell Stanton to expand the biz or shove it up your ass. Stanton would shit. Carlos would shit. The Boys *might* temporize.

It might work. It might shake them. It might serve to de-refugize. He needed it. He needed something. He needed MORE.

He got bored. He got crazed. He fretted shit.

Like: Cuba—*mucho* boat runs—no at-sea resistance.

Like: Bob Relyea—nervous and hi-amped.

He's talking trash. He's saying our work's dead. He's saying I've got work transcendent.

He went by Bob's kompound. He saw Bob with guns. He saw Bob burn three-zero codes.

Huh? What? Don't grab at straws. Don't be this skittish refugee.

He got bored. He got crazed. His pulse skipped.

DOCUMENT INSERT: 12/3/67. Bug-extract transcript. Marked: "Confidential"/"Stage-1 Covert"/"Eyes Only": Director, SA D. C. Holly.

Location: Card room/Grapevine Tavern/St. Louis/listening-post-accessed. Speaking: Norbert Donald Kling & Rowland Mark DeJohn, paroled felons (Armed Robbery/Bunco/GTA) & presumed organized-crime associates. (Conversation 14.1 minutes in progress.)

NDK: And people hear, you know. Word goes out.

RMDJ: It's like the name of this place. The Grapevine.

NDK: Yeah. The grape for the ape.

RMDJ: Guys come through, they hear, they start thinking.

NDK: They think, shit, 50 G's for a good deed, and it don't go unrewarded.

RMDJ: You do it down south, no jury would convict you.

NDK: You're right. It's like those guys in Mississippi. They wax those civil rights humps and walk scot-free.

NDK: You know who I saw here? Like in May?

RMDJ: Who?

NDK: Jimmy Ray. I bought goofballs off him in Jeff City.

RMDJ: I heard he broke out.

NDK: He did. He breaks out, then he's disappointed that there's no big manhunt.

RMDJ: That's Jimmy in a nutshell. Hey, world, notice me.

NDK: He hates niggers. You got to give him that.

RMDJ: He was tight with the guards. At Jeff City, I mean. I never liked that about him.

NDK: The guards were klanned-up. That was the attraction to Jimmy.

RMDJ: That one guard was a pisser. Remember him? Bob Relyea.

NDK: Bob the Brain. Jimmy called him that.

RMDJ: I heard he's klanned-up down south now.

NDK: Klanned-up and a snitch is what I heard. As in, he works for the Feds.

RMDJ: That could be. Remember, he left Jeff and joined the Army.

NDK: Jimmy said he might go see him.

RMDJ: Jimmy's a talker. He always talked about a whole lot of things.

NDK: He heard about the bounty. He nearly bust a gut talking about that.

RMDJ: Talk's talk. Jimmy said he fucked Marilyn Monroe, which don't mean he really did it.

(Non-applicable conversation follows.)

DOCUMENT INSERT: 12/3/67. Bug-extract transcript. Marked: "Confidential"/"Stage-1 Covert"/"Eyes Only": Director, SA D. C. Holly.

Location: Office/Mike Lyman's Restaurant/Los Angeles/listening-post-accessed. Speaking: Unidentified Males #1 & #2, presumed organized-crime associates. (Conversation 1.9 minutes in progress.)

UM #1: . . . you've heard the stories, right?

UM #2: Just glimmers. Carlos knows they're on the boat, so he sends some guys to the Keys.

UM #1: Not just any guys. He sends Chuck the Vice and Nardy Scavone.

UM #2: Oh, Jesus.

UM #1: You have to assume that he wanted to prolong things. It is well known that Chuck and Nardy work slow.

UM #2: I have heard the stories, believe me.

UM #1: Here's the good part. You'll like it.

UM #2: So tell me. Don't be a fucking cock-tease.

UM #1: Okay, they spot the boat. It's docked someplace quiet. They sneak up quiet and climb on board.

UM #2: Come on, don't string it—

UM #1: Arden and Danny see them coming. Danny starts bawling and saying rosaries. Arden's got a gun. She shoots Danny in the back of the head to put him out of his misery. She aims at fucking Chuck and Nardy, but the fucking gun jams.

UM #2: Fuck, that is rich. That is just—

UM #1: Chuck and Nardy grab her and tie her down. Carlos wants to know why they rabbited and did someone tip them off. Chuck's got his vice in a toolbox. He puts Arden's head in. He leans on the handle, but Arden won't give it up.

UM #2: Jesus.

UM #1: He cracked all her teeth and broke her jaw. She still wouldn't talk.

UM #2: Jesus.

UM #1: She bit her tongue off. She couldn't talk if she wanted to, so Nardy capped her.

UM #2: Jesus.

(Non-applicable conversation follows).

DOCUMENT INSERT: 12/3/67. Pouch communiqué. To: Dwight Holly. From: Fred Otash. Marked: "Confidential"/"Eyes Only"/ "Read & Burn Immediately."

DH,

Here's the summary on my dealings with the PROSPECT to date, including my reasoning on why I think we should use him. I hate writing things down, so READ & BURN IMMEDIATELY.

1 - Contact with PROSPECT established 8/16/67, at bar ("Acapulco") downstairs from PROSPECT's residence ("Har-K Apts") in Montreal. PROSPECT was using alias "Eric Starvo Galt." I utilized my fake appearance & Latin accent & used the alias "Raul Acias."

2 - At Acapulco I sold PROSPECT amphetamine capsules & posed as smuggler with segregationist leanings. PROSPECT & I met at Acapulco & Neptune Tavern over next several nights & discussed politics. PROSPECT admitted 2 recent robberies in states (East St. Louis, Ill. & New Hebron, Miss.) but did not mention his 4/23/67 prison escape. PROSPECT stated that he also robbed a prostitute & pimp at a "fuck pad" in Montreal shortly after his arrival. He got $1,700 but was spending $ fast & would "soon be broke."

3 - PROSPECT discussed his need to secure ID which would allow him to get a Canadian passport & thus travel to other countries. I told him I had connections & would help him. I lent him small amounts of money, supplied him with amphetamines & discussed politics with him. He frequently mentioned his hatred of M. L. King & desire to "kill niggers in Rhodesia." I stalled him per the ID papers & continued to lend him $. PROSPECT became nervous & stated his desire to return to the states, go to Alabama & "Maybe go to work for Governor Wallace." I saw that he was determined to go & improvised a plan.

4 - I told him I had some narcotics for him to drive across the

border & would pay him $1,200. He agreed to do the job. I filled
a briefcase with sand, locked it & gave it to him, then met him
on the American side. This was a test to see if he would steal
the briefcase or would prove to be as compliant as I thought he
would be.

5 - He passed the test & made 2 other "narcotics runs" for me.
I saw that he was determined to drive to Alabama & told him I
would get him his ID, a new car & more $, because I had more
"jobs" for him to do. PROSPECT stated that he wanted to spend
time in Birmingham, because of its history of "nigger bombings." I
gave him $2,000 & told him to wait for a letter at Birmingham
General Delivery. I also gave him a phone-drop # to call me at in
New Orleans.

6 - This was the risk part of the operation, because there was a
chance the PROSPECT would ditch out on me. If he didn't, it would
confirm his pliable nature & suitable nature for our job.

7 - PROSPECT called phone-drop on 8/25 & gave his address as
"Economy Grill & Rooms" in Birmingham. I mailed him $600 & a
small supply of biphetamine capsules, flew to Birmingham & surveilled him from discreet distances. PROSPECT visited the National
States Rights Party HQ, purchased right-wing leaflets & bumper
stickers & holed up in his room. I called him (allegedly long-
distance) & agreed to give him $2,000 (advance against future
jobs) so he could buy a new car. I wired the $ to him & surveilled
his purchase of a 1966 Mustang.

8 - PROSPECT secured an Alabama driver's license (9/6/67)
under name "Eric Starvo Galt" & registered the '66 Mustang. I met
PROSPECT in Birmingham, drank & talked politics with him & told
him to buy some camera equipment to sell in Mexico. PROSPECT
purchased $2,000 worth of equipment, which I told him to "sit on."

9 - PROSPECT remained in Birmingham, took a locksmith's
course & dance lessons & surreptitiously filmed women from his
rooming-house window. I remained in Birmingham & took pains
never to be seen with him. My plan was to situate PROSPECT in
various places & give him orders that would sound ridiculous
should he be captured & interrogated after our operation.
PROSPECT's need for $ & amphetamines kept him beholden to me.

10 - I wrote PROSPECT on 10/6/67 & told him to meet me in
Nuevo Laredo, Mexico with the camera equipment. PROSPECT
agreed to meet me after he "fenced the goods." Again, I promised
to secure him valid ID papers & added that I could get him a Canadian passport. PROSPECT met me in Nuevo Laredo with $ from the

equipment he fenced, at a loss. I told him I was not mad & had more "narcotics runs" for him. PROSPECT was mad that I had not yet secured papers for him, but agreed to stay in Mexico & wait for my calls.

11 - PROSPECT traveled throughout Mexico by car & called me at phone-drop in New Orleans. I forwarded sums of $ to him at American Express offices & paid him for 4 "narcotics runs" from McAllen to Juarez. I met with PROSPECT 4 times from 10/22/67 to 11/9/67 & drew him out on political issues. PROSPECT described a "Bounty" offered thru the Grapevine Bar in St. Louis ($50,000 to kill MLK), which sounded like a fantasy but indicated that he might be willing to step up for D-Day, which would upgrade his role in our plan. PROSPECT was drinking heavily, taking amphetamines & smoking marijuana in Mexico & while there got into altercations with prostitutes & pimps. PROSPECT drove to Los Angeles (without calling me) & called with address on 11/21/67. He stated he wants more work from me, is taking self-hypnosis & self-improvement courses & is visiting "segregationist bookstores." He urged me to get him his passport papers as an "advance against future jobs."

12 - PROSPECT remains in L.A. I'm L.A.-based, so I'll be able to surveil him. PROSPECT remains pliable & I'm convinced he'll work for us. Have we got a date & or location yet?

I'll pouch again when required. Again, READ & BURN.
F.O.

DOCUMENT INSERT: 12/4/67. Pouch communiqué. To: Fred Otash. From: Dwight Holly. Marked: "Confidential"/"Eyes Only"/"Read & Burn."

F. O.,
No date or location yet. Continue with PROSPECT. Will try to secure RED RABBIT's travel plans.
READ THIS & BURN.
D.C.H.

DOCUMENT INSERT: 12/4/67. Atlanta *Constitution* headline and subhead:

KING ANNOUNCES "POOR PEOPLE'S MARCH" ON WASHINGTON
PLEDGES TO WORK FOR "REDISTRIBUTION OF WEALTH"

DOCUMENT INSERT: 12/5/67. Cleveland *Plain Dealer* headline and subhead:

KING ON SPRING MARCH:
"TIME TO CONFRONT POWER STRUCTURE MASSIVELY"

DOCUMENT INSERT: 12/6/67. Verbatim FBI telephone call transcript. Marked: "Recorded at the Director's Request"/"Classified Confidential 1-A: Director's Eyes Only." Speaking: Director Hoover, President Lyndon B. Johnson.

LBJ: Is that you, Edgar?

JEH: It's me, Mr. President.

LBJ: That goddamn march. It's all over the news.

JEH: I've read the announcements. They've fulfilled my very worst fears and apprehensions.

LBJ: That son-of-a-bitch is bringing an army to protest me, after all I've done for the Negro people.

JEH: The march will unleash a bloodbath.

LBJ: I asked him to call it off, but the son-of-a-bitch refused. He's killing my chance to get reelected. He's in cahoots with that spoon-fed cocksucker, Bobby Kennedy.

JEH: I will let you in on a little-known fact, Mr. President. Bobby allowed me to tap and bug King himself, back in '63. He has forgotten his initial misgivings in his rush to embrace that Communist.

LBJ: The cocksucker wants my job. King's creating the fucking dissent that will get it for him.

JEH: I'm putting 44 agents on King. They will disseminate derogatory data nationwide. I will do everything in my power to subvert this march.

LBJ: Edgar, was there ever a better friend to the Negro people than me?

JEH: No, Mr. President.

LBJ: Edgar, has my legislation improved the lot of the Negro people?

JEH: Yes, Mr. President.

LBJ: Edgar, have I been a friend to Martin Luther King?

JEH: Yes, Mr. President.

LBJ: Then why is that cocksucker trying to cornhole me when I've bent over backwards to befriend him?

JEH: I don't know, Mr. President.

LBJ: He's a worse bane to my fucking existence than this fucking war I'm fucking knee-deep in.

JEH: I'm going to plant a Negro in the SCLC. He used to work as my chauffeur.

LBJ: Tell him to chauffeur King off a cliff.

JEH: I understand your frustration, Sir.

LBJ: I'm getting fucked from two flanks. I'm fighting a two-front war against a King and a fucking Kennedy.

JEH: Yes, Mr. President.

LBJ: You're a good man, Edgar.

JEH: Thank you, Mr. President.

LBJ: Do what you can on this, all right?

JEH: I will, Sir.

LBJ: Goodbye, Edgar.

JEH: Goodbye, Mr. President.

DOCUMENT INSERT: 12/7/67. Los Angeles *Examiner* subhead:

BUSINESS COMMUNITY ATTACKS KING FOR "POOR PEOPLE'S MARCH"

DOCUMENT INSERT: 12/9/67. Dallas *Morning News* subhead:

SPRING MARCH ON WASHINGTON "SOCIALISTIC,"
BUSINESS LEADERS CHARGE

DOCUMENT INSERT: 12/17/67. Chicago *Tribune* headline and subhead:

NIXON IN '68?
EX-VEEP TO ANNOUNCE CANDIDACY?

DOCUMENT INSERT: 12/17/67. Miami *Herald* headline and subhead:

CLERGYMEN ON WASHINGTON MARCH:
"A CALL TO ANARCHY AND RIOTS"

DOCUMENT INSERT: 12/18/67. Chicago *Sun-Times* subhead:

RFK PRAISES WASHINGTON MARCH
MUM ON WHITE HOUSE PLANS

DOCUMENT INSERT: 12/18/67. Denver *Post-Dispatch* headline and subhead:

WILL HE OR WON'T HE?
PUNDITS ASSESS LBJ'S REELECTION PLANS

DOCUMENT INSERT: 12/20/67. Boston *Globe* subhead:

KING CALLS FOR WAR PROTESTERS TO EMBRACE POOR PEOPLE'S MARCH

DOCUMENT INSERT: 12/21/67. Sacramento *Bee* subhead:

EXPECT NIXON TO RUN, GOP INSIDERS SAY

DOCUMENT INSERT: 12/22/67. Los Angeles *Times* subhead:

RFK, HUMPHREY PLAYING COY?
AWAITING LBJ'S DECISION?

DOCUMENT INSERT: 12/23/67. Kansas City *Star* subhead:

ROTARY PRESIDENT CALLS
KING MARCH "COMMUNIST INSPIRED"

DOCUMENT INSERT: 12/28/67. Las Vegas *Sun* headline and subhead:

FRONTIER HOTEL FALLS TO HUGHES
BILLIONAIRE'S VEGAS ROLL CONTINUES!

DOCUMENT INSERT: 1/4/68. Verbatim FBI telephone call
transcript. (OPERATION BLACK RABBIT Addendum.) Marked:
"Recorded at the Director's Request"/"Classified Confidential 1-A:
Director's Eyes Only." Speaking: Director, BLUE RABBIT.

DIR: Good morning.
BR: Good morning, Sir.
DIR: RED RABBIT is misbehaving. He's being a very bad bunny.
BR: I've been reading the newspapers, Sir. I think he's stepped
over the line.
DIR: He has, but not to the extent where he'll discredit himself
finitely. He is immune to that form of censure. He is riding a wave
of unjustified discontent that is bigger than any of us.
BR: Yes, Sir.
DIR: Lyndon Johnson is furious. He despises himself for the
way he's coddled RED RABBIT. He knows that this wave of silly
discord is partially of his manufacture.
BR: Yes, Sir.
DIR: I've planted a Negro within the SCLC. My former chauf-
feur, no less.
BR: Yes, Sir.
DIR: He's a sensible Negro. He despises Communists more than
the white power structure.
BR: Yes, Sir.
DIR: He tells me the SCLC is in a state of great disarray. They
are attempting to recruit an army of the wretched to compete with
Hannibal's hordes.
BR: Yes, Sir.
DIR: They will storm our nation's capital. They will urinate and
fornicate with abandon.
BR: Yes, Sir.
DIR: This display of pique will be a catastrophic disaster. It will
encourage the unruly and criminally prone and give them an
unprecedented license. The ramifications will be severe and nihilis-
tically defined.
BR: Yes, Sir.
DIR: I am at my wits' end, Dwight. I do not know what more I
can do.
BR: There's a counter-consensus brewing, Sir. I know you've
been reading the bug transcripts.
DIR: I would define that consensus as too localized, too little,
and too late.

BR: Some men are offering a bounty.

DIR: I would not be overly perturbed to see it happen.

BR: The concept is very much out there.

DIR: I would not like to be stuck with the task of investigating such an incident. I would be inclined to work for brevity and do what was best to put it behind us.

BR: Yes, Sir.

DIR: Unreasonable actions and unjustified rage serve to spark reasoned and measured responses.

BR: Yes, Sir.

DIR: I take comfort in that.

BR: I'm glad to hear it, Sir.

DIR: Is there anything I can do for you, Dwight?

BR: Yes, Sir. Could you speak to your contact and pouch me RED RABBIT's itinerary for the next several months?

DIR: Yes.

BR: Thank you, Sir.

DIR: Good day, Dwight.

BR: Good day, Sir.

DOCUMENT INSERT: 1/8/68. Pouch communiqué. To: Fred Otash. From: Dwight Holly. Marked: "Confidential"/"Eyes Only"/"Read & Burn Immediately."

F.O.,

On go. Send update on PROSPECT. RED RABBIT's travel plans to follow.

READ & BURN.

D.C.H.

DOCUMENT INSERT: 1/18/68. Pouch communiqué. To: Dwight Holly. From: Fred Otash. Marked: "Confidential"/"Eyes Only"/ "Read & Burn Immeidately."

D.H.,

Per PROSPECT's activities from 12/3/67 to present date.

1 - I met with PROSPECT 6 times. I continued to give him $ as advances "against future jobs." We discussed politics & PROSPECT frequently mentioned Geo. Wallace's presidential campaign, "niggers" & "the bounty on Martin Luther Coon." PROSPECT continued

to press me for travel papers & as previously I stalled him. PROSPECT divided his time between his apt (1535 N. Serrano, Hollywood), the Sultan's Room at the St. Francis Hotel-Apts (Hollywood Blvd) & the Rabbit's Foot Club (appropriate!!!!) also on Hollywood Blvd. PROSPECT continued to discuss his plans to travel to Rhodesia & on 3 occasions said he might "kill Coon, collect the bounty & seek political asylum in Rhodesia."

2 - PROSPECT became involved with woman at Sultan's Room, who talked him into driving her brother to New Orleans to "pick up her friend's kids." PROSPECT told me about this & asked for travel $. I gave him $1,000 & told him I would meet him in N.O. PROSPECT & woman's brother drove to N.O. (12/15/67), arrived on 12/17 & stayed at the Provincial Motel. I met PROSPECT 3 times, gave him $ & promised future jobs. PROSPECT remained in N.O. & frequented pornographic bookstores. PROSPECT, woman's brother & 2 8-yr-old girls left N.O. on 12/19 & arrived in L.A. on 12/21.

3 - PROSPECT settled into L.A. routine. I spot-tailed him on 6 occasions & met with him on 6 more. PROSPECT visited pornographic bookstores, took hypnosis courses & told me he intended to hypnotize women into acting in porno films that he would direct. PROSPECT frequented the Sultan's Room & the Rabbit's Foot Club, drank habitually & habitually used amphetamines. He frequently discussed the "bounty" & his plans to "escape" to Rhodesia. During this period PROSPECT visited the office of the L.A. Free Press & placed a classified ad seeking women for oral sex. PROSPECT also purchased liquid methamphetamine at the Castle Argyle Apts (Franklin & Argyle). He routinely stays up for 2 & 3 days at a time & I have noticed recent needle tracks on his arms.

4 - PROSPECT stated (4 occasions) that his intentions are to stay in L.A. & "do jobs" for me, join a swinger's club & figure out a way to "get the bounty & shag to Rhodesia." I've started talking about the bounty & ways to get at MLK & PROSPECT has not noticed any shift in my tone or personality, because (a) he's seriously disturbed & extremely self-obsessed; (b) he's beholden to me for $ & narcotics; (c) he's strung out & impaired by his liquor & drug use.

5 - I think I can keep him in L.A. until our go-date & then get him to the spot to either participate or work the fall-back slot. We need his prints on a rifle & some other things, which should be easy to do.

6 - He's the guy. I'm sure of it. We're buffered on him (nobody will ever believe his "Raul" stories) & we'll never let him get into custody anyway.

READ THIS AND BURN. Pouch me if you need further updates. F.O.

DOCUMENT INSERT: 1/21/68. Boston *Globe* subhead:

MARINES IN LIFE-OR-DEATH SIEGE AT KHE SANH

DOCUMENT INSERT: 1/24/68. New York *Times* headline and sub-head:

TET OFFENSIVE SHOCKS U.S. FORCES
LARGEST BATTLES OF WAR RAGE

DOCUMENT INSERT: 1/26/68. Atlanta *Constitution* headline:

KHE SANH—THE BLOODY SIEGE CONTINUES

DOCUMENT INSERT: 1/27/68. Los Angeles *Examiner* subhead:

MASSIVE VIET BATTLES SPARK U.S. PROTESTS

DOCUMENT INSERT: 1/30/68. Chicago *Sun-Times* headline and subhead:

KING CITES TET HOLOCAUST
CALLS FOR UNCONDITIONAL U.S. TROOP WITHDRAWAL

DOCUMENT INSERT: 2/2/68. Los Angeles *Times* headline and sub-head:

NIXON ANNOUNCES PREZ'L CANDIDACY
PLEDGES TO WORK FOR "HARDWORKING, FORGOTTEN MAJORITY"

<u>DOCUMENT INSERT</u>: 2/6/68. Sacramento *Bee* subhead:

KING IN MOBILIZING EFFORT FOR POOR PEOPLE'S MARCH

<u>DOCUMENT INSERT</u>: 2/8/68. Houston *Chronicle* headline and sub-
head:

RFK IN HEATED ATTACK ON WAR
CALLS FOR NEGOTIATED SETTLEMENT

<u>DOCUMENT INSERT</u>: 2/10/68. Cleveland *Plain Dealer* subhead:

HOOVER WARNS OF BLOODSHED IF MARCH PERMITTED

<u>DOCUMENT INSERT</u>: 2/18/68. Miami *Herald* headline and
subhead:

HUGE NIXON CROWDS IN NEW HAMPSHIRE
EX-VEEP ASSUMES FRONT-RUNNER STATUS

<u>DOCUMENT INSERT</u>: 3/2/68. Boston *Globe* headline and subhead:

U.S. CASUALTY RATE MOUNTS IN VIETNAM
KING BLASTS "FUTILE" CONFLICT

<u>DOCUMENT INSERT</u>: 3/11/68. Tampa *Tribune* headline and sub-
head:

WILL HE OR WON'T HE?
RFK ISN'T SAYING

<u>DOCUMENT INSERT</u>: 3/13/68. Bug-extract transcript. Marked:
"Confidential"/"Stage-1 Covert"/"Eyes Only": Director, SA D. C.
Holly.
   Location: Office/Mike Lyman's Restaurant/Los Angeles/listen-
ing-post-accessed. Speaking: Charles "Chuck the Vice" Aiuppa &

Bernard "Nardy" Scavone, organized-crime associates. (Conversation 6.8 minutes in progress.)

CA: It's what you call a coalition. Bobby's the president, but he needs the head ape to mobilize all the little apes and put him in power.

BS: Do the arithmetic, Chuck. They don't have the votes.

CA: Then you add the Jews, the college kids, the comsymps and the welfare creeps. It gets to be a very tight race with those forces in play.

BS: Bobby scares me. That I will readily admit.

CA: Bobby needs the head ape to create the unrest. Then he comes in and promises all the fucked-up people the moon.

BS: Bobby would fuck us, Chuck. He'd fuck us like he fucked us when he was AG and Jack was the prez.

CA: Bobby's only happy when he's got some made guy's dick in the vice.

BS: Watch it, Chuck. You say "vice," you give me these urges.

CA: Control yourself. There'll be more. Uncle Carlos has always got work.

BS: I'd like to put the head ape and Bobby in the vice. One squeeze and arrivederci.

(Non-applicable conversation follows.)

DOCUMENT INSERT: 3/14/68. Bug-extract transcript. Marked: "Confidential"/"Stage-1 Covert"/"Eyes Only": Director, SA D. C. Holly.

Location: Card room/Grapevine Tavern/St. Louis/listening-post-accessed. Speaking: Norbert Donald Kling & Rowland Mark DeJohn, paroled felons (Armed Robbery/Bunco/GTA) & presumed organized-crime associates. (Conversation 0.9 minutes in progress.)

NDK: This is rich. I grab the pay phone this morning and who do I get?

RMDJ: Jill St. John?

NDK: No.

RMDJ: What's her name? That cooze with the go-go boots.

NDK: No.

RMDJ: Norb, shit—

NDK: It's Jimmy Ray. He starts talking shit and says he joined a French cult in L.A. He dives muff and gets sucked off all day, and he needs money to support all his slaves, and did I know if there was a time limit on the bounty, 'cause he's got his hands full with his slaves right now and he don't know when he can get free.

RMDJ: That is hilarious. Jimmy's got his hands full, all right.

NDK: One hand, at least. At Jeff City he'd geez meth and jack off for two days at a pop. He'd read these fucking pussy books and orbit. He said the fucking pictures were talking to him.

RMDJ: Jimmy's got delusions of grandeur.

NDK: Yeah, but he hates niggers.

(Non-applicable conversation follows.)

DOCUMENT INSERT: 3/15/68. Bug-extract transcript. Marked: "Confidential"/"Stage-1 Covert"/"Eyes Only": Director, SA D. C. Holly.

Location: Suite 301/El Encanto Hotel/Santa Barbara/listening-post-accessed. Speaking: Senator Robert F. Kennedy, Paul Horvitz (senate staff mbr.), Unidentified Male #1. (Conversation 3.9 minutes in progress.)

RFK: . . . simple and matter-of-fact. That's the way my brother announced. (Pause/3.4 seconds.) Paul, you time the statement. Read it aloud, but don't try to imitate me.

(Laughter/2.4 seconds.)

PH: About the position paper. Do we publish—

UM #1: You want the abbreviated version, right? The long form's too dense, and the press guys will have to cut too much.

RFK: Condense it and let me read the final draft. And be damn sure there's nothing in there about organized crime.

PH: Sir, I think that's a mistake. It undercuts your credentials as Attorney General.

UM #1: Bob, shit. You know you'll go after those guys ag—

RFK: I intend to, but I don't intend to broadcast it.

UM #1: Shit, Bob. Good foes make for good campaigns. The war and Johnson are one thing, but—

PH: The Mob's dead as a campaign issue, but—

RFK: I'll do what I do, when I do it, but I'm not going to broadcast my intentions. Think "social justice," "end the war" and "unite the country" and forget about the goddamn Mafia.

PH: Sir, do you think—

RFK: That's enough. I've got enough on my mind without worrying about those sons-of-bitches.

(Non-applicable conversation follows.)

DOCUMENT INSERT: 3/16/68. Bug-extract transcript. Marked: "Confidential"/"Stage-1 Covert"/"Eyes Only": Director, SA D. C. Holly.

Location: Suite 301/El Encanto Hotel/Santa Barbara/listening-post-accessed. Speaking: Senator Robert F. Kennedy, Paul Horvitz (senate staff mbr.), Unidentified Male #1. (Conversation 7.4 minutes in progress.)

RFK: . . . a litigator I had at Justice. He was there for most of my moves against Carlos Marcello.

UM #1: Uncle Carlos. You deported him.

RFK: I dumped his fat ass in Central America.

PH: You're tipsy, Senator. You rarely say "ass" when you're sober.

RFK: I'm getting tipsy now because I won't be able to get tipsy until November. (Laughter/6.8 seconds.)

RFK: I'm starting to feel like a fighter before he goes into training. I'm dumping all the stuff I won't be able to talk about during the campaign.

PH: That litigator. What ab—

RFK: We were talking about the Outfit. I told him that one day I'd get my second shot, and devil take the hindmost.

PH: Is that from Shakespeare?

RFK: It's from me. It means I'm going to make those sons-of-whores pay.

(Non-applicable conversation follows).

DOCUMENT INSERT: 3/17/68. Verbatim FBI telephone call transcript. (OPERATION BLACK RABBIT ADDENDUM.) Marked: "Recorded at the Director's Request"/"Classified Confidential 1-A: Director's Eyes Only." Speaking: Director, BLUE RABBIT.

DIR: Good afternoon.

BR: Good afternoon, Sir.

DIR: You pulled me out of a meeting. I assume you have news of some import.

BR: We hit on CRUSADER RABBIT. One of my men tailed him to a bank in Silver Spring, Maryland. He has a dummy account there. I got a bank writ and checked his transaction record.

DIR: Continue.

BR: The account was opened under a pseudonym. CRUSADER uses it for one purpose, to send checks to the SCLC. I cross-checked our bank-account covers on the SCLC and determined that checks from four other accounts, in different cities and states, have been regularly sent in. They go back to '64 and they all bear CRUSADER's handwriting. He's got a different alias for each account, and he's donated close to a half million dollars total.

DIR: I am astounded.

BR: Yes, Sir.

DIR: He's embezzled the money or stolen it from some convenient source. His salaries would not sustain that degree of largesse.

BR: Yes, Sir.

DIR: He's indulging the Catholic concept of penance. He's atoning for the sins he's committed under my flag.

BR: It gets worse, Sir.

DIR: Tell me how. Fulfill my worst fears and most justified suspicions.

BR: An agent spot-tailed him in D.C. two days ago. He was heavily disguised and almost unrecognizable. He met a Kennedy staffer named Paul Horvitz at a restaurant and spent two hours with him.

DIR: More atonement. A roundelay that will not go unpunished.

BR: What do you want me—

DIR: Let CRUSADER continue to atone for his sins. Send copies of the March 15th and March 16th El Encanto bug tapes to Carlos Marcello, Sam Giancana, Moe Dalitz, Santo Trafficante and every other Mob patriarch in the United States. They should know that Prince Bobby has long-range plans for them.

BR: It's a bold and inspired gambit, Sir.

DIR: Good day, Dwight. Go with God and other felicitous sources.

BR: Good day, Sir.

DOCUMENT INSERT: 3/18/68. New York *Times* headline:

RFK ANNOUNCES BID FOR DEMOCRATIC PRESIDENTIAL NOMINATION

Part VI

INTERDICTION

March 19, 1968–June 9, 1968

106

(Saigon, 3/19/68)

You're back.

It's vivid. It's vicious. It's Vietnam.

See the troop swarms. See the displaced slopes. See said gooks talking Tet. See the boarded temples. See the truck convoys. See the antiaircraft guns.

You're back. Dig it. Saigon '68.

The cab crawled. Trucks hemmed it in. Gun trucks/food trucks/troop trucks. Tailpipe fumes windshield-high. Fume grit in your eyes.

Pete watched. Pete smoked. Pete chewed Tums.

He breached the truce. He flew overnight—Frisco/Tan Son Nhut. He lured Barb to Frisco. He pitched it as romance. He cloaked his truce override.

She nailed him. She said you're going back—I know it. He copped out. He said let me go. He said let me brace Stanton.

She said no. He said yes. It went waaaay bad. They yelled. They threw shit. They gouged walls. They scared the desk clerks. They scared the bellboys. They scared the hotel staff.

Barb split to Sparta. He roamed San Francisco. The hills bonked his heart. He drove to the airport. He sat in the bar. He saw some Carlos cats: Chuck "the Vice" Aiuppa and Nardy Scavone.

They hailed him. They bought him drinks. They got tanked and bragged. They said they clipped Danny Bruvick. It was a twosky. They clipped Danny's ex Arden-Jane. They supplied details. They supplied sound effects.

Pete walked out. Pete caught his plane. Pete ate Nembutal. He slept. The plane pitched. He saw vices snap heads.

The cab crawled. The driver grazed monks. The driver monologued: Tet kill many. Tet fuck things up. Tet kill GIs. Victor Charles naughty! Victor Charles evil! Victor Charles *baaad!*

The cab pitched. The cab lurched. Pete gagged on truck fumes. Pete's knees bumped his head.

There's the Go-Go. It's still gook graffitied. You're back. It's still ARVN-guarded. There's two Marvs door-posted. You're back.

Pete grabbed his duffel. Pete grabbed Wayne's satchel—beakers and test tubes prewrapped. Drop them off/check the lab/hit Hotel Catinat.

The driver braked. Pete got out and stretched. The Marvs snapped to. Said Marvs knew Pete—*le frog grand et fou.*

They saluted. Pete walked in the Go-Go. Pete smelled white horse residue. Piss and sweat/stale excrement/cooked dope residue.

The niteclub was *mort.* The niteclub was a dope den. It was ground-floor Hades. It was the river Styx boocoo.

Slopes on pallets. Tube tourniquets. Lighters. Cooking spoons. Dope balloons. Spikes. Fifty junkies/fifty dope beds/fifty launch pads.

Slopes cooked horse. Slopes tied off. Slopes geezed. Slopes swooned. Slopes grinned wide. Slopes sighed.

Pete walked through it. Marvs and Can Laos sold balloons. Marvs and Can Laos sold spikes. Pete walked upstairs—dig it—there's the river Styx revived.

More slopes on pallets. More tube ties. More needles. More toe-crack injections. More arm and leg pops.

Pete walked upstairs. Pete hit the lab door. Pete saw a Can Lao cat. He saw Pete. He knew Pete—*le frog fou.*

Pete dropped the satchel. Pete talked Anglo-gook:

"Equipment. From Wayne Tedrow. I leave with you."

The Can Lao smiled. The Can Lao bowed. The Can Lao reached and grabbed.

Pete said, "Open up. I check lab now."

The Can Lao bristled. The Can Lao blocked the door. The Can Lao pulled a belt piece. The Can Lao snapped the slide.

The door popped open. A gook stepped out. Pete caught a view: trays/sorting chutes/bindles prepacked.

The gook bristled. The gook slammed the door. The gook blocked Pete's view. The gook braced the Can Lao. They jabbered *en gook.* They eyed *le frog fou.*

Pete got goose bumps. Pete hinked out. Pete hinked out boocoo.

They sold balloons downstairs. They packaged two ways upstairs.

They sold bindle pops too. That implied wiiiiide distribution. That implied upscale use.

The gook walked downstairs. The gook walked fast. The gook slung a duffel bag. The Can Lao re-bristled. Pete bowed and smiled. Pete pidgin-gooked:

"Is alright. You good man. I go now."

The Can Lao smiled. The Can Lao de-bristled. Pete waved bye-bye.

He walked downstairs. He held his nose. He grazed pallets and squashed turds. He walked outside. He looked around. He saw the gook.

He's on the street. He's walking south. He's got that duffel bag.

Pete tailed him.

The gook walked the dock. The gook cut inland. The gook walked Dal To Street. It was hot. The street teemed. It's a slopehead ant farm run amok.

Pete stood out. Pete duck-walked low. Pete shaved half his height. The gook walked fast. The gook plowed monks. Pete huffed keeping up.

The gook cut east. The gook bopped down Tam Long. The gook swung down a warehouse block. The sidewalk narrowed. Foot traffic thinned. Pete saw Can Laos straight up.

Can Lao classics—goons in civvies—perched outside a warehouse. Cabs out front—good numbers—cabs perched down the block.

The gook stopped. A Can Lao checked his duffel. A Can Lao got the door. The gook walked in the warehouse. A Can Lao slammed the door. A Can Lao double-locked.

Six buildings down. Side alleys between each one. One connecting alley in back.

Pete walked.

He cut sideways. He hit the back alley. He cut down six buildings. He walked half a block.

Six warehouses/all glazed cement/all three-story jobs.

He cut back streetside. He saw first-floor windows. He heard the Can Laos out front. The windows were covered/mesh over glass/burglar-proof stuff.

Pete checked a window. Pete saw light through glass.

He took a breath. He grabbed the mesh. He pulled it back. He made a space. He made a fist. He punched the glass out.

He saw pallets. He saw tourniquets. He saw white arms tied up. He saw GIs buy bindles. He saw GIs cook horse. He saw GIs shoot up.

He slept bad. He slept weird. Jet lag plus Nembutal. He dreamed bad. He saw vices and crossbars. He saw white kids geezing up.

He woke up. He got some focus. He de-raged. He called John Stanton. He said I'm fried. I can't see straight. Let's meet tomorrow night. Stanton laughed. Stanton said why not?

Pete sedated. Pete reslept. Pete roused and jumped up. Dream shots reran wide awake—all broken-glass shots.

That boy with the tattoos. That boy with the gone eyes. That boy with the spike in his shvantz.

Pete hired a cab. Pete hunkered low. Pete ran tail ops. Cab stakeout by Hotel Montrachet—John Stanton's billet-drop.

He got more focus. The sleep helped. He totaled it all up. One GI dope den/*one at least*—kadre kode breach.

Don't sell to GIs. It's sacrilege. Sell and die hard. Stanton knew it. Stanton cosigned it. Stanton said Mr. Kao agreed. Ditto all the Can Lao.

Stanton assured Pete. Stanton assuaged Pete. Stanton puffed and mollified.

Mr. Kao ran dope Saigon-wide. Mr. Kao ran the Can Lao. Stanton knew Kao. Stanton quoted Kao: Me no push to GIs!

He had that much. That to start. "That" could go wide.

It was hot. The cab broiled. A dash fan swirled. It stirred hot air. It stirred gas fumes. It stirred tailpipe farts.

The Montrachet boomed. The MACV brass loved it. Dig the bay windows with grenade nets.

Pete watched the door. The driver ran the radio. The driver played Viet rock. The Bleatles and the Bleach Boys—all gook redubbed.

9:46 a.m. 10:02, 10:08. Fuck, this could go on—

There's Stanton.

He's walking out. He's got a briefcase. He shags a cab quick. Pete nudged his driver—tail that cab quick.

Stanton's cab pulled out. Pete's cab pulled up. A cab pulled between them. Cabs boxed them in. Cab traffic stalled and sat.

Traffic moved. They got free. They drove south. They drove slow. They snail-trailed.

The driver was good. The driver stayed close. The driver laid back discreet. They drove south. They hit Tam Long Street. They hit that warehouse block.

Stanton's cab braked. Stanton's cab stopped at *the* warehouse. Two Can Laos walked straight up.

They saw Stanton. They heel-clicked. They passed an envelope. Pete watched. Pete's cab hovered back.

Stanton's cab gunned it. Stanton's cab hauled south. Pete's cab pulled out and tailed back. A truck cut between them. Stanton's cab cut west. Pete's cab blew a red light.

Stanton's cab stopped. It's halfway down a side street. It's an all-warehouse block.

A short street/six warehouses/*good* warehouse block.

All Can Lao–guarded. Cabs perched curbside. Cabs perched down the block.

Pete watched. His cab idled. His cab hovered back.

The Can Laos ran up. The Can Laos swarmed Stanton's cab. The Can Laos dropped envelopes. A warehouse door popped. Four GIs walked out. Four GIs weaved on white horse.

Stanton's cab U-turned. Stanton's cab passed Pete's cab. Pete hunkered waaay low. Stanton's cab turned east. Pete's cab tailed it. Pete's cab tailed discreet.

Traffic slogged. Snail trail. Fucking turtle speed. Pete prickled. Pete chain-smoked. Pete chewed Tums.

They hit Tu Do Street. Stanton's cab stopped.

Pete knew the spot. One TV supply store/one CIA front. One door guard/one jarhead PFC/carbine at high port.

Stanton got out. Stanton grabbed his briefcase. Stanton walked in. Pete grabbed his binoculars. Pete framed the door.

The cab idled. His view bounced. His view settled flat. He checked the window. He saw drapes. They blocked his view.

He caught the jarhead. He got him in close. He got his carbine. He got the barrel. He got a stamped code.

He resighted. He got in *close*-close. Weird—a three-zero code—per Bob Relyea's stock.

The driver cut his engine. Pete timed Stanton's trip. Ten minutes/twelve/fourt—

There:

Stanton walks out. Stanton shags his cab. Stanton takes off.

Pete nudged the driver—you stay here now. Pete walked to the shop. The jarhead saw him. The jarhead snapped to.

Pete smiled. "It's all right, son. I'm Agency, and all I need are directions."

The kid unsnapped. "Uh . . . yessir."

"I'm new here. Can you point me to the Hotel Catinat?"

"Uh . . . yessir. It's straight left down Tu Do."

Pete smiled. "Thanks. And by the way, that code stamp on your rifle intrigues me. I'm ex-Corps myself, and I've never seen that designation."

The kid smiled. "It's an exclusive CIA allotment designation, sir. You'll never see it on regular military ordnance."

Pete got pinpricks. Pete got goose bumps. Pete got this cold flush.

He held it close. He held it calm. He didn't blow up. He hit the Catinat. He chained coffee and cigarettes. He racked logic up.

Call it:

The three-zero code/strict CIA/*non*-military.

Bob Relyea lied. Bob Relyea konned the kadre. John Stanton helped him. Bob's gun heists and "pilferings": bullshit.

Call it:

Stanton got the guns. Per some kickback scheme. His CIA pals helped. They took dope profits. They fake-purchased guns. They laundered dope cash. They paid a CIA source. Said source supplied guns. Stanton and *who else* made money?

Stanton and Bob. Carlos logically. Trace it back. Track the time line. Trust the time line logically.

Stanton knows Mr. Kao. Mr. Kao pushes white horse. Mr. Kao shares kadre lab space. Kao runs dope camps. Kao ships to Europe. Kao exports there exclusively. Kao runs Saigon dope pads. Kao excludes GIs. Kao pushes to gooks exclusively.

Bullshit.

Kao and Stanton were jungled up. They ran Saigon dope properties. Said properties serviced gooks. Said properties serviced GIs.

Warehouse dope pads/seven minimum/kadre kode breach. Death sentence/no recourse/kadre kode breach.

Backtrack:

It's 9/65. Kao starts selling dope. Kao tells Stanton this: Me bossman. I run Can Lao. We share lab space. I no hook GIs.

Stanton kowtowed. Kao *bought* lab space. Stanton told Pete. Stanton showed Pete a ledger for proof.

Stanton lubed Pete. Stanton supplied facts and figures. Stanton supplied phony proof.

Backtrack:

Tran Lao Dinh kills dope slaves. Tran Lao Dinh steals M-base. Tran Lao Dinh resists torture. Pete fries his gonads. J. P. Mesplède assists.

Tran said I steal dope. I sell to Marvs then. That all I do. Pete persisted—give me more details—Mesplède shot Tran some juice.

Tran ad-libbed then. Tran dumped his hot seat. Tran electrified.

Pete talked to Stanton. Pete told Tran's story. Pete logicked it through:

Tran stole the base. Tran sold it to Kao. Tran did not snitch Kao. Stanton bought Pete's logic. Stanton praised Pete's logic. Stanton signed Pete's logic through.

Make the jump:

Tran worked for *Stanton*. Tran roamed Tiger Kamp. Tran was *Stanton's* pet gook. Tran steals base on Stanton's orders. Tran supplies Kao. Tran fears *Stanton*. Tran won't snitch *him*. Tran fries with glee.

Kall it kold—Stanton and Kao are kolleagues. It goes back to '65. Kadre kode breach/death decree/retroactive.

Jump two:

Pete rotates. Wayne rotates. Pete moves stateside. Laurent's there. Ditto Flash. They funnel stateside. Stanton stays in-country. Ditto Mesplède. Tiger Kamp runs low-supervised. The war escalates. More troops pass through. The kadre hits Saigon half-assed.

Shit percolates. It's outside their view. It's covert supervised. Thus Stanton-vetted dope pads sell dope to GIs.

Two years in? Maybe one. Maybe Tet-time stuff.

Bogus gun sales. GI dope sales—kadre kode breach. Stanton's nailed. Bob's nailed—kadre kode breach. Who else made money? Who else gets breached?

Pete chained cigarettes. Pete sweated gobs. Pete mainlined caffeine. He brainstormed in bed. He sopped up his clothes. He soaked up the sheets.

His logic felt strong. His logic felt big. His logic felt incomplete. His pulse raced. His chest pinged. He got bips to his feet.

Stanton said, "You look tired."

Drinks at the Montrachet. Code 3 Tet Alert. More door guards. More bomb nets. More fear.

"Travel fucks with me. You know that."

"Unnecessary travel, too."

Pete seized up. Pete juked his performance. Get mad/stay mad/reveal shit.

"What are you saying?"

"I'm saying I've got eyes. You flew over to convince me to expand the business, but I'm going to say no and go you one better. I'm glad you're here, because I owe it to you to tell you to your face."

Pete flushed. Pete felt it—blood to the face.

"I'm listening."

"I'm disbanding the operation. The whole funnel. Tiger Kamp through to Bay St. Louis."

Pete flushed. Pete felt it—cardiac hues.

"Why? Give me one good fucking reason."

Stanton stabbed his swizzle stick. A piece broke off and flew.

"One, the Hughes thing has brought too much attention on Vegas, and Carlos and the Boys want to reinstate the no-dope rule. Two, the war's out of control, and it's become too unpopular at home. There's too many journalists and TV people in-country who'd love to nail some rogue CIA men for doing what we do. Three, our on-island dissidents are getting nowhere, Castro's in to stay, and my Agency colleagues all agree that it's time to pull the plug."

Pete flushed. Pete felt it—deep purple hues. *Be shocked/be pissed/be irate.*

"Four years, John. Four years and all that work for *this?*"

Stanton sipped his martini. "It's over, Pete. Sometimes the ones who care the most are the ones least able to admit it."

Pete gripped his glass. Pete snapped the rim. Ice chips spritzed and spewed. He grabbed a napkin. He blotted blood. He stanched cut residue.

Stanton leaned in. "I cut Mesplède loose. I'm selling Tiger Kamp to Mr. Kao, and I'm leaving for the States tomorrow. I'm going to disband the Mississippi end of the team and make one last Cuban run to pacify Fuentes and Arredondo."

Pete squeezed his napkin. Scotch burned the cuts. Glass shards worked through.

Stanton said, "We did what we could for the Cause. There's some consolation there."

Cab stakeout 2. 6:00 a.m./the Montrachet cab line/heat and cab fumes.

Pete hunkered low. Pete watched the door. Pete ran logic through: Stanton's disbanding/Stanton's regrouping/Stanton's kutting kadre kosts and konnektions.

Pete yawned. Pete got zero sleep. Pete prowled bars past 2:00. Pete found Mesplède. He was pissed and drunk. He was fried on his frog ass boocoo.

Stanton sacked him. Mesplède raged—*le cochon/le putain du monde.*

Pete gauged Mesplède. Mesplède gauged sincere. Mesplède gauged non-Stantonite. Pete rigged a test. Pete rigged a tour.

They drove by the dope cribs. They saw cabs pull up. They saw GIs walk out. They saw GIs bop zombified.

Mesplède was shocked. Mesplède vibed *très* sincere and *très* horrified. *On va tuer le cochon. Le cochon va mourir.*

Pete said yes. Pete amended. Pete said Die Tough.

It was hot. It was a.m.-sticky. The dash fan puffed. Pete hunkered low. Pete watched the door. Pete chewed Tums.

6:18. 6:22. 6:29. Fuck, this could go on—

There's Stanton.

With a suitcase. Errands first? *Then* the airport?

Stanton got a cab. The cab pulled out. The cab pulled out slow. Pete nudged his driver—tail that cab fast.

The driver gunned it. A cab cut him off. The driver swung around fast. Tu Do was busy. Gun trucks goosed traffic chop-chop.

Stanton's cab cut south. Pete's cab bird-dogged it. Pete's cab stuck two car lengths back. A rickshaw cut in. A coolie lugged cargo—tail cover boocoo.

Traffic slowed. They drove south. They bopped toward the docks.

Pete's cab goosed the rickshaw. The driver rode his horn. The coolie flipped him off. Pete sighted in. Pete watched Stanton's cab antenna. It wiggles/it weaves/it tracks good.

They hit the docks. Pete saw warehouse blocks. Pete saw loooong buildings laid out. Stanton's cab braked. Stanton's cab stopped. Stanton got out.

The rickshaw passed him. Pete's cab passed him. Pete ducked and looked back. Stanton grabbed his suitcase. Stanton walked. Stanton unlocked a warehouse.

He did it mock-cool. He looked around. He stepped in. He pulled the door shut.

Stanton's cab waited. Pete's cab U-turned. Pete's cab parked down the block. Pete swiveled the fan. Pete ate hot air and watched.

Time the visit. Do it now. Run your time clock.

Pete checked his watch dial. The second hand swept. Six minutes/nine/eleven.

Stanton walked out. Stanton still had his suitcase. Stanton locked the door up.

He shagged his cab. He stretched and yawned. The cab took off northbound—toward Tan Son Nhut.

Pete paid his driver. Pete got out and walked. The cab peeled off.

The warehouse stretched. It ran two football fields plus. One story/one steel door. Side walkways adjacent. Mesh-covered windows inset.

Pete pushed the buzzer. Chimes ricocheted. No footsteps/no voices/no peephole slid back. Two walkways. Side windows. No witnesses out.

Pete cut south. Pete hit the near walkway. Pete took his coat off.

He found a window. He flexed his hands. He peeled the mesh back. His bad hand tore. Glass specks got reimbedded.

He made a fist. He wrapped it up. He made a coat-fabric glove. He punched out the window. Glass blew inward.

He hauled himself up. He squeezed through the frame space. He rolled to the floor. His hand throbbed. He squeezed blood out. He patted the wall. He caught a switch. Lights went on—two football fields plus.

He saw a space. He saw a floor. He saw *merchandise*. He saw swag. He saw rows and rows. He saw piles and piles.

He walked. He touched. He looked. He counted. He inventoried. He saw:

Sixty boxes stuffed with watches—pure gold waist-high. Mink coats dumped like trash—forty-three piles hip-high. Six hundred Jap motorcycles—laid side to side. Antique furniture—twenty-three rows stretched wide.

New cars—parked side by side. Thirty-eight rows/twenty-two cars per/stretched out lengthwise.

Bentleys. Porsches. Aston-Martin DB-5s. Volvos/Jaguars/Mercedes.

Pete walked the rows. Pete ID'd booty. Pete saw export tags attached. Point of shipment: Saigon. Point of entry: U.S.

Kall it easy. Kall it kold. Kall it dead:

Swag. Black-market-purchased. Non-U.S.-derived. Swag from Europe/Great Britain/the East.

Stanton ran the gig. His CIA pals helped. They bootjacked kadre money. They laundered it. They glommed luxury shit.

Stanton's disbanding. They ship the goods now. They ship duty-free. The Boys help them. Carlos walks point. They resell near-retail. Carlos takes points. Carlos pays the Stanton guys. Cold millions accrue.

The dope plan. The funnel. Cash for the Cause. Wrong—the Cause was THIS.

Pete walked the warehouse. Pete kicked tires. Pete smelled leather seats. Pete flicked antennas. Pete buffed rosewood. Pete fondled mink.

THIS.

He tracked logic. He looked for loopholes. He got none.

And:

Stanton stopped here. Stanton lugged in his suitcase.

Why?

He dropped something off. He picked something up.

Which?

Pete walked the walls. Pete tapped the walls. Pete tapped whole cement. No wall panels or hidey holes—shit.

Pete checked the floor. Pete looked for chipped paint. Pete looked for off-color streaks. Pete got whole cement/solid/no streaks.

Pete checked the ceiling. It was solid cement. No patches/no caulking/no streaks.

No bathroom. No storerooms. No closets. Four walls/one looooong strrrretch/two football fields plus.

Something was *somewhere*. Something was *here*.

Cars/minks/watches. Motorcycles/antiques. It's a day's work. It's needle meets haystack. It's do it anyway.

He walked the rows. He plowed watch piles. He dug through mink. He grabbed. He touched. He fished.

Forty-three piles/sixty boxes—shit.

He walked the rows. He popped antique drawers. He rifled and dipped.

Twenty-three rows—shit.

His stomach growled. Hours flew. No food and no fucking sleep.

He checked the motorcycles. He opened saddle bags. He popped gas caps and peeked.

Six hundred bikes—shit.

He checked the cars. He checked row by row. He checked twenty-two times thirty-eight.

He popped hoods. He popped glove compartments. He popped trunks. He checked under rugs. He checked engine mounts. He checked under seats.

Porsches first. Bentleys next—shit.

The space went dark. He worked by touch. Volvos/Jaguars/DB-5s. He got the feel. He worked fast—Braille by necessity.

Five models down. One left: Mercedes.

He hit the top row. He braced the first car. He snapped the hood. He touched the valve covers. He touched the air cleaner. He brushed a cylinder ledge.

Wait—feel the bump—Braille by necess—

He felt the bump. He felt tape. He pulled. Something tore loose. Said something was textured and flat.

Rectangular. Paged. A long book.

He grabbed it. He reached up and popped a wind wing. He tapped the key and headlights. Good kraut autowerk—fog lights beamed out.

He got down. He turned pages. He read by fog light. One cross-columned listing ledger—names/money/dates.

Key dates. Back to late '64. The kadre ops inception.

Names:

Chuck Rogers. Tran Lao Dinh. Bob Relyea. Laurent Guéry. Flash Elorde. Fuentes/Wenzel/Arredondo.

Payouts/monthly stipends/covert. Odd spic names/cross-columned/ starred with "CM"s.

Kall it: CM for Cuban Militia. Cuban passage paid in full.

Pete scanned columns. Pete scanned dates. Pete scanned names. Names stated/names absent/names unindicted: His name/Wayne's/Mesplède's.

Money paid out. Loyalty purchased. Kadre kode breach.

Guéry and Stanton ran poly tests. They were all *lies*. Flash snuck into Cuba. It was a *lie*. Cuban dissension—one sustained *lie*. Safe runs to Cuba—one prepaid *lie*. Cuban Militia sold out as fodder—part of the *lie*. Guns sent to Cuba—funneled to where?—key to the *lie*.

Cars.

Watches.

Furs.

Jap motorcycles.

Faggot antiques.

Years gone. One heart attack. THIS.

Pete dropped the ledger. Pete flipped the car key. Pete killed the fog lights.

The dark felt right. The dark scared him. IT WAS ALL A BIG FUCKING LIE.

DOCUMENT INSERT: 3/25/68. Telephone call transcript. Taped by:
BLUE RABBIT. Marked: "FBI-Scrambled"/"Stage-1 Covert"/
"Destroy Without Reading in the Event of My Death." Speaking:
BLUE RABBIT, FATHER RABBIT.

BR: It's me, Senior. You hear those clicks?

FR: I know. Scrambler technology.

BR: Are you ready for some good news?

FR: If it relates to D-day, I am.

BR: It's connected. That's for damn sure.

FR: Have we got a date? Have we got a loc—

BR: My men found Wendell Durfee.

FR: Oh, sweet Jesus.

BR: He's in L.A. He's got a room on skid row.

FR: I hear the saints, Dwight. They're singing hymns all for me.

BR: My men make him for some rape-snuffs. You think he
developed a taste with Lynette?

FR: How could he? She always struck me as frigid.

BR: RED RABBIT's on the move. I'm looking at D-day for sometime next month.

FR: Shitfire. Let's bring Wayne in, then.

BR: My guys have got Durfee staked out. I'll wait a few days,
then have some jig stiff a call through Sonny Liston.

FR: Hymns, Dwight. I mean it. And all in stereo.

BR: You think Wayne's ready for this?

FR: I know he is.

BR: I'll patch you when I've got more news.

FR: Make it good news.

BR: We're close, Senior. I've got this feeling.

FR: From your mouth to God's ears.

107

(Mexico City, 3/26/68)

Show-and-tell:

Sam G.'s villa / the rumpus room / drinks with umbrellas.

A valet toiled. Said valet dished hors d'oeuvres. Said valet built gin slings.

Littell ran charts. Littell ran easel graphs. Sam watched. Moe watched. Carlos twirled his umbrella. Santo and Johnny yawned.

Littell jabbed a pointer. "We're getting our prices. Mr. Hughes should have all his hotels by the end of the year."

Sam yawned. Moe stretched. Carlos ate quesadillas.

Littell said, "There's a garbage-hauling business in Reno that I think we should take over first. It's nonunion, which helps. All told, we're on schedule in every area except one."

Moe laughed. "That is vintage Ward. Lay out this big preamble and stop short of the point."

Sam said, "Ward's a cock tease."

Santo said, "Ward dropped out of the seminary. They teach you to string things out there."

Littell smiled. "Mr. Hughes is insisting that we enforce a 'Negro sedation policy' at his hotels. He knows that it's unrealistic, but he's dug in."

Moe said, "The shvartzes need sedation. They're creating too much social unrest."

Sam said, "You don't rape and pillage when you're sedated."

Carlos said, "The sedation concept is stale bread. We're closing down Pete's business."

Littell coughed. "Why? I thought Pete's thing was solvent."

Sam looked at Carlos. Carlos shook his head.

"Solvent is as solvent does. It got us what we wanted, so we're cutting it loose."

Looks passed: Johnny to Santo/Santo to Sam.

Sam coughed. "We're covered in Costa Rica, Nicaragua, Panama, and the D.R. These guys I greased did not need a road map."

Santo coughed. "The U.S. dollar is the international language. You say 'casino gambling' and it paints a big picture."

Johnny coughed. "The U.S. dollar buys influence on both sides of the political line."

Santo coughed. "We've got our bearded pal to thank for that."

Moe looked at Santo. Sam looked at Santo. Santo went oops. The Boys regrouped. The Boys sipped drinks. The Boys snagged hors d'oeuvres.

Littell flipped graph sheets. Littell gauged the gaffe.

They screwed Pete. They screwed Pete per his Cuban deal—*somehow*. Guns to *Castro? Not* rightists? *Perhaps*. They greased leftists—said "Influence"—Pete's usefulness lapsed. *Maybe/somehow/perhaps*.

I won't tell Pete/they know it/they trust me/they own me.

Sam coughed. Sam cued the valet. Said valet split *rápidamente*.

Carlos said, "We're still waiting to see if LBJ runs again, but we're 99% committed to Nixon."

Santo said, "Nixon's the one."

Sam said, "LBJ can't change Justice Department policy like a new man can."

Johnny said, "Humphrey's too soft on the spooks. I can't see him or LBJ granting that pardon to Jimmy."

Santo said, "Nixon's the guy. He's a shoo-in for the nomination."

Carlos said, "You sit down with him in late June, Ward. Then you can retire."

Santo smiled. "I know someone else who's going to retire."

Sam smiled. "Yeah, per that little box of goodies we got in the mail."

Looks passed: Carlos to Santo/Moe D. to Sam. Santo flushed. Sam went oops.

The plane soared. Air Mexico—Vegas nonstop.

The summit soared. The Boys vouched his plans—no rebuttals/no controversy. The Boys made gaffes. They were niggling for him. They were troubling for Pete.

They dropped the dope biz. That implied trouble. That implied a pissed Pete. No more Cuban runs or Viet ops—*probably*.

The plane banked. Littell saw clouds. White puffs laced with grimey debris.

He called Janice. They talked last night. She was scared. Her cramps were worse. She saw a doctor. He ran some tests.

He cited trauma. It went long untreated. It was Wayne Senior's work. It masked her symptoms. It masked internal damage. It was cancer *possibly*.

She talked scared. She talked strong. She ran litanies: I'm young/it's not *that*/it can't *be*. He calmed her down. He said goodnight. He prayed for her. He said rosaries.

The plane leveled off. Littell shut his eyes. Littell saw Bobby.

Bobby announced. Bobby met the press nine days ago. Bobby said I want it. Bobby voiced policy.

Let's end the war. Let's work for peace. Let's end poverty. Domestic reforms. Peace accords. No *stated* Mob policy.

Prudent Bobby. Sage Bobby. Sound policy.

Barb called him last week. She saw Bobby announce on TV. They talked. They got misty on Bobby.

Barb met Bobby once. It was spring '62. Peter Lawford threw a party. Barb talked to Bobby. Barb liked Bobby then. Barb loved Bobby now. Pete deployed Shakedown Barb. Barb slept with JFK.

Barb laughed. Barb praised Bobby. Barb said he'd kick Dick Nixon's ass. Barb predicted a victory.

A stew walked by. Said stew pushed a snack cart. Littell grabbed a club soda. Littell grabbed the L.A. *Times*.

He creased it out. He saw war headlines. He flipped the fold. Columns jumped. He saw "Poor People's March"/"planning stages"/"momentum." He flipped to page 2. He saw Bobby.

There's Bobby caught candid. He's standing by a putting green. He's near some bungalows. The backdrop's lush. The backdrop's familiar.

Littell squinted. Wait now, what's—

He saw the pathway. He saw the door. He saw the "301." It's the bungalow. It's the "Mob meet spot." It's his gig for Dwight Holly.

Littell dropped the paper. Thoughts jumped and garbled. The Boys/that gaffe/"box of goodies."

108

(Los Angeles, 3/30/68)

Death kit:
Four hypos / full loads / pre-mixed: Big "H" and Novocain anesthetic.

One .44 mag. One silencer. One roll of duct tape. One paper-bag carry-all. One pack of moist towelettes.

We're here. We're at 5th and Stanford. It's Skid Row. It's Bum Hell.

Wayne lounged. Wayne watched the hotel. Wayne jiggled his sack. He stood outside a blood bank. Bums hobnobbed. Nurses culled donors up.

He's there. He's in the Hiltz Hotel. He's in room 402. It's four floors up.

Wayne watched the front door. Wayne savored. Wayne stalled.

He'd rotated south. He hit Bob's kompound. He found it cleaned out. It vibed raid. It vibed heedless. It vibed state cops. Bob had friends. Bob was Fed-vouched. It vibed *dumb* state cops.

Wayne flew to Vegas then. Wayne checked the Cavern. Wayne picked messages up:

Call Pete. He's in Sparta. Call Sonny.

He called Pete. He got no answer. He called Sonny. Sonny was jazzed. Sonny said, "This nigger called me." Sonny cited said nigger source.

Bam:

Sonny's guy saw Wendell. Wendell was nom-de-plumed. Wendell's now Abdallah X.

It was warm. It was eighty at noon. Skid Row was crammed up. Winos/amputees on skateboards/he-shes rouged up.

They jostled Wayne. Wayne felt zero. Wayne felt ate up. His skin buzzed. He rode eggshells. His bloodstream froze up.

He walked over.

He walked through the front door. He passed bums in the lobby. He passed a TV cranked up.

'68 Novas! Buy now! *Se habla español* at Giant Felix Chevrolet!

A wino convulsed. Wayne dodged his legs. Wayne took side stairs up. He lost his feet. He lost *his* legs. He fought gravity.

He hit the fourth floor landing. He saw the hallway. He saw wood doors inset.

He passed 400. He passed 401. He hit 402. He touched the knob. He turned it. The door popped.

He's right there. He's backlit. You've got window light. There's Wendell in a straight-back chair. There's Wendell with a short-dog.

Wayne stepped inside. Wayne shut the door. Wayne almost threw up. Wendell saw him. Wendell squinted. Wendell grinned all fucked up.

Wayne stood there.

Wendell said, "You looks familiar."

Wayne stood there.

Wendell said, "Give me a hint."

Wayne said, "Dallas." Wayne almost threw up.

Wendell slurped wine. Wendell looked bad. Wendell wore injection welts. Wendell wore needle tracks.

"That's a good hint. Makes me think you a certain husband with a grievance. I've fucking widowered more than a few of them, so that narrows it down somewhat."

Wayne scoped the room. Wayne saw empty short-dogs. Wayne smelled wine upchucked.

Wendell said, "That was some weekend. Remember? The President got shot."

Wayne moved. Wayne took two steps. Wayne kicked out and up. He hit the chair. He hit the jug. He knocked Wendell flat.

Wendell puked wine and bile. Wayne stepped on his neck. Wayne full-weight-pinned him. Wayne dug through his sack.

He grabbed a hypo. Wendell thrashed. He shot his neck up. Wendell de-thrashed. Wendell soared. Wendell went smack-back.

Wayne dropped the hypo. Wayne grabbed a hypo. Wayne shot his hands up. Wendell shuddered. Wendell resoared. Wendell went more smack-back.

Wayne dropped the hypo. Wayne grabbed a hypo. Wayne shot his hips up. Wendell grinned. Wendell soar-soared. Wendell went waaay smack-back.

Wayne dropped the hypo. Wayne grabbed a hypo. Wayne shot his knees up. Wendell grinned. Wendell sooooooared. Wendell smaaacked out and up.

Wayne dropped the hypo. Wayne grabbed the tape. Wayne pulled a strip up. He taped Wendell's mouth. He rolled three loops dense. He cinched Wendell's neck up.

He dropped the tape. He grabbed the mag. He cocked it back. He fixed the silencer. He bent low. Wendell's eyes rolled back.

Wayne grabbed his right hand. Wayne shot off his fingers. Wayne shot off his thumb. Wendell squirmed. Big "H" constrained him. His eyes rolled *waaaay* back.

Wayne dumped the shells. Wayne reloaded. Wayne cocked his piece back. He grabbed Wendell's left hand. He shot off his fingers. He shot off his thumb.

Wendell squirmed. Big "H" constrained him. His eyes rolled *mooooore* back.

Wayne dumped the shells. Wayne reloaded. Wayne cocked his piece back. Wendell puked. Bile blew out his nostrils. Wendell shit in his pants.

Wayne leaned down. Wayne aimed tight. Wayne shot his legs off at the knees. Blood spritzed. Bone chips flew. Wayne grabbed the towelettes.

Wendell's stumps twitched. Wayne grabbed a chair. Wayne watched him bleed to death.

The flight ran late. He flew numb. He dozed L.A. to Vegas. He smelled things that weren't there.

Cordite and blood. Cheap wine. Burned silencer threads.

The plane landed. He got off. He smelled things that weren't there.

Burned bone and vomit. Scented towelettes.

He walked through McCarran. He found a phone. He got an operator. She patched Sparta direct.

He heard eight rings. He got no answer. No Barb and Pete there.

He walked outside. He veered toward the cab line. Two men walked up. They flanked him. They braced him. They slammed a two-cop press.

It's Dwight Holly. It's a swarthy guy. It's that guy Fred Otash.

Shakedown Fred—skinny now—this cadaver.

They grabbed him. They led him. He felt limp. He felt numb. He saw two cars double-parked. He saw a Fed sedan. He saw Wayne Senior's Cadillac.

They stopped between cars. They patted him down. They let him go slack. He stumbled. He almost fell. He smelled Wendell dead.

Holly said, "Durfee wasn't for free."

Otash said, "We stiffed that tipoff through Sonny."

Holly said, "I've got a print transparency on you. If you say no, I'll have a guy roll it around Durfee's room."

Wayne looked at them. Wayne *saw* them. Wayne got *IT*. Wayne Senior/his hate talk/the hate-mail intercepts.

Wayne said, "Who?"

Holly said, "Martin Luther King."

109

(Sparta, 3/31/68)

TV news—breaking:

LBJ's out. The war fucked him up. He won't seek Term Two. It's Humphrey v. Bobby. The race looks tight.

Barb watched the news. Pete watched Barb. Barb dug on the Bobby aspects. The house was cold. Barb's sister was cheap. Barb's sister skimped on the heat.

He flew Saigon to Sparta. Barb welcomed him reluctant. Barb ragged him incessant. Barb ragged his travel-ban breach.

Barb flipped channels. Barb caught war news. Barb caught some Memphis strike.

Trash workers. A support march. One riot so far. Sixty injured/looter damage/one nigger kid dead. Crazy King's there. Crazy King's *between* riots. One "Poor People's" riot on tap.

Barb watched the news. Pete watched Barb. Barb watched the news rapt. Pete popped gum. Pete obeyed Barb's rule—don't smoke inside.

He chewed gum. He chewed double sticks. He fretted shit.

He called Bob's kompound. He got a weird tone. It vibed disconnect. He called the Cavern. He left Wayne a message. Wayne never called back. He punked out. He stalled his speech. He set his flight back.

Barb flipped channels. Barb caught Bobby. Barb caught Crazy King. Pete stood up. Pete blocked the screen. Pete turned off the set.

Barb said, "Shit."

Pete popped his gum. "Hear me out on some things. You'll like part of it."

Barb smiled. "You're getting ready to snow me. I can tell."

"Here's the good part. The Boys want to scuttle the biz, the funnel, and the whole operation. I'm going along with it."

Barb shook her head. "If that was most of it, you'd be smiling."

"You're right. There's mo—"

"I know there's more, I know it's bad, so tell me."

Pete gulped. Pete swallowed. Pete choked his gum back.

"Part of it went bad. I've got to pick Wayne up in Vegas and make one more Cuban run. I need you to hole up somewhere until it's over and I cut some kind of deal with the Outfit."

Barb said, "No."

Boom—case closed—like that.

Pete gulped. "I'll dump Tiger Kab and the Cavern then. We'll go someplace else."

Barb said, "No."

No drumroll—no pause—no inflection.

Pete gulped. "I can finesse it. There's some risk, sure, but I wouldn't do it if I didn't think the Boys would buy my explanation."

Barb said, "No."

No fanfare—all deadpan—no shit.

Pete gulped. Pete coughed his gum up.

"If I don't pay this off, the word will go out. The wrong guys will think, 'He knew the story and let it all go.' They'll start thinking I'm weak, which will cause us trouble somewhere down the line."

Barb said, "No. Whatever *it* is is bullshit, and you know it."

No recourse—I *know* you—that's that. No tears yet—tears pending—eyes wet.

Pete said, "I'll be back when it's over."

Charter flight: La Crosse to Vegas. Junket geeks/smoky cabin/cramped seats.

The geeks were insurance men. The geeks were Shriners and Moose. They drank. They swapped hats. They cracked jokes.

Pete tried to sleep. Pete fucked with IT.

He'd called Stanton. He called looooong distance. He called Saigon to Bay St. Louis. He brought up the Cuban run. He said I want to go. Please let me say adios.

Stanton said yes.

He mopped up in Saigon. He laid cover tracks. He bought weapons. He fixed the warehouse window. He worked on the QT. He installed new glass/new mesh. He called Mesplède. He said *I'll* handle it. He said *I'll* breach the breach.

He bought three guns: one Walther and two Berettas. He bought three silencers. He bought three inside-the-pants rigs.

Booty. Swag. Cars/furs/watches/antiques. THE BIG FUCKING LIE revealed.

The flight bumped. They ran low-pressure sweeps. The junket geeks pawed the stews. The junket geeks laughed. The junket geeks preached.

Pro-war stuff. All clichés. We can't pull out. We'll forfeit Asia. We can't look weak.

Pete shut his eyes. Pete *heard* the geeks. Pete *saw* home movie flicks.

There's Betty Mac. It's visit twelve million. There's Chuck the Vice Freak. There's Barb. She says, "No"—eyes working on tears.

We stand firm. We bong the Cong. We never surrender. We stomp the peace freaks.

It droned on. It went stereophonic. He tried to sleep. He failed. He fought this exhaustion. He got this idea:

Fuck it all. Fuck it now. Forfeit the kadre kode breach.

The plane touched down. Pete got off. Pete walked to Air Midwest.

He bought a ticket. He splurged. He booked first-class to Milwaukee/ connector to Sparta/two flights one-way.

He had a layover. He had four hours to kill.

He walked to the gate lounge. He schlepped his gun bag. He sprawled across four seats. He fell. It was soft and dark. He had newspapers as sheets.

He opened his eyes. He saw ceiling lights. He saw Ward Littell. Ward had his ticket. Ward flicked the edge.

"You were going back. Barb will like that."

Pete sat up. His newspaper sheets fell.

"Jesus, you scared me."

Ward cleaned his glasses. "Barb called. She said you were going south on some insane errand, and could I stop it."

Pete yawned. "And?"

"And I put a few things together and called Carlos."

Pete lit a cigarette. It was 6:10 now. His flight left at 7:00.

"Don't stop there. I want to see where this is going."

Ward coughed. "Part of it is from Carlos, part of it I put together my—"

"Jesus, just tell—"

"Carlos is cutting off your business. It was part of a ruse to get weapons to Castro, so that he could funnel them to rebels in Central

America. It all played into my foreign-casino plan, and I never knew any-thing about it."

Fill-in/paint-by-number/link-the-dots diverse. Stanton and Carlos/the fake funnel/the BIG LIE complete.

"It was a shuck, Ward. The whole thing."

"I know."

"Bob Relyea. What about—"

"He dropped his Klan gig and went off on another operation. Wayne's working with him, and Carlos said that's all he knows."

Pete grabbed the ticket. Ward grabbed it back.

"You flew to Saigon. You put some things together. I'm going off what you told Barb."

Pete grabbed his bag. The guns rubbed and scraped.

"You're leading me. You talked to Barb, you talked to Carlos, you found me. Let's start there."

Ward squared his glasses. "Carlos learned that Stanton, Guéry, and Elorde have been skimming off his portion of the profits. He actually *wants* you to take them and their Cuban contacts out. He said if you do that and another 'small favor,' he'll retire you."

A speaker popped. Flight 49—nonstop to Milwaukee.

"Do you think he means it?"

"Yes. They want to clean this thing up and move on."

Pete checked the gate. The flight crew stood there. Baggage carts rolled.

"Call Barb. Tell her I almost came home."

Ward nodded. Ward crumpled the ticket.

"There's one more thing."

"What's that?"

"Carlos wants you to scalp them."

110

(Memphis, 4/3/68)

Rabbits:
WILD RABBIT. RED RABBIT.
DEAD RABBIT soon.
Wayne pulled curbside.
Wayne parked. Wayne watched the New Rebel Motel.

The Mustang pulled up. Fred O. walked over. The shooter got out. There's skinny Fred O. He's starved to look different. There's skinny Jim Ray. He's starved off crystal meth.

They laughed. They huddled. Fred O. passed the box. It was long and bulky. It contained a 30.06.

Hi-end scope. Geared for soft-point bullets. Contact spread/blunt impact/bad for ballistic IDs.

Jimmy had his rifle. Bob had the same one. Fred O. had rifle 3. It was one-shot test-fired. It was print-smeared by Jimmy.

D-day was tomorrow. Jimmy might shoot. Jimmy might punk out. Bob *will* shoot instead.

Fred O. ran Jimmy. Fred O. said he'd shoot. Fred O. was sure.

The Plan:

There's a rooming house. It's a wino pad. It's across from the Lorraine Motel. King's at the Lorraine. He's in room 306. It's off a balcony. There's a wino pad vacancy. Fred O. made sure. Fred O. held said flop for a week.

He "checked in." He stayed away. He'll "check out" tomorrow. Jimmy will check in. He'll get that room. It's near a bathroom perch-site.

He might shoot. He might punk out. Thus Bob shoots instead.

There's a brush patch by the wino pad. It supplies cover. It supplies trajectory. The wino pad runs back to Main Street. The Lorraine's on Mulberry.

Jimmy shoots. Jimmy exits—way *off* Mulberry. He wipes his rifle. He drops the rifle. He drops it in a doorway.

Fred O. lurks near. Fred O. grabs the rifle. Fred O. drops rifle 3. It's print-smeared. It's smeared by Jimmy. It's smeared by transparency.

Jimmy splits. Jimmy drives to the safe house. Wayne's waiting there. It's a cheap apartment. It's furnished.

With booze empties/dope baggies/needles. With white powder/dope fits/crystal meth.

With a suicide note—forged by Fred Otash.

I flew on meth. I killed Nigger King. I'm scared now. I escaped Jeff City. I refuse to go back. I'm a hero. I'm a martyr. Hey, World, take that.

Wayne waits. Wayne geezes Jimmy up. Wayne shoots Jimmy then. Jimmy dies on a speed rush.

Panic. Suicide. Your stock "lone assassin"—gone on crystal meth.

Wayne watched the New Rebel. Fred O. stood outside. Jimmy walked in. Fred O. looked over. Fred O. saw Wayne and winked.

Wayne winked back. Wayne shoved off. Wayne drove to the Lorraine Motel.

He parked close in. He checked the lot. He checked the balcony. He checked the wino pad. He checked the brush patch. He checked the street.

The patch was thick. It flanked a cement wall. A passageway led to Main Street. They perch in the patch. They shoot or don't shoot. They walk to Main Street.

Wayne watched the motel. Negro men hobnobbed. They stood on that balcony.

No cops attendant. Dwight Holly confirmed said. Dwight Holly tapped cop frequencies. Memphis was uptight. They had riots and marches. They had cops alert on Code 3. More shit was planned. One more march boded. It was set for April 5th.

He'd be dead. Memphis would burn. Wayne *knew* it. Jimmy would shoot. Fred O. said so. Fred *knew* it.

Fred O. ran Jimmy. Jimmy ran L.A. to Memphis. Jimmy made stops in between. Jimmy was wacked. Jimmy took hypnosis courses. Jimmy went to bartender's school. Jimmy shot meth. Jimmy bought skin mags. Jimmy jacked off and read porno books.

Jimmy joined the Friends of Rhodesia. Jimmy placed swinger ads. Jimmy got rhinoplasty. Jimmy stalked Dr. King in L.A. Jimmy stalked March 16/17.

Fred O. surveilled him. Fred O. *knew then:* He'll shoot proactively. Fred O. recruited him *proactive.* Fred O. was cloaked as "Raul."

Fred had King's travel plans. Dwight Holly pouched them. They came from an FBI source.

King went to Selma. He arrived on 3/22. Fred O. and Jim Ray were there. The conditions were sub-par. Fred O. stalled D-day.

King stayed in Selma. Jimmy drove to Atlanta. He knew King lived there. King foxed him. King flew to Jew York. King had business there.

Dwight got a tip. His Fed source pouched it. RED RABBIT to Memphis. Arrival 3/28. There's a garbage strike there.

Dwight recruited Wayne on 3/30. "Raul" goosed Jimmy Ray. Cash perks and meth—Memphis dead-ahead.

It was NOW. Fred said so. Fred knew it. Jimmy was strung out. Jimmy craved the "Bounty." Jimmy craved this mock Holy Grail.

Wayne watched the balcony. Wayne saw activity.

Dwight ran death-threat checks. The Memphis Feds supplied facts. King logged eighty-one death threats. Klan threats mostly.

King blew them off. King shined them on. King scorned security.

Wayne watched the balcony. Wayne saw Dr. King. They went back. They intertwined. They had symmetry.

He went to Little Rock. He enforced integration. He saw King there. He saw that fuck film. It was FBI-shot. He saw King there. He killed three coloreds. King indicted Las Vegas. King almost went there. He killed Bongo in Saigon. King hated his war. He killed Wendell Durfee. Wayne Senior found Durfee. King served his vengeance cause.

Wayne Senior knew:

You *want* it. I *made* you. It's *yours.*

He killed Durfee. Dwight suborned him. He joined Wayne Senior's cause. It's Wayne Senior's Hate School. It's the postgrad course. Coloreds foist chaos. Coloreds breed discord. Coloreds spawn doss.

Wayne Senior said you learned. Wayne Senior said you paid. Wayne Senior said you earned this shot.

Wayne Senior bragged:

Ward Littell's retiring. Mormon heavies love me. *I'll* get his Hughes spot. It's certain. I know. I was told.

Carlos Marcello called me. We talked. We discussed Littell's retirement. We discussed general business. We discussed the Hughes spot.

Carlos said this:

Littell worked for Hughes *and* me. *You* take that full spot. Littell suborns Nixon. Littell retires then. *You* go from there. *You* work with Nixon. *You* secure our requests. *You* insure our warranty.

Wayne Senior said this:

My son the chemist. You know him. *I* know he's outgrown Pete B.

Carlos said this:

We'll find a spot. We'll bring Wayne in. It's adios to Pete B.

Wayne watched the balcony. Wayne saw King laugh. Wayne saw King slap his knees.

I hate smart. I've killed five. You can't outhate me.

111

(Bay St. Louis, 4/3/68)

Castoff—9:16 p.m. Light wind. Course south-southeast.

The last gun run. The kadre kurtain kall.

Pete walked the deck. His pants fit tight. He wore three guns in. He wore his shirt out. His gut bulged. The silencers chafed.

He flew in. They held castoff. He flew in late. He looked for Wayne in Vegas. He tapped out. Carlos called him.

Carlos was Carlos. Fuck the Big Lie. Carlos was brusque:

"You found some things out. So what? You were never dumb, Pete."

"Bob's off somewhere. He's working with Wayne. He don't get hurt like the rest."

"Don't act aggrieved. Bring me some scalps. Remember, you owe me for Dallas."

The boat pitched. The boat dipped. The boat leveled. Pete walked the deck. Pete thought it through. Pete fought butterflies.

They're below deck. Get them alone/get them together. Hit the arms locker. Get a shotgun. Choke a tight spread.

Pilot the boat. You know how to. Head for Cuban seas. Lure Fuentes on. Lure Arredondo. Kill them/scalp them/dump them. Scalp and dump the rest.

Six snuffs. Butch haircuts. Scalped per kadre kode breach.

The boat ran smooth. Automatic pilot. Glassy Gulf seas.

Pete climbed the bridge. Pete read dials. Pete ran instrument checks. It's OK. You know how. You'll do it.

He walked below. He got flutters—biiiiig butterflies. The main cabin stood full: Stanton/Guéry/Elorde/Dick Wenzel.

Pete jittered. Pete twitched. Pete bumped his head on a beam.

Stanton said, "They don't build these boats for giants."

Guéry said, "Which is my problem, too."

Flash said, "I do not have that problem."

Wenzel said, "You're a shrimp, but you're dangerous."

They laughed. Pete laughed. Pete went lightheaded.

Four men/no sidearms/good. All relaxed/sipping scotch/good.

Note this oversight. Note this fuck-up and glitch:

You *could* have brought Seconal. You *could* have spiked the scotch. You *could* have killed them asleep.

Stanton said, "We'll refuel at Snipe Key."

Wenzel said, "They're meeting us eighty knots out. It's the only way to rendezvous before dawn."

Pete coughed. "It's my fault. I was late."

Flash shook his head. "The last time. We no go without you."

Guéry shook his head. "You were always the one with the . . . *qu'est-ce que* . . . 'greatest commitment.' "

Wenzel slugged scotch. "I'll miss the runs. I hate the Reds as much as the next white man."

Flash smiled. "I am not white."

Wenzel smiled. "In your heart you are."

Pete faked a yawn. His chest pinged. His pulse raced.

"I'm tired. I'm going to lie down for a bit."

The guys smiled. The guys nodded. The guys grinned and stretched. Pete walked back. Pete shut the door. Pete ran a cabin check:

Four units/low bulkheads/four sleeping sacks. Please get drunk. Please crap out. Please crap out in shifts.

He opened the cargo hold. The boat rolled. The boat rolled *très* light. It rolled too drifty—sans-gun-ballast light.

He popped the storage door. He looked in. He hit the light.

Bam:

Empty/*no* guns/*no* ordnance packed tight.

He got butterflies. Huge now. Sized like King Kong.

No guns. *No gun run.* Loose ends scheduled up. *They* kill *you.* They dump *you.* They kill Fuentes and Arredondo.

The boat pitched. Pete dug his legs in. Pete popped the shotgun rack. He got moths—big fuckers—way up in his chest.

He pulled shotguns. He worked slides. He popped the shells chambered in. Butterfingers: four shotguns/shells popping/no hands to catch said.

Shells dropping. Shells spinning. Shells hitting the floor deck. Shells skitting and rolling free.

He grabbed them. He stuffed his pants. He stuffed his teeth. He fumbled the shotguns. He refilled the rack. He heard the cargo door creak.

He turned around. He saw Wenzel. He looked dumb. He looked *caught.* He had shells in his teeth.

Wenzel shut the door. Wenzel stepped close. Wenzel made fists.

"What the fuck are—"

Pete looked around. Pete saw the flare gun. It's close. It's on a wall hook.

He spit the shells out. He stepped back. He grabbed it and aimed. He pulled the trigger. The flare ignited. The flare hit Wenzel's face. Wenzel screeched. His hair burned. He batted his face.

The flare dropped. It burned Wenzel's clothes. It shot flames chest to feet.

Pete stepped in. Pete grabbed Wenzel's neck. Pete snuffed hair flames. He snapped left. He burned his hands. He snapped right.

Wenzel convulsed. Wenzel went limp. Wenzel's eyebrows shot flames. Pete threw him down. Pete ripped his shirt off. Pete snuffed the flames.

The flare fizzled out. The door stayed shut. *Contained* stink and flames.

Pete flexed his hand. Burn blisters popped. Pete anchored his legs.

Now.

They'll miss him. They'll need him. They'll yell. The boat's rolling. It's on auto pilot. Wenzel stays on call.

Now.

Pete clenched up. Pete listened—ear to the door.

Nothing.

He pulled his Walther. He cocked it. He opened the door. One walkway/four cabins/two per side wall.

Ten yards up: the main cabin/set perpendicular/with the door shut.

Pete inched up. Pete took baby steps—slow. He hit cabin 1. He looked in. He braced the door.

Nobody.

Pete inched up. Pete took baby steps—slow. He hit cabin 2. He looked in. He braced the door.

Nobody.

Pete inched up. Pete took baby steps—slow. He hit cabin 3. He looked in. He braced the door.

There's Flash. He's sacked out asleep.

Pete walked up. Pete aimed close. Muzzle to hairline/silencer tight. He shot once. His piece went pffft. Brains doused the bed.

Pete walked out. Pete took baby steps—slow. He hit cabin 4. He looked in. He braced the door.

Nobody.

Pete inched up. Pete ate jumbo moths and butterflies. Pete popped the main cabin door.

Nobody—all hands on deck. *Slow now*—with a deeeeeep breath.

He did it. He walked topside. He took baby steps. He got fifty-foot butterflies. His breath tugged. His hands shook. His sphincter blew. He smelled his shit. He smelled his sweat. He smelled cooked silencer threads.

Baby steps—three more now. Make the deck/watch your feet.

He pulled one Beretta. He cocked it. He climbed two guns out. His breath tugged. Baby steps slow and—

He hit the deck. His breath stopped. His left arm ripped. Pain shot heart to arm—fucked arteries.

He gulped air. He sucked spray. He fell to his knees. He dropped his left-hand gun. It clattered on teak.

He made noise. Somebody yelled. Noise boomed behind him.

Stanton.

Stanton yelled, "Dick!" Stanton yelled, "Pete!"

Down the deck. Forty feet. The aft rotor-seats.

Pete pitched forward. His left arm blew. The deck cracked his teeth. He rolled over. He gulped breath. He spit out cracked teeth.

He heard Guéry—aft and left—"I don't see him."

He heard Stanton—back-stairs aft—"I think he got Dick."

He heard slides click. He heard hammers cock. He heard rounds snap in. His left arm exploded. His left arm died. His left arm flopped free.

He sucked air. He sucked hard. It hurt bad. It burned bad. He lodged some breath free.

He crawled.

One-handed. One-armed. At one-arm speed. He brushed a rope stack. It was cover. Thick ropes stacked deep.

He heard foot scuffs. They scuffed mid-deck left. He saw pantlegs and feet.

Guéry—fast-walking—*his* way.

His breath crimped. He saw starbursts. He saw twelve legs and feet. He aimed off the ropes. He aimed low. He fired.

He popped six shots fast. He got six muzzle bursts. Double vision/tracer zips/spider legs and feet.

Guéry screamed. Guéry dropped. Guéry grabbed his feet. Guéry fired way high. Shots ripped a mast sheet.

Pete sucked air. Pete *got* air. Pete got a bead. He aimed head high. He pulled slooow.

The slide jammed. Muzzle light dispersed. He saw Guéry with stump feet.

He heard foot scuffs. They scuffed way aft. They scuffed the back stairs clear. He pulled gun 3. His pump lurched. He dropped it.

Guéry fired. Shots hit the ropes. Shots ricocheted.

Pete rolled free. Pete crawled. Pete crawled with one arm and two feet. Guéry saw him. Guéry stretched prone. Guéry fired.

Tracers—loud and close in. Over his head. Scraping the gunwales. Ripping through teak. Six shots/seven/full clip.

Guéry dropped the gun. Pete got close. Pete one-arm leaped.

He bared his teeth. He bit down. He got Guéry's cheek. He raked his fingers up and out. He gouged an eye free.

Guéry screamed. Guéry swung a fist. Guéry hit bared teeth. Pete bit down. Pete snapped bone. Pete made his good hand a V.

Guéry screeched. It was high-decibel. It was half whine/half screech.

Pete drove his hand up. Pete ripped throat tissue. Pete smashed neck bones. Pete drove up to bridgework and teeth.

Guéry spasmed. Pete yanked his arm out. Pete made a hole elbow-deep. Guéry spasmed. Pete rolled back. Pete dug in and shoved with his feet.

He kicked Guéry. He kicked hard right. He kicked him off the deck. He kicked him into the sea.

He heard a splash. He heard a scream. He sucked breath. He *got* breath. He crawled free.

He crawled. He crawled one-armed. Noise cut through deck teak.

It's Stanton. He's below deck. That's steel gnashing steel. He's in the cargo hold. He's loading shotguns. Steel's jamming on steel.

Pete sucked air. Pete rolled up. Pete made his knees. His bladder blew. His breath stopped. He sucked air in deep.

He walked. He staggered. He threw lopsided weight. He made the back steps. He smashed at the door. He threw lopsided weight.

Zero—*weak* weight—no give.

He kicked the door. He shoved the door. He threw lopsided weight.

Zero—*weak* weight—no give.

Barricade/smashproof/blocked stairs below.

Pete kneeled down. Pete laid down lopsided. Pete got echoes off the deckwood. Pete heard steel gnash steel.

It's about three feet over. It's about ten feet up. The deck's scuffed there. It's threadbare. It's breakable teak.

Pete hauled his weight up. Pete heaved for breath. Pete made his knees.

He crawled. He knee-walked. He hit the anchor hub. He stood up. He invoked Barb. He did a dead squat. He threw his right arm out. He wrapped the anchor stem. He jerked and stood up.

His breath exploded. His breath held. His left arm burned up.

He stumbled. He weaved four feet starboard. He reared up to six-five plus. He let the anchor drop.

It cracked the deck. It shattered loud. It snapped threadbare teak. It fell below. It dropped straight down. It smashed John Stanton flush.

112

(Memphis, 4/4/68)

Countdown:

It's 5:59. We're heading for checkmate—pawn to RED KING. We're close. King's outside. King's on the balcony.

He's by the railing. He's with a Negro man. Negro men mill below. King's talking to them. It's jovial. Cars sit below.

Jimmy's in the wino pad. Fred O. said so. Jimmy *will* shoot. Fred O. said so. Jimmy *will* split. I'll drop gun 3. Fred O. said so.

Wayne watched the balcony. Brush covered him. Bob Relyea ditto. Bugs crawled. Ants swarmed. Pollen spritzed.

Bob held gun 2. It was aimed up and out. It was eye-sighted in. Wayne held binoculars. Wayne zeroed in tight.

He held on King. He got King's eyes. He got King's skin.

Bob said, "He ain't walking downstairs. If Jimmy don't shoot inside a minute, I do."

Code Red/all systems clear/all systems GO. No security extant/no cops visible/Feds and Fed cars ditto. Their car was parked on Main Street. Fred O.'s car ditto.

Bob shoots or Jimmy shoots. Jimmy runs then. They run faster. They run zippo. They run through the same passageway. They're younger and swift. They cut through the wino-pad wings.

They bag their car. They split. Jimmy bags his car. Jimmy splits. Fred O. drops gun 3 in a doorway—upside Canipe Novelty.

Wayne hits the safe house. Jimmy shows up. Jimmy suicides.

Countdown—6:00 p.m. sharp—pawn to RED KING.

Wayne honed his binoculars. Wayne got King's eyes. Wayne got King's skin.

"I'm on him. If Jimmy misses or wounds, I'll tap you."

"I want him to punk out. You know that."

"Otash says he's solid."

"He's a fruitcake. Always has been."

Wayne watched King. Wayne ran outtakes. Wayne saw that fuck film. The mattress jiggles. King's flab rolls. That ashtray drops.

Wayne tingled. Bob tingled. Wayne saw his veins pop. They heard a shot slam. They saw red blood on black skin. They heard concurrent pop.

Wayne saw the impact. Wayne saw the neck spray. Wayne saw King drop.

The safe house:

A two-room apartment. Bargain-basement furnished. Three miles off South Main.

Wayne dropped Bob off. Wayne went there. Wayne sat. Fucking Jimmy schizzed out. Fucking Jimmy no-showed.

Fred O. said go there. Fred O. said meet my friend. He's got the bounty. He's got your visa. He's got your Rhodesian passport.

Wayne sat. Wayne waited. Wayne shagged walkie-talkie reports. Fred O. buzzed. Fred O. talked. Fred O. culled juicy cop talk.

He dropped the gun. He did it unseen. Jimmy bagged his sled and took off. The cops showed. The cops found the gun. The cops checked it out.

They talked to folks. They got descriptions. They put broadcasts out. Look for a white man. He's got a white Mustang.

Wrong. Jimmy's 'Stang was yellow.

Fred O. buzzed. Fred O. fretted. He's gone. He smelled shit. He shut "Raul" off. The cops have the plant gun. The Feds will take over. The Feds will obfuscate.

Soft-point bullets. Hard to ID. Ballistic holocaust. It's a 30.06. It's the murder weapon. We know that's a fact.

Trust Mr. Hoover. He'll extrapolate. Big Dwight says so. Wayne agreed. Wayne said we're covered. We *both* say so.

Bob was crushed. Bob didn't shoot. Bob the Klansman bereft. Bob laughed and hailed a cab. Bob booked for West Memphis, Arkansas.

Wayne sat. Wayne waited. Wayne gave Jimmy up.

He burned the suicide note. He flushed the crystal meth. He smashed the hypodermic. He put gloves on. He wiped the pad. He played the radio.

He heard eulogies. He caught breaking news. He heard Negroes-in-the-street bereft. Riots in progress/nationwide chaos/arson and sack.

Wayne popped a window. Wayne heard sirens. Wayne saw flames sweep and crack.

Wayne thought *I Did That*.

113

(Washington, D.C., 4/6/68)

Updates—live on TV.

Littell watched NBC. Littell caught riots and mourning. Littell watched all-day TV.

Riot dead: four in Baltimore/nine in D.C.

Riots: L.A./Detroit/St. Louis. Chicago/New York. Outrage/chain reaction/big damage stats.

Littell cracked a window. Littell smelled smoke. Littell heard bullets smack.

A newsman pitched a D.C. update. This just teletyped:

Negroes see a white man. Negroes swamp his car. Negroes kill said white man. Other Negroes watch.

Littell watched TV. Littell kept a vigil. It ran forty-eight hours plus.

He flew to D.C. He did Teamster work. He got the news. He holed up in his apartment. He lived by his TV.

He mourned. He watched TV. He ran scenarios: Mr. Hoover/Dwight Holly/BLACK RABBIT.

The Rustin shakedown. Attendant frustration. The Poor People's March provokes. Time lines/event chains/conclusions pro and con. The FBI investigates/cover-up pro and con/empirical lessons from Dallas.

He holed up. He wept some. He wondered:

The El Encanto bug. The Boys' "goody box." Bobby's bugged suite. Access to Bobby's campaign.

He ran scenarios. He connected them—King to Bobby. He watched TV. He debunked scenarios—King to Bobby. He stayed inside. He stayed safe. He called Janice.

She got the word. She learned eight days ago. The doctors said it's cancer.

It's in your stomach. It's spreading slow. It's in your spleen. Your cramps masked the symptoms. Your cramps cost you time. Your cramps skewed early detection.

You might live. You might die. Let us operate. Janice said maybe. Janice said let me think.

He told her:

You love the DI. Move in with me. Relax and play the golf course.

Janice did it. Janice moved in. They talked. Janice blasted Wayne Senior.

Janice wept some. Janice said he talked in his sleep. He asked what he said. She said you reach out for "Bobby" and "Jane."

She said no more. She zipped her lips and played coy. He consoled her. He convinced her—let them operate.

Janice showed courage. Janice said yes. Janice faced the knife next week.

Sick list:

Janice was gravely ill. Pete almost died. Heart attack/on his boat run/well out at sea.

Pete killed four men. Pete dumped the bodies. Pete turned the boat back. Pete radioed Bay St. Louis. Pete said call my friend in D.C.

Littell got the message. Littell called Carlos. Carlos pledged a cleanup crew. Pete got the boat in. Pete got lucky. No one saw *five* men embark.

The cleanup men got on. The cleanup men cleaned up. The doctors got Pete. The doctors operated. The doctors patched his heart.

Coronary thrombosis. Mid-range this time. You were lucky.

Pete rested. Littell called him. Pete said he got four. Pete said he missed the last two.

Littell called Carlos. Littell relayed the message. Carlos said fuck it. Carlos reprieved the last two.

Pete called Littell back. Pete asked favors. Don't tell Barb. Don't scare her. Let me get my shit back. Call Milt Chargin. Say I'm okay. Have him mind the cat.

Littell agreed. Littell called Pete. Littell called one hour back. A nurse came on. She said Pete checked out—"Against doctor's advice."

Pete had a visitor. Said visitor spooked him. It was "Carlos Somebody." It was four hours back.

Littell flipped channels. Littell saw Bobby. Bobby was solemn. Bobby condemned racial hate. Bobby mourned Dr. King.

The scenarios kicked in: bug jobs pro and con/collusion widespread. It got bad. It got wild. It got *real.*

Littell grabbed his Rolodex. Littell found Paul Horvitz.

He made the meet. Paul said he'd risk it. See you at 6:00 p.m.—Eddie Chang's Kowloon.

Littell weighed *his* risk.

The hotel bug. Potential upshots exponential. Risk it. Tell Paul. Have him warn Bobby.

Littell dressed up. Littell wore his beard and tweeds. Littell walked out.

He walked. He broke curfew laws. He heard sirens. He saw D.C. locked down tight. He saw flames two miles over. He heard klaxons overlap.

He walked fast. He broiled in tweed. A breeze blew soot flakes. A car eased by. A Negro yelled. He heard race obscenities.

A Negro hurled a beer can. A Negro dumped an ashtray. Cigarette butts breezed.

Littell hit Conn. Ave. Water mains erupted. Firemen lugged hoses. Cops stood by fire trucks.

The Kowloon was open. Eddie Chang was feisty. Eddie Chang fed local cops.

Littell walked in. Littell grabbed the back booth. The barman turned the TV up.

Live local feed. Negroes with gas cans. Cars belly-up.

Three men watched. They were bluff-hearty types. They had hardhats and beer guts.

One man said, "Goddamn animals."

One man said, "We gave them their civil rights."

One man said, "And look what we got."

Littell sprawled. Littell went invertebrate. Littell culled Deep South anecdotes.

Paul Horvitz walked in.

He saw Littell. He brushed his pants off. He walked over. He shook his coat sleeves. Ash dropped and whirled.

He dug his feet in. He spanned the booth. He gripped two hat posts.

"An FBI man talked to Senator Kennedy, an hour ago. He showed him a photograph of a man who looked very much like you, without your beard. He said your name was Ward Littell, and he called you a 'provocateur.' The senator heard that name and saw that picture and almost freaked out."

Littell stood up. His knees shook. He banged the tabletop. He tried to talk. He went cottonmouthed. He st-st-st-stuttered.

Paul grabbed his coat. Paul pulled him close. Paul tore his beard off. Paul slapped him. Paul shoved him. Paul knocked his glasses off.

Littell fell back. Littell dumped the table. Paul fast-walked out.

The hardhats twirled their stools. The hardhats looked over. The hardhats flashed shit-eating grins.

One man flashed a Fed badge.

One man said, "Hi, Ward."

One man said, "Mr. Hoover knows all."

114

(Los Angeles, 4/8/68)

Some crazy A-rab. Two names the same.

Wayne brought him up. Wayne said he muscled him. The A-rab stiffed the Cavern. The A-rab packed hate tracts. The A-rab packed a piece.

Wayne got his hate-mail gig. Wayne pulled hate letters. Guess what? The A-rab sent Bobby K. notes.

Craaaazy shit. "Jew Pigs"/"RFK Must Die."

Pete drove freeways. Pete looped L.A. Pete drove old-man slow.

He felt weak. He felt sapped. He felt drained. He took midget steps now. His breath sputtered. He carried a cane. He measured his steps. He got minor satisfaction. He got more wind each day.

You're young. You're strong. The docs said so. The next one kills you. The surgeon said so.

They split your chest. They cleared your tubes. They stitched and stapled you. You checked out. You bought surgical clippers. You de-stitched yourself slow. You used scotch for disinfectant. You used scotch for anesthetic. You used scotch for the pain.

Pete drove freeways. Pete looped downtown L.A. Pete drove old-man slow.

Carlos bopped to his bedside. Carlos said the boat job—bravo. Carlos mentioned the "small favor." I know you know about it. I know Ward told you.

Pete said sure. You get a favor. I get retirement.

Carlos said go to L.A. Find Fred Otash a stooge.

Carlos said I like Fred. Wayne Senior referred him. I like Wayne Senior too. He's classy. He'll get Ward's job. Ward retires soon.

Pete left the hospital. Pete flew to L.A. Pete saw Fred O. Fred O. was skinny. Fred O. said why.

He ran a stiff. He ran him for eight months. He ran the King fall guy.

Bob Relyea worked the gig. Dwight Holly played ramrod. Wayne Senior ran ops. Wayne Junior was sequestered now. Wayne Junior worked backup.

He killed Wendell Durfee. The LAPD caught it. They had questions still. The snuff vibed revenge/the vic killed your wife/we'd like to talk to you.

Pete weighed the details. Pete gauged Fred O. Pete tore the "small favor" up.

Oh shit. The Boys need a stooge. It's a Bobby hit.

Fred O. confirmed it. Fred O. named no names. Fred O. confirmed implicit. Pete recalled the A-rab. Fred O. was Lebanese. Call it synergy.

Pete dished on the A-rab. Pete dished partial stats. Fred O. fucking drooled. Pete flew to Vegas. Pete kissed the cat hello and goodbye. Pete tossed Wayne's Cavern room.

He found his hate-mail copies. He went through them. He found the A-rab's notes.

RFK MUST DIE! RFK MUST DIE! RFK MUST DIE!

He called Sonny Liston. He said where'd you brace that A-rab? Sonny said the Desert Dawn Motel. He hit the Desert Dawn. He bribed the desk clerk. He checked registration stats.

Bam: Sirhan B. Sirhan/Pasadena, California.

He flew back to L.A. He called the DMV. He got Sirhan's full stats. He called Fred O. He said sit tight. He said I'll stake him out.

Carlos called last night. Carlos waxed sly. You figured it out. Fred O. said so. You know, I'm not surprised.

Carlos waxed assertive then. Carlos said this:

Ward's soft on Bobby. You know Ward. He's liberal martyr Littell. Sever contact for now. Ward's smart. Ward smells things. Conniver Littell.

Pete said sure. I'll do it. You know I want out.

Carlos laughed. Pete saw Big D. Jack's head goes ka-blooey. Jackie dives for scraps.

Chez Sirhan: A small crib/old wood-frame/near Muir High School. Car Sirhan: A jig rig/spinners and skirts/a coon maroon Ford.

Pete pulled up. Pete parked. Pete waited. Pete chewed Nicorette gum.

He thought about Barb. He ran the radio. He got some Barb tunes. He got the news—dig it—King Killer at Large!

He thought about Wayne. Wayne the spook assassin. Jigs from Wendell Durfee on up. He ran instincts. He laid bets. Wayne Senior sandbagged Wayne. Wayne Senior recruited him. It was fucked-up daddy stuff.

He ran the dial. He got more King. He got Bobby campaign stuff.

Sirhan walked out.

He darted. He walked funny. He smoked. He skimmed a racing form. He sideswiped a tree. He face-plowed a hedge.

Two kids walked by. They ogled Sirhan—dig on *that* freak!

Sirhan walked funny. Sirhan looked funny. Sirhan had wild hair and big teeth. Sirhan dropped his cigarette. Sirhan lit a cigarette. Sirhan flashed yellow teeth.

Sirhan got in his car. Sirhan U-turned. Sirhan drove southeast.

Pete tailed him. Sirhan was a track nut. Odds on Santa Anita. Odds on the spring meet.

Sirhan drove funny. Sirhan waved his hands. Sirhan straddled lanes. Pete tailed him close. Fuck the laws of tail work. Sirhan was stone nuts.

They drove southeast. They hit Arcadia. They hit the track lot. Sirhan brodied. Sirhan parked erratic. Pete parked close up.

Sirhan got out. Sirhan pulled a pint of vodka. Sirhan took little pops. Pete got out. Pete tailed him. Pete dogged him cane-first.

Sirhan walked funny. Sirhan walked fast. Pete walked heart-attack slow.

Sirhan hit the turnstiles. Sirhan dropped change. Sirhan said, "Bleacher seat." Pete bought a cheap seat. Pete huffed for breath. Pete tailed Sirhan slooooooooooow.

Sirhan pushed through people. Sirhan pushed funny. Sirhan used darty elbows. People gawked—check that clown/what a freak!

Sirhan stopped. Sirhan pulled out his scratch sheet. Sirhan cognified.

He studied the sheet. He picked his nose. He flicked snot. He licked a pencil. He circled nags. He jabbed at his ears. He dug earwax. He sniffed it. He flicked it off.

He walked. Pete cane-walked slow. Sirhan pulled a wad of dollar bills. Sirhan hit the two-dollar window.

He bet six races. He bet all longshots—two dollars per. He talked funny. He talked stilted. He talked fast.

The cage man passed him tickets. Sirhan walked. Pete tailed him slow. Sirhan walked fast. Sirhan pulled his jug every six steps.

He took a pop. He took six steps. He imbibed again. Pete counted steps. Pete tailed him. Pete yukked.

They hit the bleachers. Sirhan studied faces. Sirhan studied faces slooooow. He stared. His eyes darted. His eyes flared and flashed.

Pete *got* it:

He's looking for demons. He's scouting for Jews.

Sirhan stood still. Sirhan stared. Sirhan saw big beaks. Sirhan smelled Jew.

Sirhan walked. Sirhan grabbed a seat. Sirhan perched by some groovy girls. The girls checked him out. The girls went ugh. The girls went P-U.

Pete took a seat. Pete sat one bleacher up. Pete checked the view: the paddock/the track/the nags at the gate.

The bell rang. The nags tore ass. Sirhan went nuts.

He yelled. He shrieked go go go. His shirttail hiked up. Pete saw a bullet pouch. Pete saw a .38 snub.

Sirhan slurped vodka. Sirhan yelled in Arabic. Sirhan beat his chest to a pulp. The girls moved. The nags crossed the finish line. Sirhan tore a bet-stub up.

Sirhan sulked. Sirhan paced. Sirhan kicked paper cups. He studied his scratch sheet. He picked his nose. He flicked hunks of snot.

Some guys sat down—jarheads in dress blues. Sirhan slid close. Sirhan talked shit. Sirhan offered his jug.

The jarheads imbibed. Pete listened. Pete heard:

"The Jews steal our pussy."

"Robert Kennedy pays them."

"That is no shit I tell you."

The jarheads yukked. The jarheads goofed on the spastic. Sirhan got pissed and reached for his jug. The jarheads tossed it over his head. The jarheads goofed double-hard.

They stood up. They stretched tall. They tossed the jug high. Sirhan was short. They were tall. They made Sirhan leap.

Keep away—*Semper Fi*—three-handed.

They tossed the jug. Sirhan leaped. Sirhan lunged and jumped. Keep away/hot potato/three hands.

The jug traveled. The jug flew shell-game fast. The jug fell and broke. The jarheads laughed. Sirhan laughed—à la Daffy Duck.

An onlooker laughed. He was fat and frizzy-haired. Dig his beanie and mezuzah.

Sirhan called him a "pussylicker."

Sirhan called him a "vampire Jew."

Pete watched the races. Pete watched The Sirhan Sirhan Show.

Sirhan noshed candy bars. Sirhan picked his teeth. Sirhan lost bets. Sirhan sulked. Sirhan picked his toes. Sirhan hassled blond girls. Sirhan dug earwax. Sirhan talked shit.

Jews. RFK. The pus puppets of Zion. The Arab revolt.

Sirhan trawled for Jews. Sirhan scratched his balls. Sirhan aired his feet. Sirhan walked to the paddock. Pete tailed him close. Sirhan hassled jockeys.

I was jockey once. I was hot walker. I hate Zionist pigs. The jockeys razzed him—fuck you, Fritz—you're a *camel* jockey.

Sirhan walked to the bar. Pete tailed him. Sirhan drank vodka shooters with candy-bar chasers. Sirhan chomped ice cubes.

Sirhan trawled for Jews. Sirhan fixed on big schnozzolas. Sirhan jumped stools. Sirhan walked to the john. Pete tailed him. Sirhan trawled urinals.

Sirhan bagged a toilet stall. Pete loitered close. Sirhan shit long and loud. Sirhan walked out. Pete walked in. Pete saw toilet scrawls:

Pigs of Zion!

Blood Licker Jews!

RFK Must Die!

Pete called Fred O. Pete said, "He looks good." Pete drove downtown. Pete hit the Hall of Justice. Pete hit the state horse race board.

He flashed a Rice Krispies badge. He conned a clerk. He cadged an employee file check.

The clerk showed him a file bank. He saw six drawers alphabetic. The clerk yawned. The clerk split. The clerk took a java break.

He pulled the S drawer. He finger-walked. He found "Sirhan, Sirhan B." He skimmed two pages. He got:

Sirhan *was* a hot walker. Sirhan fell off horses. Sirhan bonked his head repeatedly. Sirhan drank too much. Sirhan gambled too much. Sirhan defamed Jews.

He found a memo. The board sent Sirhan to a shrink. A pork dodger/Dr. G. N. Blumenfeld/out in West L.A.

Pete laughed. Pete walked. Pete found a pay phone. He called Fred O. He said, "He looks great."

He tired fast. He tired hard. It killed him. The *day* fucking killed him. Cane tails at age forty-seven.

He hit his motel. He took his pills. He snarfed his blood-thinning drops. He chewed Nicorette gum. He ate his rabbit-food dinner.

He was shot. He was dead whipped. He tried to sleep. His circuits disconnected. Recent shit recohered.

Barb/the boat/the Big Lie. Wayne/the King hit/Bobby.

Barb made sense. Nothing else. Barb dug on Bobby. Barb would mourn Bobby. Barb might link him to the hit. She might do a "Not Again" number. She might freak and split. She might leave him for Bobby *and* Jack.

It scared him. Nothing else did. No outrage or fugue for *la Causa*. No fear outside that.

My shit's too exhausting. I'm dispersed and dead whipped. I'm shot.

He checked the Yellow Pages. He got the shrink's address. He slept.

He got six hours. He revived. He went out sans cane. G. N. Blumenfeld/ office on Pico/out in West L.A.

2:30 a.m.—sleepytime L.A.

He drove out. He parked curbside. He checked the building: Stucco/one-story/six doors in a row.

He grabbed his penlight. He grabbed a pocket knife. He grabbed his Diners Club card. He got out. He tilt-walked. Where's my fucking cane?

He made the door. He flashed the lock. He tapped the keyhole. Go— the knife blade/the card/one sharp twist.

He got leverage. He applied force. The door popped.

He tilt-walked inside. He caught his breath. He pulled the door shut. He flashed the waiting room. He saw clown prints. He saw one desk and one couch.

He flashed a side door. He saw a caduceus. He saw G. N. BLUMENFELD. He walked over. He braced off the walls. His breath snagged and huffed.

He tried the door. It was unlocked. There's the shrink chair. There's the file bank. There's the shrink couch.

His breath jerked. He got dizzy. He stretched out on the couch. He laughed—I'm Sirhan Sirhan—RFK watch out!

He got his breath. He stowed the yuks. His pulse leveled out. He flashed the file bank: A to L/M to S/T to Z.

He got up. He pulled drawer handles. The file drawers slid out. M to S—be there, you fuck.

He pulled drawer 2. He finger-walked. He found him: one folder/two pages/three-visit summary.

He flashed the pages. Quotes leaped:

"Memory loss." "Fugue states." "Disoriented condition."

"Overdependence on supportive male figures."

Boffo quotes. Fred O. would swoon. Hello, you camel jockey!

DOCUMENT INSERT: 4/11/68. Atlanta *Constitution* headline and subhead:

SEARCH FOR KING ASSASSIN BROADENS
FBI IN MASSIVE HUNT

DOCUMENT INSERT: 4/12/68. Houston *Chronicle* headline and subhead:

LAUNDRY-MARK CLUE ID'S ASSASSINATION SUSPECT
SEARCH WIDENS IN LOS ANGELES

DOCUMENT INSERT: 4/14/68. Miami *Herald* subhead:

RIOT DAMAGE ASSESSED IN WAKE OF KING ASSASSINATION

DOCUMENT INSERT: 4/15/68. Portland *Oregonian* headline and subhead:

ASSASSIN'S CAR FOUND IN ATLANTA
SEARCH FOR SUSPECT GALT BROADENS

DOCUMENT INSERT: 4/19/68. Dallas *Morning News* subhead:

HUNT FOR KING ASSASSIN "#1 PRIORITY," HOOVER SAYS

DOCUMENT INSERT: 4/20/68. New York *Daily News* headline and subhead:

FINGERPRINT CHECK YIELDS PAYDIRT!
"GALT" REVEALED AS PRISON ESCAPEE!

<u>DOCUMENT INSERT</u>: 4/22/68. Chicago *Sun Times* headline and subhead:

RFK IN HUGE INDIANA PRIMARY PUSH
CITES LEGACY OF DR. KING

<u>DOCUMENT INSERT</u>: 4/23/68. Los Angeles *Examiner* subhead:

SKID ROW MURDER VICTIM DURFEE REVEALED AS LONG-SOUGHT RAPIST-KILLER

<u>DOCUMENT INSERT</u>: 5/7/68. New York *Times* headline:

RFK WINS INDIANA PRIMARY

<u>DOCUMENT INSERT</u>: 5/10/68. San Francisco *Chronicle* headline:

RFK WINS NEBRASKA PRIMARY

<u>DOCUMENT INSERT</u>: 5/14/68. Los Angeles *Examiner* subhead:

SEARCH FOR KING ASSASSIN SHIFTS TO CANADA

<u>DOCUMENT INSERT</u>: 5/15/68. Phoenix *Sun* subhead:

RFK IN OREGON-CALIFORNIA CAMPAIGN PUSH

<u>DOCUMENT INSERT</u>: 5/16/68. Chicago *Tribune* subhead:

HOOVER SAYS KING ASSASSINATION "NOT A CONSPIRACY"

<u>DOCUMENT INSERT</u>: 5/22/68. Washington *Post* headline and subhead:

LOW TURNOUT FOR POOR PEOPLE'S MARCH
KING'S DEATH CITED AS REASON

DOCUMENT INSERT: 5/26/68. Cleveland *Plain Dealer* subhead:

HUNT FOR SUSPECT RAY WIDENS

DOCUMENT INSERT: 5/26/68. New York *Daily News* subhead:

RAY DESCRIBED AS "AMPHETAMINE ADDICT—LONER"
WITH BENT FOR "GIRLIE" MAGAZINES

DOCUMENT INSERT: 5/27/68. Los Angeles *Examiner* subhead:

FRIENDS CITE RAY'S RACE-HATE HISTORY

DOCUMENT INSERT: 5/28/68. Los Angeles *Examiner* subhead:

NO LEADS IN HUNT FOR SKID-ROW KILLER
LAPD LINKS VICTIM TO RECENT RAPE-MURDERS OF THREE WOMEN

DOCUMENT INSERT: 5/28/68. Portland *Oregonian* headline and subhead:

RFK LOSES OREGON PRIMARY
MOVES CAMPAIGN TO CRUCIAL CALIFORNIA TEST

DOCUMENT INSERT: 5/29/68. Los Angeles *Times* subhead:

HUGE CROWDS AS RFK STORMS STATE

DOCUMENT INSERT: 5/30/68. Los Angeles *Times* subhead:

RECORD CROWDS CHEER RFK'S PLEDGE TO END WAR

DOCUMENT INSERT: 6/1/68. San Francisco *Chronicle* subhead:

RFK SETS BREAKNECK PACE IN CALIFORNIA CAMPAIGN

115

(Lake Tahoe, 6/2/68)

The hole-up:

Wayne Senior's cabin / four rooms / secluded. Up mountain roads. Wide views and trout streams.

Home for now. Home since Memphis.

He had a scrambler phone. He had a food stash. He had a TV. He had shit to sort out. He had time to think.

Let's wait. The Feds will get Jimmy Ray. LAPD will give up on Durfee.

Bob Relyea had his hole-up. Bob had some shack near Phoenix. Wayne got better lodging. Wayne made phone calls. Wayne watched TV.

The Feds traced Ray to England. The search tapped out there. They'll get him. They'll kill him or bust him. He'll give up "Raul." They'll say you're crazy. They'll say there is no "Raul."

The TV spieled news. Wayne Senior called daily. Wayne Senior spieled gossip.

I work with Carlos now. Carlos said he got some tapes. Mr. Hoover sent them. The tapes scared him. Bobby K.'s out to fuck us. Let's clip him fast.

Wayne Senior tattled. *See what I know?* Wayne Senior bragged.

Fred O.'s gigging it. He runs the new shooter. Pete B. runs backup. Wayne Senior gloated. *I'm an insider.* Wayne Senior bragged.

Pete killed some kadre men. Pete klipped loose ends at sea. Carlos told me that. Wayne Senior tattled. *Your daddy hears things.* Wayne Senior bragged.

The kadre biz was a shuck. The Boys fucked the Cause. Carlos told me that. Wayne hashed it out. Wayne came to this: I just don't care.

He watched TV. He caught the war. He caught politics. Wayne Senior puffed. Bobby's a dead man. I'll set Nixon up with the Boys.

Wayne hashed it out. It felt felicitous. Wayne grooved the details. Wayne foresaw the balance.

King's dead. Bobby soon. Shit will peak and resettle. The Poor People's March tanked. The riots upstaged it. Fools popped their rocks and resettled. Chaos is taxing. Fools tire quick. King's death let them roar and resettle. Bobby will go. Dick Nixon will reign. The country will roar and resettle.

The fix will work. Peace will reign. His type will run things. He saw it. He felt it. He *knew*.

And:

You'll step up. You'll get *your* piece. You *know* it. You're making calls. You're listening. You're *thinking*.

He called Wayne Senior. He let him talk. He let him tattle and puff.

Wayne Senior said this:

Littell will retire. I'll get his job. I'll span Howard Hughes and the Boys. Dick Nixon and *me*. Dick and the Boys—shitfire.

Wayne listened. Wayne prompted. Wayne dropped soft tell-me-mores.

Wayne Senior said:

I ran Maynard Moore. He was my snitch. I bankrolled most of Dallas. I sent you there. I got you close. I bought you history. You killed Moore—*didn't you?*—you *lived* history.

Wayne dodged the probe. Wayne rethought Dallas. Moore and the bankroll were old news. The hot news was contempt and hubris.

Dallas derailed your life. Dallas killed your wife. Dallas almost killed you. Wendell D. was there. You weekended with him. Cut to your last rendezvous.

Wayne Senior found Durfee. Dwight Holly helped. They found him and staked him for you. Durfee killed three more women. He killed them during that interval—*before* your last rendezvous.

Wayne Senior gloated. *Hear this now.* Wayne Senior bragged. Pete killed the kadre men. Carlos vouched the job. Carlos said Pete could "retire." Carlos lied to Pete. Carlos told Wayne Senior why.

Pete was impetuous. Pete was erratic. Pete had ideals. Pete and Barb go. Pete and Barb go after Bobby. Carlos has a guy. His name's Chuck the Vice. Chuck kills shitfire. Carlos will call Chuck *après* Bobby.

Hubris. Miscalculation. Pure contempt for YOU.

He had time. He had the phone. He had scrambled frequencies. He called out. He didn't call Barb. He didn't call Pete.

He called Janice. He listened. She talked.

She had cancer. They cut some out. Most of it spread. She had six months tops. She blamed herself. Her cramps hid the symptoms. Said cramps were Wayne Senior–derived.

She hid the prognosis. She never told Ward. She moved into his suite. She still loved the golf course. She still hit shag balls.

She was fading. Ward never sensed it. Ward was soooo Ward. Ward talked in his sleep now. Ward invoked "Bobby" and "Jane."

Ward studied ledger books. There were two separate sets. Ward had them hidey-hole stashed. Ward was secretive. Ward was heedless. She found the stash.

Teamster books. Figures and code names. One set. Anti-Mob books. Typed pages with hand scrawls. One set.

Feminine scrawl. Probably scrawled up by "Jane."

Ward mimeo'd the Jane sheets. Ward wrote cover notes. Ward filled envelopes. Ward was secretive. Ward was heedless. She watched him. She peeked and saw.

She did the pencil trick. She traced a scratch-pad sheet. She bagged a cover note verbatim. Ward wrote to "Paul Horvitz." He was on Bobby's staff. Ward pleaded. Ward groveled. Ward pressed. Ward said here's more dirt. Ward said I'm not a spy. Ward said *please don't hate me.*

It was pathetic. Janice said so.

He called her again. She disdained cancer talk. She talked about Ward.

He's guilt-wracked. He's paranoid. He's confused. He's talking crazy. He says the Feds are on me. He says the Boys might be out for Bobby.

He plays Bobby tapes. He plays them late at night. He thinks I'm asleep. He sleeps fitful. He prays for Bobby. He prays for Martin Luther King. He split ten days ago. He hasn't called. I think he wigged out.

I miss him. I might burn his stash pile. It might drive some sense home. It might wake him up.

Wayne said don't do it. Janice laughed. Janice said it was just talk. Wayne proposed a date. He said I'll pass through Vegas soon. We'll meet at Ward's suite.

Janice said yes.

He wanted her. Dying or not. He knew it. Janice got him thinking. *Everything* did.

He got an urge. It was time-travel stuff. It reached back fourteen years. He called his mother in Peru, Indiana.

The call shocked her. He let her calm down. They broke some ice. They bridged some pauses. They talked. He lied his life off. She said all good things.

You were a tender child. You loved animals. You set trapped coyotes free. You were a brilliant child. You learned complex math. You excelled at chemistry. You carried no hate. You played with colored children. You loved righteously.

I was pregnant once. It was '32—two years before you. Wayne Senior had a dream. He saw the baby as a girl. He wanted a boy.

He beat my stomach in. He used brass knuckles. The baby died. Wayne Senior was right. It was a girl. The doctor told me.

Wayne said goodbye then. His mother said God bless.

Wayne thought it through. Wayne called Janice. Wayne set up their date.

116

(Long Beach, 6/3/68)

Bobby! Bobby! Bobby!

The crowd chanted it. The crowd went nuts. Speak Bobby speak!

Bobby climbed a flatbed truck. Bobby grabbed a microphone. Bobby rolled up his sleeves.

The Southglen Mall. Three thousand fans—Speak Bobby Speak! Parking-lot frenzy. Kids on daddies' shoulders. Sound speakers on stilts.

The fans loved Bobby. The fans fucked up their vocal cords. The fans fucking shrieked. Watch Bobby smile! Watch Bobby toss his hair! Hear Bobby speak!

Pete watched. Likewise Fred O.

They watched Bobby. They watched his bodyguards. They watched the cop crew. The numbers were low. Bobby loved contact. Bobby shined on security.

Fred watched cops move. Fred watched cops scan. Fred watched cops flank. Fred nailed details. Fred memorized.

Fred met Sirhan. They "met" at the track. They "met" six weeks back. Fred staged a play for Sirhan. Fred beat up a Jew.

He was a big man. He had a big beak. He wore a big beanie. He was a *very* big Jew.

Fred kicked his ass. Sirhan watched. Sirhan dug the show. Fred dished rapport—I'm Bill Habib—I'm Arab too.

Courtship/subornment/recruitment/sheep dip.

Fred palled with Sirhan. Fred bought him booze. Fred ragged the Jews.

They met every day. They worked up a mojo. They ragged Bobby K. They met semi-private. Fred stayed skinny. Fred stayed camouflaged.

Fred tweaked Sirhan. Fred studied Sirhan. Fred learned:

How far to push him. How much booze to pour him. How much hate to stoke. How to get him talking. How to get him fuming: Kill RFK!

How to get him blackout drunk. How to get him fucked-up blotto. How to push him to memory loss. How to get him stalking rallies. How to get him talking death. How to get him talking fate. How to get him target shooting out in the hills—blasting at mock–Bobby K.'s.

Fred gauged Sirhan. Fred said:

He's drinking hard. He's drinking every night. He's drinking with and without me. He's hitting rallies. He's rally-hopping countywide. He always packs his piece. I've tailed him. I've seen it. I *know.*

He hates Bobby. His logic's warped. It's misdirected and rationalized. He hates the Jews. He hates Israel. He hates Zionist Bobby. He hates Bobby because Bobby's a fucking *Kennedy.*

He's primed now. He's ready now. He's psycho. He's blackout-prone. He's booze-atrophied.

Fred picked the spot. Fred told Sirhan. Fred made Sirhan drink. Sirhan *picked* the spot. Sirhan picked it two bottles later. Sirhan usurped the idea. Sirhan thinks it's *his* idea. It's his booze epiphany.

Tomorrow night. The Ambassador Hotel. Bobby's victory gala. Bobby to shout victory.

Bobby will be fried. Bobby will be torched and zorched—cumulatively. The kitchen's the way out. It's short and fast—serendipity. Sirhan's there. Sirhan's primed—tenaciously.

Fred knew the kitchen. Fred checked it out. Fred pumped rent-a-cops. Said cops pledged this:

Tight spaces/armed guards/tight security. That meant potential combustion/potential confusion. That meant potential insanity.

Fred's suggested drama/Fred's *predicted* lunacy:

Men draw their guns. Men shoot Sirhan. Shots bounce and hit Bobby K. Fred said he *will* shoot. Fred knew the nut turf. Fred-"Raul" ran James Earl Ray.

Pete looked around. The crowd yelled. The crowd went nuts. The crowd out-yelled Bobby.

The speakers backfired. Reverb blew wide. Bobby spoke basso-falsetto. Pete heard platitudes. Pete heard "end the war." Pete heard "King's legacy."

Barb dug Bobby. Barb dug his antiwar shit. He hadn't called her. She hadn't called him. She never wrote. No contact since Sparta. No contact post-boat trip. No contact post-coronary.

The crowd yelled. Pete looked around. Pete saw a pay phone. It was streetside. It was away from the noise. It was away from Bobby.

He pushed over. People stepped aside. People saw his cane. He made the booth. He caught his breath. He fed quarters in.

He got an operator. She patched the Cavern. He got the switchboard. He shagged his messages.

No message from Barb. One message from Wayne: Call me/Lake Tahoe/*urgent*/this number direct.

Pete dropped quarters. Pete got an operator. She patched Tahoe direct. Pete heard two rings. Pete heard Wayne:

"Hello?"

"It's me. Where the hell have—"

"Littell's on to the hit. Grab him and bring him here. And tell Barb go someplace safe."

117

(San Diego, 6/3/68)

Bobby soared.

He jabbed the air. He tossed his hair. He praised Dr. King. He co-opted him. He out-orated him. He made his praise sing.

It all worked. It all sang—the sunburn/the bray/the rolled sleeves.

The crowd soared. The crowd roared. The crowd cheered in sync. Two thousand people/crowd ropes up/parking-lot streams.

Littell watched. Littell willed Bobby: *Please look at me.*

See me. Don't fear me. I won't hurt you again. I'm a pilgrim. I fear *for* you. My fear's justified.

Bobby stood on a flatbed. The tailgate shook and dipped. Aides stood below him. Aides steadied him.

Look over. Look down. See me.

His fear boiled over. It popped two weeks back. His fear stretched and peaked. He linked fear dots. He plumbed fear lines. He read fear hieroglyphs.

The news pic/the El Encanto/suite 301. The Sam line: "Box of goodies." The Carlos line: Pete's "small favor." Fear connections/hieroglyphs/puzzle chips.

It got bad. It ate him up. It ruined his sleep. He split Vegas. He flew to D.C. He called Paul Horvitz.

Paul hung up. He called Mr. Hoover. He called Dwight Holly. They hung up. He drove to the Bureau. Door guards ejected him.

He flew to Oregon. He approached campaign staffers. Staff guards restrained him. He saw his name on a list—all "Known Enemies."

He told the guards I *sense* things. He said *please* talk to me. They said no. They manhandled him. They ejected him.

Chips dovetailed. He sensed things. Mr. Hoover *knows*—just like he knew about Jack.

He flew to Santa Barbara. He got a hotel room. He staked out the El Encanto. He watched 301. He followed wires. He found the listening post.

Suite 208/fifty yards up/manned twenty-four hours per day.

He staked it out. He wore disguises. He worked six days and nights. He waited. The post stayed manned—all day/all night.

He went schizzy. He gave up sleep—six days/six nights. He lost weight. He saw goblins. Spots torqued his eyes.

It rained on day 7. One agent stayed on-post.

Luck:

Said agent goes off-post. Said agent visits suite 63. Said agent has a prostitute.

Littell hit 208. Littell picked the door lock. Littell locked himself in. Littell tossed the post.

He found a transcript log. He found a routing log. He found transcripts stacked. He skimmed back through mid-March. He saw:

March 15/16. Two three-way talks transcribed. Bobby plus Paul Horvitz. One man un-ID'd. Bobby's voluble. Bobby's effusive. Bobby talks anti-Mob.

He skimmed the routing log. He hit 3/20. He saw tape copies routed. The tapes for March 15/16. Said tapes routed to the Boys.

To Carlos. To Moe D. To John Rosselli. To Santo and Sam G.

That was this morning. That was twelve hours back.

He tracked Bobby's schedule. He drove south. He hit San Diego. He called the Bureau office. The ASAC hung up. He called SDPD. He told his story. A sergeant blew up.

The sergeant yelled at him. The sergeant said, "You're on a list." The sergeant hung up.

He drove to the rally. He got there early. He saw sound men set up. He braced them. He braced staffers. He got the bum's rush. He left. He came back. The crowd ate him up.

Littell watched Bobby. Littell waved his hands. *Look at me please.* Bobby soared. Bobby waved. Bobby loved up the crowd. Bobby spread contact thin.

Littell waved his hands. Something jabbed him—a needle/a pin/a stick. He went woozy—BOOM like that—he saw Fred Otash thiiiiiinnn.

118

(Las Vegas, 6/4/68)

Wild Janice—frail now.

More gray hair. More black eclipsed. More lines and hollows.

Wayne walked in. Janice shut the door. Wayne embraced her. He felt ribs. He felt hollows. He felt her curves slack.

Janice stepped back. Wayne took her hands.

"You look pretty good, considering."

"I wasn't going to put on all that powder. I'm not dead yet."

"Don't talk like that."

"Let me indulge myself. You're my first date since Ward deserted me."

Wayne smiled. "You were my first date, ever."

Janice smiled. "Are you talking about the Peru Cotillion of 1949 or the one time we did it?"

Wayne squeezed her hands. "We never got a second shot."

Janice laughed. "You weren't looking for one. It was just your way to cut loose of your father."

"I regret that. That part of it, I mean."

"You mean it was good, but you regret the timing and your motive."

"I regret what it cost you."

Janice squeezed his hands. "You're leading up to something."

Wayne blushed. Shit—you *still* do that.

"I was hoping there'd be one more time."

"You can't mean it. With me like *this?*"

"You never get things right the first time."

. . .

It went soft. It went slow. It went like he wanted. It went like he planned.

Her body showed the hurt. Sharp bones over skin. Gray tones over white. Her breath tasted bitter. He liked her old taste—Salem Menthols and gin.

They rolled. Her bones scraped him. They touched and kissed long. Her breasts fell. He liked it. Her breasts used to stand.

She still had strength. She pushed him. She clutched and grabbed. They rolled. He tasted her. She tasted him.

She tasted sick. It stunned him. The taste settled in. He tasted her inside. He kissed her new scars. Her breath fluttered thin.

He got her close. She pulled back. She guided him in. He reached over. He turned on the bed lamp. The beam settled in.

It caught her face. It bounced off her gray hair. It caught her eyes flush.

They moved together. They got close and held. They locked their eyes up. They moved. They peaked close together. They let their eyes shut.

Janice played the radio. KVGS—all lounge stuff.

They hit some Barb songs. They laughed and rolled. They kicked the sheets up. Wayne dimmed the volume. The Bondsmen purred. Barb sang "Twilight Time."

Janice said, "You love her. Ward told me."

"I outgrew her. She grew up and messed with my crush."

Barb segued upbeat—"Chanson d'Amour." Janice dimmed the volume. Barb blew a high note. The Bondsmen cued her back up.

"I ran into her, about two years ago. We had a few drinks and discussed certain men."

Wayne smiled. "I wish I could have been there."

"You were."

"That's all you're saying?"

Janice zipped her lips. "Yes."

Barb segued dreamy—Jimmy Rogers' "Secretly."

Janice said, "I love that song. It reminds me of the man I was with then."

"Was it my father?"

"No."

"Did he find out?"

"Yes."

"What did he do?"

Janice touched his lips. "Be still. I want to listen."

Barb sang. Her voice held. She segued. She went upbeat. Reverb killed the mood.

Wayne killed the volume. Wayne rolled close to Janice. He kissed her. He touched her hair. He got her eyes close up.

"If I told you I could help you settle the one score that counts, would you want to do it?"

Janice said, "Yes."

She slept.

She ate pain pills. She drifted off. Wayne fluffed her hair on a pillow. Wayne pulled a quilt over her.

He checked his watch. It was 6:10 p.m.

He walked to his car. He grabbed two laundry bags. He grabbed a scratch pad and pen. He walked back. He bolted the door. He walked the living room. He pat-checked the walls. He patted and touched.

No hollow thunks/no wall seams/no panels.

He walked the bedroom. He worked around Janice. He patted and touched. No hollow thunks/no wall seams/no panels.

He walked Littell's study. He slid out a cabinet. He saw a wall seam. He found a catch and flipped it. A panel slid back.

He saw shelves. He saw a .38 snubnose. He saw ledgers stacked.

He opened the blue ones. He saw Teamster nomenclature. He opened the brown ones. He saw typed notes and hand scrawl. He skimmed the text.

Arden-Jane indicts Teamsters. Arden-Jane indicts mobsters. Arden-Jane culls anti-Mob facts.

Book 2—page 84:

Arden-Jane rats "Chuck the Vice" Aiuppa. Arden-Jane rats Carlos M. She heard a rumor. She confirmed it. She transcribed.

March '59. Outside New Orleans. Carlos gives "Chuck the Vice" work. A "cajun fuck" fucked Carlos. Carlos says clip him.

"Chuck the Vice" obeys. "Chuck the Vice" kills said fuck. "Chuck the Vice" buries him.

Across from Boo's Hot-Links—six miles from Fort Polk. Look there—you'll find the bones.

Wayne pulled page 84. Wayne grabbed his scratch pad. Wayne wrote a note:

Mr. Marcello,

My father bought Arden Breen–Jane Fentress's file from her before she left Ward Littell. Ward has no idea that such a file exists.

My father plans to extort you with information contained in the file. Can we discuss this? I'll call you within 24 hours.

Wayne Tedrow Jr.

Wayne checked Littell's desk. Wayne found an envelope. Wayne dropped the page and note in.

He sealed the envelope. He addressed it: Carlos Marcello/Tropicana Hotel/Las Vegas.

He grabbed the ledger books. He filled a laundry bag. He walked out. He killed the bedroom lights. He kissed Janice.

He touched her hair. He said, "I love you."

119

(Lake Tahoe, 6/4/68)

News flash! It's over! Bobby K. wins!

The TV ran figures. Percentage points and precincts. It's Bobby decisive. It's Bobby's big win.

Pete watched. Ward watched near-comatose. Ward watched shell-shocked.

They got Wayne's tip. They jumped him. They spiked him with Seconal. Pete drove him up. They hid in Wayne Senior's lodge.

Wayne was in Vegas. Fred O. was in L.A. Fred O. was priming Sirhan.

Ward slept crypt-style. Ward slept sixteen hours. Ward slept cuffed to a bed. He woke up. He saw Pete. He *knew.* He refused to talk. He said zero words. Pete knew he'd want to *see.*

Pete cooked pancakes. Ward ate zero. Pete ran the TV. They waited. Ward watched election news. Pete twirled his cane.

He'd called Barb. She said Fuck You. I won't run. I won't hide.

Pete babied Ward. Pete said talk to me please. Ward shut his eyes. Ward shook his head. Ward cupped his ears.

News flash! The Ambassador live! Bobby proclaims victory!

A camera cut to close-up. Bobby's all tousle-haired. Bobby's grinning all teeth.

The phone rang. Pete grabbed it.

"Yeah?"

Wayne said, "It's me."

Pete watched the TV. The picture skipped and settled. His pulse skipped. Bobbyphiles cheered Bobby.

"Where are—"

"I just talked to Carlos. He had plans for you and Barb, but I talked him out of it. You're free to do whatever you want, and Ward is retired as of now."

"Jesus Chr—"

"Dallas and up, partner. I pay my debts."

The picture skipped and settled. Pete put the phone down. Pete felt his pulse skip.

Bobby splits the podium. Bobby waves. Bobby steps away. The camera pans a doorway—Bobby adieu—the camera cuts back.

The camera pans Bobbyphiles. A mike gets the gunshots. A mike gets the screams.

Oh God—

Oh no.

No not *that*—

Senator Kennedy has been—

Pete hit the remote control. The TV bipped off.

Ward cupped his ears. Ward shut his eyes. Ward fucking screamed.

120

(Lake Tahoe, 6/9/68)

Reruns:
> The eulogies. The High Mass. The funeral scenes. Wakes plural—King and Bobby.

He watched. He watched all day and night. He watched four days on.

Reruns:

The kitchen chaos. The cops with Sirhan. The Feds with James Earl Ray. Caught in London. "I'm a patsy." A familiar theme.

He watched TV. He watched four days on. It would end soon. The news would shift. The news would move on.

Littell flipped channels. Littell saw L.A. and Memphis.

He was hungry. His food was gone. Pete stocked for two days. Pete left four days back. Pete cut the phone lines free.

Pete said walk to Tahoe. It's six miles tops. Catch a Vegas train.

Pete was disingenuous. Pete knew he wouldn't. Pete knew he'd stay. Pete caught the drift. Pete left his gun behind. Pete told him straight:

They killed King too. You should know that. I owe you.

Littell said goodbye. One word and no more. Pete squeezed his hands. Pete walked away.

Littell flipped channels. Littell caught The Triad: Jack/King/Bobby. Three funeral shots. Three artful cuts. Three widows framed.

I killed them. It's my fault. Their blood's on me.

He waited. He watched the screen. Let's try for all three. He flipped channels. He got one and two. He lucked on all three.

There—old footage. It's pre-'63.

They're in the White House. Jack's at his desk. King's standing with Bobby. The image held. One picture/all three.

Littell grabbed the gun. Littell ate the barrel. The muzzle roar shut off all three.

121

(Sparta, 6/9/68)

The cat hissed. The cat snarled. The cat paced his cage.

The cab hit ruts. Pete bounced. His knees bumped the cage. Sparta in bloom. Mosquitoes meet Lutherans and trees.

He flew unannounced. He brought truce papers. He brought seller's deeds. He sold the Cavern. He took a loss. He sold Tiger Kab to Milt C.

The cat hissed. Pete scratched his ears. The cab cut due east.

His wind was back. He ditched his cane. He still tired easy. He was fried/fragged/*frappéed*. He was frazzled and free.

He tried for regret. He fretted the bad shit on Ward. He ran his fears for Wayne T. Nothing jelled persistent. You're fried/fragged/*frappéed*. You're frazzled and free.

The cat snarled. The cab cut south. The driver read address plates. The driver pulled over. The cab grazed the curb.

Pete got out. Pete saw Barb. She's pruning fucking trees. She heard the cab. She looked over. She saw Pete.

Pete took one step. Barb took two steps. Pete jumped and took three.

122

(Las Vegas, 6/9/68)

He's home.

The lights are on. The shades are up. One window's cracked free.

Wayne parked. Wayne walked up. Wayne opened the door and walked in.

He's upside the bar. It's ritualized. He's got his nightcap. He's got his stick.

Wayne walked over. Wayne Senior smiled. Wayne Senior twirled his stick.

"I knew you'd be by."

"What made you think that?"

"Certain allegedly unrelated events of the past few months and how they relate to this burgeoning partnership of ours."

Wayne grabbed the stick. Wayne twirled it. Wayne did a few tricks.

"That's a good place to start."

Wayne Senior winked. "I'm sitting down with Dick Nixon next week."

Wayne winked. "No, I am."

Wayne Senior laughed—faux rube/yuk-yuk.

"You'll meet Dick in good time. I'll get you a box seat at the inauguration."

Wayne twirled the stick. "I've spoken to Carlos and Mr. Hughes' people. We've come to some agreements, and I'm assuming Ward Littell's position."

Wayne Senior twitched. Wayne Senior smiled in slow-motion. Wayne Senior built a slow-motion drink.

One hand's clenched. It's on the bar rail. One hand's pure free.

Their eyes met. Their eyes held. Their eyes locked shitfire.

Wayne pulled his cuffs. Wayne freed a ratchet. Wayne snared one wrist. The cuff snapped on. Wayne Senior jerked back. Wayne jerked him back in.

Wayne flicked the spare cuff. Wayne freed the ratchet. Wayne cuffed the bar rail crisp.

Good cuffs/LVPD/Smith & Wesson.

Wayne Senior jerked. The cuff chain held. The bar rail squeaked. Wayne pulled a knife. Wayne flicked the blade. Wayne cut the bar phone cord.

Wayne Senior jerked the chain. Wayne Senior dumped his stool. Wayne Senior spilled his drink.

Wayne twirled the stick. "I reconverted. Mr. Hughes was pleased to know that I'm a Mormon."

Wayne Senior jerked. The ratchets scraped. The bar rail held strong. The chain links went *screeee.*

Wayne walked out. Wayne stood by his car. The Strip lights twinkled waaay off. Wayne saw incoming beams.

The car pulled up. The car stopped. Janice got out. Janice weaved and anchored her feet.

She twirled a golf club. Some kind of iron. Big head and fat grips.

She walked past Wayne. She looked at him. He smelled her cancer breath. She walked inside. She let the door swing.

Wayne stood tiptoed. Wayne made a picture frame. Wayne got a full window view. The club head arced. His father screamed. Blood sprayed the panes.

AMERICAN TABLOID

We are behind, and below, the scenes of JFK's presidential election, the Bay of Pigs, and the assassination. FBI men Kemper Boyd and Ward Littell work every side of the street, jerking the chains of made men, street scum, and celebrities alike, while Pete Bondurant, ex-rogue cop, freelance enforcer, troubleshooter, and troublemaker, has the conscience to louse it all up. Mob bosses, politicos, snitches, psychos, fall guys, and femmes fatale are mixing up a molotov cocktail guaranteed to end the country's innocence with a bang.

Crime Fiction/0-375-72737-X

CRIME WAVE

Los Angeles: in no other city do sex, celebrity, money, and crime exert such an irresistible magnetic field. With this fever-hot collection of reportage and short fiction, James Ellroy portrays his native habitat as a smog-shrouded netherworld. From his mother's unsolved murder to the killing of Nicole Brown Simpson, Ellroy investigates true crimes and restores humanity to their victims. He also enlists the luminaries of a vanished Hollywood in two baroquely twisted novellas of slaughter, smut-mongering, and corruption.

True Crime/Crime Fiction/0-375-70471-X

MY DARK PLACES

In 1958 Jean Ellroy was murdered, her body dumped on a roadway in an Los Angeles suburb. Her killer was never found, and the police dismissed her as a casualty of a cheap Saturday night. James Ellroy was ten when his mother died, and he spent the next thirty-six years running from her ghost, attempting to exorcise it through crime fiction. In 1994, he went back to Los Angeles to find the truth about his mother—and himself. *My Dark Places* is an epic of loss, fixation, and redemption, a memoir that is also a history of the American way of violence.

Memoir/True Crime/0-679-76205-1

WHITE JAZZ

It is 1958 and the heat is on LAPD lieutenant Dave Klein. He not only works the mean streets, he helped make them that way. Murder, bribery, scams, shakedowns—he's done it all in the line of duty. But now, with the Feds on the tail of blue corruption, Klein is hung out to dry as a bad example, and it's pay-up time. Telling his own story—his voice clipped, sharp, often as brutal as the events he's describing—Klein plunges into a nightmare world of greed, blood, and twisted sin—a monstrous world he created. But now the monster has turned on its creator.

Crime Fiction/0-375-72736-1

VINTAGE BOOKS

Available at your local bookstore, or call toll-free to order:
1-800-793-2665 (credit cards only).